The Flame Priest

KIRALYNN EPICS

THE FLAME PRIEST

BOOK TWO OF

THE SILK & STEEL SAGA

Karen L. Azinger

KIRALYNN EPICS

Published by Kiralynn Epics L.P. 2011

Copyright © Karen L. Azinger 2011

First published in the United States of America by Kiralynn Epics 2011

Front Cover Artwork Copyright Greg Bridges © 2011

Second Edition 2017

Celtic Lettering used with permission of Alfred M Graphics Art Studio

The Author asserts the moral right to be identified as the author of this work

All characters in this publication are fictitious and any resemblance to real persons living or dead, is purely coincidental.

ISBN 978-0-9835160-2-6

Library of Congress Control Number: 2011960619

ACKNOWEDGEMENTS

My dream of an epic fantasy continues, and like the first book, it takes a lot of people to make the saga come true. First and foremost, to my husband Rick, who is always keen for the next adventure and always believes no matter the odds. To my best friend, first reader and sword sister, Danae Powers, who listened from the very first chapter. To my writer friend, Peggy Lowe, a critique circle of one. To my first editor, Bill Johnson, a story really is a promise. To my alpha readers, Mike, Nick, Diane, Mary, John, Stewart, Tanya, Chris, Cheryl, Bob, and Gina, your enthusiasm kept me going through all the bleak times. To Greg Bridges for the totally awesome front cover and the book spine. To Peggy Lowe, graphic artist extraordinaire, for the back cover, the two maps and the logo, well done! To Violet Lowe for my author photo. To all of my readers who eagerly followed the saga to the second book, I write for you. And to my mom, for everything, I so hope you know.

ACKNOWLEDGMENTS

Prologue

A voice seared her mind, *"Come to me!"* The Priestess of the Oracle stirred in her sleep, a sheen of sweat beading her naked body. A breeze laden with the sweet scent of flowering nightshade blew in through the marble columns, yet it did little to sate her heat.

"Come to me!"

Awakened by a god's call, the Priestess rose flushed with ardor. Slipping into a robe of sheer purple silk, she ran her fingers through her raven-black hair. Silk against skin, every movement became a caress, deepening her need. Barefoot, she followed her master's command. Guards snapped to attention and torches sputtered as she passed. Hungry stares followed but none dared interrupt. Reaching the rear of the villa, she stepped from the confines of cultured marble into the tangled wildness of the garden.

Night prevailed. A silver crescent rose low in the east, marking the lateness of the hour. Shadows and darkness painted the garden with mystery, but her footsteps were sure. Moon-blooming flowers lined a path to the grove, their musky scent providing a heady perfume. The tangled blossoms crowded close, as if yearning for her touch. Deep-throated foxglove and spiky-white baneberry sat amongst the gray-green leaves of bloodroot, and nestled along the back, her favorite, the lush purple pendants of nightshade. She knew them all, by name and by nature. Some were aromatic, others beautiful, but all were poisonous, her garden of deathly delights. The Priestess smiled, appreciating the dual nature of her dark garden. Beauty could be *so* deceiving.

Gliding through the blossoms, she reached the grove of hawthorn trees. Gnarled and twisted, the ancient trees stood as guardians to the Oracle, their limbs raised like tortured hands grasping at the night. Tangled branches swallowed the sounds of the surrounding swamp, the croak of frogs smothered to an expectant stillness. The Priestess followed the path to the inner sanctuary, intent on the summons from the Dark Lord.

The trees fell away to reveal a small clearing. A ring of black basalt stones waited at the center. So old, the ancient well reeked of unimaginable Darkness. The Priestess shivered, feeling the pull of the Oracle.

She bowed low in homage and then knelt, leaning across lip of the well. Cold from the stones seeped through the thin robe, invading her flesh. Shivering with anticipation, she stretched forward, peering into the Oracle. Her raven-black hair cascaded around her face, forming a veil to block out the feeble starlight. Mirror-flat, the water of the well was deep, and dark, and mysterious.

Infinite Darkness beckoned.

"I am here, my Lord."

A throbbing power emanated from the waters, seductive as sin. Her heart pulsed to the dark rhythm. Her breath plumed to a cold mist, the warmth of humanity surrendered as an offering. She felt a sharp tug deep within her soul. Her hands clutched at the lip of the well, fingernails scrapping against black stone. Her back arched as power spiked through her. A groan of ecstasy escaped her lips. The Priestess writhed across the cold stones, consumed by passion laced with pain. A scream ripped through her, but then the spasms subsided, leaving her thrumming with power. Gasping for breath, she gloried in the fullness of the Dark Lord. More than mortal, she was the Priestess of the Oracle, a vessel of Darkness...and now her cup runneth over.

The Dark Lord withdrew.

She reclaimed control, feeling the power centered in her loins. Staring into the well, she cast her powers upon the waters. The well awoke. Images danced across the water. Colors and shapes stilled to clarity, giving her a bird's-eye view. She leaned forward, keen to scry the secrets of Erdhe. A stranger's face appeared on the waters, a young man with close-cropped blond hair lying asleep on a small cot. He seemed ordinary enough, plain of face, wearing simple woolen robes, but the Priestess watched, knowing the Oracle held some deeper purpose. The young man stirred. His eyes flew open, releasing the red light of hell. The Priestess recoiled, a gasp on her lips. Understanding pierced her surprise. Intrigued, she leaned forward to memorize his face.

The voice of the Dark Lord rumbled through her mind, "*Witness the Awakening! My servant, the Mordant, is reborn!*"

Her heartbeat quickened. "So, the time is at hand!"

"*Behold my Emissary to Erdhe. He comes to divide my enemies, watch and learn.*"

The Priestess stared into the well, watching as the night gave birth to the Dark Lord's grand design. *The oldest harlequin, a thousand years of evil hidden beneath an innocent face...and she knew his secret!* Spellbound, she watched as the Ancient One left his cell. He walked through strange hallways, unlike anything she'd ever seen. The floors were colored a rich golden hue, the walls illumined in flowing script, but it was the Mordant who consumed her gaze. Young of face, his eyes still rimmed with a hellish light, yet he dared to stride through the corridors, shunning stealth. Fascinated, she watched as he encountered a knight in a powder-blue surcoat. She yearned to hear the exchange, but the Oracle's power yielded only sight. A blond-haired woman approached, sleep-tousled and unsuspecting. The Priestess watched as the knight slew the woman and then slew himself, and all the while the Mordant looked...indifferent. The Priestess shuddered, appreciating the coldness of the kill. She studied his face, wondering at the power hidden beneath the youthful visage. Leaving the dead puddled in their own blood, the Mordant roamed the golden corridors. Avoiding the midnight-blue doors, he made his way to the cell of a dark-haired woman. He slit her throat as she slept, removing a golden chain from her neck. The Priestess craned forward, watching as the Mordant held the amulet aloft. Even blood-spattered the rune-carved gold was clearly a thing of power. Covetous, she watched as he slipped it in his pocket. Making his way back through the corridors, he strode towards the outer gates.

A ripple disturbed the Oracle, marring the view. The waters clouded, the vision blocked by a strange, impenetrable whiteness, like staring into the milky eye of a blind beggar. She hurled a command at the waters. "Sianth tabeth anous!" The ancient words hissed from her tongue. The very air crackled with power but the Oracle remained clouded.

"*Sianth tabeth anous!*" A burnt smell hung over the well, but the view remained obscured. A finger of fear trickled down her back; she'd never before been denied.

Swallowing her alarm, she kept a wary vigil; more than one power was at work this night. Clutching the stone rim, she stared into the well, a contest of wills. Thunder rumbled in the distance, the first hint of an approaching storm, but the Priestess remained vigilant, striving to pierce the white shroud. Black tendrils slowly crept across the water, repulsing the white. The Oracle began to clear, the vision sharpening to clarity. The Mordant emerged from a dense fog. A white mist swirled behind him yet he seemed unscathed, the golden amulet shining at his breast. The Priestess sighed, the Light had meddled but Darkness prevailed.

The view widened. Like a bird of prey hovering in the sky, she watched as the Ancient One made his way down a mountain path, melting into the wilderness. The Priestess smiled. Wherever his starting point, she knew the Mordant would make his way north, to his fortress-city beyond the Dragon Spine Mountains. Laughter bubbled from her ruby lips. Death was loose in the lands of Erdhe and only a handful knew it. The images from the Oracle were bound to turn bloody. The Priestess had much to look forward to.

Curious to see what other Darkness plagued Erdhe on this night of destiny, she invoked her powers, willing the scene to change. Her thoughts turned toward Coronth. A single ripple shimmered across the water. Snow-capped mountains disappeared, replaced with a view of the Flame God's capital city. Since his visit to the Oracle, the Priestess had studied Steffan's rise in power. As the counselor to the Pontifax, he used the religion of the Flame to twist the people of Coronth toward the Dark, building an army of fanatics. The use of religion to work the will of the Dark Lord was a stroke of genius, a genius worth watching.

Concentrating, she willed the image to focus. The Oracle showed her an opulent bedroom. A familiar dark-haired man slept entwined in silken sheets. Even in sleep, his handsome arrogance was apparent. A predatory smile crossed her face as she remembered the night of Steffan's initiation. She'd pushed him past the bounds of his imagination, taking as much pleasure as she gave. She'd only had one night with him...but one night was all she *ever* needed. She purred with delight, knowing her hooks were sunk deep. Steffan's choice of lovers told her that he still dreamt of her. She smiled, knowing that he would never find her equal. When the time was right, she would set his desire ablaze. Passion was such a relentless power...and such an ultimate pleasure. The thrill of the hunt coursed through her. She had much to look forward to...once her work on the Isle was finished.

Darkness blazed across the Oracle.

The Priestess hissed, singed by the backlash of power. Gripping the cold stones, she watched as the Dark Lord claimed Steffan with a taste of hell. Pain twisted his face. His back arched, his mouth stretched in a wordless scream. He writhed across the bed, clutching his chest, the silken sheets sodden with sweat. The Priestess gave a throaty laugh, enjoying the show. Pain and pleasure had so much in common, but all too soon his torment ended, leaving him gasping in bed.

The Dark Lord withdrew and her interest waned. Reaching for her power, she caused a ripple in the waters. She wondered about the enemy, the servants of the Light, but the Oracle only revealed acts of Darkness. She found plenty to watch. Faces and distant places flickered across the waters, revealing fresh souls bent toward the Dark. Most of the young ones never knew the direct touch of the Dark Lord, yet they served anyway, they all served. The followers of her god were legion. Erdhe was rife with seeds of Darkness. The Priestess memorized their faces, tracking their deeds, deciding how best to use them. Sensing the possibilities, she yearned to join in the dark dance of destiny, to take her turn at manipulating the young. Leaning forward, she breathed upon the waters, her voice husky with desire. "When, Lord? When will you release me?"

She held her breath, not expecting an answer.

The Oracle throbbed with Darkness. A deep voice rumbled in her mind, *"Not yet. You are my Dark Huntress, groomed for the kill. Watch and prepare. Each of my servants has their appointed task. All will be needed for the coming war."*

The Priestess bowed her head in acceptance, but plans churned in the back of her mind. She was eager for her chance at immortality.

The voice of the Dark Lord boomed within her mind. *"Look to the night sky. Behold the sign of my coming!"*

Breaking her gaze from the Oracle, she looked toward the stars. A red comet tore a bloody gash across the heavens, a sign of the Dark Lord's ascendancy. A hungry eagerness thrummed through her. The Priestess whispered a fervent prayer, "May the Dark Lord's pleasure reign...over all the lands of Erdhe."

1

Katherine

A stubborn sun skulked above the snow-capped mountains. Kath trudged along the narrow path, bone-weary, feeling as if the very sun mocked her. It seemed an eon since this morning, so much had changed. Despite the bloody sun at dawn, the sky had turned a crystal blue. On such a clear day, Kath could see forever, yet the way forward had never been so treacherous. She threw a weary glance aloft. Even in the light of day, the comet was visible, a scorching red scar across the vaulted blue, proof the nightmare was real. Kath gripped her sword hilt and made the hand sign against evil. She'd come to the monastery for answers and now she followed death.

The funeral procession wound its way up the south face of the mountain. Such a long way to come for a burial, but Kath and her companions kept their silence, their breath frosting to white plumes in the harsh mountain air. Four blue-robed monks carried the body on a narrow litter while Master Rizel led the mourners in death's wake. Kath's gaze followed the body. Stripped of armor, surcoat and sword, the body was wrapped in a white winding sheet and bound to the litter. Borne aloft, it looked like a snow moth's chrysalis, like something waiting to be born instead of buried. Kath shivered at the strangeness of the thought.

A stone skittered off the ledge, falling to oblivion.

Death changed everything.

The monastery was supposed to be a haven not a trap. Kath wondered if the gods even cared. She trailed a hand along the rock face, trying to avoid the ice, but her gaze kept flicking to the heavens. The comet haunted her. She gripped the crystal dagger sheathed at her belt. After escaping the Mist, she'd sworn to carry it always, but a dagger seemed a feeble weapon against a thousand-year-old evil. Memories from the Mist assailed her mind, the battlefield strewn with corpses, and all the dead wore maroon. Somehow she had to warn Castlegard...to warn the king. She wondered if he'd listen. The knights scorned prophecy...and the messenger alone might doom the message. Her lord father was never one to heed the words of a daughter, especially a daughter who'd disobeyed. The thought opened a chasm in her mind. Willfulness in a son might win praise from the king, but never in a daughter. The distaff gender could be such a curse, but she had to make him listen, especially with so much at stake. Her boots slipped on ice.

Kath fell hard, sliding toward the precipice. She flailed for a hold.

A strong hand caught her arm. "Steady."

Duncan lifted her to her feet, holding her till her boots found purchase. For half a heartbeat, she leaned into his strength. Regaining her footing, she flashed him a grateful smile. "My thanks," but the words were swallowed by the wind.

Duncan leaned close, his one-eyed gaze intense. "Tread your own path. You will find a way."

Her breath caught, as if he'd heard the worries plaguing her mind. *"How?"*

"Your gaze follows the comet instead of the trail. Beware the danger close at hand."

Her face flamed red. Chagrined, she spared a quick glance for the two knights plodding behind and then turned and trudged up the steep trail, rushing to catch the monks. Skirting the ice, Kath tried to focus on the path, but her mind skittered like a wild horse. She'd asked Master Rizel why the burial was so rushed, but he just gave her a look that brooked no questions. So they followed the monks skyward, passing from the alpine spring of the monastery back into winter's harsh bite. Kath walked with her head bent and her cloak pulled tight against the blistering cold. No one spoke. The small procession remained grief-quiet, nothing but boots crunching on snow. A bitter wind snatched at Kath's long blond hair, obscuring her vision, obscuring the tears that would not flow. The dead deserved grief, but all she felt was anger. She'd liked Sir Cardemir. Liked his ready smile and his honey-smooth voice, a master of sword and lute, a boon traveling companion...but more than that, she owed him a debt for saving Jordan at the glacier. And then she'd found them both felled on the monastery floor. Memories from the morning cut like glass. A bloody dagger and a bloody sword, as if the two friends had fought. *A bold-faced lie!* Anger roared through her. They should have been safe. She should have come sooner.

A cold wind slapped Kath in the face.

She staggered, realizing the path veered away from the mountain. A fist of stone jutted from the mountainside, nothing but snow-capped peaks and empty air waiting beyond. Duncan and the two knights crowded behind. She heard Blaine mutter, "We're not going up that?"

As if in answer, a monk climbed the fist, his blue robes flapping against the gray granite. A rope snaked back down. They used the rope to haul the body up the stony fist. Kath watched in silence, thinking a stone cairn would be so much easier. And then it was her turn to climb. Deep footholds were worn in the rock. *Worn,* not carved. Kath wonder how many thousands of monks had trod this path, more proof the Order took the long view. A cold wind snatched at her cloak, buffeting her against the rock, but Kath clung to the handholds. She reached the top and learned she was wrong. It wasn't a fist of stone, but a flat ledge, like an open hand held palm upwards to the sky. And in the center, chiseled deep in the stone, was a Seeing Eye. Kath shivered, as if she stood exposed to the gods.

The monks set the litter next to the Seeing Eye. Untying the lashings, they moved the shroud-wrapped body directly onto the carving. Kath half expected to see a flash of light or a spark of magic, but nothing happened.

Two monks moved to the far side of the ledge, to a shelf of stone that lay like a thumb along the side of the hand. Inset in the shelf was a long narrow wooden door, the size of a jousting lance. And the color of that door was midnight blue.

The monks opened the door and removed a horn, but it was like no horn Kath had ever seen. Long and tapered like a lance, the copper horn was ringed in silver, narrow at one end and flanged to a wide bell-shaped mouth at the other. Runes were etched into the copper, a delicate swirl running the length of the horn. A third monk unrolled a small, tasseled rug on the cold stone hand. The first monk sat cross-legged on the rug, holding the horn's mouthpiece. The second used a small silver chain to suspend the horn's bell out over the stone fingertips, pointing the sound towards oblivion. Kath and her companions watched spellbound, waiting for the voice.

The monk took a deep breath, his cheeks puffed full, and then he blew. A deep-throated drone hummed through the thin mountain air, powerful and otherworldly. Like the voice of a god, Kath felt the sound shake her very bones.

Master Rizel gave her a knowing smile. "Ragdon has a mighty voice." He gestured towards the sky. "The horn calls the eagles."

And then she saw them, great roc eagles, spiraling overhead, their wings spread wider than a man stands tall. Shadows swooped across the open palm, drawing a circle around the dead. "But why..." and then she understood. Her breath gasped in horror, "You'll feed him to the eagles?"

The master watched the soaring wings. "It is a sky burial. It is our way." But then he turned and saw her face. "We do this to honor him. His flesh will soar with eagles, one step closer to the gods, while his bones, his armor, his sword, and his lute will be returned to Lanverness. Sir Cardemir will be honored. He will be remembered."

Kath could only stare, shocked by the barbarity.

The master's gaze narrowed. "Would you rather be food for worms, or eagles?"

His rebuke made Kath reconsider. Put that way, the sky burial made a strange sort of sense. She turned to gaze across the stone palm, out towards the endless jumble of mountains crowned by a vast blue sky. The view was exhilarating, the heavens near enough to touch. A sense of awe flooded her. "I think I understand."

The master gave her a solemn smile. "The gods are near."

The great horn continued its deep-throated drone, her whole body quivering with sound. More eagles gathered overhead, carving majestic circles in the pale blue sky. Master Rizel lifted his hands and began to chant, his deep baritone weaving words around the thrum of the horn. Kath strained to listen, but the words hid their meaning, buried in an ancient tongue. Yet the more she listened, the more she felt a sense of enduring peace, like the balm of the gods. All too soon, the chant ended and the horn fell silent.

Master Rizel turned towards Kath. "It is time to say your farewells."

Kath looked at the others, uncertain what to do.

When no one spoke, the master intervened. "Our customs are strange to you, so I will go first." He turned and offered a deep bow towards the linen-wrapped body. "Sir Cardemir, we thank you for the words of your queen. Know that they will be answered in a way that matters." He bowed a second time. "We ask for your pardon. Our monastery should have been a sanctuary not a threat. The Kiralynn monks honor you for facing the Order's oldest enemy. A debt is owed to you and yours." He bowed a third time. "Go in peace to meet the Lords of Light."

The master retreated. Kath looked to the others. Sir Tyrone gave her a solemn nod and then stepped forward, his maroon cloak snapping like a banner in the wind. The black knight's voice was steady and sure. "Sir Cardemir, I thank you for the gift of your music, and the way your lute made the leagues pass. You will be missed."

Sir Blaine went second. He hesitated, as if uncertain what to say, but then he unsheathed his blue steel sword. Raising the gleaming blade to the heavens, he said, "I sparred with you on the way south and learned the worth of your sword despite the noise of your lute. Valin will claim you as one of his own, a warrior in life and in death." Saluting the body, he sheathed his sword.

Kath thought Duncan would go next, but when the archer made no move, she realized it was her turn. Stepping forward, she stared at the shroud-wrapped body. Stripped of his armor and his seahorse surcoat, Sir Cardemir seemed diminished by death...but Kath swore his deeds would not be forgotten. "I too thank you for your music. But most of all, I thank you for saving my sword sister at the glacier." Thinking of Jordan, a single tear escaped her eye, but then an image of the bloody dagger assaulted her mind. Her voice hardened, "and whatever evil befell you in the monastery, *I will not believe the lie.*" Kath shook with conviction, staring at the dead.

Duncan put a warm hand on her shoulder. She gave the archer a heartfelt look and then retreated. Duncan took her place, standing before the dead. For a dozen heartbeats he remained statue-still, black leathers beneath a wolf-skin cloak, the wind tugging at his long dark hair. Eventually he spoke, his voice gruff, "Jordan was mine to protect. I thank you for the mountain pass but I question the monastery hallways." His voice dropped to a hoarse whisper and Kath strained to hear. "But either way, you remind us to drink deep, for life is all too often cut short." He turned and flashed Kath a look that she could not fathom, but then his face closed and he strode to confront Master Rizel. "We've honored the dead; now take us to the living."

Sorrow creased the master's sun-weathered face. "Her wounds were grievous, so close to death."

A savage anger flared on the archer's face. "You said your healers would save her."

Kath's breath caught, afraid to hear the answer.

"I said, our healers would do all they can." The master glanced toward the pale sun skimming the mountaintops and then back to Duncan. "They've had time enough to try. Come. We've honored the dead. Let us return to the monastery."

Numb from the cold, and battered by the events of the day, Kath followed the master back down the rock face. Behind them, the horn resumed its deep-throated sound, mourning the seahorse knight, but Kath refused to think about death. She pressed for speed, needing to know if Jordan still lived.

2

Liandra

Threats crackled the air like summer lightning. Liandra, the sovereign queen of Lanverness, sat at the casement window in the Queen's Tower, alone in the eye of the storm. Death stalked her, a queen's intuition, yet even at this late hour, Liandra was unsure from whose hand the blow would come. Through a stroke of good fortune she'd learned of the Red Horns' plot to steal her crown and put a king on the Rose Throne but the identity of the traitors remained undiscovered. To tease the Red Horns into the open she'd taken the risk of sending Prince Stewart along with her most trusted squad of the army to a distant corner of the kingdom...leaving her crown exposed as bait. It was now, when her throne was most vulnerable, that the Red Horns would strike.

She needed more information. The Rose Court swirled with political intrigue, much of it of her own making. She'd spun a number of webs, but she had yet to catch her intended prey. While her webs remained empty her throne was vulnerable.

A sharp knock interrupted her thoughts. With a nod she gave the page permission to respond.

The Master Archivist, a tall gray-haired man dressed in dour robes of black, entered the chamber and bowed low. The queen acknowledged her shadowmaster with a brief smile, the one man in the Rose Court whose intelligence and cunning nearly matched her own.

"Pardon your majesty, but there is someone here you should see."

His excessive formality set off alarm bells in the queen's mind yet her face remained impassive. With a regal wave she gave the master permission to continue.

He glanced pointedly at the page.

The queen dismissed the page, gaining a prudent privacy.

The master stepped close. "One of your loyal subjects has uncovered a plot against the crown. I think it best you hear the details."

Liandra kept the hope from her voice, "Do the details provide a trail to the source?"

The master frowned, his dark eyes troubled. "It deepens the complexity of the plot."

A fist of anxiety tightened within her; the leader of the Red Horns was too clever by half. "Perhaps complexity will be his undoing." When her spymaster did not respond, the queen asked, "Who is this citizen who sees plots?"

"A goldsmith, your majesty. Master Saddler to be exact, the same goldsmith who designed your majesty's Royal Ruby necklace."

Intrigued, she raised an eyebrow asking for more.

"He approached one of my deputies begging an audience. The deputy was wise enough to bring the artisan to my attention. The man awaits your pleasure. I think it best you hear his tale."

Schooled in the ways of remembering faces, the queen recalled the short stout goldsmith who had so admirably fulfilled the royal commission regarding the dark red rubies. Master Saddler was a fine craftsman and now it seemed an even better citizen. Having remembered the man, Liandra wondered how a simple goldsmith could uncover a plot that her own shadowmen had not detected. It seemed unlikely but not unwelcome; chance favored the nimble player. Determined to steal advantage from the opportunity, the queen rose from the window seat and moved to sit in the wood-carved throne. Ever mindful of her image, she arranged the folds of her beaded silk gown before nodding to her shadowmaster.

The master opened the door and ushered the short heavyset man into the queen's presence. "May I present Master Saddler, a goldsmith and loyal citizen of Lanverness."

Dressed in a green velvet jacket brushed to a shine, the stout goldsmith bowed his way across the floor. His final bow left him peering at the hem of her gown.

"You may rise."

The goldsmith straightened but did not speak.

The queen took note of the fine sheen of sweat coating the goldsmith's balding pate; the man feared to be the bearer of grim tidings. Knowing that truth seldom flourished under a cloak of fear, the queen chose a warm, regal voice to welcome the goldsmith. "We are pleased to see you, Master Saddler. We remember your excellent work on our Royal Rubies. Your craftsmanship transformed the dark gemstones into the prevailing fashion of the court. We thank you again for your service to the crown."

The goldsmith flushed with pleasure, giving the queen a deep bow.

Having put the man at ease, the queen turned to the heart of the matter. "Now it appears that you have come to serve the crown a second time. We are told you have knowledge of a plot against the Rose Throne. We are keen to hear your news."

The goldsmith swallowed, visibly gathering his courage. "I beg pardon for bringing this to your majesty's attention, but it's something a goldsmith would notice before all others. At least I haven't heard any rumors in the marketplace, so there may still be time." Shrugging, he said, "Best if I just show you." Fumbling at his waistcoat he produced two gold coins and handed them to the queen.

Puzzled, the queen examined the coins. Both bore the twin roses of Lanverness on one side and a likeness of the queen on the other. Turning the coins, Liandra detected no discernible flaw. She checked the rims for illegal shavings but the edges were clean and uncut. The two coins appeared to be like any other coins of the realm...but then she noticed the subtle difference. Her breath caught in her throat. Liandra willed her face to remain still. Her gaze slipped toward the Master Archivist. Her spymaster's normally opaque eyes flashed with anger, confirming that he understood the magnitude of the threat. Not only was Lanverness at risk but the plot threatened the stability of all the southern kingdoms. Wearing a mask of calm, the queen turned her penetrating gaze toward the goldsmith. "Where did you get this?"

The stout man took a step backward as if avoiding an onslaught. In a fearful voice he said, "S-so...you see the d-difference. The two coins bear the same face, yet one is pure while the other is tainted." The goldsmith took a labored breath. "I came across the first in a pub, the Green Briar, and then I began to notice more. I melted one down in my shop. One part in twenty is silver, causing only a slight dilution of the gold color. It is enough to devalue the coin without being blatantly obvious. But once you know what to look for, the muted color cannot be missed." The goldsmith fell silent, a mixture of fear and pleading on his face.

In a level voice the queen asked, "To the best of your knowledge, have any others seen this difference?"

Trembling, the stout man cast his gaze to the floor and muttered, "I am ashamed to say that m-most of the other m-members of my guild have noticed. They plan to keep the knowledge to t-themselves, hoarding the true coins while using the diluted coins to pay their accounts. They seek to gain an extra measure of profit by knowing the difference."

The queen sat back in her throne, stunned by the magnitude of the plot. Destroy the people's faith in coins and the kingdoms would be driven back into barter. Debts would cause disputes. Chaos and suspicion could lead to war. The Rose Crown might even be blamed, yet one honest man had seen the danger and dared to speak up in the hope of making a difference. It was amazing how great events could sometimes turn on the decisions of a single soul. Perhaps the warning came early enough to turn the tide. Liandra prayed for it to be so. "Master Saddler, you have done the realm and the crown a great benefit by warning us of this threat. The kingdom of Lanverness is well served by loyal citizens of your honesty. We will see you suitably rewarded once the threat is averted. In the meantime, we need you to work in the service of the crown."

"*Me?*" The goldsmith's eyes widened. "But I am only an artisan..."

The queen gave the goldsmith a beguiling smile. "You are the best of our citizens, an honest man."

The goldsmith flushed crimson.

"We would keep such honest men in our service."

The stout goldsmith fell to his knee. "I am yours to command."

The queen reached out and tapped him on both shoulders as if anointing a fresh-sworn knight. "Your fealty is accepted." Having bound the man to her service, the queen said, "Now rise, Master Saddler, for we have much to discuss." Liandra waited till he gained his feet. "We have a royal commission for our most honest servant. We command you to do the opposite of those in your guild." Seeing the puzzlement on his face she explained, "You will hoard the diluted coins, exchanging them for coins of solid gold. It is imperative that the false coins be taken out of circulation, before the common people take notice of the difference. We would have you approach the guild and enlist their aid in quietly gathering the diluted coins. Assuming that the guild works in total secrecy, the crown will exchange seven coins of solid gold for every five that are tainted. If the dilution factor is as you say, then the exchange represents a profit of nearly fifty percent." She paused to let the goldsmith consider the magnitude of the reward.

His eyes grew wide. "A very generous offer, your majesty."

"We expect to be well served by the profit. You and your guild must work with the utmost secrecy. Panic in the marketplace will benefit no honest merchant or citizen of Lanverness." She lowered her voice. "Panic will terminate our royal offer...and those who hold the coins will be the poorer." She studied the goldsmith. "Do you agree?"

He blanched pale. "Hard but fair." His face turned thoughtful, "But the guild won't believe me."

"You shall have our royal writ to convince them...in exchange for an oath of secrecy. Breaking the oath will be considered treason and we are not in the mood to extend clemency to traitors. Are we understood?"

The goldsmith swallowed. "Y-yes, your majesty. The guild knows how to keep a secret."

"See that they do." Adding a touch of gracious warmth to her voice, she said, "You have done well in bringing this scheme to our attention. Foil the plot and we shall see that you are richly rewarded. We would have men of your honesty elevated to the Peerage."

A gasp escaped the goldsmith, a stunned look on his face.

"The Rose Crown rewards those who are loyal. We value honesty in our court."

The goldsmith straightened, his face flushed with pride.

The queen extended her ringed hand. "You are dismissed with our thanks. The Master Archivist will see to the drafting of the writ and the administration of the oath. Go with our thanks."

Bowing, he reverently kissed her emerald ring of office. With a dazed look, he followed the master from the chamber.

The queen sat wrapped in stillness, her mind plumbing the depths of the plot. Instead of unveiling the identity of the Red Horns, the dire news only served to deepen the complexity. The dilution of the coins had to be linked to the Red Horns. Such a devious plot was worthy of her adversary. With one fell stroke the traitors harvested gold from her royal treasury to fund their rebellion while threatening economic ruin across the realm. Simple yet elegant, the plot had far reaching consequences. Liandra seethed at the threat. Building the prosperity of Lanverness had been her lifelong goal. Everything she'd achieved could be undone by a single plot. Rage boiled within her. The threat had to be contained and the mastermind brought to the scaffold. It was time to end this treason.

The door to her solar opened to admit the Master Archivist. The fact that he had not knocked indicated the depth of her counselor's unease.

"My deepest apologies, majesty, for not having seen the plot myself."

"We were both looking elsewhere. Your shadowmen watch for people not coins. Now it appears they must look for both. Our resources will be stretched thin but it must be done." The queen stabbed at the heart of the problem. "Clearly the royal treasury is compromised."

"Do you suspect Lord Wesley?"

"No, our Lord Treasurer does not have the imagination or the subtlety for this plot."

"I concur." Lowering his voice, the master said, "The question now is whether to act on the knowledge and tip our hand to the Red Horns or to wait until we know the traitors' identity."

In a grave voice, the queen said, "There is nothing to debate. This plot goes beyond the threat to our throne. Lanverness provides the coinage for all the southern kingdoms. Should word of the false coins spread, it will spark panic and chaos across all of Erdhe. War and economic ruin are the surest outcomes." Shaking her head, the queen said, "We must nip this plot in the bud, even at the risk of our crown."

The master's voice showed rare emotion. "You dare not take the risk!"

"The leader of the Red Horns has called our bluff. We must act before panic spreads across the kingdoms."

The master grimaced, "Then we must stop the mint in a way that does not alert the Red Horns."

Fingering the strand of pearls at her neck, the queen said, "We must act without seeming to act."

Nodding, the master crossed his arms, his brow furrowed in thought, a pillar of shadow anchored to the center of her solar. Tugging on his thin gray mustache, he said, "I can think of only two ways to halt the production of the false coins. The first is to commission a new die for the royal coins, one with an updated visage of the sovereign. The minting of coins could be halted until the new die is cast." Lowering his voice, he added, "The second solution is less eloquent. Assuming that those who work in making the false coins are equally guilty of treason, my shadowmen could arrange for 'accidents' to occur in the mint. Working with molten metal is very dangerous. The workmen could be replaced with men more loyal to the crown, ensuring the production of pure coins."

The queen gave her spymaster a sharp glance. "We will not loose assassins against our own people."

Her spymaster had the grace to blanch at the rebuke.

The queen stared into the hearth. "But suddenly announcing the commission of a new die is too blatant. The Red Horns would spring their trap before we are ready." She shook her head. "We must hide our actions beneath subterfuge. Halting work in the mint must be blamed on chance and happenstance rather than calculated design." The queen paused in thought, considering her own words.

Lightning cracked outside the casement window, startling both the queen and her advisor. A storm raced across the spring sky, dark clouds on the horizon.

The queen stared at the open window, considering the inclement weather. "We need a fire in the heart of the mint, a fire that is caused by accident rather than a deliberate hand. Something fierce enough to put the mint out of commission until the plot of the Red Horns is foiled." Gesturing toward the window, the queen said, "A lightning storm could provide the perfect spark for the blaze...assuming it strikes the proper place." The queen stared at her spymaster. "The sooner the minting of the false coins is stopped the better."

Bowing, the master said, "It shall be as you command. In the meantime, my shadowmen will keep a close watch on those who work within the mint. Perhaps they will lead us to the Red Horns."

"Pray that something leads us to our enemies. Time grows short and the leader of the Red Horns has proven to be a most cunning adversary. It is past time your shadowmen found the clues needed to unmask this traitor."

"I shall do my best." The master bowed. "With your majesty's permission, I shall see to your 'lightning bolt'."

The door clicked shut and the queen sat in silence, the spring storm thundering outside her window. Unclenching her hands, she stared down at the mismatched coins. The motive for the false coins screamed of avarice but Liandra sensed an underlying stench of Darkness. Her opponent was both dangerous and cunning, but this plot reached beyond a single kingdom, threatening chaos on a grand scale. Staring at the coins she realized her opponent was more than dangerous...he was evil, as if she faced the Dark Lord himself.

Outside the casement window, lightning cracked across the evening sky as if to confirm the queen's suspicions.

3

Justin

The sun was warm and bright and half way across a brilliant spring sky, too fair a day for murder. Justin kept his face composed, guarding his thoughts, following the crowd through narrow cobblestone streets. He'd heard the refugees' horror-filled tales so many times that he knew them by heart, but now that he was in Coronth, he had to see the worst for himself. He couldn't put it off any longer.

Clad in an emerald-green jacket accented with faux gold piping and matching hose, he wore the gaudy plumage expected of minstrels, but the fabric was poor, even threadbare at one elbow, all part of the disguise. The prince hid in plain sight, just a poor struggling minstrel, trying to earn a living and advance his craft. The threadbare garments disguised his royal lineage, his skill with the harp hiding his intent to topple a false religion. He laughed at himself but the sound held little mirth. He expected a lot from music, but he believed in his craft...and in the justice of his cause.

The street grew crowded, citizens pouring out of houses, stores, and taverns, heeding the call of the priests. Justin joined the crowd, a short, plain-faced man in a sea of many, following the human tide toward the city's ash-filled heart. He was a stranger to Balor, but no one gave him a second look.

Minstrels and bards were welcome across the kingdoms of Erdhe, even in the Flame God's city. To the common people, bards meant music to cheer the soul and ease the chill of life, harp and song, lute and lyre. But there was more to being a bard than just playing songs. A secret throbbed at the heart of his craft, a secret that turned a mere musician into a true bard. All great bards were witnesses, first, foremost, and always. Witnessing life, and sometimes death, bards studied commoners as well as lords, searching for the pivotal moments that mattered most, moments that brought a tear to the eye or hope to the heart. Life was the secret ingredient true bards wove into their songs, the secret that made each listener feel the song was meant for them alone. Life was the magic that made a soul resonate with melody, a heart beat to the rhythm, or a mind soar to the lyrics. It was past time Justin witnessed the ritual that beat at the heart of the Flame God's religion. He'd come to witness the Test of Faith.

For two weeks he'd avoided the ritual, exploring instead the cobblestone streets and back alleyways of Balor, spending as much time in the rich sections as the poor. He took short engagements playing his harp in taverns where the patrons paid in coppers not golds. He strummed his small harp and sang popular, well-known tunes, always playing to observe never to influence or impress. His craft served him well, letting him play in all the city's taverns, just a middling minstrel trying to earn a meal. He made contacts and earned a few coins, but mostly he learned about life in Balor.

What he learned chilled him to the bone.

Balor was flush with the faithful, the chosen, the beloved of the Flame God. They carried themselves with a righteous confidence he'd rarely seen outside of royalty. More than arrogance, it was almost a feeling of invincibility, as if the Flame God himself intervened on their behalf. The faithful of Coronth believed they deserved everything and that nothing was beyond their grasp. It was a dangerous combination, reinforced by the rabid rantings of the red-robed priests.

It was the perfect combination for a holy war.

Chilled by his observations, Justin explored the city, searching for an antidote to the Flame God. Just as the refugees had said, he discovered another side to Coronth, a side that lurked in the shadows fearing to be seen. Most hid in the alleyways and the poor quarters of the city, but others tried to mingle with the faithful. They ate in taverns, worked in shops, and some even attended temple services, but to a bard's knowing stare their eyes always gave them away. At best their eyes were dull, annealed to the dangers around them. At worst their eyes were haunted, reflecting the cruelties of the Flame God. Justin kept a lookout for the ones who lived on the fringe, making note of the taverns and taprooms where they dared to be seen. When the time was right, he hoped to rouse them with his music and change Coronth from within. But first he needed to witness the worst of their fears.

The pace of the crowd increased, eagerness flashing through faithful like summer lightning, spreading an infectious excitement. They pressed against him, rich and poor, old and young, a relentless tide of people sweeping him toward the temple square. Justin angled sideways, moving with the flow but trying to stay on the edge. He didn't want to get too close to the flame pit. In truth, he didn't know if he could stomach watching such a gruesome death. Besides, he'd come to observe the crowd as much as the ritual, a place at the back would do just fine.

Breaking away from main stream, he made his way to a stone wall on the north side of the square. Others had the same idea, already sitting perched along the top. Justin flashed a smile, plying a bard's charm. "Is there room for one more?"

His minstrel's garb earned him more than one welcoming smile. A large, beefy man with a callused grip offered a hand up. Justin accepted, taking a seat perched between the man and a matronly woman holding a fidgeting boy on her lap. The presence of the youngster bothered Justin, but he buried his concern beneath a voice pleasant. "Your son, madam?"

The woman blushed like a maid. "Oh no, 'tis my grandson, Simon, and a right fine lad he is."

"He's lucky to have his grandmother's eyes."

The woman's blush deepened, her dimpled smile hinting at younger days of beauty.

Justin risked his question, keeping his voice light. "Does Simon often come with you to the Test of Faith?"

"Oh by heaven, yes! The good priests say the young ones need ta see the miracle for themselves." Pride filled her voice. "Only in Balor, the Flame God's own city, can ya see the true miracle of the Test of Faith." She gave him a knowing nod. "We're blessed ya know, truly blessed by the presence of the Flame Priest." The woman wrapped her arms around her grandson, a pious smile confirming her beliefs.

Justin wondered how long her beliefs would hold if one of her loved ones was condemned to the flames...but he hid his thoughts behind a polite smile, now was not the time.

The drums of the temple began a rhythmic pounding, a monstrous heartbeat thundering through the square. The crowd stilled to a hush. Expectant faces turned toward the temple doors, bodies swaying to the rhythm of the drums.

The brass doors opened, disgorging a procession of red-robed priests. Incense burners swayed as they walked, spewing clouds of holy smoke. The double line of priests snaked through the crowd, making the sign of blessing while chanting, "Feed the Flames...Feed the Flames."

The crowd took up the chant, the words throbbing through the square. "*Feed the Flames! Feed the Flames!*"

Justin watched, appalled by the intent, but awed by the showmanship. The audience was primed, ready for the main players.

A large man appeared on the temple steps, a burly priest draped in rich red robes, holding a flaming torch aloft. From Samson's description, this had to be the Keeper of the Flame. Justin studied the high priest. A square jaw, a smooth-shaved head, a thin slash for a mouth, he carried the massive torch with ease, prowling through the crowd with a brawler's muscle-bound stride. The Keeper was physically intimidating, an enforcer of the faith, but Justin knew this man could never mesmerize a crowd; the master puppeteer had yet to make an appearance.

The Keeper made his way to the charcoal pit and lowered the torch.

Fire erupted from the pit, sucking air like the inhalation of a dragon. Flames roared skyward, five times the height of a tall man. The faithful nearest the pit pushed back, retreating from the pulsing heat.

The temple drums stilled.

Expectation seethed through the crowd, every face turned towards the temple.

The great brass doors swung open. A single figure emerged. Tall and stately, with long white hair and a flowing beard, the patriarch stood arrayed in robes of gold, an enormous red ruby sparkling at his breast. His robes caught the sunlight, the gold cloth competing with the brilliance of the flames, creating a dazzling vision. Justin leaned forward; so this was the Pontifax, the showman who came to mesmerize a kingdom.

The Pontifax descended the temple steps making the sign of blessing. He moved with a stately dignity, benevolence shining from his face.

The crowd fell to its knees as the Pontifax passed. Adoring followers reached out to touch the hem of his robe. Mothers held their children up, hoping for a special blessing. Women swooned as he passed. The puppet master had arrived.

The Pontifax took his time, working the crowd. He wound his way to the fire pit and then climbed the dais, gaining a vantage above a sea of heads. Spreading his arms wide in blessing, his voice carried to the farthest corner of the square. "My people! We come here in humility to worship our beloved Flame God! Feel his boundless love wash across each of you! Feel his love pulse like the heat of a flame! Know that you are all worthy."

Justin reeled backwards, almost falling from the wall. The man had the voice of a bard! But he used the gift to subvert, to deceive, to enslave. Justin gripped the wall, fingernails scrapping against stone, appalled by the corruption of his craft. He took a steadying breath, struggling to keep his face composed. Closing his eyes, he blocked out the charlatan's words, focusing on the voice instead, studying the rhythm, the pitch, the cadence...the undertones of deceit. The voice was rich and complex, the pitch perfect, the cadence seductive...but there was something not quite right. Justin strained to listen. The voice changed from seductive to strident revealing a subtle flaw; the transitions were slightly off, not as smooth as they could be, leaching some of the power from the oratory. Justin shook his head, amazement mingling with relief. The man had the gift but he wasn't bard trained. Justin opened his eyes to study his adversary. The Flame Priest played his part well. The benevolence of his face reinforced the power of his voice, while the richness of his robes lent him a royal authority. The Pontifax was a consummate showman, a master of religious seduction.

A commotion on the edge of the crowd drew Justin's attention. A flatbed wagon surrounded by a small troop of soldiers trundled into the square. A figure in white was chained to the stocks mounted on the wagon bed. Justin's jaw dropped. *A woman!* They were going to burn a woman!

Justin glanced at his neighbors, expecting to see his own horror reflected in their eyes...but what he saw sickened him. They leered at the woman with a fascination bordering on naked lust.

An elbow jabbed Justin in his ribs. The man beside him leaned close, his voice rich with triumph. "I know this one!" He winked, a conspirator sharing a secret. "My cousin's in the priesthood." He pointed toward the chained captive. "This one's a prostitute! She refused to share her bed with a priest!" He barked a laugh. "Imagine, a prostitute refusing a priest! Now she'll get what she deserves!" He raised his voice to a yell. *"Burn, sinner, burn!"*

Justin stared at the man, stunned as much by his cruelty as his twisted logic. *A priest and a prostitute...virtue where you'd least expect it.* Justin looked away lest his eyes betray him. He sent a silent prayer to the Lords of Light, wishing there was a way to save the woman.

Murmurs rippled through the crowd, drawing Justin's attention back to the heart of the ritual.

The Pontifax knelt by the flames, an acolyte removing his gilded sandals.

Justin leaned forward, needing a better view. Samson had told him about the miracle of the Test of Faith, but there had to be a trick, an illusion, some grand sleight of hand. He studied the charlatan, determined to uncover his secret.

Barefoot, the Pontifax stood before the bonfire, his face solemn. The flames snapped and crackled, towering into the afternoon sky, an inferno of heat beating against the faithful. A hush fell over the crowd. The Pontifax gripped the ruby at his breast and marched into the flames.

Justin stared slack-mouthed. *He walked into the inferno!* If there was a trick, he could not see it.

The flames enfolded the Pontifax, turning bright crimson surrounded by gold.

Beside Justin, the matron cried, "It's a sign! A sign of his blessedness!"

Minutes passed. The Pontifax walked the length of the fire pit, immune to the blaze. He emerged on the far side, unscathed, not a hair on his head singed. Women swooned at his feet. Men reached out to touch the hem of his robe. The crowd celebrated the miracle, an electric tension in the air.

Justin shook his head in denial. He refused to believe that this charlatan had the divine favor of a god. A cold thought gripped him. If a god meddled in Coronth, it had to be the Dark Lord of hell. Only the Dark Lord would pervert worship into human sacrifice. Justin shook his head in denial, but then he had another thought. If not a god, then it must be magic! But this brazen display was unlike any he'd ever heard of, an abomination, an obscene perversion of power. As a prince of Navarre, Justin was no stranger to magic, but the magic of Navarre was both secret and subtle, allowing the queens of Seaside to give safe birth to the tuplets required for the royal succession. The Test of Faith *had* to be magic. Justin studied the Pontifax. Somehow he'd find away to discredit this charlatan and free the people of their religious delusion.

A chant rippled through the crowd. *"The Sinner! The Sinner!"*

Bile rose in the back of his throat.

Soldiers dragged the woman from the wagon.

Understanding struck Justin like a hammer blow; the woman was the proof, proof of the potency of the flames! So clever and yet so evil, he wondered how many innocents had died to further the charade.

The soldiers prodded the woman towards the flames. She screamed for mercy, beseeching the people around her, but the crowd slavered for the kill. Justin did not want to watch...but he was a bard, a witness of life and of death. He stilled his face to a mask, determined to give the woman his best.

The captive sagged in the arms of the soldiers, dragging her feet, tears cascading down her face. The crowd enjoyed the show, clamoring for her death. Soldiers passed the dark-haired woman between them, half carrying her towards the flames. She screamed and writhed to no avail. A soldier thrust her into the flames, while the others prodded her with spears.

A hideous scream ripped through the temple square.

Her dark hair caught fire, a banshee screaming in the flames.

Justin looked away, turning his gaze on the crowd, measuring the depth of their depravity. The faithful capered around the fire pit, drunk on the spectacle of death, their faces twisted in religious ecstasy. Their reaction sickened him; he wondered if Coronth could be saved. The whole city deserved be put to the torch, but then he remembered the victim, a prostitute who had dared reject a priest. He had to find the ones worth saving.

A breeze blew through the square, catching the dark smoke billowing from the pit. Greasy and black, the smoke blew his way. Justin gagged. Bile pushed at the back of his throat, betraying his true feelings. He had to get out of the square or the faithful might claim a second victim. Jumping from the wall, he pushed his way through the frenzied crush. Holding his cloak to his face, he tried to filter out the stench, but the reek of roast flesh was everywhere, in his clothes, in his hair, in his nostrils. A wave of nausea ripped through him, but he fought it down.

He staggered out of the celebrating masses, retreating down an empty side street. Gulping fresh air, he got as far as the first corner before his stomach gave out. Gripped by convulsions, he bent double, heaving his breakfast onto the street. Images of the woman's death lashed at his mind, prodding his stomach to a second upheaval.

A man's voice intruded. "You must be new here, minstrel." Smooth and confident, the man's voice carried an undercurrent of power.

The voice sent a shiver of warning down Justin's spine. He caught a glimpse of expensive boots polished to a mirror shine. Swallowing, Justin straightened, struggling to regain a mask of composure.

The boots belonged to a tall, dashing nobleman in a long black cape, a silver-tipped walking stick in his right hand. Justin lifted his gaze to meet the man's stare. Coal black hair framed an aristocratic face, a hawk nose, a generous mouth and thick black eyebrows. A single lock of white hair at his temple added a touch of distinction to a handsome face. The man's smile exuded charm but his slate-gray eyes were dark and fathomless, menace cloaked in elegance.

Justin bobbed his head in homage, keeping his voice subservient. "I'm new to the city, m'Lord. Just a minstrel looking for an honest living." He stole a glance toward the emblem blazoned on the man's cape. *A black raven on a field of red.* Fear spiked through him, so this was the Lord Raven, the counselor to the Pontifax. Justin held his breath and kept his head bent, hoping the man would pass him by.

"Your first Test of Faith?" The voice was casual but the stare was keen.

Justin bowed. "Yes, m'Lord." He fell silent, praying to escape.

"And what do you think of our ritual?"

Drawing on his bard's training, Justin widened his eyes and infused his voice with awe. "A true miracle, m'Lord! I saw it with my own eyes! The Pontifax walked through the heart of the flames! Not a singe to his hair! Not a smudge to his robes." He lowered his voice and threw an earnest glance at the man. "It's what I came for Lord, a chance to set the miracle to song! To craft a ballad so others will believe the truth." He added a touch of avarice to his argument. "A ballad that will line my pockets with gold!"

The Lord Raven's stare narrowed, his hand gesturing toward the mess spewed on the ground. "And what of your breakfast? Minstrels are said to have silver tongues, perhaps the truth lies exposed on the cobbles?"

A fist of fear tightened in Justin's stomach. He dropped his gaze and tried to look chagrinned, hiding behind a mask of embarrassment. "T-the smoke, Lord. The wind shifted and I got caught in the brunt of it...I couldn't stomach the smell. I've always had a weak stomach."

Feeling the man's hard scrutiny, Justin kept his gaze on the ground, just a harmless minstrel beneath the notice of a wealthy Lord.

"Minstrels always have a favorite instrument, what's yours?"

"The small harp, m'Lord."

"Show me your hands."

The command brooked no argument. Justin held his hands out, palms up. The Lord Raven knew what to look for. He ran his fingertips across Justin's thumbs and the tips of his first two fingers searching for the ridged calluses that all harpers carry as a legacy of their music. Justin had earned the calluses before the age of ten; his hands confirmed his story, proving the value of hiding behind the truth.

A flicker of disappointment flashed in the lord's gray eyes. "So you've come to raise a ballad about the Test of Faith?"

"Yes, m'Lord."

"Minstrels are always welcome in the Flame God's city. Sing well, harper, and help us spread the true faith." His velvet voice lowered a notch. "But make sure you sing the right tune...or you'll find yourself fed to the flames."

Justin kept still, a hare hiding from the hawk.

"As to the smoke, well, sinners always smell like roast pork." He chuckled. "Just a hearty serving of spit-roasted pork."

The Lord Raven made a dismissive gesture and then turned and sauntered down the street, an elegant darkness gliding through the Flame God's city. A shudder ran down Justin's spine. Beneath his cloak, he made the hand sign against evil, watching as the Lord Raven turned the corner. Alone again, he leaned against the wall, his face slick with sweat. Justin thought he understood the Pontifax, but the Lord Raven was something else, something worse, a shrewd mind cloaked in a noble's smooth elegance. For the first time, he wondered if music would be enough.

4

Katherine

The journey back down the mountain seemed to take forever. Kath and her companions followed close behind Master Rizel, shuffling down the knife-edged trail. The ice was treacherous, but they were keen for answers. Huddled beneath fur-lined cloaks, no one spoke. From the distant heights, the great horn Ragdon still blared. A shiver raced down Kath's spine, but she refused to think about death, willing her sword sister to live.

They finally reached the base of the trail, only to face one more challenge, the wall of magical Mist. Kath dreaded passing through the Mist, but this time the white proved empty, nothing but cold fog. Perhaps the crystal dagger kept the spirits at bay, or perhaps they had nothing more to say. Either way, she emerged safe from the Mist, surprised to find two blue-robed monks stationed at the monastery gates. Grim-faced and watchful, the monks both bore stout quarterstaffs. *Guards at the gates, so magic is no longer enough.* It seemed an ill omen. Kath gripped her sword hilt, wondering if the gods would help.

Master Rizel coiled the guide rope while Kath and her companions stomped their boots, knocking clods of snow to the ground. Battered by wind and cold and loss, they climbed the hill to the monastery. At a nod from the blue-robed master, the guards eased the great gates open.

They passed between the Seeing Eyes, a swirl of cold air following them inside. After the chill of the mountaintop funeral, the warmth of the monastery was shocking. Heat rose from the golden floors, warm and welcoming, but comfort could not dull Kath's fear. As the others shrugged off their furs, Kath confronted Master Rizel, "We need to see Jordan."

He gave her a solemn nod. "Follow me." The master turned and led them into the depths of the monastery. Their jangle of weapons seemed at odds with the knowledge inscribed on the illuminated walls, but Kath kept her hand on her sword hilt. The beauty of the monastery remained undeniable, every wall a masterpiece of calligraphy, but the feeling of peace was shattered, every shadow filled with threat. Kath half expected to find blood still staining the floor. *The Mordant is reborn and the world is filled with shadows.*

Spatters of snow fell from their cloaks, melting like teardrops on the warm floors. The monastery was a maze, adding to Kath's frustration. Anxious to learn Jordan's fate, she nearly trod on Master Rizel's heels. The master turned and gave her a knowing glance, "Almost there." Descending a long stairway, the air grew thick with the scents of herbs and ointments, the unmistakable smell of a healery. Kath took a deep breath, but if death lurked in the hallway, she could not tell.

The master led them to a small room, an antechamber with gold-colored doors set in every wall. Master Rizel gestured to a row of benches. "Please wait here."

Duncan snarled, "We've waited long enough."

The master raised his hand in a gesture of peace. "I ask you to wait one moment more. You dare not interrupt the healing magic."

The archer gave a terse nod and the master slipped beyond the far door.

Sir Tyrone and Blaine hovered near the outer door, while Kath stood statue-still, numb with worry. She gripped her gargoyle, silently beseeching Valin's aid, watching as Duncan paced the small room. His every step tightened the tension of the chamber till Kath thrummed like a bowstring. The question burst out of her, "Surely they must know something by now?" but her companions had no answer.

The inner door opened and a pudgy healer in midnight-blue robes emerged. He gave them a weary smile. Kath was afraid to hope.

Duncan stopped his pacing. "Will she live?"

The monk sighed, his voice weary. "I need to explain."

"Will she live?" The archer loomed over the portly monk like a thunderstorm threatening to strike.

"I believe so, but I must explain."

Kath sighed, and Sir Tyrone put a steadying hand on her shoulder, but Duncan was relentless. "What do you mean, you believe so?"

"Be at peace." He raised his hands in entreaty. "Nothing is certain, yet there is much to be hoped for." He gestured them towards a bench, but none of the companions sat. "The princess nearly died before she even reached the healery. Master Garth saved her life, but only because of his magic. The cost of such a powerful working is grievous, extracting a heavy toll on the wielder. Healer and healed have both fallen into a deep sleep, a sort of hibernation." Pausing, the monk said,

"Princess Jordan lives but she will not respond to touch or voice. We won't know how well the healing has taken until she wakes."

Duncan hissed. "How long?"

"Given the severity of her wounds...six full turns of the moon or more."

Duncan swore, "By the nine hells! Why so long?"

"She was spared from the very brink of death, but such a great healing takes time." The monk's face softened with sympathy. "If you wish, you may see her now."

They followed the monk through the golden door, into the depths of the healery, to a small windowless chamber. A second monk kept watch over two figures lying in narrow beds along the wall.

Kath gasped when she saw Jordan. So pale, her sword sister looked the same as when she'd found her lying in the corridor, soaked in a pool of her own blood. Ghost-pale and still as death, Jordan looked as if she'd already passed beyond the gray veil. A cold fear gripped Kath. "Is she?" The question clogged in her throat.

"She lives."

Kath stared down. If Jordan still breathed, she could not tell.

Duncan touched Jordan's throat.

The monk whispered, "I assure you, she still lives."

Duncan gave a terse nod. "Thank the gods."

An icy fist released Kath's heart.

The monk approached the bed, his voice soothing. "You must see her wounds to appreciate the magnitude of the healing." He eased back the blanket, revealing an angry v-shaped scar snaking across Jordan's abdomen.

Kath shivered, recognizing a mortal wound, a soldier's worst fear.

Blaine muttered, "A bloody miracle."

"Not a miracle, just magic." The monk replaced the blanket. "When Master Garth uses his focus, the healing is usually so complete that no scar remains. This scar proves how close the princess came to death's door. Had she been found only a moment later, she would have died."

Kath shivered, knowing it was a gift from the gods.

The monk gestured towards the other bed. "Master Garth risked his life to attempt this healing."

An old man with a mane of white hair and a kindly face lay beneath a thick blanket, both hands clutching an amulet on a chain around his neck. Still as death, his face was a mask of peace. Feeling the need to pay her respects, Kath was drawn towards the healer. She owed this monk a debt for saving her sword sister. It was a debt she would not forget. Kath bowed low in homage, "Thank you for saving my sword sister."

Straightening, Kath noticed a swath of bright velvet crumpled on the floor, her sword sister's cloak. Retrieving the cloak, she settled it across Jordan's still form...a fallen warrior lying beneath the battle banner of Navarre. "Heal well, for your sword is still needed."

Behind her, a familiar voice said, "We need to talk."

Kath turned to find Master Rizel standing in the doorway. The blue-robed master had a knack for appearing unannounced. Kath searched his face for answers but the master was too hard to read. It was Duncan who understood, "What word of the attacker?"

A grim look claimed the master's sun-weathered face. "Not here."

Kath glanced toward Jordan and then followed the master to the outer chamber. Her companions crowded close behind like a pack of wolves starving for answers.

Gesturing to the benches, the master said, "Please be seated and I'll try to explain."

None of them sat. Duncan growled, "What's to explain? Have you found the attacker or not?"

The master sighed. "We've sealed the town of Haven and our monks search the mountainside but it is too soon to tell."

Duncan glared, his hands balled into fists. "How did a murderer escape the Mist? I thought your monastery was safe."

"He murdered a Guide and stole an amulet. More was lost this day than you can imagine." The master made a weary sigh, sitting on a bench while the others stood. "Let me explain. To gain admittance to the monastery each of you had to pass a test with a Dahlmar crystal, but you may not have understood the reasons behind it. The greatest servants of the Dark Lord are rewarded with more life. Their life spans are lengthened and when they die, the favored few are reincarnated with full memories of their past lives. These reincarnated evils are called harlequins. Dahlmar crystals are the only known way to detect an Awakened harlequin." The master paused staring at each of them. "Last night, a very ancient evil, the worst of the harlequins, awakened within the walls of the monastery."

Duncan's voice blazed with anger. "By all the gods, how could this happen?"

"Not by all the gods, just one, the Dark Lord." In a patient voice, the master explained, "The evil seed is planted at birth, but the Awakening does not happen until the host is mature. No parent would knowingly raise such an abomination. Instead the seed lies dormant until a time chosen by the Dark Lord. To the best of our knowledge, the

Awakening occurs sometime between the ages of eighteen and twenty-five. We believe the host is an innocent victim, crushed by the older soul." Pausing, he added, "The Dahlmar crystal can only detect a harlequin *after* the Awakening has occurred." A look of sadness cloaked the master's face. "The Dark Lord chose a host who was already within the monastery, an accepted member of our community."

"I saw him."

Her companions turned, pinning her with sword-sharp stares. Kath flamed red. With all the death and confusion, she'd only told Master Rizel. "After I found Jordan and Sir Cardemir, I raced to the outer gates and saw him."

Duncan clutched the dagger sheathed at his belt. "Does this evil have a name?"

A shiver ran through Kath. "His name is Bryce, an acolyte of the monastery...but the Mist said otherwise."

Master Rizel came to her rescue. "He wears the face of Bryce, a healer and an initiate of our Order, but in truth, he is the Mordant Reborn."

Sir Blaine drew his great blue sword, a hiss of steel on leather, but there was no one to attack.

Sir Tyrone asked, "How can this be?"

The master sighed. "The Dark Lord plays a shrewd and terrible game. The Mordant now wears the face of one of our initiates."

Sir Tyrone stared. "One of yours?"

"Yes." The single word held a world of weariness.

Duncan growled, "Will you kill him?"

The master said, "It is not that simple. Only the crystal dagger can truly slay a harlequin."

Kath felt the weight of their stares. She fingered the crystal dagger, the call of duty warring with her sense of justice. "But Bryce wanted to be a healer! And now he walks with Death? The gods are cruel!"

The master whispered, "The gods have their own reasons."

Kath glared at the master, not satisfied with his answer. "And now I'm supposed to kill him?"

"To slay the Mordant, yes, else the visions of the Mist will come to pass."

His words struck a hammer-blow to her heart. The visions haunted her...the death of the Octagon...the death of her father. Her stare dropped to the floor, her hand gripping the crystal dagger.

Sir Tyrone intervened. "Can the Mordant claim the memories of this initiate?"

The master hesitated. "We believe so, yes. And therein lies the greatest danger. With the amulet in his possession, the Mordant can return through the Guardian Mist. For the first time in our long history, the monastery is vulnerable to evil."

Kath whispered, "Beware the Ancient Evil that wakes behind the safest walls."

Master Rizel gave her a keen look.

Kath bit her lip, shocked by the sudden memory. "The gods gave warning but I did not understand." Seeing the look of puzzlement on the master's face, she tried to explain. "On the Isle of Souls, the god, Valin, spoke to me through a fortune teller. Valin told me to beware the Ancient Evil that wakes behind the safest walls." She shook her head, drenched in guilt. "The gods gave warning, but I did not listen!"

Sir Tyrone put a comforting hand on her shoulder. "The message was too cryptic. We both heard the god but neither of us understood enough to heed the warning."

Master Rizel studied her with an eagle's keen gaze. "I am not surprised the god spoke to you. It proves there is more at work here than just Darkness."

Kath's eyes widened. "Then why don't the gods just say so?"

"To give you a choice." His eyes crinkled in wry amusement. "There is always a choice, for it is the very vanguard of the Light."

Duncan growled, "What choice did Jordan have?"

The master answered, "That remains to be seen. I suspect her life was spared for a reason. A reason none here can yet foresee."

Kath swayed on her feet, suddenly felled by a great weariness. The master must have noticed for he offered her a compassionate smile. "You should get to bed. It has been a long and trying day, full of blood and death, warnings and hope."

"Hope?" Duncan shook his head. "I do not see much hope."

"We are forewarned. We know the Mordant's new face. And wherever a few dare to stand in the Light, there is always hope." The monk and the archer traded stares. Kath was surprised when the archer was the first to look away.

Sir Tyrone said, "Come, Jordan lives and there is naught more be done but fall asleep on our feet."

Kath started to turn, but Duncan said, "Wait." He locked stares with the master. "Our sleeping cells are scattered throughout the monastery. From now on, we stay together."

"You don't trust us?"

Duncan replied, "For good reason."

The master gave a terse nod. "Understandable. Adjacent quarters will be found." His crystal-blue stare turned to Kath. "Sleep well, for tomorrow we begin."

Kath met the master's stare, but instead of clarity, she found only endless layers of riddles. "Begin?"

"To defeat the Dark."

Kath's breath caught, feeling the call of destiny.

5

Liandra

The sand grains fell, marking time, prisoners of the hourglass. The queen paced her solar, caged by time and circumstance, searching for another way. Outside her casement window, the moon set on the edge of night, the last darkness before dawn. The time for options had run out. The queen stopped pacing, resolved to the bitter truth. In this most obscure of hours, when honest folk still slept, it was a time for risks and reckonings on a royal scale.

A polite knock heralded the entrance of her ladies-in-waiting. Six women rudely roused from sleep, curtseyed to their queen, their faces full of questions.

Bristling with hard edges, the queen set her women to work. "We'll have the dark green velvet gown, the one worked with seed pearls."

Mouths dropped open and sleep-filled eyes stared in alarm.

Impatient, the queen clapped her hands. "There is no time to dawdle! Attend us!"

Her women scattered like mice, each to their appointed tasks.

The queen sat on the stool before the massive mirror, stern and unmoving. Her ladies-in-waiting circled like bees attending the hive-queen. Each had their appointed duties: tighten the corset, arrange the hair, anoint with perfume, apply the powders, prepare the gown. The women worked at familiar tasks but worried glances darted between them, filling the chamber with anxiety. Questions hung in the air but none were foolish enough to broach them, she'd chosen her women well.

The queen sat stiff and erect, examining every detail of her own reflection. The unforgiving glass showed a face leached by strain, eyes etched deep with shadows, and skin pale and wan, the color of death. Her own face betrayed her. Liandra narrowed her eyes in anger. Pale was a telltale sign of fear. Pale spoke of shock or loss. Pale would never do for a monarch, especially a sovereign queen. Liandra gestured to the mirror. "More rouge." Ever critical, she watched to be sure the color was applied feather-light so as to appear natural instead of painted. Even at this dire hour, the queen would not give up the image she had worked so hard to create. Making the guards wait, Liandra resolutely sat before the mirror until the reflection equaled her ideal of a sovereign queen.

Powders and paints covered much, but the queen could still see the strain beneath the facade. Never-the-less her women had done their best. Her royal regalia would have to do the rest. Liandra gestured toward the ironbound casket. "Lady Sarah, our jewels."

Her senior lady-in-waiting sputtered, "B-but your majesty!" Shock rippled across the faces of her women; the crown and scepter were only used for state occasions, not the dead of night.

The queen brooked no argument. "Lady Sarah, our jewels."

Pale and trembling, Lady Sarah unlocked the ironbound chest. Freed from swathes of velvet, the circlet of gold roses encrusted with emeralds glittered in the candlelight. The heavy crown was settled on Liandra's head, the royal scepter placed in the crook of her arm. Sword-straight, she carried the weight of her kingdom, the hope of her people. The weight had never seemed so heavy. Bejeweled and crowned, the preparations were complete. Armored with the full regalia of her office, Liandra was ready to face the traitorous Red Horns.

Rising from her place before the mirror, the queen addressed her women. "You have done your work well, now it is time that we do ours." Her women knelt before her, their faces reflecting a mixture of confusion and fear. Taking pity on them, Liandra summoned a reassuring voice, "Keep quiet and remain within the royal bedchamber. Whatever the events of the night, remain here."

Amy, the youngest of her women, broke under the tension, weeping over the queen's hand.

In a controlled but kindly voice, the queen said, "Do as you are bid and no harm will come to you."

Fixing her mind on the task ahead, the queen left the sanctuary of her bedchamber. A knot of grim-faced guards waited outside. The captain barked an order and the soldiers drew their swords, surrounding the queen with a ring of naked steel. She kept her face impassive and held her head high, walking with measured steps through the torch-lit corridors. The hallways were empty, devoid of life. In the small hours of the morning, the castle slept, leaving the hallways as still as a grave, a fitting setting for the grim tableau.

Her escort took the back passageways, walking unhindered from the Queen's Tower to the Throne Room. Approaching the antechamber she saw the first bodies. Lying haphazard and twisted, soldiers littered the approach to the Throne Room, bloody swords scattered across the marble floor...and all the fallen wore the green and white of Lanverness. *Her men, her people,* the queen studied the fallen but said nothing.

One of her guards rushed ahead to open the Throne Room doors...but there were no heralds or grand announcements for this bitter entrance. Surrounded by guards, the queen crossed the threshold. Flaming sconces lined the long walls casting pools of light into the cavernous room, but the torches waged a losing battle. Shadows claimed the chamber, the vaulted ceiling lost to darkness, pressing down with an ominous weight. Diamond-paned windows acted as mirrors, eerily twisting the reflected torchlight. It was a room meant for sunshine, but the distortions of the dark seemed fitting for the deed ahead.

Soldiers in the green and white of Lanverness lined the walls, the only witnesses. The queen played her part, advancing across the black and white checkerboard floor to the raised dais. The throne stood empty. Liandra climbed the steps, feeling the stares of the guards shadowing her every move. Slow and deliberate, she surrendered the royal scepter to the cushioned seat. Reaching up, she removed the heavy, gold crown, gently laying it on the velvet. Scepter and crown, the gold and emeralds glittered in the torchlight. Liandra gazed down at the royal regalia, counting her losses. She'd sacrificed much for the crown but her stewardship had served her people well...yet the challenges and sacrifices never seemed to end. Gazing at the golden circlet, the queen hardened her resolve. The crown of roses was not without its thorns. She knew better than anyone how deep those thorns could bite, how bitter their price, yet she would not willingly give up her reign. The Rose Throne was her prerogative, her destiny.

Tightening her hands into fists, Liandra was reminded of the rings on her hands, the Great Emerald on her right and the golden Seal of State on her left. She'd gained the rings on her coronation, and in all the years of her reign, the two had never left her hands. She would not remove them now. Only death would part her from the royal rings and all that they implied. Clenching her fists, Liandra banished the dark thoughts. She needed to keep her wits for the task at hand. The bitter act needed to be done, and done well, with everything accomplished before the coming dawn.

Wearing poise like a cloak, Liandra submitted to the guards.

Soldiers encircled her, swords sliding free from scabbards, and all the points faced inward, towards the Spider Queen.

6

Katherine

The swords met with a clang, echoing in the practice yard of the monastery. Kath disengaged and tried a different line of attack. She feinted to the left and then lunged for the opening in Blaine's guard. He whipped his shield around, catching her blade and deflecting the blow.

He growled a warning, "Your sword feinted left but your eyes gave you away! Never let your eyes betray you!"

Kath stepped back and wiped the sweat from her brow, weary from the long hours of training...but there was always more. Sir Blaine and Sir Tyrone kept at her, insisting on weapons practice whenever she wasn't studying with Master Rizel. Her mornings were spent with the monks, her afternoons with the knights, and her evenings with Master Rizel. She understood the urgency but the constant training wore thin. Kath couldn't remember the last time she'd gotten enough sleep.

Blaine gestured with his sword. "Try again, only this time, keep me guessing." He took a defensive stance, his silver surcoat glinting in the afternoon sun, the maroon octagon a perfect target.

She gripped her sword and danced left, baiting him with her shield, searching for an opening. Sweat burned her eyes.

Across the practice yard, an arrow thunked into a target.

Blaine rolled left, his shield dipping down. Kath lunged forward. Her sword snaked in but Blaine beat it away at the last instant. He barked his displeasure, "Too slow! Speed is your greatest advantage. You're better than this."

She glared at him, so tired she could barely stand...but he didn't seem to notice.

"Perhaps you're bored with the sword. Let's try the battleaxe next. You must be proficient against every weapon."

Kath struggled to suppress a groan.

Thunk! Another arrow struck the target.

Blaine exchanged his short sword for a battleaxe, a half-moon blade etched with runes. They'd discovered a cache of weapons in the monastery. Some bore ancient designs and strange embellishments, their edges blunted by time. But a solid blow could still break bones, more than sufficient for practice sessions.

Thunk! Another arrow struck the target.

Blaine advanced, swinging the axe, cleaving circles of threat. Kath adjusted her stance, dancing away from the half-moon blade. The battleaxe was a fearsome weapon. She dare not try a direct parry, better to step away and attack in the lee of the swing. Footwork, speed, and patience were the keys to defeating a battleaxe, but the menace of the axe made patience difficult.

Thunk! Another arrow struck the target.

Kath flicked a glance toward the leather-clad archer on the far side of the yard. Questions gnawed at her mind.

The battleaxe cut the air with a keening whistle.

Hearing the warning, she jerked sideways, her heart pounding.

The axe whistled past, a narrow miss.

Blaine slowed the axe and glared. "You're not concentrating! If your mind wanders in battle you're dead!"

Thunk!

Kath shook her head, feeling harried from all sides. "I know." Her voice sounded weary. She studied the knight's face, a young man with too many scars but his eyes were always honest, her first weapons master. Grateful that he cared so much, she softened her voice, "You're right, but I need a rest."

"You'll get no breaks in battle."

Kath just stared, a bead of sweat escaping from beneath her helm.

Blaine gave her a reluctant nod. "Enough for this afternoon. We'll practice your throwing axes after dinner." His voice held an edge of urgency, "You need to prepare. There's no telling what we'll face once we leave the monastery."

Always the reminder that time slipped away, as if the bloody comet was not warning enough. Her shoulder's tightened into a fierce knot; her sword arm ached.

Thunk!

She sighed. "After dinner then."

Blaine nodded, a smile transforming his face. He stowed the practice weapons and slung the harness of his great sword across his back. "Are you coming?"

"In a moment."

She watched him walk away, the hilt of the sapphire blue sword riding above his right shoulder. Somehow Blaine wasn't complete without his great blue sword.

Thunk! Another arrow struck the target.

Kath sheathed her sword and set her shield next to the bench. She removed her half-helm and shook out her long blond hair, the mountain air cool against her face. Aching in every part of her body, she longed for a soak in the monastery's hot springs.

Thunk!

Her gaze was drawn to the archer. Black leather stretched across a broad back, muscles rippling with the pull of the longbow, his black hair tied at the nape of his neck, clasped by silver. She watched him move with a feral grace, setting the arrow to the string and drawing the bow to a kiss, all in one smooth, powerful motion.

Thunk! The arrow found the target's heart, a heart crowded with arrows fletched in black swan feathers.

She needed an answer; her time in the monastery was growing short. The two knights would come, their blades sworn to her service, but the archer remained a mystery, a tantalizing mystery. She needed to know what Duncan would do. He'd grown taciturn since the attack on Jordan. She missed his company, his wry smile and his surprising insights. Kath crossed the practice yard, her gaze fixed on the archer, iron drawn toward a lodestone.

Thunk!

A riddle wrapped in black leathers, Duncan filled her mind and tugged at her heart, spurring memories of another time. She wanted this man beside her, wanted a chance to find out what he meant, what he could mean. Approaching on his right, she avoided his blind side. Need warred with anxiety, making her heart thunder. She wondered that he did not hear the wild drumbeat.

Thunk!

She waited but he seemed lost in the art of the bow. Draw and release, he never missed the target's heart.

Thunk!

"Duncan!" She cringed, too much heart in her voice.

He lowered his longbow and turned to face her. Rugged and tanned, his face gave little away. His right eye was the deep blue of a mountain lake, a lake with no bottom, a lake to drown in. His left was covered by a leather patch, dark and mysterious, adding to his allure.

"Yes?" The word was polite but nothing more.

She stared, hoping he would understand, hoping to break the frosty wall that had sprung between them. The moment stretched thin.

Her question came in a tumbled rush, "Will you come?" Chiding herself for blurting it out, she waited on his answer.

"To the north?"

She nodded.

His face hardened into bitter lines. "I am the companion of Jordan's Wayfaring, yet I failed her." His voice cut like a knife. "The best way to protect her now is to recover the stolen amulet and kill the Mordant." He fingered the fletching of an arrow. "Yes, I'll come...and see the quest to its finish."

Kath remembered to breathe.

"We'll need to leave soon. We've already waited too long. There'll be no trail to follow."

Anxiety tightened across her shoulders. "I know. The monks say I'm almost ready."

He nodded. "When you're ready, and not before." He chose an arrow from the quiver belted at his waist.

Kath yearned for more, but Duncan had already set another arrow to the notch. Turning to the target, he pulled the string to his lips, his muscles corded beneath black leather, the massive longbow bent to his will. Feeling dismissed, Kath turned to go, but at the last moment, she looked back to watch the arrow's flight.

Thunk! Another heart.

7

Danly

"Your majesty!" The words invaded Danly's sleep.

"Please wake, your majesty!"

Persistent, the words won through to Danly's sleep-fogged mind. Angry at the disturbance, he struggled to wake, intending to throttle the annoying culprit. His head ached from too much brandy. He squinted against the lantern light. "What do you want?"

Danly caught a glimpse of a soldier, a soldier in armor looming over his bed!

Jolted awake, he shrank back into the pillows, fear lodged in his throat. One word screamed through his mind, *betrayed!* Someone had betrayed him, betrayed the Red Horns, but then the words of the soldier sank in. *Majesty* was a title reserved for a queen...or a *king!* Blinking to clear the sleep from his eyes, Danly muttered, "What did you say?"

Bowing low, the soldier said, "Your majesty, I beg your pardon for waking you, but the queen has been taken! The Red Horns have won! The Rose Crown is yours by right!"

The queen has been taken! The words flooded Danly's mind, leaving elation in their wake. At last, the Rose Crown was his! Throwing off the covers he rose from bed. "Call my valet; I must dress for the throne!"

Six guards dropped as one to their knees, their heads bowed in the presence of their king. A flush of pleasure rushed through Danly. So this was what it felt like to be king. He had gone to sleep as the second son, the spare heir, and woke to claim his destiny. Triumph swelled through him, the day he'd long dreamed of was finally at hand.

Eager to claim his throne, Danly glared at his valet. "Hurry, Talbert!" Frail and bent, the old man had served him since childhood, but now that Danly was king he deserved better servants. "I need my best silk shirt and the emerald vest of crushed velvet trimmed with gold. Be quick about it. You serve a king!"

As the valet hastened to obey, Danly looked down at the kneeling guardsmen and used what he hoped was a regal voice. "You may rise." Remembering to use the royal 'we' that his mother was so fond of, Danly nodded toward the ranking guardsman and said, "Captain, we require a full report on the uprising."

The young captain bowed his head. "As you wish, sire."

Danly smiled at the captain's quick compliance; royal authority was such a splendid thing. He listened to the captain's report while his valet fussed to ease him into his best hose and riding boots.

"The Red Horns rose at midnight. Knives in the back slew those who would not join your cause. We took them by surprise, capturing many asleep in their beds. The only fighting to speak of was at the Queen's Tower and the Throne Room. The battle to capture the queen was fierce, but in the end, your royal mother surrendered when she realized the cause was lost. The Rose Throne is yours, sire."

His valet approached with a straight razor and a basin of rose-scented water, but Danly waved the razor away. His left cheek still throbbed, too sore for a shave. The five claw-marks from the virgin-wildcat had festered, refusing to heal. Rather than face the pain of shaving, Danly intended to grow a beard, a manly beard for a reigning king. Fingering the painful marks, he silently vowed to see the whore tortured and killed...but that pleasure would have to wait for another day. Turning his attention back to the captain, Danly asked, "And what about my royal mother? What about the queen?"

"She was given leave to dress and now waits to make her formal surrender to you in the Throne Room."

"Excellent." A pleasure that was almost sexual rushed through him. He was going to enjoy having his royal mother kneel before him. In his mind's eye Danly imagined what the royal bitch would do to save her own life. Eager to discover which of his fantasies would prove true, Danly snapped at his valet, "Talbert, move quicker or you'll find yourself serving in the kitchen." Accepting an emerald green cape to complete his attire, Danly turned to the captain and said, "We are ready. You may escort us to the Throne Room."

Saluting, the captain barked an order and the five soldiers drew their swords, forming an honor guard around their king. Protected by steel, Danly walked through the empty hallways of Castle Tandroth. The hour was early, well before the first light of dawn. The castle slept, still shrouded in darkness. Torches cast eerie shadows in the empty halls, giving the passageways a sinister look. Danly kept to the center of his escort, wondering if any resistance remained.

They came across the first bodies in the hallway to the Throne Room. Corpses lay strewn across the floor in various poses of death, the smell of blood heavy in the air. Witnessing the carnage, Danly appreciated the protection afforded by the guards. One of the guards sprinted ahead to throw open the great double doors to the Throne Room. As Danly crossed the threshold, the guard snapped to attention and announced, "All hail his royal majesty, King Danly, the rightful ruler of Lanverness!" Soldiers lining the Throne Room echoed back the refrain, *"All hail his majesty, King Danly!"* The accolades rolled on a tidal wave of male voices, crashing against him.

A triumphant thrill gripped Danly. Buoyed by the soldiers' adoration, he swelled with the pride of a king. Danly crossed the checkerboard floor, eager to claim his victory.

His stare focused on the royal prisoner caged by swords at the foot of the empty throne. Circling the guards, Danly studied the captured Spider Queen. Bedecked in a green velvet gown ornamented with thousands of seed pearls, she stood haughty and stiff despite her defeat. His royal mother had taken the time to dress for the part...but all of her precious powders could not rescue the severe, pinched look of her mouth or the deep shadows beneath her eyes. The strain of defeat was showing. The royal veneer had cracked.

A smile filled his face and his loins stiffened with pleasure. Laughter bubbled from Danly's throat. "So the great Spider Queen falls prey to another's webs! Defeated by superior plots, the Royal Intellect is at last laid low by the genius of mere men. How does it feel to lose, mother? How does it feel to be stripped of the crown?"

Her face remained a mask of ice. The queen stood mute, a stone statue surrounded by a ring of drawn steel.

Disappointed, Danly sneered, "What's the matter, mother, have you lost the royal 'we'?" Amused by his own wit, Danly chuckled. "I shall enjoy finding ways to make you talk." He dropped his voice to a hiss, "I warn you mother, I won't be denied my pleasures."

He spied the empty throne and mounted the dais. The rose crown and scepter waited on the velvet seat, gold and emeralds gleaming in the torchlight. His eyes widened in delight. "What's this, mother? Presents for me?" Lifting the heavy gold circlet high into the air, Danly pivoted to stare down at the captured queen. The woman stood with her back to the throne, ignoring his triumph. Anger pulsed through Danly. "Turn around mother." His voice held a deadly edge. "You will not ignore our victory."

He thought for a moment that she would refuse...but then she began to pivot. Stiff with irritating dignity, she moved with a glacial slowness that sapped the warmth from the chamber. He half expected to hear the marble floor grind beneath her feet. Coming to a stop, she stared up at him with unrelenting eyes, her arms held stiff at her side, her hands clenched in fists.

Even defeated, she tried to steal his glory...but he would not be denied. His anger boiled over, years of hatred welling within him. Pinning his royal mother with his stare, Danly slowly lowered the Rose Crown onto his head. "I crown myself, Danly, king of Lanverness, sovereign ruler of the Rose Court!" His voice rang hollow in the marble chamber....but then the soldiers answered their king with a cheer. "All hail Danly, the rightful king of Lanverness!" The refrain shook the room but there was no reaction from the queen. His royal mother stood still as a statue carved of frozen marble.

Danly claimed the throne. He draped his left leg over the gilded arm, making the throne his own. Fondling the royal scepter, he stared down at his mother. "I wear your crown and sit on your throne yet you say nothing."

An accusing glare was her only response.

Seeking to punish her stoic silence, Danly decided to twist the knife further. "Perhaps you don't realize the extent of your loss. The signal for the Red Horns to rise was the untimely death of my dear brother, Stewart, killed in an ambush by mercenaries." His voice became a knife seeking the queen's heart. "Even as we speak, my dear brother's head graces the portcullis of Castle Tandroth."

The queen's mask wavered. For a half a heartbeat Danly thought she might behave like a natural woman and swoon, but the queen remained rooted to the marble floor, staring up at him with accusing eyes.

"So, you won't even shed a tear for the shiny knight? And I always thought you loved him best." Willing the queen to break, he said, "Perhaps I should have a guard fetch the grizzly trophy so you can give your first-born son a final kiss." Anger burned within him. Rising from the throne, he glared at his mother and shouted, "Damn it to the nine hells, is there no woman left in you? Are you so unnatural that you care nothing for either son?"

Her eyes never wavered; her face never changed.

When his outburst gained no response, Danly roared, "On your knees woman! You will kneel before your rightful king, or I will have your head as a second trophy for the castle gates! Kneel!"

The ring of guards tightened the noose of swords.

He almost hoped she would not obey...but the stiff-backed queen slowly sank to her knees, her face a cold mask. Despite the bent knee, her posture screamed of unrelenting pride.

His anger exploded. "Speak or I will have you killed." He would break this woman in death if not in life...but before he could issue the command, she broke her stony silence.

"Why?"

The single word lanced him like a bolt of ice.

Danly teetered on the edge of rage. One word had saved her from oblivion. Mollified, he reined in his anger and barked a laugh. "You ask why? Isn't it obvious, mother?" He resumed his seat on the throne. Throwing one leg over the arm, he toyed with the scepter. "Women are not meant to rule. No real man will long bend the knee to the weaker sex...but then you have never been a true woman, have you, mother? It is past time you learned. Stripped of the crown all that is left to you is your sex. You kneel before me, devoid of power, nothing more than a woman. How does it feel to be merely female?"

Cold eyes stared back at him. Even on her knees, the woman seemed indomitable.

A killing rage rushed through him. "Answer me, woman! Your king commands it!" Gripping the scepter, he took a step toward her, murder in his stare.

The queen glared, her voice a knife in the dark, "Who designed the plot? Where is the one who defeated me?"

Danly gaped in shock, amazed that she did not know. A bark of laughter erupted from him. "Even now you do not know? He weaves his plots so deftly that even in victory his identity is disguised!" He shook his head, his voice incredulous. "You sat beside him on your royal council. Madam, you are too easily deceived! Small wonder you lost the throne." He laughed, the irony of the moment gripping him. Recovering himself, he spoke to the guards. "Where is the noble councilor? He should be here to witness the triumphant crowning of his king."

The guards shuffled, but no one answered.

Danly spied the captain who had first brought him news of the victory. "You there, captain, where is the councilor? He should be here in our hour of triumph."

Blanching, the captain bowed low and stuttered a reply, "Y-your m-majesty, I last saw him at the...Queen's Tower. I had orders to wake you and bring you safely to the Throne Room. I assumed he would be here awaiting your triumph."

Puzzled, Danly gestured toward the captain, "Well go and fetch him! It is past time our dear councilor rushed to our summons for a change. Tell him that the king demands his presence in the Throne Room."

The captain bowed low and made a hasty exit.

Turning his attention back to the captured queen, Danly said, "While we wait for our advisor, you will entertain your king." Reclaiming his seat on the throne, Danly struck a regal pose. "It is time to put aside your stiff-necked pride and beg for your very life." He extended his booted foot. "You may grovel before us, begging for our mercy...or you will take a turn on the rack." He thought he spied shock in her eyes. Pressing his advantage, he said, "Yes, Madam, torture. Lanverness will resume the practice. A king must be strong in the face of his enemies, something you never understood." Thrusting his right foot forward, Danly said, "You may kiss our royal boot and beg for your life. If your pride will not allow it, then you will go to the dungeons and beg after a turn on the wheel...or perhaps we should order one of the guards take you here on the steps, a reminder that you are nothing more than a mere woman." His voice turned to a sneer. "Grovel well, mother, and avoid the pain."

A deathly stillness settled over the room.

The queen remained on her knees, cloaked in stern dignity. "Anger and cruelty will not avail you."

The woman's haughty arrogance was impossible. Danly exploded out of the throne. *"I said grovel!"*

Footsteps approached from behind. Confused, Danly turned.

From the shadows behind the throne, a dark figure emerged. The flickering torchlight revealed the stern face of the Master Archivist.

8

Katherine

All doors were forbidden to her, both the golden-yellow and the mysterious midnight-blue. Kath's doeskin boots whispered down the hallway, the maze of the monastery growing familiar. The warmth of the floor increased, a telltale sign that she neared her destination. Descending the steps, she found the golden door with the glass pane shaped like a diamond...but the door was closed. She stared hard at the challenge. So easy to turn the knob and enter, but somehow they'd know. The monks had their own way of training. Magic could be even more exhausting than sword practice, yet she dared not miss a lesson. She'd need every weapon for the fight ahead.

Resigned to the task, she placed her left hand on the stone wall next to the door. Wood was impenetrable to her magic but not stone. Shivering with apprehension, she gripped her small mage-stone gargoyle. Kath leaned against the wall, a solid barrier, yet the monks had taught her another way. She stared at the wall, summoning the courage to try. In her worst nightmares she became trapped in stone, her mouth forever frozen in an endless scream. Banishing her doubts, she closed her eyes and concentrated, reaching for the magic within.

A deep vein of power throbbed at the heart of her gargoyle. Kath felt the pull of magic, the seductive call of stone to stone. Leaning forward, she pressed against the wall, pushing into it, pushing through it, needing to get to the other side. Mage-stone surrounded her with a hard embrace. Solid, sedentary, stubborn...streaks of granite and veins of quartz, the stone called to her, trying to hold her in place, offering her permanence, a whispered dream of eternity. The stone sang its siren's song, enduring, constant, forever. So hard to be herself, hard to remember...hard to move yet she needed to push through, needed to breathe. Refusing to be a prisoner, she pressed forward. *Crack!*

Like a flash of lightning, the world returned in a rush. Kath staggered into air. She gasped, remembering to breathe, hungry to fill her lungs. She checked herself, two arms, two legs, flesh not stone, her heart thundering in living proof. Damp with sweat, she sighed, her muscles quivering with strain, but she was whole and on the other side. Kath sagged against the wall, breathing hard, wondering if it would ever get easier.

The moist warmth of the garden embraced her, the rich fragrance of living green. She breathed deep, welcoming the scent of life, relishing the lushness of the garden. Even for the monastery, the Garden of Contemplation was a marvel. Heated by piped water from underground thermal springs and flooded with sunshine through a vaulted ceiling of glass panes, the garden was both a refuge of green and a sanctuary of art. Statues peered out from among the fronds, a story or a lesson behind every one. Kath followed the stone path along the reflecting pool. Her fingertips brushed the verdant green as she gazed at the secluded art.

Reaching the far end of the narrow pool, she took a seat on the stone bench. The statue of the three monk-keys peered out from the fronds. She studied the carving, remembering her first meeting with the master, only a moon turn ago. So much had changed, the weight of destiny felt heavy on her shoulders.

"Power begets power."

Kath jumped, her hand reaching for her sword...but it was only Master Rizel. Her mentor had a knack for suddenly appearing. She meant to catch him but never did. She wondered if it was magic but knew better than to ask.

Amusement crinkled the corners of his eyes, as if he knew her question and dared her to ask. But Kath knew from experience her questions would only lead to a maze of riddles, so she kept quiet, waiting for the lesson to began.

He took a seat on the bench, sharing her view of the monk-keys. He gave her a sideways glance, his sun-kissed face lined with deep laugh lines, his jewel-blue eyes hiding as much as they revealed. "Power begets power...the saying is true for magic as well as for politics."

Kath sighed; the day's lesson always began with a riddle. Easing back on the bench, she considered the master's words. Daring a sideways glance, she searched his face for clues, but he gave nothing away. The masters of the Kiralynn Order were sparing with their explanations, forcing their apprentices to puzzle out the full truth from mere kernels of wisdom. Master Rizel had explained it as a type of sword play of the mind, but sometimes Kath found it slow and frustrating...especially since the sands of time were slipping away.

The master raised an eyebrow, drawing her back to the lesson at hand.

Tumbling his words within her mind, Kath thought out loud, "Power begets power...magic begets more magic. So you're saying that because I have the ability to unleash the power of my gargoyle, I may be able to do other types of magic?"

"Just so. Magic is an innate gift, born to only a few mortals. For each person, the gift takes different forms but most magics can only be unlocked with the enhancing powers of a focus."

Kath smiled with victory...but her triumph was short lived.

"And?" The word held a challenge.

She shook her head in frustration. One layer of understanding was never enough. The monks offered riddles wrapped in endless layers of logic. It was the student's task to peel back the layers, exposing the wisdom hidden within. She fondled her gargoyle and searched her mind for the next step in the lesson. "Power...magic...focuses. So, if I find another focus, besides my gargoyle, I might be able to use it?"

"It's possible, yes, but first you will have to establish a bond, like the one you have with your gargoyle. Without that affinity, you will never be able to unlock the magic within."

More magic? The possibility stunned Kath. *How much magic was in the world?* Nightmares of the magic-sniffing goblin-man invaded her mind. *Kidnapped by the captain...all because of my gargoyle.* Connecting the ideas, Kath's eyes widened. "That's why the Mordant is so powerful, isn't it? He's spent the ages collecting focuses?"

"Yes, but magical focuses are the least of his powers. The Mordant has the divine favor of the Dark God. It is rumored that the Dark Lord endows his dedicates with powers and special favors. Favors that do not require the use of a focus."

Kath made the hand sign against evil, her voice a hesitant whisper. "What powers does he have?"

"Rumors shrouded in history...none have ever lived to tell the truth of the tales."

An icy touch feathered down Kath's back.

"Even more dangerous than his magics, you must never forget what you are dealing with. As the oldest Harlequin, the Mordant has served the Dark Lord for more than a thousand years." His voice became heavy with thought. "It is hard for any of us to imagine a thousand years of memories, a thousand years of evil."

Hearing the unexpected catch in the master's voice, Kath asked, "Do you wish for it? Do you yearn for a thousand years of life?"

Rocking back on the bench the master gave her a shrewd look offset by a light laugh. "Who is the master and who is the apprentice?" Shaking his head, Master Rizel said, "Such a span of years is not natural. I would never trade my soul for more life. But, to have the wisdom of a thousand years, that *is* tempting...to any monk of the Order." His voice sank to a whisper. "For you see, the Kiralynn Order seeks that kind of wisdom, but we do it within the Light, always within the Light. We collect, preserve, and study the histories and learnings of those who have gone before us. By standing on the shoulders of others, we dare to reach for a wisdom that is far beyond our years."

The clouds shifted in the afternoon sky, flooding the garden with sunlight like a blessing from the gods. Smiling into the warmth, Master Rizel said, "But I am forgetting myself. There is a practical aspect to today's lesson. The Grand Master has given permission for you, and each of your companions, to be tested, though we doubt the others will succeed."

Curious, Kath watched as the master removed a folded square of fur and a cloth bag from his pocket. Spreading the fur on the stone bench between them, he upended the bag, spilling an assortment of odds and ends across the fur.

It looked like a thief's harvest, but Kath knew otherwise. "These are focuses, aren't they?"

"Some are and some aren't. It is all part of the test...a test that is normally reserved for sworn members of the Order...but these are dire times." The master distributed the items, creating a space between each one. "None from among the Order has been able to bond with any of these focuses, and so we offer you the chance to extend your abilities." He waved toward the items. "We offer you our treasures. Take your time and examine each of the items. Feel them with your mind, your heart, and your magic. See if any of them speak to you."

Kath studied the collection of odds and ends, a strange mixture of the unusual and the ordinary. Some of the items were miniature works of art, carved by master craftsmen, while others were costly, encrusted with jewels and gold, but most could have come from a peasant's hut. Skeleton keys, smooth pebbles, odd colored stones, rings, bracelets, amulets, a broken bit of antler, loose gems, carved figurines, a seashell, an ordinary spoon, all lay in a jumble on the fur, as if a thief had picked the pockets of kings and paupers alike. She studied the jumble, wondering what they did, wondering which were true and which false.

Of all the pieces, the most exquisite was a small dragon carved of turquoise. So detailed, the dragon looked as if it could take wing. Gesturing toward the turquoise carving, Kath said, "May I?"

"Yes, of course."

She picked up the dragon and held it cradled in her palm. The carving was magnificent, as if the tiny dragon could breathe fire and take wing. She marveled at the craftsmanship, but it did not spark anything within her. Disappointed, she returned the tiny dragon to the fur and examined the others. She considered each one, but her hands always found their way back to a small pyramid carved of golden amber. The amber felt warm to the touch and there was something fascinating about the way the translucent gemstone caught and held the light.

Beside her the master said, "You are drawn to the pyramid?"

"Other items are more beautiful...but there is something about the warmth of amber and the perfect shape of the pyramid."

With a grace more common to a warrior than a man of letters, the master rose from the bench. "Then we shall see if the pyramid is truly meant for you." From the pocket of his robe, he produced a long golden sash. "First, you must be blindfolded."

"But why?"

"There is no other way."

Kath nodded and held still as the master secured the golden silk.

"Now give the pyramid back to me."

Kath was surprised to find that she still clutched the pyramid. Reluctant to relinquish it, she forced her fingers to uncurl. The master took the pyramid. Her hand felt empty. She sat in darkness, her senses telling her that he rearranged the items displayed on the fur.

A hushed stillness settled over the garden.

"Stretch out your hand but do not touch any of the items." The master's voice held a note of command. "Use all of your senses to find the pyramid. Take your time, and when you are sure, reach down and snatch the pyramid from the bench. You have but one chance to find the focus. Touch anything else, and you fail. Move only when you are ready. Let the magic be your guide."

Another test, the monks were overly fond of them. Kath yearned for the pyramid but the task seemed impossible. Blindfolded, and granted only a single touch, there was no way she could find it. Shrouded in darkness, she scowled, befuddled by the test. The monks expected too much. If the pyramid could help defeat the Mordant then why not just give it to her?

The master's whisper pierced the darkness. "You think too much. Stop relying on your eyes alone. Use your other senses. Listen to your inner voice. Still the clamor in your mind and find the magic within. If it is meant to be, the pyramid will call to the magic within you. Relax, for if you cannot find the pyramid then you will never be able to wield it."

Kath struggled to still her mind and quell her doubts. Taking deep calming breaths, she stretched her senses. The garden's lush green scent surrounded her, a heady perfume of life. The stone bench felt cool beneath her. The warmth of the sun caressed her face. She felt the rhythm of her own heartbeat. Her left hand curled around her mage-stone gargoyle. Magic throbbed within her gargoyle but Kath pushed it away, seeking something else, something kindred but different. She stretched out her hand, yearning for the pyramid. A pinprick of magic tugged at her awareness. Kath focused on the pinprick, like a candle guttering in the dark. She willed the spark to grow, to blaze bright. Suddenly sure, she reached down and snatched the magic from the fur. Her fist tightened, sensing the amber pyramid within. A smile of triumph filled her face.

The master released the blindfold. Kath blinked at the light.

"I knew you would succeed." His voice was warm with pride.

She gazed down at the small pyramid. "What does it do?"

"This focus is the Order's gift to you, to help in the fight against the Mordant. Use it well."

"But what does it do?"

Gathering up the baubles and returning them to the cloth pouch, the master said, "Some focuses have a history that is known to the Order, while others are a blank slate. This pyramid is one whose history is lost. But even if we knew what it did, there is no guarantee that it would perform the same feats for you. Magic is always a combination of the abilities of the person and the abilities of the focus. Every combination is different."

"I don't understand."

"Take for example, Master Garth. You've seen for yourself the great works of healing he can perform with his amulet, but when the master passes from this life, the next person to bond with the amulet may only be able to use the focus to heal burns or to cure simple fevers, nothing more. It is just as possible that the next person may be able to work even greater feats like healing the blind or the deaf. The master's amulet is clearly keyed to healing, but the exact nature of the magic depends on the innate ability of the person bonded to the focus."

Kath considered the master's words, pieces of the puzzle falling into place. "So that's why the captain and his men kidnapped me instead of just stealing my gargoyle?"

"Just so. If necessary, they would have killed you to get your focus, but they prefer to take the prize intact, in order to study your magic...and twist you to the service of the Mordant."

Kath shuddered.

The master's voice softened. "You did well to escape that trap."

She fingered the crystal dagger sheathed at her belt. "And now I have to chase the Mordant into the north, into his lair." Searching the master's face, she whispered, "Is there any hope of defeating him?"

"There is always hope. Despair is the ally of evil."

For a moment, the master reminded her of the knight marshal. The one-eyed marshal would have said the same thing, but it seemed a slender answer against the power of a thousand years of evil. "But how can such a monster be defeated?"

The master stilled, closing his eyes, a look of contemplation on his face. "The Book of Prophecy says that the companions will find among themselves the right combination of swords and magic, of mind and heart, to defeat the demon that walks in the guise of a man." Opening his eyes, the master said, "Evil always has weaknesses. The Mordant is very old, and very powerful...and therefore very arrogant. Trust to yourselves, and you will find a way."

Kath scowled. "Just words and cryptic messages."

"Words have power." He raised an eyebrow against her skepticism. "Arrogance is the Mordant's most obvious weakness, which may explain why the gods chose you to find the crystal dagger."

She stared at him, hungry for understanding.

"Think about it. The Mordant has lived for over a thousand years. With the arrogance of so many lifetimes, he holds mere mortals in contempt." His voice dropped to a whisper. "If he holds men in contempt, how much more will he underestimate the worth of a young woman?"

His words struck with the power of lightning. She sat stunned. This was a lesson she already knew, an advantage she'd already claimed. It had worked against the oily captain and his men, but she hadn't thought to use it against the Mordant. She studied the master's face, wondering what else she'd missed, what else she didn't understand. "But why can't the gods just say what they mean? Why give us nothing but riddles?"

The master laughed, "Always so impatient."

She stared at him, insistent.

He nodded. "We've discussed this before. The Lords of Light gave you a mind and a free will; they expect you to use both."

Kath muttered, "Sometimes I'd trade a bit of free will for a direct answer."

"No you wouldn't." His rebuke cut like a sword. "To give up your free will is to become a slave. A woman who dares all tradition to take up the sword would never submit to a slave collar."

Kath's face flamed red.

A familiar look crossed the master's face, signaling a lesson to come. Gesturing toward the carved marble nestled among the leaves, the master said, "Do you remember the first day we met? I told you the story behind that statue, the story of the Three Monk-keys?"

Kath's stare was drawn to the marble carving of three creatures, mythical animals that seemed to be caricatures of men. "I remember. The empire was destroyed because the people refused to see, hear, or speak evil." After a pause she added, "You said it was one of the oldest pieces of art in the Order's collection and one of your favorites."

The master flashed a satisfied smile. "Ah, then you were listening."

Kath could not help but return his smile.

Settling into the bench, the master said, "After the fall of the empire, the people commissioned the statue to always remind them of their duty to face evil whenever it comes among them...but I have often wondered why the artist chose to carve the lesson with three monk-keys instead of three men?" Pinning her with his stare, the master asked, "Do you know the reason why?"

Accepting the challenge, Kath studied the statue. The carving was amazing; three mythical animals with long tails and flattened faces, yet the artist had given each of them very human expressions. One covered its eyes, another its ears, and the third its mouth. Kath stared at the statue, but the answer remained locked in stone. Stymied, she shrugged. "I don't know master, but I'm sure you'll tell me."

"Impertinent as well as impatient."

"Yes, but I'd still like to know the answer."

"The artist carved monk-keys instead of men because the people of the empire surrendered their free will and forgot to think for themselves. They behaved like animals that mimicked, instead of men who think. By throwing away the two greatest gifts of the Lords of Light, free will and the power of thought, the people of the empire nearly became slaves of the Dark Lord." His jewel-blue gaze pierced her. "Remember this when you face the Mordant lest you become his slave." Confused, Kath dropped her gaze to the still waters of the reflecting pool. She did not understand how the monks' clever teachings would help slay the Mordant. Swords made more sense.

"Your time in the monastery is almost done."

A knot tightened in her shoulders.

"You have learned much but your first reaction is always to reach for the sword. It will take more than swords to defeat this evil."

Kath shivered, for his words held the ring of prophecy. She stared into his sun-kissed face, searching for answers. She'd come to depend on his wisdom and insights. Her voice dropped to a whisper, "The more I learn, the more impossible it seems..."

"You must never stop learning. Knowledge is always an advantage, a potent weapon against the Dark."

"And thus your Order hoards knowledge."

He chided her with a glance. Raising his right hand, he revealed the Seeing Eye tattooed in blue on his open palm, the symbol of the Kiralynn Order. "Seek knowledge, Protect knowledge, Share knowledge...as we have shared so much with you."

She avoided his rebuke, reaching out to touch the glassy surface of the reflecting pool. A single touch sent a ripple in all directions, shattering the mirrored image of the garden. Sometimes life seemed like a reflection, easily shattered. She glanced sideways at the master, afraid to ask but needing to know. "Will you come?"

The question hung between them, too much revealed in her voice.

Exposed, Kath rushed to shore up the naked question with a compelling argument. "If knowledge is such an advantage, then who better to join in the fight against the Mordant?"

His hand slipped across hers, a reassuring warmth that was all too brief. "The Book of Prophecy warns of wars not battles. The Dark Lord will draw on every resource of hell to win this war. We have prepared you as best we can. You go to fight the most important battle, but others must stay behind to fight the war."

Disappointment hit hard. Kath tightened her grip on the amber pyramid and kept her gaze fixed on the reflecting pool. "So you're saying the Mordant will start a war?"

"The war has already started. Sir Cardemir was not the first to die."

A chill shivered down her back.

His face was solemn, his eyes reflecting pools of infinite blue. "You came by way of Lanverness, from Queen Liandra's court. Surely you heard of the horrors of Coronth?"

She nodded, unsure where this was going.

"Look beneath the Flame God's religion and you will find the seeds of evil."

"A war not just a battle," she began to see Erdhe as a battlefield between Light and Dark. "But if the war is already started, what will the Mordant do?"

His face was grim. "If history serves, the Mordant will play the role of the Deceiver, dividing those who serve the Light, turning ally against ally, brother against brother...till the kingdoms of Erdhe run with blood and chaos."

"But what of my visions in the Mist?"

"Memories of the past, echoes of the future."

"But will it come to pass?"

"Nothing is foreordained. What you saw was possible, not certain." Master Rizel's voice grew thoughtful. "But for the Guardian to choose that vision...such a future must be ripe with chance."

Kath's fear annealed to iron. "Castlegard must be warned."

"The Octagon Knights will be called to battle, but swords alone will not prevail."

"They don't even know he walks the southern kingdoms."

"So much has been forgotten. The Mordant is an ancient and insidious enemy. He will sow lies and turn ally against ally.

Kath's voice dropped to a whisper. "Divide and conquer...the first rule of war."

"Exactly, but this war will be unlike those that have gone before. This war will be waged for hearts and minds and souls."

Frustration boiled through her; the monks were nothing but words. "But how do you fight such a war?"

He smiled, but the smile did not reach his eyes. "With knowledge, and free will, and a steadfast heart." His voice held a warning. "You must know your enemies and never forget your friends."

Kath shook her head and stared into the depths of the reflecting pool. The fading ripples distorted the view of the garden, mirroring her confusion.

The master sighed. "You chafe at these lessons, thinking they are merely words, but even your Octagon Knights would say that you must understand your enemy in order to defeat him." His voice dropped to a whisper. "You must understand the true nature of evil in order to be victorious."

She sat still as a statue, watching his face in the reflecting pool. "But I don't understand."

"You will. You are capable of more than you know. And help will be found along the way. A few who dare to make a difference can do much against the Dark. And always remember, the Lords of Light work under the guise of chance and happenstance. Help will be found in the most unexpected places."

She nodded, silently vowing to do her best despite the odds.

As if he read her mind, the master whispered, "Even the Lords of Light cannot ask for more than your best."

Kath met his jewel-blue stare, trying to look past the surface. She wondered if the Lords of Light would truly help...or if they would merely watch from above, letting ripples of Darkness shatter the kingdoms of Erdhe.

9

Steffan

The Lord Steffan Raven stood at the back, studying the beast he'd help create. The crowd roared, slavering for the kill. A smile crept across his face, the beast did not disappoint.

The temple drums pounded, heightening the tension. At a signal from the Pontifax, the guards pressed forward, spears and swords forcing the sinner into the flames. The young man had a giant's build, burly and muscular, yet he fell to his knees, sobbing for mercy. Steffan smiled, for mercy was never part of the Test of Faith.

The soldiers did their jobs well, relentlessly jabbing with their spears. The flames crackled and snapped, releasing a fierce heat. Forced backwards, the sinner teetered on the edge, horror scrawled upon his face. A spear snaked forward tipping the balance. Arms flailing, he fell into the pit. A rush of golden flames roared heavenward, accepting the offering. Hair and skin and cloth caught fire, creating a human blaze. Howls of agony split the air. The doomed figure writhed in the flames, a fiery jester entertaining the faithful. The crowd roared its approval. The sinner had exceptional stamina, lasting longer than most...but all too soon the screams subsided, the jester collapsing into a charred lump. A pillar of oily smoke belched into the afternoon sky.

The sinner was dead, yet a shimmer of ecstasy sparked the crowd.

A wild-haired young man standing near the flames threw his head back and screamed, "I feel the Flame God! I feel his pleasure!" Waving with his hands in the air, he mimicked the death throes of the sinner.

The frenzied dance proved contagious, rippling out from a single source. Arms raised, heads tipped back in ecstasy, the crowd twisted and howled in a macabre imitation of death. The temple square convulsed, a sea of bodies caught in a death dance.

The Lord Steffan Raven smiled. The crowd was a beast, a wild animal addicted to the Test of Faith. Drunk on spectacles of ritualized death, the people of Coronth proved easy to manipulate...but wild beasts often have a nasty habit of turning on their masters. Steffan studied the crowd, knowing he needed to keep the beast chained. The best remedy was surprise; keep the people off-balance, forcing them to change while lulling them with religious spectacle. Like beasts, people needed to feel the whip as well as taste the sugar, and Steffan had a plan to do both.

Having weighed the crowd's reaction, Steffan cut a dark path through the frenzy. People melted away before him, fear and deference in their eyes. Their reaction pleased him. Few knew his face but almost all knew his symbol, a black raven emblazoned on a red disc. By design, the Lord Raven stayed out of sight at most religious rituals, yet rumors of the Raven's influence seeped through the city, instilling fear and wary obedience in the people. The situation suited Steffan perfectly; better to influence from behind the throne than to rule from the front, a lesson taught by the Dark Lord, may his pleasure reign.

Beyond the square, the narrow cobblestone streets were empty, devoid of life, the shops and taverns temporarily closed in honor of the Flame God. Citizens attended the rituals or they hid...there wasn't much in between.

Steffan strode through the back streets, making his way to the rear of the temple. The massive structure overshadowed the city, brooding columns topped by a gilded spire. He climbed the steps to the rear doors. Guards snapped to attention, spears glinting in the sunlight as he passed inside. Incense and the coolness of cloistered stone surrounded him. Red-robed acolytes rushed to be of service. Steffan waved them away. Striding through the marbled halls, he made his way to the Vestment room.

The small gilded chamber served as the Vestiary to the Pontifax. Opening the doors, Steffan startled a half dozen priests and acolytes waiting to serve the Enlightened One. The acolytes stared in confusion while the priests blustered, protesting the invasion of their domain. Steffan stilled their bleating with a wave of his hand. "You are all dismissed. I will see to the Pontifax myself."

The senior priest, Clavin, made a show of protest. "You have no authority here."

Steffan knew the old man played the toad for the Keeper, whispering secrets against the other priests and acolytes...no one would mourn his loss. He stared at the priest, letting his voice drop to a whisper, "You can be replaced. Now go!"

The priest's mouth puckered into a sour scowl but he scurried out the door with the rest. Steffan smiled. Toads liked to bluster but they had no teeth.

Steffan closed the doors and went straight to an ornate sideboard, pouring three glasses of the finest Urian brandy.

The double doors burst open admitting the Pontifax and the Keeper of the Flame. A fawning entourage followed. Priests and acolytes crowded the Vestiary, the smell of incense and burnt flesh clinging to their robes. Steffan ignored the entourage and focused on the Pontifax. Tall with a flowing white beard, the Pontifax had a dignified bearing and a benevolent face befitting the secular and religious ruler of Coronth, the perfect showman for their religious charade. The square-jawed Keeper, on the other hand, was burly and bald, radiating a thug's threat despite his sumptuous red-velvet robes.

Bowing low, Steffan approached the Pontifax, offering a glass of brandy. Leaning close he whispered, "Dismiss your priests and give me the honor of serving you."

The Pontifax raised a bushy eyebrow. Accepting the brandy, he waved the others away. "You are all dismissed. Our counselor will assist us with our holy vestments."

Priests and acolytes bowed their way out of the chamber, more than a few darting jealous stares at Steffan before closing the doors.

The Pontifax sipped the brandy, studying his counselor. "You've ruffled the feathers of my priests, I trust it is for a good reason?"

"They grow complacent in your favor. Sometimes change is good."

The Keeper growled, "They serve, and serve well. If change is needed, you should talk to me, counselor."

Steffan turned and bowed, acknowledging the burly Keeper. He offered the priest a glass of brandy, making a show of serving the big man his daily dose of deference. The Keeper accepted, his dark eyes glaring in challenge as he downed the amber liquid in a single swallow. Steffan kept his face still, letting the big man wallow in his illusions. Finishing the brandy, the Keeper sprawled back in a chair, a smug sneer on his face.

"You asked for the honor of serving me?" The Pontifax held his arms out, emphasizing the heavy vestments, but his eyes were amused. The old man was shrewd in his own way, understanding the value of a house divided.

"Yes, Holy One." Steffan nodded and stepped behind the Pontifax. Assuming the role of a servant, he began unlacing the complex ties that bound the gold vestment.

"We looked for you at the ritual this afternoon." The Pontifax's voice was congenial but Steffan sensed an underlying goad. "I caught a glimpse of a dark figure skulking at the edge of the crowd." The velvet voice deepened. "You have earned a place at my left hand yet you always watch from the rear. Why is that?"

Steffan infused his voice with humility. "Because I serve you best from the rear, Holy One." He loosened a knot and released the final set of bindings. "By standing in the back, I can best measure the crowd's true emotions. If the ecstasy of the ritual reaches to those on the fringe then we know we have succeeded." Steffan lowered his voice, leavening his argument with a dash of deference. "Besides, the people wish to see their Pontifax and the Keeper of the Flame, not the shadowy counselor."

The Keeper barked a laugh. "Ha! I know the true reason you skulk in the back. You haven't the stomach for death! The Lord Raven, like his name sake, is a carrion feeder, always lurking at the edge of death but never daring to make the kill!"

Steffan eased the heavy gold robe off the shoulders of the Pontifax, hiding his smile. Keeping his hands busy and his face averted, he baited the Keeper with silence.

The burly priest took the bait, his voice barbed. "Tell us Lord Raven, from your perch at the back, how did you enjoy today's ritual?"

Unfastening the padded tunic worn beneath the gilded robe, Steffan replied, "The ceremony was excellent as always." Flashing a pointed smile in the Keeper's direction he added, "Today's heretic was especially good. The young man had plenty of stamina, putting on a fine show. The crowd was enthralled. Who was he anyway?"

"A peasant farmer from a village on the outskirts of the city. Body of a bull but the mind of a child." The Keeper's voice held a smug edge of self-satisfaction. "General Caylib's men reported him to one of my acolytes. The farmer was too stupid to join the army, so we made an example of him." Barking a crude laugh, the Keeper added, "The general won't be having any more problems recruiting from that village."

It was the opening Steffan had been waiting for. Helping the Pontifax into a lush silk robe of the deepest purple, he said, "Perhaps there are others, besides the general, who know of sinners deserving of the Flames."

The Keeper sat up, a dog protecting his bone. "My acolytes find plenty of tinder for the Flames."

"But do we use the ritual to our best advantage?"

"We keep the Flames fed, what more is there?"

"Perhaps there is a way to get double the value from each death."

The Keeper narrowed his gaze. "You squawk a lot, raven, but the sounds are nothing but nonsense!"

The Pontifax intervened. "Let the counselor speak. I assume he has a suggestion else he would not have joined us in the Vestiary."

Steffan bowed toward the Pontifax acknowledging his insight. The Keeper glowered but held his silence. Freed of his ceremonial robes, the Pontifax took his ease in a cushioned chair next to the Keeper, his feet resting on a stool, his hands caressing the ruby amulet that was always around his neck. "Tell us what you have in mind, Lord Raven."

Steffan reached for the brandy and refilled each man's glass. "I see many things from my perch at the back. Just as we planned, the people of Balor are addicted to the spectacle of death. The trick now is to keep them enthralled while also keeping them cowed." Taking a sip of brandy, Steffan said, "We need to ensure a steady supply of sinners to the Flames, the spectacle in the temple square cannot stop."

A bark of a rude laugh erupted from the Keeper. "Is this all the famous counselor has to offer? Of course we must keep the Flames fed! My acolytes have never failed to provide sinners for the ceremonies. I don't see what you're complaining about."

Knowing that he was treading on the Keeper's domain, Steffan made his smile deferential. "I am not complaining...I am merely suggesting that we put a fresh twist on an old tale."

Anger swept across the Keeper's face but the Pontifax looked intrigued. Fingering his ruby amulet, he said, "Tell us more."

Steffan inclined his head, swallowing a smile. "Let the people choose the sinners for the Test of Faith."

Silence smothered the chamber.

The Keeper was the first to react, his face flaming an angry red. "Have you lost your mind? Why would we give the people that kind of power?"

"We only give the people the *illusion* of power...what we actually give them is fear and mistrust."

The Pontifax stared at Steffan with hooded eyes. "Explain."

"The possibilities are truly delicious. We invite the people to inform on their neighbors, their friends, and their families. Anyone reporting a heretic to the priests garners favor with the Flame God, and of course, those favored by the Flame God need never take the Test of Faith. For the sake of their own survival, the faithful will rush to confess the sins of their neighbors, all in the name of piety. With one stroke, the temple gains tens of thousands of eyes and ears throughout the city, helping to enforce the will of the Flame God. It may seem like a gift of power, but in reality, this new policy will sow fear and mistrust on a rampant scale." Pausing he added, "Don't you see the beauty of it? Those who fear will always obey and those who mistrust will never band together to threaten their masters. We will feed the beast and cow him at the same time, securing the silken shackles of religion."

The Pontifax studied his counselor with shrewd eyes. "Lord Raven, we trust that your devious mind will ever work for us...never against us."

Humbly bowing his head, Steffan said, "Ever your servant, Enlightened One." His words hung in the chamber like an oath. Steffan kept his head bowed, waiting, wondering if he'd gone too far.

"And how would you propose to implement this plan?"

He stifled a smile, knowing the hook was set. "It starts with you, Enlightened One, from the pulpit at temple worship." Gesturing toward the Keeper, Steffan said, "Create a new order of priests, the order of confessors, led by the Keeper of the Flame. Specially chosen from among the priesthood, the confessors will go out among the people, gathering reports of blasphemy, heresy, and other crimes against the faith. This information will be reported to the Keeper, who will, of course, make the ultimate decision as to which sinner will walk in the Flames." Steffan paused to watch a slow smile spread across the Keeper's face. "Under this new policy, the temple will keep its fingers on the pulse of the people while ensuring a steady stream of sinners for the Test of Faith."

As expected, the Keeper leaped at the chance to expand his powers. "I like this new idea! It will tighten the temple's hold on the people."

Steffan kept the smile from his face, watching the Pontifax, waiting for approval.

Caressing his ruby amulet, the Pontifax said, "Your plan has merit. We will adopt the Lord Raven's suggestion." Turning toward the Keeper, he added, "Since you will lead this new order, we entrust you with the task of recruiting the confessors from among the priesthood. We suggest you choose the zealous and the shrewd, both should make excellent confessors."

Nodding, the Keeper said, "I know several priests who will do well in the new order."

"Good, see that it is done." Turning back to Steffan, the Pontifax said, "We will miss your insights and advice while you are away with the army. How soon will you leave?"

"Since the coming of the comet, new recruits flock to the standard of the Black Flames, but it will take time to train them. Meanwhile, with your permission," he inclined his head toward the Pontifax, "I will work with the Keeper to create this new order of confessors. Once the confessors are in place, the Flame God's grip will tighten to a stranglehold and your rule will be secure. Only then will I take the army south, to plunder Lanverness."

The Pontifax smiled, his eyes shining with a hunger for power. "The sooner the confessors start their holy work the better."

Raising his glass, Steffan said, "A toast to the new order of confessors!"

The three men clinked their glasses in salute, the undisputed rulers of Coronth.

Observing his co-conspirators, Steffan had to laugh within his mind. Neither man understood the trap he'd set. Kings, emperors, and religious rulers did well to always give their people something to love and something to hate. The people of Coronth revered the Pontifax for the miracle of the Test of Faith. In time, the people would come to hate the Keeper for administering the confessors. Their hatred for the Keeper would make the people love the Pontifax all the more. Something to love and something to hate...while the shadowy counselor worked in the background, progressing the will of the Dark Lord. And if the grand scheme ever failed, if the mob rose against the Flame, then they'd turn on the one who betrayed them. They'd turn on the one they loved, always the one they loved...leaving the shadowy counselor to slip away unnoticed. Steffan raised his glass, silently toasting the genius of his god. May the Dark Lord's pleasure reign, over all the lands of Erdhe.

10

Liandra

Emerging from the shadows, the Master Archivist glided across the dais. A vengeful wraith in black robes, he hovered behind the throne, his eyes cold, his face a mask of menace.

"*You!*" All color fled from Danly's face. "What are *you* doing alive?" His face contorted into a snarl. "Guards, seize him!"

"I think not." The master's voice carried the bite of a deep winter frost.

Rising from her knees, the queen issued a single command, "Guards!"

Pale-faced, the soldiers caging the queen rushed up the dais, re-forming around the throne. Growling, the soldiers crowded the prince, a ring of naked steel enforcing the reversal of fortunes.

Danly sputtered, "What is this? I am your rightful king! Obey or heads will roll!"

The master replied with controlled menace, "The only head in danger of rolling is yours."

Standing at the foot of the dais, the queen watched the scene play out, a frozen pillar of ice.

The ring of soldiers parted, admitting the queen's spymaster. "Relinquish the crown and scepter. The royal regalia should not be dishonored by the touch of a traitor."

Danly sputtered, "*Traitor!*"

The word hung in the air like a death knell.

Danly's eyes went wide and wild, flooded with panic. "But the bodies, the dead soldiers in the entrance way, I saw them!"

The Master Archivist smiled. "Soldiers arranged in poses of death, pig's blood fresh from a butcher, all done before the dawn, before the castle wakes...a mummer's farce fit for a prince...or a traitor."

The queen watched as terror claimed the face of her second son. Danly's gaze raced around the Throne Room, a mouse frantic for a bolt hole. Finding no escape, his stare fixed on the queen. A wounded animal desperate for help, he wailed, "Mother *please?* I am your *son!*"

She made her voice as hard as stone, "And such a filial son you are. You were given much yet squandered everything." The queen stared up at her second son, as if seeing a stranger. She'd long overlooked Danly's frivolous spending habits and his addiction to the bordellos, unwittingly blinding herself to the hate that simmered just beneath the surface, a hate that had been easily twisted into treason. Now she paid the price for her mistakes. *Another mistake, another sacrifice,* Liandra knotted her fists in anger, her nails biting into her palms, drawing blood. As the sovereign queen, it was her bitter duty to witness Danly's fall, but she would leave the interrogation to the Master Archivist. Drawing a deep breath, she gave a grim nod to her shadowmaster.

Stepping up to the prince, the Master Archivist pressed, "Relinquish the royal regalia."

Danly shrank backwards, but his dark eyes held a shrewd glint. He pointed an accusing finger at the shadowmaster and hissed, "You're the one! You bewitched my mother with your austere habits, worming your way into her confidence, and then you hatched this plot against me." He drew himself up, his voice ringing with righteous indignation, "What evidence do you have to stage this mummer's farce against a royal prince?"

The master's voice was cold with reason. "The testimony of a courtesan. She overheard you plotting treason in the bordello."

Shock convulsed across Danly's face. His hand covered the telltale scratch marks on his cheek but his voice was full of bluster. "Ha! You'd take the word of a whore over a prince?"

"With a plot of high treason, the testimony of one citizen is more than enough reason to put the question to the test. But the damning evidence came from your own mouth. You are condemned of treason by your own words and actions."

"No!" The prince lunged for the master, but the soldiers were quick to intervene, sword tips holding him back.

Constrained by steel, Danly's voice was a low hiss. "The Red Horns will rise."

"More evidence of your guilt." The master removed a scroll from the pocket of his robe. "And now we come to the heart of the matter...the sentencing." Snapping the scroll open, he read, "Prince Danly Tandroth, second son of the sovereign queen, you have been found guilty of high treason against the Throne of Lanverness. In accordance with the laws of Lanverness, you are hereby sentenced to die a traitor's death."

"Nooooo!" Danly's scream echoed in the cavernous room. He looked toward the queen, his eyes begging.

Liandra kept her face a mask of stone.

"The traitor will be hung by the neck until nearly dead. Revived from this ordeal, four horses are used to stretch the limbs toward the four directions of the kingdom. After the stretching, the executioner uses blunt knives to quarter the body while the heart still beats. The butchering is prolonged for as long as possible. The heart is the last thing to leave the body. The remains are then burnt, so that nothing is left to contaminate the soil of Lanverness." The scroll rolled snapped with a grim finality.

Danly swayed, his face ghost-pale, his eyes desperate. *"Mother, please!"*

Liandra remained rigid as stone, her clenched fists drawing blood.

The master leaned toward the prince. "A horrible way to die. A death that befits only the vilest of traitors." The master tapped the scroll against the prince's chest. "Of course, the crown could be persuaded toward leniency, *if* you provide the identity of the Red Horns. Give us the leader's name and things will go much easier for you."

Fear and panic warred across Danly's face. "You're bluffing. Such torture hasn't been used in Lanverness in generations!"

"There has never been a traitor prince."

Danly threw a desperate look toward the queen, *"Mother please!"*

Steeling herself, the queen replied, "You will receive justice from the throne, nothing more."

"But I am your *son!*" The cry echoed through the Throne Room.

Stepping between the prince and the queen, the master said, "Give us the names!"

Danly snarled, "I pray to all the gods that the Red Horns rise! I will spit on your dead bodies when I take my rightful place on the throne!"

"Bind the prisoner!"

Two burly prison guards stepped out of the shadows and approached the throne. Working around the swords, they seized the scepter and crown, handing them to the shadowmaster. Iron chains clanked as the first guard placed heavy manacles on the prince's wrists while the second seized the prince's throat forcing a leather gag into his mouth. Danly squirmed but he was no match for the guards. The stench of hot urine flooded the dais. With the prisoner bound and gagged, the guards stepped away awaiting further orders.

In a low voice, the Master Archivist said, "I will have his signet ring as well. This one has no further right to the royal symbols of house Tandroth."

One of the guards twisted the prince's gold signet ring, yanking it from his hand. The master pocketed the ring.

Danly stood trussed in shackles, a leather gag stuffed in his mouth. His eyes wide and wild, his hose wet with urine, he panted through his nostrils like a cornered beast.

The queen stared at her fallen son, willing him to give up the names.

The master stepped close to the captured prince, his voice dropping to a whisper, "Time is of the essence. You have but two days to yield the names. To help you think, you will be taken to the deepest dungeons of Castle Tandroth. Your gag will be removed and you will be chained and lowered into the traitor's pit. You will find the pit a dark, snug fit, with only rats and other vermin for company. If you decide to yield the names you need only call to the jailor. The jailors have orders to summon me." The master paused, "Lest you hold to silence hoping for rescue by your traitorous friends, you should know that only a few loyal men will ever know your exact location. If the Red Horns rise, you will likely starve in the pit." He dropped his voice to a whisper. "If you stay in the pit, death is inevitable." Glancing toward the prison guards, the master said, "Take this traitor away, the rats of the dungeon are waiting."

A hood of rough leather with slits for eyes was yanked over the prisoner's face. The guards emptied his pockets and used a knife to cut the royal emblems from his clothes. A soiled cape of homespun wool was draped around his shoulders, covering the emerald green of his garments with peasant brown. When the guards were done, nothing royal remained.

Caged in a ring of naked steel, the hooded traitor was escorted from the Throne Room. The queen watched the exodus, her back rigid, blood streaking the palms of her hands.

The doors of the Throne Room clanged shut.

The queen wavered. Her resolve exhausted, she swayed with strain.

The Master Archivist rushed forward. Strong arms reached for her, offering support.

She leaned into him for a moment, just a heartbeat of stolen comfort, and then she stepped away, her face a mask, her royal resolve hardened once more. She told herself it had to be done. *One son lost, stolen by traitors.* The Rose Crown had many thorns, but she had a kingdom to save, a crown to protect...and the leader of the Red Horns remained a mystery. She stared up at the empty throne, her voice full of steel. "And so it begins." Time was not her friend.

11

Katherine

The world was vertical. Harsh and stony, the snow-capped mountains thrust against a pale blue sky. The horses blew hard, struggling to pick their way up the last of the switchbacks, steam rising from their sweat-streaked flanks. Rivulets of ice-melt trickled across the trail, confirming the spring thaw. Heeding the warning, Kath scanned the sky to gauge the hour. A silver half moon rode among thin fingers of clouds, a welcome sign that morning still lingered.

Six riders and two packhorses raced the sun to the mountain pass. Driven by the threat of the red comet, they dared risk Drumheller Pass despite the dangers of springtime, but none wanted to tempt fate by crossing at noon.

Stretched out along the trail, they rode in pairs: four companions with two strangers bringing up the rear. Duncan and Blaine rode in the lead, black leather and the silver surcoat of the Octagon. Kath kept to the middle with Sir Tyrone, her throwing axes strapped to her back, a sword of good Castlegard steel belted to her side. She stared across the valley, trying to catch a last glimpse of the Kiralynn monastery, but too many clouds intervened. Perhaps it was the Mist. She shivered, remembering.

Her horse snorted and shied sideways. Kath firmed her grip on the reins. The wonders of the monastery were behind them, the dangers of the prophecy lay ahead. They chased an ancient evil across the mountain pass, returning to a world where swords mattered more than words. Staring across the distance, Kath felt the keen loss of Master Rizel's wisdom, but even more, she missed having her sword sister at her side. *"Heal well, sword sister."* Raising her hand, Kath saluted the far mountains and all that lay hidden in their distant peaks.

"She will be well cared for."

Surprised to hear own thoughts echoed, Kath glanced over at the black knight riding even with her mount. Dark ringlets of shoulder-length hair framed an ebony face lined with leagues of experience. Sir

Tyrone wore the silver surcoat of the Octagon Knights, the hilt of a great sword jutting over his right shoulder.

"We all miss her, but the monks are Jordan's best hope." His voice hardened with resolve. "Jordan needs to heal and we need to catch the spawn of hell who attacked her."

Kath nodded, the attack on Jordan made the hunt personal. "The Mordant will be hard to catch. The trail's gone cold, even for Duncan."

"True, but if the monks have the truth of it, we race to confront the demon in his lair not to catch him on the road. Still, I'd rather slay him before he crosses the Dragon Spine Mountains. I've seen the Dark Citadel from a distance and I'd just as soon avoid the dark-cursed fortress."

Kath glanced at the black knight, surprised once again by his travels. "At least we have the advantage of knowing the Harlequin's face...though it's hard to believe the Mordant lurks within Bryce."

"You know his face. To me he was just one monk among many."

Falling silent, Kath thought back to her first day in the monastery. She'd liked the young monk-initiate. Bryce had wanted to be a healer and now he walked with Death. Kath shook her head, angry at the unfairness of it all. What had Bryce done to deserve such a fate? Or Jordan for that matter? Did the gods even care? It seemed so unfair...but at least her sword sister still lived. Kath took heart from the thought...and from the all she'd learned at the monastery. She gripped the small gargoyle tied by a leather cord around her neck and then checked the amber pyramid nestled deep her pocket, but the weapon that suited her best was the sword. *Magic and steel,* she wondered if it would be enough. The monks had solved the riddle of her gargoyle, but her time in the monastery had fled with so many questions unanswered and so many more unasked. The last days were a fevered blur of advice, pouring over scores of maps, studying obscure passages from the Book of Prophecy. If knowledge was a sword against the Dark, Kath had left a whole army of weapons behind. She felt naked despite the sword belted to her side and the axes strapped to her back.

"I was surprised that Master Rizel didn't join us." Sir Tyrone intruded, his baritone voice carrying above the steady clop of the horses. "Given the store the monks put in their Book of Prophecy, I thought he'd come."

The unspoken meaning in the knight's words drew Kath's gaze to the rear of the column. Two strangers from the monastery rode at the rear, both thrust on them at the last moment, an old man and a girl, one sullen and the other reluctant. With the rush to leave, there'd been little chance to learn much more than their names. At least Zith wore the midnight-blue robes of a master. Kath hoped the old man harbored some vital store of forgotten knowledge, but he did not radiate the confidence she'd come to expect from the wise. Riding hunched in the saddle, his chin tucked down against his silver-streaked beard, the old man seemed broken and withdrawn, wrapped in a cloak of misery. Of all the monks in the monastery, Kath wondered why the Grand Master had chosen this sullen old man to join them on the quest north.

His companion was even more of a puzzle. Of a similar age to Kath, Danya kept to the rear, huddled beneath a brown cloak of plain homespun wool. The small, dark-haired woman wore a brown tunic and a peasant's wool leggings, but as far as Kath could tell, she rode without a single weapon belted to her side. Neither a monk nor a warrior, it remained to be seen how she'd contribute to the fight ahead. At least the girl had a good seat on her horse, which was more than Kath could say for the monk.

Turning back to the black knight, Kath muttered, "I know what you mean. I don't know why the monks saddled us with those two." After a pause she added, "Before we left, I asked Master Rizel to join us."

The black knight raised an eyebrow.

"He spoke of wars not battles...that the Dark Lord will draw on every resource of hell to claim all of Erdhe. He said that the battle against the Mordant is key, but while we travel north, others must stay behind to fight the war."

Sir Tyrone nodded. "Makes sense. Generals seldom fight from the front."

Kath's eyes widened at the insight. Master Rizel had always seemed like a learned chess master, full of wisdom and insights, but perhaps a chess master was just another name for a general. If the prophecies did indeed herald a great war, Master Rizel would make an excellent general...though she would miss his counsel and his friendship.

The switchbacks leveled off marking the summit of Drumheller Pass. The horses blew hard, struggling to catch their breath, pulling against the reins. Hooves stamped and bridles jangled in protest. The horses wanted a rest but the riders held them to the pace, not daring to waste the last hours of morning.

Kath glanced skyward, checking the sun's passage, but her gaze was snared by the red comet. Time was against them. She'd felt it in the monastery, the need to learn warring with the need to leave. She wondered what the delay would cost them. "The Mordant has more than a full moon-turn lead. Do you think we'll catch him?"

The black knight shrugged. "All we can do is try."

His answer left her unsettled. Her hand crept to the crystal dagger. "How much havoc can he cause in a single moon-turn?"

"Depends on the man...or the fiend."

And that was the problem, for none knew the Mordant's true powers.

A sharp bend in the trail brought them into the throat of the pass. Overhead, a great fist of sapphire-blue ice shadowed the trail, death poised in frozen form. Kath shivered at the sight, remembering Jordan's peril. The glacier glinted in the sunlight, the sparkle of a thousand diamonds, but instead of a frozen beauty, they found a beast wakened by spring. The vast ice field stretched and groaned like a bear roused from winter sleep. Melt dripped from the overhang, teardrops plunging into the chasm with the sound of harp strings plucked one note at a time. Kath's breath caught in her throat, it would have been achingly beautiful if not for the threat.

Kath angled her horse next to Duncan's, her gaze moving from the glacier to the narrow pass. What she saw made her gasp. Spring had claimed the pass. Great swords of blue ice impaled the bridge of stone, creating a gauntlet of frozen death.

A sundering sound split the air, like the crack of broken stone. Kath's horse shied, but she held him firm. As the companions watched, a great sword of ice split from the glacier, plunging down, narrowly missing the pass.

Kath stared, awestruck by the power of the ice swords.

Beside her, Duncan said, "We've come too late. Spring is already here. The pass is a death trap."

Kath said, "If there's any justice in the world, the body of the Mordant should lie crushed beneath one of those ice-swords, felled by the hand of the gods."

"Why should the gods lift their hands when they have men to do their dirty work?"

His voice was bitter, but Kath refused to give up hope. Her stare searched the pass for signs of a broken body but she found only rock and ice. Disappointed, she conceded the archer might have a valid a point.

Glancing at the sky, Duncan said, "At least we've beaten the sun to the pass, we shouldn't tarry." His stare turned to the two strangers among them. "Does anyone wish to go back? Best decide before we risk the crossing."

No one spoke.

"Then let's cross before the danger deepens."

No one argued.

"Sir Tyrone, you take the lead followed by Kath. Once you two are safely across, I'll send the monk and the girl with their horses. Sir Blaine and I will bring up the rear with the packhorses." Turning toward Sir Tyrone, Duncan said, "Walk your horse across, but if there's any problem, leave the horse and get yourself to safety. Horses can be replaced."

The companions dismounted, waiting to take their turn at the crossing. Sir Tyrone checked the tack on his horse and then gathered the reins, giving his horse a reassuring pat. All eyes watched as he advanced under the threat of the glacier. The steady drip of melt water sounded like a celestial harp, seductively peaceful, belying the danger. Kath held her breath, but the black knight and his horse made it to the far side without incident.

Kath led Dancer out onto the thin finger of rock. Ignoring the threat of the twin chasms, she stared at the great shards of ice impaling the pass. Standing twice the height of a tall man, the shards resembled great blue swords. Kath could imagine Valin wielding the swords against any who dared breach the peace of the mountains. She shivered as she neared the first. The ice radiated a bone-numbing cold but the deep sapphire-blue was mesmerizing. Kath blinked and forced her stare away, leading her horse around the frozen swords. They passed three more ice-swords before stepping out from under the glacier's shadow. Grateful for the sun's warmth, Kath stood next to black knight, watching as the others crossed the chasm.

The monk was next.

Tall and thin with long silver-blond hair, the monk led his piebald horse out across the narrow pass. Leaning on a stout quarterstaff, he walked with his head bowed and shoulders hunched, as if he carried an immense weight. Kath wondered what memories could be worse than the menace of the ice. The monk and mare reached the first ice shard. The piebald mare skittered sideways, eyes rolling, but the monk forged ahead, heedless of the horse's fear.

Crack! A thunderous noise split the peace of the mountains.

The glacier groaned, releasing a shard of blue ice.

The piebald mare reared, hooves flashing in terror.

The monk fell to his knees, pulled off-balance by the horse.

Time stopped as the ice fell.

A sword of blue ice plunged towards the pass. Chips of ice rained down, solid pellets of pain. The mare screamed in terror. The blue sword slammed into the pass, ice grinding against stone, narrowly missing the monk. The stone ledge shook. The mare bucked wild with panic, the whites of her eyes showing, her muzzle flecked with foam. The monk lay prostrate beside the plunging hooves.

A streak of brown raced from the far side of the pass. Danya ran to the side of the mare, hands raised in supplication.

The mare skittered backwards, front hooves slashing toward the new threat, mad with fear. The horse snorted and squealed, dancing close to death.

Kath held her breath, expecting to see blood, but Danya dodged the hooves, reaching up to lay her hands on the neck of the piebald mare. A shudder rippled through the mare, her eyes showing brown instead of white. Her coat slick with sweat, the mare settled onto four legs. Quivering and blowing hard, the piebald mare nuzzled Danya. Peace returned to the pass.

Kath had never seen anything like it. She thrust the reins of her horse into the black knight's hands and sprinted back across the knife-edged toward the fallen monk. She slowed as she neared the trembling mare, not wanting to spook the horse.

Danya's voice was soft but sure, "The mare will be fine. Help the monk."

Kath knelt next to Zith. "Can you walk?"

Blood trickled from a deep cut across his forehead. His hazel eyes were dazed with shock. "W-what happened?"

"The glacier. We need to get you to safety. Can you walk?"

Duncan appeared next to Kath, reaching down to help. Together, they got Zith to his feet. The old man had more weight to his frame than Kath expected. The monk staggered like a drunk but they held him upright, steering him to the safety of the far side. Danya followed with the mare.

Duncan settled the monk next to a boulder. Kath ran to get a skin of water and a pouch of healing herbs from her saddlebag. Returning, she was surprised when Duncan took the pouch and began to tend the monk. Kath watched as he chose a sprig of dried lavender. Crushing the purple flowers, he held his fist close under the monk's nose. Zith snorted, a bloom of color rushing to his face.

A soft voice from behind said, "Will he live?"

Startled, Kath turned to find Danya standing close. Deep brown eyes, the color of earthy loam, met and held Kath's gaze. They were of the same height and nearly the same age. Kath nodded, acknowledging the woman's bravery. "You saved them both."

Relief washed across Danya's face. "The mare didn't mean it you know, she was just spooked by the ice."

Kath searched the young woman's face. Brown hair framed an oval face, a small nose and a generous mouth...nothing extraordinary or unusual, yet there was something more here. "How did you do it? How did you get the mare to calm so quickly?"

Fear flashed across Danya's face, quickly buried beneath a rising blush. Danya ducked her head and mumbled, "It's nothing. I just have a way with animals."

Another riddle. Kath let her go, but she suspected there was more to the two strangers than anyone guessed. She prayed it was so. From what she'd learned at the monastery, they'd need all the help they could get to slay the Mordant.

12

Micah

Sunlight streamed through the high trees, sending a few shafts of golden light all the way to the forest's needle-strewn floor. Micah threaded a path through the great trees, cedars, redwood, and pine, dancing his way through the beams of light that pooled on the forest floor, collecting luck as he went. He caught the first pool of sunlight next to the waxy dark-green leaves of a holly bush and then scrambled over a fallen redwood, thick with moss and mushrooms, eager to reach the second. His Nana had told him that any light beams that reached all the way to the forest floor were lucky and any boy who danced in their pools was sure to have a long life rich with golds. He knew that he was lucky, his Nana said so, but he was still waiting for the golds. In all of his seven years he'd never held a gold in his hand, nor a silver for that matter, only coppers and it took a lot of coppers just to buy one meat pie at the village fair. Still it was fun to catch the sunbeams and some day the golds would come, he was sure of it; his Nana had said so and she was old and wise and had a story about almost everything.

He ran through the forest, wondering what type of story Nana would tell tonight. His favorites were about knights in bright armor mounted on warhorses but perhaps tonight it would be something different, something about a boy besting the fearsome sea serpents of the lake in order to win four prized rainbow trout for his family's supper. The four fish dangling on his pole were smaller than the ones in his imagination, but at least one of them truly was a trout, the best eating the lake had to offer. His family would feast tonight, thanks to his skill with rod and worm, and it had only taken him half the morning to make the catch.

Dodging to the left, he decided to tag one more pool of light before heading home when he heard the voice, *"Something bad is coming."*

Fear shot through him, the voice was never wrong.

Dropping to his knees, Micah crouched behind a thick redwood trunk, slinking into the loam of the forest floor. The silent voice rarely spoke but when it did he listened. His Mam didn't believe in the voice but old Nana did. Nana said that the silent voice was a gift from the forest gods, a gift of warning that should always be heeded. Micah tried to listen for more, but it was hard to hear anything over his heart's wild pounding. Peering from behind the tree, his stare flicked to shade and shadow searching for wolves or a rare mountain cat, but he saw no sign of either. Fearful of claw and fang, he kept to his hiding place, his hand searching out a rock among the pine needles. The rock fit perfectly into his palm, making a much better weapon than his slender fishing pole. The rock gave him courage and his racing heart stilled. The silent voice remained silent and no threat appeared. Perhaps the danger had passed. Micah stepped out from behind the redwood, alert to any danger, but none came. Relieved, he raced for home, no more sun pools today.

His bare feet sped through the forest, taking the shortest way. The fish dangling from his pole made wet slapping sounds against his back, beating out a rhythm as he ran. He reached the edge of the forest, the trees giving way to the small meadow surrounding their cottage, when the voice came again, *"Hide, hide now!"*

Micah froze, still as a deer, searching for danger, searching for a place to hide. So close to home, he was sorely tempted to run to their cottage. The thatch-roofed cottage stood alone in the middle of the sunlit meadow, the door open and welcoming. He could hear his mother singing as she churned the butter she planned to sell at market. His mother's sweet song drifted across the meadow, proving there was no danger, yet Micah hesitated. Old Nana said he should always obey the voice...yet home was so close. He longed to race across the meadow and burst through the open door, but the voice had said to hide. Deciding to obey, Micah moved off the path and crouched behind a fallen pine. He held his breath, trying to be as still as a mouse.

Inside his mind the voice screamed, *"No! Hide better! Hide better now!"*

Terrified, Micah scrambled in search of a better hiding place. He spied a large blackberry bramble nestled next to a boulder. Dropping his fishing pole, he ran to the brambles and lay on the ground, worming his way into the tangled thorns. Squirming on his back, he followed a rabbit run that snaked its way inward. He was too big for the run, but he forced his way through, heedless of the thorns. Scratched and bleeding, he stopped when he reached the bramble's heart, pressing his back against the cool stone of the boulder. Half afraid to look, Micah peered through the thorns trying to spy the danger.

"Stay quiet, stay safe!"

Micah's breath caught in his throat, the voice had never said so much before. The last time he'd heard it he'd been hunting truffles. Finding a plump patch of the tasty black 'shrooms growing on the underside of a felled tree, he was about to reach for the prize when the voice had warned him. It was only then that he saw the wood adder, coiled and ready to strike. Wood adders were a sure and painful way to die, but the voice had only given him *one* warning. Micah shuddered to guess what *four* warnings could mean. Fueled by Nana's tales, he imagined slavering werewolves or shambling ghouls raised by an evil wizard. Pressing his back against the boulder, Micah made himself small and quiet, a rabbit hiding in the thorns.

He caught a flicker of movement in the forest.

Afraid to look, Micah strained to see.

A lone man approached, walking through the woods. Tall and lean, he wore long flowing robes of a rich yellow-gold color, like the pools of sunlight on the forest floor. He walked with a long, easy stride, using a quarterstaff for a walking stick, a leather rucksack on his back. His robe was travel-stained but the rich gold color marked him as a wealthy noble. No one from the village could afford a dye like that. But a nobleman without guards or even a horse was a riddle, not a danger. Perhaps the voice warned of something else. Puzzled, Micah watched from the brambles.

The stranger followed the path that led to his family's cottage. Micah bit his lip, worried. He knew he shouldn't look, but his stare locked on the stranger. Nana always said he was too curious for his own good.

The stranger stopped as if something had caught his attention. He glanced around and then moved toward a fallen pine tree.

The hairs bristled on the back of Micah's neck.

The man stooped behind the log and rose holding Micah's abandoned pole, the four fish still dangling on the line. Surveying the forest, his gaze swept toward the brambles.

Micah held his breath, watching the stranger. The man had short-cropped blond hair and blue eyes and the faint beginnings of a beard. From the fairness of his face, Micah guessed the stranger was high-born...until he caught the full brunt of the man's stare. Like getting doused with freezing water...only worse. Something cold and evil stared out of the stranger's eyes...something very wrong...something far worse than all of Nana's stories combined. Micah shivered, pressing his back against the boulder, wishing he could disappear.

Trapped by the man's gaze, Micah found it hard to breath. His stomach clenched into a fierce knot and sweat poured out of him, drenching his clothes. The man's stare urged him to speak, to give himself away. He fought, trying to close his eyes, to reject the stranger, but his eyelids would not obey.

A shout teetered on the edge of Micah's lips.

"Stay quiet, stay safe!"

The silent voice broke the spell. Micah swallowed, holding his yell inside.

The man's stare moved on.

Micah breathed again, short and shallow, fearful that even the smallest breath would draw the man's attention.

The man finished his slow survey of the forest, leaving Micah to wonder if the golden-robed stranger had truly seen him. He shuddered to think how close he'd come to betraying his hiding place.

The stranger shouldered Micah's fishing pole and resumed walking toward the sun-drenched meadow...toward the cottage, toward *home*.

Micah's heart thundered; he had to warn his Nana and his Mam. Fear for his family warred against his fear of the stranger. He screwed his eyes shut and told himself that a knight wouldn't hide in the brambles, a knight would find a way to save his family. His fist closed around the rock that had never left his hand. A single tear escaped, running down his cheek. He wasn't a knight, he was just a boy with a rock, but he had to try. He started to crawl back through the rabbit run when he heard the voice, *"Stay hidden, there is nothing you can do."*

Micah froze, afraid to do nothing, afraid to disobey.

The singing stopped...and the screams began.

Micah had never heard anything like it. Screams raced out of the cottage and across the meadow impaling his mind like daggers. Such agony could not come from a human voice but he knew it did. His mother's voice, his Nana's voice, he stopped his ears, but it did no good. Thrashing to escape the screams, the thorns flayed his flesh. His mind tried to flee his own body, but there was nowhere to go. It wasn't until the sun set that the screams finally stopped.

Micah lay in a stupor, impaled by the brambles, unable to do anything but watch.

Smoke rose in lazy curls from the chimney. The smell of fried trout wafted out of the door as if to taunt him. The smell sickened him.

Convulsing, he emptied his stomach onto the dirt, trying to disgorge the memories of the screams.

The stars came out overhead. He found the Big Ladle, the fire breathing Dragon and the Great Bear. He wondered if these were the same stars that his Nana told stories about, but they couldn't be. How could those same stars shine on something so evil? Micah stared at the stars demanding an answer, but he passed out before they replied.

He woke the next morning, stiff and sore, afraid to open his eyes. He wanted to be safe in his bed, the ordeal nothing but a nightmare, but his body told him otherwise. Shivering with cold and caked in blood from countless cuts, Micah opened his eyes to the brambles. It was real, it was all real, but something told him he hadn't seen the worst. He turned his head to stare at the cottage.

The man in the golden robes stood in the doorway.

It was almost as if he was waiting for Micah, but Micah refused to move.

The boy's heart beat loud in his ears, marking the passage of time. He waited, too afraid to even pray.

The golden stranger shrugged on his rucksack, picked up his staff and left the cabin. He passed to the far side of the meadow, disappearing into the woods, whistling a tune as he walked.

Micah waited. He waited till the sound of the whistling faded into the forest. He waited till he heard the robins and the jays singing in the branches again. He waited till the sun was high in the sky and his throat was parched with thirst. Finally, when his mouth was so dry that he could barely swallow, he bulled his way out of the brambles, heedless of the clawing thorns.

Pulling free of the brambles, he stood at the edge of the meadow and called to his Nana and Mam. It was a weak, croaky call but it didn't matter. In his heart he knew they would never answer.

The silent voice spoke again, *"Don't go to the cottage. Turn away, else the evil will spread."*

But this time Micah couldn't obey; he had to see for himself. Clutching the rock, he crossed the meadow and stood before the door. The stranger had left the door closed, a bloody mark painted on the wood. It was crudely drawn but clear nonetheless. Scrawled in red, scrawled in blood, was the mark of the stranger, the mark of evil. Micah made the hand sign to ward off the Dark Lord, knowing it was too late. Gripping the rock tight, he pushed the door open and walked into a bloody nightmare.

His mind shuddered and stopped.

Someone was screaming.

He recognized his own voice.

He began to run, chased by his own screams. Barefoot and bloody, he ran through the forest, desperate to escape the cottage. He didn't remember crossing the stream or running along the dirt lane but somehow he got to the village. He ran to the center, to the old well, yelling and screaming despite his parched throat.

Villagers tumbled from their homes, the forge, and the tavern. They gathered around, shock on their faces. Some tried to help, but he pushed them away, the tale bursting out of him. He told them about the golden-robed wizard and his spells of evil. He told them about hiding in the brambles and hearing the screams. Through a veil of tears, he told them about the horrors of the cottage. Dropping to his knees, he scrawled in the dirt, drawing the wizard's sign. Remembering the bloody mark on the door, Micah drew the sign of evil. He drew a man's open hand and on the palm was a seeing eye.

13

Samson

A rat scurried across the alleyway, brazen in the sunlight. *Rats*, Samson hated rats. The Flame God's city was full of them, especially in the back alleys. He turned his head, not wanting to see the reason the rat risked daylight but his nose betrayed him. Something rotten, something more than the usual refuse, something dead laced with decay. He held his sleeve to his face and walked faster. The stench was another reason to hate the back ways, but the alleys were safer than the streets. He'd never seen a red-robed priest in the alleys, or the bright-eyed faithful for that matter...the grime might tarnish their holiness. Samson chuckled but the sound was bitter. Compared to the priests, the rats were good company.

Samson threaded his way down the dirt lane, doing his best to avoid the yellow puddles. The alley narrowed, the buildings on either side becoming a better quality, stone instead of wood, a sure sign the back way was coming to an end.

He paused in the shadowy exit, scanning the intersecting street, searching for the telltale red of a priest's robe or a guard's tabard but found none. Relieved, he stepped into the cobblestones, joining the noon-time crowd, trying to look innocent...worried that he didn't know what innocent meant anymore.

Hands in his pockets, he strolled the street of chandlers, wooden signs displaying tapered candles. He shook his head, amazed that merchants with the same wares flocked to the same street, as if they found profit in numbers. It was the same for cobblers. He wondered how their little shop would fare away from the other boot makers, but then they hadn't returned to Coronth to earn golds...or to make boots. Samson sighed, wishing he was still in Lanverness.

He tried to blend in, making sure to walk at the same pace as the others, women returning from markets, merchants delivering bundles, boys running errands. His beard itched, too hot for the summer, but it was his only disguise; small wonder he preferred the safety of the back alleyways.

The street came to an intersection and he turned right, always scanning for red. Two more turns and he came to a small, open square lined with inns, taverns, and narrow stone houses, a respectable section of the city but not wealthy. The kind of place where people paid in silvers not golds.

Samson squinted at the sun and saw that he was early. He found a shadowy corner and leaned against the wall, staring at the tavern across the square. The well-kept wooden sign named it "the Jolly Penitent". The name didn't make any sense to Samson. In the Flame God's city penitents were either burnt alive or in hiding, rarely jolly. He stared at the sign and realized the tavern's name had never bothered him before, back when he had a normal life, back when he was a city guard, back before all the nightmares.

The tavern door opened and he saw her, long raven-black hair, skin as light and soft as cream, and a smile to brighten the sun, his Lucy. He drank in the sight like a man starved for food. Lucy was living proof of his past life, the girl he'd courted before the priests burned his father in the Test of Faith, before everything changed. He'd spied her in a crowd three weeks ago and had been following her ever since, trying to get up the nerve to meet. He longed to talk with her but he didn't know if he dared, didn't know if he should, now that he was a fugitive from the priests and a deserter from the guards. If truth be told, he wasn't sure if she'd even remember him, but he didn't want to think about that.

He watched from the shadows, waiting to see which way she'd turn. When she turned left, he knew she was heading for the spice markets; she went there once a week. He followed, not too close, not too far.

Once, just once, he dared get close enough to brush against her, to lean close and sniff her scent. A hint of lilac on her skin, the smell brought a rush of memories. He used to save his pay and buy her soaps infused with lilac, back before everything changed. Heady with her scent, he nearly said something, nearly whispered her name, but he kept walking past, brushing against her sleeve at the last moment. She glanced up at him but there was no recognition in her light brown eyes. Maybe it was the beard, or all the weight he'd lost, or maybe the lack of a uniform, she'd always liked his guard's uniform.

Samson kept walking, circling the market, circling Lucy. Cinnamon, nutmeg, pepper, basil, a rush of smells pressed against him. He breathed deep, enjoying the rich mingling of scents while watching Lucy meander through the market, a feast for the senses.

The market was crowded, a crush of women and a smattering of men, haggling for small packets of spices. The haggling was heaviest around the salt merchants; everyone needed salt. He lost sight of Lucy in the press. Rushing forward, he tried to find her. He caught a flash of her dark hair to the left and angled in that direction. He broke through the crowd and skidded to a stop.

"Alms for the temple!" A short, bird-eyed priest glared up at Samson. "Ease your sins by giving alms to the Flame God."

Fear strangled Samson's throat. He stared at the red-robed priest, wanting to run but afraid to move.

The priest thrust a black lacquer bowl at Samson's chest, his voice insistent. "You look like a man with sins on your soul. Give alms to the temple and lessen your burden."

Samson struggled to breathe. Frantic to escape, he fumbled in his pocket, desperate for a coin. Without looking, he flung one into the bowl, praying it was silver.

The priest's stare followed the coin till it chinked among the others. He glanced up at Samson, a neutral smile on his face. "Blessings of the Flame God be upon you." He turned away, searching for another donor.

Samson sagged in relief; it must have been a silver. A copper coin and the priest would have harassed him for more. A gold coin and the priest would have fawned all over him. A silver was the only safe offering, the only way to escape.

Shaken by the encounter, he fled back to the market, seeking to disappear in the crowd. He scanned the stalls, looking for red; priests usually traveled in packs. Glimpsing red robes to the left, he ducked low and worked his way to the far edge of the market, slipping into the first alleyway. Free of the crowd, he found himself running, needing to get away.

He took two wrong turns but eventually found his way back to their cobbler shop. He paused, trying to still his ragged breathing; he didn't want the others to see him this way. When his racing heart finally calmed, he straightened his jerkin and stepped out into the street. A fresh painted sign showed a gentleman's black boot on a field of green. Samson opened the door and stepped into a workshop cluttered with tools and a few pairs of finished boots. A whiff of fresh-baked apple pie competed with the smell of worked leather. Mouth-watering, he followed the smell past the stairs to the large stone kitchen at the rear. The soothing sound of knitting needles made him smile, the tension of the streets melting from his shoulders.

"Come in dear, there's no sense hovering in the doorway."

The silver-haired old lady had a habit of inviting poor folk home, offering them a meal at their table. She was always saying, "You need to feed their bodies before you can change their minds." But today she was alone, sitting in a rocking chair by the hearth, her hands busy with knitting needles. Grandmother Magda looked harmless enough but Samson knew she had at least one sharp-edged butcher's knife tucked away in the yarn bag at her feet. The old woman could take care of herself. She looked up from her knitting, her eyes keen, her voice warm. "Come and have some tea. The kettle's on the fire and there's corn bread in the warming pan."

He never saw her cooking but there was always something fresh baked, waiting in the oven. Apple pie was his favorite, the smell of apples always made him feel safe. He took a mug from the hook and lifted the kettle from the fire. "Will you have a cup with me?"

"Thanks but I'll wait for the others." The knitting needles kept at a steady, rhythmic clacking, the sound of safety.

He settled onto the bench by the table and wrapped his hands around the mug. "When will they be back?"

"Ben should return soon; he's delivering a pair of boots. Justin is harping at one of the taverns; he won't be back till late."

The mention of taverns sent a shiver of guilt down Samson's back. He shouldn't have followed Lucy, shouldn't have gone to the Jolly Penitent. "Which tavern?"

"Oh the Thirsty Saint, or the Hungry Sinner, the names all sound alike to me." Her gray eyes twinkled in the firelight.

He chuckled at the joke; the old woman was sharp as a knife, never missing a trick.

The rocking chair creaked in a steady rhythm, the knitting needles clacking. "How was your day, dear?"

The question brought a ration of guilt. Instead of searching out citizens who hated the priests, he'd squandered his morning following Lucy. He was supposed to be scouring the city for allies, but he found it hard to approach the ones with haunted eyes. So hard and so dangerous...so much easier to find other things to do. He hid behind the mug, taking a long drink of tea.

"Have you found anyone, dear?"

He sputtered and choked, his face turning red, the question too close to the bone.

The rocking chair stopped, but not the knitting needles, never the knitting needles.

He hid from her gaze, staring into the mug. "So much has changed. The city is worse than I remember." He thought about Lucy, about the life he'd lost, about the way he felt when he followed her through the markets. The old woman knew what it was like to lose family. She'd lost everything to the Flame God; surely she'd understand his need to be loved. Samson raised his gaze and stared at the silver-haired grandmother, the shawl wrapped tight around her shoulders, the lines of wisdom etched deep on her face. He wanted to tell her about Lucy, wanted to ask her advice. He leaned forward, struggling to find the right words.

Snap! The fire cracked, spitting a spark.

Samson jumped, his heart hammering as if he'd seen a priest, his secret clogged in his throat. He shook his head, and tightened his grip on the mug. He couldn't tell anyone about Lucy. The moment was lost.

The rocking chair started again, the low creak keeping time to the knitting needles. "Have a piece of pie, dear, you'll feel better."

Samson reached for the pie and cut a thick slice. He breathed deep, wrapping himself in the smell of cinnamon and baked apples. He needed to feel safe, needed to believe the kitchen was a haven. He knew it was an illusion, but he held tight to it anyway, otherwise the reality of Coronth was just too damn scary.

14

Liandra

Mired in worry, the queen paced in front of the mullioned window. "Has he yielded the names?"

The Master Archivist bowed his head. "He spewed plenty of names when we first put him in the traitor's hole, all of them false."

The queen wore a path in the carpet. "You're sure they're false?"

"Prince Stewart? Myself? And then he started on more obscure names."

"Such as?"

"Madam Stock."

"A woman?"

The master grimaced. "The madam of an expensive bordello. The prince named half the whores in Pellanor."

The queen shuddered. "More proof he is not worthy." Liandra massaged the half-moon cuts on her palms, scars from the scene of betrayal. She forced the memory from her mind; she had a kingdom to secure. "So whom does he name now?"

"He's fallen silent. Perhaps the dungeon is finally taking its toll."

"Danly was always one to wallow in luxuries. We expected a single day in the dungeons to break him. He japes at us by naming whores." Glancing out the window, she watched the sky darken, ominous with storm clouds. "We need those names. Time grows short. The ruse that Prince Danly has taken ill with the flux wears thin." She tightened her hands into fists, aware of the rings on her fingers. "When the Red Horns learn the truth, they will have but two choices, retreat and try to escape, or to spring their trap and attack. Judging from the way the leader of Red Horns has so far played the game, we expect him to fight rather than flee." The queen turned to stare at her spymaster. "We can feel it in the very air. We are but a hair's breath away from bloodshed."

The master nodded. "What would you have me do?"

"Your jailors have tried and failed. It is time for different tactics." She fingered the string of pearls at her throat. "We will go to him."

"No!"

The queen raised an eyebrow in warning.

The master's face contorted in worry, a rare sign of emotion from the stoic counselor. "It is far too dangerous. The safety of the sovereign is paramount. My shadowmen can best protect you in the Queen's Tower."

"Time is running out. We have made up our mind." Picking up a hand bell, the queen summoned her lady-in-waiting.

A petite blond-haired woman answered the summons. Curtseying, she waited for the queen's command.

"Lady Sarah, is everything ready?"

Blanching, the woman replied, "Yes, your majesty, all is in order."

Turning to her shadowmaster, the queen said, "See to it that the guards are waiting at the servants' entrance in one turn of the hourglass and do not forget the password."

His face grim, the master objected, "There is no need for you to do this. Let me try again. It is too dangerous for you to leave the Queen's Tower."

"The game is nearing checkmate; we must make a daring move to save our crown." The queen turned a gilded hourglass, setting the sands coursing. "You have an hour to prepare. We will go to Danly and get the traitors' names."

"Everything will be done as you have planned." With a final bow the Master Archivist left the solar.

Turning to her lady-in-waiting the queen said, "Now you must help us with our disguise."

Lady Sarah worked with quiet efficiency, divesting the queen of her royal raiment.

Liandra sat statue-still, enduring the transformation. She watched through narrowed eyes as the armor of her image was stripped away. The glitter of wealth was the first to be removed; pearl necklaces, gold bracelets, and diamond hair studs, all divested, leaving the queen unadorned. The delicate swirls of her raven hair were next, combed out and tied back in a simple peasant's knot. Layers of the finest silk were exchanged for a dull butternut frock of plain homespun wool. The artful powders accenting her cheeks, lips, and eyes were stripped away, revealing her inner face. As a final touch, a simple shawl was draped over her head and around her shoulders, the coarse brown wool scraping against her face.

The queen studied the results, feeling vulnerable. A commoner stared back from the royal mirror, a woman older than the queen and far less captivating. Liandra mourned her youth and the armor of her image. Suppressing a shudder, she steeled her resolve. Desperate gambits often required extreme measures. Turning away from the harsh truth, the queen rose, ready to make her next move.

Lady Sarah curtseyed. "Pardon me, your majesty, but your rings?"

She stared at the royal rings gracing her hands. "You are quite right, Lady Sarah, but these rings shall never leave our hands...not till death takes them from us." Twisting the Great Seal and the Royal Emerald, the queen adjusted the rings so that they appeared as two plain bands of thick gold. "That will have to do." Looking closely at her lady-in-waiting, the queen said, "Do you understand your role in this play?"

"Yes, your majesty."

The sands of the hourglass had run out. Outside the window, the sky was dark, the storm nearly upon them. "Then let us be away, and remember, once we leave this chamber you are to refer to us as your 'cousin'. We cannot be the queen beyond this chamber."

Turning pale, Lady Sarah bowed her head and murmured, "As you wish, your majesty."

The queen paused, infusing her voice with warmth, "We are entrusting you with our life, Lady Sarah. Are you equal to this task?"

Color bloomed on the woman's cheeks. "Yes, majesty."

"Then lead the way. Your simple 'cousin' from the country follows behind."

The queen hid her face within the shawl and slumped her shoulders, trying to shed her royal posture. With a final curtsey, Lady Sarah opened the door to the hallway, forsaking the safety of the queen's solar. Guards snapped to attention but they relaxed once they saw the women, allowing them to pass without comment.

Using back passageways frequented by servants, they wound their way through the tower, trusting to the simple disguise of being merely women. The queen kept her face deep within the shawl while Lady Sarah chattered on, explaining the ways of the court to her country cousin. The queen, accustomed to having stares follow her every move, was amazed at the freedom of the disguise. Despite the presence of guards at most doors, the two women reached the servants' entrance at the rear of the tower without challenge.

The evening was cool and full of shadows, dark clouds roiling above. The queen lingered in the doorway, watching as Lady Sarah ventured into the courtyard. Soldiers and young men loitered in the cobblestone yard, waiting for girlfriends and lovers to finish their shift of work. A handsome young man approached Lady Sarah, taking her arm. Words were exchanged and then the lady let out a peal of laughter that echoed against the walls of the castle.

Hearing the pre-arranged signal, the queen pulled the shawl tight around her head and dared to leave the safety of the tower. Her glance darted around the yard, wary of foes. Halfway across, a captain in the emerald tabard of the royal guards fell into step with her, gallantly offering his arm. Leaning his head toward her in a familiar fashion, the captain whispered, "White's Gambit".

Relieved, the queen took the captain's arm, hoping the gesture looked natural. She studied her escort, pleased to find him tall and handsome as well as good mannered; her shadowmaster had chosen well.

The captain threaded a muscular arm around her waist, walking close as a lover.

The queen bristled but then forced herself to relax.

The captain whispered, "I beg your pardon for the familiarity, but the master's orders were explicit. My name is Captain Durnheart of the Rose Guards and I will see you safely to your destination."

His voice was soothing but the rigid tension of his arm screamed of danger. Keeping her voice to a whisper, the queen asked, "How many others are there?"

"Shadowmen lurk in every doorway along the route, protecting our back as well as the way forward. The Master Archivist leaves little to chance."

The queen nodded, pleased with her spymaster, but her gaze never stopped raking the courtyard, trying to judge friend from foe.

They walked at a leisurely pace, blending in with servants leaving the castle. They followed the crowd toward the western gate, but before passing out of the inner yard, the captain steered her away toward the great kitchen. Avoiding the kitchen at the last moment, they ducked into an unlit passage linking the inner yard to the soldiers' barracks. Pausing in the shadows of the covered passageway, they scanned for threats. A group of soldiers patrolled the barracks yard, marching in formation. When the soldiers reached the far corner, the captain tightened his grip around the queen's waist and briskly walked her toward the short squat tower that marked the entrance to the dungeons.

Castle Tandroth's dungeons lay below ground, a deep delving of black cells and hidden chambers, a place of buried misery, the one place in the castle the queen had never been. Pulling her shawl tight, she bowed her head, hiding her face from the guards.

The captain whispered a word and the prison guard jumped to open the heavy iron door, giving the pair admission to the underworld. The queen shivered as she passed through the portal. Behind them, the ironclad door clanked shut like the jaws of a metal beast. The sound grated on the queen's nerves. The captain released his hold and stepped away, giving her the space due a royal. She missed the comfort of his arm.

Cold stone closed in around them, dank and dark and menacing. The queen and the captain descended the ramp. A horrid stink smacked them in the face, rank with all the smells of human fear, a warning of the cruelties that lay below. The queen pulled her shawl across her face as if the coarse wool could insulate her from the stench.

Emerging from the sloped tunnel, they entered a well-lit guardroom, torches and weapons racks lining the walls. They found the Master Archivist in conversation with one of the jailors. Tension melted from the queen's shoulders at the sight of her spymaster.

The master turned, barely flicking a glance in her direction. "There you are, Durnheart. I see you've found the rogue's doxy. Perhaps her pleading will convince him to talk."

The master's curt dismissal struck Liandra like a slap. It was all part of the ruse, yet it hurt to be ignored, especially by him. The queen bridled her temper, forcing herself to play the part of a mere woman. In the game of kings most women barely counted as pawns.

Turning his back on the queen, the master addressed the burly jailor. "Paulus, we'll need the keys for the lower dungeon."

Scratching an itch at his crotch, the pot-bellied jailor leered at the queen. "Lest she's goin' to raise her skirt, a woman won't much matter to the men in here."

"I'll be the judge of that." The master's retort cut like sharp steel. "Now be quick about it, and get the keys."

"No need to get angry, m'Lord," the jailor groused as he selected a thick ring of keys from the rack along the back wall. "It'll be darker than hell down there, so you may be wantin' a torch or two."

The master turned to two soldiers waiting in the shadows. "You two grab extra torches and bring up the rear. Captain Durnheart, follow me. Bring the woman along and watch your step, the floors are slick with slime."

The captain moved to the queen's side, tightening his grip on her arm.

This time the queen welcomed his touch.

He steered her forward, following directly behind the spymaster. Two soldiers with torches brought up the rear. Hinges creaked as the jailor unlocked a massive ironbound door. The door revealed a long stone passageway lined with cells. A low stone ceiling pressed down, cramping the space, swallowing light and life, strangling the senses. They walked into the belly of the dungeon, the air rank with the stench of urine and unwashed bodies. The queen fixed her gaze on the master's back, trying to avoid any glimpse of the cells. Hairy arms thrust out from between iron bars making grabbing gestures. The prisoners jeered, hurling lewd comments. The queen refused to flinch. Shutting her ears, she kept to the center, walking a gauntlet of obscenities.

The jailor clattered his keys against the iron bars. "All right you scum, quiet down. There'll be no skirt for the likes of you." But the din continued, perhaps threats no longer mattered to these men.

An eternity later, they reached the second door. The jailor fumbled with the keys. Shadows danced in the flickering torchlight. The rusted hinges screeched, opening to a steep staircase, the stones coated in a green slime. They worked their way down the tight spiral, the air stagnant with the smell of festering mold. The queen lost her footing, but the captain was quick to catch her. She gripped his arm, grateful for his strength.

The stairway led to a second row of cells, only this time a pounding silence assaulted the queen's ears. Her own heartbeat sounded loud, an intrusion of the living in a tomb of stone. The silence was chilling, as if any semblance of humanity could not survive the murky depths. The queen shivered, her gaze fixed on the Master Archivist, afraid to see what lay rotting in the cells.

The cellblock ended in a rusted door. Muttering, the jailor said, "Don't use the torture chambers no more, pity that." Jiggling the key into the lock, he added in a louder voice, "Only opened this section of the dungeon for the new prisoner. Must've done something really wicked to earn the hole."

The queen shuddered, unable to imagine what type of hell lay below.

The door opened onto a balcony of heavy wood beams. Stepping onto the balcony, they gained a view of a cavernous room hewn from bedrock. The air held a cold dampness that leached the soul. Liandra shivered, longing for the warmth of her solar.

Torches lined the walls along the wooden staircase, casting flickers of light into the gloom. She clutched the railing as they descended, staring down into the cavernous void. Strange devices lurked like misshapen monsters on the crowded floor, threatening the imagination with the stuff of nightmares. The queen consoled herself with the knowledge that torture had not been used in more than three generations of Tandroths. She prayed to the Lords of Light that it would remain that way.

Skirting the main floor, the jailor led them to a side room where two guards sprang to attention, their swords drawn. Seeing the Master Archivist, they sheathed their weapons. The queen kept her face hidden within the folds of her shawl, as much a disguise as a refuge from the stench.

Turning to the jailor-guide, the master said, "Paulus, you can wait for us here, Barkley will take us the rest of the way."

Shrugging, the jailor slumped into a chair and said, "As you wish m'Lord."

"Barkley you lead the way, Collins, stay here and keep watch. I do not wish to be disturbed for any reason. Do you understand?"

The older of the two guards nodded while the younger unlocked an ironbound door. Waving them through, he locked the door behind them. The quiet was otherworldly, the weight of stone pressing down like a sepulcher. No one spoke. The guard led them past a row of solid iron doors, finally stopping at the door at the end of the narrow passageway. Rust coated the iron door like a sheen of dried blood. A pair of grim-faced guards stood at attention. The queen shivered, finding the cold dankness oppressive.

The master said, "Durnheart, you and the others remain here on guard."

Nodding, the captain relinquished the queen into the care of the Master Archivist.

In a curt voice, the master said, "Open the door."

The hinges protested. The door swung open. The queen and her spymaster stepped through. A single guard with a drawn sword met them on the other side. Recognizing the spymaster, the guard sheathed his sword, closing the door behind them.

The metal clang reverberated in the small spare chamber. The queen felt buried alive. Swallowing her unease, she studied the chamber. Iron chains dominated the room. Heavy links ran from a rectangular grate set in the floor, up through hooks in the ceiling and then over to a huge winch built into the wall. A shiver ran down the queen's back. She'd expected to find her prisoner-son, but instead found only chains and rough rock walls. Her mind froze, unwilling to speculate on the function of the chains...or the apparent absence of her son.

While the queen surveyed the chamber the marshal interrogated his man. "Has he said anything?"

"Not today."

"Has he received food and water?"

"He is raised three times a day and offered both. He takes the water but has so far refused the food."

With a curt nod the master said, "Raise him up, I would speak to him."

The guard's stare slid toward the queen.

"Just do as you are ordered and then leave us alone with the prisoner."

Bowing, the guard took up a position by the winch. He unlatched the wheel and began to wind the iron chains, the muscles on his arms and neck bulging with strain. The wood of the winch creaked in protest. The chain grew taut, slowly hoisting the metal grate from the stone floor like a sword eased from a scabbard. Two pale hands appeared, manacled to the underside of the plate. The queen gasped, suddenly understanding the meaning behind the words, "traitor's pit". The slit in the stone floor was just wide enough for a man to stand. The queen watched in horror as her second son was raised from the traitor's tomb of cold stone.

Naked except for a filth-encrusted loincloth, Danly was manacled in a spread-eagle position against an iron plate. His eyes were sunken, his face haggard, open sores on his legs hinted at vermin within the pit. He reeked of stench but the queen refused to flinch. Three days in the pit and her son no longer looked the prince. The prisoner screwed his eyes shut, wincing at the sudden light, but otherwise he gave no reaction.

The guard latched the winch and threw a bucket of cold water on the prisoner. As Danly sputtered, the guard held a dipper to his lips, letting him drink his fill. When the dipper was empty, the guard bowed toward the master and then retreated to the outer corridor. The door clanged shut, leaving them alone with the prisoner.

The Master Archivist stared at the queen, waiting for orders.

The queen lowered her shawl and stepped forward to stare into the face of her second-born son. She steeled herself to his suffering, remembering that Danly had planned to murder his brother and anyone else who blocked his path to the Rose Throne. This second son had been nothing but evil since the day of his birth.

"Danly, how did it come to this?"

At the sound of her voice, he squinted into the light. "Is that you mother?"

"Yes, we are here."

Straining to see, Danly said, "It cannot be. The queen would never soil her gowns with the prison's stench. It must be a dream. My royal mother even invades my worst nightmares."

"Open your eyes and believe."

He peered at her, studying her face. "So it is you, plucked of your royal plumage. Beneath the paints and powders you're quite an ordinary woman, best stick to being queen, mother."

She ignored his barbs. "We have come to you, even to the depths of the dungeon, to convince you that this suffering is senseless. End this agony by giving us the names of the traitors."

Danly barked a laugh. "My dear mother, you ordered me here."

"Actions have consequences. When you chose the way of the traitor you tempted a traitor's fate. What consequence did you expect?"

"I expected a throne, mother, and a crown on my head. Surely you can understand the all-consuming need for power." He lunged toward her, rattling the chains but unable to reach more than a few inches.

"You had power and wealth as a prince of Lanverness. If you wanted more then you need only earn it through service to the people."

He groaned. "Spare me your lectures on service, mother. Monarchs rule they don't serve. Perhaps your crown would be more secure if you understood that. But either way, you would never have given more to me. You never gave me anything but the scraps from your plate. It was all for my brother, the shiny knight, none for me, none for Danly the despised second son."

Slap! The sound echoed through the chamber.

She'd forgotten about her rings. The great emerald left a gouge on his cheek, opening the claw marks of the prostitute. Puss oozed from the side of his face, as if he rotted from within. She'd learned much about her son in the last three days, all of it ugly, too ugly for a mother but she was the queen. The evidence of Danly's perversion only increased her ire. "Does your brother, Prince Stewart, still live?"

Danly gave her an insolent smile. "Why should I bother answering? What will you do, mother, cast me into the dungeon?"

From behind her, the Master Archivist growled, "Answer the queen if you care for your life."

"Madam, your dog barks." Danly shrugged as much as the chains would allow. "If my dear brother's head does not grace the portcullis then it may still be on his shoulders. But that would be a pity." His voice dropped to a malignant hiss. "Think about it mother, if the shiny knight loses his head, then *I* am your only heir." He railed against his chains, his voice rising to a shout. "And this is how you treat your son, your spare heir. *Nothing for me, mother, never anything for me!*"

Liandra staggered backward, the pain of the past erupting within her. Anger and hurt poured into her voice, "Why should I give *more* to you when all you have ever done is *take* from me?"

"When have I ever taken anything that mattered to you?" His voice was incredulous. "I spent plenty of your precious golds at the dicing tables, yet you never seemed to care."

The queen struggled for composure, but the long buried secret erupted. "You killed my only daughter!"

"What?"

In a strangled voice, the queen whispered, "You were born a twin. But your selfish, evil nature prevailed even in the womb. You emerged healthy but your twin sister was blue, *your* birthing cord wrapped tight around her neck. She died before ever taking her first breath, before ever feeling the arms of a mother's love. *You killed my only daughter! You strangled your sister in the womb!*"

Danly gaped. "A womb killer...and I never knew."

"I saved your life that day." Liandra choked on the words. "The midwives wanted to smother you in the cradle lest a seed of the Dark Lord chance to sit on the Rose Throne, but I stayed their hand. Having lost a daughter I could not bear to also lose a son. I swore the women to secrecy on pain of death. I gave you life twice in one day...and you repay me with betrayal."

Danly sagged in the chains. "Blamed from birth..."

"I spared you from the taint of your first foul deed, your first *murder,* yet now I rue my mercy. Instead of a son, I nurtured a viper at my breast!" Liandra turned away, sickened by the sight of her traitorous son. Struggling with the past, she fought to regain her composure. When she turned back to the prisoner, she was once more the queen. "We have come to claim payment for the life of our daughter. Give us the names of the traitors."

"You never told me."

"We spared you the knowledge, hoping that you might grow straight and true. But instead you turned to the Dark, raping women and plotting to steal the Rose Throne."

Danly's eyes widened, his guilt written upon his face.

"We have learned much of your true nature in the last few days." The queen lowered her voice, "Give us the names of the traitors."

His voice was small, "Did you ever love me, mother?"

He stabbed at her heart, but she kept her face stony.

When she did not answer, something hardened in his eyes. His voice sank to a sneering whisper, "I dreamt of you mother...with every whore."

The Master Archivist intervened, his fist smashing against the prisoner's face.

Danly's head snapped back, a trickle of blood at the side of his mouth. "Your dog hits hard."

"You are speaking to the *queen!*"

"Oh, I thought she was my mother."

The queen forced herself to study the true face of her son, but she saw only the traitor. He belonged in chains. "Spare yourself this agony and give us the names."

"I see the queen is back...if there ever was a mother." Danly strained against the chains but fell back, defeated. "You win, mother. You always win." His words said one thing but a sly look hung in his dark eyes. "What if I told you that the leader of the Red Horns is none other than your own precious spymaster?"

Slap!

Her hand stung from the blow. She'd never struck him as a child but twice the man had goaded her to violence. The queen felt as if she was unraveling. "Spare us your lies."

A trickle of blood ran from Danly's mouth. He shook his head. "I bring out the best in you, don't I mother?"

She glared, unrelenting. "Give us the names."

"Or what? I'm your son, your spare heir, mother!"

He pushed her too far. "Enough of this liar! Put him back in the hole!"

Her shadowmaster moved to unlock the wench mechanism. Chains rattled and the iron platform began to descend.

Fear scrawled across Danly's face. *"No! Don't do this!"*

The queen watched, unrelenting. Danly lunged against his chains but he remained caught. Howling in fear, his stare became frantic as the device lowered him into the stone tomb. *"I'll tell you!"*

The queen signaled and the mechanism came to a halt. Danly's face and bound hands remained in the light, the rest of him sheathed in cold stone. *"I'll tell you, but don't put me back!"*

"Speak and do not lie, for we shall know."

Danly craned his neck to stare up at her. His gaze was wide and wild. "Lord Turner. The leader of the Red Horns is Lord Turner, the Knight Protector, the man charged with the safety of the queen." He rattled his chains. *"Now let me out!"*

The queen looked to her shadowmaster, shocked by the depth of betrayal.

The master nodded a grim assent.

"Let him up."

Chains clanged as the platform emerged from the stone floor. The metal rack lurched upwards, slowly drawing even with the queen. Drenched in sweat and ripe with fear, Danly hung spread-eagle in his shackles. His face rippled with emotion, finally settling on a twisted sneer. "Isn't it ironic, mother? The man charged with your protection is the one man who cannot stomach to serve a mere woman. He sits on your council controlling the royal guards, perfectly positioned to lead the rebellion." A mocking laugh erupted from him, spittle flying from his lips. "He may yet beat the vaunted Spider Queen!" Danly rattled his chains. "Careful, mother, or you could end up dangling in another's webs." Laughter bubbled from the fallen prince, a laughter that skirted the edge of madness.

The queen took no triumph in the revelation, only shock at the depth of betrayal.

Danly giggled, hanging like a fly caught in a metal web.

Liandra wondered if they were all nothing more than flies, caught in a cruel web of fate. She tightened her fists in anger, her rings of office biting deep into her palms. The pain reminded her of her duty; she had a kingdom to care for. Turning to her spymaster, she ordered, "See to it that he is freed of this device. Clean him up and put him in a better cell. His identity must remain hidden but there is no need for this barbarous cruelty. We would have him treated with dignity despite his crimes."

Danly laughed, *"Dignity, dignity for the prince."*

The master said, "It will be as you command, but first I must see you to safety. And then I have a traitor to catch."

Shaken by the confrontation and shocked by the identity of the traitor, Liandra could only nod. Wrapping the shawl around her head, she shrank back into the posture of a mere woman.

The Master Archivist knocked a rhythm on the ironbound door. It swung open, easing the pressure in the queen's ears, something she hadn't noticed before.

The master issued commands, "Keep the prisoner above ground. Give him food and water but wait for my orders." Without waiting for a salute, he shepherded the queen back through the grim labyrinth. This time, she did not notice the stench or the catcalls, her mind preoccupied with strategies of vengeance.

The jailor opened the door to the last level, a long walk through darkness and stench. Prisoners rattled their chains, hurling jeers, but the queen paid them no mind. They passed out of the depths into the main guardroom, torchlight flickering along the walls. Whatever the master said to the jailor, the queen did not hear, wrapped in her own bleak thoughts.

Captain Durnheart took her arm and steered her toward the ramp. The stone ramp seemed steeper, the horrors of the dungeon nipping at her heels. Her clothes itched, as if lice-ridden. The stench of the underworld clawed at her soul. She felt soiled by the deeds of her son. Liandra gripped her skirts and hurried, feeling a sudden need for fresh, clean air, feeling the need to be queen.

They reached the outer doors. The guard fumbled with the keys. Liandra willed him to hurry. She bit back a harsh command, struggling to remember the charade.

The door swung open to admit the cool night air...and the sounds of battle. Lightning flashed over head as the storm unleashed a downpour. The courtyard rang with the chaos of swords. A rallying cry, "For the king!" echoed against the castle walls. The queen gaped at the chaos. Her shadowmaster appeared, pulling her back into the dungeon, shielding her with his body...but the bloodshed was imprinted on her mind. The traitor's name came too late. The Red Horns had risen.

15

Katherine

Stars crowded the night sky, a spray of jewels strewn across a dark vault. Perhaps it was a trick of the mountains, but it seemed to Kath that she could almost reach out and touch them. She sought the familiar patterns, the swan flying due south, the knight pointing the way north, and the dragon with his wings stretched half way across the heavens. It would have been a perfect night sky, if not for the red comet ripping an ugly scar across the dragon's wing. Kath dropped her gaze to the campfire, her hand seeking the crystal dagger. She needed no reminders of the Mordant.

A gust of wind howled down from the glacier, causing the fire to sputter. Shadows and light danced unevenly across her sleeping companions. After the perils of the crossing, Duncan had decided to camp on the trail just below Drumheller Pass. It was a grim place for a campsite, but a night's rest would give the monk a chance to recover. Luckily, his injuries weren't serious. A warm meal and a night's sleep should restore his strength for the long ride ahead.

Sir Blaine and Sir Tyrone had set up camp while Kath gathered firewood and Duncan took his bow to search for game. It was scarce, so they had to settle for a stew made from dried meat and vegetables from their travel rations. Subdued by the near tragedy of the pass, the companions ate a quiet meal and then sought the warmth of their bedrolls. There was little conversation.

Kath drew the first watch. She sat on her bedroll tending the fire, running a whetstone along the edge of her sword. Questions ran through her mind. The incident at the pass deepened the mystery of the two strangers. Kath had to admit that she was impressed with Danya. Quick to respond to the mare's terror, the young woman had risked her own life on the narrow bridge of stone. Danya had proven her courage, but it was passing strange how she'd calmed the mare with just the touch of her hand.

The fire crackled, spitting a harmless spark.

Kath felt a stare crawl up her back.

Drawing her sword, she whirled to face the threat.

From the edge of the firelight, a pair of green eyes glowered. *Animal eyes...predator eyes.* Kath crouched in a fighting stance. Transferring the sword to her left hand, she reached back for a throwing axe.

A low growl rumbled from the dark.

Kath gripped the handle of the axe.

"No! Don't!" Danya's voice cut like a knife.

The others woke, scrambling for weapons, bright steel glittering in the night.

Danya leaped from her bedroll. *"Bryx, to me!"*

The wolf's eyes glittered cold and keen...but it did not attack.

Kath stayed her hand.

Danya stepped toward the beast. "He won't hurt you."

A low growl turned into a chuff. A massive mountain wolf stepped into the light, a monster of fur and teeth. Six feet from nose to tail, a thick ruff of bluish-black fur around his neck, the wolf bared its teeth at Kath and then sauntered toward Danya. Sniffing the young woman's outstretched hand, the beast settled at Danya's feet, tongue lolling from the side of its mouth like a tame dog. Kath had the strangest impression that the wolf was laughing at her. "A wolf that acts like a dog?"

Flashing a shy smile, Danya said, "I told you I had a way with animals." Dropping her glance to Kath's sword, she added, "You can put that away, Bryx won't hurt anyone."

Kath stared at the wolf but the wildness of a moment ago was gone. Her gaze sought Duncan. The archer shrugged, "He looks tame enough."

"Please, all of you," Danya hugged the wolf, her gaze circling the companions. "Bryx won't hurt you."

The monk stirred in his bedroll, his eyes bird-bright in the firelight. "The wolf is her companion. He won't harm you unless you harm Danya."

Strange and stranger, but she'd come to trust the monks. Kath sheathed her sword but kept her hand on the hilt.

Blaine said, "That's the biggest damn wolf I've ever seen," but he lowered his sword as well. The others sheathed their weapons and crawled back into their bedrolls. Kath suspected they kept watch, their swords near at hand.

Keeping a wary eye on the wolf, Kath resumed her seat by the fire. Glancing at Danya, she said, "How did you come to tame a wolf?"

"It's a long story."

"I've time to listen."

An awkward silence settled between them.

Kath added more branches to the fire. "I've kept the kettle warm. Join me in a cup of tea and we can trade stories." Without waiting for a reply, she sprinkled herbs and ground tea into two metal mugs. Reaching for the kettle, she poured the water. The rising steam carried a welcoming hint of lemongrass. Kath passed one mug across to Danya, careful not to bring her hand too near the wolf.

Cradling the mug with both hands, Danya sat cross-legged on her bedroll, the wolf lolling by her side. She gazed at Kath, her face thoughtful. "The monastery was full of rumors about the princess of Castlegard and the fabled Knights of the Octagon. I watched while you practiced with your throwing axes and sword, but I never thought I'd be joining you. I never wanted to leave the monastery."

"So why did you come?"

Danya shrugged, "When the Grand Master asks you don't say no."

It was an answer Kath could understand. She picked up a branch and poked at the fire, a mystery of unanswered questions hanging between them. The wolf yawned and the fire crackled. Kath took a sip of tea, giving Danya time to spin her story. When nothing more was said, she tried another tack. "So how did you come by the wolf?"

Danya lowered her eyes, a flush spreading across her face. "The wolf's part of the long story."

Kath sipped her tea, waiting.

Danya let out a long sigh. "I might as well tell you. You'll probably understand better than the others." She reached down to ruffle the wolf, her hand sinking deep into the blue-black fur. "My Da was just a hedge knight who sold his sword for services. We never had much but Da wanted more for my brother, Robert. Word came that a local lord was looking to add retainers. Robert had the chance to swear his sword to the baron, to win a name and a shield for himself, but it turned out the high and mighty lord only accepted the fealty of knights who came equipped with full armor and a trained warhorse. Da needed coin to equip my brother. Problem was, the only thing Da had left to sell was me, his only daughter."

Kath stared in horror. "What happened?"

The brown-haired girl hugged the wolf, her eyes dark with memories. In a toneless voice that spoke of deep hurt, she said, "Da knew a tavern keeper who'd buried three wives and was looking for a fourth. He was older than Da and there was a sour smell about him but he had the coin Da needed. The man agreed to Da's bride price." Danya shrugged and said, "There wasn't even a blessing. It was just a peasant wedding, a cup of ale, a song or two...and then the bedding." Danya's brown eyes flashed in the firelight. For a moment, the girl's eyes looked more feral than the wolf's.

Kath whispered, "How old were you?"

"I'd seen ten winters. Hadn't even had my first blood yet. S'pect Da got more coin cause I was so young."

Kath shivered and looked away. She'd always feared her father would marry her off to some faceless lord...but this was far worse than any marriage Kath had ever imagined. "So you ran away." It was a statement, not a question.

Danya nodded. "Ran the first chance I got. Had nowhere to go and didn't really know how to fend for myself...but I learned." A touch of pride crept into the woman's voice. "I fled to the forest and lived off of nuts and berries. I was always hungry, always wet, always cold, but I refused to go back. I worked my way deep into the forest, becoming well and truly lost. Probably would have died, 'cept it was summer and a hermit found me and took me in. Master Martin was ancient, the oldest man I've ever seen, but he was kindly and shared what he had with me. We lived in a snug cave, deep in the woods. He taught me my letters and how to live in the forest. I was happy for more than two years...but then Master Martin took sick with the black wasting. He had no family, no one to care for him. I did the best I could but it wasn't enough."

The wolf chuffed and licked Danya's face...almost as if the beast offered sympathy. Kath looked away, focusing on the fire, poking at the glowing embers. "So how did you find the wolf?"

Danya's voice softened, "Master Martin had two treasures and no one but me to leave them to. The first treasure was his life's work, a set of scrolls he'd labored over for scores of years. Before he died he begged me to take them to an apothecary who lived in a village on the edge of the forest. It's strange, but I think he feared losing the scroll's knowledge more than he feared dying." Danya shrugged, pausing to sip her tea and then said, "His second treasure was his gift to me." Danya set the mug on the ground and slowly rolled up her left sleeve.

Silver glittered in the firelight. An ornate cuff of worked silver covered her arm from wrist to elbow. The workmanship was amazing, silhouettes of animals incised in the silver. Scores of animals, wolves, horses, eagles and bears, capered from her wrist to her elbow.

Kath touched the small gargoyle hidden at her throat. Reassured, she said, "It's a focus isn't it?"

Danya nodded. "I thought you might understand."

The two women locked eyes.

Kath knew it was a test of trust, a trade of a secret for a secret. She hesitated but then reminded herself that Danya had been chosen by the Grand Master. Suddenly wanting the young woman's friendship, Kath tugged the leather thong at her neck, revealing her stone gargoyle. "I found it in Castlegard, but I didn't understand the magic till I came to the monastery."

Danya nodded, a warm smile of friendship spreading across her face. "The monks taught me as well."

Kath returned the smile, wondering if she'd found a different sort of sword sister.

Danya's gaze dropped to the silver cuff. She traced her fingers across the animals, pausing at a howling wolf. "I felt the magic as soon as I put it on, though I didn't really understand it at the time. Of course, the monks recognized it instantly. Turns out it's a special kind of focus, a type of magic the monks thought was long lost, destroyed during the War of Wizards." Danya looked up from the cuff and stared into Kath's eyes, "When the monks saw the cuff they gave me a new name."

"What name?"

Her voice dropped to a whisper. *"Beastmaster."*

Kath rocked back in her seat, making the hand sign against evil. The single word conjured a primal fear, images of slavering werewolves and fearsome dire beasts stealing children in the dead of night. In many parts of Erdhe, the mere rumor of a shape shifter earned a burning at the stake. Kath forced the images away, refusing to give in to superstition. She studied the small woman sharing her fire. She seemed human enough. Kath tried not to judge but her hand crept to the hilt of her sword.

"I know what you're thinking. I've heard the tales too, but it's not that way."

Kath stared at the woman and wolf, not trusting her tongue.

"Look, there's nothing to fear, I can't turn into anything. It's not like that." In a strained voice, Danya said, "I'm human, I'm not a beast." Her voice dropped to a hush. "Sometimes I understand what animals are feeling, what they fear, or need. Like the mare at the pass."

"So you talk to animals?"

Danya shook her head, "Not really, not like you and I are talking. It's more a jumble of feelings or needs, a rush of scents and images. The only animal I can truly talk to is Bryx. I raised him from a pup, rescued from a hunter's snare." Shrugging Danya said, "Bryx and I are family, a pack of two."

Kath stared in confusion.

Danya rushed to explain. "The monks thought the magic was lost. There hasn't been a Beastmaster since before the War of Wizards. Some of the monks took it as another sign of the Prophecy...a sign of hope from the Lords of Light."

Kath's head was spinning, there was more here than just a woman and a wolf. Leaning forward, she said, "So you're here because of the Prophecy?"

"I'm here because of the Grand Master." Danya sighed and dug her hands into the wolf's thick fur. A low rumble of pleasure came from the beast. "The monks couldn't agree. They argued for more than a fortnight. Some wanted me to stay, to help protect the monastery, but others argued that I should be sent with you, to help fight the battle in the far north." Dropping her voice to a whisper, she added, "And a few wanted to take the silver away from me." Danya shuddered, searching Kath's eyes for understanding.

Kath's hand closed protectively around her gargoyle. Now that she was linked to the magic, she couldn't imagine giving it up. "Why did they want to take it? It doesn't seem like something the monks would do."

Danya's voice dropped to a hesitant whisper. "Because I can't really use it." Her face flamed red. "The monks say I'm only using a fraction of the powers locked within the silver. They argued that a gift so powerful shouldn't be squandered on someone with so little talent...especially now that the comet has come." She stared at Kath, her voice bleak. "The monks argued for weeks, but in the end, the Grand Master decided."

The fire waned, letting the shadows encroach. Feeling the tale was better told in the light, Kath tossed fresh kindling into the fire's heart. Branches crackled with flames, releasing a spray of red sparks. Light pulsed from the fire, pushing back the darkness. From the corner of her eye, Kath caught a subtle movement. She glanced toward the bedrolls and met Duncan's one-eyed stare. He nodded and Kath understood. The archer listened but didn't want to interfere. Kath returned her gaze to the fire. Reaching for the kettle, she said, "More tea?"

Danya held her mug out. "Sure, why not."

Kath liked tea, having acquired a taste for it in the monastery. She took her time filling the mugs, swirling the fragrant leaves into the steaming water. The simple task gave her a chance to sort through the questions crowding her mind. Handing a mug back to Danya, she decided go straight to the heart of the matter. "So why did the Grand Master decide to send you?"

"The Grand Master agreed with those who saw the return of a Beastmaster as a sign from the Lords of Light."

"A sign from the gods?" An unexpected wave of hope washed through Kath. Perhaps the Lords of Light cared after all. Looking across the fire, Kath found Danya staring at her, a searching look on her face.

"The Grand Master said that in days of old, before the wizards broke the world, at least one Beastmaster always fought at the side of the Star Knights. The master said it is a sign that the ancient powers, those who have long lain dormant, are awakening for the battle to come. He said it was time for the forces of Light to fight together again."

Kath reeled as a door opened in the back of her mind. For a moment she stood in the Star Tower, when it was whole and unbroken. She caught a glimpse of knights in silver readying for battle...and Kath knew she belonged among them. A shiver ran through her. She yearned for that other time, but the door slammed closed, sealing the vision. Kath scrambled to find her way back...but it was lost, nothing but a wisp of memory. A long sigh escaped her.

An urgent hand gripped her shoulder. Kath opened her eyes to find Danya peering at her, alarm on her face. "Are you unwell? You turned pale and swayed. I thought you were going to fall face-first into the fire."

Kath rubbed her forehead in confusion. "I'm fine...it's just that your words confused me. What do you know of the Star Knights?"

Danya released Kath and settled back on the bedroll next to the wolf. Shrugging, she said, "I don't really know. Just some knights I suppose. Heraldry and houses don't mean much to me."

Kath scowled in frustration. The past mattered; she needed to understand the visions.

Danya's voice was soft with apology. "I bet Zith would know if you asked him. There doesn't seem to be much the blue-robed masters don't know."

Reminded of the monk, Kath whispered the question that had plagued her since the monastery gates. "Of all the monks and masters, why did the Grand Master choose to send an old man like Zith?"

Danya hugged the wolf. "I heard the monks arguing about him as well. Some said he was chosen by the gods." She glanced toward the sleeping monk and then dropped her voice to a whisper, "Master Rizel said that Zith had a role to play in killing the Mordant."

"But why him?"

"Don't you know?"

Kath shook her head, puzzled.

Danya leaned forward and whispered, "Because of his son."

Kath stared in confusion.

"Zith's son is Bryce...the one the Mordant took."

16

Justin

A moonless night, a perfect time for skullduggery. Cloaked in velvety darkness, Justin slipped through the back alleys of Balor's poor quarter. A master of sounds, he walked with a hushed, uneven rhythm, his soft doeskin boots mimicking the scuffling of a rat. A stray cat stalked him part way down the lane, proof his performance was appreciated. Melting into the shadows, he threaded his way through the city's back ways, trying to avoid the sharp eyes of pious informers. His cloak, a deep enough blue to almost be black, covered him from head to heel. His face and his hands were darkened with lampblack, part disguise, part showmanship, and all of it part of the hiding. Beneath his cloak, he hugged his small harp tight against his side like a lover. It wasn't his best harp, he'd left that sweet voice safe behind the stout walls of Castle Seamount, but this harp, the twenty-one string Cloyne, was almost as dear.

Lantern light and lewd language spilled from the backdoor of the Praying Maiden. A badly weathered sign revealed the Maiden had once been the Bawdy Widow, proof that religious miracles occurred even in the poorest quarters of the Flame God's city.

Pulling the deep cowl of his cloak forward, Justin hid his face in shadow and climbed the stairs to the rear door of the tavern. Exposed to the kitchen lights and the cooks' curious stares, he added to the disguise by hunching his shoulders to obscure his height and dragging his left foot like a cripple. Peering out from under the cowl of his robe, Justin greeted the scullery women, knowing most of them by name.

Bev, the prettiest of the bunch, gave him a gap-toothed smile. "So, the Dark Harper is back to grace us with his music." With a wink and a leer she added, "Why don't ya ease back that cowl so we can have a peek at your face? If ya look half as bonny as ya sound, ya can warm me bed tonight!"

The kitchen erupted in lewd offers and hasty wagers, giving Justin the perfect response. "A grand offer Bev, but if I was to go home with you I'd be breaking too many hearts, best if I just keep close to my lady the harp."

"Go on with ya then. Your stool is set where ya like it and I'll be bringing ya a tankard of ale and a cut of meat off the spit for the Harper's portion."

"The ale will do just fine, I've eaten already."

Justin had learned the hard way that meat on the spit in taverns like the Maiden often turned out to be dog or rat, the staples of the back alleyways. He'd stick to a tankard of ale. The brew was always worth drinking or the tavern would be out of business.

Passing from the kitchen into the great room, he was hit with the rank smells of unwashed bodies and stale ale. The Maiden had a full house tonight; perhaps he'd find fertile ground for his songs.

He took a seat on a high stool set in the shadows of the back corner near the door to the kitchen...it always paid to have an escape route handy. From beneath the cowl of his robe, he studied the patrons. Mostly men, mostly working poor, and mostly well into their cups, it was the usual crowd for the Maiden. Tom, the barkeeper and owner, bowed his head in Justin's direction giving the Harper a half smile. The man was taking a risk by letting the Dark Harper play, but he also stood to gain a pretty profit. Good music made the ale flow faster. The Maiden, with its poor patrons and poorer fare, wasn't the type of tavern frequented by minstrels. The barkeeper's half smile told Justin that his greed still exceeded his fears, so for now, the Dark Harper was welcome.

Justin scanned the room for informers, looking for eyes that were too bright, too confident, too keen, and much too interested. Finding nothing to arouse suspicion, he settled the small harp on his lap and let his fingers caress the strings, sending a ripple of chords through the great room.

Surprise followed by a hushed expectation settled over the crowd as the Maiden's patrons turned their attention towards the bard, thirsty for a song.

Justin took his time tuning the harp, gauging the audience. An old wives' tale said that the eyes are the windows of the soul and Justin believed it. *So much pain in their eyes, if only they could see it for themselves.* Most were haunted with fear, some were angry, and the rest were weary, crushed by a drudgery that was the lot of the working poor. Nothing more than tinder for the Flame God, and most of them knew it in the depths of their souls, though they did their best to hide from the knowledge. Their eyes spoke volumes, telling Justin he'd come to the right place. He was here to pull their fears out of hiding, to warn them of the dangers of doing nothing, but first he had to help them laugh and then he had to give them courage.

Accepting the challenge, Justin launched into a playful tune with bawdy lyrics about a lonely farmer, a milkmaid, and a dairy cow. The crowd roared with laughter. Feet began tapping a rhythm and tankards clanked on tabletops.

Keeping the music light, Justin kept the crowd laughing, playing a dozen songs with ribald lyrics and lively tunes. Familiar melodies swept through the tavern, enfolding the crowd with a warm embrace. Even the reluctant and the tone-deaf gave in to the merriment of the songs.

Having warmed the room, Justin stilled his harp strings, taking a minstrel's break. The crowd shouted for more music, but they also shouted for ale. Serving girls moved among the tables, carrying frothing tankards and trenchers of roast meat. The ale flowed and so did the coins. The profit was a measure of safety for Justin, the owner collected silvers and the Dark Harper kept his welcome, a fair enough bargain.

Quietly sipping his ale, Justin waited for the tables to be served but not long enough for the crowd to lose interest. Judging the time to be right, he set his fingers to the strings releasing a burst of melody. Eager faces turned his way; the audience was his once more.

Changing the tempo of the night, Justin ripped into a fury of chords and loosed his tenor voice in a rousing ballad that told of the battle of Raven Pass. Spinning visions with words set to melodies, the music brought the battle to life. His fingers flew across the strings creating a vision of the Mordant's hordes swarming up the narrow pass where a few dared to hold off many. Harp strings screamed with discordant notes and the desperate battle was joined. The tempo became frantic as the heroes struggled against the odds. The lyrics soared up an octave as the vanguard of knights arrived to push the hordes back, saving the southern kingdoms. A single stirring note soared to the rafters, drawing the tale to a close. Stilling the strings, the Harper sat back to watch.

A ragged cheer rose from the patrons, as if they'd fought the battle themselves. Fists pounded on tables, demanding more. Bowing his head to the audience, the Dark Harper set his hand to the strings and gave them songs of war. He flooded the great room with tales of heroes from history and legends. One after another, he sang songs where victory and justice triumphed over near impossible odds. Fingers blistering across the strings, he kept the tone bold, the rhythm strong, and the cadence fearless. He played till the men's eyes burned, kindled with the light of courage...and then he stopped.

Released from the music's spell, the men reeled backwards, temporarily lost. It seemed as if the entire tavern took a deep breath...and all the while the Harper watched. The magic of the music held. Their eyes stayed bright and a roar woke from the throats of men who had moments before been mere mice. Bold shouts called for more ale and more songs. Buoyed by the music, they became men of large appetites, demanding more from life.

The Dark Harper gave the serving girls time to pass the ale before he started on the last round of songs. This time he kept the harp quiet, using muted tones and hushed words. Having caught his audience, the Dark Harper made them strain to listen; he made them work to hear. This time he gave them something that was hard to listen to...this time he gave them the truth.

Haunting melodies and penetrating words warned of the dangers of the Flame God. Loved ones burnt in the flames, women and children, not just men. Laden with truth, the ballads clawed at the heart while the words worked on the mind, exposing the lies of Coronth's religion. The slightest offense sent peasants to the flames while those who served the priests prospered. Blending lyrics with melody, the songs told how the religion of the Flame God was a matter of obedience rather than faith, a matter of golds rather than grace. The words cut close to the bone and the mood in the tavern darkened. Many hardened their gaze and looked away, refusing to listen, but a few heard the truth, their eyes smoldering in silent rage.

The Dark Harper watched closely, gauging the impact of the songs, wanting to make the men think but not wanting to push them too far. Warned by the darkening mood, Justin began to draw the last song to a close.

A loud crash came from the back of the tavern.

A bench overturned and a mountain of a man stood to glare at the Harper. Bulging with the muscles of a blacksmith, his voice boomed through the tavern. "Your songs are blasphemy, Harper! If we listen to you, we'll end up dancing in the Flames while you stay safe, hiding your face within that dark cape. Show your face, heretic, or still your blaspheming tongue!"

Dark mutterings filled the room.

Justin stilled the harp strings and surveyed the crowd. Shame filled a few faces, but most hung in the balance, timid sheep, waiting to see which way the wind would blow. Turning his full attention to the blacksmith, Justin answered, "Not just words, Sir, but the truth." Using his bard's voice he reached for the crowd, "Each of you dances with death at every Test of Faith. Since you don't have the coin to bribe the priests, you're only a dice roll away from walking the Flames." He pointed to those who wavered. "You could be next, or you." He dropped his voice to a hush. "The Flames wait for all of you, hungry for more death. You can go to the Flames as sheep, or you can rise against it. The choice is yours."

He'd set the spark to the kindling. The tavern erupted in argument.

The blacksmith gave up on words and started hammering with his fists. The argument became a brawl, an angry whirlpool of violence.

In the midst of the chaos, an urchin-boy burst through the outer doors, a wild look on his face. Justin recognized the dark-haired lad, the one that he'd paid to act as a lookout.

Seeking to avoid whatever danger followed, Justin tucked the small harp under his arm and scuttled back into the kitchen. Remembering to drag his left foot, he lurched around the scullery women and past the bread ovens to peer out the backdoor. Finding the alleyway empty of soldiers, he made his escape. Perhaps another night the men of the taverns would be ready to hear his words, but not tonight...tonight the Dark Harper would run and hide and hope to harp another day.

Shouts rang out from the far end of the alley.

Hunted, the Harper fled into the darkness. Forsaking his limp, he raced through the back alleyways, his dark cape flaring behind. Pressing for speed, he held to his escape route, two lefts and three rights, then squeezing through a narrow opening between a boarding house and an abandoned stable. The stench of the back alleys intensified, rotting garbage and puddles of urine, but Justin welcomed the reek, knowing the awful stench was one of the best defenses of the alleyways. Running flat out, he rounded the corner without hearing any sounds of pursuit, perhaps he'd lost them.

Nearing his bolt hole, he skittered to an abrupt stop. Three silhouettes stood at the far end. Justin hesitated, anyone lurking in the back alleyways at this hour was either a soldier or a thief...and he preferred to avoid both. Shrinking into the shadows, he retreated back around the corner. Mentally recalling the map of the city, he set off at a hard run, choosing a different route.

His feet slipped out from under him. Skidding on something greasy, he fell, twisting at the last moment to shield the harp. He landed hard on his back, cushioning the harp from the impact, but knocking the wind out of him. A loud clatter echoed down the alleyway. Cursing his luck, Justin froze, listening to the night.

The silhouettes rounded the corner; only this time there were five of them. They surrounded Justin like a pack of alley dogs hounding prey.

"Ho lads, looks like we caught a lone pigeon in the night!"

Justin caught the glint of steel, but they carried daggers not swords. A measure of relief washed through him, he faced the lesser threat of thieves not soldiers.

"Since you dare to walk these alleyways at night, you can pay our price, pigeon. Hand over your purse or we'll take our payment in blood."

The words were tough but the voice was young, they were a gang of lads posing as hardened men. Relieved, Justin reached for his purse. "You can have my purse. I want no trouble with you."

The tallest one snatched the purse from his hand but it was the smallest who said the words that chilled Justin. "And whatever you're hide'n bundled beneath your cloak, we'll be taking that too."

Justin's left arm tightened protectively around the Cloyne, while his right hand stole to the dirk on his hip. He would forfeit the coin without a fight but not the harp. "It's only a harp. You have my purse without a fight, settle for that. You won't have the harp."

The tallest one leaned forward, menacing his dagger in Justin's face. "There are five of us, pigeon. We'll bloody well take what we want. Hand over the harp."

He did not want to fight but he could not give up the harp. Before Justin could slide the dirk from its sheath, the smallest one said, "Wait Red, I know this one. You're that Dark Harper ain't you? You're the one that sings them songs against the Flame God?"

Surprised to be recognized, Justin saw no point in denying the truth. Tightening his grip his dirk, he said, "Yes, I am the one they call the Dark Harper."

One of the lads let out a long, low whistle.

An awkward silence filled the alleyway.

Justin tensed, preparing to fight or flee but hoping to do neither.

Finally the small one said, "The Dark Harper is a hero in the back alleys." Dropping his voice to a hush, the lad added, "Me Da died in the Flames. Me Mam used to say that the soldiers took him 'cause it's a sin to be poor in the Flame God's city."

A different voice said, "They burnt me Dad as well. Me Mam and sister were hauled off in chains to the slave blocks but me and me brother escaped to the back alleys. Been hide'n from the soldiers ever since."

The tallest lad, the one who seemed the leader, offered an open hand to Justin. "If you're truly the Dark Harper, then you're welcome in the back alleyways. Most of us have good reason to hate the priests and the soldiers." In an undertone the leader added, "You can keep the harp, but we need the coin to get by, food in the city is dear."

Accepting the lad's hand, Justin got to his feet. In the darkness, he stared at the ragged street urchins who knew the music of his harp.

The smallest one said in a quiet voice, "We could help you, Harper."

Surprised by the unexpected offer, Justin waited, listening to the emotions behind the words.

"No one knows the back alleyways better than we do. We could help keep you safe, Harper."

Justin stared at the lad, stunned by the sincerity of the boy's offer. He'd been harping in the Flame God's city for nearly a full moon-turn and the first real offer of help came from a rag-tag band of urchin boys forced to thieve to survive. Touched, Justin said, "Helping the Dark Harper means helping a heretic."

Five pairs of eyes stared at him, faces eager.

He studied each of them, rag-tag clothes and skinny frames marking them as orphans of the alleyways. They all needed more meat on their bones and a better purpose than thieving the alleys. The bold bravery of their faces won him over. "You know you're right, the Dark Harper could use the help of quick lads who know the alleyways like the back of their hands."

Pride crept across the lads' faces, confirming Justin's decision.

"I could use lookouts posted at the taverns and guides to show me the best hiding places. Like you, I mean to avoid the soldiers and the priests. I doubt the Dark Harper could find better eyes and ears than yours." Pausing he added, "In return for your help, I'll hand over my Harper's wages for each night that you work, a purse of mostly coppers with a few silvers, but steady pay nonetheless." Focusing on the tall leader, Justin said, "What do you say, will you join forces with the Dark Harper?"

The leader studied him and then said, "Eyes and ears, we could be that...and steady coin would help." Holding out his hand the tall lad said, "Me name is Red and you've just bought yourself the finest pack of petty thieves in the back alleyways."

A muffled cheer rose from the lads.

Accepting Red's hand, Justin smiled. In the back alleys of Balor, he'd found unexpected allies. A rag-tag band of street urchins would fight against the Flame God while adults cringed and cowered, fooling themselves to the danger. Truly the Lords of Light moved in strange ways.

17

Liandra

"*Seal the doors!*" The Master Archivist shielded the queen with his body, but she'd already seen the bloodshed.

The dungeon doors clanged shut.

A startling silence prevailed, as if the rest of the world ceased to exist...but there was no denying the truth. *The Red Horns have risen! The traitor's name comes too late!* The queen watched the men around her, watched the heavy timber slide into place to bar the dungeon doors, but she said nothing, her mind grappling with strategies and plots.

The Master Archivist barked commands. "Stand guard and let no one enter." The guard saluted, but her shadowmaster did not wait. Gripping her arm, he ushered her back down the stone ramp into the gloom. Captain Durnheart followed, his sword drawn.

The tension in her shadowmaster's grip screamed of danger. The queen let him lead, her mind fixed on the rebellion.

They burst into the guardroom, catching the head guard, Paulus, guzzling from a bottle, the sour odor of cheap wine sickening against the dungeon's stench.

Thrusting the bottle behind his back, he sputtered, "Back again? What da'ya want now?" Red wine dribbled down his double chin.

The master's voice snapped like a cold whip. "I need three of the guards stationed in the lower levels, the ones guarding the special prisoner. Get your keys and escort Captain Durnheart back down to the lower dungeons while I wait here." Turning to the captain, the master said, "Inform the men of the situation and return with Collins, Barkley, and Dent. The others should keep to their post."

Durnheart saluted and turned to harry the reluctant jailor. The jailor grumbled, keys rattling, but he eventually got the door open, retreating back into the bowels of the dungeon.

The door clanged shut, leaving the queen alone with her shadowmaster.

"Wait," the master raised a finger to his lips. Grabbing a torch, he swept the alcoves with light. Returning the torch to its bracket, his voice dropped to a harsh whisper. "The traitor's name comes too late. The fate of the Rose Crown now rests with the sword." His face was grim. "I had hoped to protect you in the Queen's Tower but that plan is now foiled. I need to rally the loyalists while you remain hidden, safe within the prison. No one will think to look for the queen within her own dungeons. Captain Durnheart and the three guards will protect you until the worst of the fighting is over."

"No."

"Madam, there is no time to argue!"

The queen stood erect, dropping the pretense of an ordinary woman. "We will not cower in the dungeons while brave men die for our throne."

"Madam, there is nothing you can do! The time for politics is long past. All will be lost if you are killed or captured. You must remain hidden, where my shadowmen can protect you."

"We have no intention of being killed or captured but we cannot cower like a rat in the dungeon, we must lead in order to rule."

The master's face blazed with frustration. "Majesty, you are a brilliant queen with rare gifts for manipulating politics and multiplying golds, but for all that, you are still a *woman*. What can a *woman* hope to do against *swords*?"

"We cannot and never will let our sex interfere with our duty." She gave him a withering glare. "But this is more than mare pride or duty...it is good strategy."

He hesitated, a shrewd gleam returning to his gaze. "What strategy?"

"We must find advantage where it is least expected."

"How?"

"We will fight with our wits...as we always do." Annoyance leached into her voice. "It has been our observation that whenever swords and men mix, wits vanish."

She watched the barb hit home.

Taking a measured breath, the master said, "I will hear your plan."

The concession was a start. Moving straight to the practical, the queen said, "Tell us where the greatest concentration of loyal troops is located."

"The Queen's Tower. Those with unquestionable loyalty were assigned to guard the sovereign. Some are in uniform but most are hidden in the guise of servants. Caches of weapons and supplies are also stocked in the tower. The plan was to protect the queen while using the tower as a base to lead the fight against the rebels."

"Then it is in the Queen's Tower that the sovereign must be seen."

"This is insane! The rebel forces will have the tower completely surrounded. You will be killed or captured before you get near the doors."

"We do not plan to use ordinary doors."

"What?"

"Castle Tandroth has secrets known only to the sovereign and the heir."

A shrewd look stole across his face. "So there's truth to the legends."

She nodded. "Memories fade to legends, adding to the advantage. We will put those legends to good use. Your shadowmen need only get us to the great kitchen. From there, assuming the passageways have withstood the test of time, we will make our way to the Queen's Tower."

"And once in the tower?"

"Concealed in the tower is a chamber designed to serve as a royal bolt hole, a place where a monarch can hide for moon-turns if needs be. But we do not intend to merely hide; we will be a thorn in the side of the Red Horns. The tower walls are honeycombed with passages that can be used to launch ambushes or facilitate an escape. Castle Tandroth is a labyrinth for good reason, all the better to hide a royal secret."

"And how is it that your shadowmaster is only now learning of these hidden ways?"

The queen smiled. "The Tandroths were ever shrewd and rarely trustful. The secret is held only by the sovereign and the heir."

"So Prince Danly does not know?"

Her voice bristled with frost, "Danly was never our heir."

"Thank the Lords of Light for that."

Shouts from the prison cells intruded. Warned, the queen pulled the shawl tight around her face and dropped her stare to the floor, shrinking back into the disguise of an ordinary woman. The master turned his back to her and stood facing the inner door, his hand on a knife-hilt sheathed at his belt.

Keys rattled in the lock. The door opened and the turnkey, Paulus, ambled into the guardroom followed by Captain Durnheart and three of the master's guardsmen.

Nodding toward the Master Archivist, Paulus said, "Got yer men for ya, just as ya asked." The jailor scratched at his groin, his gaze raking the queen. "If his Lordship is not needin the woman, ya could always leave her here with us...a bit of skirt makes a nice reward for the men."

Liandra could feel his lewd stare crawling through her shawl. The queen struggled to still her rage, wondering how ordinary women stomached such pigs.

The master snapped, "The woman is with me! You'd best keep your small mind to your own matters." Crossing the room, the master yanked opened the doors to a weapons rack and removed a sheathed sword and a pair of daggers. Strapping the sword around his waist, he tucked the daggers in his belt and then turned to face the burly jailor. "Trouble stirs in the castle. Once we leave, I want the doors to the dungeon sealed. No one is to enter without the correct password. The password will be *Darkened Sun*. Do you think you can remember that?"

Turning pale, the jailor stuttered, "W-what trouble?"

"There's no time for questions. Just do as you're ordered or instead of guarding the traitor's hole you'll find yourself in it. Now escort us to the outer doors and be quick to seal the dungeon once we leave." Not waiting for a reply, the master turned on his heel and strode up the ramp.

The queen hurried to keep pace, anxious to be quit of the dungeon despite the dangers above. Captain Durnheart stayed by her side, the three guardsmen and the jailor following behind.

At the top of the ramp, the two jailors shouldered aside the timber sealing the outer door. Cracking the door open, the master peered into the courtyard. The queen strained to hear, relieved that the sounds of fighting seemed distant.

"It's clear for the moment. Now is as good a time as any to leave." Turning to the captain and the three shadowmen, the master said, "We'll make for the great kitchen. This woman holds information vital to the crown. She must be protected even at the cost of your lives. Cut down any who stand in our way, we cannot take any risks. Am I understood?"

The men unsheathed their swords their faces grim.

To the jailor, the master said, "Bar the door once we leave and let no one enter without the password. Repeat the password."

Confused, Paulus stuttered, "D-darkened sun."

The master nodded. "See that you remember." He glanced toward the queen, a thousand warnings in his stare. Her breath caught at the intensity of his gaze, but there was no time for words. He pulled a knife from his belt and slipped through the doorway. Darkness beckoned, but the queen refused to be cowed. Lifting her skirt, she followed. Captain Durnheart and the three guards stayed close on her heels.

Night embraced her. Cooled by the rain, the night air felt refreshing, yet the darkness was full of threat. She breathed deep, vanquishing the stench of the dungeons, staring at the debris of war. Broken bodies littered the cobblestones, every one of them in the green and white tabard of Lanverness. So much blood, so much death, the moans of the wounded sent a shiver down her spine; the traitors had much to answer for.

A hand grabbed her arm. "Stay close."

Startled, the master's words drew her back to the dangers at hand.

Her shadowmaster led the way, prowling around the side of the tower. He moved with a fluid grace she'd never noticed before, like a shadow flowing across stone, his black robe blending with the night. It struck Liandra that her spymaster thrived in the shadows. Corded muscles hidden beneath dark robes, he was a man of strategy *and* action.

The master rounded the curve of the squat tower, moving out of sight.

Feeling clumsy in her long wool skirt, Liandra did her best to follow. She rounded the tower, hugging the side of the wall. The far side was untouched by fighting, yet the master skulked in the shadows.

He whispered a command, "Collins."

One of the shadowmen moved to stand at the master's elbow.

Pointing to the tunneled passageway on the far side of the courtyard, the master said, "Search the passageway and signal if it is safe."

The guard moved like a silent wraith, crossing the courtyard and entering the dark passage without challenge. An eternity later, he stood at the entrance and waved them forward.

The master whispered, "Swords at the ready." He stepped out of the shadows, sword in hand, and sprinted for the entrance. The queen gathered up her skirts and ran to keep pace, her breath ragged in her ears. Captain Durnheart took her elbow, hurrying her into the tunneled passageway.

The tunnel's darkness fell like a cloak. Blinded, the queen groped her way along the wall.

A hand grabbed her ankle.

Stifling a scream, she skittered backwards.

The hand released her. A wounded soldier moaned, "Help me. Please, help me."

The queen struggled to regain her composure, the cold wet touch imprinted on her ankle.

Her shadowmaster took her arm, his grip full of urgency. "Come."

The queen's voice was whisper thin, "Can't we help him?"

"There's no time." He steered her around the soldier, ushering her toward the tunnel's gaping mouth.

Swords clanged against swords as the sounds of fighting grew louder. Peering from the entrance, they found the main courtyard in chaos. The stables blazed, an inferno of flames licking into the night sky, casting an eerie glow across the courtyard. Soldiers in the green and white of Lanverness crossed swords in a bitter battle, brother against brother. The shouts of men mingled with the screams of horses, as if a doorway had opened onto the very halls of hell.

A battle line snaked across the courtyard, bending and contorting like the death throes of a giant serpent. Banners fluttered overhead, brightly colored moths caught in a dance with death. The queen recognized the Black Rose, the Tangled Thorns, and the Twin Roses, wondering which were loyal and which were false.

One of the banners faltered and fell. The battle line convulsed around the fallen standard, the strong consuming the weak. The slaughter sickened the queen, confirming her abiding hatred for war.

Her shadowmaster gripped her arm. "This is too dangerous!"

Odd how she did not feel the danger, only a deep need to end this awful waste and bring the traitors to justice. "We must see this." Her command brooked no argument. The master fretted by her side, his sword held at the ready.

A trumpet blared and reinforcements flying the battle banner of the Bloody Rose arrived from the west gate. Soldiers charged, surging into the line. With a mighty roar, they pushed the battle past the great kitchens and into the heart of the castle, toward the Queen's Tower.

The battle swept out of sight, the clash of swords becoming muffled. An eerie hush followed the battle's wake. All across the courtyard, the injured struggled to retreat from the killing field while the mortally wounded lay moaning in pools of blood. Appalled by the bloody harvest, the queen swore to see the traitors to justice. Any pity she'd felt for Danly drowned in the bloodshed of the yard.

Her shadowmaster hissed in her ear, "Let me take you back to the dungeon where my men can protect you."

The queen was resolute. "Fate has opened a path to the great kitchen, we must dare the crossing now."

The master glared at her but then bowed his head in resignation, "As you wish." To the men he said, "We'll cross in the lee of the battle.

Surround the woman and keep her safe." He gripped her arm. "Wait, the wind is changing."

She had not even noticed the wind.

Smoke from the fires billowed into the yard, stinging her eyes, obscuring the dead and dying. The gray pall hid everything.

"*Now!*" A sword in one hand and a dagger in the other, the master ran into the smoke. The queen followed. Holding her shawl to her face, she raced to keep the master in sight, a dark shadow flitting through the smoke. Liandra danced left, avoiding the bodies puddled in blood. The smoke thickened, laden with the smells of burning wood and singed horseflesh. The harsh tang made it hard to see, hard to breathe. Liandra stifled a cough.

A sword cut toward her face.

Liandra staggered backwards, her eyes held spellbound by the blade. Time slowed, as if the sword cleaved molasses instead of air. A second sword leaped to block the first, turning death away. Her shadowmaster stepped in front of her, his dagger slicing the enemy. A bloody gash opened in her assailant's throat...like a reaper's grim smile. Dead, he crumpled into the swirling smoke. Time resumed with a rush.

"*Hurry!*" Her shadowmaster raced forward.

Her heart hammering, the queen scrambled to keep pace. Her long skirts threatened to trip her.

A breeze blew and the smoke began to clear. A single soldier blocked their path to the kitchen doors, a swarthy captain brandishing a bloody saber. The master hurled his sword at the soldier's head. Steel clanged on steel. The soldier parried the thrown sword. Laughing, he raised his saber to attack. "Come on, old man," but then his eyes began to glaze, puzzlement scrawled across his face. The soldier toppled forward like a felled tree, the master's throwing dagger lodged in his throat.

Liandra stared; she'd never seen so much death.

Running past the fresh corpse, the master retrieved his thrown sword. "*Hurry!*" He lunged toward the kitchen, throwing his shoulder against the double doors. The stout oak shuddered but held. Captain Durnheart and the two guardsmen rushed to pitch their weight against the barrier. The queen cringed; the pounding seemed loud enough to wake the dead. Desperation won. The doors groaned, opening just wide enough for a single person. The master slipped inside. The queen followed.

Pushing past a barricade of tables, they won through to the kitchen, staggering into an island of calm. The master growled, "Secure the doors."

The queen swayed to a stop. Aromas of fresh baked bread and spitted lamb surrounded her like a warm blanket, a stark contrast to the death of the courtyard. In the sudden normalcy of the kitchen, Liandra wasn't sure if she wanted to weep or retch. She'd seen the underbelly of war and faced death in a whispering blade; life would never be the same. Taking a deep breath of comfort, Liandra forced her mind to the matters at hand.

Her shadowmaster growled, "Where's Dent?"

Captain Durnheart answered, "Dead. He took a sword in the belly during the crossing."

Liandra stared, a man had died for her and she hadn't even noticed.

"Barricade the doors."

While the men pushed tables and chairs against the outer doors, Liandra surveyed the great kitchen. Frightened faces peered back at her. Hiding behind overturned tables, the kitchen folk stared at the intruders.

A tremulous voice asked, "M-majesty, is it really you?"

Shocked to be recognized, Liandra realized she'd lost her shawl in the terror of the crossing. Her masquerade was broken. She stood exposed, without paints and powders, without shimmering jewels, without the trappings of royalty. The queen summoned her royal poise. Standing sword-straight, she met the stares of her people. "We seek sanctuary from the fighting."

Rising from behind an overturned table, a stout man in a flour-stained apron doffed his cap. "When the fighting broke out, we didn't know what to think. So we sealed the doors."

Putting a name to his face, she recognized the master baker, a hard-working man who ruled the great kitchen with a soft hand. Infusing her voice with dignity, the queen said, "The crown sees you, Master Carl. What would you ask of us?"

The baker blanched and bent the knee, his round face as pale as pastry dough. "So it's really you, majesty?"

She heard the doubt in his voice. Twisting the rings on her fingers, Liandra held out her hand, presenting the Great Emerald. The square-cut jewel flashed green in the candlelight. "Your queen is here."

A sigh of amazement rippled through the kitchen. A dozen flour-dusted cooks rose from behind overturned workbenches. Many clutched knives or cast iron skillets, their faces a battleground of hope and fear.

She did not blame them for their fear, for the common people oft became fodder for wars. The queen met their gaze, projecting a sense of royal confidence. "Traitors have risen against us, but victory will be ours."

Questions hung in the air, but hope won out. The kitchen folk relinquished their makeshift weapons, emerging to bow to their monarch. Their honest homage humbled the queen. For the sake of loyal subjects like these, she needed to end the bloody rebellion and return her kingdom to the prosperity of peace.

"We thank you for sharing the sanctuary of the kitchen, but now we must command you to silence. The rebels must never learn that your queen was here on this night. We charge you to keep our secret safe."

A murmur of assent swelled from the kitchen staff, pride and wonder on their faces.

Her shadowmaster stepped forward, grim in his dark robes, blood on his sword. "A group of rebels wearing the tabards of Lanverness has risen against the Rose Throne. Loyal soldiers are holding the rebels at bay but the fighting is fierce. Remain in the safety of the kitchen until the rebellion is put down." Deliberately sheathing his sword, the master added, "And now Master Carl, we need your services. The queen wishes to inspect the storage rooms below the great kitchen."

Caught off guard, the baker stuttered, "The s-storage rooms?"

"Yes and there is no time to waste. Bring a torch and lead the way."

Befuddled, the baker reached for one of the torches lining the walls. Gesturing toward the rear of the kitchen he said, "This way m'Lord."

The master crossed the room to follow the baker but the queen lingered by the doors. Noting the confusion on the faces of the kitchen folk, the queen realized they needed reassurance...and hope. "We thank you for your loyalty and your silence. We go now to put an end to this rebellion. It is our royal wish that you keep to the safety of the kitchen, Lanverness needs all of her people."

Cooks and serving wenches melted to the floor, kneeling before their queen. "The Lords of Light save her majesty the queen." The murmur spread through the kitchen.

Tears crowded Liandra's eyes. The loyalty of her people was the perfect balm to the bloodshed of the courtyard. Picking up her skirts as if they were made of silk instead of homespun, she followed the baker and her shadowmaster to the rear of the great kitchen.

Stone stairs descended into shadows. Torchlight glimmered on the walls as the master baker led the way. The steep stairs emerged onto a wide hallway with three stout wooden doors. Warmth laced with the scent of fresh baked bread permeated the cellars. The baker stopped by the first door, a ring of keys in his hand. "There are three storerooms, which would you see?"

The queen hesitated, recalling memories of her father's voice. A secret rhyme from childhood hummed through her mind. She hoped her memory and the rhyme both held true. "The third one."

Obeying, the baker led them to the end of the hallway and opened the third door. Cooler air and the tangy scent of aging cheese cloaked the storeroom. Lighting torches bracketed along the stone walls, the baker revealed a long narrow room filled with grain sacks, stacked casks, and heads of cheese hanging from hooks in the ceiling. Bobbing his head, the baker said, "This is the cheese room, we also use it to store grains and sometimes sides of smoked beef or ham."

It was not the contents of the room that interested the queen, but rather the architecture. The stonework was exceptionally fine, especially for a mere storeroom. Beveled vaults ran along the north wall sheltering recessed alcoves cloaked in shadow. Stone columns crowned by carved shields separated each alcove. The stonework of the shields was clearly the work of a master mason. The queen smiled; so far the rhyme of her childhood proved true.

Turning to the master baker, the queen said, "Master Carl, we thank you for your assistance. Surrender your torch to one of the guards and then return to the kitchen. Forget that you ever saw us here. Go with our thanks." The queen offered her ringed hand.

Clearly confused, the baker handed the torch to the captain. Bowing low, he kissed the great emerald of her office and left the storage room with a dazed look on his face.

Nothing more was said until the door was closed. "Captain Durnheart, we ask you and the two guardsmen to wait outside the door. We have matters to discuss with the Master Archivist."

The captain bowed and said, "As you wish, your majesty."

With the others gone, the master turned to the queen and said, "So now that we are alone among the cheeses, how do we find this hidden passage of yours?"

"With a rhyme from childhood." She walked the length of the storeroom, reciting from memory.

"Kings are served from kitchen stores,
Beneath the ovens take the third door,
Emblazoned heraldry is the key,
First stag then stallion and finally bee."

"And the King's Tower was renamed at your coronation."

"Exactly."

The queen read aloud the heraldic devices etched on the stone shields, "A boar, a stag, a bee, a bear, and finally a stallion. Depress the stone shields in the order of the rhyme and we believe the hidden door will open."

"You believe or you know?"

"We saw it once as a child, but only once. The rhyme was a secret between ourself and the king. The hidden passageways are meant to be used only in the most dire of times."

"The times are certainly dire, so let us see if the passageway is myth or fact." Going first to the stag, the master set the heel of his hand against the stone shield and pushed. For a moment nothing happened, then the shield slowly depressed two finger-widths into the wall. "Which one is next?"

"The stallion and then the bee."

The shield of the stallion behaved in the same fashion as the stag. Depressing the bee, a low grinding noise rumbled from the rear wall of the alcove. Stone scrapped against stone and a narrow doorway eased open at the back of the alcove, exhaling a long-held breath of stale air.

"It seems we have found your passage."

"The very stones of Castle Tandroth will fight against the rebels. Bring a torch and summon the others, it is past time we put a stop to this rebellion. We will not have our kingdom sundered by bloodshed."

"I will not be going with you."

The queen stared at her shadowmaster, ambushed by his decision. The notion of going without him left her feeling strangely bereft. "We would have you by our side."

"I can best serve Lanverness from the outside. I will rally the loyal troops and even raise the people if needs be. With your majesty working from within, we will crush the rebel forces between us."

Reluctant to be parted from the one man she trusted, Liandra hesitated. "Your plan has merit...but we need you to stay safe. We would not lose our ablest advisor. We cannot..." Her voice choked on emotions, revealing far more than she intended.

Bowing his head, her shadowmaster whispered, "And I would not lose my queen."

He came forward and knelt, taking her ringed hand.

The intensity of his touch rippled through her, something long understood but never acknowledged. She gently pulled away, it could not be, but he held her hand captive, turning it over and kissing the hollow of her palm. The perfect blend of tenderness and ardor. Liandra shivered with emotions long denied, but the weight of the crown sat heavy on her brow. She was always the queen. Reluctant to move, she withdrew her hand, "This cannot be..."

He rose and nodded, his face a stone mask. His voice turned brusque, nothing but duty. "Take Captain Durnheart and Collins with you, they are both good men. They will see you safely to the tower or die trying." He stared at her as if memorizing her face. His voice softened, "Keep safe, my queen." He saluted and turned, leaving her alone in the storage room.

"And you..." But he'd already gone. She froze her face, froze the tears in the corner of her eyes and tried to remember to breathe. Short, sharp breaths that pierced her to the core. She had a kingdom to care for, a crown to save...but there was always a price, always. Resolute, the queen turned to face the darkness of the hidden passage.

18

Duncan

A ring-necked pheasant broke from the brush, rising in a rush of feathers. Duncan raised his bow. An arrow fletched with black swan feathers took the pheasant before it breached the forest ceiling. He angled his mount toward the kill but the mountain wolf beat him to it. Nosing the bird, the wolf gave the archer a satisfied grin and then loped back into the summer-green of the forest. Duncan had to smile; the wolf was turning out to be a valuable hunting partner. Flushing game during the day and keeping watch at night, the wolf proved his worth as a welcome companion, but Duncan had his doubts about the other two.

Dressing the bird, he stuffed the pheasant into the game bag, leaving the offal for the wolf. Urging his horse to a gallop, he returned to the main trail. His companions made enough noise that he had no trouble finding them. Horse and rider emerged from the dense brush, startling the others. Hands slid to scabbards and then fell away. Raising his bow in greeting, he cantered to the front, resuming the lead.

Duncan felt a hunter's stare on his back. Heat crept up his neck. He did not have to turn to know it was Kath. Gripping his bow, he fought the urge to meet her leaf-green eyes. The girl was like iron to a loadstone...but if truth be told, the pull went both ways. Taking a deep breath, he focused on the task at hand.

Glancing behind, he checked on each of his companions. He could count on Kath and the two knights in a fight, but the two from the monastery were a worry. The wolf-girl, Danya, claimed a rare magic but she had no fighting skills and refused to carry a weapon. Beyond bringing the wolf, Duncan couldn't see how the girl would help against the Mordant. At least she had a way with horses and was proving to be a competent traveler.

The monk, on the other hand, remained a riddle. Keeping to the rear, the old man rode hunched in the saddle, hiding beneath his midnight-blue robes. Whatever his secrets, the monk held them close. The man's sullen silence gnawed at Duncan like an aching tooth. He didn't trust the monks; they hadn't kept Jordan safe, and now this one played possum, hiding behind a stony face. Duncan understood the need for secrets but not if those secrets got others killed. He kept a close watch on the monk, intent on flushing the man out of hiding.

With supper in the bag, Duncan urged his gelding to a canter. They rode till twilight, hoping to gain ground on an enemy they could not even track. As darkness fell, he chose a spot near a brook for their camp. Sir Tyrone used his skills with spices to prepare the pheasant and a brace of quails while Danya and Sir Blaine settled the horses. Blaine had developed a sudden interest in tending the horses, helping Danya rub the mounts down with handfuls of grass, picking their hooves, and seeing to the watering. The two worked well together but the brown-haired girl seemed oblivious to the spell that she'd cast on the lanky knight. Duncan chuckled, amused that the two young people couldn't see what was right in front of them.

Filling the kettle with creek water, Duncan turned to find Kath standing behind him. The girl always seemed to be underfoot, but this time she had a distracted, worried look on her face. In a low voice he said, "Looking for something?"

"Do you think we made the right choice?"

"What choice?"

She gestured to the west. "Back at the fork in the trail, the decision to avoid the Isle of Souls and ride for Tubor instead?"

"Will the Mordant hide amongst people or trees?

"I...don't know."

"Just so. The best trackers know their prey. Since we don't know the beast, we can't anticipate its path." Duncan shrugged, "Time and the spring thaw have erased any signs of the Mordant's passage. With no trail to follow and no way to predict his actions, one way is as good as another. All we can do is hold the horses to a trot and keep them pointed north."

She stared at him as if she were trying to peer into his soul. He knew what she wanted...he felt it too, but it could not be.

In a quiet voice Kath asked, "Do you believe in the prophecies?"

"I came, didn't I?"

Hurt danced in her eyes.

He regretted his hasty retort. Cynicism had gotten the better of him since the attack on Jordan. Kath deserved better. "Sit with me." He straddled a fallen tree while she settled on a moss-sheathed stone.

Considering his words, he tried to explain, "It's a matter of coincidence."

She stared at him, listening.

He struggled to explain. "Finding the crystal dagger, the return of the Mordant, the attack on Jordan, the red comet tearing across the heavens, too many things have happened for it all to be coincidence. And despite the monks' tight-lipped reticence, they don't lie." He lowered his voice and leaned toward her, "I believe there's a truth buried in the prophecies, but I wonder if we're wise enough to understand the meaning."

"Do we have a chance against the Mordant?"

He held her gaze. "I don't know, but I intend to find out."

She nodded. "In the monastery, it all made more sense. The monks know so much but their explanations are so..."

"...convoluted."

She flashed him a knowing grin but her green eyes remained serious, deepening to a rich moss color. "Every answer leads to another question...and so much is left unsaid."

The girl had a habit of echoing his own thoughts. "The monks are a secretive lot. Makes a man wonder if he's being helped or used." He watched her face, but she did not take the bait.

"Do you believe in free will or a fore-ordained destiny?"

She stared at him, her gaze full of questions and challenges. She had a way of making him look past the surface. "I believe in balance. When evil rises, the balance must be restored. We all hope the gods will lean down from the heavens to fix the world, but the gods are a fickle bunch, rarely bothering to lift a finger. It always comes down to ordinary men making the choice to step forward and set the balance right." Duncan shrugged and said, "I guess this time, we're the ones chosen to the task."

Kath sat cloaked in stillness.

Sensing she needed more, Duncan added, "I'll tell you this, if the fate of the southern kingdoms rests with the crystal dagger, then I'd rather be counted among those trying to set the balance right than leave it to others. At least this way we have a hand in steering our own fate."

Kath whispered, "I guess I feel the same." A warm smile filled her face.

Before more could be said, the black knight yelled for the kettle.

Sharing a laugh at the irony of the mundane, Duncan and Kath returned to camp.

Smells of roasted pheasant swirled around the fire. The black knight knew how to ply his store of spices. The companions circled the fire. Sitting on bedrolls, they savored the crispy skin and juicy slices of spit-roasted pheasant. Stories were traded and laughter shared but there was one who always sat apart. The monk hid behind his midnight-blue robes like a shield wall, impervious to friendship.

Duncan respected the monk's right to privacy, but if Zith had a reason for joining the group, they all needed to hear it. Tired of waiting for the monk to pick his moment, he stared at Zith and said, "Is it true?"

To Duncan's right, Kath gasped, knowing what was asked.

Duncan kept his gaze focused on the monk.

An awkward tension swirled around the campfire.

The wolf whined, disturbed by the mood.

Zith kept his head bent, staring into the fire.

Duncan asked again, "Is it true that the Mordant took your son?"

Zith shrugged. The cowl of his midnight-blue robe fell backwards. Long silver-blond hair framed a face etched with sorrow. Hazel eyes, heavy with sadness met Duncan's gaze. "Yes."

"I'm sorry for your loss."

Murmurs of condolences circled the fire.

Duncan said, "So, you joined us for revenge?

The monk's eyes widened in surprise, "Revenge? No. I've come for something far more dear than revenge. I've come to free my son."

Sir Tyrone gaped, "Is that possible?"

Anguish washed across the monk's face. "It's not what you think. Only the crystal dagger can free my son. Slay the Mordant with the dagger and his soul will be cast back into the pit of hell, never to be reborn. The dagger will also take my son's life...but any soul who has not willingly joined with Darkness will be freed to go into the Light." Dropping his voice, the monk added, "My son was trained by the Kiralynn Order, I know he will hold true." A hint of steel leached into his voice, "I've come to see that my son's soul is set free, to return him to the Light."

Duncan respected the monk's loss, but he couldn't let the old man retreat to his walls of silence. "So how can you help in the fight against the Mordant?"

The monk's hazel eyes flashed in the firelight. For a moment, the heavy cloak of sorrow dropped away, revealing a hidden determination. Stretching out his right hand, the monk exposed his open palm. A Seeing Eye tattooed in dark blue stared at them. "Seek knowledge, Protect knowledge, Share knowledge." Closing his hand into a fist, the monk said, "For those who have the wisdom to use it, knowledge is a great power."

The monk slumped back against his bedroll, resuming his mantle of sorrow, but Duncan refused to let him hide. "What knowledge do you carry?"

"What knowledge do you need?"

The sharp retort parried further questions, but Kath dared to break the silence. Pulling the crystal dagger from the sheath at her belt, she held the milk-white blade up to the firelight. The blade caught and held the light, almost as if it glowed from within. "Master Rizel explained the purpose of the crystal dagger, but for whose hand was it forged?"

The monk stirred. "Carved from the heart of a Dahlmar crystal and imbued with the powers of the Light, the daggers were created for the Star Knights."

The Star Knights. The words whispered in Duncan's mind, achingly familiar yet somehow unknown.

Kath asked the question that hovered on Duncan's lips. "And who were the Star Knights?"

The monk nodded as if he expected the question. "The Grand Master told you of the Orb of Seeing. Long ago, the scholars of the Orb foresaw a great war that would destroy the civilizations of Erdhe, a ruin that would push the race of man back into barbarism. The Kiralynn Order sought to oppose this threat, to change the thread of time, but the way forward was not clear. The Grand Master called a conclave of the wise, but the masters could not agree. The majority argued that the role of the Order was to preserve knowledge, to keep the lamp of civilization lit against the Darkness. Others argued that the Order needed to take up the sword, to openly oppose the threat. The argument sundered the Order, causing the Great Schism. Most of the monks retreated deep into the seclusion of the Southern Mountains, building the monastery and preserving the knowledge of the world. But a smaller group of mages, beastmasters, and warriors raised a battle standard against the forces of Darkness. That battle standard bore the eight-pointed star."

The fire crackled, sending a shower of sparks into the dark.

Enthralled, Kath whispered, "What happened to them?"

The monk stared at her from across the fire. "They were betrayed."

The wolf rose to his haunches and tipped back his head, hurling a mournful howl into the night. The eerie wail scraped down Duncan's spine. Danya tried to calm the beast, to no avail. Rising to all fours, the wolf shook his fur and stalked off into the night, as if the beast refused to hear more of the monk's grim tale.

Disturbed by the wolf's behavior, the companions re-settled around the campfire. The black knight was the first to speak. "So the Star Knights failed and the great war happened anyway?"

The monk nodded. "The world was broken by the War of the Wizards."

A grim hush settled across the campfire.

Blaine said, "And now we chase the Mordant into the north."

Kath's gaze narrowed. "The Mordant isn't the only harlequin, is he?"

"No."

Duncan stared at the monk. Such a clipped answer begged for more questions.

Kath must have felt the same, for she pressed the monk for answers. "The Mordant is the oldest harlequin, the bane of the north, the enemy of the Octagon...but why must he be killed before all others?"

"How little you understand. The Mordant is not just the oldest harlequin; he is the right hand of the Dark Lord." The monk paused, staring at each of the companions in turn. "So much has been forgotten, yet you dare not underestimate the enemy we chase. In the time before the War of the Wizards, the counselor who goaded the kingdoms to war went by the name of *the Mordant*."

A shiver ran down Duncan's spine.

Kath stared slack mouthed, her face ghost-pale.

Sir Tyrone made the hand sign against evil.

The monk gave a solemn nod. "The Mordant started the War of Wizards. Our legends are his memories."

No more questions were asked.

Sir Blaine rose to throw more wood on the fire and then drew his great blue sword to stand guard. The sapphire-blue blade gleamed in the firelight, a sharp edge against the Darkness. Duncan stared at the blue sword, a promise of protection yet it suddenly seemed an illusion. Despite the vigilance of the Octagon Knights the Mordant roamed the southern kingdoms. Duncan checked his bow and his long knife before crawling into his bedroll. He noticed the others kept their weapons close. The monk had given them much to think on, perhaps too much. Unable to sleep, he stared at the sky, but he found no solace in the stars.

19

The Mordant

Sunlight streamed through trees, releasing the sharp scent of pine. Summer lay soft on the lands of Erdhe, lulling the people with peace, sheep oblivious to the wolf in their midst. The Mordant smiled as he walked. The comet heralded his coming, but few understood its portent. Soon they would learn, they would all learn. The Mordant lengthened his stride, following the dirt road north, always north.

He considered stealing a horse but walking suited his needs. This simple act strengthened the bond between mind and body, fusing his will to flesh and bone, making him whole. He gloried in his new life, a thousand years of memory packed into a body twenty-two years young. Youth was such a heady elixir. Legs that walked leagues without tiring, a heart that brimmed with stamina, and senses that delivered a flood of tastes, smells, and carnal delights. The Mordant laughed. It took an old soul to truly appreciate the wonders of youth...all in the service of the Dark Lord.

Knowing his eyes had lost the red glow of hell, he gained the appearance of a young man wandering the land in the golden robes of the Kiralynn Order. The Mordant reveled in the irony of his rebirth. Seeking fresh ways to damage his oldest enemy, he took the time to lay a fair few traps for those who were sure to follow. Seeds of chaos planted along the way, he wondered which would bear bitter fruit. Pity he wouldn't be there to witness the harvest, but he'd learned long ago that the best traps were those sprung from a distance.

Setting a ground-eating pace, he strode through forests and villages, comparing reality to memory. Much had changed. Wyeth, the once proud stronghold of the Star Knights, was overgrown with dark forests, empty except for the occasional village full of superstitious peasants. The ancient heart of Erdhe was hollow, soft and ripe for the taking. He laughed thinking of the victories to come.

Spying a rocky outcrop, he climbed to the summit to scout the land ahead. His body took the steep slope in stride, barely breaking a sweat. The Mordant gloried in his vigor. Reaching the summit, he gained a sweeping view of the summer-cloaked land. The forests of Wyeth gave way to the fields and vineyards of Tubor, a patchwork of green and yellow farmland flush with bounty. A small village lay nestled below the ridge, stone chimneys sending tendrils of smoke into the clear morning sky.

He scanned the horizon, searching for landmarks, trying to match the map in his mind to the view. Eye Lake lay to the west, a shroud of fog obscuring the volcanic mount at the lake's heart. His young eyes served him well, but they could not pierce the unnatural fog. A slumbering power inhabited the ancient waters, something gray and unpredictable and better left undisturbed, hence his decision to take the eastern route, by-passing the lake. He averted his gaze, seeking a more pleasing sight. To the far north, the distant peaks of the Dragon Spine Mountains marked the northern limit of the southern kingdoms...and the start of his domain. Snow-covered even in summer, the mountains made a formidable barrier, but once crossed he could summon an army of servants. A powerful pull drew him to the north, a yearning to renew his power at the Dark source. Taking a deep breath, he quelled the need, focusing on the task at hand. Pulling his stare from the north, he searched in vain for a great city in the east. A blanket of unbroken forest stretched as far as the sunrise. Memories drew his gaze to the northeast. Trees of an unnatural height towered where the city should have stood. Grotesquely overgrown, the evergreen sentinels were something new, something unnatural...something unexpected. The Mordant fixed his gaze on the forest. Unexpected usually meant a rival for the Dark Lord's favor...or tampering by the cursed Lords of Light. Either way, it posed a possible threat. Threats could not be permitted. He needed more information.

The Mordant prodded the soul trapped within his mind, *Awake monk, I have a use for you.*

No! Leave me be, I will not aid you! I saw what you did to those women! With my own hands, with my own body, you tore them apart and spattered their blood upon the walls! No one should die such a death! You are a fiend, a monster! I curse you! The captured soul pulsed with horror.

The Mordant smiled, he'd forced the monk to witness his handiwork, giving the young man a taste of the Dark. *Come now monk, you know you enjoyed it...especially when I took the young girl.*

I walk in the Light! I walk in the Light!

The monk was amusing in his stubbornness, but he would eventually break, they all broke, succumbing to the allure of the Dark. *Come monk, I offer you the chance to see through my eyes, to walk in the sunshine, to feel the summer breeze upon my face, to smell the sun-warmed pine. Would you pass up this chance to taste the world?* The Mordant flooded the captured monk with the sights and smells of summer. The monk resisted, fighting longer than most, but his will eventually crumbled under the sensual onslaught. It was always this way. Isolated from all physical senses, the captured souls yearned for the world they'd lost. It was so easy to torture the damned. The Mordant smiled and mentally stepped aside, permitting the monk to see through his eyes.

The monk's soul flared with emotions, reveling in the luxury of sensations.

Obey me, monk, and you will be well rewarded. The Mordant gave the monk a few moments to bask in the view, before reminding him of his chains. *Tell me monk, what is the virulent green that grows to the east? How does a forest come to reach such an unnatural height?*

How can I answer when I have never seen this before?

The monk spoke the truth yet he sought to deceive. Walls slammed down, forcing the captured soul back into isolation.

The young man howled for all that was lost.

You disappoint me monk. You must learn to be of service. Tell me what you know or I will rip the thoughts from your mind.

The monk became quiet and small, a pitiful attempt to hide.

You cannot hide from me, monk. Serve me or prepare to be raped. There is no other way.

He gave the monk time to consider.

I spoke the truth. I have lived all of my life in the Southern Mountains. I have never seen this place before.

A shallow evasion. I asked what you know, not what you have seen. Surely your precious Order knows of this forest. The Mordant focused his will upon the captured soul, a painful threat hanging by a slender thread. *One last time, monk, tell me what you know.*

The monk cowered in a dark corner, a jumbled knot of fear and loss wrapped around a kernel of defiance. The Mordant struck, punishing the monk with waves of pain.

The captured soul wailed. *I will tell you what I know, but it is not much.*

The Mordant stayed the lash, studying his captive.

I have heard tales of a forest called the Deep Green. It grows where an ancient city once stood. Rumors say the trees grow unnaturally fast, reaching more than four times the height of an ordinary forest. Some believe the unnatural growth is due to residual magic soaked into the land from the War of Wizards. The Deep Green is a mystery that few dare to penetrate.

The Mordant considered the monk's words. He knew of places steeped in residual magic...but a strange taint emanated from the towering trees, making the Mordant suspect that the Lords of Light had somehow meddled. He prodded the monk. *Tell me, monk, do any people live in this unnatural forest?*

When the monk did not answer, the Mordant ripped the knowledge from his mind. What he learned enraged him. *So the Light had meddled, threatening to undo his greatest triumph.* The forest sounded too much like the Pit of the far north...a ruined crater where the Mordant bred ogres and twisted dwarves from human stock. He could only assume that the forest people possessed some type of wild and unpredictable magic...a threat against the Dark.

The Light tampered with his triumph, but the Mordant walked the southern kingdoms, unknown and undetected, a perfect chance to foil the threat. Staring at the forest, he recalled the monk's words. Hate and fear already existed between the forest-folk and the commoners of Erdhe. Hate and fear were two of the Dark Lord's favorite tools. Possibilities tumbled through his mind.

He made his decision, but for his plan to work he would have to shield the Darkness within. The red light of the Awakening had long since faded, but mortals who were god-touched or strong in the old magics could sometimes sense the Darkness lurking behind his eyes. Unwilling to take the chance, he forced the Darkness deep, burying it beneath his mortal shell. To the simple village peasants his pale blue eyes and open face would project nothing more than a young man enthralled with life. Satisfied, he set off at a brisk pace for the village below the ridge.

His long stride covered the distance quickly, yet he did not reach the village until early evening. The sun set in a bloody blaze as the Mordant walked up the dirt road. Wagon ruts ran deep, the stink of horse dung mingling with the faint aroma of fresh baked bread. A dog howled and a sow squealed, but no one looked his way.

Simple wooden cottages gave way to larger buildings made of mud daub and mitered logs. He passed an inn, a store, a stable, a blacksmith's shop and a tavern. The Mordant slowed his pace, giving the villagers a chance to observe the stranger in their midst. The rich golden color of his monk's robe drew curious stares. Despite the mud spatters and travel stains, the robe's deep color spoke of a luxury beyond the reach of most farmers. The Mordant smiled and nodded to the villagers. None saw past his robes or the façade of his youth.

Setting a smile to his face, the Mordant climbed the steps to the door of the tavern. Faded paint on a weathered sign named it "The Rusty Plow". Dimly lit and drafty, the tavern's great hall was crowded with the smells of spilled ale, greasy meat, and unwashed men. Wooden kegs lined one wall and a stone hearth with a smoldering fire filled the other. Tradesmen, farmers, and the odd traveler mingled together on crowded benches. The tavern did a good business despite the smallness of the village.

The Mordant took his time choosing a table, choosing the human tools for his next trap. Breathing deep, he searched for the spark of Darkness that so many mortals carry in their souls, some deeper than others. Rowdy laughter caught his ear, drawing his attention to a table in the back. Half a dozen young men of peasant stock sat at a long table sharing a jest and a pitcher of ale. The Mordant studied the young men, looking for a thread of Darkness. Loud and full of themselves, they were of an age similar to the monk but their lives were yoked to the plow. Their raucous laughter and crude jokes hid an undercurrent of discontent and resentment, small seeds of Darkness waiting to be nurtured, the perfect prey for his plan.

Beaming a broad smile, he fished a gold coin from the pocket of his robe. "I've coin for a pitcher of ale but no one to drink with. Would you share your table with a foot-weary traveler?

Wary eyes became welcoming once they took in his rich robes and the gold in his hand. Young men jostled along the bench, making space for the mysterious traveler, never suspecting the threat they invited to their table.

The Mordant took the offered seat and tossed the gold coin onto the table. Declaring a hearty thirst, he ordered a bottomless pitcher of ale. The single gold coin bought a table full of friends. Peasants were cheap and so predictable, mortals never seemed to change.

Introductions were made and the inevitable questions asked. As tempting as it was to blame his intended deeds on the Kiralynn Order, this time the charade would not suit his purpose. Instead he claimed to be a storyteller from Lanverness, a journeyman wandering the kingdoms in search of fables and legends.

A roar went up from the table, for storytellers were always welcome.

The young men toasted their good luck and demanded a story from their new-found friend. The Mordant obliged, drawing on centuries of experience. Delving into his own memories, he ensnared the lads with tales of magic and wizards of old. And all the while he kept the ale flowing. As the night wore on, he seeded their minds with stories of injustice, weaving tales where younger sons broke their backs on land they could never hope to inherit. The stories found their mark, lancing a boil of Darkness deep within their souls. As the night lengthened, tongues loosened, and the young men admitted to being third and fourth sons of landed-peasants with no hope of inheriting any future. They roiled with the injustice of their lot. To peasant-farmers land was wealth, and there was never enough land to go around. The Mordant hid his smile; the wheel of time turned yet the plight of peasant-farmers never changed.

The Mordant let the young men talk, filling their mugs and fueling their discontent. Righteous anger swirled round the table. Having prepared the ground, the Mordant planted his seed. Using a congenial voice, he struck the spark to dry tinder. "There's plenty of land for the taking, why not look to the forest?"

Roland, a curly-haired young man with the shoulders of a blacksmith, scowled. "The forest belongs to the Duke, a royal hunting preserve. We daren't touch the land."

Tully, a gap-toothed red-head on Roland's left added, "Our necks would be stretched by the noose if we cleared the Duke's forest."

Similar warnings echoed the length of the table. They wanted the land but not enough to risk the Duke's wrath.

When the protests subsided, the Mordant seeded his true intent. "I didn't mean the Duke's forest. I meant the other one, the Deep Green, the forest infested with the cat-people."

Eyes widened and hands made the sign against evil.

The Mordant hid his smile, amused by their superstitions. With a little prodding, stories of the forest-folk spilled out. The young men competed to tell the most gruesome tales, conjuring images of rituals where devils mated with beasts and human children were served as delicacies at dark feasts. They told of careless hunters wandering into the tangled green, never to be seen again. They spoke of homesteads cursed by the cat-folk so that crops failed and calves died at birth.

The Mordant nurtured the stories of hate and fear. When their emotions reached a fevered pitch, he struck flame to their tinder. "Why let the cat-people infest the very land you deserve, good land that could be used for rich new homesteads?"

A hushed stillness settled across the table.

In a voice thick with ale, Roland said, "But what about the Duke?"

"The cat-folk are a curse on the land, an unnatural blight infesting the forest. I'm sure the Duke would reward those who freed the forest from evil. Reward them with rich land hungry for the plow."

Stares shifted around the table, unsure.

Reaching for his most persuasive voice, the Mordant whispered, "It could be done quietly, under cover of darkness so that no man is accused yet the deserving benefit. You will all gain more land, rich land, soil that has never been touched by the plow."

Their eyes glistening with hunger, the young men leaned forward. "Tell us more."

The Mordant hid his smile. "Wait for a dark night when a stiff wind blows due east, then kindle fires along the forest's edge. Fortify the flames with casks of oil so the fires burn hot and true, a raging inferno. In just one night the tangled green will be reduced to ash, clearing the land for planting. The cursed cat-people will be driven off, or better yet, killed by the flames. In a single stroke, an evil blight is wiped from the forest and good land is freed for the taking, ready for the plow."

Their eyes widened, entranced by the plan.

His task done, the Mordant sat back and listened. Keeping their tankards full, he let them talk, stoking their courage and priming their anger. He could have used compulsion, but he reveled in the art of persuasion. Acts of Darkness were always more potent when leavened with free will. In the end, he stayed three nights, always sitting with the same young men, nurturing the seed of Darkness, fanning their anger and fortifying their resolve.

On the fourth day he rose early with the first cockerel's crow. He left the village, striding along the dirt road to the north. To the east, a false dawn flamed along the edge of the forest. Fed by a stiff wind, the line of fire licked at the towering trees, orange consuming green. Columns of black smoke roiled into the morning sky, dark pillars of destruction. The air stank of burnt trees...and triumph. The Mordant smiled as he walked, leaving seeds of chaos behind him and a dark destiny ahead.

20

Samson

Nightmares chased him from his bed, but for once Samson wondered if his dreams would be safer than the day. He dreaded the morning, his stomach clenched into a fist, his nightshirt sodden with sweat. Realizing more sleep was hopeless, he rose and pulled on his clothes, fumbling in the dark, wishing he could run away but knowing there was no place to go. A soft snore rose from the other bed. Samson shook his head in mute amazement. Ben always slept soundly, no matter what the Harper had planned. Finishing his toilet, Samson descended the narrow staircase, trying to be quiet, surprised to catch the smell of fresh baked apple-bread rising from the kitchen.

He found Grandmother Magda and Justin deep in conversation, the clacking of the knitting needles filling the kitchen with a soothing rhythm. Justin gave him a blazing smile. "Good morning, Samson."

The bard was insufferably cheerful, but his smile was hard to resist. Samson took a mug from the hook and made an attempt at a smile but it turned into a yawn.

"There's fresh apple-bread in the warming pan, dear. Help yourself." The silver-haired matriarch sat in her rocking chair, her knitting needles in constant motion, firelight glinting off her hair.

Samson shook his head. "Just tea this morning, thanks." She knew he loved anything with apples in it, but this morning the smell made his stomach roil. He filled his mug with tea and avoided the bread, afraid his stomach would betray his fear.

Taking a seat on the bench, he stared at the bard. Justin looked strange without his gaudy minstrel's plumage but there would be no bright colors today, nothing to ensnare the eye, nothing memorable, just butternut wool and brown leather jerkins. The plan was to look like any other peasant...except the peasants of Balor were going to be asleep in their beds, not risking their lives.

As if sensing Samson's unease, Justin flashed a wide smile, raising his mug of tea in salute. "Today we beard the Pontifax! Today we beat him at his own game and strike a blow for the freedom of Coronth!"

Samson stared at the bard who was also a prince, wondering if royal blood came with an extra dollop of courage, or if it was just a minstrel's show of bravado. His doubt must have showed on his face.

Justin laughed. "Cheer up, my friend, as long as we're quick there'll be no danger today."

Amazed by the bard's confidence, Samson had to ask, "How so?"

"Their arrogance has made them blind. Like a dragon sleeping safe in its lair, the priesthood thinks no one will dare interfere. We're about to prove them wrong." His face sobered. "The danger will come later, once we wake the fire-breathing dragon."

Samson shuddered. He didn't want to wake the dragon; he didn't want to be a hero, he just wanted a quiet life.

Footsteps clattered down the stairs, announcing that Ben was finally awake. The sergeant seemed to fill the staircase. A solidly built man with a face tanned to leather and a head of close-cropped salt-and-pepper hair. He looked more like a soldier than a boot maker, but some things could not be easily disguised. "Any word from the boys?"

Justin shook his head.

Ben loosened the floorboard on the third step. Reaching into the secret space, he removed three short swords in leather scabbards. Replacing the floorboard, he handed a sword to each of the men. "We'll be wanting these today."

The sight of the swords was sobering. Citizens of Balor were forbidden to carry weapons, but that would be the least of their problems this morning. Samson strapped one around his waist, drawing courage from the steel. At least he'd have a chance to defend himself.

A knock came from the cupboard next to the stairs.

Hands moved to sword hilts but the clacking of the knitting needles never stopped.

The door creaked open and a dark-haired lad peered into the kitchen. "It's me, Jack! We found him!"

Justin surged out of his chair, eagerness on his face. "Well done! Which part of the city?"

The boy entered the warmth of the kitchen, a skinny scrap of an orphan lad, hardly a day over ten, the youngest of a gang of street urchins Justin had recruited as eyes and ears. The boy gave Justin a blazing smile, and nodded to Grandmother Magda, but his gaze kept darting to the apple-bread in the warming pan. "He's in the street of tanners, way on ta other side of town, so we'll have ta run."

"Have a piece or two dear, it's fresh out of the oven."

The boy's hands struck like a twin snakes, one piece going into his pocket, the other crammed into his mouth for a single, bulging bite.

While the boy struggled to swallow, Samson and the others pulled on long brown cloaks to hide their swords and add to the disguise. Ben returned from the front workroom carrying a leather satchel that clanked of tools. Justin beamed a smile at the boy. "Come on Jack, we need you to lead."

The boy swallowed his mouthful and flashed a gap-toothed smile, hero-worship in his eyes.

Samson caught the look and shook his head; hero-worship could get you killed.

"Have a good day, dears." The matriarch stayed by the fire, her knitting needles making a steady clacking.

Three men and the boy stepped through the shallow cupboard to a secret door that opened onto the back alley. They startled a stray cat, but otherwise the alley was empty. Setting off at a trot, they followed the boy through the back ways of the city. The stars had already faded but the sky was still dark. They picked up the pace needing to finish before dawn.

The boy led them through the twists and turns of the back ways. Jack seemed to know every short cut, never once hesitating. At one point, he led them through a burnt building, bridging the distance between two parallel alleys. They kept to the back ways, avoiding the city guard.

The last alley spilled out into a muddy lane crowded with timbered workshops. A horrible stink rose from the street, urine and lye and other foul smells, the tanners were one of the lowest trades. They crouched in the alley mouth, searching the street for soldiers. It proved empty of red, but a man's keening wail beat against the buildings. Fear mingled with rage, the wail scraped down Samson's spine. He shuddered, making the hand sign against evil; this was too much like his nightmares.

Justin paused to question the boy. "Are the other boys in place? Do they know the signals?"

Jack nodded. "Yep, they're hiding at both ends of the street. Willie's on the roof across the way. He'll keep a lookout for soldiers."

A figure melted out of the shadows. Tall and gangly, a young man with a shock of unruly red hair approached Justin. "About time you got here, Harper."

"Red." Justin offered his hand to the leader of the orphan boys. "Is everything ready?"

"Just as you asked. But the soldiers will be back with the first light."

Samson flung a fearful glance to the sky. "There's color in the east."

"Then let's get this done." Like a general to battle, Justin led them into the street.

A flatbed wagon, empty of horses, crouched in the center of the street like a misshapen monster. A framework of timbers jutted from the wagon bed. The stocks held a large man captive, arms spread wide in the shape of a cross, chains wrapped around his neck and hands. The man bucked and fought against the chains, his twisted scream echoing down the street. The neighbors must have heard but no one stirred, leaving the sinner to his fate.

They raced down the street and climbed on the back of the wagon.

The man fell silent, eyes wide and wild, hope and disbelief warring across his battered face.

Justin spoke first, his voice calm and soothing. "We're here to save you. We'll soon have you out of those chains."

The man trembled, his voice a hoarse whisper, "Nobody ever helps a heretic."

A bright smile broke across the bard's face. "That's about to change, my friend. But you best keep screaming till we get your chains undone."

The man complied, howling for help, but to Samson's ears the tenor seemed false.

Ben removed a hammer and chisel from the bag and set to work on the chains. Samson reached for the second set of tools.

Justin stepped close to the man. "Do you have family in this street?"

The man's voice broke, "A wife and three little ones."

"Which house?"

The man pointed. "The one on the left."

Justin jumped from the wagon, "I'll see to them. Red, with me."

Hammers beat against chisels, pounding at the locks, a rhythm of steel against steel. The sinner yelled, trying to drown out the din, but it seemed a futile effort. Samson cringed at the noise. Hammer blows rang in the street but thankfully no one intervened. The people of Balor were well and truly cowed, sheep hiding behind shuttered windows. Samson wondered how long their luck would hold. Tightening his grip on the hammer, he wielded it with a madman's strength, desperate to break the locks.

Samson spared a glance for the sinner. His face was bruised and battered; he must have fought the soldiers. This one didn't belong among the sheep.

Clang! The lock shattered. The man's right hand came free.

Samson dropped to his knee and began working on the leg shackles. He spared a glance at the sky. *Too much light in the east,* fear shivered through him. "We're running out of time!"

Ben's voice remained rock-steady. "Keep at it, we're almost done." A second lock shattered, but there were two more to go.

Justin and Red returned with a thin, pale-faced woman and three small children, tears on their faces, fear in their eyes. The bard kept a steadying hand on two of the children, a bedraggled boy and a weeping girl. "How much longer?"

The dawn light broke in the east, lining the street with gold.

Samson flailed at the lock, fear renewing his strength. The chisel slipped, and he gouged the wagon floor, narrowly missing the man's naked foot.

Shatter! Ben broke the lock at the man's neck, pulling the chains free.

A sharp whistle echoed from the rooftops.

Red hissed, *"They're coming!"*

Panic flared in Samson. For the second time, his blow missed the chisel, denting the wagon bed. Ben shouldered him out of the way and began working on the last lock.

Justin issued an ear-piercing whistle, signaling the lookouts to scatter. "We've got to get the wife and kids away. Red and I will see to the family. Finish the locks and disappear into the alleyways!" The bard ushered the children down the street.

The man strained against the last shackle binding his foot.

"Stand still!" Ben swung the hammer, attacking the last lock.

Samson peered over the edge of the wagon, his heart thundering. "We're running out of time!"

Crack! The last lock shattered.

The man stumbled free of the stocks.

From the edge of the alley, Jack hissed, *"Hurry!"*

They jumped from the wagon, the man nearly falling. Ben threw an arm around him, half carrying him down the lane. Samson grabbed the tools and ran for the alley. He thought he heard the tramp of soldiers marching but it might have been the frantic beat of his own heart.

Jack waved them on, his face twisted in worry.

An urgent whistle echoed from the rooftops.

They rushed into the alleyway. Jack sprinted ahead, *"Follow me!"* They ran, not waiting to see if soldiers followed. The boy led them on a convoluted route, slipping between buildings and dodging down narrow lanes. Samson lost track of the turns, struggling to keep pace. His heart thundered and his breathing became ragged, a sharp pain lancing his side.

They rounded a turn and Jack slowed. Samson staggered to a stop, gasping for breath. "Why have we stopped?"

"The sun's up. If we keep running, we'll attract attention."

Samson raked a worried glance across the windows, wondering if the faithful watched.

Ben finally caught up, the escaped sinner leaning on him for support.

Jack said, "It's time to split up. Can he walk?"

The man tottered to a stop, his bare feet bloody. "I'll run to hell and back if I have to."

Jack looked at Samson. "Do you know where we are?"

Samson studied the narrow lane, recognizing one of the dilapidated buildings. "Behind the vegetable market?"

Jack nodded, looking older than his years. "I'll take him to the hiding place. You lead Ben back to the shop."

Samson nodded, this he could do. He started walking down the alley, but the man cried, *"Wait!"* Samson turned. The man's face rippled with emotions, his stare bouncing between Samson and Ben. "I need to know why?"

Ben answered, "Because someone has to stop the madness."

Tears streaked down the man's face. "I owe you my life."

Ben nodded, "Then help us save others."

"My family?"

"We'll keep them safe. Help them find a way out of the Flame God's city."

Hope kindled in the man's eyes. He offered his hand. "My name's Daniel, I'll stay and help."

Ben shook his hand.

Samson met the man's stare, ashamed that he'd been afraid.

Jack rocked from one foot to another, his voice impatient, "We need to be hiding." The boy tugged on the man's soiled nightshirt, pulling him into a side alleyway.

Samson agreed with the boy, they could talk later. He turned and led Ben toward the east. He forced himself to walk at a measured pace, keeping his cloak closed to hide the sword. They met others using the back ways and always averted their gaze, obeying the unspoken law of the alleys, not to see or be seen.

The alleyways became increasingly familiar. They made a final turn and reached the narrow lane behind the cobbler shop. While Ben kept watch, Samson found the hidden latch and opened the secret door. He stepped into the cupboard and stooped to stare through the knothole. The kitchen was peaceful, Grandmother Magda sitting in her rocking chair, her knitting in her lap. Relief washed through him. Samson knocked on the door and entered the kitchen, Ben following behind.

"Welcome home, dears. I trust the morning went well." The smells of bacon and cornbread drew them to the warmth of the kitchen.

Samson smiled, suddenly starving. "One less sinner for the Flames."

A satisfied smile spread across the old lady's face, her knitting needles keeping time to the creak of the rocker.

The men hung their cloaks on hooks and Ben collected the swords, hiding them under the third stair. Samson poured mugs of tea and heaped two plates with servings of bacon and bread. They fell to eating, talking between bites, taking turns explaining the morning while Grandmother Magda worked on her knitting. Food had never tasted so good, the bacon salty and the cornbread sweet. As they cleaned their plates, the tale grew bolder with the telling.

Still hungry, Samson rose to fix a second helping when a knock came from the cupboard door.

The talking stopped but not the knitting.

The door opened to reveal Justin and Jack, triumph on both their faces.

"Come in, dears, we were just talking about the morning."

Justin swirled the cape from his shoulders and hid his sword. He joined them at the table, excitement shining from his face. "We've struck the first blow! Saved the first life!" He looked at Ben and then at Samson. "You both did well."

Samson grinned, surprised at how much the bard's praise mattered to him.

Justin winked, gesturing at Samson's full plate. "I see you've found your appetite. Saving a life is hungry work and Daniel was worth saving." He turned to Jack. "Get yourself a plate, Jack!"

The boy pounced, grabbing a plate and heaping it with bacon and cornbread, a hungry smile on his soot-stained face. Ben made room for the boy on the bench, giving him his usual spot. The gang of orphans took turns joining them for meals.

Justin rose from the table and began prowling the hearth, as if the small kitchen could not contain him. He walked with a boundless energy, his face alight with determination...and something else, something Samson could not put a name to.

Justin talked as he paced, his voice filling the kitchen with rich undertones. "Today we did more than just talk, more than just sing. Today we took action and we made a difference." The bard paused and turned, clapping Samson on the back. "Who'll join me at this morning's Test of Faith?"

The bacon suddenly sat heavy in Samson's stomach.

Ben said, "Do you think it wise?"

The clack of the knitting needles seemed loud, counting the heartbeats of hesitation.

The bard nodded, a slow smile on his face. "We'll just be a few among many, hiding in a sea of people, but I need to gauge the crowd's reaction when there is no death. I need to see if the people will turn on the Pontifax and his red-robed priests."

The rocking chair creaked. "One life saved will not be enough." The old woman's words had the ring of certainty. "The people see the Test of Faith as a miracle. It will take a miracle to defeat a miracle."

Justin's face stilled. "True enough, but I need to see for myself."

Jack stared at the bard, mumbling past a mouthful of food, "I'll go with you, Harper."

The bard beamed a smile at the boy. "Stay and enjoy your meal, there's not enough meat on your bones to interest an alley rat!" The bard's piercing gaze turned to Samson. "Will you come?"

Samson studied his plate, his stomach roiling. "I'll stay with the boy."

Justin nodded, a hint of disappointment in his voice, "Then I'll be going."

The rocking chair stopped...and so did the knitting needles. "I'll join you." The old woman thrust her knitting needles into the bag of yarn at her feet. Pulling a worn shawl around her shoulders, she tucked the bag under her arm and stood. Her face was serene, her back unbowed despite her age.

Samson stared, slack mouthed.

Grandmother Magda met his gaze. "It's what I've come for, dear. Revenge and justice, two things that are oft times the same, especially in the eyes of a bereaved mother...or a kinless grandmother." She nodded, her eyes cold as steel. "It's only the start, dear." Her voice dropped to a hushed whisper. "I'll have my share of justice and bear witness for all the women who grieve."

Samson shivered; the old woman's face was still kindly, still wisdom-worn, but an implacable hatred shone from her steel-gray eyes. He did not know how she intended to strike a blow against the Pontifax, but he was certain it would be something terrible, something he couldn't imagine.

The bard intervened, rescuing him from the old woman's unrelenting gaze. Justin offered his arm to the silver-haired grandmother, like a gentleman leading his lady to a dance. Samson watched them go, justice and vengeance walking arm in arm...moving to a dance that dared death.

The shop door closed and the silence seemed suddenly ominous. The knitting needles had stopped. The illusion of safety was shattered. They'd struck a blow for freedom, tweaking the tail of the dragon...but Samson shuddered, knowing the fiery breath of the beast was still to come.

21

Liandra

The secret passage gaped open, a chance to defeat the rebellion. Captain Durnheart entered first, cutting a trail through the cobwebs and lighting the way. The queen followed close behind. The shadowman, Collins, guarded the rear, bringing a second torch. Torchlight flickered against narrow walls, a dance of shadows and light.

Just inside the secret door, the queen found what she was looking for, a small stone shield carved with a heraldic bee. Even here, in this hidden passage, the quality of the stonework was excellent. Her ancestors never stinted when it came to the castle.

The queen set the heel of her hand against the shield and pressed. A grating noise rumbled behind her. The secret door ground shut, closing off the scent of aging cheeses, leaving nothing but stale air and darkness. "The way is hidden once more. Castle Tandroth keeps its secrets." She gestured and the captain continued up the narrow passage.

Cold and dark and long unused, decades of dust caked the passageway. They walked single-file, disturbing spiders and mice. The queen shrank from the narrow walls yet the cobwebs still found her, clinging to hair and clothes. Liandra shuddered; she'd need more than one bath to wash away the filth of this misbegotten day. Lifting her skirt, she followed the torchlight, her gaze searching the walls for more carvings.

The captain paused at a crossway.

The queen trusted her memory from childhood. "Keep straight."

Darkness threatened to choke their torchlight. The walls narrowed, one of them weeping moisture. Liandra could almost feel the weight of the castle brooding above. They walked close, keeping within the circle of torchlight. Behind her, the shadowman sneezed, disturbing a quiet that rivaled a tomb.

They reached steps that spiraled upwards.

"Wait." The queen's command echoed against the stone. "Pass the torch along the wall." The captain waved the torch, illuminating a carving, a king's crown of roses. The queen caressed the stone crown. Carved for her grandfather's great grandfather, the Tandroths were ever devious, hollowing their castle with secret ways. The queen nodded. "This way is right. The stairs lead to the Queen's Tower."

Their ascent was slow, a series of spiral steps, steep ramps, and narrow passageways honeycombing the outer walls of the tower. After the first spiral, faces began to appear on the inner wall. Carved from stone, each face was unique, a jester, a maiden, a prince. Young, old, happy, sad, each face was so expressive it seemed as if the stone might waken to smile or wink. Most had carved onyx insets for eyes. Several had keyholes cut into the recesses of their open mouths. The queen paused at the first face with onyx eyes. The captain shielded the torchlight while the queen gently pried loose an onyx plug. Peering through the eyehole, she gained a view of an inside corridor. What she saw chilled her blood. Torches guttered along marble hallways, revealing three soldiers crumpled in pools of blood. The rebellion had breached the outer doors to the tower. Worry gripped her. *"The enemy is in the tower."* Replacing the onyx plug, she fretted over the floors above. Liandra prayed she was not too late.

Their progress slowed. The queen insisted on checking every spy hole, needing to understand the extent of the threat. The second floor revealed a shocking surprise. Peering through a spy hole, the queen found herself staring straight at the traitor. The Lord Turner stood tall and arrogant, issuing orders to soldiers of the rebellion. A pillar of command, he wore the uniform of the Royal Guard, the uniform he betrayed. Burning with anger, the queen stifled a hiss. Everything about the traitor screamed of ambition, from the arrogant tilt of his head, to the belligerence of his stance, to the way he gripped his sword hilt. Liandra wondered that she hadn't seen it before. She'd trusted this man with her life, with her kingdom. Rage erupted within her, venom in her glare. If stares could kill he would be dead.

The Lord Turner whipped his gaze in her direction.

Liandra snapped her eyes closed, but kept her face pressed firm to the spy hole, lest the torchlight betray her. Trapped against the stone, she chided herself for the hatred of her stare. Her heartbeat thundered. Eyes closed, she waited, wondering if a dagger would pierce the spy hole, pierce her eye and pith her brain...a terrible way to die. Liandra strangled her imagination, refusing to move, refusing to succumb to fear. An eternity later, she dared a second glance. The traitor had turned away, conversing with his men. Her hands shaking, she replaced the onyx insert. She leaned against the wall, drinking up the coldness of the stone, struggling to still her racing heart.

"What is it, majesty?"

"The traitor...I saw him." The queen shuddered, gripped by wild surges of relief and rage. Hatred boiled within her...but beneath the hate a plan brewed. She turned to the shadowman. "Collins, is it?"

The shadowman stood to attention. "Yes, majesty."

"We have an important mission for you."

The shadowman nodded, his gaze eager.

"Retreat back down the passageway and find the Master Archivist. Tell him, and him alone, that the Lord Turner lurks on the second floor of the Queen's Tower. Tell him to rouse the troops and seal the tower. If we trap the traitor between us, we may force a swift end to this rebellion."

"The Lord Turner is the *traitor?*"

She heard the disbelief in his voice. "Do you doubt your queen?"

Her shadowman flushed. "No, majesty."

"Then do as we command." She considered her plan, knowing it hinged on what she found above. "Tell him, the queen will play the anvil to his hammer, trapping the traitor between us." She prayed her loyal men still held the top floors. "Now go with the Light, and see the message gets to our shadowmaster."

Collins saluted and turned to make his way back down the gloomy passageway.

Captain Durnheart said, "You take risks, majesty."

She raised an eyebrow in question.

"To rely on just one sword."

Her voice softened. "One sword that we trust."

"Two would be better."

"Two will make little difference. If the message is delivered in time we may yet quell this rebellion." She gestured up the passageway. "We must learn what lies above."

The captain led the way, a single torch against the dark. They passed a dozen faces before the queen was willing to dare another spy hole. Steeling her courage, she removed an onyx plug and pressed her face to the cold stone. *Nothing...an empty sitting room.* Her questions remained unanswered. Three spy holes later she found the fighting. Swords clashed as her loyal men defended the hallway, a chaos of blood and death...but it meant the upper levels had not been compromised. Relief washed through her, there was still time.

Needing speed, she left the faces untouched until she reached the sixth floor. She tried the jolly face wearing a minstrel's cap but it was not the right room. A cherub's face was next, the eyeholes revealing a sumptuous sitting room. As the queen watched, a young dark-haired woman in a close-fitting gown of deep blue, swept into the room, a strung bow in her left hand, a quiver of arrows belted to her side. The queen smiled, Princess Jemma was the perfect protégé, a petite beauty with a scorpion's sting. A wave of fierce affection swept through Liandra. Here was a daughter to replace the one who hadn't lived, a daughter to make up for a traitorous son. Liandra made her decision. Replacing the onyx plug, she reached for the gold skeleton key cradled in her bodice. The key unlocked the secrets of the tower, a key she always kept close. Moving to the companion cherub with the deep laugh, she inserted the key into its mouth. She needed both hands to turn the key. The lock clicked and the outline of a narrow door appeared in the wall. Removing the key, the queen whispered, "Wait here." Before the captain could answer, she slipped through the doorway, stepping from dust and shadows into the luxury of the sitting room.

Princess Jemma spun, a startled look on her face, her hand reaching for an arrow.

The queen's voice rang with authority, "Princess Jemma, you know us."

The princess stared, her eyes wide in astonishment. "Your *majesty?*"

"We have come to offer you safe haven."

"They're fighting in the lower floors, talk of a rebellion." Her eyes narrowed. "A secret passage?"

"Even the walls of the castle aid us. Come, there is no time for talk. Bring your guards and anyone else you trust. We must be away."

The princess nodded. She ran to the outer doors, returning with two Navarren guards. "There's no one else."

"Then come and bring your bow." The queen led them to the doorway hidden in the wood paneling. They slipped into the dust-choked passage, pulling the door shut behind them.

"Captain Durnheart, lead us to the end."

The captain climbed the narrow stairs, the torch sputtering against the dark. They passed the marker for the seventh floor and still the passage continued upward. The captain gave the queen a puzzled look. "Majesty, there are only seven floors in the tower of the queen?"

The queen smiled. "There only appear to be seven floors. The eighth is a secret space reserved for monarchs. From the eighth we will retake our castle."

They rounded the final turn, the narrow passage ending in a stone doorway shrouded in cobwebs. Waving the torch, the captain set the cobwebs to sizzle. Released from the white shroud, a crowned king stared from the door. Liandra touched the stone-cold face. Legend said the visage was that of King Barrick, the first great king of the Tandroth line, a wily monarch known for devious strategies. Liandra hoped the old codger was still full of tricks. She inserted the gold key into the king's mouth. Even using both hands the key would not turn. "Captain Durnheart, your strength is needed."

The captain grasped the key and turned. The stone door shuddered opened.

"Come, we are nearly at the end."

The thick stone door opened into a round, windowless chamber. The single torch cast glimmers of light into the gloom. The queen knew the chamber from memory, a secret hidden away for dire times. "You'll find torches lining the walls, light them, and the candelabra over the table as well."

Captain Durnheart moved from torch to torch, throwing the chamber into light. The stone ceiling was low but not confining. Six wooden doors ringed the chamber with an alcove leading to steps on the far side. A heavy oak table dominated the room, an iron chandelier full of candles hanging overhead. The round table had seats for twenty, a map of Erdhe painted in the center. A moth-eaten tapestry depicting the green and white shield of house Tandroth graced the north wall, the only sign of luxury in the spare room.

Princess Jemma ran her finger across the painted map, a look of surprise on her face. "It's not dusty."

In stark contrast to the narrow passageway, the chamber was fresh-swept and clean, as if waiting for a specific purpose. The queen smiled. "This chamber is always prepared for the worst. You'll find provisions behind one of the doors and weapons behind another."

Princess Jemma broiled with questions. "But what is this place? And why are you dressed like that?"

The queen had to laugh for fashion was suddenly the least of her worries. "This chamber is a legacy from our ancestors, a bolt hole for a beleaguered monarch, a secret sanctuary...and now, our war room. We have come to reclaim our kingdom from traitors. But first, we must assemble our loyal forces." She turned to the captain. "Captain Durnheart, with me. The rest of you wait here. You'll find supplies behind the first door on the right, casks of wine, water from the cistern above, and stores of food."

She turned and led the captain to the far alcove where one set of steps led up and another down. She took the stairs leading down, descending to a second stone door. The door bore the carved face of another king, another ancestor, but this king had onyx eyes. Removing the onyx, she peered through the king's eyes spying on the queen's solar.

At first the room appeared empty but then a figure passed by the spy hole. Lady Sarah waited alone, pacing the chamber, her face a mask of worry.

The queen replaced the onyx eyes and unlocked the door.

Lady Sarah stifled a scream and then curtseyed when she saw the queen. "Your majesty! I feared you were *dead*!"

The honest concern touched the queen. "We are not dead yet."

"But majesty, the rebels have attacked the castle! They hold the bottom floors. They say the fighting is terrible. Some whispered..." the Lady blanched, her voice going hoarse, "Some claimed the queen is dead!"

"Dead, eh?" Her mind churned with the implications. "The traitors will be disappointed." Seeing opportunity in the rumor, the queen laughed, but her laughter had cutting edge. "We shall be a vengeful ghost! One they will not soon forget." She gestured for the lady to rise. "But come, there is much to be done. Are the others waiting?"

Rising, Lady Sarah nodded, color returning to her cheeks. "In the sitting room, as you commanded."

"Summon them. All are needed."

Lady Sarah returned with two other ladies-in-waiting and six of the master's shadowmen dressed as servants to the crown. Relief washed across their faces as they saw their queen.

Liandra infused her voice with royal confidence, "Come. Join us in the war room above, where we will hear your reports." She did not give them time for questions. Turning, she led them to the secret door and up the narrow stairs. Over her shoulder, she said, "Captain Durnheart, see that the door is closed behind you."

Returning to the hidden chamber, she found the others seated at the table, the room brimming with light. She waited for the rest to assemble and then turned her gaze to the senior shadowman, a compact, swarthy man with salt-and-pepper hair. "Major Telcore, we would have your report."

The major bowed, his voice gruff, "*Traitors*." He made the word was a curse. "There must have been traitors among the guards at the tower's main entrance. They opened the doors at midnight, allowing the rebels to swarm our defenses. Many were taken by surprise, murdered at their posts, but our forces rallied. We make the traitors pay for every step into the Queen's Tower, but we're outnumbered. The battle line has fallen back to the fourth floor."

The queen blanched, the noose tightened faster than she thought.

"Without reinforcements, it is only a matter of time." The major's face turned grim, his voice earnest, "Majesty, I don't know how you came to be in the tower, but however you managed it, you must leave.' His voice dropped to a whispered plea, "Leave before our lines break."

Tension threaded through the chamber like forked lightning.

She felt the weight of their stares, the weight of a kingdom. "We have come to fight."

"But majesty..."

Silencing him with a wave of her hand, the queen turned her stare to Princess Jemma. "We must take this risk, but not you. Captain Durnheart shall escort you from the tower and see to your safety."

Princess Jemma stood full of dignity. "I prefer to stay."

"But it is not your fight. We would keep you safe from harm."

"Majesty, my father is a king. He did not raise his children to run from a fight." Her eyes sparked with mischievous pride. "Besides, I believe you will find a way to win...and I have come to learn from the best."

The queen smiled, a mixture of gratitude and pride. *Steel beneath velvet, surely this was the daughter she had lost.* "Then stay close to us and see how we vanquish those who reach for our throne."

The queen surveyed the loyal few gathered round the table. Her plan had many risks; she would need each of them to rise to their best. Infusing her voice with the power of her throne, she assumed a regal stance. "We have come to fight...with our wits, and our determination, and our secrets. The enemy has underestimated us. The very walls of Castle Tandroth will give us the advantage we need." Her voice flushed with righteous conviction. "We will not leave this tower unless it is in victory." Her gaze circled the room, giving confidence to each. "Will you fight with us? Will you help us vanquish the rebels?"

Captain Durnheart was the first to reply, *"For the queen!"* The others echoed his response, a shout of courage defying the odds.

Their conviction was like an elixir to the queen. "With such loyalty we can not fail." She flashed a smile of courage and determination. "Listen and we shall tell you how to weave a web to catch a viper." She explained her plan, assigning tasks to each of them. Liandra did not believe in war but now that the battle was joined, she would not shirk from it. It was past time the traitors felt the Spider Queen's venom.

22

Duncan

Redwoods, cedar, and spruce gave way to the lighter greens of birch, alder, and aspen. As the companions rode north the trees thinned, slowly giving way to farmland. Sunlight streamed through the branches and birdsong rode the air. The forest seemed peaceful enough, but something itched at Duncan's senses, a vague unease. He scanned the forest as he rode, but the threat remained elusive, a dread lurking just out of reach. He kept his short bow strung and his gaze alert but the peace of the forest remained unbroken. Riding in the lead, he took the risk of lifting his eye patch, using all of his senses to search for the danger, but he found no target for his arrows. Frustrated, Duncan thrummed his legs against the gelding, hoping to outrun the lurking dread.

A rider approached on his right. Duncan swiveled in the saddle and found Danya urging her cream-colored mare forward. The girl rode the pale mare with a fluid grace, almost as if she'd been born to the saddle. He wondered if it was part of her magic.

She drew even, her voice rising over the drumming hooves. "Blaine's charger has a loose shoe. We should find a blacksmith."

He turned and studied the knight's warhorse, unable to detect any flaw in the charger's gait. "How do you know?"

"I just know."

Magic. He trusted his own senses more than any magic, but the knight's battle-trained charger could not be risked. Duncan nodded, "Best if we find a village and get the warhorse properly shod." He took a deep breath, tasting the air. The scent of wood smoke rode the wind but the horizon was empty of chimney smoke.

"Bryx says there's a village to the east. If we keep to a steady trot we should get there by noon."

"The wolf *told* you this?"

Danya's face clouded. "Well not in so many words, just the stink of too many people in the direction of the rising sun." Danya shrugged. "It's more feelings and smells, than words."

The mountain wolf chose that moment to lope out of the brush, a wide grin on his face.

"Sometimes I think that wolf is laughing at me."

Danya chuckled, flashing a smile.

Duncan gave up and said, "Tell the wolf we'll follow him to the village, but once there, it would be best if he stayed out of sight. Most villagers don't take kindly to wolves."

"Don't worry, he knows. Besides, Bryx doesn't like the stink of towns. He'll stick to the forest and fields."

The wolf yipped and set off toward the east at a ground-eating lope. They followed at a steady trot, riding for the better part of the morning. The forest fringe faded away to farm fields and vineyards, a patchwork of gold and green, peaceful and content. Beyond the fields, tendrils of chimney smoke scored the summer sky, marking the location of the village. The wolf grinned back at them and melted into the fields, disappearing into the summer green.

The riders followed a sunken dirt lane toward the east. A pair of fortified towers rose in the distance, marking the seat of a minor lordling. A purple banner emblazoned with three golden spears streamed from the tower rampart. Duncan recognized the banner and scowled. Baron Brannock carried a reputation as a cruel and petty tyrant, a tight-fisted lord with a thirst for his neighbor's lands. They'd do well to avoid the baron and his men.

The road split into a fork. Duncan turned the gelding toward the village, avoiding the twin towers. Deep cart ruts and clumps of manure marked a path leading straight to the village. Duncan slowed the gelding to a walk as a sign of courtesy.

Thatch-roofed cottages clustered close, the smell of wood smoke heavy in the air. They rode past a group of women gathered at a well, a few knee-high children clutching at homespun skirts. Duncan nodded hello but the women avoided his stare, herding the children away. He caught a look of fear in one woman's glance, something far more than the usual distrust of strangers. The fear puzzled him, but they needed to get the warhorse shod.

Duncan followed the road into the heart of the village. A few stone buildings stood among the wooden cottages. A chicken fluttered across the road in a squawk of feathers. Faces turned to study the strangers, none of them welcoming. A sense of unease shivered down Duncan's spine, as if the dread of the forest had followed them to the village. If they hadn't needed a blacksmith, he would have kept riding, but the warhorse would be valuable in a fight, it shouldn't take long to get the horse shod.

A column of sooty smoke marked the forge. Duncan dismounted and tied the gelding to a post. He followed the beat of a hammer to the forge. A sweat-soaked blacksmith worked a bar of hot metal against an anvil. A bellows boy kept the forge glowing cherry-red. The big man glanced at Duncan, his voice a deep rumble. "Somethin' I can do you for?" The words were welcoming but the glance was not.

Duncan kept his voice friendly. "I've got a horse outside that needs re-shod and seven more horses I'd like you to have a look at. We've a long road ahead and we're anxious to be off."

The hammer rang against the iron, never missing a beat. "Four shoes for a silver and I'll see the color of your coin first. Course you'll have to wait till I finish this piece."

Duncan reached for his coins, flashing gold to the blacksmith. "Two golds if you'll do them all now."

"Eight horses?"

"But only one that definitely needs shod."

The hammer stopped. The blacksmith plunged the rod into the glowing coals, the smell of hot iron heavy in the air. "I'll take your gold. Be back in a few hours and I should have them done." The coins disappeared into the blacksmith's fist. "Show me your horses."

The big man followed Duncan out into the sunshine. They found Danya checking the rear hoof of Blaine's warhorse, the lanky knight hovering at the girl's side. Danya nodded toward the blacksmith, her voice soft but sure. "The shoe needs replaced and there's a hairline crack starting at the side of the hoof. Just as well we stopped."

The blacksmith shouldered the knight aside and examined the hoof. "The crack's not too bad. Just needs filed. A bit of glue and a new shoe and the horse will be fine."

Satisfied to leave the horses in the care of the blacksmith and the wolf-girl, Duncan said, "We've a few hours to spend while the blacksmith does his work. Who'll join me for a meal and some gossip at the tavern?"

Blaine was predictable. "I'll stay and help Danya."

Duncan kept the smile from his face.

Sir Tyrone said, "I'll visit the market and see if there's anything good for the cook pot."

Duncan nodded. "Don't take too long." He turned to Kath and the monk. Kath looked at the monk and said, "We're with you."

They left the blacksmith shop and strolled down the lane toward the tavern. They passed a carpentry shop loud with hammers. A pair of men worked to repair a thatched roof but otherwise they met only women and small children. Duncan smiled but the women shied away, crossing to the far side of the lane and making the hand sign against evil. Duncan stretched his senses, trying to understand the villagers' fear but he found no answers.

He leaned toward Kath and whispered, "Stay sharp. I've a bad feeling about this place."

She nodded, her hand resting on her sword hilt, her eyes scanning the village.

He liked that she heeded his warning without questions.

A timber-framed longhouse served as the tavern, a weathered sign over the double doors. They climbed the stairs and entered the great room, eyes adjusting to the smoke-filled gloom. The tavern was stuffy with the smell of spilled ale and spitted meat.

The low rumble of conversation came to a sudden stop. The tavern was crowded with men. Soldiers in the purple livery of the local lord and sellswords in patched leathers and chainmail turned to stare at the strangers. A few of the stares were curious but most were hostile...a much rougher crowd than he'd expected.

Duncan lifted his hands in a gesture of peace and nodded to the barkeeper. He chose an empty table near the door and sat with his back to the wall. Kath sat on his right, the monk on his left. Flashing a gold coin, Duncan caught the attention of the portly barkeeper.

Wiping his hands on a grease-stained apron, the barkeeper ambled to their table. "Whad d'ya want?"

"A meal and information."

Eyeing the gold coin, the barkeeper said, "The gold will buy ya a loaf of white bread, three mutton pies and a pitcher of ale, the best fare in town. Any answers will depend on yer questions."

"Then I'll ask the questions first."

The barkeeper shook his head, a stubborn look on his face. "In this town, strangers pay first."

Duncan didn't like flashing gold in room crowded with sellswords but he wanted answers. He slid the coin across the table.

A meaty palm slammed down, trapping the coin. "Whad d'ya want ta know?"

"Why so many sellswords?"

The barkeeper shrugged, "The Baron's anxious. Anxious lords attract sellswords."

"What's there to be anxious about?"

The barkeeper squinted, a suspicious look on his face. "Where d'ya come from that ya haven't heard?"

Duncan felt it best not to mention the monastery. "From Lanverness, we're just passing through. Stopped to get a horse shod."

The barkeeper stared at the leather-clad archer, disbelief on his face.

Kath leaned forward, her voice surprisingly soft. "Please, sir, we'd really like to know."

The barkeeper looked at the girl, his face softening. "Ya best keep ridin. Somethin evil's been stalkin the farms and woods around these parts. Cottages drip with blood and whole families are found dead, their flayed skins nailed to the walls. There's talk that one of them cursed wizards of old has returned to haunt the land." The man's fear-filled eyes slid toward the monk. "The baron's offered a bounty for the wizard's head. The bounty's lured sellswords to town like flies to carrion. Best if ya finish yer business and move on."

Duncan kept his face neutral and passed a second coin across the table. "We'll have the standard fare and a flagon of ale."

The barkeeper backed away. "I'll send the girl with yer ale."

Duncan glanced at Kath.

Her face was grim. "Perhaps the Mordant has left a trail after all."

"Or set a trap." The menace he'd felt in the forest made more sense. Turning to the monk, Duncan whispered, "If the peasants fear a wizard then I'm guessing the Mordant is still garbed in a robe from the monastery. Perhaps you should find something else to wear."

The monk stared, anger etched across his face.

A serving girl approached with a pitcher of ale and three tankards. Blonde and buxom, her hands shook as she served the tankards. She scuttled back to the bar without making eye contact.

The low rumble of conversation resumed, but too many stares were still turned their way. Too many hands rested on sword hilts, Duncan didn't like the odds. "We'll have our meal and leave. I'd rather sleep under the stars than spend a single night in this town. This place reeks of fear. And the sellswords might decide to collect our heads without bothering to check who they belong to."

Zith leaned toward Duncan. "The local lord might have information about the wizard. The sooner we catch the Mordant the better."

"Better to avoid Baron Brannock. We ride as soon as the horses are shod."

Zith gave Duncan a searching look. "Then how will we find the Mordant?"

"We'll try another village, one with less sellswords." He shook his head with the irony of it. "We were looking for tracks on the ground when we should have been searching for fear." Duncan tightened his hands into fists. "Follow the fear and we'll find the Mordant."

The serving girl returned balancing a tray laden with bread and steaming meat pies. The girl edged the tray onto the table and served each of them a small pie in a deep dish. Zith reached to help, but the girl flinched away, her gaze dropping to the monk's outstretched hands.

A scream split the tavern. The tray clattered to the floor, the plates shattering.

Pale-faced and wide-eyed the girl backed away. Pointing at the monk, she screeched, "The Evil Eye! He bears the mark of Evil on his hand!"

Swords slid from scabbards.

Kath reached for her sword, but Duncan stayed her hand. He rose from the table holding his open palms out. "We're peaceful travelers. We've done no harm and want no trouble."

From the back of the room a man yelled, "*I seen what the wizard did! I seen with my own eyes what was left of my kin!*"

The sellswords stalked forward, like hounds on the hunt.

Duncan kept his back the wall, shuffling towards the door.

The nearest sellsword growled a warning. "Where do you think yer going?"

The tavern door swung open and Sir Blaine stood on the threshold, sunlight glinting on his silver surcoat.

The sellswords froze.

Duncan almost laughed; who better to come to the rescue than a knight of the Octagon. Sir Blaine drew his great blue sword and held the doorway by shear intimidation. The three companions reached the door. They cleared the tavern without violence and sprinted for the smithy.

Sir Blaine caught up to Duncan and said, "What was that?"

"A trap. Seems we've followed in the Mordant's footsteps. A serving girl saw the tattoo on the monk's hand and claimed it as a sign of evil. We need to get out of here before the villagers start burning strangers." Glancing at the knight, Duncan added, "Is your horse shod?"

"Yes but Danya wanted the blacksmith to check the rest of the horses."

"No time for that."

They raced to the smithy and found Sir Tyrone and Danya in conversation with the blacksmith, looking at the hoof of one of the packhorses.

"Get to your horses, we ride now!" The urgency of Duncan's tone brooked no argument.

The companions scrambled to tighten cinches and secure the leads on the packhorses. One packhorse shied and bucked, refusing the bit. Duncan shouted, "Leave him if you can't get him settled."

Danya laid a hand on the horse and got him settled. The wolf-girl was the last to mount up. Duncan led them out into the lane.

A crowd of peasants and sellswords had started to form.

Duncan nosed his horse forward, pushing his way through the grim-faced crowd. The villagers parted just wide enough for the black gelding to pass. He felt their stares, fear mingled with hate. Hearing their muttered curses, Duncan half expected to be stoned.

His horse cleared the crowd, but he held the gelding to a walk. If they ran they'd look like prey and running prey always raised the bloodlust of predators. He didn't want the crowd to become a mob, bad enough there were sellswords among them.

They reached the outskirts of the village and Duncan nudged his gelding to a trot. He listened behind but heard no sounds of pursuit. Passing the first field, Duncan gave the gelding his head, urging the horse to a gallop. They rode through rolling farmland and back into forest, racing toward the northeast, eager to put the village behind them.

They kept the horses to a hard gallop for the better part of an hour. Crossing a shallow stream, Duncan called a halt. The horses stamped and blew hard. Sweat-streaked from the run they reached for the water, but their riders only allowed them a short drink. Kath started to say something but Duncan held his hand up for silence. He strained to listen, stretching his senses back toward the village.

In the stillness of the forest, he caught the faint thunder of galloping hooves.

Duncan swore. "The sellswords have found their courage." He scanned the terrain searching for an advantage. "There's a ridge in that direction. Head for the high ground."

Duncan kicked the black gelding to a gallop. Riding cross-country, he led them through the thinning forest to an open field. The gelding raced across the fallow field and jumped a low stone wall. On the far side of the wall, he found a narrow dirt road that led up the ridge.

Duncan slowed the gelding, turning to watch the others. Kath and her chestnut stallion sailed effortlessly over the wall. The two knights followed close on the stallion's heels, but the others lagged behind. Duncan cursed. The mountain horses were bred for stamina not speed. Danya emerged from the forest, coaxing her mare, but the monk and the two packhorses lumbered behind. Zith bounced in the saddle, an awkward rider, ruining the gait of his mount.

Duncan swore. *"Hurry!"* Leaping from the saddle, he strung his longbow.

Danya's mare cleared the stone wall. One of the packhorses followed but the other balked.

"Leave it! Ride for the ridge!" He nocked an arrow.

A triumphant shout rang from the edge of the forest. Three score sellswords thundered into the field, a rabid hunting pack bristling with weapons.

Duncan loosed three quick arrows, enough to give the sellswords pause.

The monk reached the wall, his face pale but determined, hands gripping the saddle horn. The mountain horse gathered for the jump, barely clearing the stones. Landing hard, the horse nearly threw the old man. Duncan swatted the horse with his bow. "Ride for the ridge!" He leaped to his own mount, spurring the gelding to a gallop. The black surged forward, overtaking the mountain horses and galloping up the steep slope. The ridge was a jumble of sharp rocks and boulders, the narrow road the only way to the top. Duncan grinned. The ridge offered the archer the advantage he needed.

He reached the top and found Kath and the two knights waiting, their swords drawn.

Pulling even with Sir Tyrone's charger, Duncan yelled, "I'll hold them from the ridge. You keep the rest going. Ride for the Mother Forest, the sellswords won't dare follow you there." Seeing puzzlement on the black knight's face, Duncan yelled, "Cross over the ridge and ride to the east. You'll know the forest when you see it. Don't stop for anything."

The black knight nodded.

Duncan dismounted and pulling two quivers of arrows from his saddle.

Danya and the monk rode past, but Kath wheeled her horse around, riding back to Duncan's side.

The archer set an arrow to the string.

The sellswords galloped hard across the field.

Kath yelled, "What are you doing? There's too many of them!"

"The mountain horses can't outrun the sellswords. A single archer can hold them from here. Follow the others."

He took aim at the lead sellsword and let the arrow fly.

Kath dismounted. "I'll not leave you!"

The arrow found its mark and the lead horse crumpled.

Duncan reached for a second arrow.

Kath grabbed his arm. "I won't let you fight alone!"

Angry, he turned on her, but he bit back his words, shocked to find a woman instead of a girl, a woman with fire in her stare, one who cared enough to fight beside him. His breath caught in his throat. Perhaps he'd found the one thing he'd never had...but it came too late. He banished the thought. "No, you don't know me!"

Her green-eyed gaze consumed him. "I know enough!"

He heard the sellswords galloping up the ridge. "No time for this, you have to ride!" He wanted to pull her close, to wrap her in his arms and kiss her lips, but instead he pushed her away. "You have to live! *Now ride!*"

Emotions raced across her face. Hurt settled in her green eyes and stubborn anger on her mouth. He had a wild impulse to kiss the anger away, but instead he turned his gaze to the enemy and made his voice as hard as stone. "You're the one from the prophecy. It's your duty to slay the Mordant. *Now ride!*" He drew the bowstring to his lips and picked another target.

She leaped to the saddle, but he heard the tears in her voice. "Promise you'll follow!"

The sellswords brandished their swords, braying for the kill.

Duncan loosed at the new leader. Horse and rider tumbled, making an obstacle for the others. He reached for another arrow. Without taking his eyes from the approaching sellswords, he growled, "I'll do my best."

"I'll hold you to it!" Frustration and anger laced her words, but she thrummed her mount to a gallop.

He relaxed as she rode away.

Peace settled over him and he fell into the rhythm of the bow. The ridge forced the sellswords to bunch in the narrow road, making easy targets, but there were too many of them. His only hope was to wilt their courage with a hail of arrows. Needing every advantage, he flipped the leather eye-patch up. He took his time and made every arrow count. Accuracy could be a terrible weapon. One arrow struck an eye; another impaled an open mouth, sowing death as well as terror. Screams echoed across the ridge. The road clogged with carnage, slowing the advance...but they kept coming. The bounty must be high for the sellswords to risk so much. It was only a matter of time till they gained the summit.

The howl of a lone wolf broke from the forest below. A black streak raced across the field to harry the sellswords from behind. The horses reared, screaming in terror. Hooves slashed the air and riders tumbled. Panic shuddered through the sellswords.

Duncan flashed a hunter's smile. Perhaps a mountain wolf and a lone archer would be enough. He nocked another arrow and let it fly. All they could do was try.

23

Steffan

Priests and acolytes fled like cockroaches escaping a booted foot. The temple roiled with fear and confusion. Steffan strode through the marble corridors, cutting a dark swath through the sea of panicked red. He watched the priests' faces as they scurried past, fear and doubt reflected in their eyes. Fear was acceptable, even encouraged, but never doubt...doubt was the bane of religions...the Lord Raven had work to do.

He reached the Vestiary and paused in the doorway, studying the two high priests.

Anger thundered through the gilded chamber. The Pontifax railed at the Keeper, his face a thunderstorm of wrath. "Whose idea was it to leave the heretics unguarded in the stocks?" The Pontifax wielded his finger like a dagger, jabbing each word into the chest of the burly Keeper. "You're responsible for the sinners. You're responsible for getting the heretics to the ceremony. It isn't a true Test of Faith without a *sacrifice!*"

The Keeper cringed under the tongue-lashing despite his muscle-bound frame.

"The people expect death and *you're* supposed to give it to them! *I* do the miracles, and *you* supply the death!" The Pontifax balled his hands into fists. "I want to know who did this! I want them rounded up and consigned to the Flames! I want to see them *burn!*"

The Keeper showed a flash of backbone, his voice belligerent. "It was your idea to keep them in the stocks. You said it would cow the others into submission. Don't blame me for your ideas."

Steffan shook his head; the big man never knew when to keep his mouth shut.

The Pontifax's face flamed red, rage on the verge of eruption.

The argument needed to be stopped before more damage was done. Steffan glided into the room, radiating calm. He kept his voice soothing, like cool water poured on a fresh burn. "Gentlemen, there is no need to argue." He punctuated his interruption by closing the double doors with more force than was necessary. Gaining their attention, as well as a prudent privacy, he said, "When the religious leaders argue in public it causes doubt to ripple through the faithful. *Doubt* is the one thing a religion cannot afford." He lowered his voice a notch, "Never argue in front of the hired help, it puts us all in jeopardy."

The Pontifax rounded on his counselor. "Did you see the crowd? Did you see their faces when they realized there would be no sacrifice, no death?" A hint of desperation leached into the old man's voice, "For a moment I thought they would turn on me! *Me*, their beloved Pontifax!"

The old charlatan was rattled. The crowd had been disappointed and confused but never dangerous. Religion still held the people of Balor in thrall. "You handled it well." He stroked the Pontifax with his voice, willing the man to calm. "You saved a bad situation and turned it to our advantage." The Pontifax had preformed brilliantly in front of the crowd, but now that he was away from the stage, the cracks of fear were beginning to show. "Choosing a child from the crowd and carrying her through the Flames was brilliant. You defused the tension, giving the people two miracles instead of one death." He flooded his voice with admiration. "You did well. You turned the tide. Never underestimate the value of a good miracle. You are the Pontifax, beloved of the Flame God and his people." His stare moved between the two men, his voice dropping to a hush. "But we cannot afford to argue among ourselves...not in front of the people, not in front of the priesthood."

The Pontifax took a steadying breath, calm returning to his face. "You're right. The act never ends, we are always on stage." His hands clutched at the ruby amulet, a mask of calm benevolence settling over his face. "But these rebels, whoever they are, need to be stopped."

The Keeper nodded. "We'll change the procedure and imprison the heretics in the dungeons instead of the stocks. They can wait under lock and key until the start of the ceremony." His voice was gruff. "After today, there'll be no shortage of sinners for the Flames. You'll have your sacrifices."

Steffan moved to the sideboard and poured three glasses of brandy. "The Keeper is right. There must always be sinners available for sacrifice." He served each man a glass of dark amber liquor. "But we cannot deviate from the routine. The heretics must spend their time in the stocks, contemplating their sins before the Test of Faith."

"Are you mad!" The Keeper's face blustered red. "The stocks were a stupid idea, like dangling fresh meat in front of a starving dog." He shook his head. "The stocks make it easy for the rebels to free the sinner."

"Then we'll make it harder." Steffan sipped the brandy. "We'll follow the Keeper's plan and hold spare sinners in the dungeons but we'll also continue to use the stocks."

The Pontifax reclined in a chair and studied his counselor with a narrowed gaze. "Why?"

Steffan raised his glass in salute. "The Pontifax is always god-inspired and therefore never wrong. We will not admit a mistake by changing our tactics." He re-filled each of the men's glasses. "The sinners will spend their time in the stocks, sending a warning to the populace...while serving as bait for the rebels."

The Keeper flashed a predator's smile. "Bait, I like that."

Steffan nodded. "The rebels have tipped their hand, displayed their tactics. We'll give them a chance to do it again...only this time, soldiers will be waiting."

The Pontifax said, "A worthy plan, but who are these rebels? And why now?"

Steffan leaned against the wall, his arms crossed. "You've seduced a kingdom with a divine miracle and shackled the people with religion, achieving the most subtle form of conquest. But in every religion, there will always be disbelievers who become rebels." He infused his voice with confidence. "We'll tease the rebels out in the open and give them a taste of divine justice."

The Pontifax's eyes glowed with interest. "But how?"

"The confessors are the key, thousands of eyes and ears searching for sins against the Flame God." He made his voice thoughtful, "Next time you preach from the temple pulpit, you must make confessing a virtue. All sins great and small must be confessed to the priests of the Flame...for only the virtuous will avoid the Test of Faith."

The Pontifax fondled his amulet, a pleased smile on his face. "I can do that."

Steffan turned to the Keeper. "How many confessors have you recruited?"

"Almost two dozen."

"A good start but we'll need more." Steffan made his voice warm and inclusive, a brotherhood of conspirators hatching a grand plot. "A holy acolyte should be assigned to each confessor. The acolyte will serve as a scribe, documenting the details of each confession. We'll tell the people that the scrolls will be burnt in a holy bonfire, a symbolic cleansing of sins, an offering to the Flame God, but in reality, we'll keep the scrolls and sift through the details to find sinners worthy of the Flames. The people themselves will hand over the rebels, serving them up as an offering to the god."

The Keeper grinned. "I like it."

The Pontifax studied Steffan with a shrewd look on his face. "But won't the people be afraid to confess?"

"We'll make it clear from the temple pulpit that they're not confessing their own sins...they're confessing sins they see around them."

"But shouldn't the confessions be anonymous?"

Steffan shook his head and smiled. "That's the beauty of it. Those who confess are proving their devotion to the Flame God by purging Coronth of sin. As their reward, the devout will avoid the Test of Faith. So those who confess will *want* the priests to know their names. They'll clamor to be counted among the faithful, the chosen of the Flame God."

The Pontifax fondled his ruby amulet, a satisfied smile on his face. "Very clever, Lord Raven. We let the people hunt for the rebels, securing our grip on Coronth."

Steffan bowed. "Just so, Enlightened One."

"Tell us, Lord Raven, is there anything else we should do to create this new sect of the priesthood?"

Steffan made his voice thoughtful. "They'll need distinctive vestments to mark them as confessors, the acolyte-scribes as well. And we should have a ceremony in the temple to consecrate the priests in their new roles." He gestured toward the Keeper. "And the Keeper of the Flame should be installed as the leader of the confessors. We'll devise a grand ceremony to mark the importance of his new office."

The Keeper's voice rumbled with pleasure. "A grand ceremony, I like that."

Steffan acted the servant, filling each man's glass. "The confessors will change the very nature of Coronth, each citizen confessing the sins of his neighbors, ensuring that only the faithful survive."

The Pontifax smiled. "The rebels will have nowhere to hide."

"Just so, Enlightened One."

The Pontifax raised his glass. "To the confessors! To the defeat of the rebels and the triumph of the faithful!"

The men chinked their glasses.

Steffan stifled a smile. The two men would play their role but he doubted either understood the impact of their decisions. The confessors would help catch the rebels, a thorn that needed to be eliminated, but more importantly, they would change Coronth forever, sowing mistrust and hatred among the people. The faithful would start by betraying their enemies and their rivals, then their neighbors...then members of their own family. The steep slope of betrayal would create a society of fear...and fear was fertile soil for the will of the Dark Lord. Create enough fear and people would commit any atrocity. Steffan raised his glass in silent salute, may the Dark Lord's pleasure reign...over all the lands of Erdhe.

24

Liandra

The queen prepared for battle, donning the trappings of war. Her armor and weapons were vastly different from other monarchs. Instead of chainmail, she chose a gown made of cloth of gold to bedazzle the eye. The bodice was close-fitting, the dagged sleeves nearly reaching the floor, every aspect designed to accentuate her hourglass figure. Glowing in the candlelight, the golden gown created a vision of royalty that exceeded most men's imaginations. Her raven-black hair was teased to a lustrous shine, her face painted to remove the years and draw attention to her emerald-green eyes. And on her brow, the royal crown to impart authority, the shining symbol of her sovereign power. *Beauty to beguile,* it should have been the motto beneath her coat-of-arms. Liandra scrutinized the mirror, needing all of her weapons to win the fight for her throne. Victory or death, there was no other choice for a sovereign monarch, especially a queen.

"Do we look dead to you?"

Nervous laughter tittered from her women.

The queen turned before the mirror. "We shall be a vengeful ghost."

An urgent knock sounded on the outer door, sending shockwaves through her women.

Princess Jemma answered the door, taking a message from the soldier.

The queen stood statue-still as her women made the final adjustments. "We need your best work. We must be our most regal, a vision of sovereign splendor, a monarch anointed by the Lords of Light...a queen worth fighting for."

Princess Jemma closed the door and approached. The petite young royal wore a close-fitting gown of deep blue, a quiver of arrows belted at her waist. Her face blanched pale but her voice held steady. "Your majesty, the fighting has reached the sixth floor."

A glass vial shattered against the stone floor, flooding the chamber with the scent of roses. Lady Martha gasped, "Only one floor below!"

The queen kept her voice iron-calm. "Any word from our other forces?"

The princess shook her head. "None, your majesty."

Lady Amy knelt to clean the broken glass but the rose scent prevailed, overbearing and sweet.

Liandra glanced at the casement window. Dawn was still hours away. "Time for us to play our part. We dare not tarry any longer." Liandra stood sword-straight, her face composed. Her women fluttered about, arranging the heavy folds of the golden gown, perfecting the royal image. Lady Sarah knelt and clutched the queen's hand, kissing the emerald ring of office, tears on her face.

The queen spared a moment for her ladies. "You have all served us well. Wait for us above, in the secret chamber. We would see you kept safe." She dismissed them with a small smile and then set her mind on the task ahead.

The gown was stiff and heavy but the queen glided forward, maintaining a royal posture designed to bear the heavy crown. Princess Jemma opened the door and the queen stepped into the outer hallway.

A gasp rose from the handful of soldiers guarding the door. The men dropped as one to their knees.

The queen studied their upturned faces, satisfied that her beauty still held sway. "You may rise."

Captain Durnheart approached, his voice a low whisper. "Your majesty, we don't have the numbers to hold the rebels. You must flee the tower while there is still time!"

She kept her voice calm. "What news of our forces?" Against the better judgment of her senior military men, the queen had split her loyal soldiers, sending the greater number into the secret passageways to attack from the rear, counting on the element of surprise to make up for the disparity in numbers.

The captain paled. "Still no word from the lower floors."

"Then we will continue to hope." The captain looked to argue the point but the queen raised an eyebrow forestalling him. She turned to one of the soldiers. "There is a footstool in our solar. We bid you to bring it." The soldier looked confused but leaped to obey. The queen turned back to the captain. "You may escort us to the fighting."

"But majesty, you must flee!"

She gave him a stern look. "If a monarch flees, why should soldiers stand and fight?" She softened her voice. "In order to rule, we must lead. We will do what we can to buy time." The queen's voice brooked no argument.

Captain Durnheart swallowed hard, a resigned look on his face. "Majesty, if this is your will, then allow us to escort you to the battle."

The queen gave him a gracious smile. "The honor is yours."

The captain barked an order and the soldiers unsheathed their swords, forming a protective ring around the queen.

"Majesty, I wish to join you!" Princess Jemma held her bow in her hands.

The queen admired the young woman's courage. "Walk with us. We will show them the courage of royal women." The soldiers reformed around the princess and the queen. Liandra set the pace, balancing the heavy crown upon her brow. She walked to war with an escort of five soldiers and an archer princess, a thin hope but Liandra knew guile and beauty might win where swords failed. The rebels whispered rumors that the queen was dead, killed in the uprising. The blatant lie might be the rebels' undoing.

At the end of the hallway, she heard the faint clash of swords. The sounds of war echoed in marble halls that had only known the flattery of courtiers, the queen silently cursed the rebels.

At the staircase, the battle sounds intensified. Captain Durnheart looked her way. "Majesty, are you certain?"

She gave him a terse nod. The captain led the way down, his sword held at the ready. Wounded soldiers lined the lower half of the stairs, crimson stains marring their emerald tabards, pools of blood staining the marble floor. Many were grievously wounded, some missing limbs. Most stared with vacant eyes while others moaned in agony, the awful price of war. One of the wounded glanced her way. "The queen comes! The queen *lives!*"

The cry was echoed by other wounded, a herald that ran ahead of the queen. Faces turned her way, desperate for a glimmer of hope. Liandra gave them a radiant smile, her voice full of confidence. "You've fought with honor. You deserve better than this. Make your way up the stairs to our royal solar. Our ladies-in-waiting will do their best to bind your wounds and ease your pain." The gratitude in the soldiers' eyes clutched at the queen's heart. She wished there was a way to protect them all, to end the bloodshed.

The sounds of fighting intensified, proof the battle was near.

The queen took a deep breath, hardening her resolve.

The staircase opened onto a long hallway. Chaos claimed the far end, soldiers crammed into the narrow hall, fighting with swords and spears. A din of screams and a clash of swords, the emerald line retreated as she watched. The fighting was fierce. More wounded fell, trampled beneath the line of combat.

"This must stop."

A soldier retreated from the line of battle, running to meet the queen. Major Telcore bore a sword cut across his forehead and was missing an ear but otherwise he seemed whole. "Majesty! I gave orders for you to leave the tower. We will not hold much longer."

"Major, you are a brave man but one does not order a queen."

"Majesty, it is not safe!"

"We do what we must."

A wave of desperation passed across the major's face.

The queen raised a hand, forestalling his argument. "When swords fail, we must try other ways."

The major's face darkened. "Surely you won't surrender?"

"We shall try a queen's gambit, a feint within a feint."

The old soldier narrowed his stare. "What would you have of me?"

"Stand with your men at the front line and watch the enemy. This gambit could yield a victory...or further treachery, be prepared for both."

He raised a bloody sword in salute. "As you command."

The queen turned to the soldier carrying the footstool. "We must move closer to the lines of battle. We need to be seen by both sides." Armored in regal calm, she moved toward the fighting, drawing close enough to smell the battle, a terrible mix of sweat and blood and grim determination.

Soldiers near the rear of the frontline flicked quick glances backward, amazement on their faces. Cries of "The queen!" mixed with the sounds of battle.

She gestured to the marble floor. "This will do." She needed help stepping up onto the small platform. Captain Durnheart provided a steadying hand. She found her balance on the small stage and released his arm. Sword-straight, she stood armored in a shimmering gown of gold, a royal sun rising before the dawn. Staring above the heads of her loyal soldiers, she sought the attention of her enemies, looking for familiar faces among the traitors...but she found none. Three officers directed the rebel forces but none were lords. The leaders of the rebellion were absent, cowards hiding behind the bloodshed of others. Their absence was her opportunity. The queen pitched her voice to carry. "*Soldiers of Lanverness! This bloodshed must end!*"

The clash of swords continued, claiming a bloody harvest.

"*Soldiers of Lanverness, we would speak to you!*"

The ferocity of the swords lessened. A hesitation hung in the air. A few soldiers on the far side of the battle lines looked up and stared at her, surprise on their faces. A low murmur spread through the ranks.

The queen seized the moment. *"Soldiers of Lanverness put up your swords and let us speak!"*

"The queen lives!" The words echoed on both sides of the battle.

The swords came to a stop. Soldiers on each side drew back, creating a narrow strip of neutral ground. Suspicious faces stared up at her, but she'd won her chance to speak.

She stood tall, giving them a chance to see what they opposed, to see the glory of their rightful queen. "It is a grim day when brothers fight brothers. You are all brave men...but your bravery is wasted." She studied their faces, noting their surprise at her praise. "Rumors whisper that the queen is dead...but *we are here!*" A ragged cheer rose from her loyal troops. She waved them to silence, focusing on the rebels. "We dare our own life to save your lives, the lives of our soldiers. We would stop this bloodshed. Even now, we would pardon every one of you, every soldier who puts down his sword and swears fealty to our crown. We will not spare the lords who lied but we will spare the soldiers who were misled."

One of the rebels yelled, "Don't listen to the witch!" but other voices shouted him down. A rebel officer turned and ran back down the far hallway, her time was limited.

The queen raised her voice, using all of her skills of persuasion. "Look behind you! Where are your leaders? Where are your lords? They cower while you fight. They grasp for glory by risking your blood. They *lied* to you about our death. *What else have they lied about?"* A murmur rose among the rebels, confusion and anger on their faces. The seed of doubt had taken root.

"Save your lives and the lives of your fellow soldiers. Put down your swords and swear fealty. Let peace return to Lanverness."

A hush settled over the hallway. A grizzled sergeant shouted a challenge, his voice skeptical. "You'd pardon us all, every one?"

She kept the hope from her face. "Every soldier who lays down his sword and swears fealty." Doubt shadowed their faces. She made her voice solemn. "You have our royal word."

Arguments broke out among the rebels.

The queen rushed to persuade, but this time she made her voice a soft, feminine hush. "We have heard what they say about us."

The orator's trick worked. Her soft words teased the soldiers, stilling their argument. The rebels turned and stared at her, their faces a mixture of curiosity and wariness. Knowing the tide could turn either way, she kept her voice teasingly feminine. "They say a woman cannot rule." She shuffled on the stool, the ripple of movement causing her gown to shimmer in the light, a calculated vision of splendor. "We are only a woman yet we keep the taxes low and find ways to grow the wealth of Lanverness, a wealth that benefits all our people. Is any other kingdom more prosperous than Lanverness?"

Her loyal men shouted, "*No!*"

Their answer echoed down the marble halls.

"We are only a woman, but a queen is also a mother. We know the value of each life. We guard the peace like a lioness because we refuse to needlessly risk the lives of our soldiers...*your* lives. We would keep the sons of Lanverness safe."

Her loyal men drummed their swords against their shields, a soldier's salute.

She made her voice a woman's plea. "*Sheathe your swords and swear to keep the peace!*"

She'd won them over; she saw it in their eyes.

The rebel sergeant knelt. The others cleared a space around him. He extended his sword toward the queen, hilt first, remorse on his face. "Pardon me for fighting against my true queen. Accept my sword in fealty."

A low murmur raced through the rebels.

The queen extended an open hand toward the sergeant. "We do accept."

"*No!*" Footsteps raced from the far end of the hall. A minor lordling led a fresh squad of rebels. Their battle cry echoed through the hallway, "*Kill the witch! Fight for the king!*"

The battle line roiled in confusion.

Major Telcore rushed to the queen's side. "You must be away!"

She stood her ground, needing to see the outcome.

The wave of rebel soldiers slammed into the battle line, pushing their way to the front, their faces contorted in hate. They struck the loyalists with a ferocious clash of steel. The fighting resumed but all was not lost. Some of the rebels kept their word and switched sides, fighting for the queen. From her perch on the stool, she saw the drill sergeant cut down the rebel lordling. Other rebels swarmed the sergeant, seeking revenge; she hoped the man survived.

The major hissed, "*You must leave!*"

A bowstring thrummed. Princess Jemma loosed an arrow into the rebels.

The queen stepped down from the stool. "Yes, it is time for us to leave." She met the major's stare. "We will retreat to the hidden floor.

Hold for as long as you can and then join us there. We will keep the door open, waiting for you and your men."

Anger rode in the major's steel-gray eyes. "Majesty, you should flee the tower. If the queen falls then all is lost."

A second arrow thrummed into the rebels.

The queen's voice was full of steel. "We will not flee." She turned before he could argue and glided down the hallway. Captain Durnheart hovered at one side, Princess Jemma at the other.

She reached the stairway and found it empty of wounded soldiers but the bloodstains remained. Liandra stared at the stains, wondering if the marble would ever come clean, forever stained with treachery and heroism, a dark day for Lanverness. She would show clemency to the soldiers but never the traitorous lords.

The walk back seemed to take forever, the sounds of battle raging below. Reaching her solar, she found the chaos of a makeshift healery. Her women tore bed linens and undergarments into strips creating bandages for the wounded. Lady Sarah made the rounds, offering wine to the soldiers, bloodstains on her silk gown. The soldiers were stoic, eyes glazed with pain, lying silent on thick wool rugs.

The queen held her head high and glided into the small chamber as if she entered the throne room, seeking to give her people courage by her own bearing. More than one soldier stared in awe.

She made her voice warm and full of confidence. "You have all served well, but we must retreat to the floor above. We have prepared a secret redoubt, a stronghold from the rebels. Come with us to the floor above." She unlocked the secret door and gave orders for the strong to help the weak.

They settled the wounded in the central chamber of the eighth floor, taking bandages and flasks of wine with them. When the last of the soldiers was moved, the queen commanded Lady Sarah and Captain Durnheart to return with her to the solar.

The sounds of battle seemed closer but the queen held firm to her intent. She removed her crown and placed it in an ironbound chest along with the scepter and the other royal regalia, retaining only her two rings of office. "Captain Durnheart, we charge you with protecting the crown jewels. Take this chest to the eighth floor. If the stronghold should fall, we order you to get the jewels out of the tower and into the hands of Crown Prince Stewart." Her voice hardened. "The crown jewels must not fall to the rebels."

The captain saluted. "As my queen commands." He gathered up the chest and retreated to the secret floor.

"Lady Sarah," the queen turned to her most trusted lady-in-waiting, "gather up the rest of our jewels. We will not leave them as plunder for the rebels."

Pale-faced, the lady curtseyed and went to work, gathering the queen's jewels into an embroidered pillowcase.

The queen turned to her desk. Unlocking the top drawer, she removed the scrolls from the Kiralynn monks and placed them on the cold grate of the fireplace. She used a candle to set the monks' words ablaze. Opening her scroll cabinet, she removed more messages from other monarchs and ledger scrolls detailing the financial holdings of the Rose Crown. The ledgers would go with her into the secret chamber, but the rest she heaped on the fire, throwing a goblet of wine onto the scrolls just to be sure. The stack of parchments crackled with flames, her secrets becoming smoke.

Lady Sarah peered into the outer hallway. Clutching the bulging pillowcase, she hissed a warning. *"The fighting has reached the seventh floor!"*

Liandra let her gaze roam her solar. There was more she would do, but time had almost caught her. "We have done all we can." She nodded toward Lady Sarah. "Time to retreat to the stronghold of our ancestors."

Captain Durnheart and another soldier waited with swords drawn inside the secret door. She gave the men their orders. "Hold the door open for as long as possible. Give every loyal soldier a chance to escape but then make sure the door is closed and the locking mechanism triggered. This door is our last defense."

The captain saluted, his face grim.

The queen climbed the stairs to the main chamber. The wounded lay along the walls, her women working among them.

Soldiers began to stream into the chamber, all of them bearing wounds. The clash of swords echoed up the stairs, the fighting had reached her solar.

The queen tensed, listening.

More soldiers stumbled up the stairs, most of them wounded. Major Telcore was not among them.

A shout rang out and then an eerie quiet descended.

Captain Durnheart appeared at the top of the stairs. He nodded toward the queen and then went to stand by the ironbound chest containing the crown jewels. His ghost-pale face told her that soldiers had stayed behind on the other side of the hidden door...a brave few who would never get the reward they deserved. Liandra vowed to learn their names and find a way to repay their families.

The queen stood in the middle of the chamber, dressed in cloth of gold, peerless elegance hiding among the cobwebs. Her kingdom was reduced to a few score soldiers and a hidden chamber. The Spider Queen had spun her webs and laid her traps...now all she could do was wait.

25

Katherine

Kath clung to her stallion, urging the horse to speed. The shouts of the sellswords receded with each stride. Kath's world blurred. She blamed it on the wind, on the chestnut mane whipping against her face, on anything but the tears crowding her eyes. Crouching low in the saddle, she let the horse choose the path, asking only for speed, desperate to get away. The stallion answered her need, leaping to a blistering gallop. They passed the others, racing down the north side of the ridge.

Kath felt torn. For one brief moment, she'd breached Duncan's walls, but then he'd pushed her away, forcing her to leave because of duty. *Duty*, the word curdled like a curse in her mind. She knew Duncan was right, the crystal dagger couldn't be lost on some nameless ridge in the backlands of Tubor...but it hurt to leave. *It hurt*. Kath had never imagined that duty would require her to run, to stand and fight, yes, but never to run. And worse yet, to leave *him*. Thirty against one, the stubborn, noble, fool-of-a-man bought them time to escape, a chance to fight another day...but the price was too dear. A sob escaped her; duty had never seemed so hard. Kath crouched in the saddle, burying her emotions beneath speed.

She rode in a blind fury, letting the stallion have its head. Perhaps she'd made a fool of herself on the ridge, but it wouldn't matter if Duncan didn't survive. Kath drummed her heels into the horse. The stallion lengthened his stride. Kath plunged into the rhythm of speed, ignoring everything but the need to ride, the need to fly. The countryside became a blur.

Leagues later, the acid tang of smoke slapped her face. Kath pulled on the reins and wiped her eyes dry, not believing the sight.

She'd ridden straight into hell.

A scorched land stretched in every direction, still smoldering from a wildfire. Charred trees towered overhead, reduced to dark skeletons, accusing fingers pointing toward an indifferent heaven. Smoke smoldered from fallen logs, adding a grim pall to the devastation. Kath rode through a forest of ash. A legion of crows worried the blackened ground, searching for roasted carrion. Squawking, they swarmed the burnt carcass of a deer. Kath looked away, making the hand sign against evil. The crows were the only sign of life in the charred nightmare.

Muffled hoof beats followed behind.

Kath drew her sword and waited, almost hoping the sellswords followed.

Sir Tyrone galloped through the pall, his face grim, his horse lathered. The others rode behind, strung out in a tattered line.

Kath looked for Duncan but the archer wasn't among them. Her heart tightened into a fist.

Sir Tyrone rode straight toward her, pulling on the reins of his charger as he drew even. His dark eyes flashed like daggers, his voice gruff with anger. "What were you thinking to race ahead like that? Duncan's sacrifice would be wasted if you fell into a trap!"

His words cut like a knife.

Sir Tyrone shook his head, his voice a low growl. "You want to be a knight. Knights don't run."

Shame flooded through her.

"I don't know what demon gripped you back on the ridge, but we must all keep our wits if we're to have a chance against the Mordant."

Kath felt her face pale with shame. In her haste to get away she'd let the others down. She tightened her grip on her sword, furious at her own weakness. "I'm sorry."

"Do you even know where you've led us?"

Not trusting her voice, Kath shook her head. Another failing.

The others crowded around. Their horses quivered with strain, their heads hung low, their hides drenched in sweat. Kath realized her own stallion was just as spent as the others; she shouldn't have ridden him so hard.

Blaine glared. "Where the hell are we?"

Sir Tyrone answered. "I got a view from the ridge top. Burnt farmland stretches to the west, but it seemed only the outer fringe of forest is destroyed."

"Well, we can't stay here. If the sellswords follow we'll be too exposed."

Kath gripped her sword hilt. "Duncan will hold them."

Sir Tyrone said, "Perhaps. But Blaine is right, we need to keep moving."

Blaine nodded. "Which way?"

"Duncan said to head into the depths of the forest, so we'll ride east, looking for living trees."

Kath struggled to keep her voice even. "Shouldn't we wait for Duncan?"

Sir Tyrone gave her a piercing stare. "If the archer lives, he'll find us. That man can track like a wolf." He dismounted. "We'll need to walk the horses or we'll lose them. We head east, to the cover of the forest." The black knight turned his gaze towards Zith and Danya. "Can you two keep up?"

Zith nodded, his face pale but determined. "I'll walk to the nine hells and back if needs be."

But Danya swayed in the saddle, her eyes glazed.

Blaine forced his horse next to hers. "Are you well?"

Danya stared at the knight, her eyes wide and wild. *"I can't feel him!"*

Sir Tyrone said, "Feel who?"

"Bryx!" A sob escaped her lips. "I called the wolf to help, but now I can't feel him! There's only emptiness, only darkness..." Danya swooned in the saddle.

Blaine caught the wolf-girl, pulling her across to his horse. He settled her in his lap, his arms around her, her head nestled under his chin. Blaine gave the black knight a grim stare. "I'll take care of Danya, but if the wolf's lost, we need to gain more distance."

No one mentioned the archer.

Kath and Zith dismounted, leading their sweat-streaked horses. The black knight took the lead. Blaine rode behind him with Danya cradled against his chest. Zith took the reins for the lone packhorse. Kath walked last, her hand on her sword hilt. Determined to make-up for her lapse of judgment, she strained to listen for sounds of pursuit but heard nothing.

The charred forest was deathly still. Blackened trees towered around them, mute sentinels to the devastation. Embers glowed among the smoldering trunks, gleaming like red-eyed demons. Death surrounded them, a scorched landscape. A flock of crows took wing. Flapping feathers and harsh caws filled the gray spaces between the dead trees. Kath shuddered, wondering if the ruined forest truly was a glimpse of hell.

Soot and ash dampened the sounds of their passage. Everything was black and burnt and dead...and then suddenly green. Almost like magic, they crossed a line, passing from death's dominion into an explosion of living green. Vibrant with colors and sounds, the forest hummed with winged insects and songbirds. Trees towered overhead, branches thick with leaves, blocking out the sky. Underbrush and vines pressed close, enveloping them in a swath of wilderness. The companions quickened their pace, heartened by the vibrant forest, but their passage soon slowed to a crawl, impeded by the dense tangle.

Sir Tyrone unsheathed his great sword and began hacking at the underbrush. Kath joined him, venting her anger on the dense green.

The forest resisted. Armored in wicked thorns, the tangled green snagged at exposed skin and soft cloth, drawing blood. Splinters and spikes jabbed at hands and eyes. Only chainmail proved impervious to the green bite. Kath slashed at the dense tangle, hacking her way forward. She sliced a vine and it recoiled like a whip, lashing nasty thorns till it finally fell still. Kath whispered, "What is this place?"

A squeal came from behind.

The packhorse reared, its eyes white with fright. Zith pulled on the reins, barely avoiding a lashing hoof.

Kath saw the problem. "There's a vine wrapped around its rear leg!" She leaped to sever the vine. Her sword sliced clean through. One half whipped backwards, flailing thorns, but the other half remained entwined around the horse.

The packhorse reared, blood staining its leg, its eyes mad with fright.

"The vines are stranglers! How do I get it off?"

Sir Tyrone tossed her an armored gauntlet. "Try this!" He grabbed the reins from the monk, trying to still the plunging horse.

Kath pulled on the gauntlet. Dodging hooves, she gained the horse's side and grabbed the vine. Wicked thorns pierced the horse's hide. Embedded deep, they drew blood. She yanked at the vine, but blood and flesh came with it.

The horse went wild.

Stripping the reins from the black knight's hands, the horse charged headfirst into the tangled green. It did not get far. Squealing in pain, it sagged forward and lay still.

Kath looked at Sir Tyrone. The black knight shrugged. Together they hacked at the green, trying to reach the horse. They found the horse impaled on a spiked branch, speared through the heart. The branch belonged to a dark gray tree, its trunk and branches bristling with five inch long dagger-like spikes. "What is this place?"

"Deadly."

Blaine said, "Look behind us."

The way back was sealed with green. The forest had surrounded them.

Blaine said, "The forest is alive!"

Kath said, "It's more than that." Reaching beneath her leather jerkin, she grasped her stone gargoyle. Holding the focus tight, she closed her eyes and quested with her inner senses. Using lessons learned in the monastery, she probed outward, searching for magic. What she found nearly dropped her to her knees. A vast sea of green swamped her tendril of thought, surrounding her with a pulsing power. The forest thrummed with wild magic, something old and potent, something fierce yet sentient...something that stared back at her with golden cat-slit eyes. Kath's eyes shot open. She staggered backwards, releasing her gargoyle, breaking the contact. Shivering, she stared at the forest. Leaves and bark hid a potent power. Staring up at the impossibly tall trees, she put a name to the forest. *"The Deep Green."*

Sir Tyrone hissed, "You know this place?"

"I've heard of it." Knowledge of the name brought with it the feeling of hostile eyes. The words of the cat-eyed archer came back to her. *"Sheathe your sword!"* Kath sheathed her own blade but the black knight just stared at her in puzzlement. "Sheathe your weapon *now!*"

The black knight obeyed.

Kath raised her hands and pitched her voice to carry. "We come in peace! We seek a ranger to guide us. We wish you and the forest no harm."

She felt the forest watching, judging.

Kath and her companions waited, peering into the trees, hands well away from weapons. The dense brush seemed to tighten around them, a threatening strangle of green. Kath pivoted, feeling stares from every direction. Her shoulder blades itched with warning. She longed to reach for a weapon but she kept her hands raised and her face calm.

Green-clad archers melted out of the forest.

And all of them had golden cat-slit eyes.

Eyes of the forest, Kath counted twenty archers staring from behind nocked arrows. The hatred in their gaze was palpable.

Kath searched their faces looking for a leader, surprised to find several women among them. She raised her hands higher in a gesture of peace. "We come in peace, invited to visit the Deep Green by the archer, Jorah Silvenwood."

A bearded man stepped forward and snarled, "White-eyes aren't welcome here."

Kath ignored the anger in his voice. "I've a token given to me by Jorah. He said the token would grant me safe passage into the forest."

"Tokens are easily stolen from the hands of the dead."

"Kill them now, Jenks, and be done with it."

Another voice growled, "Aye, blood for blood!"

Bowstrings tightened.

Seeing death in the arrows, Kath inched her hands toward her axe handles. The odds were bad, but she'd rather die fighting. Beside her, the black knight tensed for battle.

"*Stop!*" The command rang through the forest, causing warriors on both sides to pause. All eyes turned toward the blue-robed monk. Zith held his right hand out, palm forward, revealing the blue tattoo of the Seeing Eye. "A master of the Kiralynn Order seeks an audience with the Treespeaker."

Murmurs that were equal parts anger and amazement rippled through the archers.

The bearded leader stared at the monk, easing back on his bowstring. "You've come at an evil time, white-eyes, but by invoking the name of the Treespeaker you've delayed your fate. Submit to being bound and we'll provide safe passage through the forest."

The monk nodded, "We submit."

Sir Tyrone glanced her way and nodded. Kath understood. It was better to live and fight another day.

One of the archers hissed, "Jenks, you can't trust the white-eyes!"

The bearded man snapped, "I don't trust them. Now put up your bow and see that their hands are bound tight."

The leader's authority held. A handful of leather-clad archers stepped forward with lengths of rope.

Blaine dismounted, holding Danya in his arms.

The leader stared at Blaine, "Can the woman walk?"

"No."

The leader nodded, "Carry her then." To one of his men he added, "Leave his hands untied but tether a noose around his neck."

Blaine snarled but Sir Tyrone intervened. "We have no choice." The blond knight submitted to the noose, anger broiling in his stare.

Kath lowered her hands, holding them out to be bound.

A young archer looped a coarse rope around her wrists, jerking the cord tight enough to draw blood.

Kath hissed at the harsh treatment.

The archer sneered, "It's much less than you deserve, white-eye."

She wondered at the hatred in his voice.

Their weapons were taken, swords, axes, and daggers. Kath flinched when they took the crystal dagger, her gaze following it to the belt of one of the archers. She felt naked without it, but at least her captors had ignored the gargoyle tucked beneath her jerkin and the amber pyramid hidden in a deep pocket.

Blaine balked when they reached for his blue steel sword. "*No!*"

Bowstrings tightened, arrows fixed on his heart. Blaine submitted with a low growl. "I'll have that back!"

A cat-eyed archer flourished the blue sword.

The bearded leader yelled, "Let's go."

Kath was jerked forward, almost falling. Bound and tethered, the companions followed the cat-eyed people into the depths of the forest. The green tangle parted to reveal a narrow pathway threading through the dense brush. They walked single file beneath stands of redwood, cedar, and spruce. Kath scuffed her feet to mark the trail, hoping Duncan followed. She kept glancing backward, hoping for a glimpse of him.

Towering trees hid the sun, cloaking the forest in dappled shadows. Their captors forbade talking. They marched in silence, but now and then one of them imitated the call of a woodlands bird. Kath suspected the calls were signals to other watchers. She wondered at their numbers.

They crossed other footpaths, proving the forest was more tamed than it first appeared. Kath tried to memorize the twists and turns but after a while the trees all looked alike. Peering into the undergrowth, she caught fleeting glimpses of fallen columns and ruined walls choked by vines, deepening the mystery of the forest. She paused to stare at a ruined bit of statue that lay near the path, a woman's face carved on a keystone, hauntingly beautiful. Kath wondered at the ruins, at the lost beauty carved in stone. The butt of a bow jabbed her in the back. "Keep moving!" Kath staggered forward, struggling to keep her balance.

Their captors kept at a ground-eating pace, leading them deeper into the forest. Without a view of the sun, it was hard to judge how long they walked. Kath's hands were numb and useless by the time they emerged from the underbrush into a clearing of sorts. The dense brush and saplings were stripped clean, cleared away to yield a smooth needle-strewn floor, but the towering grandfather trees remained, standing like majestic columns in the grand hall of a forgotten king.

Tendrils of smoke curled up from the heart of the clearing. A village of ornate wooden cabins clustered around the base of the trees. From the number of cabins, Kath judged the village to hold a hundred or so.

The escort of archers whooped a cheer. Women straightened from cook fires and men stopped their chores to stare, all of them with the strange yellow eyes of a cat.

Welcoming smiles changed to hatred at the sight of the captives. Women gathered up their children, herding them into cabins, while men reached for weapons, watching with wary eyes. Hatred and mistrust swirled through the village. Kath hoped they would not regret the decision to yield their weapons.

The archers led the companions to the center of the village, to a white-haired man seated by a small fire. He whittled a flute from a length of wood, his hands making long sure strokes with a carving knife.

The troop leader acknowledged the white-haired man with a deep bow. "Greetings of Leaf and Bark, Cenric."

The white-haired man looked up from his craftwork, studying the strangers with a golden stare. A deep battle scar ruined the right side of his face, belying the peaceful work of his hands. He pointed his carving knife at the captives, his voice deep with the power of command. "How dare you bring white-eyes to our village?"

The leader of the archers moved to speak, but the white-haired man forestalled him with a raised hand. Keeping his seat by the fire, the leader studied the captives while the villagers gathered around. An old woman emerged from a cabin carrying a long cape of emerald green feathers. Purple eyes shimmered and winked the length of the feathered cloak, a garment fit for a king. The woman draped the magnificent cape across the man's shoulders. With a show of ceremony, she took a seat next to him by the fire. A hush fell over the villagers. Kath felt as if she stood on trial before a judge, but she didn't know the crime.

The white-haired man spoke with the formality of command, "The leader of Clan Hemlock sits before the hearth fires cloaked in the power of the Green. We are ready to hear your report."

The archer gave a half bow. "We were patrolling the green edge near the burned lands of the Cedars when we found these white-eyes hacking their way into the forest."

"And you did not leave them to the Green Death?"

"We watched from the cloak of the forest, but the blond-haired woman acknowledged the Deep Green, claiming to come in peace."

The leader's golden stare found Kath's face. She met his strange gaze without flinching.

"Who are you and why do you come to the Deep Green?"

Kath took a half step forward. "I am Princess Katherine of Castlegard. I was invited to the Deep Green by the archer, Jorah Silvenwood. He gave me a leather token of safe passage."

Murmurs of shock and outrage rippled through the villagers. Several made the hand sign against evil.

The leader stirred beneath his feathered cape. "You claim the welcome of the dead."

Shock hit her like a hammer blow. "Jorah is *dead?*"

"As are many of our people. Taken by the fires set by the cursed white-eyes."

Their hatred and hostility made sudden sense. "That fire was *set?*"

"An attack against the forest, an attack against our people, set in the dead of night."

Kath could hardly imagine the horror of such a fire, towering flames burning everything, nothing left but blackened ashes. "I am sorry for your loss."

Whispers swirled around the fire, some in anger, most in disbelief.

"Why does a white-eyed girl speak the name of one of our dead?"

"Jorah saved my life. I called him friend." Kath raised her stare to the clan leader, willing the truth into her face.

The leader gave her a crooked half-smile, his grin distorted by the ugly scar. "Faces can lie. Especially those bearing white eyes. We shall see if the truth rides the winds." He gestured and two men grabbed Kath's arms from behind. Sir Tyrone yelled, "Leave her!" but Kath stilled him with a glance. The men walked Kath around the fire, forcing her to kneel before the leader. Despite her bound hands, she kept her back straight and defiant.

The clan leader leaned close, his face stopping a hand span from hers.

Kath forced herself to remain still, meeting the scrutiny of his golden gaze.

"Who is Jorah Silvenwood to you?" The leader's voice was a command, his golden stare penetrating.

"He was a friend. I owe him my life."

Murmurs circulated the fire, but Kath kept her gaze on the clan leader.

Flaring his nostrils, the leader closed his eyes and took a deep breath as if testing her scent. He sat swaying under the feathered cloak, his eyes closed, his face thoughtful. His rocking motion caused the cape's feathered eyes to glisten and wink in the firelight, as if a thousand beasts peered from the emerald-green feathers, all of them judging her. Kath shivered, trying to dispel the illusion.

The leader exhaled, his golden eyes opening. "The wind tastes of pride...and stubbornness...and truth."

"*No!*" A young man shouldered his way through the crowd, his face contorted in hate. "The wind is full of ashes! Dead trees and dead clansmen! The white-eyes should pay for their deeds! I claim tauth against the intruders for the death of my family!"

Anger sparked around the campfire.

The old woman, the one who'd brought the feathered cloak, replied, her voice stern with rebuke. "Ronah, we all grieve for the dead, but the winds have been tested and judgment has been passed. You dishonor yourself with this outburst."

"Are we animals who cower or men who fight? If we hadn't been hiding in the depths of the forest, we might have stopped the white-eyes before they lit their cursed fire."

"*Enough!*" The old woman glared.

"No, it will never be enough." The young man spat on the ground and turned his back on the leader, pushing his way through the crowd. A murmur of disapproval followed but none barred his way.

Ignoring the outburst, the clan leader picked up his whittling knife. With a quick slash, he cut Kath's bonds. Pain assaulted her hands as the ropes fell away. Villagers reached out from behind to help her stand.

The clan leader stood with the lithe grace of a warrior despite his age. "The winds are choked with burning and death, but this white-eyes speaks the truth. There will be no tauth claimed against these strangers. Release their bonds."

Kath resumed her place among her companions, trying to work some life back into her pain-pricked hands.

The white-haired leader stared at her. "The question remains, why have you come to the Deep Green?"

Kath stared at the leader, fumbling for an acceptable reason, unsure how to answer. The monk saved her. Holding his open hand up to display the dark blue tattoo, Zith said, "I am Master Zith of the Kiralynn Order. My companions and I seek an audience with the Treespeaker."

Protests rippled around the fire. A woman's voice hissed, "*Blasphemy!*"

The feather-cloaked leader lifted his hands, stilling his people. Peering at the monk, he said, "You speak a name not mentioned outside of the Deep Green."

"I speak a name whispered to me by the Grand Master of my Order."

The leader shook his head. "By Leaf and Bark the five of you pose a strange riddle. You ride out of the burnt lands speaking a name you should not know. A woman leads claiming friendship of the dead, one knight bears a sapphire-blue blade, and another has skin the color of soot. If the wind did not tell me otherwise, I would mark you as dangerous enemies. You are not of the Green yet we grant you hearth-welcome, but no more than that. The Treespeaker will decide your fate."

The monk nodded. "We accept your welcome."

"In the meantime, you will have food and shelter and healing if you need it."

Blaine said, "Return our weapons."

"As a gesture of peace, we will keep your weapons till the Treespeaker decides."

Kath said, "You may hold our weapons of steel in safekeeping, but return the crystal dagger."

"What is so special about this dagger?"

"It is a weapon of the Light, meant for a specific evil. I won't be parted from it."

He stared at her as if peering into her soul.

She met his golden gaze, shocked by the rush of green power rising behind his eyes. It was the same power that thrummed through the forest, something proud and untamed...and sentient. That power stared back at her, the golden eyes widening with recognition...and warning.

An owl hooted in the depths of the forest.

The clan leader broke his stare and nodded.

Kath staggered backwards, released from the power.

The clan leader's voice was rich with undertones. "The forest agrees. The crystal dagger is best left in your care." He glanced at her companions but his gaze returned to Kath. "My name is Cenric, leader of Clan Hemlock. You will be given the courtesies of the hearth until the Treespeaker decides your fate." He gestured to the bearded ranger. "Jenks will show you to the stone house and will see to your needs." Staring at Danya's limp form he added, "Do you need a healer?"

Cradling Danya against his chest, Blaine shook his head, "Just rest and food."

"That you shall have." Cenric's stare roved the crowd. "Sefforth, return the dagger."

An archer pushed through the crowd, anger in his eyes, yet he offered the crystal dagger to Kath.

She snatched it from his hand and sheathed it at her belt, her fist locked on the hilt.

"Jenks?"

The bearded archer appeared at Cenric's side.

"Show our guests to the stone house and provide for their needs. Put a guard on the door for our safety as well as theirs."

The archer inclined his head and turned to the companions. "This way."

The villagers parted to let them pass, their stares a mixture of curiosity and mistrust. More than one made the hand sign of evil.

Jenks led them away from the fire and through the cluster of cabins to the far side of the clearing. On the edge of the underbrush they found a small stone building half covered in vines. Three steps led down to an open doorway. Jenks ushered them into a small, rectangular room of white marble with no windows, only a door, as if the building had once been a tomb. A caved-in hole in the center of the ceiling provided the only light. A scattering of leaves, twigs, and broken stones littered the floor. A musty scent of wild animals lingered in the air. The room was barren of furniture but timeworn carvings covered the four walls, hinting at an ancient glory.

Blaine settled Danya on the floor, spreading his maroon cloak across her. Kath was drawn to the walls. The carvings depicted a royal hunting party, subtle yet beautiful in the dim light. One of the figures wore a crown. She traced her fingers across the stone frieze. "What is this place?"

Jenks shrugged, "Something best forgotten."

Zith said, "The past may be forgotten, but the present is always shaped by what has gone before."

Kath looked at the monk, but his face provided no explanation for his words.

Footsteps clattered down the stone stairs. Cat-eyed men entered the room bearing the companions' saddlebags and bedrolls. Another brought wood and tinder, starting a small fire in the center of the stone floor. Their golden cat eyes glowed strangely bright in the firelight.

Jenks said, "Food and water will be provided. If you need anything, ask the guards at the door."

Blaine said, "Our weapons?"

"If the Treespeaker decides." Pausing, he added, "You picked a poor time to claim a hearth-welcome."

Zith asked the question that nagged at Kath. "Who started the fire?"

"*White-eyed cowards!*" Hatred flashed across Jenk's face. "The deed was done in the small hours of the morning. The dawn sky was clear of lightning, just a hard wind blowing east. There was no reason for a fire, yet a wall of flames roared into the forest, destroying everything in its path. The fire burned so fierce and was so widespread that it must have been started by torches and oil, a coward's weapons." His voice turned bitter. "Raging flames consumed an entire clan village while they slept. Women, children, and homes...all destroyed, reduced to nothing but cinders." The archer's eyes narrowed in hate. "But the Goddess of the Green intervened. The wind changed direction and the flames turned away from the forest, feeding on the farmlands of the white-eyes instead. The Goddess turned the wrath of the fire against those who set it. Evil was repaid in kind. The inferno ravaged the farmlands of the white-eyes, leaving the rest of the forest untouched." Making the hand sign against evil, the archer's voice dropped to an angry hiss. "It was a dark day when those fires were lit, dark and cowardly."

Zith nodded, "Darker than you know, archer. An ancient evil is loose in the lands of Erdhe. It will not respect the borders of your forest."

"Our arrows bite deep, old man. Next time we'll be waiting." The archer turned his back on the companions, striding through the open door, unaware that his words rang hollow in the ancient tomb.

Zith shook his head. "And so it begins."

Kath stared at the monk. "What begins?"

"The Dark Divide."

She gave him a puzzled look.

The monk took a deep breath. "It's what the Mordant does. By setting fire to both the forest and the farmlands he pits two peoples who should be allies against one another. Hatred is a bitter divide."

Kath whispered. "Divide and conquer."

"Just so."

The monk's words sounded like a doom. Kath gripped the crystal dagger. "We'd best make ourselves comfortable." The companions arranged their bedrolls around the fire. Little was said, for the guards listened at the door. They shared a meal of roast venison and pan-baked flat bread provided by the villagers. The venison was juicy but Kath had little appetite. She ate but there was no heart in it, like sitting at a fire that had no warmth. Thoughts of Duncan haunted her.

Blaine coaxed Danya into drinking some water but the young woman refused any food. She sat slumped against the knight, her face pale and her eyes glazed as if staring at something in the distance, something only she could see. Kath wondered if Danya saw the ridge where Duncan stood against the sellswords. Perhaps the girl saw the battle using her link with the wolf. Kath leaned toward her, needing to know. "Danya, what do you see?"

The question hung in the marble tomb like a ghost. Kath swallowed, fearing to hear the answer but needing to know.

The other companions sat statue-still, faces frozen, waiting.

Danya stared over their heads, as if seeing another world. Kath thought she wouldn't answer, or hadn't heard...but then Danya spoke, her voice haunted by grief. "I can't feel him." Her face was full of despair. "Only darkness...all is lost."

A cold hand clutched at Kath's heart. She found it hard to breathe.

Blaine wrapped a blanket around Danya's shoulders but the girl seemed oblivious to his care.

The fire snapped, spitting sparks.

Questions hung in the air but so did weariness. Numb from the trials of the long day, the companions sought their bedrolls.

Kath burrowed into her blanket but sleep was elusive. Troubled by Danya's words, she stared at the ancient hunting scenes. Duncan was an excellent tracker; he should have caught up to them by now. She banished the traitorous thought. If she believed it hard enough, surely the gods would let him live. A single tear slid down her cheek, betraying her fear.

26

Samson

The Flame God's city baked under the summer sun, the cobblestone streets radiating heat. A trickle of sweat ran down Samson's back, but it wasn't due to the heat. The city was full of spying eyes. Every stare seemed suspicious, every glance hostile, a city of watchers, all of them spying for the priesthood. The confessors changed everything. Samson scanned the street, trying to blend in. Everywhere people watched people, an entire city caught in a sticky web of deceit and betrayal. The confessors ensnared both the rich and the poor, the devout and the skeptical, everyone looking for a way to avoid the Flames. If they couldn't find a sin to confess, they invented something. No one was safe.

Samson mingled with the crowd, trying to hide among the citizens heading to market, but he couldn't shake the feeling of being watched. His neck prickled in warning but he did not turn. He'd have to get used to the feeling...but old habits died hard. Every day it grew harder to tell the innocent from the faithful. The confessors gave everyone an equal chance to betray. The price of salvation was the confession of your neighbor's sins. Most of Coronth thought the price was cheap. Neighbor turned on neighbor. Families broke apart, betraying secrets to garner favor with the priests. Betrayal was rampant. The proof came in the night, a knock on the door heralding prison, and then a fiery death. No one ever came back. Samson shuddered, staring at the people around him, knowing they were all conspirators to murder. Balor had become a waking nightmare with no way out but death.

Samson quickened his stride, desperate to find Lucy. He needed a refuge, a haven of sanity, someone to go to when the knitting needles stopped. Lucy filled his dreams like a talisman against the madness of the city. Perhaps today he'd finally find the courage to speak to her.

The market was crowded. A pungent scent of green hung over the stalls, vegetables over-baked in the sun. The price of food was dear. Many came to the market late, hoping to save coppers by purchasing vegetables ruined by the heat. Samson tried to blend in, just another hungry citizen looking for a bargain.

He caught snatches of gossip as he wove his way through the stalls. The street gossip had changed and not for the better. Talk of love or money was replaced with tales of false accusations and injustice. People feared the confessors, but no matter the complaint, Samson heard the same words whispered over and over again, *"If only the Pontifax knew."* They chanted the phrase like a prayer. Blame was placed everywhere, on the priests and the temple, on the Keeper and the confessors, everywhere except the Pontifax. People deluded themselves into trusting the father figure, the benevolent miracle worker. The depth of the delusion scared Samson. It made him feel as if their fight against the Flame was hopeless, as if they fought to douse a raging inferno with only a teacup of water. The sense of futility compounded his fear. All the more reason he needed to find Lucy.

He came to the end of the stalls and rounded the corner. Passing a wagon of cabbages stinking in the sun, he caught a glimpse of her raven black hair. His breath caught in his throat. He followed the blue-black hair like a shimmering beacon, his heartbeat quickening with hope.

She wore a simple dress of brown wool. It clung to her figure in the heat, accentuating every curve. Her long hair was tied back with a green ribbon, giving him a glimpse of the milk-white nape of her neck. She looked fresh and lovely, better than any dream.

Following, he threaded his way through the crowd. She paused at a stall selling carrots. She selected a small bunch and paid for it, laughing at something the merchant said. Samson envied the merchant, wishing he'd overheard the comment, wishing he had a chance to make her laugh.

She moved on to other stalls and he followed, not too close, not too far. He drank in every detail while his stomach churned with indecision. He didn't know how to approach her, didn't know if he should. He couldn't imagine what to say...or how she'd react...but he knew he needed her, like a drowning man needs air.

She stopped at a stall selling apples and he took it as a sign. He closed the distance without thinking and stood close behind her, close but not touching. He breathed deep and smiled at her scent, lilac and soap, fresh and clean, just like his memories.

Her voice was soft and lilting, sending a shiver down his spine. "How much for your apples?"

"Two coppers apiece or a dozen for two silver."

Lucy returned the apple to the crate. "Why are apples so dear?"

The merchant shrugged. "These come from cooler climes and times are hard. If only the Pontifax knew how much the temple tithes hurt the farmers and the merchants." He shook his head. "A man has to eat."

Samson leaned past Lucy. "I'll take a dozen apples for the lady."

She gazed at him, her face a mixture of surprise and puzzlement. "Do I know you?"

He nodded, staring into her dark eyes, willing her to remember.

The merchant interrupted. "That'll be two silvers."

Samson fumbled with the coins, paying with coppers, knowing any other coin aroused too much attention. Handing the merchant his due, he turned to Lucy. "Help me pick them out?"

They lingered over the apples, searching for the plumpest fruit. She kept glancing up at him, puzzlement on her face. He savored every moment, enjoying her company but saying nothing of consequence. They placed the apples in her basket, hands inadvertently touching. He gazed down at her, and for once, he wasn't afraid. "Walk with me?"

She nodded, a shy smile on her face.

He had to laugh. "You always did like presents."

Her face was puzzled but her dark eyes sparked with questions. "Do I know you?"

He steered her toward the edge of the market, looking for a less crowded street. "I used to bring you soap laced with lilac." He'd courted her for half a year but he'd always known he was one suitor among many. "And flowers. Daffodils in the spring and roses in the summer, pink roses not red, your favorite color." A blush crept across her face but her eyes remained puzzled. "And on your naming day I gave you a rosewood box to hold the combs and ribbons for your glorious hair..."

She came to a sudden stop, her eyes wide in disbelief, "Samson?"

He nodded, searching her face, praying for acceptance, hoping for more.

"But I thought...we all thought...that you were *dead*!"

He felt other people beginning to stare. A thread of fear shivered through him. He leaned toward her, urgency in his whisper. "Walk with me and I'll explain everything.

She nodded but her eyes were tinged with fear, her face ghost-pale.

"This way." He shepherded her away from prying eyes, into a street less crowded, walking close to her but not quite touching. No public place was truly safe, so he kept walking, hoping to limit the watchers to nothing more than a passing glance. Staring down at her, he fumbled for a way to start. "I've missed you. When I saw you in the market I just had to talk to you."

She stopped and stared at him. "We all know about your father. He was burnt as a *heretic!*"

The word seemed to echo in the street.

Samson broke out in a cold sweat.

A hunchbacked old woman stared at Samson with eyes that were too interested.

Needing to escape, he grabbed Lucy's arm and propelled her into the nearest alleyway. She tried to pull away, but he kept a tight hold. "Don't say that! You'll get us both killed!"

She stared up at him, her dark eyes wide with fright.

He released her and stepped away, shamed by his actions. "I'm sorry. I didn't mean to hurt you." He shook his head. "I just wanted to talk with you. I guess I've made a mess of it."

She took a step away from him, but she did not run. "Tell me what happened. Where have you been?"

"They burnt my father, so I had to run." His voice was thick with emotions. "I had to get my mother out of the city. We left that night, escaping in a farmer's wagon." He shrugged. "We walked most of the way, hiding during the day and traveling by night. The journey was a nightmare but we made it to Lanverness."

"Lanverness?" Her face was skeptical, her eyes wary. "Then why did you come back?"

This was the part he couldn't really explain...yet he longed to earn her trust. He stared down at her, drinking in the sight of her dark eyes and lustrous blue-black hair, knowing Lucy was his one chance for something normal in a city of nightmares. "I trust you, Lucy...with my life."

Her eyes widened.

"Does your father still own the Jolly Penitent?"

She nodded.

"Sometimes the Dark Harper plays in your father's tavern."

She gasped and stared in disbelief. "Papa won't let me work on the nights the Harper plays...but I've listened to his songs...and I've heard the rumors." Her voice dropped to a hush. "It's dangerous to even speak his name."

"I came back to work for the Dark Harper." His heart thundered at speaking the secret. He watched her close, praying for acceptance, hoping for understanding.

Her face was incredulous, her voice breathy. "You're one of the heroes of the Harper's songs?"

He had to laugh. He'd never thought of himself as a hero. "I help, yes."

"You free heretics?"

He nodded.

Emotions rippled across her face. Her dark eyes held a spark of interest. "Then you're a hero!"

Relief washed through him, relief and pride, two things he hadn't felt in a long time. He wanted to take her in his arms but he resisted. "When I saw you in the market, I had to speak to you." A strand of dark hair escaped her ribbon. With a tentative hand, he smoothed it back behind her ear, silken beneath his fingertips. "I just want to see you, to walk with you in the markets, to talk with you..."

"And you're not afraid to be seen?"

"Sometimes the best place to hide is in plain sight." His voice grew husky with need. "If I meet you in the markets, will you walk with me?"

"You're truly one of the heroes?"

The admiration in her dark eyes filled him with pride, easing his fears. He yearned for more of that look. She made him feel brave. Courage made him reckless. "We freed a man from the stocks just two nights ago, over on the street of cobblers. Another innocent saved from the Flames...but every night it gets harder. The soldiers set traps hoping to catch us but the Dark Harper is full of tricks. We do what we can to make a difference." He leaned toward her, drinking in the scent of lilac. "So will you walk with me in the markets?" He held his breath, daring to hope.

A blush crept across her face. "I'll walk with you. Tomorrow, in the spice market, a turn of the hourglass after noon."

Triumph flooded through him.

"Till tomorrow then." She gave him a coy smile and then turned and left the alleyway for the sunshine of the cobblestone streets.

He watched her go. Watched her till she rounded the corner, savoring the memory of her smile and the way the wool dress clung to her curves. He'd found his courage, a talisman against the city of madness. He wanted to shout for joy but he settled for a smile. Noticing an apple lying in the dirt, he picked it up and burnished it against his tunic. It must have fallen from Lucy's basket. Plump and juicy, apples were always lucky for him. He took a bite...but then spit it out. Rotten inside, the apple was full of worms. One worm was half eaten. Gagging, he threw it away in disgust. A shiver of dread passed through him. Samson told himself that he didn't believe in omens. He fled the alley. Sometimes the gods asked for too much.

27

Liandra

A battering ram pounded against stone door, the relentless voice of doom. The rebels sought entrance to the secret chamber but so far the stone door held. Liandra's ancestors had wrought well. The queen paced the chamber, watching the faces of her loyal few. The slow pounding throbbed like thunder, eroding courage and multiplying fears. They all knew the door could not hold forever.

Her ladies-in-waiting tended the soldiers, binding their wounds with embroidered linens and lace. The wounded lay on the floor or leaned against the wall, stoic in their silence, swords within reach. The queen kept a brave face and a stiff back, providing courage for all.

The waiting was its own torture. Liandra paced the chamber like a caged lioness, examining options and strategies, searching for a way to snatch victory from seeming defeat. Only a handful of soldiers were fit enough to fight so the sword was not the solution. The passageways that honeycombed the tower offered a possible escape route, but the queen had sent the majority of her loyal soldiers through the secret ways hoping to ambush the rebels. If her loyal troops had failed then the passageways could be compromised, becoming a deadly trap. Stay or flee, the conundrum was enough to drive her mad.

The tempo of the battering ram increased, the rebels grew impatient.

The tension in the chamber tightened. Her women threw worried glances toward the queen, looking for reassurance.

Liandra balled her hands into fists, desperate for a solution. She needed something better than escape. She needed a checkmate. The queen paused in mid-stride. If she could capture the Lord Turner, the leader of the rebellion, then perhaps she could claim the field and end the fighting. A plan formed in her mind, thin and desperate but a chance all the same. "Captain Durnheart, we would speak to you and any men who are fit enough to fight."

The captain saluted and made the rounds, speaking to those who were the least wounded.

The queen turned to Princess Jemma. "We have a plan, but it is fraught with risks. With so few men, your bow might make the difference."

The princess smiled, her dark eyes sparkling. "My bow is yours." Her face blushed red. "But majesty, I must warn you, I'm only a middling archer. I can hit the target but rarely the heart."

Liandra had to smile; candor and courage in abundance, the young woman had the makings of a good queen. "You Navarrens are made of stern stuff. We are pleased to have you by our side."

The princess flashed a radiant smile, beauty enough to dazzle any court.

Captain Durnheart approached with seven soldiers. Four of them bore wounds, badges of courage stained red with blood.

The queen met each man's gaze testing his mettle. A grim determination echoed in their faces. Eight brave men would have to be enough. They gathered around the queen, hands on swords, waiting for orders.

The queen voice was steel coated with velvet. "We will not act the prey but instead be the hunter. We will strike at the heart of the rebellion and end this bloodshed. Will you take this chance with your queen? Will you be hunters instead of prey?"

The soldiers' faces blazed with eagerness. Captain Durnheart said, "Sound the hunt, our swords are yours."

"The hunt is sounded." The queen dared a small smile. "We will use the tower secrets to hunt for the rebel leader. Capture or kill the leader and we may yet gain a checkmate and end the uprising. Are you with us?"

"*For the queen!*" The soldiers' cheer drowned out the steady beat of the battering ram.

The queen turned to a young soldier with coppery hair. "In the storage room, you'll find some shuttered lanterns. Bring two and light them."

As the soldier moved to obey, Liandra faced the rest of her loyal subjects. She took a moment to memorize each face. "We are *not* abandoning you. And we are *not* retreating. We go to fight, to take a desperate chance against the enemy." She felt their stares begging for hope. "We will take these few who are fit and lead them back into the secret passageways, seeking an end to this conflict." She wanted to give them hope but they deserved honesty. "If we fail, the passageways will not be safe. We give each of you leave to make your own choice. Wait here and surrender when the door fails or attempt escape via the passageways. The choice is yours."

The soldier returned with two lanterns. She took one, leaving more hands to hold swords.

She stared at the faces of those who had been most loyal. "We thank you for your loyal service. May the Lords of Light protect us all."

One of the wounded banged the hilt of his sword against the stone floor. *"The queen!"* The chant echoed through the room.

The queen turned away lest her composure fail. She removed the onyx plugs from the face of the carved king and stared into the hidden passageway. Darkness and uncertainty waited beyond but she would dare the risk. Turning to the soldiers, she said, "Keep your swords ready, the passageways could be compromised." Replacing the onyx plugs, she unlocked the door and led her handful of loyalists into the secret ways.

She paused on the threshold. Flinging her senses down the stairs, she listened for an ambush, but heard nothing. If treachery awaited, she could not tell.

The lantern cast a soft glow on the stairs, just enough light to see by. She led them down the staircase, through the cobweb-shrouded passages. Time was against her. She couldn't afford to check all the spy holes, so she relied on instinct instead. She knew her prey. The Lord Turner was too much of a coward to risk his own blood. If the traitor remained in the tower, she'd find him someplace safe, someplace opulent.

The queen led her small band around the tower, descending three floors without opposition. She paused at a stone face carved like an old woman, wrinkled and careworn. "Shutter the lanterns." Prying the onyx eye plugs loose, she checked the room. She'd guessed wrong. Replacing the plugs, she tried five more faces before she found what she was searching for. The queen stared through the spy holes and smiled. She'd found the royal audience chamber...and her prey.

The traitor leaned against a gilded table, sipping from a jewel-encrusted goblet. *How confident!* Hatred shuddered through her. She'd trusted this handsome viper, showing him favor by seating him on her council and giving him command of the royal guard. Venom flooded her stare, but Liandra had learned her lesson. She slammed her eyes shut, refusing to be caught by the intensity of her own stare. Taking a deep breath, she opened her eyes and forced her gaze to circle the chamber. She counted ten soldiers. *Ten that she could see.* Her loyal band would be outnumbered but desperate times required desperate gambits.

Putting her finger to lips, she warned the others to silence and then motioned Princess Jemma to the spy hole. "Look through and see the traitor. Tall and handsome with shoulder length blond hair, he has a thin mustache and gold braid on his uniform. Mark him well."

The princess stared through the spy holes and then nodded toward the queen.

Liandra took a last look and then replaced the onyx plugs. She turned to address her loyal band, her voice a low hush. "The Lord Turner is the traitor leading the rebellion."

More than one soldier gasped in surprise.

The queen nodded, her face grim. "This is our chance for checkmate. The traitor uses our private audience chamber as his command post. Ten soldiers guard him but we have the element of surprise." She looked at the princess. "Prepare your bow. We would ask you to go first. Aim your arrow at the traitor's heart and advance toward him. We hope to take him alive, but if he does not surrender, aim to kill."

The young woman turned ashen.

The queen softened her voice, "Can you do this?"

"I've never loosed at a living target let alone a man."

"But you fired in the hallway?"

The young woman's face flamed red. "I loosed several arrows...but I did not aim." She shrugged. "I thought the diversion might help."

The queen was impressed with the young woman's pluck. "Can you do this?"

The princess swallowed, her voice low, "I will do what needs to be done."

Liandra gripped the young woman's arm. "We will not forget this." The queen turned to study the faces of her soldiers. "We will go second, urging the rebels to surrender. The rest of you follow behind." Her voice hardened to steel. "If the rebels fight, they must be defeated. If they flee, they must be cut down. We will capture or kill their leader and then retreat into the passageway. Take care that none of you comes between the archer and her prey. Do not break the line of fire." She looked toward the captain. "Captain Durnheart, we will trust you to disarm the traitor. Be prepared for tricks. He will not come quietly."

The captain nodded, his face determined.

"Leave the lanterns in the passageway and prepare for battle. May the Lords of Light grace your swords." The queen set her lantern on the floor and then removed the golden skeleton key from her bodice. The lock proved stubborn. The queen strained to turn the key. It turned with a click that seemed far too loud, but the time for caution was past.

The queen looked to the princess.

She nocked an arrow to her bow, her face was pale but determined.

The queen pushed the secret door open. Bow drawn, the princess rushed into the chamber, an arrow aimed at the traitor's heart. The queen hastened to follow, her soldiers on her heels.

Time slowed. Every detail was etched clear as crystal in the queen's mind. She saw the shock in the rebels' eyes and the snarl of hatred twisting the Lord Turner's face. The princess closed on the traitor, keeping her bow taut, a slight tremor in her arm. The Lord Turner froze, transfixed by the arrow's threat, a calculating look in his gaze. The rebels reached for their swords. Her loyal soldiers sprang to meet the threat.

Regal in her golden gown, the queen strode to the heart of the conflict, her voice a royal command. "Put down your swords!" She sought to dominate the room with her presence. "We have come for the traitor who misled you but we will pardon any soldier who swears allegiance to the crown. This rebellion is ended."

The rebels hesitated. Her men moved into position.

The traitor snarled, *"Seize her!"*

The queen's voice was certain as stone. "Speak again and die."

The bow creaked with strain but the arrow held on target.

One of the rebels lunged to the attack. A loyal soldier parried the stroke, plunging his sword into the rebel's chest. The rebel made a wet, gurgling sound and then slumped to the floor. Blood stained the marble.

"Stop!" The queen used the voice of command. "There is no need for more death. Keep your hands away from your swords and you will all live."

The Lord Turner seethed with anger yet the arrow's threat was enough to keep him silent.

The rebel soldiers obeyed the queen, holding their hands high, their faces confused.

Captain Durnheart disarmed the traitorous lord without breaking the archer's aim. A dagger and a gold-hilted sword clattered to the marble floor. The captain grasped the lord's hair from behind and jerked his head back, holding the edge of his sword to the traitor's exposed throat. A thin cut of crimson reinforced the threat.

The Lord Turner glared at the queen, a killing rage in his gaze.

The queen ignored the traitor, focusing on the rebel soldiers, willing them to stillness. "Captain Durnheart, get the prisoner into the passageway. Princess Jemma, you follow."

A ripple of unease passed across the rebels.

The queen pitched her voice to carry. "We want all of you to live." Her stare passed to each of the rebels, making the message personal. "We will pardon every soldier who lays down his sword and swears fealty to the crown. Spread the word to your comrades. The traitor is captured and the queen lives."

A shout came from the far doorway. More rebel soldiers poured into the chamber.

The queen fled for the secret door.

Swords clashed behind her.

She reached the passage with two loyal men on her heels.

Captain Durnheart yelled, "Shut the door!"

"No wait!" The queen turned but it was too late. The door had slammed shut. *More men lost.* The queen leaned her forehead against the cold stone walls, drawing strength from the castle. A strange mixture of triumph and fear flooded through her, *so this is how battle feels*.

From out of the darkness, the Lord Turner hissed, "You won't succeed."

Captain Durnheart growled, "Quiet or I'll cut your throat."

The queen lifted a lantern and studied the traitor, amazed that she'd ever thought him handsome. Even captured, he did not relent, his face twisted by naked hatred.

Staring into the cold, blue eyes of her enemy, she whispered, "*Checkmate!*"

Confusion roiled across his face.

"You had the swords but we outplayed you." She stood regal within the dusty passageway, feeling the strength of her ancestors in the castle walls. "We are only a woman, but the queen is ever the most powerful piece on the chessboard."

The traitor hissed, "It's not over."

Captain Durnheart tightened his grip. The traitor gasped, a trickle of blood running down his throat. The captain looked to the queen. "Up or down?"

She considered the risks and the advantages. Having no information about the integrity of the lower passages, she decided to take the known risk. "Up. We will proclaim victory from the ramparts of the Queen's Tower." She nodded toward the captain. "And if the traitor balks, you have our royal permission to slit his throat. We only need his head to prove the rebellion is over."

"*Bitch!*" Despite his outburst, the traitor blanched pale, the stink of fear flooding the passageway.

"A command I will be happy to obey." The captain's voice held a keen edge. He shoved the prisoner up the stairs, holding his sword as a threat.

They reached the eighth floor without hindrance. Her small band passed through the king's door with their heads held high in triumph. They'd lost three men but gained a traitor. A heartfelt cheer greeted their return...but the pounding of the battering ram did not abate. The queen hid her unease beneath a mask of courage, providing strength for her people. Her gambit had worked. She'd captured the red king but the knights and pawns fought on. War was not as neat as chess. The game was far from over. She ordered the traitor to be bound and gagged. Wits against swords, the Spider Queen vowed to keep her throne.

28

The Knight Marshal

The knight marshal watched the recruits practice, blades clanging against shields and helms. They fought with edged weapons to better prepare for combat, but the rhythmic clang of Castlegard's practice yard was a far cry from the chaotic din of battle. The marshal watched, wondering who would be heroes and who would lie among the fallen. Their fates lay in the hands of the gods and in their own skill of arms, but of one thing he was certain, these young men would see battle.

An urgent tension gripped Castlegard. Veterans kept their swords sharp and the knight candidates trained with renewed vigor. Even the raw recruits felt the looming shadow of war. The red comet affected them all. Rumors whispered it was a sign of war, an omen of bloodshed, an end to the long, uneasy peace. The marshal was not a superstitious man. He did not believe in omens, but he could feel the coming war in his bones, in the throbbing ache of old war wounds. Battle was coming, fierce and terrible, glory and honor, his last war.

The marshal walked the length of the practice yard, barking criticisms when needed but most of the time a stern look was sufficient. He drove the new candidates hard, honing their skills. There could never be too much preparation for war...and time was drawing thin.

Hearing someone approach on his blind-side, he turned and waited, his hand resting on his sword hilt.

Sir Malvoy was a fresh-sworn knight, resplendent in his new silver and maroon surcoat, his First Weapon, a battleaxe, belted to his side. The knight saluted, fist against chest. "Sir, there's a man at the west gate, requesting an audience with the king." The young knight extended a sealed scroll.

The marshal studied the scroll's unbroken seal, knowing he held the harbinger of war. "Describe him."

"A tall man in his late forties, dressed in a dark blue robe, carrying no weapons...or at least none that can be seen. He says his name is Aeroth. He claims to be a monk of the Kiralynn Order and asks to see the king."

"He came alone, without any entourage?"

"Not even a horse, sir."

The marshal raised an eyebrow. Rumors said the monks hid their monastery deep in the Southern Mountains, a long way for a man to walk. "You're sure?"

"Yes, sir."

He tapped the scroll against his palm. "Find Sir Abrax and have him escort the monk to the king's solar. Tell him to keep a close watch on our visitor."

The knight thumped his chest in salute. "As you command."

The marshal strode across the practice yard, passing into the heart of the great castle. Soaring towers and crenellated battlements marked the inner castle, all made of impossibly smooth mage-stone. The marshal appreciated the military value of the inner castle but the wonder had long since worn off. He made his way to the King's Tower, accepting the crisp salute of two knights stationed at the outer doorway.

A spiral staircase wound through the tower's thick walls, the mage-stone steps smooth and even despite more than thirty generations of use. Spears of sunlight lanced through the arrow-slit windows casting stripes of light across the stairs. Even here, in the King's Tower, military advantage dictated the castle's design. Castlegard was built for war.

The marshal reached the twelfth floor, breathing easy despite the long climb. A knight snapped to attention and opened the door to the antechamber. The room was small and spare, steeped in the proud history of the Octagon Knights. Passing beneath tattered battle banners, he knocked on the inner door.

"Come."

The marshal obeyed the voice of his king. He found the silver-haired king of Castlegard seated at a round table, pouring through the latest dispatches. The warrior-king wore battle-scarred leathers and burnished mail, his great sword always by his side. The king looked up and smiled, years of decision etched deep in his tanned face. "Ah, Osbourne, have you seen the dispatch from Raven Pass?" The king's steel-green gaze raked across the marshal. "But you did not come to discuss the dispatches. Why such a grim look on such a fair day?"

The marshal raised the scroll in response and offered it to his king. "A messenger at the west gate, a monk from the Kiralynn Order."

King Ursus handled the scroll as if it contained a viper. "It's been a long time."

A chill feathered down the marshal's spine. "A long time between scrolls, but never a monk messenger."

"The comet has flushed them out of the mountains."

The marshal nodded. "A harbinger of war." A knowing look passed between the king and his marshal. "We'll be ready, sire."

The king nodded, breaking the scroll's seal.

The marshal waited, wondering. The king's face gave nothing away.

The scroll rolled shut with a snap. "There's nothing here but an introduction. The monk must carry the message."

"I've ordered Sir Abrax to escort the monk to your solar."

The king's eyes narrowed. "Sir Abrax is one of our best, quick with a sword but even of temperament. What's spooked you about this monk?"

"He arrived without a horse."

"*Magic!*" The king made the word a curse.

"Only a guess, but it's a long walk from the Southern Mountains."

"We trust in the truth of steel, never the trickery of magic." The king stroked his silver beard, a stern frown on his face. "Bring him here rather than our solar."

"Here, sire?"

The king gestured to the arms and armor lining the walls, to the tattered battle banners hanging from the vaulted ceiling. "We will meet him here, among the glories of war. What better place to learn why the monks have come down out of their lofty mountain?"

"As you wish, sire."

"And find my squire, Baldwin, and have him bring bread and salt and wine."

"And Sir Abrax?"

The king's eyes narrowed. "Osbourne, the two of us should be more than enough for one monk."

"Our swords are sharp but our quickness is long tarnished. You've often said that quickness is the only remedy to magic." The king scowled but the marshal persisted. "Sir Abrax should stand guard."

The king waved his hand in dismissal. "Then make it so."

The knight marshal bowed and retreated before the king could change his mind. He went in search of Baldwin, knowing the lad would not be far. Tall and skinny, with a shock of bright red hair, he found the king's squire burnishing a helmet that already gleamed. He gave the lad his orders and then made the rounds of the tower, checking on the alertness of the guards. He ordered two additional knights to stand guard inside the king's antechamber, one could never be too cautious, especially when it came to the monks.

Judging that he'd delayed long enough, the marshal turned his steps toward the king's solar. He found Sir Abrax standing guard just inside the door. Broad of shoulder but lean of waist, Sir Abrax had a lightning quickness that made him one of the deadliest swordsmen to wear the maroon. The knight saluted the marshal, his gaze never leaving the blue-robed monk.

The monk stood with his back to the door, staring out of an arrow-slit window. Tall and lean, his shoulder-length hair carried more gray than black, his robe a deep midnight blue.

The knight marshal kept his voice neutral. "Welcome to Castlegard."

The monk turned, showing a lithe grace even in such a small movement. His face was fair as a nobleman's, his smile open, his hazel eyes deep but warm. If there was something magical about the monk, the marshal could not see it.

The monk bowed. "Thank you for your welcome. I am Aeroth, a master of the Kiralynn Order."

He felt the monk's gaze studying his face, the crisscrossed scars and the empty eye socket. At least the monk did not gape like so many others who had never seen war. The marshal's voice was gruff with pride. "Scars of battle, taken against the Mordant's forces. I wear them with honor."

"As you should."

The marshal listened but he heard only honest respect in the monk's voice. "I am Sir Osbourne, the Knight Marshal of the Octagon. I will escort you to King Ursus." He gestured toward the door.

The monk obliged. Sir Abrax followed behind, a silent sentinel. The marshal led the monk down the hallway to the antechamber, guards snapping to attention at the door. They passed beneath the bloodstained battle banners and entered the inner council chamber.

The king stood on the far side of the round table, sword-straight, shoulders square, his maroon cloak brushing the floor. King Ursus wore no crown or sign of rank, only burnished fighting leathers, his sun-weathered face etched with lines of decision. His blue steel sword, Honor's Edge, lay unsheathed across the center of the table, the point facing the door. A single shaft of sunlight spilled across the sword, causing the sapphire-blue blade to gleam like a naked threat...or an open promise.

The king stared across the table, across the sword, his steel-green gaze fixed on the monk.

The monk bowed and then held his arm straight out, his hand open, a blue Seeing Eye tattooed across the palm. "Seek knowledge, Protect knowledge, Share knowledge." Balling his hand into a fist, he lowered his arm. "My name is Aeroth and I bring a message to King Ursus of Castlegard from the Grand Master of the Kiralynn Order."

"I would hear this message, but first let me offer bread and salt and wine, as a sign of peace between us."

"You honor me."

The king gestured and his squire stepped from the shadows. Dressed in a plain gray tunic the color of unpolished steel, the lad bore a tray laden with two golden goblets, a small loaf of bread, and a plate of salt. The squire offered the tray to the monk.

The monk tore a small piece of bread from the loaf, dipped it in salt, and ate. He reached for the goblet and drained the wine, accepting guest's rights. A small measure of tension leached from the chamber.

The squire circled the table and offered the tray to the king. The king completed the ritual, partaking of everything offered. Draining the goblet, he dismissed his squire, waiting until the door closed before speaking. "Now that guest's rights have been offered and accepted, we would hear your message."

The monk nodded, his face solemn. "I bring a warning from the Grand Master of the Kiralynn Order."

The king's smile was full of irony. "Of course you do."

"The Mordant has been reborn in the southern kingdoms. Look for him to cross the Dragon Spine Mountains, seeking to regain his power in the north. If he can be stopped before he reaches the Dark Citadel, a terrible war may be averted."

The king raised his hand, interrupting the monk. "You said, *reborn*? What do you mean, by reborn? The Mordant is a title, like a king, or an emperor, the ruler of the Dark Citadel."

"If the Octagon has forgotten then the Order has stayed hidden for too long."

The king's eyes narrowed. "Forgotten? What have we forgotten? You speak in riddles."

"Forgive me, your majesty. I will do my best to explain." The monk paused, a look of concentration on his face. "An immortal battle is being waged between the Light and the Dark. The Lords of Light reward their followers in heaven, in the after-life, but the Dark Lord offers something different. To those who please him, the Dark Lord offers tangible rewards in this lifetime, wealth, power, and long life. But to the few who serve him best, the Dark Lord offers more than one life."

Sir Abrax gasped, disbelief on his face. The marshal rebuked him with a stern look.

The monk continued as if he had not heard. "A select few are reborn back into this world...with full knowledge of their past lives. These monsters that walk in the guise of men are called Harlequins." The monk's voice deepened. "The Mordant is the oldest of the Harlequins. We believe he has seen more than a thousand years of life...more than a thousand years of evil."

The king's voice cut like a sword. "This is madness!"

The monk parried the king's words. "Magic is rare, but it exists. You want to deny it, but you need only look to the walls of Castlegard to know it is true. If magic exists, then so can the Harlequins."

"What proof do you have?"

"None save my word."

"The word of a monk."

"The gods meddle in the mortal world. You dare not ignore the Grand Master's warning."

"I *dare* not?"

The marshal knew the monk's words curdled in the king's mind. "Sire, perhaps we should hear him out."

The monk raised his right hand, exposing the Seeing Eye. "I swear by the Light and by the Seeing Eye that what I have told you is true. Knowledge of the Harlequins is one of the core teachings of the Kiralynn Order." He closed his hand and lowered his arm. "I am the herald of forgotten truths."

"Why now?"

"The coming of the red comet portends a terrible war. The Order seeks to avoid that war."

The king reached for his great sword, lifting it with a single hand. "Now we come to it." The sapphire-blue sword gleamed in the fading light, beauty and death crafted into steel. "War we know very well. Tell us, monk, how can you help us stop a war?"

"The Knights of the Octagon patrol the Dragon Spine Mountains, but all of your eyes face north, watching for the Mordant's hordes. We ask that you spare some men to look south, to stop the Mordant before he crosses the mountains."

"And what guise does he wear, this evil of many lives?" A trace of mockery rode the king's words.

The monk scowled. "The Mordant was reborn as one of our own. He wears the guise of a young monk-initiate, a young man of twenty-two, tall and fair of face, with short blond hair and pale blue eyes. He left the monastery wearing the golden robes of a monk-initiate but clothing is easily changed. He will seek to cross the Dragon Spine Mountains and reclaim the power of the Dark Citadel."

"So, you have lost one of your own." The king gripped the hilt of his sword, his voice as keen as his blade. "And does this Mordant-monk know the secrets of your Order?"

"Bryce was trained in our ways of thinking. He studied in our outer libraries, training to become a healer, but he was not a full monk. He never had access to our true secrets."

"...or your powers?"

The monk bowed his head in acknowledgement. "You see beneath the words."

"So you would have us kill this Mordant-monk, doing your work for you, protecting your secrets?"

"Not kill but capture."

The king's eyes narrowed.

"If you kill the Mordant, he will only be reborn in another body. The unknown may be worse than the threat that is known. The only way to stop this evil is by using a weapon of the Light, a dagger made of Dahlmar crystal. Capture him and the bearer of the crystal dagger will be sent to you."

"And where is this wondrous weapon, this crystal dagger?"

"The bearers of the crystal dagger always choose their own path."

The king scowled. "Magical weapons and reborn ghouls, this sounds like a mummer's farce!"

"I assure you, it is not. The Grand Master merely asks that you keep a watch for a young blond-haired man trying to make his way into the north."

The marshal said, "It seems a simple enough request."

The monk nodded. "If you capture him, you would do well to gag him and hold him in your deepest dungeon lest he find a way to turn brother against brother."

"Lest he tell your secrets."

The monk stared, "Caution is advised."

"Your caution, our blood." The king's eyes flashed steel-green. "What else should we know about this Mordant-monk?"

"He carries an amulet the size of a man's fist, a golden oval incised with runes along the edge and the Seeing Eye and the eight-pointed star in the center. It was stolen from our monastery and is dear to the

Order." The monk's voice softened to a request. "The Order would be most grateful to see it returned."

"Now we come to the truth of it. You've lost one of your precious secrets."

"The amulet is no threat to you or yours. The magic is of no use away from the monastery."

The marshal studied the monk's face, looking for deception but found none.

"And if we capture this Mordant-monk, how will we get word to you?"

"Fly a blue pennant from the highest tower and word will reach us."

The king's gaze flashed to the knight marshal, understanding passing between them. The king set his sword on the table, the point facing the monk. "The Dragon Spine Mountains are vast. To find and stop a single man from crossing into the north will take the luck of the gods. As a favor to your Grand Master, we will turn a few eyes south and look for a stranger seeking to cross. If we catch anyone similar to your description, we will fly a blue pennant from our ramparts." The king narrowed his gaze. "Meantime, we prepare for war...for that is the true message of the comet, is it not?"

"If the Mordant crosses the mountains, look for war from the north."

The king glared across the table. "We doubt your story, but we will do what we can to catch this rogue monk."

"You have the thanks of the Grand Master." The monk bowed toward the king. "May the Lords of Light be with you." His voice deepened. "There is a second part to the message. A warning and an offer of aid."

The king waited, his face like chiseled stone.

"The Mordant may not be the only Harlequin to walk the lands of Erdhe. The Dark Lord is stingy with his favors, so there are never more than a handful of the reborn. Given the magnitude of the coming battle, there may be more than one monster loose in the lands of Erdhe...though none are as old or as potent as the Mordant."

"And how does this warning apply to Castlegard?"

"Castlegard is said to be invulnerable to attack...but what if a traitor lurked within, waiting to lower the drawbridge, to open the gates when an army waits outside the walls? What if one of the Awakened wore the surcoat of the Octagon Knights?"

The king's voice cut like steel. "The knights are loyal to a man." His voice dropped to an angry growl, a bear baited in his own den. "Be careful whom you name traitor."

The monk raised his hands in a placating gesture. "It is not a matter of loyalty. Harlequins are awakened within the minds of men in their early twenties. The host has no choice in the matter, a victim crushed beneath the older mind, subsumed by a great evil. Once awakened, the Harlequin can masquerade as the host knight until the time of the Dark Lord's choosing." Reaching within the pocket of his midnight-blue robe, the monk extracted a milk-white crystalline shard, the length of a small dagger. "This is a Dahlmar crystal, a gift of the Lords of Light. In the hand of an awakened Harlequin, this crystal will glow bright red." The monk set the crystal on the table. "The Order uses Dahlmar crystals to test monk initiates, ensuring that no Harlequin ever gains access to our deepest secrets." He gestured toward the crystal. "You have heard the second half of the warning. This crystal is the Order's offer of aid. If your majesty so wishes, I will use the crystal to tests the knights in your service before I leave."

The king stared at the crystal as if it were a coiled snake. "And why should we trust this tale of magic? Why should my loyal knights submit to this test?"

The monk's face saddened. "Because our warnings have always borne the weight of truth."

A perilous stillness settled over the chamber.

The king lanced the monk with his stare. "Is there a traitor among us?"

The words coiled like venom in the small chamber.

"It is a possibility, not a certainty. Hosts for the Harlequins are chosen to give the Dark Lord every advantage. To place one of his minions among the Octagon Knights seems logical."

The marshal said, "The Dark Lord targets his strongest enemies."

The monk nodded. "Just so."

The king gestured toward the crystal. "What is involved in this...*test*?"

"Each knight need only hold the crystal in his hand. If a Harlequin lurks within, the crystal will glow cherry-red." The monk picked the crystal up and held it in his fist. "It is a simple test, with no harm or ill effect to mere mortals."

Seeing the king's doubt, the knight marshal stepped forward. "I'll take this test. Try your magic on me." He looked to his king for permission. "We need to understand how it works."

The king gave a grim nod, his hand on his great sword, his eyes wary.

A fine tension threaded through the chamber.

The monk handed the marshal the crystal. "Hold it in your fist so that half the crystal is exposed. By tradition, the person taking the test proclaims their name and their position."

The marshal accepted the crystalline shard. It seemed nothing more than an ordinary crystal. "My name is Sir Osbourne and I am the knight marshal of the Octagon."

There was no change in the crystal.

The monk retrieved the shard. "You have passed the test. There is no Harlequin within you."

The marshal shared a glance with his king.

The king turned his stare to the monk, his voice grave. "We need time to consider your request."

"As you wish. But Dahlmar crystals are rare and I must take this with me when I leave.

The king nodded. "We will talk more about this in the morning, but only behind closed doors. I'll not have rumors of traitors dividing my men, especially on the eve of war."

"As you command."

The king fingered his silver beard. "Will you share meat and mead at my table tonight?"

"I would be honored, your majesty, but I can only stay a few days. Others need to be warned of the threat."

The king nodded. "Sir Abrax will see you settled into a guest chamber in the Marshal's Tower. He'll see to your needs while you remain at Castlegard."

"Thank you, your majesty. Your welcome is most generous."

The king waved his hand in dismissal. The monk turned to follow the knight. When they reached the door, the king said, "One more thing."

The monk turned.

"We received a scroll from Lanverness. My daughter, Princess Katherine, was invited to your monastery for fostering. Is she there? Is she safe?"

The monk turned ghost-pale. "The monastery is vast. I know of your daughter but we never met."

A slow anger burned in the king's eyes. "This fostering was arranged without my blessing. She is only a girl, but she is a daughter of Castlegard. Her marriage will bring an alliance and a wealthy dowry to the Octagon. I will have a proper accounting of this fostering from your Grand Master or I will have the girl sent home. Am I understood?"

The monk bowed, his eyes wide. "I will see that your message is conveyed to the Grand Master."

The king nodded. "You have our leave to go."

The monk bowed and followed Sir Abrax out the chamber.

The marshal secured the door and then waited, watching his king. The king went to the sideboard and poured a goblet of wine. He drained it in long pull and then refilled it with more merlot. He gestured toward the marshal, "Don't just stand there stone-faced. What do you think?"

"It's a strange tale, even for the monks." He moved to the sideboard and poured himself a goblet. "It's a hard tale to swallow...but the monks' warnings have always carried weight."

"The monks are like crows, carrion birds with a sixth sense for the carnage of war." The king took a seat, his face thoughtful. "But they're only telling us a fraction of what they know."

"Always." The marshal nodded. "They want their amulet back. Whatever it does, it is precious to them. But do you believe their tale about a renegade monk being the Mordant reborn?"

"Impossible...yet it might explain the long peace."

The marshal stared, startled by the idea. "It might at that...but it still sounds like a bard's folly." He lowered his voice. "And what of this talk of a traitor among us, one of these Harlequin devils?"

"The monk slights our honor." The king banged his fist against the table. "The rumors alone would ruin morale, making brother distrust brother." He scowled. "And he wants to test my knights with his magic! It is an insult, an outrage!"

The marshal risked his king's ire. "But what if it's true? What if this crystal is the only way to know?"

"A grim choice. I would sooner trust to swords."

"So would we all, but that is not the choice." The marshal refilled the king's goblet. "I watched the monk's face when he told his tale. I swear he believes it is true."

The king swirled his goblet, taking a long drink. "The monk seemed open and honest...except when it came to Katherine. But why be evasive about a mere girl? And why invite her to their monastery? Do you think they hope to gain leverage over Castlegard?"

"If it's an alliance they want, they should have approached you directly. Whatever the monks want, it is nothing simple." The marshal shook his head. "The monks are a riddle unto themselves. They make uneasy allies."

The king shook his head. "No, Osbourne, the monks are never allies. Allies share the risk; they fight at your side, risking their blood with yours. The monks hide in their mountain monastery and watch, hoarding their secrets. They give warning but they do not take risks. They've endured for centuries while so many others have fallen to dust."

"If they are not allies, what are they?"

The king stroked his silver beard, his face thoughtful. "Messengers. They seem to me like messengers of the gods..."

"So do we trust the gods?"

The king barked a laugh, a mixture of defiance and amusement. "We trust in steel, Osbourne, steel and honor and courage." His voice sobered. "But we'll listen to the gods, when they care to speak."

"So we'll search for this Mordant-monk?"

The king nodded. "We'll search for their renegade. If we catch the devil, perhaps we'll squeeze the truth out of him. Prepare a dispatch for each keep and castle in the Domain. Order the captains to keep a sharp lookout for anyone who tries to cross."

"And what about this test of crystal?" The marshal shrugged. "I felt nothing when I held it. It seemed harmless enough, no more than an ordinary quartz shard."

"If the monks are truly messengers of the gods, then we must take their test." The king's voice hardened. "But it will not be a test of loyalty. I'll not let the monks impugn our honor." He rubbed his forehead in thought. "We'll make it a dedication to the Light, a blessing against the threat of the red comet, a talisman for safe-keeping. Anything but a test for traitors. Hell, it might even improve morale, an antidote to the red comet." The king stood. "Meantime, we gird for war." His voice lowered to a whisper. "I can feel it in my bones, Osbourne. If it comes to war, it will be like none we've yet seen. A war that eats men like a ravenous beast."

The marshal nodded. "I feel it too, sire. Even the young ones look at the comet and know that time is running thin."

"The monks know it too. The threat must be dire to chase them down out of their mountains." The king gave the marshal a knowing look. "No man wishes for war...but," a fire burned in the king's steel-green gaze, "we'll have one more chance, Osbourne. Instead of fading into old age, we'll have one more chance at honor and glory."

The marshal saluted his king who was also his friend. "You have my sword, sire. Lead the way and we will sweep our enemies before us."

The king nodded. "Like the battle of Raven Pass, when a few stood against many and won." He raised his goblet in salute. "To honor and the Octagon...and whatever the gods throw our way."

29

Katherine

Yellow cat-slit eyes stared back at Kath. *Eyes of the forest*, full of knowledge and wisdom and warning. Kath struggled against the golden scrutiny, but she could not move, caught by a power she did not understand. The yellow eyes peered down at her, close enough to touch, close enough to strike. Startled, Kath woke to find a cat-eyed archer looming over her. She reached for her sword...but there was none to grasp. Fighting off sleep, she stared up at his golden gaze, trying to separate dreams from reality.

"Don't be afraid." The words were a whisper.

Putting a name to the bearded face, she recognized Jenks, the captain of the cat-eyed archers. "What do you want?"

He sat back on his haunches, studying her. His eyes glowed like lamps in the firelight, making him seem otherworldly. "You must all rise and bring your belongings. You are summoned to meet with the Treespeaker."

Kath heard awe in the archer's voice. "But we only got here late yesterday."

A knowing smile spread across his face. "The summons came before Cenric had a chance to send a message bird."

Kath shivered, remembering the mysterious power that invaded her dreams.

The archer nodded. "The Treespeaker is one with the forest. Now wake the others, there is no time to waste." The archer rose with a lithe grace and moved toward the open doorway. He glanced back at her, a flash of golden eyes in the dawn light, and then he was gone.

Kath roused her friends, explaining the summons. With a bit of coaxing, Danya woke as well. Pale-faced and haggard, the girl seemed well enough to walk, but the pain in her eyes held the companions at bay. The young woman paid a great price for her magic, grieving for her wolf.

No one mentioned Duncan.

Kath kept her hope to herself.

The five companions ate as they worked, stuffing belongings into saddlebags and binding up bedrolls. Kath's mind raced, caught off-guard by the sudden summons. Needing to know more, she sidled close to the monk, keeping her voice to a whisper. "Who is this Treespeaker and why do we want an audience with him?"

An ironic smile creased his face. "*Her* not him, the Treespeaker is a woman, a very old woman, steeped in ancient power." Zith tugged on his silver beard, his face apologetic. "My knowledge of the Deep Green is limited. It was never one of my areas of study." His voice took on the pedantic tone. "The Deep Green is in many ways a riddle. It is both an old and a new power, one that arose with renewed vigor from the ashes of the War of Wizards. Some say it is something more than mere magic, almost a god. As the Order understands it, the Treespeaker is the mortal manifestation of that power. A priestess, a witch, a seer of sorts, she is revered by the Children of the Green. Her word is law within the forest."

"So why did you ask to meet with her?"

"Aside from avoiding bloodshed at the forest's edge?"

Kath had the grace to blush.

"You flatlanders are always quick to violence." Zith sighed. "Before we left the monastery, the Grand Master spoke of the Deep Green. He said that if we found ourselves within the forest's boundaries, we should ask for an audience with the Treespeaker."

"So what are we meant to do at this audience?"

"Seek and offer aid."

Kath rocked back on her heels, surprised by the answer. "But what aid can we offer the Treespeaker?"

"Knowledge is a sharp sword in the right hands."

She stared at him waiting for an explanation.

"Perhaps we are meant to warn the Treespeaker of the Mordant's return."

Kath considered his words. "So the Grand Master foresaw this? He expected us to come to the Deep Green?"

"Expected, no. A possibility, yes." Zith buckled his saddlebag and said, "The bearers of the crystal dagger always choose their own paths. You charged down the ridge and we followed in your wake. Did you lead us here or was it chance that brought us this way? The hands of the gods are often cloaked in chance and happenstance. Perhaps we were meant to come here."

His words sparked anger within her. "Not at the cost of Duncan's life!"

Zith dropped his gaze, crushed once more by a mantle of sorrow.

Too late, Kath remembered the monk's son.

Sir Tyrone intervened. "There are always risks and always sacrifices, especially in war. It is the duty of the living to turn the sacrifices of those we love into advantages for the Light." Shouldering his bedroll, the black knight added, "We should join the villagers. I, for one, am curious to meet this Treespeaker. Let's see what we can gain from this meeting, chance met or otherwise."

The black knight's words set Kath to thinking, stoking her curiosity.

Gathering up their saddlebags and bedrolls, the companions abandoned the marble tomb, their guards trailing behind. The village roiled like a kicked anthill. Banked cook fires sent wisps of smoke into the canopy. Men shouldered bows and large packs while women groomed children in their best clothes. It seemed the entire clan scrambled to answer the summons. Kath took the presence of children as a reassuring sign. She hoped the Treespeaker would be more benevolent than the eyes staring in her dreams.

They found Cenric at the heart of the village, a commanding presence in his long cape of emerald-green feathers. His cloak shimmered in the dawn light, the feathered eyes dancing with every movement, making him appear like some mystical lord of the forest. Cenric acknowledged them with a nod. "The Treespeaker has granted your request for an audience...an honor rarely given to white-eyes."

Kath gave the clan leader a half bow. "We look forward to the meeting."

Cenric studied her with his golden gaze. "One wonders at the urgency of the summons. It is almost as if you were expected."

Kath kept her face neutral, unsure how to reply.

Cenric's stare narrowed. "You and your companions are to march at the front of the line with an escort of archers."

"Are they escorts or guards?"

"That depends on the Treespeaker."

Prisoners or guests, Kath felt naked without her weapons, but there was nothing to do but comply. The bearded captain, Jenks, approached and directed Kath and her companions toward the front. They took their place, surrounded by a dozen leather-clad archers.

The swirling chaos quickly resolved into a long line of people, women and children, young and old, each with a pack on their back, many with strung bows in their hands. Cenric strode to the head of the procession. Cupping his hands to his mouth, he made a bird-like trill that echoed against the canopy. Waving a carved staff, Cenric led his people into the forest.

They left the clearing, heading east toward the rising sun. The forest crowded in around them, the thick underbrush narrowing the trail. The brush was dense despite the dappled shade, massive trees supporting a soaring ceiling of green. Branches and leaves rustled overhead, giving the impression of whispered words. Kath gripped her gargoyle and stretched her senses, straining to listen but the green language eluded her.

Golden eyes stared into her mind.

Shocked, Kath staggered backwards, releasing her gargoyle. Sir Tyrone put a steadying hand on her shoulder. "Are you well?"

"Yes." Kath tucked her gargoyle beneath her jerkin, deciding not to pry.

They walked in twos down a well-worn trail, all talking left behind. The dawn song of woodland birds rose to fill the forest. The flood tide of song surprised Kath. A hundred villagers marched along the trail yet their passage did not disturb the birdsong. Listening for the sounds of marching, she realized even the babes in arms were quiet. The extreme stealth amazed Kath until she puzzled out the underlying message. The cat-eyed people were used to being hunted. Stealth in the forest was their protection. The understanding made Kath more forgiving of their hostility, but she still felt naked without her weapons.

The path wound through the forest, threading through a maze of green. Kath tried to keep track of the twists and turns but there were no clear landmarks, just endless trees. She kept glancing backwards, hoping Duncan followed. Scuffing her boots as she walked, she held to the belief that the archer still lived...and somehow he'd find her.

The path seemed endless. They walked for the better part of the morning, always heading east. Sunbeams pierced the canopy, sending shafts of light slanting to the forest floor. Birdsong trilled from the upper branches, flashes of bright colors flitting among the dense green. The underbrush thickened and the girth of the grandfather trees spread to immense proportions. Kath saw several trees wide enough to hide a horse. She marveled at the lushness of the forest and the gigantic scale of the trees. Dwarfed beneath the towering green, the lives of men seemed insignificant. Humbled by the trees, Kath appreciated the cat-people's reverence for their forest home.

The trail turned steep, winding up the side of a rocky ridge, sword ferns sprouting among the rocks. Cenric maintained a brisk pace, his feathered cape flashing like an emerald beacon, a lord of the green at home in the forest.

By the time they reached the ridge top the sunbeams had turned vertical. Cresting the summit, Kath paused, stunned by the view. The far side fell away to an open crescent of tiered seats, a green amphitheater carved into the ridge, everything covered in vines and ivy. The sloping gallery of tiered benches formed an elegant crescent-shaped symmetry unexpected in the forest depths. Despite the perfect evenness of the steps, Kath saw no stone, only a lush carpet of green. Even more impressive, was the tree. A massive redwood claimed the heart of the amphitheater, sheltering the entire gallery under the shade of its branches. Soaring out of sight, the redwood made all the other grandfather trees seem like mere saplings. The great tree had a majestic presence, evoking the image of a green god. Kath gave the tree a half-bow, honoring the god of the forest.

A cat-eyed archer, one of their escorts, stepped close behind Kath, his words a whisper laden with venom. "Your face betrays your surprise, white-eye. You thought we were just a simple forest folk, nothing but savages." His voice became a sneer. "Few white-eyes have ever lived to see this. Appreciate what little time you have left."

The threat jerked Kath back to vigilance. An audience with an unknown power could easily turn into a trial...or an execution. Tightening her grip on the crystal dagger, she quickened her steps, descending the ivy-cloaked stairs.

Movement caught her eye. Other clans emerged along the ridgeline, descending to fill the crescent-shaped gallery. Bright feather-cloaks in all the shades of the rainbow marked the other clan leaders. Kath counted more than two score cloaks. The presence of so many clans was unexpected...and slightly ominous, boding for something far more than a mere audience.

Kath followed Cenric down the steps, guessing the amphitheater could hold several thousand people. If things turned ugly their only hope would be to flee.

The steps were steep but surprisingly even, made by man not nature. Kath sensed a riddle beneath the ivy.

Cenric led them to the heart of the amphitheater, gesturing to seats in the first tier, close to the great tree. Kath sat next to Zith, Sir Tyrone on her left. Blaine stayed close to Danya, keeping a steadying hand on the dazed wolf-girl. Guards were stationed behind the five companions, an open threat.

Kath's stare roved the gallery while her fingers explored the ivy growing across the bench. Parting the leaves, she discovered white marble beneath the living green. A shiver ran through her. The forest grew across the bones of some ancient civilization.

Zith noticed her interest, keeping his voice to a whisper, "A great city once stood here, destroyed by the War of Wizards."

Intrigued, she wanted to hear more, but a warning hiss from Cenric silenced her. She glanced back up at the filling gallery. A sea of golden cat-slit eyes stared down at her, a wave of hostility waiting to break.

A horn sounded from the heart of the amphitheater, a high clear note that echoed in the gallery. A young cat-eyed man, clad in a long robe of leaf-green, stood beneath the tree holding a curved antler-horn to his lips. Three times the horn sounded, stilling the murmurs of the crowd.

Overhead, the massive boughs of the great redwood rustled, adding a subtle voice to the horn's call.

Kath shivered, feeling the power of the forest.

A tall and stately woman stepped from behind the redwood, a carved staff in her ringed hands. Her long silver hair was bound by a wooden circlet, an emerald diadem set at her brow. A magnificent cloak of snow-white feathers cascaded from her shoulders to the ground, shimmering as she walked. Her face was serene and unlined, making her age difficult to guess, but her most striking feature was her eyes. Her eyes were pure gold, unmarred by any pupil. She should have been blind, but she moved with the grace and confidence of the sighted, radiating a sense of power and dignity. There was no doubt in Kath's mind that this was the Treespeaker.

The Treespeaker stood before her people and opened her arms wide in a maternal gesture of welcome. "We greet you in the name of the Forest!" Her voice had a rich, smoky timbre that carried through the amphitheater.

The gallery shook with the reply of the clans, "Greetings of Leaf and Bark to you Treespeaker!" The words held the cadence of ritual.

The Treespeaker closed her arms, enfolding the greeting to her breast like a beloved child.

Kath sat transfixed, awed by the power of the simple gesture.

The branches of the redwood rustled overhead but there was no wind.

"Strangers have come amongst us, trespassing the boundaries of the Forest."

A murmur of anger rippled through the gallery.

Kath stirred in her seat, missing her weapons.

The Treespeaker raised her hand, stilling the crowd. "The strangers come under the guidance and guard of Clan Hemlock. It is fitting that Clan Leader Cenric be the first to speak."

Cenric rose to his feet and bowed low to the Treespeaker, his feathered cape shimmering emerald-green in the dappled sunlight. Gesturing toward Kath and her companions, he spoke with the authority of a leader. "Rangers patrolling the fringe of the forest near the burned lands, found these five hacking their way through the underbrush. The rangers watched, intending to leave the strangers to the Green Death, but the blond-haired woman sheathed her sword and claimed hearth-welcome from the Deep Green. When the rangers questioned her claim, the blue-robed monk asked for an audience with the Treespeaker."

Murmurs of outrage rippled through the crowd.

Cenric glared, waiting for quiet. "The rangers escorted the strangers to my village, where the princess of Castlegard claimed the friendship of a dead clansman of the Cedars and the blue-robed monk renewed his request for an audience with the Treespeaker."

Cries of "Blasphemy!" and "Tauth!" erupted from the crowd.

The Treespeaker raised her staff and the disruption quieted.

Cenric turned toward the crowd. "I understand the anger of the clans. Some of my own people claimed tauth against the strangers for loved ones lost in the fire. As clan leader, I tested the winds and discovered the strangers speak the truth. Clan Hemlock offered the strangers hearth-welcome pending a decision from the Treespeaker."

A hum of conversation swirled through the gallery. Kath judged most of the voices to be hostile.

Cenric resumed his seat while the Treespeaker spoke with calm authority. "The strangers have asked for an audience. The request has been granted." Looking at the companions, she said, "Who among you will speak before the Mother Tree?"

Kath felt the Treespeaker's strange golden eyes staring at her. It was as if the woman wanted something from her, but Kath did not know how to reply. Zith must have sensed her unease for he stood, extending his tattooed palm toward the Treespeaker. "I am Zith, a master of the Kiralynn Order." The monk stood proud in his midnight-blue robes, his cloak of mourning cast aside. "I bring you greetings from the Grand Master of my Order. He bid me to offer friendship to the Children of the Green."

Shock and surprise rippled through the gathering.

The Treespeaker inclined her head toward the monk. "Long have we waited for an offer of friendship from the clans of the white-eyes." Her voice deepened, carrying a note of warning. "Friendship is highly prized among the clans, for we survive by trust. While we welcome the offer of your Grand Master...we suspect other reasons brought you beneath the shade of the Mother Forest."

Zith bowed his head. "You have seen the truth of it. We bring a dire warning to the people of the Forest. A great evil has been reborn, loosed into the world by the Dark Lord."

The Treespeaker stilled, her face unreadable. "We would hear this warning."

"The Mordant has returned. Cloaked in the guise of a young monk, he walks the southern kingdoms spreading chaos. The Dark Lord is rising, marshalling his forces. Be warned, the god of the hells intends to bring war to the southern kingdoms."

Angry whispers filled the gallery.

Half way up the tiered seats, an orange-cloaked clan leader shot to her feet and shouted, "You white-eyes have ever been a curse to the Deep Green. You come here offering friendship with one hand but your true aim is to embroil *our* people in *your* war! Keep your friendship and your war and leave us to the peace of the Forest!"

Arguments cascaded down the gallery, but Zith shouted over them. "You cannot hide in the Forest! The shadow of evil has already touched you in the form of a great fire! Do you think that fire was an accident?"

An elderly white-haired woman wearing a cloak of blue jay feathers stood. Wizen and wrinkled, yet she stared daggers at Zith, her voice full of venom. "That fire was set! We name it *murder*."

"Murder!"

The crowd erupted in rage, *"Death to the white-eyes!"*

Zith tried to shout above the din but his words were drowned out.

The horn sounded, cutting through the anger. When order returned, the Treespeaker spoke. "You offer friendship, yet you speak of a fire that robbed us of kith and kin, leaf and bark." Her voice held a dangerous edge. "We would hear what you know of this fire."

Kath felt the crowd coil like a snake waiting to strike. She hoped Zith knew what he was doing.

Zith remained a pillar of calm. "I know very little of the fire, but I suspect much." The monk took a deep breath, like a man preparing to plunge into a bottomless pool. Turning to face the crowd, he spoke with the solemn cadence of a sage. "Since the War of Wizards, the Kiralynn Order has hidden in the depths of the Southern Mountains. The rugged remoteness helped to preserve the Order through dark times, but the choice of seclusion had a steep price. The memory of the Order has faded to myth. Now the Mordant turns that choice against us." The monk held his hand out, showing his tattooed palm to the gallery. "In the lands of Erdhe, the Seeing Eye once symbolized knowledge, wisdom, and peace. Less than two days ago, the mere sight of this tattoo sparked violence in a small village in Tubor. *Violence* and *hatred* spawned by a single tattoo. Twisting good into evil has long been the hallmark of the Mordant."

The monk paused, his face lined with weariness. "Seven of us were sent from the monastery to slay the Mordant. Two of our companions are missing, but we five continue." Zith stared up into the crowd. "I do not know how the Mordant accomplished it, but I know the hatred in that village was a clever trap set against the Order. That trap proves the Mordant passed this way, passed within striking distance of the Deep Green." Zith pointed toward the east. "The inferno that raged into the Forest also destroyed a wide swath of farmland. The fire was a weapon of evil, loosed to drive a wedge of hatred between neighbors, between the white-eyes and the Children of the Green. That fire serves the Mordant by dividing those who might otherwise fight for the Light. The dark divide has begun." The monk's stare searched the crowd. "Can't you feel the hatred sown in that fire? The Mordant has already poisoned your forest."

Chaos erupted in the gallery.

The horn sounded a third time.

The shouting dimmed to the angry drone of a kicked hornets' nest.

Up in the tiered seats, the white-haired old woman cloaked in blue jay feathers remained standing, her leathery face twisted in rage. "*Hatred!* How dare you speak of hatred! You white-eyes rape our daughters and lynch our sons, treating us like vermin instead of people. And now you set fire to the Forest, our Mother, our home, and our refuge! If it is evil you seek, white-eyes, then you need look no further than the nearest mirror! *Death to the white-eyes!*"

The chant echoed through the gallery.

The crowd verged on becoming a mob.

The horn sounded a frantic call but the people were past reason.

Kath scanned the amphitheater, searching for an exit. Escape seemed the only option.

A stone flung from the upper seats struck Zith in the temple. More stones followed.

The monk staggered backwards, blood on his forehead. Kath and Sir Tyrone rushed to shield the monk. Sir Blaine stood, reaching for a sword that wasn't there.

Zith wiped blood from his forehead. "It's only a flesh wound."

Kath hissed, "We have to get out of here before they kill us!"

Overhead, the boughs of the massive redwood began to bend and sway...but there was no wind. A sound like a thunderclap split the air...but there was no storm. The tree shuddered and swayed, emitting a mighty groan. Tree limbs gnashed together, beating the air. Green needles rained down, pricking flesh like sharp darts. Exposed roots writhed across the ground. The earth shook, quaking beneath the great tree. The mighty redwood woke like a vengeful god.

Kath and her companions cowered to the ground, spellbound by the great tree.

The cat-eyed people fell to their knees, pale faced and shaking.

Only the Treespeaker remained standing, serene beneath the quaking tree. Shimmering in her cloak of snow-white feathers, she raised her arms and began to sing. The song had no words, yet the lilting melody carried the balm of summer sunlight filtering through green leaves. Calm and soothing, the melody swirled around the tree and out across the people, lifting anger and restoring harmony.

The great redwood settled to stillness, sunlight streaming through the upper branches.

Whispers of awe filled the gallery. The people rose from their knees and resumed their seats, bowing their heads in reverence.

Kath whispered, "What was that?"

A voice answered inside her head. *There are more powers in this world than you know!*

A shiver feathered down Kath's spine. She looked up at the Treespeaker meeting her strange golden eyes.

The Treespeaker nodded. *Yes, the Forest has seen you, Warrior of the Light. You carry the crystal dagger, the bane of evil. Much depends on the choices you will make. Will you hold true? Will you see the task to its end, no matter the sacrifices?*

Kath clutched the crystal dagger, thinking of Duncan.

Yes, there will be sacrifices, more than you know.

Kath shivered at the certainty of her words.

Hold true to your path, no matter the price, or much that is good will fade to dust!

Kath dared a question. *What do you know?*

I know the touch of evil. I know how it twists the truth.

The golden gaze released her. Kath sagged against the ivy-covered ground. Questions flooded her mind, but she wasn't ready to know the answers.

The Treespeaker turned her gaze to the gallery, her voice raised to the clans. "We are the Children of the Green, the Children of the Forest, but we are also the children of *men*. We live protected by the shade of Leaf and Bark, nurtured by the Mother Forest, but the world beyond is changing. The east winds are laden with the ashes of the dead, of kith and kin, of leaf and tree. But the winds did not bring the first warning. The taproots of the old trees run deep, tasting the marrow of the world. The great trees shudder with the bitter changes. Evil seeps into the land, twisting those that grow in the Light. And now the shadow of evil has dared to touch the very heart of the Mother Forest." The Treespeaker stood rooted to the ground, splendid and ominous in her feathered cloak. "*Blasphemy* has been committed in the shade of the Mother Tree! *Blood* was drawn from a hearth-guest! The Mother Tree quakes with anger at the weakness of her Children."

The air around the Treespeaker crackled with power, the emerald diadem at her brow pulsed with light.

"You sit in the shade of the Mother yet you allow yourselves to be twisted by evil. You shame your roots! It is time to put old hatreds aside. Saplings grow true or they are cut down and fed to the fires for kindling. The Children of the Green must either retreat into the Forest and hide forever, hoping that others win the fight, or they must go out into the world and confront the evil. It is time for the clans to choose!"

The Treespeaker dropped her arms and the power dimmed and faded. The silver-haired woman bowed her head, resuming a mortal façade.

Her silence released the clans. A waterfall of words cascaded down the gallery, but now the voices ran clear, a debate of reason replacing a babble of hate.

The Treespeaker approached the five companions.

Kath and her companions scrambled to their feet, bowing low.

The Treespeaker spoke to the monk. "The promise of hearth-welcome was broken, a debt is owed. Ask for a favor, and if it is within our power, it will be granted."

Zith bowed. "You are most generous. I will think on your offer."

Her golden gaze studied the companions. "Your visit was ill-timed. The fire caused a terrible loss, stirring old hatreds. A dangerous time for white-eyes, yet you speak the truth. And now you warn of an ancient evil, speaking a name we have not heard for over a thousand years."

Kath stared in awe. *Are you immortal?*

The Treespeaker gave an enigmatic smile. *Immortal, no, but we share the age of the great trees.* Aloud, she said, "Forgive the harsh words of my people. Sometimes a viper must be flushed from the grass before it can be destroyed."

Zith said, "Will your people join the fight?"

"Conviction is best gained by consent not commands. The debate will rage for days, perhaps weeks, it is our way. In the meantime, you will be our honored guests." Turning to the green-robed youth holding the antler horn, the Treespeaker said, "This is Martyn, he will see that you are given food and provided with a place to sleep. He will do his best to see to your needs."

Sir Blaine stepped forward. "Our weapons?"

The Treespeaker nodded. "Will be returned to you. Martyn will see to it."

The freckle-faced youth bowed toward the companions and said, "Follow me, honored ones."

Zith and the others began to follow, but something caused Kath to linger.

The scream of a hawk rent the sky.

A twitter of birdcalls followed.

Tension forked through the crowd like summer lightning. Swords were drawn and arrows were fitted to bows.

Kath reached for her only weapon, unsheathing the crystal dagger.

A band of cat-eyed rangers emerged from the forest to stand along the top rim of the amphitheater. One of the rangers trilled a flurry of birdcalls. The tension in the crowd seemed to ease.

Confused, Kath remained wary.

The rangers on the ridge parted and a black gelding appeared at the crest...but the horse was without a rider.

Kath recognized the gelding, her breath caught in her throat.

Beside her, Danya whispered, *"Bryx!"*

Clad in bloodied black leathers, Duncan stood on the ridge, the limp form of the wolf cradled in his arms.

A dam of emotions broke within Kath. *"I knew it! I knew you'd come!"* She found herself standing at the bottom of the steep stairs, waiting for him. Their eyes met. Duncan smiled and Kath felt his blue-eyed gaze caress her face. A jolt of joy passed through her.

Cradling the wolf against his chest, he began to descend the steps, a warrior returning with a fallen comrade.

Danya's whisper became an anguished shout, *"Bryx!"*

Duncan reached the bottom of the stairs. Danya rushed past Kath, wrapping her arms around the limp form of the wolf. Duncan gently lowered the blood-spattered wolf to the ivy-covered floor, surrendering Bryx to Danya's arms. Crouching beside the wolf, Duncan spoke to Danya but his words carried to Kath. "The wolf saved my life. He attacked the sellswords from the rear, panicking their horses and stalling their advance. The chaos gave me time to pick most of them off with my bow, but in the thick of the fight, the wolf was kicked by a horse." Duncan put his hand over the wolf's heart and looked at Danya. "His heart still beats, but I haven't been able to rouse him. Perhaps he will answer to your voice...or else find peace in your arms."

Danya sobbed, wrapping her arms around the wolf.

Duncan rose and turned to face Kath.

She drank in the sight of him. Blood marked his black leathers but other than a sword cut on his left arm he seemed unharmed. Kath reached out to touch his arm, needing proof he was real. Her hand curled around his forearm, feeling the braided muscles beneath black leather. A second jolt coursed through her. Unable to speak, she stared into his face.

He gave her a familiar, wry smile. "I promised I would try my best." His voice dropped to a whisper, "...but I didn't know it would take so long to find you."

The world shifted. For a moment, they stood alone in the Star Tower.

A shrill voice broke the spell, yanking them back to the present. *"Duncan Treloch, are you ashamed of your people?"*

The accusation cracked like a whip in the stillness of the gallery.

Duncan rocked back on his heels, like a man taking a punch to the gut.

Halfway up the tiered seats, the wizen old woman cloaked in blue jay feathers stood rigid, her hands clenched into fists. Like a bright-eyed vulture she glared down at Duncan, her face twisted in loathing and hate. "You shame us all!"

Kath stared at the woman in confusion, turning to Duncan for an explanation.

Duncan stilled his face to stone, his one-eyed gaze turning ice blue. He inclined his head toward Kath and whispered, "Forgive me. I would have done this differently."

Kath shook her head in confusion.

Duncan ripped the leather eye patch from his face. The eye beneath was golden, with the vertical slit of a cat.

Kath took a step backward, shocked by Duncan's mismatched eyes, one sapphire-blue and the other cat-eye yellow.

A bitter smile twisted Duncan's face. "And now you know." Before Kath could say anything, Duncan squared his shoulders and looked up toward the old woman. His voice rang with challenge. "No, Grandmother, I am not ashamed of my people...*my mother's or my father's!*"

The gallery erupted in chaos.

30

Liandra

Wars were not as easily ceded as chess. She'd captured the rebel leader but checkmating the enemy was not enough. The battering ram boomed through the hidden chamber, a looming threat. Liandra needed a way to proclaim victory and end the fighting. Time was against her. The battering ram's relentless pounding proved the grim truth.

The door would not hold forever.

The queen paced the secret chamber, desperate for a strategy, her head pounding to the rhythm of the battering ram. Communication was the problem. Trapped within the tower, her enemies isolated her from both friend and foe. She needed to send a signal to prove the queen still fought. Her gaze settled on the large tapestry filling the north wall, the only sign of luxury in the otherwise spare chamber. Moth-eaten and threadbare on one corner, the tapestry depicted the coat-of-arms of house Tandroth, two white roses crossed on a shield of emerald green surmounted by a golden crown. Despite the wear of time the colors were still vibrant and the size was perfect. The queen fingered the embroidered edge, wondering if some distant ancestor had foreseen her need. Liandra smiled, the game was not yet done.

She turned and surveyed the faces of her loyal followers. Despite their wounds, many still held hope. In the face of such loyalty, Liandra refused to lose.

She strode the length of the hidden chamber, torchlight glinting off her golden gown. Infusing her voice with confidence she roused her people to action. "Come, we have one last gambit to play. We must announce our victory to friends and foe alike. We must be our own herald. Will you join us in this venture?"

Her words roused a ragged cheer.

She gave them a regal smile. "Then we have work to do." She turned to Captain Durnheart. "We give you responsibility for guarding our prisoner. Bind the traitor tight and gag him, but he must be able to walk. If needs be, we will flaunt him from the tower rampart." Her stare turned to the Lord Turner. "If the traitor gives you any trouble, you have our permission to bleed him. If the rebels breach the tower, we expect you to take his head." Her voice hardened to stone. "The leader of the rebels will not outlive us."

The Lord Turner glared, hatred in his eyes.

The captain tightened his grip on the prisoner. "It will be my pleasure."

The queen nodded. "Good." She turned to survey her people. Most of the soldiers were wounded but a few remained hale. "We need two stout men to carry this tapestry. Who will bear our banner of victory?"

A handful of soldiers stepped forward, vying for the honor. The queen smiled, pleased by their eagerness. "We need brawn for this task, the banner must not falter." She chose the two with the broadest shoulders. "Remove the tapestry from the wall but keep it on the rod. Both will be needed on the roof."

While the soldiers stepped to the task, the queen addressed the rest of her people. "We ask all who are able to light a torch and follow us up to the tower rampart."

One soldier raised a hooded lantern. "What about the lanterns, your majesty?"

The queen shook her head. "Leave the lanterns and bring torches instead, there should be plenty in the storeroom. Raw fire provides the better spectacle."

The chamber swirled to activity. Two soldiers wrestled the tapestry from the wall, furling the thick embroidery around the hanging rod. A gray-haired sergeant distributed torches from the storeroom. Her ladies-in-waiting each took one. Princess Jemma held a torch in her right hand, her bow in her left. Even the soldiers who bore wounds rose to help, reaching for torches, some of them asked for two. The chamber glowed with the light of twenty-four torches. The queen hoped it would be enough to signal a new dawn.

The pounding of the battering ram quickened, as if the enemy sought to check her next move. The queen raised her voice, shouting to be heard over the boom. "Come, we have little time. Bring the traitor and the tapestry and as many torches as you can carry."

She led the way to the alcove, choosing the stairs that led upward. An ironbound door flush with the stone ceiling blocked the way. The heavy door was bolted, not locked, but the bolts were rusted shut. "We need a soldier's strength."

The queen pressed against the cold stones, giving a redheaded soldier room to pass. The rusted bolt proved difficult. The soldier hammered the pommel of his sword against the stubborn bolt.

The pounding of the battering ram echoed in the stairwell.

The queen hissed, "Hurry!"

The soldier redoubled his efforts. The bolt gave way in a shower of red flecks, a rusty tang heavy in the air. Hinges creaked in protest as the soldier shouldered the door upwards. The trap door swung backwards, admitting a rush of fresh air and the faint dawn light.

They scrambled to the roof, crenellated battlements circling the tower top like a king's crown. The queen rushed to the eastern battlement, desperate to learn the fate of her castle, the fate of her kingdom. The tower gave her a bird's-eye view. Gripping the carved stones, she leaned out, peering down into the courtyard. An eerie silence echoed from below. Death claimed the courtyard, the dead and dying scattered across the cobblestones like fallen leaves, but all the soldiers wore Lanverness green. The queen railed against the ruin of the rebellion...all because of her gender, a queen instead of king. She turned away from the grim sight. There was nothing she could do for the dead; she needed to find the living.

Princess Jemma called from the far side of the tower. "Your majesty, the battle is here!"

The queen crossed the rooftop to join the princess, her heart thundering. Leaning on the tower battlement, she peered below.

War claimed the western courtyard, a swirling chaos of swords. Green against green, soldiers fought soldiers, with no way for the queen to tell the rebels from the loyalists. The fiercest battle raged in a tight knot at the base of the Queen's Tower, a bitter clash of steel. Screams echoed from below. One side had the advantage of numbers but the queen could not tell friend from foe.

A horn sounded from below. Citizens and soldiers stormed toward the tower, joining the fray. Homespun brown fought alongside the bright colors of nobles and the green tabards of soldiers. *Her people rallied to her need!* A flush of gratitude swept through the queen.

Her voice rang like steel. "Time to proclaim our victory!" She gestured to the two soldiers carrying the tapestry. "Unfurl our banner over the battlement. Let our people know that the queen holds the tower top!"

Soldiers hoisted the tapestry to the top of the notched battlement. Holding the rod, they unfurled it over the edge. The heavy embroidery slapped the side of the tower with a dull thud, releasing a cloud of dust.

Defiant in the morning light, the emerald coat-of-arms stood vibrant against the tower walls.

The queen said, "The rest of you wave your torches with wild abandon."

Her people obeyed, waving their torches out over battlement, crowning the tower with a halo of dancing flames. The queen stood above the tapestry, her golden gown reflecting the torchlight. Liandra held her breath, willing her people to look up, willing the numbers to be in her favor.

At first there was no reaction...but then a few faces looked up...and then a few more began to point toward the tower top. A murmur rippled through the fighting and then a cheer rose from the throats of many, proving the loyalists far outnumbered the rebels.

Relief and pride washed through her. She'd kept her crown, the kingdom was still hers to guide.

"*Your majesty!*" The urgent words came from behind.

Turning, she found a young soldier hobbling toward her. Blood-soaked lace bound his right shoulder. "Your majesty! The battering ram has stopped! The rebels have broken through!"

A cold fear gripped the queen, *defeat on the very edge of victory!*

Captain Durnheart took command. "Protect the queen!"

A thin bristle of swords surrounded her. The queen stood with her back to the crenellated battlement.

The iron door clanged open and rebels poured onto the rooftop.

The queen pushed to the front. "*Stop!* Or the traitor dies!"

Captain Durnheart forced the bound traitor to kneel beside the queen. Gripping the Lord Turner's blond hair, he held his sword to the traitor's throat.

The rebels hesitated, a menace of swords claiming the rooftop.

"Remove his gag." She glared at the traitorous lord. "Tell them to surrender or I'll have your head!"

Turner hesitated, till the captain's sword drew a thin edge of blood. "Enough! Lower your swords, the queen has won."

The rebels held their ground, a grim stalemate.

The queen summoned her most regal voice. "Greedy lords misled you, shedding *your* blood for *their* gain. Lower your swords and you shall be pardoned. We will spare the soldiers, punishing only the traitorous lords."

A murmur rose among the rebels.

The queen waited, willing their surrender.

A minor lordling stood among the rebels. "*Kill the queen and victory is ours!*"

A sword sprouted from the lordling's chest. A gray-haired sergeant stepped from behind the dying lord. "I'll take your pardon." His bloody sword clattered to the rooftop.

The others followed, lowering their weapons.

The queen nearly sagged in relief. Summoning the last of her strength, she stood sword-straight. "Lady Sarah, lead our women to collect their swords." Victory so narrowly won could be easily lost. Surrounded and outnumbered, Liandra knew she needed to keep control of the rebels. The queen remained with her guard while her women disarmed the rebels.

A shout came from the far side of the battlement. "I seek the queen!"

The rebels parted and a troop of soldiers strode towards the queen. The commander dropped to his knee, proffering his sword hilt. "Captain Ranoth with men from the Rose Squad. The Queen's Tower is secured."

The Rose Squad, so her message had gotten through. Liandra dared to hope, but she needed to be sure. "If you serve the prince then you know the password."

"White's Gambit!"

The password was correct, but the crucial question remained. She stared at the captain, noting the spray of blood on his tabard. "What news of crown Prince Stewart?" Liandra struggled to keep her face impassive while fear gripped her heart. The mother feared for her son, the queen feared for her only heir.

"The prince commands the castle. He sent me to ensure your safety."

Liandra closed her eyes in relief. Her son lived and her kingdom was secure. Her desperate gambit had paid off.

"For the queen!"

The salute roused her. She opened her eyes to find that her women had sunk to a deep curtsey while her loyal men knelt. The queen gave them a radiant smile, bestowing a heartfelt thanks on each of them. "We shall never forget the loyalty you showed your queen on this most dire of days."

"Long live the queen!"

Liandra felt suddenly gay...and young, as if the weight of twenty years had lifted from her shoulders. She laughed and the sound was light and cheerful. Perhaps this was the battle euphoria that the soldiers spoke of. "Come, all of you! Rise up and come with us. We have won a great victory! But there is still work to be done. We must care for the wounded and bury the dead and set our kingdom to rights, but then we shall celebrate in a manner that none shall soon forget."

Liandra led her people back down into the tower. She had traitors to punish and loyalty to repay...and a kingdom to steer towards peace and prosperity. The crown was her destiny and none would part her from it.

31

Steffan

The fortress crouched on the north side of the Flame God's city. Fashioned of ugly gray stones and brute architecture, it looked like a hungry beast waiting to pounce. Steffan smiled at the imagery, for the beast's appetite was truly insatiable, the lower dungeons crammed with heretics waiting to dance in the Flames. The people of Balor feared the fortress, and rightly so. Fear was useful, especially in a theocracy...but today he visited the fortress for other reasons, today he pursued a dark vision that stretched far beyond a single kingdom.

Guards snapped to attention as Steffan approached the gate. His long black cape with the bloody badge of the raven prominent on the right breast drew quick salutes. A sergeant offered to accompany him to the general's quarters, but Steffan waved him away, preferring privacy.

He passed beneath the iron portcullis, into the inner yard. The fortress rang with the clang of halberds, the weapon favored by the army of the Flame. The dread weapons were designed to skewer, cleave, and chop. On the battlefield, they'd be used for much more than just killing. Soldiers of the Flame were trained to decapitate, dismember, and disembowel the enemy, sowing fear as well as death. Fear would be the vanguard of Steffan's army.

The new recruits practiced on leather pells stuffed with straw. Hacking at painted heads, they spilled straw-innards across the cobblestones, making a mangle of their enemies. They started with pells but they'd soon progress to live prisoners. The confessors kept the dungeons well stocked with heretics, more than enough to feed the Flames.

The Lord Raven crossed the training yard, a dark shadow amongst the swirling red. He climbed the steps to the commander's quarters and paused on the battlement to gaze beyond the city's walls. The view was impressive. Rows of tents stretched in every direction, campfires scoring the sky with pillars of smoke. The Fortress of the Flame proved too small for his burgeoning army, just as a single kingdom was too small for his ambitions. Soon it would be time to unleash war upon Erdhe, time to transform the counselor into the conqueror...all in the service of the Dark Lord.

Steffan hid his smile and buried his ambition, a chameleon skilled at shades of darkness. Turning from the view, he knocked on the door to the commander's quarters.

A gruff voice replied, "Enter!"

The chamber was small and spare, a camp bed and an army trunk along one wall, a cold fireplace and a weapons rack along another. A thick wooden table and two long benches took up the middle of the room. A small window and a cluster of candles provided a dim light.

General Caylib sat at the table, a booted foot sprawled the length of the bench, one arm resting on the tabletop, the other holding a dispatch. He was a large, brute of a man, with short iron-gray hair, a pockmarked face, and an old scar that twisted the right side of his mouth into a perpetual scowl. He wore scarred fighting leathers and a short sword belted to his side, scorning any signs of his rank. Steffan approved. He'd chosen the man for his ruthlessness and strict discipline as well as his ability to take orders; so far he'd not proved Steffan wrong.

The general glanced up and said, "Ah, counselor, come in. You're just in time for supper." He used his foot to shove the bench on the opposite side of the table, wood scrapping against stone, a soldier's lack of ceremony.

Steffan nodded and removed his cape, hanging it on a peg behind the door.

Tempting smells of spitted meat and garlic swirled through the chamber. A servant finished setting the table, placing a platter of roasted onions and potatoes next to a haunch of roast beef still on the bone. Pouring beer from a flagon, he filled two pewter goblets and then bowed to the general and retreated from the chamber, closing the door behind him.

Steffan took a seat on the bench opposite the general. He lifted the goblet in salute and sampled the beer, dark and strong. It was always black beer with the general, never merlot or brandy; the general was a man of crude tastes and plain talk. Steffan preferred finer fare, but he took a long pull from the goblet and wiped the back of his sleeve across his mouth, blending in with his surroundings, all the better to influence. "How goes the training of the troops?"

"Another lot of fumble-footed farmers, but we'll soon have them trained. They'll learn to wield a halberd or die in the process." The general used his dagger to slice a long sliver of rare meat from the haunch. He ate straight from the dagger, grease dribbling down his chin.

Steffan mimicked the general, skewering a roasted potato. "And the recruiting? How are the numbers?"

The general barked a laugh. "You were right, counselor. Once the confessors started plying their trade, young men from across Coronth flocked to join the army, seeking a haven from the Flames. We've almost doubled our numbers in the past turn of the moon. The tent city is nearly full." He spat a wad of gristle onto the floor. "I guess the priests have their uses after all!"

Steffan nodded, plans within plans. "The priests minister to the people, but not the army." He pointed the tip of his dagger at the general. "Make sure you keep the confessors away from the troops. The confessors are a force to divide, a force to create fear...neither is good for an army."

"I'll keep the pox-faced confessors away from my men, never fear." The general reached for the flagon, refilling his goblet. "I've issued orders that any confessor who wants to minister to my men must first learn to wield a halberd." He barked a crude laugh. "You should have seen their lily-white faces when they heard the order. I swear one of them soiled his smallclothes!" The general grinned and skewered a potato with a vicious jab. He lowered his voice and gave Steffan a sideways glance. "The chief priest is asking for more men."

"The Keeper?"

"Aye." The word was a half-growl. "His confessors rule the lower dungeons. They enjoy the torture but they like their victims in chains. They won't risk their precious necks to capture the heretics. They fear the rebels and say it's a job for the army not the priesthood."

"The rebels will fall in time. The confessors will catch them, betrayed by the very people they strive to protect."

The general grunted. "So do I give the Keeper more soldiers?"

Steffan chewed a strip of meat. It was tough and stringy but the garlic added a savory flavor. "The confessors have their role to play. Give the Keeper the men he asks for. Consider it a training exercise. But rotate the men assigned to round up the heretics. I don't want any of them becoming too comfortable with the priests." Steffan stabbed another potato. "And don't give the Keeper any of the Black Flames. The Black Flames are reserved for the battlefield."

The general nodded. "As you say. But I can't stomach the bloody Keeper." He sliced another strip of beef, blood-red juices running down the side of the haunch. "The success of the confessors has gone to his head. The man struts around like a puffed up adder, spewing commands at my men as if he controls the army." The general dropped his voice to a low growl. "His bloody arrogance goes too far. The people love the Pontifax, but there's many a soldier who'd gladly slip a knife in the Keeper. It could be arranged."

The general was shrewder than he looked, he'd have to keep a closer watch on the man. Steffan shook his head, his voice calm, smoothing the waters. "The Keeper is pompous ass but he does a good job with the confessors, and he serves a greater purpose. The people need someone to hate, takes their minds off of other things." He filled the general's goblet with more beer. "Let the Keeper have his moment. Give the man a ladle's worth of deference and he's easily managed."

"*Deference.*" The general sneered, making the word a curse. "I'd sooner the Keeper and his god-cursed confessors stay the hell away from my army."

Steffan didn't bother correcting the general as to whose army it was. "Train the army, general, and I'll manage the Keeper."

The general grunted, his mouth full of meat.

Steffan sipped his beer. "How long till the army is ready?"

"You asked for ten thousand. I'll give you twenty-five thousand, fully trained, in another two turns of the moon."

Steffan nodded, impressed. The man was a crude bore, but he had his uses. "What about equipment?"

"I've got every armorer and blacksmith in the city working late into the night. The men will be armed and ready."

"And provisions?"

"That's the biggest worry. The army eats like a plague of locusts. I've billeted some of the trained squads at villages outside of the city. It makes the priests think there's less soldiers and eases the strain on the city stores. I've ordered my men to put a levy on the farms. The farmers grumble but they can't argue with the bite of a halberd."

Steffan nodded. "Prices in the local markets are soaring but the peasants will find a way to eat, they always do." He fingered the pewter goblet. "We'll have to march before the last harvest and forage along the way."

"The army will be ready."

"And Lanverness ripe for the taking."

"More ripe than you think, counselor."

Steffan cocked an eyebrow. "What have you heard?"

"Rumors from a merchant. Whispers of a rebellion against the queen."

Steffan sensed the Dark Lord's hand and wondered if he had a rival. Burying the thought, he gave the general a deliberate smile. "Win or lose, the chaos will work to our advantage." He finished his beer and stood. "Train the army well, general. I want the troops quick to obey and brutal in the execution."

The general flashed a wolfish grin. "Bloodthirsty and ruthless...the surest way to victory." His grin twisted into a crooked smile. "I'll give you an army that'll make widows weep and bards raise a lament for kingdoms crushed. Erdhe will run with the blood of our enemies."

Steffan approved of the naked bloodlust in his general's eyes. The man was hungry for war, a valuable tool, but a sword could cut two ways. The chamber suddenly seemed close and confining, the smell of rare meat overpowering. "I'll see you in a fortnight. Make sure everything goes as planned." He swirled his black cape around his shoulders and left the general to satisfy his hunger with the bloody haunch.

Steffan stepped out of the chamber and into the summer night, a shadow in the darkness. He stood on the battlement watching the blazing campfires below. The glow rivaled the stars. A sense of power swelled within him. He'd built an army of fanatics in the heart of Erdhe and he controlled Coronth with a religious stranglehold, but there was still so much to be done. Soon he'd have his chance to reach beyond a single kingdom, to reach for the ultimate reward. One lifetime was not enough.

32

Duncan

Duncan stood in the center of a raging storm, both eyes uncovered.

Shouted arguments cascaded down the tiered seats, a waterfall of anger.

Nothing had changed. Bitterness welled within him, *always the half-breed, always the outcast.* Duncan stood beneath the deluge of anger, his mismatched heritage written upon his face.

The Treespeaker intervened. "This is a matter for the clans. Remove the hearth-guests and see to their comfort."

The anger quieted to a dull roar.

Four green-clad attendants leaped to obey, ushering Kath and the rest of her companions from the amphitheater. Blaine carried the wolf, Danya hovering by his side. The monk cast a questioning glance toward Duncan, but the archer kept his stare fixed on Kath. She'd recoiled at the sight of his mismatched eyes but it could have been shock...or it could have been loathing. He watched her go, longing to follow, needing to know the truth, half afraid of the answer...but instead he stood his ground. He had to deal with his past before he could pursue his future.

He turned to face the gallery of golden eyes, kith and kin, friend and foe. His birth-home held a tangle of sore emotions, a nettle of memories armed with great, nasty thorns. Given a choice, Duncan would have avoided the Deep Green, but the gods, or fate, had brought him back. Standing in the heart of the amphitheater, he squared his shoulders and faced the bitterness of his past.

Lifting his gaze, he met the stare of the wizen old woman cloaked in blue jay feathers. Her white hair was thin and wispy, her leathery face wrinkled and lined with equal parts age and spite. "I see you, Grandmother, I see you with both eyes, white and golden." His mismatched eyes had always brought out the worst in the old harridan but Duncan was tired of hiding. "And I see that nothing has changed."

The leader of clan aspen leaned on her staff, her bird-bright eyes keen as a raptor sighting prey. "It has been a long time, Grandson. You return to the Forest, yet you hide your heritage beneath a black eye-patch. Are you ashamed of your people?" Her voice dripped with venom. "Or have you become one of the hated white-eyes?"

Duncan pitched his voice to carry. "I remember my heritage, Grandmother. I remember how you hounded my mother into taking her own life because she was raped by a white-eyes. You never spared any pity for the victim, Grandmother, only hatred for anything touched by the white-eyes." The old harridan maintained her withering glare, but Duncan refused to be cowed. "I remember how you shunned me as a boy, merely because of my mismatched eyes." He scanned the gallery looking for the scarlet cloak of clan redwood. "And I remember how I was not permitted to marry the woman I loved because my blood was tainted." Duncan swallowed a mountain of bitterness. "You revile the white-eyes for their prejudice, but are you so different?"

Outrage ripped through the gallery, but Duncan was not done with them. He shouted above the din. "The heritage of the Forest allows us to taste the wind, to sense the truth, while the white-eyes walk through the world blind, unable to tell the truth from a sea of lies. You know the truth, Grandmother, yet still you hate. Your hatred shames the Forest!"

Anger leaped through the gallery like wildfire set to dry tinder.

He'd shown them a mirror they dared not face. The truth had sharp, nasty edges.

Duncan stood like a rock, enduring the crash of hatred.

A gentle touch penetrated his defenses. The Treespeaker rested her hand on his shoulder, her touch feather-light. The soothing balm of the Forest flowed into him. Duncan turned and stared into her unblemished eyes, finding serenity and wisdom in the depths of her golden gaze.

Her voice whispered like rustling leaves in his mind. *Welcome home, Duncan Treloch. You have faced many cruel storms, yet the tree has grown straight and true. You bring honor to the Mother Forest.*

The words healed a jagged hole in Duncan's heart. He dropped to one knee and bowed his head in homage.

The great redwood rustled overhead, stilling the angry voices in the gallery.

Rise and let your people gain from your experience. Let your voice be heard in the clan council.

Duncan rose to stand next to the Treespeaker. Squaring his shoulders, he stared up into the gallery of golden eyes.

The Treespeaker spread her arms wide in benediction. Her white feather-cloak shimmered in a shaft of sunlight, as graceful as a forest stork. Her voice rose on wings to fill the gallery. "One of our sons has returned bringing experience from beyond the Forest. The Children of the Green stand upon the cusp of change. We must decide to withdraw from the realms of Erdhe and retreat into the Forest depths...or go out into the world and take up arms against the gathering evil." Her voice deepened, rich with the timbre of old trees. "Know that this threat of evil is real. This decision will echo through the ages, the Trees have tasted it, the deep roots know." The Treespeaker gestured toward Duncan. "This son of the Forest has spent more time among the white-eyes than any other. Perhaps the Mother called him home to help with this decision." The emerald diadem at her brow began to glow with a soft light of living green. "Listen to this son who has lived among the white-eyes. Learn from his experiences." The emerald glow intensified and the Treespeaker's voice held an undercurrent of storm. "But never doubt that the Mother Tree claims Duncan Treloch as one of her own!"

The Treespeaker lowered her arms and retreated to the base of the giant redwood, a sentinel judging the clans.

Murmured whispers passed through the crowd.

Duncan turned to seek out his Grandmother's stare. The blue-robed harridan sat rigid with her arms crossed, throwing poisoned daggers with her glare, but at least the shrew's tongue was stilled.

Duncan waited, wary of the crowd, the half-breed's voice had never been welcome at clan council.

Near the bottom of the gallery, a burly man cloaked in the black feathers of Clan Ash, stood. "Greetings of Leaf and Bark to you, Duncan Treloch."

His face was older, etched with lines of responsibility, but Duncan still recognized the square jaw and honest gaze of his childhood friend. Duncan gave Bran the half-bow owed to clan leaders. "I greet you, Bran Caldon, leader of Clan Ash."

The clan leader nodded, his face neutral. "The Treespeaker has charged the clans with a difficult decision. You have lived beneath the shelter of the Forest and also out among the white-eyes. What path should the clans tread?"

Duncan rocked back on his heels, struck by the simple honesty of the question. He stared up at the gallery of golden eyes, considering his words. A wall of hostility waited, poised to fall, but he dared to give the clans the truth, hoping it would make a difference. "I can tell you that the threat of evil is very real. My companions and I have seen the handiwork of the Mordant. He sows the land with evil, leaving a wake of hatred behind him. Though they may never ask for it, the southern kingdoms will need help to defeat this enemy. I believe help should be given." A tide of argument rose against his advice, but Duncan talked over it. "The Light must stand against the Dark, no matter the differences between us." Duncan paused, surveying the gallery, finding a few who listened. "As to living outside of the Forest, I have found as much good in the outside world as evil. Perhaps the white-eyes only fear what they do not understand. If we leave the Forest and fight beside them, raising our bows against this evil, then perhaps the Children of the Green will be welcome among the kingdoms of Erdhe."

A thoughtful murmur raced through the crowd.

The shrill voice of his Grandmother slashed like a knife, sharp with hatred. "The white-eyes hunt us like animals. Now evil hunts the white-eyes. Let the cursed white-eyes be consumed by their own evil! Let them kill each other off so that only the Children of the Green remain."

A male voice yelled, "Death to the white-eyes!" The ugly refrain echoed through the amphitheater.

The leader of clan ash remained standing, unruffled in his cloak of raven feathers. He raised his wooden staff, asking for quiet. "Clan ash retains the right to speak!" The anger of the gallery dulled to a hush, the rules of the council held. Bran returned his gaze to Duncan. "There are too many ill-deeds between the Children of the Green and our nearest neighbors, the farmers of Tubor. Neither side will soon forgive the other for the fire." Nods of agreement rippled through the gallery. "If we leave the Forest, we must seek other allies. Which leader of the white-eyes will receive us as equals? How can we best use our bows?"

Duncan nodded. "In my wanderings of Erdhe, I have met two rulers with uncommon wisdom. If the Children decide to leave the Forest, make your way to King Ivor of Navarre or to Queen Liandra of Lanverness."

Whispers of disbelief raced through the gallery.

Puzzlement scrawled across Bran's face. "You mean to say there is a white-eyed kingdom ruled by a queen?"

Duncan had to smile. Clan leaders were a mix of men and women, but under the steady leadership of the Treespeaker the Children favored a matriarchy. It was another difference they could never understand about the white-eyes, a difference they considered barbaric. "It's true, most white-eyes have a backwards view of their women, but the queen of Lanverness is so extraordinary that she rules undisputed from a single throne."

Bran's voice deepened, "And is she wise enough to see past the color of our eyes?"

Tension rippled through the gallery.

Duncan felt the weight of the question, knowing it could tip the argument. He fixed his gaze on the face of his oldest friend and offered the harsh truth. "If Queen Liandra cannot see our value, then none can."

Bran nodded, his stare hard. "You say you've met these rulers, but does either of them know your true heritage?"

He gave Bran a wry smile. "I learned more than enough about prejudice and hatred here in the Forest. None of them know the truth behind my eye patch."

The black-cloaked man gave Duncan a half-smile and then resumed his seat.

Arguments ignited from all sides. He'd set the spark to the tinder, now all Duncan could do was watch.

A dozen clan leaders rose to claim the floor, including his Grandmother. Her shrill voice led those opposed to leaving the Forest but several of the other clans argued against her. Some wanted to end the hatred and the persecutions while others wanted better opportunities for the young. A few voices recognized the evil of the fire and the threat to the Forest. The debate ebbed and flowed, for and against, heated on both sides, a raging thunder of disagreement.

Duncan stood in the eye of the storm, the half-breed son once again forgotten by the clans.

The soft whisper of the Treespeaker filled his mind. *Duncan Treloch, son of the Forest, you have done well. You have risen above hatred and prejudice to find honor in both worlds. You give your people hope, a bridge to a better future. Go now, and join your companions. They also have need of you. One in particular, waits for you in the high meadow.*

Her words lifted a weight from his shoulders. Duncan turned and bowed low to the Treespeaker.

Released from the debate, he followed his heart out of the amphitheater.

33

The Mordant

The night wind carried a thin thread of Darkness. The Mordant paused in mid-stride, tantalized by the scent. It came from the northwest, strong enough to draw his notice but not Dark enough to be a dedicate. He breathed deep, tasting the scent, rolling the Darkness across his tongue like a vintner tasting a fine wine. Darkness came in many different shades: the depraved, the malevolent, the vicious, the greedy, the cruel, the debauched, the murderous...so many different forms of corruption, each with its own particular taste, its own particular use. This thread tasted sharp and vicious, a tool waiting to be wielded by the will of a master.

The Mordant followed the thread, intent on claiming a servant. Leaving the road, he cut across an open field. Moonlight cast a silvery glow across the farmland, peaceful and unsuspecting. He followed the thread through a vineyard and across an empty pasture. By the light of the crescent moon, he climbed a small hill and found a collection of rooftops huddled in the valley below, the smell of wood smoke hanging heavy in the night air. More than a village, the cluster of stone and wood buildings had the look of a town posing as a city. The Mordant smiled, sensing a fertile hunting ground.

He pulled the deep cowl of his golden robe forward and followed the dirt road down into the heart of the town. Lamplight glowed from the houses, music and laughter spilling from the open door of a tavern. He strolled down the main street, keeping his head bent and his eyes averted, avoiding the villagers.

The scent of Darkness grew stronger, drawing him past the tavern and into a side alleyway. A woman's sob confirmed the direction. The Mordant paused at the mouth of the alley, studying the scene. Three men subdued a young couple—robbery and rape—two petty acts of Darkness. One of the ruffians moaned and writhed in the dirt, a knife protruding from his belly. A second thug searched the limp body of the male victim. The leader, a swarthy swordsman, unlaced his codpiece, preparing to mount the woman. Darkness clung to the swordsman like a cloak; he'd found his prey.

The Mordant advanced toward the swordsman, a soft swish of golden robes. Lamplight from the main street sent his shadow stretching down the alley like a sinister wraith. The shadow touched the swordsman. The Mordant rasped, "Attend me!"

Startled, the two thieves swung to face the intruder. Hands reached for weapons, jackals defending their kill. The leader stuffed his manhood back into his codpiece and drew an ugly short sword. Keeping one foot on the woman's back, the swordsman growled, "You're bothering the wrong man, boyo. Be gone, or I'll flay you alive for the sheer pleasure of it!"

The Mordant studied his prey. The swordsman wore a map of dark deeds etched across his face. A stubborn jaw and a nose made crooked by too many brawls...but the darker truth lay in the twin scars branded deep into his face. Each cheek bore the scar of a broken Octagon, the brand of an unmade knight. The Mordant smiled, amused by the irony. He nodded toward the swordsman, his voice a whisper, "I have a use for you."

Anger roiled across the swordsman's face. Leaving the woman, he advanced on the Mordant, his sword poised to strike. "Never bother a man when he's taking a woman, boyo. Now hand over your purse and there better be more than coppers in it or I'll have your head for interrupting my pleasure."

The Mordant whispered, "You don't yet recognize your true master."

"I have no master." The swordsman raised his blade, little realizing that the Darkness in his soul gaped open like an invitation to conquest.

The Mordant shrugged the cowl away from his face. Dropping his inner shields, he let the full Darkness of his soul ascend to his eyes. A thousand years of evil poured forth into his gaze, boring into the swordsman. Darkness fed on Darkness, overwhelming the swordsman. The Mordant exerted his will, a molten fist searing the mortal's soul.

Gasping in pain, the swordsman fell to his knees. His eyes widened in fear, the sword falling useless from his hand.

The Mordant whispered, "Yes, like knows like. The corruption in your soul kneels to my greater Darkness." The Mordant seared the soul, marking it with his own brand. An inhuman scream echoed in the alleyway. A burnt smell hung in the air.

Trembling, the swordsman stammered, "L-lord, who are you?"

"I am your master, the Mordant reborn." He sifted through the man's soul, examining the dark deeds of his past. The unmade knight reeked with bitterness and envy. In the deepest part of his soul he carried a penchant for cruelty and murder...a valuable combination.

The Mordant eased his stranglehold on the soul. The unmade knight carried enough Darkness to be compelled, but a willing bargain was always more binding...even if that bargain was never kept. The Mordant's voice was low and compelling. "I know you Raymond of Radagar, Raymond of the Octagon."

The swordsman gasped, surprise written across his face.

"The darkest secrets of your soul lie open to me. You long for revenge against those who wronged you...and you covet the great sapphire blades wielded by the favorites of the Octagon." The Mordant drew Darkness to him like a cloak, wrapping himself in power. He loomed above the kneeling man, a vision of his true self, a vision of a thousand years of evil. "Serve me and I will exceed the deepest wishes of your soul. Serve me and you shall vanquish those who cast you out. Serve me and I will make you a Dark Knight, a wielder of a legendary sword...one capable of shattering blue steel."

The unmade knight stuttered, "B-but t-that's not possible!"

"Serve me and I will give you Sir Boric's blade to wield."

Raymond gaped. "The first blue sword! But that blade is lost to legend, lost when..."

"...when Sir Boric sought the head of the Mordant...over six hundred years ago."

The unmade knight stared at the Mordant with wide eyes. Fear engulfed the alleyway.

The Mordant laughed, the sound carrying the weight of ages. "Your legends are my memories. Now you begin to see why no mortal man will ever defeat me."

"But what of the sword?"

The unmade knight proved courageous in his greed; the Mordant approved. "The sword waits in the Dark Citadel, along with other treasures. Serve me and you shall wield Boric's lost sword against my enemies."

Desire for the fabled sword flooded the man's soul.

"Will you serve me of your own free will?"

The unmade knight saluted, his fist striking his chest. "I so swear!"

The Mordant smiled, mortals were so easy to manipulate. "Now rise and serve your true master."

Raymond wiped the spittle from his mouth and scrambled to his feet. Retrieving his short sword, he sheathed the weapon and bowed low. "W-what would you have of me, lord?"

Releasing the knight from his gaze, the Mordant turned to study the second thug. The skinny thief cowered next to the body of his unconscious victim, gibbering in fear. Peering into the thief's soul, the Mordant found only a mere splinter of Darkness, just a petty thief who stole for food without any real passion for the Dark. This one would be of no use.

Turning back to the unmade knight, the Mordant said, "Do you have a mount?"

"No, lord."

Reaching into the pocket of his robe, the Mordant produced a purse thick with coins. "Buy or steal three horses, two saddled for riding and one for supplies. Stock the packhorse with clothing and food for the mountains. Choose the horses for stamina rather than speed. Meet me at the north edge of town before the sun rises. See to it that you are not followed."

"I could serve better if I knew our destination."

The Mordant studied his servant. In his early thirties, the knight was tall and well muscled with a low cunning in his dark eyes. Watching the man's face, the Mordant said, "We go to Cragnoth Keep."

The man blanched. "B-but the Frozen Keep is held by the Octagon."

"Loyalties can be deceiving."

"B-but I'm marked for death if I return to the Domain."

"Only if you are caught." The Mordant's will poured into the eyes of the knight. "Remember your vow." Letting iron leach into his voice, the Mordant said, "Whom do you serve?"

Fear and terror warred behind the knight's eyes.

The Mordant's shadow loomed large.

Dropping to his knee, the unmade knight bent his head in homage. "I serve the Mordant."

"And so you should. Now see to my commands, but first, kill the others. I will leave no witnesses."

"All of them?"

"Yes, all of them. The weak are of no use to me."

A wicked grin crossed the knight's face as he eased his sword from its scabbard.

The Mordant pulled the cowl of his robe up to shadow his face. He'd claimed his first servant of this lifetime, an unmade knight of the Octagon; the irony appealed to him. He'd use his enemy's castoff, turning the sharpened weapon back on the maker. Soon he would cross the Dragon Spine Mountains and claim tens of thousands of servants...but first he had one more trap to set, one more seed of chaos to plant. Turning his back on the unmade knight, the Mordant walked from the alleyway, leaving death in his wake.

34

Danly

The cell reeked of piss, and sweat, and mold, and festering fear...but at least there was light. Not the light of the sun, the cell was buried too deep for sunlight or fresh air or any touch of life, but this new cell had the luxury of torchlight. Torches lined the outer hallway, sputtering and glowing, casting pools of light against the cold stones. Danly became enchanted with the flickering torchlight, the way it striped the iron bars and dared to invade the crouching darkness. After the traitor's pit, Danly appreciated light.

They'd pulled him out of the hole, doused him with cold water, and handed him rough peasant-clothes to cover his nakedness. A scratchy coarse wool tunic and pants, both infested with lice and the sour stink of the previous owner. As if that indignity were not enough, they shackled his hands and legs in heavy irons and marched him at sword point out of the cell. At least they marched him the right way, heading up, out of the bowels of hell.

His chains clanking, Danly shuffled past the long line of ironbound doors, through the guardroom and across the cavernous chamber filled with the moldering devices of torture. The great devices lurked like beasts in the shadows, starving for a victim, hungry for a traitor, a nightmare waiting to pounce. Danly hurried as much as his chains would allow, hobbling up the great wooden staircase, fleeing the underworld.

Every step upwards was a victory. Up was good. Up was full of hope. Up was closer to light and life, to fresh air and sunshine. In hell, up was the only direction that mattered. But they didn't take him far enough.

They stopped on the next level, shoving him into a small cell, a lonely cell, cold and dank but at least he had the comfort of torchlight. A slops bucket, a hard pallet for a bed, and stale rushes became his kingdom, beady-eyed rats his only subjects, the prisoner-prince.

At first he'd hollered and yelled, hurling threats and bribes, commands and pleadings, but no one ever came. He learned to save his voice and nurture his hatred. Six steps by ten, he paced the limits of his domain, and every step he said a name. He lost count of the steps, but never the names. Some days he held out hope that the Red Horns would rise and the crown would still be his. They'd carry him out of the dungeons and set him on the throne, his enemies cowering at his feet, awaiting his royal wrath. That dream was sweet. On other days, he cursed the Lord Turner and his whispers of treason, damning the day he'd joined the Red Horns. But there was always one he hated above all others, his royal mother, the Spider Queen. The bitch, the witch, the unnatural woman he called mother. If he ever got his freedom, he'd have his sweet revenge...but first he had to survive.

Every day was the same. Cold slimy walls, cold lumpy gruel, cold silent hallways. The sameness wore at his sanity. At least he had light, but the torchlight never changed, never bright, never dark, no way to tell the tread of days...except by the food. Cold oatmeal gruel and a heel of dark bread in the morning...gray, lumpy stew and a heel of dark bread at night, always served with silence. His jailors ignored him, not even bothering to put him to the question. It was as if Danly did not exist, as if he did not matter. He slammed the empty bowl against the far wall, screaming his rage at the shadows. "I'm a prince of the realm! I demand to see the queen! I deserve better than this!"

A prince of the realm...the queen...deserve better than this...

The twisted echo came back to haunt him...always a mocking taunt, never an answer. He slumped to the floor, his head in his hands, clinging to sanity.

A sound pierced the silence, a sound that wasn't part of the sameness. A lock clicked and a rusty door groaned...too soon for the evening meal. Footsteps echoed down the long hallway. Hope danced within him...but fear was right behind. He was afraid to look but he needed to know. Danly pressed his face to the bars, straining to see, watching the islands of light beneath the torches.

He spied emerald green, the tabard of soldiers and swore under his breath. They never sent the prison turnkeys, always soldiers. Stern-faced, incorruptible creatures of the queen's shadowmaster, another man he swore to hate.

A captain flanked by two soldiers strode the long hallway. They stopped in front of his cell. "Move away from the bars."

Danly stood his ground, afraid to relinquish his kingdom. "Why?" His voice was rusty from disuse.

"You're to be moved." The captain's voice deepened to a growl. "Move away from the bars."

Danly told himself that moving was good; it had to be. The last move had gotten him out of the pit and up to a cell with torchlight. Perhaps the next move would give him a real window, a glimmer of sunlight. He clung to the hope and moved back against the far wall. "What happens above?"

"No questions!"

It was always the same. Danly yearned to hear what transpired in the castle. Hoping for a crumb of information, he held his silence, waiting, watching, his back pressed against the far wall.

Keys clattered in the lock. The hinges of the door screeched in rusty protest. The captain drew his sword, the steel bright in the torchlight.

Danly shrank against the cold stones, fearing murder.

The captain must have seen his fear. "Come, you're to be moved to a different cell."

The soldiers grasped his arms, one on each side. Danly shuffled forward between them, watching the naked sword. Seven steps and he passed beyond the confines of the bars, beyond his domain. He turned to the right, toward the way up...but the soldiers pulled him back. "No, this way."

They were leading him down!

"No!" His scream echoed in the hallway. "I won't go down!" He hung like deadweight between them, dragging his feet, tears streaming down his face. But the soldiers were strong. They half carried, half dragged him down the corridor.

A stream of hot urine pissed down his leg, the stench of fear flooding the dungeon...but the soldiers did not stop. Relentless, they dragged him down the great wooden stairs, down past the torture devices, down into the depths of hell. He'd walked defiant the last time they'd brought him to the lower depths, but now Danly knew better. He squirmed, fighting to get free. "Not the pit! I won't go there!"

The captain turned and struck him across the face. The shock of the blow silenced Danly, the salty taste of blood on his cracked lip. The captain growled, "You're not going to the pit, that's reserved for another traitor."

That's when Danly knew. The Red Horns had risen...and failed. He began to shake, his chains clanking, his legs turning to water. They opened an ironbound door and shoved him in, a glimpse of stone walls and pale rushes and an unimaginable stench. The door slammed shut and darkness descended, deep and dark, absolute black, the darkness of a tomb. And then the screaming began. Danly knew the wails came from a ghost...the ghost of a prince, buried alive...lost in the depths of hell.

35

Liandra

The stones of the castle gave up their bloodstains easier than the souls of men. The corpses were removed in cartloads, the loyalists sent to heroes' graves and the traitors to a mass pyre. The pyre burned for days, creating a grim pall that hung over the city, a stain against the summer sky, a stain against honor and duty, a stain that marred the soul of Lanverness.

An army of servants labored to restore the great castle, scrubbing floors, repairing the tower doors, re-hanging the tapestries. Gold and hard work restored the luster of the Rose Court, but the castle was the least of Liandra's worries. The Spider Queen had debts of loyalty and treason to settle, debts she intended to pay in full measure.

A knock sounded on the door to her solar. The queen waved her hand and a page leaped to answer. Her two most loyal advisors entered, the Master Archivist in his severe robes of black, and her royal son, Crown Prince Stewart, in the emerald tabard of an officer, a short sword belted to his side.

The queen's breath caught at the sight of her son's face, still startled by the brutal change. An angry, red scar sliced from his hairline to his jaw, just missing his left eye...a grim reminder of how close she'd come to losing her first-born son...her only heir.

The queen welcomed her two loyal men and then dismissed the servants, gaining a prudent privacy. "Be seated, we have much to discuss."

The prince sat in a chair on the far side of the chess table, his long legs sprawled across the carpet, while the Master Archivist stood rigid in front of the cold fireplace, his arms behind his back.

The rebellion had changed them both. She supposed it had changed them all. Her royal son had become a man, marked by the scars of war, a blooded warrior. The queen mourned the ruin of his handsome face but she'd also seen the way the veteran soldiers revered her royal son, praising his prowess in battle. Liandra supposed the soldiers saw the scar as a mark of valor...a valuable asset for a future king...especially since men so often rule by the sword.

The Master Archivist, on the other hand, stood as a pillar of shadow in the sun drenched room. Always lean, the rebellion had stripped the veneer from the man, revealing the steel beneath the intellect. His hawkish face seemed more chiseled, his dark gaze more penetrating, his presence more virile. Before the rebellion, her master of shadows had been a cloaked dagger, poised to strike from the shadows, but now he was a sword unsheathed, a naked threat...but still loyal to her hand. She studied his face, wondering at the thoughts beneath. So much had changed, so many debts to be paid.

The queen fingered the strand of Royal Rubies at her neck, the cold stones dark like drops of frozen blood. "The castle has been set to order. It is time to do the same with the traitors." She turned toward her son. "But first we would hear a report on the status of the army." She narrowed her gaze. "If nothing else, we have learned the value of a strong sword."

The prince nodded. "The rebellion has cost us dear. Nearly a thousand men died in the uprising, roughly a third of the soldiers quartered in Pellanor, the pride of the army. And the problem is not just the loss of numbers. The officers have been decimated, most of them knifed as they slept, murdered by traitors who acted as assassins." The prince shook his head, his face grim. "The lower hallways of the Queen's Tower were choked with blood and severed limbs, bodies stacked like cord wood along the walls, a royal charnel house."

The prince's words evoked vivid memories of the bloody gore. The queen had insisted on inspecting the site of each battle before the servants began their work, needing to know the true price of her crown. The images stayed with her. She carried the weight of so much death, so much senseless slaughter. "The dead will be remembered, but now we need a strong sword to protect the living. We asked for a report on the status of the army."

The prince straightened in his chair. "We have two thousand swords fit and trained here in Pellanor, and another three thousand spread across the kingdom with the largest contingent barracked at Kardiff." He nodded toward the queen, his face solemn. "We wouldn't have half that many if you had not pardoned the lower ranking soldiers. That was well done, Mother."

She'd kept her royal word, holding the ceremony in the great yard of the castle, accepting oaths of fealty from each soldier before the blood could dry...knowing every sword would be needed for the trials ahead. But even with the pardon, the numbers were grim. "Not enough, not nearly enough."

"Especially with the threat from the north." The master's words held the weight of doom. "The refugees from Coronth have ground to a trickle, but Prince Justin still manages to get a few messages out. The Pontifax prepares for war. A tent city of soldiers has sprung up beyond the walls of Balor. The messages warn of more than twenty thousand swords."

"*Twenty thousand!*" The prince paled. "There hasn't been an army of that size since Igor the Cruel!" The prince looked to the master. "Does Justin know the intended prey?"

The queen rose from her chair and crossed the chamber to stand by the casement window. "Where else but Lanverness?" Her voice sounded weary. "The richest prize in the southern kingdoms." She looked toward the west, the black pillar of smoke from the funeral pyres still scarring the sky. "We've lit the beacon ourselves. The smell of carrion will attract predators from every quarter. It is only a matter of time." She turned from the window, her voice velvet steel. "We must rebuild the army. We must gain the swords required to protect our kingdom." She stared at her royal son. "We look to you, our heir, our warrior-son, to do this task."

If the prince was surprised, his face did not show it. The queen approved. Her son was learning. "General Helfner is too old for this challenge. We shall retire him with honors to a manse in the country. Henceforth, the crown prince shall lead the army of Lanverness. We shall make the proclamation at the victory feast."

The prince paled. "Your majesty, I have but one victory to my credit..."

"Two victories," the queen was quick to correct her son, "the ambush in the woods and the retaking of the Queen's Tower." Her voice became pedantic. "You must learn the value of image. The soldiers hail you as a natural born leader with a sixth sense for battle. You must embrace this image and use it to strengthen your men. Confidence in leadership is critical to victory...on the battlefield or the audience chamber."

The prince gave her a look of wry amazement.

The queen gave her son a calculated laugh. "Never a soldier, yet we've waged many a battle. The strategies are often the same, whether one fights with wits, or gold...or swords."

"I look forward to learning from a master."

She detected no irony in his voice. Her eldest child had always been a stalwart supporter.

His face sobered. "But you've set me a daunting task. Twenty thousand swords!"

"Start with the constable force."

"They're not soldiers."

"Then make them soldiers." Her unrelenting stare drilled into her son. "Over three thousand men, trained to the sword and loyal to the crown. They serve as individuals instead of a unit, using wits before steel. They know the countryside and the people." Her voice deepened. "Take them and make them your own. Mix them with veterans and form them into a fighting unit."

"Yes, it could be done."

"And we'll offer a signing bonus to new recruits, enough to draw young men from farms and shops." The queen began to pace, her thoughts racing. "We'll use the bards to rouse the country folk to arms, commissioning songs about the prince who won the battle for the Queen's Tower." Her son flushed bright red but the queen persisted. "The very soul of Lanverness has been damaged by the rebellion, a bloody stain against honor and duty. The stain must be expunged. Heroism offers the best tonic." She stared at her son, her voice a command. "We will use every advantage available to us."

The prince gave a grim nod but a storm of argument lay behind his eyes.

The queen claimed the victory and pressed on. "We must have new tabards for the men...and bright battle banners steeped in pride. Our soldiers must look and think like an army greater than the sum of their numbers."

The prince's voice held caution. "It will cost money and take time."

"Gold we have, time we have not."

"What about allies? Or are we left to our own resources?"

"A good question." She gave him a smile of approval. "King Ivor of Navarre is a staunch ally but his army numbers no more than two thousand, most of them archers."

"And Navarre shares a border with Coronth."

The queen nodded. "Just so. Navarre is a trusted ally but they may not have soldiers to spare."

"There is another option." The master's voice cut through the discussion.

The queen stopped her pacing and studied her shadowmaster.

"The mercenaries of Radagar."

"No!" The prince bolted from his chair, his hand on his sword. "It was mercenaries we faced in the woods on that moonless night. Garbed in red, they were thinly disguised as soldiers of the Flame...but they bore the curved swords of the mercenary kingdom. They broke and ran once the victory became apparent." Anger flashed across his face. "Swords bought by gold can never be trusted."

The master's voice carried a thread of calm. "I seldom advise trust, my prince, but bought swords can have their uses. They might provide the quickest way to even the numbers."

The prince looked to the queen. "Majesty, as the general of your army I must advise against it. Let loyal swords defend Lanverness, not bought dogs."

She liked the way her son assumed the mantle of command, but she waited, sensing the argument was not done. The Master Archivist did not disappoint. "Majesty, there is another consideration."

She gestured for him to continue.

"Radagar boasts ten thousand trained swords...if Lanverness does not hire them, who else might?"

The prince countered. "Who else but the Rose Court can afford to hire the ten thousand?"

The master's voice held an edge. "Not all contracts are paid in gold. Mercenaries often fight for a share of the spoils...and Lanverness is rich with plunder."

The queen's voice turned grim. "And so our prosperity becomes our undoing." Both men stared at her waiting for a decision. She resumed her seat, fingering the strand of rubies at her throat. "You have given us much to think about. Let us first see how many swords we can raise within Lanverness before we look to mercenaries. We will consider your arguments...but for now, other decisions must be made."

Neither man looked satisfied but they both nodded, waiting on their monarch.

The queen steered the discussion to the next problem. "The army is the first priority...dealing with the traitors is the second. The dungeons burst with officers, lordlings, and noblemen, traitors all. A public example must be made. The price for treason must be visible and it must be high...but the question is how?"

The Master Archivist shrugged. "The penalty for treason has long been established. Traitors are drawn and quartered in public view, the worst of deaths. Hung by the neck until nearly dead, the body is then stretched on the rack before being dismembered. The beating heart is the last to leave the body, followed by beheading. The remains are then burnt, so that nothing is left to contaminate the soil of Lanverness."

The queen shuddered. "A barbaric death."

The master inclined his head. "A death by torture. Reserved for traitors, it is deliberately designed to deter further acts of treason." The master fingered his thin gray mustache. "And since there has been no treason in over three generations of Tandroths, one might argue the effectiveness of the deterrent." The master stared at the queen, suspicion on his face. "Surely, the Lord Turner merits a traitor's end?"

"Merits it, yes, of that there is no doubt...but one wonders how such an execution will reflect on Lanverness? What type of stain will it leave on the kingdom?" The queen looked at her two advisors. "We have built our reign on the justice of reason and the prosperity of gold, eschewing the might of swords. We have sought to be civilized in a world that is often brutal and cruel. If we choose this form of execution, do we not then begin the slide towards barbarism?" Her voice rang with conviction. "We guide this kingdom, and we would never willing steer Lanverness toward cruelty and barbarism."

The prince protested. "But majesty, the loyal soldiers who fought for you expect to see justice. They expect the traitors to be punished."

The queen nodded. "Justice they shall have, in full measure. The punishment will fit the crime...but let us not descend to such depths." She looked to the master. "What other forms of death are proscribed for traitors?"

"The chronicles tell of two other forms of execution which predate the practice of drawing and quartering. The most common of these is burning at the stake, said to be an excruciating way to die."

The queen frowned. "Lanverness shall never emulate the horrors of Coronth. We would hear the other method."

"The other is more rare, originally designed to execute priests and royals so that no drop of blood is shed. In this method, the traitor is boiled alive."

A grim silence settled over the chamber.

The queen rose from her chair and walked to the window, needing to feel the warmth of the afternoon sun. "And there is no other way? No other choice?"

"For lesser crimes, nobles are executed by beheading, but this is said to be a relatively painless death. Commoners are executed by hanging; an insult to a nobleman but such a sentence would seem light for the crime of treason. The people expect a grisly spectacle, something more than a mere hanging." The master's voice softened, carrying a note of concern. "Majesty, I understand the importance of image, and your desire to avoid barbaric acts, but you cannot be seen as lenient. The crown must be strong and decisive. The punishment must be dire, befitting the crime."

She turned towards the window and stared at the summer sky, a perfect blue vault scarred by the pillar of black smoke. The sky needed to be cleansed, the kingdom set to rights. "The traitors need to be punished and justice served." Making her decision, she turned to face her two advisors, her back sword-straight, her voice as hard as duty. "By royal decree, the traitors will be stripped to loincloths and paraded in chains through every street and alleyway of Pellanor. Let the people see how low the traitors have fallen. After the parade, the lesser traitors will be hung by the neck until dead. The Lord Turner will be the last to die. After witnessing the death of his supporters, he will be boiled alive. Their bodies will be thrown on the pyre and burnt rather than poison the soil of Lanverness." She looked to the Master Archivist. "We charge you to arrange the proceedings. We want the executions accomplished within four days."

The master bowed, a grim set to his mouth.

The queen stood tense, waiting for the storm to come.

The master cleared his throat. "Majesty, there is one other traitor to be dealt with."

Liandra raised a finger in warning. "We know of whom you speak. We have not forgotten the traitor-prince."

"Majesty, even in the depths of the dungeons, Danly is a threat." The master's voice became insistent. "The soldiers of the rebellion, the ones whose oath you took in the castle yard, they know of Danly's involvement. It is only a matter of time till the people know as well."

She willed herself to stone.

"Justice will not be complete until Danly pays for his treason." The master's voice dropped to a harsh whisper. "Majesty, you cannot forget or forgive the way he behaved in the audience chamber!"

"We have not forgotten." Her words struck like a whip. "We know our duty...but he is still our son." She fought to keep her voice level. "Death is very final." She looked toward her first child, her soldier-son, her heir. "What say you?"

The prince met her gaze, his face solemn. "The Master Archivist speaks the truth; the soldiers know. Danly is a traitor to the throne and must pay for his crimes." He shook his head. "But boiled alive..."

The master interposed. "For the prince, beheading would be sufficient."

She gave the master a cold stare. She'd heard all the reasons, all the logic, but she was not yet ready to make the decision. Sentencing her own son to death seemed monstrous...despite the foulness of his deeds. Liandra shook her head, her voice firm. "Danly will remain in the depths of the dungeon." She gave her shadowmaster a commanding stare. "Proceed with the other executions and leave the traitor-prince in chains."

The master shook his head in warning, a thunderstorm behind his dark eyes.

The queen knew she'd only delayed the argument...but for now that was enough.

Liandra crossed the chamber and resumed her seat, artfully arranging the folds of her gown, wishing her problems could be smoothed as easily as silk. Forcing her voice to calm, she turned to the next issue. "Punishment accounts for only half of the debts owed. We also have loyalty to repay, a happier duty. The crown will not stint when it comes to recognizing loyalty. Even those who serve in the great kitchen and kept our secret will be rewarded." She paused, considering the cost. "But we need not beggar the treasury. Titles, lands, and holdings will be stripped from the traitors and distributed to those who are worthy." She fingered the rubies at her throat. "We want the names of soldiers who served bravely and the names of citizens who rushed to our defense."

The prince nodded and the master said, "It will be done."

"We intend to host a great victory feast, open to all the people of Pellanor. An abundance of wine and roast ox and suckling pig, something the people will talk about long after the traitors are forgotten."

The master nodded. "As you wish. But there is other news worthy of consideration. A contingent of Octagon Knights has arrived in the city, requesting an audience with the queen. The smiths of Castlegard have completed their commission."

"Ah, the blue steel swords." The queen sat back in her chair. It seemed another lifetime when she'd ordered the blue blades.

Prince Stewart leaned forward, his face blazing with interest. "Blue steel blades will help us rally recruits for the army. The blades could not have come at a better time."

Even her royal son was not immune to the hero's spell of blue steel. "We will award the blades at the victory celebration. The people need signs of hope to banish the evil of the rebellion." She turned to the Master Archivist. "Arrange a meeting with the knights. We look forward to receiving the blades."

The master nodded.

"And now we each have tasks of great import which need attending." She held her ringed hand out, ending the meeting. Both men bowed and kissed her ring of office before taking their leave.

When the two men reached the door, the queen said, "Lord Highgate, we would speak with you for a moment."

The Master Archivist closed the door and returned to stand before the queen.

She made him wait, studying him through hooded eyes. He stood tall and straight, his arms behind his back, his face carefully neutral but his dark eyes burned with a fierce intelligence, and beneath the intelligence, a deep wanting. There had always been a tension between them but before the rebellion it had remained subtle, manageable, teasingly enjoyable, always proper...but now the tension had grown to a bonfire. She felt its heat and feared its ruin. She chose her words carefully. "Lord Highgate, you have always been our ablest advisor, our wisest counselor, our most trusted confidante...but during the rebellion you came to mean even more to us."

"You will always have my sword, majesty." The tension in the chamber thickened.

"In the days to come, we shall reward loyalty with blue steel swords, with promotions and titles, with land grants and manses, and with purses of gold. Yet, our ablest advisor asks for nothing. How shall a grateful queen reward you, Lord Highgate?"

The mask of neutrality fell away, revealing the steel, the intellect, and the raw passion hidden beneath. "Once an eagle has flown free it can never again be trained to hunt from the fist. I have served other masters, and in serving those others my wings have always been clipped because the one who held my tether had limited intelligence, limited vision, and no taste for daring." His voice deepened to a rough husk. "But under this queen, whose intelligence and daring exceeds my own, I soar!" He dropped to his knee. "Madam, I will never serve any other prince. To be held in your confidence, to serve as your shadowmaster, is all the reward I shall ever need."

His words said one thing but his dark gaze seared her.

Heat flashed through her. She gripped the arms of the chair, seeking a safe anchor.

He reached for her ringed hand. Lightning leaped between them.

She sat statue-still, struggling for control, struggling to be solely the queen. "You must understand," her voice betrayed too much. "We will never again accept the yoke of marriage. And we will never put off our crown, never be less than queen." Her voice dropped to a husky whisper. "And the queen must always be proper."

He cupped her hand, kissing the hollow of her palm, tender and ardent.

The kiss shivered through her, threatening her control.

He closed her hand into a fist, as if to hold the kiss tight, and then backed away and stood, placing a wall of distance between them. His face closed but his voice was a rough whisper. "Given the choice between the queen or the woman, I will always choose the queen...for only the queen allows me to soar, and having known the joys of flight, I will never be tethered." His dark gaze burned. "But if the queen ever wishes to be a woman, even for a single night, I would be there for her."

His words sizzled in her mind, the perfect answer, the perfect temptation. He understood her so well...even choosing the queen over the woman...but it could not be.

He saluted, his fist to his heart, his face once more the neutral mask of her shadowmaster. "If your majesty has no further need of me, there is much to be done."

She waved him away, not trusting her voice. The door closed and she was once more alone. *So alone.*

She sat in the chair long after he was gone, feeling the weight of her crown, fighting against her own desires. She'd long ago buried the needs of the woman beneath the imperatives of the crown...but those needs were still there, clamoring for a taste of life. She reached for the steel within her soul. The needs of her kingdom must always come first.

Having regained a measure of calm, she rose and went to the window, drawn to the view of her kingdom, the splendor of the castle, the sprawling city, and the green fields beyond. Except for the pyre of smoke, it looked peaceful enough, sunlight glinting off of stone and field...but a storm was coming, something terrible and sure, a darkness on the horizon. She'd worked hard to bring peace and prosperity to Lanverness...but now she must use her wiles and her golds to forge swords. She shook her head. It always came back to war, the eternal struggle of plunder over production, of the Dark over the Light. But perhaps she'd outfoxed fate when she'd ordered three blue steel swords. The kingdom of Lanverness would soon have need of heroes...heroes to push back the threat of Darkness. Liandra hoped three blue blades would be enough.

36

Duncan

Duncan strode through the sacred grove, past the domed tents and green-robed attendants, his mind fastened on a single goal, an arrow seeking a single heart. Hope warred with doubt as he climbed the trail to the high meadow. She was a princess, he was a half-breed bastard, it could never work, yet he found himself lengthening his stride. He rushed to see Kath, ignoring his doubts. He'd had many lovers but only one love. This new chance had taken him by surprise.

The path wound upward, through cedars and spruce and pine, the trail familiar despite his long years away. Slanting beams of afternoon sunlight filtered through the canopy releasing the rich musk of cedar and the sharp scent of pine, the smells of summer in the deep forest. Sunlight played across the leaves, creating a thousand shades of green...but for once, he saw none of it. He walked with both eyes open, the white and the golden, but his gaze was turned inward, wrestling with a thousand questions and a single hope.

The trail crested and he rounded a bend...and found Kath in the heart of a sun-warmed meadow. She sat on a fallen log in a sea of knee-high wildflowers, the last rays of sunlight gilding her hair to a silken glow. He paused in the shadows, watching her face, searching for answers. She sat sharpening her sword, the steady scrape of stone against steel, her face deep in thought. The sword was a part of her, like the talon of an eagle. And the thoughtful look on her face was achingly familiar, reflecting a soul deeper than her years...but he wondered if she would spurn him now that she knew the truth.

Bracing for scorn, he deliberately stepped on a twig. The crack sounded loud to his ears.

Her sea green eyes snapped to his face, meeting his mismatched stare without flinching. *"Duncan!"* She leaped from the log and ran towards him.

Elation swept through him. Racing towards her, he scooped her into his arms, and kissed her, long and deep.

Her arms wrapped around him, hungry with need. "I thought I'd lost you."

He kissed her back. "You'll never lose me." He laid her in the meadow, on the sun-warmed grass, wildflowers tangling in her hair. One kiss led to another. She melted into him. He held her close, feeling the beat of her heart. His hands caressed her, memorizing every touch, the softness of her cheek, the silkiness of her hair, the tenderness of her lips. She moaned with pleasure and he deepened his kiss. His hand found the gentle curve of her breast.

She stiffened beneath him. "I've never..."

"I know." He caressed her face. "There's no need to rush. We have all the time between us." He kissed her again, taking care to keep the bulge in his leathers well away from the press of her body. His restraint only made him harder, but he refused to give in. Kath quivered beneath his caress, tentative at first, but then his fingers roused her passion, till he felt his own heat reflected in her. She moaned beneath his touch, her back arching. Lithe and graceful, she molded herself to him, leather against leather, heat to heat. Her flaring passion excited him. *"Duncan,"* she moaned his name. He covered her mouth with a kiss.

#

Later, much later, they lay in the wildflowers, watching the sun set on the forest. Duncan leaned on an elbow and stared down at her. Her clothing was rumpled, her face flushed, her hair tousled, a wildflower tangled in the golden strands. He longed to stay in the haze of pleasure but the words needed to be said. "There's a chasm of differences between us." He stared at her, looking for rejection but her leaf-green gaze never wavered. "You've seen the reaction of my kin." His voice dropped to a harsh whisper. "I am bastard-born, a half-breed, a child of rape, despised by both peoples."

"Yet noble enough to stand alone on a ridge and buy the lives of your companions."

"A bastard's life is not that dear."

Her green eyes deepened. "It is to me."

He shook his head in disbelief.

Her voice never wavered. "I see you, Duncan Treloch. I see a man who risks his life for his companions. I see a man who would not abandon the wolf to die. I see strength, and courage, and purpose." Her voice dropped to a hushed whisper. "I look at you and I see the man of my dreams."

Hope burned within him, yet he kept his voice hard. "You are royal-born." He shook his head. "A bastard half-breed and a royal princess, it cannot be."

She looked up at him, her green eyes wide with honesty. "I was born to the sword."

He waited for the meaning beneath her words.

"My mother died birthing me. I never knew her touch, never knew her voice. I soon learned that there was no place in Castlegard for a girl. Growing up in the shadow of swords, I was nearly invisible, always yearning for a blade but never allowed to hold one." She reached through the wildflowers till her hand found her sword. Sunlight glinted along the edge. "My father is the king of Castlegard, the king of swords...yet he never granted me a blade. He never saw me."

Her voice reflected the loneliness of her choice... and the mountain of prejudice set against her. He shook his head at the king's folly. Better to take the claws from a lioness. "You were meant to hold a sword." His voice betrayed more than he intended.

"And holding a sword, I do not belong." She stared at him as if trying to see into his very soul. "Except, perhaps, with you..."

A shiver passed through him, but he held himself rigid, tight behind his walls. "I am a half-breed bastard without a home."

"A cat-eyed archer saved my life."

She ambushed him with surprises. "When?"

"In a meadow, in the wilds of Wyeth, before I met you." A strand of golden hair fell across her face. She brushed it back behind her ear. "He told me that among the Children of the Green, women are free to choose their own path in life, to choose the bow...or the sword...or even to lead."

Duncan nodded

"Do you know how much that choice would mean to me?" She leaned toward him, her green eyes ablaze with light. "Don't you see? To me, your heritage is a boon not a burden!"

His walls crumbled. Only once before had a woman accepted the whole of him, the white eye and the golden.

She smiled, her eyes bright with promise. "I felt it the first time I saw you, that early morning on the rampart of Castle Tandroth. I did not even know your name, or anything about you, yet I knew."

He held her close, needing to make the words real. "What would you have of me?"

"Everything."

The single word shivered through him, leaving a blaze of heat, but Duncan refused to give in. "Your father will never approve."

Kath sighed. "No, he will never approve." She sat up and plucked the wildflower from her hair, tugging at the petals. "I've always disappointed him. He never approved of the sword...and he will never approve you." She stilled, her gaze drinking him in. "Perhaps like the sword, I should make my own choice?"

He saw determination in her face...and just a touch of fear. She was brave, and lovely...and young.

She looked away. "But there are other obstacles."

"What?"

"Duty." Her green eyes pleaded for understanding. "On the ridge, when I thought I'd lost you, I rode away in a blind fury. I forgot about my companions...I forgot about duty...I fled without thinking..." her voice faded to a hush, "I can't lose you again."

He waited, sensing there was more.

"Yet I have sworn to slay the Mordant."

He nodded. "So have we all. We take a warrior's risk, and in return, are given a chance to make a difference, a chance to defeat a great evil. Isn't that what you want?"

Steel returned to her voice, "Yes."

He smiled and whispered, "My Lioness!" He did not want to lose this second chance, this chance to be whole. Taking a deep breath, he made a decision for them both. "The gods made us to be warriors, you with the sword and me with the bow."

She nodded, her face solemn.

He made his voice certain. "Then we'll chase the Mordant north, as warriors, as comrades in arms...and when the task is done, we will have each other."

A glint of doubt remained in her eyes.

He thought he understood. "You needn't fear for me."

She whispered, "How can I not?"

He gave her a wry smile. "Because a cat has nine lives...and after the ridge I've at least eight left!"

She smiled then, a smile to rival the sun. "I'll hold you to that!" Her gaze flicked to the twilight sky. "The others will be wondering." Her smile turned shy. "I'd rather stay."

"But duty calls?" They reclaimed their weapons, sword and axes, dagger and bow. For a moment it seemed as if the world came between them. But then he offered her his hand. "Walk with me?" Her hand slipped into his, their fingers entwining, a perfect fit.

37

Samson

Samson huddled in the alleyway, crouched next to Justin, one of seven men daring the risk. They hid in the dark, cloaks covering swords, faces darkened by lampblack, lying in wait for a chance to save a sinner.

A keening wail cut through the darkness, clawing at nerves already frayed.

Samson held his breath, straining to listen past the sinner's lament. The cobblestone street seemed sleepy enough but somewhere out there soldiers lurked, ready to pounce, a game of cat and mouse. Samson hated being the mouse. He gripped his sword for courage, feeling that his luck was running thin. He'd tried to talk the bard into laying low for a few days but Justin refused, arguing that words alone would never be enough. The bard needed daring deeds to shake the people out of their religious torpor, and so the raids continued...and each raid the risks got worse.

This time there were seven men: a bard, a refugee, an ex-drill sergeant, three men rescued from the stocks and one swayed by songs, a ragged handful of idealists pitted against the soldiers of the Flame. Samson shook his head in despair. They didn't have the numbers for a fair fight, so they relied on tricks and sleight-of-hand. Problem was, each ruse only worked once...and Samson knew the bard's bag of tricks was running low. They'd lost three men on the last raid, three lives lost to free one man. Freedom wasn't cheap. Samson tightened his grip on his sword, wondering when it would be his turn to pay the price.

A tow-haired boy emerged from the shadows, tall and skinny, all arms and legs, one of the orphan boys. Willie had a knack for climbing, using the rooftops like the other orphans used the alleyways. He nodded to Samson but his gaze sought Justin, hero-worship written across his freckled face. "You were right, Harper." Admiration filled the boy's hushed voice. "They put a sentry up on the roof this time, but I found him."

"Just one?"

The boy nodded. "Just one, Harper, easy to see the red even in the dark."

"What about the rest of the soldiers?"

"There's a troop of thirty over on Cobb Street, reckon they'll come from the west once the hammers start."

Samson shuddered, seven against thirty; he prayed the bard had the good sense to retreat but he wasn't hopeful.

"Good work, Willie." Justin turned to the men crouched behind. "Ben?"

The ex-drill sergeant stepped forward and crouched at Justin's side. He moved like a stalking cat, his hand on his sword, his gaze sharp. Samson envied the big man his confidence, wishing he felt like a predator instead of prey.

The bard kept his voice to a whisper. "Willie's found a sentry on the roof."

Ben nodded. "I'll take care of him."

Justin gripped Ben's arm. "Be careful, my friend, and return when you're done. We'll need your sword."

"I'll be quick about it, Harper. Just be ready for my signal." Ben turned to the boy. "Lead the way, Willie." Man and boy melted into the shadows.

A sick feeling settled in Samson's stomach; the bard would take the risk despite the grim odds.

Justin turned and faced him. "Samson?"

He nodded a wordless reply, his mouth suddenly dry.

The bard must have sensed his unease, placing a steadying hand on Samson's shoulder. "We'll need our secret weapon." He prodded the bulging leather sack at Samson's feet. "Willie says the soldiers will come from the west. For the surprise to work, the soldiers will need to see us. Set the cord in front of the chandler's shop. Blanket the street with our surprise and then join us at the wagon." Justin gripped his arm. "But wait for Ben's signal."

They waited, crouched in the stink of the alleyway. Samson's heartbeat measured the moments, loud in his ears. He clung to thoughts of Lucy, remembering the light in her eyes when she named him a hero. The memory gave him courage. He clung to it like a talisman against the grim odds.

The waiting seemed forever. A faint blush of color painted the eastern sky, a warning of the coming dawn. Samson shuddered, wondering if Ben had failed.

The harsh caw of a raven filled the street.

Justin stood, his hand on his sword. "Ben's taken the sentry! Now be quick about it, each to his task, and we'll free the sinner before the soldiers know we're here."

The others followed the bard into the street, running for the wagon, leaving Samson with the bulging leather sack. Wary of the iron spikes, he hefted the sack away from his body, running with a swaying lope. His arms ached with strain by the time he reached the chandler's shop. He dropped the bag, the clink of iron muffled by leather. Removing a hammer and two iron spikes, he knelt, searching for a place to set the spike. The baseboard of the timber-framed shop was perfect. He placed the spike low to the ground and held the hammer poised, sweat dripping from his forehead. Samson hesitated, his stomach clenched with fear. Killing the sentry bought them time but the sound of hammers would bring the soldiers running. Samson shook his head and swore; he had no choice. He swung the hammer, putting the weight of fear into the blow. A single blow set the spike. Looping a braided cord around the spike, he played the line out to the far side of the street. Setting the second spike, he pulled the trip cord taut.

The frantic beat of hammers echoed down the street. The others worked on the locks, desperate to free the sinner. The sound was enough to wake the dead...yet the doors and shutters remained shut. The faithful hid rather than know the truth, another reason to hate this god-cursed city.

Knowing time was against him, Samson hurried to finish the trap, spreading the caltrops across the street. The wicked, four-pronged spikes were usually used to stop horses but the bard reckoned they'd skewer flesh even easier than hooves...assuming the soldiers did not see the trip cord. Samson emptied the bag and then ran to join Justin and the others at the wagon.

The street rang with a desperate beat, four men hammering at four locks. The bard worked to calm the sinner, his voice a soothing balm beneath the frantic hammers. The sinner, an old man with a shock of white hair, strained against the chains, his eyes wild and wide.

Samson yelled, "What can I do?"

Justin pointed to a timber-framed shop. "The man says his wife is in the apothecary. Get the old woman out and away."

Samson swallowed, not liking the order, but he moved to obey.

A faded wooden sign showed a mortar and pestle. The door beneath it gaped open like the mouth of a dead fish. Samson hesitated, peering inside. The wood-beamed ceiling was low, the timbers hung with drying herbs, but he saw no signs of life. Unsheathing his sword, he entered. The scents of sage, juniper, and basil mingled with the smells of liniments and lotions. Tall shelves full of stoppered ceramic jars marked with runes lined the walls, neat and orderly, but the rest of the room was in shambles. A table was overturned, a chair smashed to kindling. A mortar and pestle lay shattered on the floor, a spill of green powder marked by footprints, a trail of chaos in a room dominated by order.

Against his better judgment, Samson moved deeper into the shop. He would have called to the old woman but a sixth sense warned him to keep quiet. Hanging herbs brushed against the back of his neck, skeletal hands grasping at life. Samson stifled a shout and ducked low, his heart racing. He reached the far doorway and peered into the inner room, a small kitchen with steep stairs leading up. Glowing embers in the hearth gave the room a dim red light. A gray-haired old woman sat slumped in a rocking chair, a bright-colored shawl wrapped around her shoulders. There was something odd about the woman, something not quite right.

Samson moved past the stairs and crossed in front of the hearth, throwing a shadow across the woman's face.

The woman did not stir.

Anxious to be gone, he shook her shoulder.

Her head toppled sideways, severed to the spine, a bloody gape of red beneath the shawl.

"*Samson, it's a trap!*" The bard's warning echoed in the small room.

Footsteps clattered down the stairs, a flash of red.

Samson whirled to see Justin and Ben rush through the doorway, swords drawn. They stopped the soldiers at the base of the stairs, a ferocious clash of steel. Samson ran to join the fight but the stairway was only wide enough for one. The narrowness kept the soldiers confined, a bottleneck limiting the odds. If they lost the stairs they'd be overwhelmed.

Ben took the brunt of the fight, pushing up the stairs, his sword dancing in the dim light. Soldiers clogged the stairway, stumbling over the dead, but it was only a matter of time. Justin fought behind Ben, thrusting his sword at the soldiers' legs. The bard hissed, "We need an advantage! Something to tip the odds."

Samson's stare raced around the kitchen but he found nothing to help...just kitchen implements and crockery and a dead woman.

The bard shouted, "The embers from the fire! Use the shovel to cast them up the stairs!"

Samson sheathed his sword and ran to the fireplace. He grabbed the hearth shovel and scooped up the embers. Returning to the stairs, he used the shovel like the arm of a catapult, heaving the embers over Ben's head and into the soldiers above.

Screams echoed down the stairs.

Ben took advantage of the chaos, lunging up with his sword, spattering the walls with blood.

Samson reloaded the shovel, launching the glowing coals into the soldiers. A spark fell short, landing in his hair. He beat it out and went for a third load of embers.

Fire leaped up the stairwell, tongues of orange and yellow licking at the walls. Smoke billowed across the ceiling. The soldiers shrieked and retreated, the smell of burnt flesh tainting the air.

Justin yelled, "Back to the street!"

Samson hurled the shovel into the inferno and then raced for the door. He stumbled out into the crisp, clean air...and the eerie quiet of the street. The hammers had stopped and so had the wailing. The chains of the stocks hung empty. A pair of rebels held the old man upright, his nightshirt soiled and stained, his face dazed.

A piercing whistle echoed from the rooftops, a warning from the orphan lookout.

Justin yelled, "Into the alleys, the soldiers are coming!"

Samson ran for the nearest alley, fear giving wings to his feet.

The tramp of boots came from the west, a wall of soldiers marching with swords drawn. An officer shouted a command and the line of red charged, yells hurtling down the street.

Samson ducked into the nearest alleyway. Skidding on something slick, he fell hard, slamming his knee into the cobblestones. Ignoring the pain, he struggled to stand, listening for the tramp of boots.

Out in the street, the roar of the charge changed to shrieks of pain.

Samson risked a glance. Soldiers writhed across the cobblestones, a clog of red impaled on the caltrops.

Relief washed through Samson, he'd have his chance to escape. Hobbling into the depths of the alleyways, he forced himself to hurry despite his throbbing knee. Always listening for footsteps from behind, he sought his own hiding place. The ramshackle house leaned like a rum-soaked drunk. Abandoned long ago, the house had an ominous air, the doors and windows nailed shut, but Samson knew it was more solid than it looked. He squeezed into the two-foot gap on the right side and began climbing the clapboard siding to the attic. Reaching for familiar handholds, he pulled himself through the topmost window and flopped onto the floor, trying to catch his breath. The attic seemed undisturbed. His small sack of supplies hung from a nail. The morning sunlight streamed through missing shingles, throwing a patchwork of light across the dusty floor.

Samson sprawled on the floor, his head propped against the wall. His breath came in ragged gasps, his knee ached and he stank of fear. He shuddered remembering how close he'd come to death. The apothecary was a trap, proving the soldiers had tricks of their own. If Ben and the bard hadn't followed he'd be dead...or worse, captured. A shiver raced down his spine. He'd never let the priests capture him, for their cruelty knew no bounds. The image of the old woman's severed neck haunted him. He owed the bard his life and his allegiance...but all he wanted to do was hide.

A rustling noise came from the far side of the attic.

Samson gripped his sword and held his breath.

Dark, beady eyes stared back at him...but it was only a rat. Laughter bubbled out of him, a hero hiding among the rats. The bard never put *that* in his songs. Irony gripped him and he laughed till he cried. The laughter brought a clarity that chilled Samson to the bone. Coronth was nothing but a trap...and they were all rats, waiting to be caught, waiting to be killed...it was only a matter of time.

38

Liandra

The herald pounded his iron-shod staff against the marble floor. "All hail her majesty, Queen Liandra, the White Rose, the sovereign queen of Lanverness!"

A path opened before her, a sea of loyal subjects bowing on either side. The queen glided between them, the heavy gold crown balanced on her brow, the jewel-encrusted scepter nestled in the crook of her arm. Shimmering in a cloth-of-gold gown, Liandra presented a vision of royal splendor. The tight-fitting bodice highlighted her petite figure while the dagged sleeves lined with emerald silk accentuated her every gesture. Crowned and bejeweled, the queen crossed the checkerboard floor, sealing victory with celebration.

Her subjects crowded close, eager for royal favors. Courtiers and nobles, soldiers and politicians, merchants and commoners, they shouldered together in the audience hall, bedecked in their best finery. The queen offered a smile and a wave as she passed, greeting more than a few by name.

She reached the dais and took her seat upon the Rose Throne, surveying the chamber. Sunlight flooded the diamond-paned windows sending fractured rainbows dancing across the court, painting a vision of promise and optimism. Her kingdom was meant for sunshine and prosperity. Liandra vowed to find a way to hold back the darkness.

She gestured and a hush settled over the crowd. "We have called you here to laud your loyalty. We hold the Rose Throne by the grace of the Lords of Light and by the loyalty and love of our people. Join us in celebrating our victory!"

A cheer roared through the crowd. "The queen! The queen!"

She smiled, acknowledging her people, basking in the warmth of their affection.

When the cheering subsided, the ceremony began. Over two hundred loyalists were called forward, the queen binding each one with gifts of gratitude. Titles and offices were bestowed along with land grants, manses, and purses of gold. Honors were granted to commoners and noblemen, to servants and soldiers, to lords and ladies. No service of loyalty was too small. The queen even remembered those who worked in the Great Kitchen, granting purses of gold to those who kept the queen's secret.

The greatest number of honors went to the army. Corporals were promoted to sergeants and sergeants to captains, each by the queen's own hand. Those who had shown extraordinary valor were raised to the title of knight. Forty-three knights were raised in one afternoon, each one receiving a newly forged sword from the hands of their queen.

Even a few commoners were raised to the rank of lords. Chief among them was the honest goldsmith, Willard Saddler. Short and rotund, the goldsmith blushed mightily as the queen settled the chain of office around his neck. With a single gesture, she raised an artisan and a guild master to the rank of lord, fulfilling a commoner's dream and a nobleman's nightmare. "By your actions, you prove that one honest man can make a great difference." If only her noble-born counselors had proven half as loyal. "Arise, Lord Saddler, and serve us well, our new master of the coin."

Beaming a broad smile, he turned to face the assembly. A restrained applause greeted the newly made lord, a subtle objection to an artisan joining the nobility.

The queen chose to ignore the snub, valuing honesty and loyalty above all else.

If the newly-made lord noticed the dampened reaction, his face did not show it. He took his place on the side of the hall with her other counselors, staring in wonder at the heavy gold chain.

Next to be called was Princess Jemma of Navarre. A petite vision of loveliness in a tight-fitting gown of scarlet accented with gold, the princess glided down the aisle to avid murmurs of appreciation. The Rose Court had an eye for beauty.

The young woman knelt before the throne, grace in every movement.

"Not of our realm, yet you are like a daughter to us." The queen pitched her voice to carry. "Accept this broach as a token of our affection and thanks. Let all who see it know that Princess Jemma of Navarre holds our highest esteem." The queen pinned the jeweled broach above the young woman's right breast. The broach bore the coats of arms of Lanverness and Navarre, a design calculated to create welcome rumors.

A roar of applause filled the hall. The princess turned to acknowledge the crowd, a blush intensifying the beauty of her face.

The herald announced the next name. The honorees came forward to kneel before the queen. The afternoon light began to wane and the crowd grew restive, but the queen had saved the best for last. She gestured and the herald announced, "The throne acknowledges Prince Stewart, heir to the Rose Crown, general of the Army of Lanverness and the hero of the battles of Tandrin Woods and the Queen's Tower!"

The double doors opened and the prince strode into the audience chamber, his emerald cape flaring behind him. Resplendent in silvered chainmail, his dark hair cascading to his shoulders, the prince appeared as the very flower of knighthood.

The queen flushed with pride, at least her eldest son had grown true. Her gaze roved the crowd, studying the reaction of her people. A mixture of respect and hero-worship shone from the soldiers' faces, while the women blazed with longing, a fitting response to the heir to the throne. Only her counselors remained unaffected, a calculating look on most of their faces.

The prince reached the dais and knelt, the scar on his face adding gravity to his handsome good looks.

The queen stood, pitching her voice to carry. "Heroes are most needed when Darkness threatens. Prince Stewart's battle intuition saved his men at the ambush of Tandrin Woods, turning a possible rout into a decisive victory. He then pressed for speed, returning in time to defeat the rebels and liberate the Queen's Tower. Prince Stewart is a hero of Lanverness!"

Cheers cascaded through the chamber followed by a thunder of applause.

The queen gestured and a page approached carrying a large platter cloaked in emerald silk. The crowd stilled to a hush. The queen swept the silk away in a dramatic flourish. Using two hands, she lifted the four-foot long sword, sunlight glinting on the sapphire-blue blade.

Gasps rippled through the crowd. Cries of, "A hero's sword!" and "Blue steel!" echoed through the chamber.

The queen waited for the crowd to settle. "Lanverness has many heroes, but for the first time in our long history, a prince of the realm will wield a sword of blue steel! *A hero's sword for Lanverness!*" She lowered the sword, extending the hilt toward her son.

The crowd began to chant, *"Blue steel! Blue steel!"*

Prince Stewart glowed with pride as he accepted the sword. Grasping the hilt, he executed a flurry of crosscuts. The sapphire blade gleamed in the sunlight, a stunning display of deadly skill and martial beauty. The crowd watched, spellbound. Making a final slash with the sapphire blade, the prince raised the sword to the heavens. *"For the Queen and Lanverness!"*

The people echoed their prince, *"The Queen and Lanverness!"*

Accolades thundered through the chamber, a balm to heal the wounds of the rebellion. The queen basked in the applause, a thunder of loyalty and optimism, a force against the Dark.

When voices began to dim, the queen gestured for a second page. The lad bore a leather scabbard, stained emerald green and worked with golden roses. The queen belted the scabbard to her royal son's waist.

The prince sheathed the blue steel blade and then took his place to the right of the queen, one step below the throne.

The queen reclaimed the attention of the crowd. "We have one more man to honor, one more hero of Lanverness." Whispers of curiosity threaded through the crowd. "This man proved his loyalty by protecting the queen during the danger of the rebellion. The crown summons Captain Garth Durnheart, a soldier of Lanverness, to be raised to the rank of Knight Protector, the queen's champion and her captain of the queen's guards!"

The double doors opened and the captain strode into the chamber, tall and dark-haired, handsome in the emerald tabard of Lanverness, the twin roses emblazoned on his chest. He approached the throne and knelt before the queen.

The queen accepted the jeweled sword of state from a page. She held the sword aloft, her voice solemn. "Captain Durnheart, do you swear before the Lords of Light to protect the queen, your sovereign, with your very life, and to put the monarch's safety above all else?"

"I do so swear!"

She dubbed him on the left shoulder and then the right. "We anoint you a knight of the realm and name you Knight Protector." She handed the ceremonial sword to the page. "Arise, Sir Durnheart!"

Polite applause greeted the newly made knight.

The queen gestured and two pages approached bearing an immense serving tray draped in emerald silk. Large enough to hold a roasted boar, the massive tray spurred whispers through the crowd.

Her voice rose to fill the hall. "The queen's champion must have a sword worthy of the realm." She swept the cloth away. "Sir Durnheart, take up your sword and serve the realm well!"

The knight lifted the great blade from the tray.

Gasps of awe echoed through the chamber.

The two-handed great sword was five feet of sapphire-blue steel, the hilt worked in the shape of crossed roses. Light rippled along the length of the blade, a gleaming weapon of beauty and death, a hero's sword to inspire courage and fear. The knight raised the sword high into the air, the double-edged blade straight and true.

The crowd roared its approval.

The queen smiled; the mystique of blue steel served to unite her people, restoring courage and conviction eroded by the rebellion. Liandra judged the benefit to be well worth the price.

Sir Durnheart sheathed the great blue sword in a shoulder harness, the sapphire hilt rising above his right shoulder, visible to all. He descended to the base of the dais and stood to attention, taking up his post as the protector of the queen.

The queen raised her hands, gathering the people's attention. Two squires came forth with a long cape of black velvet. They settled the cape across the queen's shoulders, eclipsing the reflected light of her golden gown. Liandra stood straight and firm, her face solemn, transforming herself from the Queen of Gratitude to the Queen of Vengeance. She stared at her people, filling her voice with steel. "You have witnessed the gratitude of your queen. Now witness our royal wrath. Loyalty and treason will both get their just rewards in the kingdom of Lanverness." She made her voice a command. "Come and bear witness to the justice of the crown. See what fate awaits those who plot treason against their sovereign queen."

The queen descended the dais and swept the length of the chamber. Prince Stewart followed a step behind on her right, Sir Durnheart on her left. The people bowed low as she passed and then joined in the procession.

She led them through the castle, down the tower stairs and out into the afternoon sunshine. Knowing justice was best served in the light of day, she'd ordered the spectacle to be held in the castle's western courtyard. Guards snapped to attention and banners fluttered overhead.

The courtyard had been transformed. Wooden stands lined the east side, providing tournament seating for the lords and ladies. A central stand, higher than the others, stood caparisoned in royal colors, providing shade from the sun. Across from the stands, a long row of scaffolds lined the western wall. Nooses hung empty and ominous; black-hooded executioners waited to do their duty. In the center of the yard, a bonfire burned beneath a great black cauldron, steam rising from the top. A platform stood to one side of the cauldron, built level with the lip of the great black pot. The stage was set for justice, needing only the victims and the witnesses to see the play to its bitter end.

The queen proceeded to the royal box, taking a seat on a throne-like chair. Sir Durnheart stood behind the throne, a deterrent against any threat. The Master Archivist appeared at the queen's side, signaling that all was prepared. Her counselors and other nobles jostled for seats in the royal box. Nervous voices whispered through the stands, for none had ever seen a royal punishment on such a scale.

Drums beat a rousing rhythm as royal soldiers marched into the great yard, a flourish of emerald tabards and burnished steel. Every soldier barracked in the capital was required to witness the fate of the traitors. Liandra intended the grim lesson to take firm root.

Orders echoed through the courtyard as the soldiers formed into disciplined ranks. They stood at attention in long lines beneath the viewing stands, each soldier facing towards the cauldron and the scaffolds. Prince Stewart rode among the ranks, his hand on the hilt of his sapphire-blue sword, a general inspecting his men.

Spectators began to pour into the yard, commoners in butternut brown mixed with minor nobles in bright colors. Summoned by the town criers, they came from the city, merchants and artisans, masters and apprentices, men and women, young and old. They filled the spaces between the stands, jostling for position, a sea of humanity come to witness the queen's justice.

They did not have long to wait. The steady pounding of the drums announced the arrival of the traitors. A troop of mounted soldiers entered from the western gate. Behind them came the drummers, beating out a slow, ominous march, marking the steps to death. Behind the drummers came the condemned, one hundred and forty-eight officers, lordlings, politicians, and soldiers...traitors all, a grim harvest for the executioners.

The clank of chains could be heard clear across the courtyard. The prisoners shuffled into view, their hands and feet shackled. Stripped to nothing but loin clothes, they walked with their heads bowed, their skin blistered by the sun, their feet bloody from the long march through the city streets. Some bore the stains of rotten fruit and hurled dung, gifts from the citizens of Pellanor, marks of shame and dishonor.

Last in the long line of misery was the leader of the Red Horns, the chief architect of the rebellion. The Lord Turner bore a heavy yoke across his shoulders, his hands shackled to the wooden beam. Stripped to a loincloth, his lily-white skin blazed with sunburn, the marks of a whip crisscrossing his back. He shuffled to the beat of the drums, but unlike the other prisoners, he raised his head as he passed below the royal stands, glaring hatred at the queen.

Her nobles gasped at the traitor's brazen arrogance, but the queen remained statue-still. She watched through hooded eyes as the prisoners were paraded around the yard and then brought to a halt in front of the royal pavilion.

The drums came to a stop and a stillness settled over the yard.

The queen signaled and a herald rose to read the royal decree. "Having foresworn your oaths of allegiance and rebelled against your sovereign queen, you are hereby stripped of all lands and titles, all rights and privileges. Having faced the wrath of the people, you are condemned to die a traitor's death, to hang by the neck until dead. Once dead, your bodies will be burnt in a pyre lest they poison the soil of Lanverness. May the Lords of Light have mercy on your souls."

The drummers beat a loud tattoo.

With the exception of the Lord Turner, the prisoners were prodded toward the scaffolds. Some marched with stoic resignation, others fell to their knees, weeping and pleading to be spared. All were forced to their fate, herded toward the scaffolds.

The crowd watched in silence, many gaping in shock, unaccustomed to the spectacle of so much death.

The black-hooded executioners worked with grim efficiency, setting the noose and then dropping the trap. The legs kicked and twitched but all soon came to a halt, stilled by death. The ropes were freed of their dread burdens and the next traitors shuffled into place. The sun sank to the horizon. Orange light streaked across the sky by the time the work of the scaffolds was finished. Only a single traitor remained standing.

The attention of the crowd turned toward the Lord Turner. He stood shackled but unbowed, standing in front of the boiling cauldron, seemingly indifferent to his fate.

The queen gestured and the herald read the final decree. "Lyndon Turner, once known as the Knight Protector, once known as the captain of the queen's guards, once known as a lord of Lanverness and a member of the queen's council, you have betrayed your oaths to queen and kingdom. Foresworn, you instigated treason against your sovereign monarch. More than a thousand deaths are charged against your soul. What say you to these charges?"

The prisoner began to laugh. Not the insane laughter of the condemned, but the laughter of a man who will have the final jest.

Unease rippled through the crowd.

A guard jabbed the prisoner with his spear.

The laughter came to an abrupt halt. The traitor bent forward, blood seeping from the fresh wound at his side, but then he straightened and glared at the queen. "You have no idea what you face!" His voice was loud and defiant. "You think you've won, but this is only the beginning of your fall. No woman shall be allowed to rule from a throne, not when he comes. You will be pulled from the throne and Darkness set in your place."

Gasps of anger rippled through the crowd.

The queen gestured and two soldiers muzzled the prisoner, ending his rant.

The herald finished reading the royal decree. "Lyndon Turner, as the architect of treason and the leader of the Red Horns, you are condemned to be boiled alive. Once dead, your body will be burnt, your ashes spread to the wind. May the Lords of Light have mercy on your soul."

Soldiers forced the prisoner up the steps. The traitor walked with dignity until he reached the top. The sight of the boiling cauldron must have melted his resolve. He began to back away, squirming against the soldiers' grip. One of the soldiers removed his gag while the others removed the yoke. They forced the prisoner toward the steaming pot. The traitor struggled to hold his position, but he did not have the strength. Pushed from behind, he toppled into the boiling cauldron.

A hideous scream split the air. The traitor splashed in the frothing boil, as if attempting to walk on water. His skin glowed bright red, his face contorted in a howl of agony. Waves lapped over the side of the cauldron, only his head and upper arms free of the boil. Screams shrieked from the cauldron, the traitor's arms flailing the water. The boiling water frothed pink with blood. The screams subsided. The flailing arms stilled, falling back into the frothing water. The death struggles came to an end.

Bloated and blistered, the corpse floated in the center of the cauldron.

A soldier prodded the body with his spear. Blood spurted but the corpse remained still.

A sigh of relief swept through the crowd.

The queen sat back, releasing her fierce grip on the arms of the throne.

The corpse sat up in the water. A baleful red light streamed from its eyes. The mouth began to laugh, mocking and hateful...but then the sound twisted to a strangled wail. *"No Lord, you can't! Don't do this to me!"* Parboiled hands clawed at the air, as if seeking purchase on something no one could see.

Screams of terror rent the courtyard.

Prince Stewart raced up the stairs, his blue sword gleaming in his hand. He swung the sword toward the corpse, striking the head from the body with a single cut. The strength of the blow sent the head flying, bouncing to the foot of the cauldron. The body of the corpse sank back into the boil, a froth of blood in the water.

A soldier spiked the head on a spear and lifted it into the air. The baleful red light was gone, leaving nothing but a bloated, parboiled head.

The prince held his blue sword aloft, shouting to be heard over the panic of the courtyard. *"Do not be afraid! Death has taken the traitor!"*

Casting off the black cloak of vengeance, the queen rose from the throne, revealing a figure of golden authority.

The crowd wavered on the edge of mindless flight.

The prince brandished his sword, a flash of blue steel against the twilight sky. *"The Light will always conquer the Dark! Look to your Queen to lead you."*

Liandra reached for the voice of command. "We have defeated the rebellion!" She pointed toward the prince. "Blue steel has defeated Darkness!" She raised her arms in entreaty. "The people of Lanverness must remain steadfast in the Light! With courage and loyalty we shall ever be victorious!"

Someone shouted, *"Long live the Queen!"*

The chant began to ripple through the crowd.

The queen stood statue-still, a source of strength for her people. Order triumphed over panic, but in the queen's mind, she shuddered at the image of the animated corpse, demon eyes staring from a traitor's head. Darkness had reached into the heart of her kingdom. Darkness had threatened her throne.

39

Steffan

Steffan stayed out of view, leaning against the wall, the man behind the silk curtains. Hidden by folds of fabric, he listened as the wealthy of Coronth made their confessions to the Keeper of the Flame.

Steffan made it his habit to eavesdrop on the Keeper, sifting through sins, searching for clues to the identity of the rebels. The rebels had proven a crafty foe, evading traps and setting some of their own. The last incident had cost the lives of more than forty soldiers, some trapped in a flaming building, while others lay wounded by caltrops, a foul trick. The pesky rebellion was becoming annoying. It was past time to put an end to the rebels.

Peering between the curtains, Steffan observed the ritual of confession. The red-robed Keeper sat ensconced on a gilded throne, a smug look on his face, clearly smitten with his own importance. A young acolyte sat at the Keeper's feet, a feathered nib scratching across a roll of parchment, scribing every sin. The penitent, a wealthy merchant, knelt on a velvet pillow at the base of the dais, recounting a litany of sins, all of them committed by others.

The horse-faced merchant had a contrite voice but his eyes glowed with avarice. "Lord Keeper, it grieves me to confess this sin, but Merchant Rasint, the pudgy wine seller on Cobb Street, the owner of a shop called the Holy Grape, is hoarding casks of wine. He has a secret space beneath his cellar steps where he hides his best casks, evading the temple's tithe collectors." He took on a look of false contrition. "Merchant Rasint cheats the temple. He does not give the Flame God his due."

The Keeper roused himself, scratching his baldhead. "Yes, a grievous sin, you do well to report it. The temple has need of every coin...for all the good works we do." He made a languid gesture with his hand. "You may continue."

The merchant bowed his head. "Holiness, I do not often visit houses of prostitution, but sometimes a man has needs…"

The Keeper smiled. "We all have needs. Visiting women of the night is not a sin."

"Thank you, Holiness, but the last time I felt the need, I overheard the madam of the house speaking against the Keeper of the Flame."

The Keeper sat up, his voice suddenly sharp. "Speaking against me?"

"Yes, Holiness. I am loath to repeat what she said, it was so…foul."

"You must confess. It is your duty!"

The merchant bowed. "As you command." He ran his hands down the front of his velvet doublet, a nervous gesture. "The madam talked about the death of her brother. He died cleansed in the Flames but the madam claimed he was innocent. She claimed," the merchant's voice dropped to a hush, "that her brother was falsely accused by the Keeper so that…so that your Holiness could claim his beautiful wife for a body slave…"

The Keeper sat forward, his voice a low growl. "What's the name of this slut?"

The merchant's head bobbed. "M-madam Lillian, the owner of the Devout Virgin."

The Keeper's face flamed dark crimson, putting truth to the tale. Steffan shook his head, the Keeper had too many weaknesses, too many liabilities…but for now, he served.

Steffan let the curtain fall back into place, obscuring the view. Angry at the waste, he scowled at the Keeper's stupidity. The burly priest heard confessions day after day, lapping up sins like a fat cat with cream on his whiskers, yet he never bothered to bestir himself unless he heard of a personal slight, never realizing the opportunities that trickled through his fat fingers. Tired of listening to trivial offenses, Steffan decided it was time to inject a higher purpose into the holy ritual of confession.

He stepped from behind the curtains, a dark shadow behind the gilded throne.

The merchant's voice stuttered to a stop. He stared at Steffan with wide-eyed fear.

The Keeper turned, following the merchant's stare, an indignant expression blooming on his face. His eyes widened when he saw Steffan, his face scowling with angry suspicion.

The Keeper knew that Steffan often listened to the confessions, but he'd always remained hidden behind the curtains, never infringing on the big man's show. Steffan knew his sudden appearance would plunge the Keeper into a fit of jealous rage. Keen to mollify the Keeper, he bowed low towards the burly priest. "Pardon me, holy one, but I could not bear to hear this sinner waste your precious time."

Confusion washed across the Keeper's face, forestalling the burst of anger.

Steffan grasped the moment. Turning his glare to the kneeling merchant, he filled his voice with righteous indignation. "Merchant Gilden, you have the privilege of confessing to the second highest priest in the service of the Flame God...yet you squander this holy opportunity."

The merchant gasped like a fish out of water. Steffan pressed the advantage. "You're a smart man, Merchant Gilden, you know what I'm talking about."

"N-no." The man's gaze bounced from the Lord Raven to the Keeper and back again, traces of panic filling his voice. "I've done my duty, I've confessed the sins of those around me...I don't know what you mean."

Steffan plucked the scroll from the acolyte's hands, reading the list of confessed sins. "Hidden wine casks and the gossip of a whore? Is this the best you can do? It's true all sins must be confessed...but these sins are petty." He glared down at the man. "Sins like these should be told to ordinary confessors. Surely you don't mean to waste the Lord Keeper's time with trivial sins?"

"No!" The man's voice took on a pleading wail. "I didn't know! Tell me what you want me to confess!"

The merchant was a quick study. Steffan smiled and made his voice as smooth as warm honey. "The Lord Keeper's time is most precious. He waits to hear the most grievous of sins, sins against the Pontifax and the faith...sins of rebellion."

The merchant began to tremble, his eyes wide in fear.

"We know that a man of your stature, an important merchant, a staunch contributor to the temple, would never be involved in something so heinous as rebellion."

The man nodded, a faithful dog begging for a bone.

"But the Flame God expects his devoted followers to be vigilant to sin. He expects them to report heretics who plot against the temple. To confess the names of those who rebel against the Pontifax." He pointed toward the Keeper, his voice full of righteous anger. "The Keeper waits to hear the sins of rebellion! If you dare to come before his Holiness in confession, then bring sins worthy of his exulted station!" He gave the cringing merchant a withering glare and then tossed the scroll to the acolyte.

Steffan bowed low toward the Keeper. "Pardon me for the interruption, Holiness, but I could not bear to see this man waste your time."

The Keeper sat on the throne like a stunned ox, his squinty gaze darting between Steffan and the merchant, as if he wasn't quite sure if he'd just been flattered or insulted.

Steffan did not give the Keeper time to decide. He turned, a swirl of black, and strode across the audience hall to the far doors, his cloak flaring behind him. Reaching the doors, he flung them open with all of his strength. The heavy doors crashed against the marble walls like a clap of thunder, a fitting exit for a vengeful raven.

A long line of wealthy citizens waited beyond the doors. They stared at him like startled deer, unsure whether to flee or hide.

Steffan made his face dark with disapproval...and then he pointed back toward the gaping doorway. "Think before you pass through these doors. The Keeper waits to hear serious sins. He waits to hear sins of rebellion. Think first, before you waste his time with trivial confessions."

He strode through the waiting crowd, leaving the sinners trembling in the hallway.

Steffan hid his smile. He preferred to lead from the back, manipulating from behind the curtains...but sometimes the citizens of Coronth needed to feel the Lord Raven's stern hand. Thinking of the startled faces in the hallway, he nearly laughed...sheep trembling before the wolf...but the sheep would learn to bleat a different tune. The confessions would soon bear better fruit. He was looking forward to reading the acolyte's scrolls. Suspicion had become a way of life in Coronth. The citizens would confess to save their own lives. He'd soon have the names of the rebels...it was only a matter of time.

40

The Priestess

The Dark Lord's voice thundered through her mind, "*It is time!*" The Priestess dismissed her servants, her heart leaping with anticipation. *At last!* Eager to answer the summons, she made her way through the marble corridors to the secluded garden at the rear of the villa.

"*It is time! Come to me!*"

Moonlight silvered the midnight blossoms. Clad in a sheath of sheer black silk, she walked barefoot through her garden, past the purple pendants of flowering nightshade and the white spiky flowers of baneberry and the elegant knee-high foliage of hemlock. Her garden was in full bloom, ripe with death. Subtle and sure, the blossoms and vines waited like their mistress for the chance to kill. "*Soon, so soon,*" she crooned to her dark beauties, reveling in their musky scent, a promise of death in the night.

Beyond the garden, she reached the gnarled hawthorn trees. The creatures of the surrounding swamp serenaded the half moon but the sounds fell away within the grove, smothered to a dark solitude.

A ring of basalt stones formed the Oracle, a black mouth gaping open to the night sky. The Priestess bowed low and knelt by the ancient well, leaning across the dark stones. The eternal cold of the stones sucked the warmth from her body, an offering to the god. She gazed into the water, her raven-black hair cascading around her face like a veil. "I am here, my Lord." Her voice was a throaty whisper.

"*It is time!*"

Power spiked through her like a sword thrust. She arched her back, fingernails scraping against stone. Each thrust deepened her power, her heart quickening to the dark rhythm. A scream hovered on her lips. She threw her head back in tortured ecstasy, pain and pleasure becoming one. The moment stretched to an eternity.

The Dark Lord withdrew. Her spasms slowly subsided...but the brimming power remained. The Priestess thrummed with potent possibilities. Taking a deep breath, she cast her power onto the dark waters. Images danced across the surface. She expected to see the Mordant weaving a trail of blood and chaos across the eastern kingdoms, but the waters of the well showed her something else, something unexpected. The image resolved into a courtyard of a great castle, scaffolds lining the far wall, a great black cauldron set to boil over a bonfire. The image sharpened, showing her the face of the prisoner. Her breath caught in surprise. She watched spellbound as the captured one struggled against the soldiers, only to be thrown into the bubbling cauldron. His death was messy. Flailing arms and parboiled skin, he screamed in agony. She held her breath and leaned forward, knowing that death would not be the end. The image did not disappoint. The floating corpse sat up, the eyes bright with the baleful red light of hell. But instead of triumph she witnessed eternal defeat.

"Watch and be warned. This one failed me."

The Dark Lord revoked his favor. The horror of hell collapsed across the harlequin's face, never to be reborn again, paying the ultimate price for his failure. Dread shuddered through her. She told herself that he was young and inexperienced, but the lesson could not be denied. There were no excuses, no leniency with the Dark Lord. One served and succeeded or faced the eternal damnations of hell. Her voice was a low whisper. "I will not fail you, Lord."

"See that you don't. Now watch and remember. There is much to be done to make up for the failure in Lanverness."

Images flashed across the surface of the waters, faces of those tainted by Darkness. She saw a young man, shackled and chained, screaming in the depths of a dungeon. She saw a turbaned prince, eyes dark with cunning, scheming for a chance to gain a golden throne. She saw the Pontifax walk through the Flames, the crowd screaming in religious ecstasy, seduced by the miracle.

The scene shifted and she saw images of the future, ripe with dark possibilities. Some scenes were familiar, but others were new. The Dark Lord revealed his plans, a complex tapestry woven of dark deeds and darker details. She saw her part in the great design. Every image brought something new, a flood of complexities. She stared into the water, memorizing faces and places, marking turning points and triumphs, a myriad of dark details in the grand design.

The images stilled, the colors fading to absolute black. Dark as a starless sky, dark as a tomb, the water lay mirror flat, an inky darkness laden with mystery and menace.

The Dark Lord's voice rumbled in her mind. *"And now the test. Thrust your hand into the water."*

Fear shivered down her back. She'd heard rumors about the nature of the water...none of them good. Yet she dared not fail, or even hesitate, she'd witnessed the consequences. Leaning forward, she lowered her right hand into the inky darkness. The water swallowed her hand like an offering, closing around her wrist like a hungry mouth.

Cold bit her hand.

A thousand daggers of freezing pain pierced her to the bone. She bit back a scream and willed her hand to endure. She tried to move her fingers, to clench her fist, but if her hand obeyed, she could not tell. The pain intensified. She felt the skin flayed from the hand, flesh peeled from the bone. Agony ripped into her. Fighting against every instinct, she refused to remove her hand. Sweat beaded on her brow. She clenched her teeth in defiance, knowing better than to ask for mercy from the Dark God. "Y-your...w-will...Lord."

Something grabbed her hand, jerking her further into the well. The dark water closed around her elbow. Pain ripped into her, like hungry mouths tearing at her flesh. The hand was gone, devoured by cold...and now the pain feasted on her lower arm, flaying away the skin, eating her by inches. She clung to the lip of the well with her left hand, panic in her grip, afraid of being pulled in...but her will held. Her right arm remained in the water, consumed by pain. A scream ripped out of her, but she kept her arm in the water. So much pain, she doubted there was anything left but bone dangling below the dark surface, the gnarled claw of a skeleton.

A great power thrust her backward, flinging her from the water. She hit the ground hard, staring up at the half moon. Struggling to sit, she was afraid to look at her hand, afraid she'd find nothing but a bony claw...but she found flesh instead. Her hand was whole and unharmed, clasped tight into a fist. She stared at it in amazement, her beautiful hand...the pain only a searing memory.

"Open your hand. You have gained the reward of obedience."

Her fingers refused to unclench. She willed them open. Lying on her palm was a smooth, oval moonstone, pale as a winter moon. She gasped with recognition, staring in wonder, a dark legend long thought to be lost. Her words were a whisper of reverence, "The Eye of the Oracle!"

"Use it well. And now it is time for you to take up your role in the great dark design."

She clutched the pale moonstone to her breast. "I will not fail you, Lord."

"You are released from the duties of the Oracle. My Priestess is inflicted on the lands of Erdhe!"

She knelt before the Oracle. "May your pleasure reign, Lord."

"See that you remember."

The thrust came without preamble. The Dark Lord claimed her for his own. Power spiked through her, deep and hard and relentless. Consumed by passion, the Priestess shuddered, overwhelmed by the ecstasy of absolute Darkness.

41

Katherine

Kath walked with Duncan beneath the great trees. Domed tents glowed with lamplight, looking like giant mushrooms clustered around the massive trunks. A sparkle of fireflies blinked between the tents, weaving trails of tiny lights. Night had fallen, yet the sacred grove was alive with light and life. Kath drank in the sights, captured by the magic of the forest. She even thought she heard laughter coming from the green vault overhead. Stopping to stare into the heights, she whispered to Duncan, "Do you hear it? Even the trees laugh!"

He echoed the laughter, a rich warm sound, full of depth and life. She liked his laugh; she wanted to hear more of it. He stood close behind her and pointed upward, guiding her sight. "It's only the children."

She thought he was joking. "You jest!"

"No!" He chuckled. "Watch and perhaps you'll see."

"But it's pitch dark and some of those branches are impossibly high."

"You underestimate them. Golden eyes see as well in the dark as you see at the height of day."

She turned and stared at his mismatched eyes, wondering what other differences lay undiscovered. "So why do they scale the trees at night?"

"To capture birds while they sleep. It is the children's task to collect the feathers for the capes of the clan chiefs. Only two specific feathers are taken, and then the birds are released, unharmed. The birds fill the forest with song and color while they re-grow their feathers. It takes a lot of birds to make a single cape...and by then, the children are grown sure-footed in the limbs of the great trees, one with the forest."

The simple tale matched the magic of the place. Kath smiled, "I can imagine you as a child among the tree limbs, the first to make a cape."

The smile fled from his face, replaced by something hard. "Feathers gathered by a half-breed are unworthy."

She gripped her sword hilt in anger, prejudice again, the thorn that ruined paradise.

He pointed to the right. "This way."

The mood was broken. Instead of meandering, he led her straight to the tent they shared with their companions. A gift from the clans, the domed tent was large and spacious, a fire crackling in the center. Danya sat on one side, her arms wrapped around the wolf, crooning a wordless tune to the still form. The two knights sat across from her, the hilts of their great swords looming over their right shoulders, their silver surcoats glinting in the firelight.

Kath stared at Danya, worried about her friend. Glazed eyes and a deathly pale face, she sat in a trance, as if her life dwindled with the wolf's. Two days had passed and still the wolf did not stir. And every day that passed, Danya fell deeper into her malaise...and every day delayed gave the Mordant a greater lead. Kath felt torn between the needs of her companions and the need to pursue evil.

She circled the fire and crouched beside the two knights. "Any change?"

Blaine shook his head. "She sings a wordless tune and dribbles broth in the wolf's mouth, but if there is any change, I do not see it." His voice dropped to a whisper, worry written across his face. "It's not natural. The girl is almost as far gone as the wolf. It's as if she's under a dark spell." He made the hand sign against evil. "She doesn't talk and she barely eats. Unless the wolf wakes soon, we may lose them both."

"No!" The word rushed out of Kath with fierce conviction. "We can't lose either of them. The wolf saved Duncan's life and Danya was chosen by the Grand Master. They're meant to be with us. There must be some way to save them."

Blaine's face was bleak. "I've never heard of anyone trying to heal a wolf."

Kath stared at the blond-haired knight, finding wisdom beneath his words. She looked for the monk. "Where's Zith?"

Sir Tyrone answered, "Walking with the Treespeaker. Those two have grown as thick as moss on a shady log. Makes you wonder what they have to talk about."

As if summoned, the monk ducked beneath the tent flap. The old man stood tall in his robe of midnight blue, his face lined with determination. He seemed changed, as if he'd shucked off the cocoon of grief, becoming somehow stronger. Kath wondered if it was the influence of the Treespeaker.

Zith nodded to Kath. "It is good to find you here."

He stepped aside and the Treespeaker entered. Tall and stately, with long silver hair and a serene face that belied her age, the Treespeaker's presence filled the tent.

Kath scrambled to stand, startled by the visit. "You honor us with your presence." She felt the weight of the Treespeaker's strange golden stare, eyes without pupils, eyes of the forest, old eyes, peering into her very soul. Images flashed through Kath's mind, the crystal dagger, Danya and the wolf, the Kiralynn monastery, Duncan in the meadow. Suddenly released, Kath staggered backwards. She took a steadying breath, wondering what thoughts the tree-witch had plucked from her mind.

The Treespeaker's gaze passed to each of the companions, staring the longest at Danya and the wolf. Tension rippled through the tent. Her golden gaze returned to Kath, her face impossible to read. "The Kiralynn monk is owed a debt for the breaking of hearth-welcome beneath the Mother Tree. The monk has asked that we attempt to heal the wolf."

Hope leaped in Kath. "Can you do it?"

"Two are broken here, not just one. The girl is lost in the dreams of the wolf. Both are caught in the gray veil, in the realm between this life and the next. Something Dark holds them in thrall. Both will be saved or both will be lost."

"But can you help them?"

"You have more enemies than you know." The green diadem at her brow flashed in the firelight, as if to dispel the darkness. "There is more at work here than a simple injury. The woman and the wolf are both lost to the in-between, stuck between life and death, held captive by Darkness. A companion, someone familiar to the wolf and woman, must enter the veil and bring them back. One of you must take this risk...or there will be no healing."

Kath stared at Danya, at her gaunt face and the desperate way she clutched the wolf. She couldn't let her slip away without a fight, but she wondered if Danya would respond better to Blaine's voice. The two had grown close...or at least the knight was smitten if not the woman.

I know you hear me.

Startled, Kath stared at the Treespeaker.

The blond knight cares for the girl but he has no affinity for magic. You are the one who must enter the veil.

Why me?

You carry the crystal dagger and your mind is attuned to magic. You are not of the Forest, yet you feel the rustling power of the towering green. The Forest stares at you and you stare back.

Kath shivered, remembering the golden eyes invading her dreams.

The woman and the wolf require a champion. Their bodies will die unless their souls are returned. The choice is yours to make.

And the risk?

The Treespeaker gave her a knowing smile. *You are wise to ask, for magic always carries a risk.* She peered at Kath as if measuring her soul. *Something Dark reaches through the wolf to trap the woman. If you enter the wolf's dreams you too may be trapped by the Darkness, your soul locked in the gray veil while your body dwindles and dies.*

Kath gripped her sword hilt. This was a fight of a different sort, something she did not understand and could not predict.

"I will do what I can to aid you, but the decision is yours."

Kath fingered the crystal dagger, certain that Danya and the wolf were both meant to see the quest to the end. "I won't let them die. I choose to try."

The Treespeaker nodded. "Then come with me. Their bodies wear thin. We must call them back before they are forever lost." She clapped her hands and a green-robed attendant ducked to enter the tent. "Bring the wolf."

Blaine said, "I'll carry him." But the Treespeaker motioned him to stillness.

The attendant crouched to gather the wolf in his arms, muscles bulging against the beast's dead weight. Danya murmured a weak protest but then stood as if in a trance, her eyes glazed, her hand clutching the wolf's fur.

The Treespeaker spoke to the others. "The rest of you must wait here. Your presence will only be a dangerous distraction." Her words were a command but Duncan dared to step forward. "You named me a son of the Forest." His gaze held the Treespeaker's.

"And so you are. But only clan leaders are called to the hidden grove."

Duncan's eyes widened with something that verged on awe…or perhaps fear. Offering the Treespeaker a half bow, he stepped back to stand beside Kath.

The Treespeaker slipped from the tent.

Kath met the stares of her companions, the naked worry in Blaine's face and Zith's concerned glance, but it was Duncan she spoke to. "I'll be back."

Duncan gripped her arm, lightning in his grasp.

She met his mismatched stare. "I'll do my best."

His smile was wry but his gaze intent. "I'll hold you to that."

She felt awkward in front of the knights, but need won out. She gave him a quick kiss and then fled the tent.

The Treespeaker waited outside, her golden gaze unreadable. Moonlight glinted on her silver hair and white-feather robe, anointing the lady of the forest in a pale white light. "Follow me." Serene as a falling leaf, she wove a path through the mushroomed domes, moving beyond the tents and deeper into the sacred grove. Light from the campfires dwindled and the gentle hum of conversations fell away, replaced by the glow of fireflies and the serenade of tree frogs. Starlight filtered through the breaks in the canopy, a peaceful night, but Kath felt the forest watching, judging, as if something of importance would be decided this night.

They passed through a stand of head-high aspens, the leaves of the saplings silvered by moonlight. The young trees formed a living curtain, dividing the campsite from the inner grove. Leaves brushed against Kath's face and arms, as if they memorized her features.

They emerged to walk beneath forest giants. Immense redwoods towered in two straight rows, massive columns forming a long hall roofed with living green. Between the trees, two bonfires crackled, filling the grove with flickering light and the soothing scent of pine. Flat moss-covered stones formed an oval of low seats around the fires. Feather-cloaked clan leaders sat waiting on the stones, their backs straight as swords. For a heartbeat, the clan leaders seemed like massive birds of prey, their hungry stares fierce and golden. Kath shook her head to dispel the illusion.

The clan leaders stared at her, a few in welcome, but most shot baleful glares toward her. Their cat-eyes glowed in the firelight like predators, but Kath refused to flinch.

Danya was already present, sitting in the mossy space between the two bonfires, cradling the wolf's head in her lap. Kath nodded to Danya but the wolf-girl did not respond.

The Treespeaker turned to Kath. "Sit here, next to the wolf."

Kath sat cross-legged, one hand on the hilt of her sword, the other buried in the wolf's thick blue-black fur.

You must enter the dreams of the wolf and find your friends. Release them from the Dark and return to the living side of the veil.

We will work to hold the gateway open but you must not tarry. Remember, to linger beyond the veil is to risk being lost forever.*

"But I don't know how."

Open your mind to your magic. Seek the eyes of the Forest. The Forest will guide you, linking your thoughts to the wolf's dreams. Find your friends and return. But be warned, to die beyond the veil is to die in the mortal world. Guard your life well and return to us. May the favor of Leaf and Bark be with you.

Kath relinquished her grip on her sword hilt and grasped her gargoyle instead. She'd rather trust the surety of steel than the mystery of magic, but the choice of weapons was not hers to make. She looked at Danya, her face ashen and her eyes sunken. Kath sent a silent plea to the Lords of Light. "I'm ready."

The Treespeaker gestured and a green-robed attendant offered Kath a wooden goblet. "Drink deep the nectar of the forest and open yourself to the power of the green."

The golden liquid smelled of leaf and bark, of summer in the forest. Kath raised the goblet and drank. A rush of tastes flooded through her, pine and nut and leaf, all the flavors of the forest, deep and green and brimming with life. She drained the goblet, expecting to feel something, but nothing changed.

"And now it begins." The Treespeaker raised her arms, stretching her staff toward the treetops. The diadem at her brow glowed bright green, a beacon in the forest. "A debt is owed to a hearth-guest." Her voice carried the strength of the redwoods. "The clan leaders are called to raise the power of the Mother Forest. Reach for the strength of leaf and bark and hold open a pathway to the dream world."

The clan leaders began to hum, a deep, sticky tone that clung to the clearing like sap to the tree. The Treespeaker added her voice, a song without words, a melody rich and complex, evoking images of the forest. Overhead, the grandfather trees began to sway, adding the rustle of leaves and the creak of branches. Together they wove a tapestry of tones, something familiar yet otherworldly.

Kath sat in the center of the grove, at the heart of the gathering power. A feeling of warmth thrummed through her. Power prickled along her skin. Her vision shifted and the forest seemed to brighten though there was no change to the light. Every detail of leaf and bark became crystal clear, etched in her mind. She stared at the rough trunks of the redwoods, entranced by the pattern of the bark. She studied the needles of the trees, sharp and distinct, each one unique. She sat mesmerized by the play of moonlight on the treetops, the silver light evoking a thousand shades of green. Even the scent of the forest seemed richer, more complex, the subtle scents of spruce and redwood mingled with boldness of pine and cedar. Kath marveled at the beauty. The forest glowed with magic and wonder and life.

Now! The Treespeaker's command intruded, drawing Kath back to her purpose. *Reach for your magic and leap to the veil.*

Confused, Kath tightened her grip on her gargoyle and reached for the magic within. Golden eyes of the Forest stared back at her, waiting, watching, full of mystery and ageless wisdom. This time Kath did not turn away. She welcomed the wisdom of the green, falling into the golden gaze, succumbing to the spell of the forest.

A wave of dizziness swept over her. She closed her eyes and clutched her gargoyle, needing an anchor. A roaring sound, like the beat of a thousand wings surrounded her. A chime sounded...and then a sudden silence.

Kath opened her eyes and stifled a gasp. The forest was gone, replaced by the walls of a cave. She stood alone in a tunnel of rock, a vaulted cavern of gray stone stretching into the murky dimness. There was no source of light yet she could see well enough, as if she walked in twilight. Her fingers scraped against the stone walls, rough and hard. The cave seemed real enough. Taking a deep breath, she tested the air, and was overwhelmed by the rush of scents. A tangled web of information hid beneath the scents. Surprised, Kath shook her head, amazed by the scents and her ability to discern each one. Perhaps it was part of the wolf's dream, or a gift from the Forest, either way she'd find a way to use her enhanced senses.

Breathing deep, she studied the tangled scents. The air held the damp mustiness of dark places, the loam of earth and the salty, stony smell of rock, but she also caught the sharp tang of wolf. Her nostrils flared, reading emotions in the wolf's scent, feelings of anger, and confusion...and fear. Startled, Kath surveyed the cavern, wondering what could cause so much fear in a wolf. Taking a deeper breath, she strained to understand...and found a horrid wrongness, something that smelled like wolf but wasn't, something twisted, something vicious...a hungry, malevolent predator reeking of Darkness.

Kath reached for her sword...but the scabbard was empty. She grabbed for an axe...but they were missing. She wore the same clothes as before, a leather jerkin and dark green breeches tucked into knee-high boots, but her weapons were gone. A shiver of fear rushed through her; she couldn't fight a demon without a weapon. She reached to her belt, relieved to find the crystal dagger in its sheath. Steel was denied her, but at least she had the crystal blade. She drew the dagger, needing to hold a weapon in her hand.

Kath gasped in surprise. The crystal blade glowed like a shard of frozen moonlight, a weapon of the Light against the Dark. The gods hadn't abandoned her.

Drawing strength from the glowing blade, she set her mind to the task. She searched for footprints but found none, leaving scent as her only guide. Pacing the cavern, she drank in the scents. Deciding the wolf-smell was strongest to the right, she turned and followed.

The cavern proved to be a complex maze of twisted shunts and side passageways, an easy place to get lost. Feeling time was against her, Kath considered calling to Danya, but a sixth sense cautioned against it. Something evil lurked in the cavern, an unknown enemy. Kath kept her silence, weaving her way into the rock labyrinth.

Time had no measure in the cavern but she felt the need to hurry. The scent of the wolf grew stronger, but it also changed. The fear deepened to a suffocating scent, threatening to infect her. Kath fought the feeling, tightening her grip on the dagger.

A noise came from the right, a low growl full of menace. Kath followed the sound into a narrow passageway. Shoulder-tight, the passage felt like a trap. Scents of fear and wrongness clawed at her mind, but Kath refused to flee. Clutching the dagger, she pressed forward, praying her friends still lived.

The passage widened, opening into a small cave. Stalactites hung from the vaulted ceiling, frozen teardrops of gray stone. Kath edged towards the opening, keeping to the shadows. Growls rumbled through the cave, an angry threat of fang and claw. A great black wolf, the size of a horse, snapped and snarled at the base of a small boulder. Monstrously large, the wolf reeked of wrongness, something dark and evil. The beast leaped, teeth snapping at prey trapped atop the boulder.

Her friends were the prey!

Danya sat hunched atop the boulder, her face ashen, her brown hair a wild tangle, Bryx crouched by her side.

The dark wolf leaped and snapped, slavering for the kill.

Danya threw rocks at the wolf, but the rumbling snarls only intensified.

Kath studied the wolf. Freakishly large and blindingly quick, the beast was a monster. She might have stood a chance with her axes, but a dagger was an invitation to death. Kath shuddered, making the hand sign against evil. Desperate for another weapon, she scanned the cavern looking for an exit or an advantage, but found neither. A steep slope of rubble filled the far end, blocking the way. The cave was a trap, the wolf the stopper in the bottle.

Faint words sounded in Kath's mind. *Hurry! The gateway threatens to close!*

The Treespeaker's warning spurred Kath to action. She studied the scree slope, noting the large boulder halfway up the side, a slim chance but better than nothing. Sheathing the crystal dagger, Kath stepped out of the shadows, willing Danya to see her.

The wolf-girl lifted a hand in greeting, surprise and hope flickering across her pale face.

Kath gestured to the scree slope, trying to signal her intent, hoping Danya understood. Ducking behind a fallen stalactite, Kath crept towards the slope, using the rubble to hide from the wolf.

Danya must have understood. Standing atop the boulder, she yelled insults and hurled stones at the wolf.

The beast leaped and growled, a snarl of savage anger echoing through the chamber.

Kath quickened her pace, her heartbeat loud in her ears. She gained the base of the slope and began to climb. Rubble shifted beneath her. Using her hands for purchase, she scrambled up the steep slope. If she could reach the large boulder, she might be able to start a landslide and crush the wolf. Kath stretched for a handhold, but it gave way. Stones clattered down the slope, releasing a shower of rocks.

The beast whirled. Quick as dark lightning, it raced up the slope, a fury of snarling teeth.

Kath scrambled to climb out of reach, but the wolf was too quick. Teeth ripped at her boots. She glanced down and froze. The wolf's eyes glowed red, the eyes of a demon, the red light of hell. Something intelligent stared back at her, the red eyes glowing with purpose...and hate.

Kath kicked at the beast.

The wolf lunged, a slavering mouthful of teeth. Kath scrabbled backwards but the scree gave way. She clung at the rubble but everything began to slide. A landslide roared down the slope. Swept downhill with the wolf, Kath tumbled against the stones. Battered from all sides, she landed on her back, the breath knocked out of her. Bruised and hurting, she clawed her way out of the rubble. Dust clouded the air. Kath fought to swallow a cough. Blinded by the dust, fear shivered through her, she couldn't see the wolf. She forced herself to a crouch, straining to see.

A black shape charged, knocking her onto her back. Teeth snapped at her face, a fury of drooling fangs and glowing red eyes.

Kath got her left arm up, driving it deep into the gaping jaws. Teeth clamped on her forearm, piercing to the bone. White-hot pain seared her arm. She screamed against the agony. The wolf shook her like a rag doll, pain ripping up her arm. She fumbled for the hilt of the crystal dagger. The wolf's jaws snapped open but she sacrificed her left arm, forcing it deeper into the wolf's maw, keeping the jaws occupied. Teeth clamped down, ripping through skin and sinew, sending ragged waves of pain up to her shoulder. Kath bit her lip, fighting against the shock. Her right hand found the dagger's hilt. The wolf's breath fouled her face, blood and slaver drooling from the jaws. She thrust the dagger upward, praying to find the heart. Light flared. The crystal blade sliced into the beast like hot iron into butter. The wolf shuddered. Its red eyes blazed bright, the wicked teeth clamping on her shattered arm, locked in a death spasm. Pain nearly claimed her. With the last of her strength, Kath drove the blade deeper. A roaring sound filled the cavern. The wolf convulsed, the red eyes going dark, snuffed like the flame of a candle. Dead, the wolf slumped on top of her, a suffocating weight.

Pain blazed through Kath, proving she still lived. She yelled for help, a weak sound, but no one answered. Pushing against the wolf's carcass, she struggled to get free. Agony raced up her ravaged arm. She screamed as she pried her arm from the wolf's death-bite.

The wolf disappeared in a swirl of gray.

Astonished, Kath sat up. Agony claimed her. The wolf was gone but her arm was still savaged. Bloody and mangled, the flesh was torn to the very bone. Pain ripped through her, lancing her very soul; a one-armed warrior was of no use. Kath cradled her torn arm and stared at the swirling fog, shivering with cold. "Danya?" Her voice sounded feeble. Kath didn't want to give up, but she didn't see the point in trying to crawl. Every direction looked the same, a cold gray void. Consumed by pain, Kath lay sprawled on the ground.

Hurry! The gate is closing!

Kath struggled to remain awake.

Hurry!

The voice refused to let her rest. Kath tried to remember, but her mind was fogged by pain. She reached for her gargoyle but it was gone, perhaps lost in the landslide. Despair threatened to crush her.

Come now!

A one-armed warrior was of no use, yet Kath fumbled across the ground, seeking the crystal dagger. Her hand found the hilt. A moon-bright glow beat back the darkness. The light of the blade cut through the pain fogging her mind. The crystal blade was needed in the mortal world. If nothing else, she had to return the dagger to the living. She struggled to think. A memory of Master Rizel in the Garden of

Contemplation prodded her mind. Hope flared through her. Sheathing the dagger, she reached for the pouch tied to her belt. Using her teeth, she opened the leather ties. The amber pyramid tumbled into her palm. Kath closed her fist around the pyramid and reached for the magic within.

Golden eyes stared back at her, the eyes of the forest.

We see you warrior of the Light.

A rush of beating wings surrounded her. Kath closed her eyes against the dizziness, her fist tightening on the amber pyramid. A roaring sound filled her ears. A brilliant white light beat against her closed eyelids, warmth chasing away the bone-numbing chill. A chime sounded...and then she heard the morning song of a bird. She opened her eyes and the forest was back, the Treespeaker hovering over her.

"You have done well, warrior of the Light. The Darkness lurking in the gray veil has been vanquished, releasing your friends."

Questions flooded her mind but Kath didn't have the strength to speak. Weary with pain, she fell into sleep's oblivion.

42

Liandra

Red eyes haunted the queen, the red eyes of a demon, the glowing eyes of the undead. *"What was that thing?"* Liandra paced her solar, images of the animated corpse plaguing her mind. "The public executions were meant to finish the rebellion, but instead they raised the specter of a darker threat. Perhaps we should have ordered a beheading instead of the cauldron."

Prince Stewart sprawled in an arm chair, his uniform rumbled, his dark eyes shadowed with lack of sleep. "Nothing should have survived the boiling cauldron. Yet the dead traitor capered in the water, as if he mocked death." He made the hand sign against evil. "The Lord Turner must have been some kind of demon, a servant of the Dark Lord."

The queen shivered. "That *thing* was a member of our royal council, a lord of Lanverness, yet we suspected nothing."

"And all of Pellanor witnessed those glowing red eyes, a parboiled corpse defying death."

The queen stared at her royal son, disappointed that he only saw one move ahead. "Witnessing the demon is not the problem." She shook her head. "In fact, it may work to our advantage."

The prince looked skeptical. "Rumors run rampant in the city. They're saying the red comet marks the end of days. That the gates of hell will open, disgorging an army of undead to conquer the lands of Erdhe for the Dark Lord."

She fingered her necklace of black pearls. "We need answers not rumors. Where is Lord Highgate? We ordered him to attend us?"

"He was called away on an urgent summons."

Her patience snapped. "More urgent than *our* summons? He should be here when we need him."

The prince stared, his eyes wide in astonishment.

His surprise stopped her like a slap in the face. She ceased pacing and reached for a facade of calm. The undead traitor had unnerved her more than she cared to admit...but the queen could never lose control, always a rock of confidence for her kingdom. She settled herself in the ornate chair, arranging the folds of her crimson gown, her face returning to chiseled stone. "We need answers not speculation. We must know what we fight."

The prince rose from his chair, pacing in front of the cold fireplace. "But aren't you worried about panic? About the rumors raging through the city like wildfire?"

She studied the angry red scar that ran the length of his handsome face. Her royal son had proven valiant with a sword, but he had much to learn about ruling. "The people saw a demon defy the cauldron's boiling death...but they also saw a prince kill that same demon, taking its head with a single stroke of blue steel." She gave him a chance to consider her words. When he said nothing, she prompted him with a question. "How goes the recruiting for the army?"

Puzzlement scrawled across his face. "The numbers are up, more than double from a fortnight ago. Why?"

Liandra nodded. "If anyone doubted the presence of evil, that doubt died in the courtyard. The people of Pellanor saw tangible proof that Darkness stalks our world, a force to be reckoned with. But by beheading the demon you proved that Darkness can be defeated. Men flock to join the army because they recognize the need to fight...and they trust in their warrior-prince and their queen to lead them to victory." She shook her head. "The people of Pellanor are not the problem."

"Then what has you so worried?"

She took a deep breath, deciding to give him the bitter truth. "Our problems are legion." She gestured toward the chessboard in mid-play, white beleaguered by red. "Our army is decimated by the rebellion, making Lanverness a rich prize for our neighbors. We scramble to rebuild our forces but we may not have enough time. And now we have more than just swords to defeat." She stared at the empty seat on the far side of the chess board. "The Dark Lord plays against us...by rules we do not understand. The game has changed. How can a demon defy death? What powers do they have? How do we defeat them? How can we fight what we do not understand?" She reached for a defeated castle, the carved ivory cool against her skin. "And one question, above all others, plagues us at night."

He stared at her, waiting.

Her voice carried the weight of a kingdom. "Whom do we trust?"

His eyes widened. "More of those things?"

"Where there is one, why not two? That thing sat at our council table, at our right hand, yet we never suspected." She set the chess piece on the table, deliberately knocking the ivory castle on its side. "One demon nearly toppled our throne. How much more damage might two cause?"

His gaze narrowed. "Whom do you suspect?"

"Easier to list those we trust." Her voice dropped to a whisper. "And there is one traitor who has yet to face justice."

"*Danly!*" The prince made the name a curse.

"Just so." Liandra shuddered to think that she might have birthed a demon. She locked that thought in her private vault of nightmares and stared at the chessboard, forcing her mind to the problems at hand. "But if Danly is a demon, then the Dark Lord missed a great opportunity."

Prince Stewart's voice held a shred of hope. "How so?"

"Had we executed Danly in the courtyard, in full view of the people, and had he proved to be a demon, then the royal family would be tainted by evil, proof that we carry the spawn of Darkness." Her voice deepened. "Never forget, we need the trust of the people to rule. The Dark Lord missed a second opportunity to topple our throne."

The prince nodded, his face thoughtful. "Then the Dark Lord is not infallible." He gave her a smile brimming with admiration. "You will find a way to win, Mother, you always do."

She did not shatter his illusion. Liandra kept her face confident, but inside she wondered how a mere mortal could thwart the God of Darkness.

A knock sounded.

Liandra startled, her nerves taut. She hid her lapse by gesturing toward the door. "See to that."

The prince answered the door.

The Master Archivist swept into the chamber, his dark eyes blazing. He bowed to the queen and extended a scroll. "Majesty, you have a visitor."

Puzzled, she accepted the scroll. Her eyes widened when she saw the dark blue seal. She broke the seal and read the message. Her stare slid to her shadowmaster. "There is nothing here but an introduction."

He nodded. "A Kiralynn monk seeks an audience with the queen of Lanverness."

She sat back in the chair. "At long last the mysterious monks come down from their mountain monastery. Perhaps Sir Cardemir met with success." She stared at her counselor. "He came alone, no entourage?"

"Alone and on foot, seeking an audience with the queen. The gate guard alerted one of my shadowmen. I thought it best to see the monk for myself."

The queen tapped the scroll against her palm. "Perhaps this monk can solve the riddle of the demon."

The master nodded, a shrewd gleam in his dark gaze. "Where will you meet him?"

She considered the options. "Make him welcome. Offer him meat and mead, the best of both. We shall meet with him in two turns of the hourglass in the throne room."

"A formal audience?"

"We shall treat with him as one power to another, formal but private. The Kiralynn Order may be the ally we need in the fight against the Dark Lord...but we must not be seen as a supplicant."

"Who will you have in attendance?"

"Our heir and our master of shadows." She gestured to the two men. "And Sir Durnheart with his great blue sword for a show of strength. We want this meeting to be both private and discreet. See that it is arranged and then return to escort us to the throne room."

The master saluted. "As you command."

The prince and the shadowmaster took their leave. The queen rang a hand bell. Lady Sarah was the first to respond, dropping into a deep curtsey. "Yes, your majesty?"

"Attend us. We must prepare for an audience." Liandra considered her wardrobe. "We will have the deep purple gown with the dagged sleeves and the deep v-neck of gold. We must look our most regal."

The queen gave herself over to the comforting ritual of image. She sat before the mirror, her women busy like bees attending the hive queen. Liandra studied the mirror as her women combed and coiffed her raven-black hair, the soft lustrous curls falling to her shoulder in a sensual temptation. Feather-light strokes added accents of paint beneath her eyes and a faint flush to her cheeks, signs of youth and beauty covering her true age. For jewels, Liandra selected a long strand of emeralds set in gold, a show of wealth combined with elegance. When all else was done, the crown of state was settled on her brow, a heavy circlet of golden roses adorned with emeralds, the symbol of her sovereign power.

The queen stepped back from the mirror to study her reflection. A vision of beauty, elegance, and power stared back at her, the perfect image for a sovereign queen. "We are pleased." She gestured to the door. "You may admit our escort."

Lady Sarah curtseyed and opened the outer door.

The crown prince wore a dashing surcoat of emerald green, his blue sword belted to his side. The master wore his usual robes of dour black, always the shadow no matter the occasion. The two men bowed low.

The queen studied their reaction, the best test of any woman's image. The prince's face reflected admiration and pride...but the master's stare smoldered. Heat washed through her, this forbidden passion would be her undoing. Liandra made her voice abrupt. "Come, we have a monk to greet." She swept from her solar, the two men following behind.

The throne room was empty, sunlight glinting off of polished marble and gleaming gold. She crossed the checkerboard floor, climbing the stairs to the Rose Throne. The prince took a position on her right, one step below the throne, while her shadowmaster stood at the foot of the dais. Liandra took the time to arrange the silk train of her gown and then signaled the herald.

The double doors opened and a small procession entered. Sir Durnheart led the honor guard, his great blue sword held erect as a precaution and a show of strength. A guard of ten soldiers followed, a proud flourish of burnished steel and emerald tabards. The queen's gaze locked on the monk. Tall and lean, in a robe of midnight blue, his shoulder length hair carried more gray than black, his face as fair as a noble's. If there was anything magical about the man, the queen could not see it.

Sir Durnheart reached the base of the throne and bowed. He took a position on the side of the dais, a protector of the throne, and then dismissed the honor guard.

The monk approached and bowed low.

The queen studied his face as he straightened. The monk's eyes widened, his gaze darting across her bejeweled cleavage before rising to meet her stare. The queen hid her smile; it was only a small lapse but it proved the monk was not immune to a woman's charms.

The monk extended his right arm, revealing a dark blue Seeing Eye tattooed on his open palm. "Seek knowledge, Protect knowledge, Share knowledge. My name is Aeroth and I bring you greetings from the Grand Master of the Kiralynn Order."

The queen gave him a gracious smile. "Welcome to our court, Master Aeroth. We have long desired to meet one of your Order, to meet a face behind the mysterious scrolls."

He nodded, his face grave. "Seclusion once served our purpose but no longer. We have stayed hidden for too long. The war is more advanced than we thought."

"War?"

"The Grand Master sends a warning of war to the rulers of the southern kingdoms. Portents predict that the Dark Lord is rising, marshalling his forces for an assault against the kingdoms of Erdhe."

The queen considered his words. "The red comet that tears a scar across the night sky?"

"That and others." His face turned grim. "The Mordant has been reborn into the body of one of our own monk-initiates. He escaped the monastery and makes his way across the southern kingdoms seeking to reclaim his seat of power in the Dark Citadel."

The monk spoke in riddles. "Reborn? What do you mean by reborn?"

"It would seem that you have already met one of the reborn."

Hope quickened in the queen, perhaps the monk held the answers she needed. "The Lord Turner was a traitor. He raised a bloody rebellion against us. We condemned him to death but it took two executions before the body lay still. We assumed he was some sort of demon or devil, a servant of the Dark Lord."

The monk nodded. "I've heard the rumors in the city, a par-boiled corpse with glowing red eyes. The traitor was a harlequin, a powerful servant of the Dark God."

"Prince Stewart severed the demon's head. The second death was final." The queen watched the monk's face, finding no hint of surprise at the grim tale; perhaps she was right to worry about more than one demon.

The monk questioned the prince. "When the corpse rose from the waters, did it seem triumphant or anguished?"

The prince looked puzzled. "It reached upwards, as if grasping for something. It screamed but I don't remember the words."

Her shadowmaster answered, his voice certain. "It said, 'Don't do this to me', and then succumbed to the prince's sword."

The monk's eyes widened. "Then I have my answer." The monk bowed low to the queen. "Your majesty, I offer apologies from the Grand Master for coming late to your court. It seems you play a larger role in this war than anyone thought."

She studied the monk with hooded eyes. "We welcome your offer of aid, but first and foremost we need answers. What was this thing that took two deaths to kill?"

"The beheading was unnecessary. The harlequin was already dead."

The queen tired of riddles. "Explain."

"The Dark Lord tempts his servants with promises of more lifetimes. At their death, the Dark Lord's greatest servants are reborn into new bodies with full memories of their past lives. In this way, the reborn may gain two lifetimes...or a hundred. These demons that walk in the guise of men are called harlequins. A harlequin's body is subject to death like any other mortal, but at death, their true nature is revealed, the red light of hell shining from their eyes. We believe the Dark Lord judges each harlequin at its death. If the harlequin has served well, he is reborn into a new body to live another lifetime. If he fails, the soul is condemned to eternal hell. The traitor failed to take Lanverness. The Dark Lord is never lenient. The traitor's soul is most likely consigned to hell for all eternity, never to be reborn." The monk stared up at the queen, his face grim. "To find a harlequin in the Rose Court proves that the Dark Lord wants your throne."

The monk's words echoed in the throne room like a death knell.

Having reached the same conclusion, the queen found cold comfort in the warning. "If the Dark Lord wants the Rose Throne so badly, why are *we* not one of these harlequins?"

The monk made a half-bow. "An astute question. The Order has no certain answer, but there are two possibilities."

The queen nodded, waiting.

"It is thought that some souls are steeped in the Light. The Dark Lord can seek to twist, tempt, or corrupt these souls but he cannot usurp them, he cannot crush them beneath the soul of a harlequin."

"And the other reason?"

He gave her a half-smile. "Women rarely gain or keep power in Erdhe, hence they are of little or no use to the Dark Lord."

She gave him an ironic smile. "Saved by prejudice. Even the gods are infected by it." Her voice held a bitter edge. "There are advantages to being underestimated...but sometimes we grow weary of it." She studied the monk, her voice velvet steel. "What aid can the Kiralynn Order offer to the Rose Throne?"

"We offer knowledge long forgotten." He reached into the pocket of his robe and withdrew a shard of milk-white quartz. "With this crystal, I offer a means to detect an awakened harlequin...to learn if another lurks within your court."

Liandra leaned forward, hope in her gaze. "How does it work?"

"In the hands of a harlequin, this crystal will glow bright red."

The queen met the Master Archivist's knowing stare and nodded. "There is one other traitor locked in our dungeon. We would have this test performed on him."

"As you wish. It is one of the reasons I have come to your court."

"*One* of the reasons?" The queen arched an eyebrow."

"Yes." The monk sighed. "I bring the condolences of the Grand Master. Your emissary, Sir Cardemir was slain by the Mordant Reborn, the first casualty of this dark war."

"*Slain?* In your monastery?" The queen struggled to understand.

"Sir Cardemir was buried with all honors. His sword, his armor, and his lute are being conveyed to Lanverness."

"But how?"

"There were no witnesses. He was found impaled on a sword, the Princess Jordan by his side."

Prince Stewart made a strangled sound but the queen ignored him. "And the princess?"

"Nearly disemboweled, she was saved by our master healer. The princess remains locked in a healing sleep. The details of the attack will remain unknown until she awakes."

"But she lives? You're sure." The prince stared at the monk, his face ashen.

The monk nodded. "I assure you, she lives. Our master healer uses more than just lore."

The queen eased back in her throne, shocked by the revelations. "Her sister fosters at our court."

"Then I owe her word of her sister's fate."

"Princess Jemma is dear to us. We will break the news ourselves."

"As you wish."

The queen stared at the monk. Talking to him was like peeling back the pages of a thick tome. She wondered what other nightmares lurked beneath his words. "So you've come to us with grim tidings and a crystal?"

The monk nodded. "I bring you a chance to detect other harlequins before they can fulfill the will of their god."

The Master Archivist asked the question the queen had been avoiding. "If the traitor in our dungeons proves to be one of these harlequins, what should be done with it? Is one death enough?"

"One death is enough for the body, but the soul is another matter. To ensure the soul is never reborn, the harlequin must be killed with a weapon of the Light, a dagger made of Dahlmar crystal. If another harlequin is found, it should be gagged and locked away in your deepest dungeon, to await death by a crystal dagger."

Prince Stewart interrupted. "What about blue steel? Will a blue steel blade put an end to these demons?"

The monk shook his head. "Blue steel will kill the body but it will not stop the rebirth of the soul."

The queen studied the monk. "And do you have one of these weapons of the Light, one of these crystal daggers?"

"There is one, yes, but it is not mine to wield."

A cryptic answer, but she let it pass. "Have other harlequins been found?"

"None so far."

The monk was sparing with his secrets. The queen probed in a different direction. "So you've come to warn of a dark war?"

He raised his right hand, revealing the Seeing Eye. "I am the herald of forgotten knowledge. I have come to bring warning that the Dark Lord is rising. If the Mordant crosses the Dragon Spine Mountains, war will come from the north. But the Order believes the war for the southern kingdoms has already started...in Coronth and here with the rebellion against the Rose Throne."

It was just as she'd feared; her true opponent was the Dark Lord. "We have long been concerned with the twisted theocracy on our northern border. We have seeded rebels into Coronth in an attempt to topple this false religion."

The monk's eyes lit with interest. "Perhaps the Order can be of help with this endeavor?"

His response told her that the monks did not know everything. Perhaps the alliance she sought would not be so one-sided. She nodded. "It seems we have much to share." Liandra needed the knowledge of the monks, but she also needed a measure of control. "But we must insist on maintaining two secrets."

The monk waited, his face neutral.

"The people of Pellanor witnessed the double death of the traitor. They saw the animated corpse rise up in the boiling cauldron, its eyes glowing red. It is imperative that the people continue to believe that the crown prince killed the demon with his blue sword. The people need a hero and they need to believe that Darkness can be defeated."

The monk nodded. "There is merit in your argument. You have my word not to say otherwise."

She glanced at her royal son's face and saw a storm brewing. She would speak to him later; her heir was prickly with his honor.

"And the second?"

"If our prisoner proves to be one of these harlequins, you must swear to keep this secret, known only to ourself and our two closest advisors."

The monk shook his head. "Any harlequin must be reported to the Grand Master. But if the demon remains secure in your dungeon, then no one else besides the bearer of the crystal dagger need ever know."

The answer was not satisfactory; this secret could put her throne at risk. "We are owed for the life of our emissary."

He gave her a half-bow. "You shall have our aid against this common enemy, but if a harlequin is found, the Grand Master must be informed." He spread his hands wide in supplication. "The Order has kept secrets for thousands of years. You can rely on our discretion."

"Yes, you've been very secretive...with your own secrets." His answer did not reassure her, but the truth was already on the table. She needed the monk's knowledge yet she had little to offer in return. "Then we must rely on your discretion." She gave him a gracious smile. "An alliance then, between the Rose Throne and the Seeing Eye?"

He nodded. "The Kiralynn Order serves the Light. We will do what we can to help."

The monk was as slippery with his words as a greased weasel, offering aid but not an alliance. The queen studied the monk, wondering how much she could trust the mysterious Order. Perhaps beggars could not be choosers. If the Dark Lord truly sought her throne, she would need all the help she could get.

43

Steffan

Religion proved a powerful tool but Steffan needed to ensure the faithful did not stray from the Dark Lord's plan. Of late, he'd sensed a change in the tension of the crowds, something more than the daily struggle for food, or the paranoid fear of the confessors. Perhaps the rebels stirred discontent, or it could be something else. Steffan needed to keep a careful watch, for religions had a way of running amok.

Sifting through the back alley whispers, he found one that snared his attention. Rumors told of a preacher, a holy man, come to spread the word of the Flame God. No one knew where the preacher came from. He just appeared one day, preaching in the back alleyways, ministering to the beggars, whores, and thieves. At first, the preacher was little more than a curiosity, a sideshow in the back alleys, but if rumors were to be believed, this so-called holy man had gained a following in the city's shadows. Fanaticism was good, but only if it conformed to Steffan's plans.

Steffan needed to see this preacher for himself and determine if the man was a threat. He followed Pip to the back of the mansion, to the servants' quarters, where a trunk of castoff clothing was kept. The redheaded lad opened the trunk, rummaging through the odd assortment. "What will you be, m'lord? A peddler, a drunk, a tanner, a priest, a..."

"...beggar." Steffan settled on a straight-backed chair and began to strip down to his breeches. "A beggar will blend in best. After all, we go to see a beggar-priest."

The lad smirked, his blue eyes full of mischief. "Yes, m'lord." The boy delved through the trunk, choosing a baggy tunic the color of mud, a filthy patch-worked cloak and a leather bag stuffed full of rags.

Pip knelt to ease off Steffan's knee-high boots. Steffan watched as the lad did his work. He'd fished the orphan-boy off the streets of Balor, buying his services for a fist full of silvers. A sometimes thief and a frequent beggar, Pip had proved quick of hand and mind and grateful for a better life. The lad served as a valet, a messenger, a collector of rumors, and a spy; a useful servant well worth the silvers. "What rumors chase the back alleyways?"

"Much the same, m'lord. Grumbles 'gainst the cruelty of the Keeper and fears 'bout the confessors and worries 'bout the rising price of bread. You already know 'bout the preacher. Most think he's a holy man sent by the Flame God to purge us of our sins." The boy began wrapping Steffan's bare feet in a collection of rags, creating beggar's boots. The lad wrinkled his nose. "Phew! These stink to the clouds. Are you sure I can't be getting' you cleaner rags, lord?"

The rags reeked of sweat and dung and piss, the perfume of the back alleys. Steffan shook his head. "The smell is a potent part of the disguise. The stench alone will turn away the gaze of the wealthy or divert the interest of thieves and soldiers alike. A healthy reek is nearly as good as invisibility."

The boy nodded, wrapping a length of twine around the rags, creating a diamond pattern to hold them in place. "I'm hearin' more and more whispers about that Dark Harper. They say he appears and disappears at a blink of an eye, playin' his harp in the taverns late at night, always harpin' against the Flame God and the Pontifax. Singin' songs 'bout heroes who steal sinners from the Flames."

Steffan had heard reports from the confessors about a bard who sang songs of sedition, stirring the people to rebellion. The confessors didn't have enough specifics to act...but it was only a matter of time till one of the wretches in the dungeon sang a different tune. "Do they say who this harper is, or where he hides?"

Pip wound the rags to the middle of Steffan's thigh, high enough to hide the breeches beneath. "Nobody seems to know, lord. Some say the harper's a phantom, disapperin' like smoke in the night. Others say he has a thousand bolt-holes, places the soldiers never look." Pip quirked a smile. "And some say he sleeps with a different woman every night. Them bards are lucky that way." The lad finished with the rags and stood. "What color for your hair, lord?"

"Make it gray, and be sure to hide the white streak in front." He tilted his head back and let the boy work the alchemist's potion into his hair, adding streaks of gray to his dark locks. "I'm interested in this harper, Pip. Bring me his name and a purse of golds is yours. If you can't find the name, then bring me a list of the taverns where he plays. I've a burning interest to hear his music."

The lad grinned. "I'll find him for you, lord." The boy finished adding the color, wiping his hands on a rag.

Steffan stood and pulled on the mud colored tunic and the patchwork cloak, completing the disguise. The coarse wool scratched against his skin. He hoped the itching was only the wool, he couldn't abide lice. "Bring me the dirt."

The boy brought him a basin of dirt. Steffan plunged his patrician hands into the soil, working the dark loam under his fingernails and smearing some on the side of his face. "That should do." The boy took the basin away and Steffan melted into his role. His back curved and his shoulders hunched. He hung his head down, gritty gray hair falling across the side of his face. Holding out his palm, he made his voice a weak quaver. "Alms for the poor?"

Pip laughed. "With that stink, you're likely to get a kick instead of a coin."

"Is there no charity in the Flame God's city?" Steffan tucked a second dagger into his belt and pointed toward the door, his voice sobering. "Lead the way. I want to see this back alley preacher for myself."

They slipped out the back door into the afternoon sun. Pip led the way, familiar with the tangled maze of narrow alleyways. Steffan followed at a discreet distance, walking with a limp, his head hung low, nothing more than a beggar of the back ways.

They found the preacher in the alley behind the vegetable market, the stink of rotting green hanging heavy in the air. The lane was crowded with people, mostly the poor, but he saw a few tradesmen in leather aprons, and even a soldier in the red tabard of the Flame.

Steffan threaded his way into the crowd, the stench of his clothes opening a space around him. He wormed his way into the knot of people until he had a view of the preacher. The old man stood on a crate, a skinny scarecrow in a soiled sackcloth, using a branch for a staff. Painfully thin, with a bald head and a long gray beard that fell in tangle to his knees, the old man looked one step away from the grave. Frail and old, the man looked inconsequential till Steffan heard his voice. The preacher had an orator's voice, deep and compelling, the kind of voice that could sway a crowd.

"Children of the Flame, you must repent! A dark time is coming, death and chaos and suffering. Only the love of the true god can save you from the torments of eternal damnation!"

Steffan watched the crowd. They seemed entranced by the mad man's ravings.

The preacher pointed to the soldier standing in the rear of the crowd. "You there, a soldier of the Flame! You wear the holy symbol of the Flame God! Your first duty must be to protect the faithful! Only sinners must burn, never the innocent. Can you tell a sinner from a saint? Beware, lest those you love burn in the Flames."

The soldier blanched pale, but others crowded forward. "Choose me! Tell me what you see!"

The preacher's hand roamed back and forth above the heads of the crowd, like a divining rod searching for water in a desert. The hand came to a stop, the finger pointing at a peasant woman with a gaggle of children clutching her skirt. "You woman, the Flame God sees you! Stand by your husband or your children will go hungry! The trials ahead will test us all, but if we believe, if we follow the truth, then the faithful will survive!"

Steffan hid a smile. The old man put on quite a show, part preacher, part fortuneteller, a perfect mummer's farce.

The preacher's hand resumed roaming, only this time, the hand pointed directly at Steffan. For the first time, Steffan got a good look at the preacher's eyes. Pale milky-white eyes, clogged by a film of blindness...yet the man stared straight at Steffan. The blind man *looked* at him. "You, beggar! You are not what you seem!"

A shiver raced down Steffan's spine, as if some meddling god of Light sought to unmask him.

"You wear the rags of the alleyways but you are more than you seem!"

Steffan reached for the dagger hidden beneath his tunic.

"The god's hand lies heavy upon you, yet those who lie are often themselves deceived. A crossroad is coming. Follow the light and your life will be spared! Fall to evil and you risk eternal damnation! Darkness is coming! Darkness to smother the Flames!"

The milky gaze passed Steffan by, looking for another victim.

Steffan released his dagger, angry at his own reaction. The old fool was nothing more than a charlatan. Determined to unmask the showman's secrets, he shuffled to the front, seeking a better view. As he suspected, the truth was in the details. An urchin-lad sat huddled at the preacher's feet, his fist holding tight to the man's sackcloth tunic. Clearly the boy was acting as the old man's eyes. It was all an elaborate con. Little wonder the peasants thought him a holy man.

Steffan listened long enough to be sure the preacher was not a threat. Having seen enough, he eased his way out of the crowd and signaled to Pip. The lad peeled away from the crowd and led the way back through the maze of alleys.

Steffan kept to his disguise, shuffling at a beggar's gait, mulling the words of the preacher in his mind. Easy enough to have the old man rounded up and consigned to the Flames, but the charlatan seemed harmless, no need to deprive the people of the show. Still, for a moment he'd felt something, as if the Lords of Light meddled. Steffan shook his head at the absurd thought. Everything was going according to the Dark Lord's plans. If there was any impediment, it was the rebels and their elusive bard. Steffan wasted his time chasing back alley rumors when he should be chasing songs. He'd find this dark harper and feed him to the Flames. Then they'd be nothing to stop him, nothing to impede the Dark Lord's plans. Steffan smiled; may the Dark Lord's pleasure reign...over all the lands of Erdhe.

44

Katherine

A song pulled Kath from sleep. But it wasn't really a song, more like a deep, rich hum. The melody hovered on the edge of hearing, teasing her mind, tugging her to wakefulness. She cautiously opened her eyes. Tree bark formed a low vault overhead, burls, and knots, and swirls of patterned wood, the smell of cedar strong in the air...as if a tree had swallowed her. Confused, she looked for the source of light. She found the Treespeaker sitting cross-legged, tending a small fire ringed by stones.

"Ah, she wakes."

Kath tried to make sense of her surroundings. The space was no bigger than a small tent, cozy and warm like a well-sealed cabin, but the walls and the low vaulted ceiling were made of rough burled wood. "What is this place? Am I dreaming?"

The Treespeaker's voice was full of warmth. "This is the Heart Tree. You have slept within the hollow of the tree's trunk for three days, held safe within the dreams of the great tree."

Kath tried to make sense of the Treespeaker's words. "The humming?"

The Treespeaker smiled. "So, you can hear the tree. Your experience in the gray veil has drawn you closer to the Forest."

She remembered the cave and the dark wolf, the glowing red eyes and the snapping fangs...her arm! Kath flexed her left hand and felt the fingers obey...only a faint memory of pain. "But how?" Half afraid to see the truth, she tugged the blanket away from her arm. An ugly mangle of white scars crisscrossed her forearm...but the flesh was healed, the arm was whole. Staring in wonder, she flexed her hand. Relief washed through her. She had a shield arm, she was still a warrior. "How?"

"You came back to us covered in blood, your left sleeve in tatters. But when we searched for a wound, we found only scars. The Lords of Light must have intervened on your behalf."

Kath remembered the flash of bright light and the sudden warmth. "But I don't understand." She sat up and the blanket slipped down, revealing her nakedness. Suddenly vulnerable, Kath clutched at the blanket.

The Treespeaker laughed, a sound like rustling leaves. "Child you amaze me. You defeat a demon in the in-between yet you fear to be naked!"

Kath felt her face blaze red.

"Your clothes were bloody and torn. They have been washed and sewn."

She remembered her missing weapons. "My sword and axes?" Her throat tightened. "The crystal dagger?"

"There, beside you."

A small pile of belongings sat against the far wall. Her twin axes in their harness of tooled leather sat on top, the red hawk embossed with wings wide and talons extended. Next to the axes lay her short sword of good Castlegard steel...and the crystal dagger in a leather sheath. She reached for the dagger and found her mage-stone gargoyle, the leather cord tangled in the sheath. Kath snatched up the gargoyle. "I thought I'd lost this!" Relieved, she settled the leather loop over her head, the small figurine nestled between her breasts...and then she remembered the amber pyramid. She searched among her things but it was not there. A frantic fear gnawed at her. "There's something missing. Did you find a small amber pyramid?"

"They tell me a dagger was found hidden in your right boot, but there is nothing else."

"But I had it in the cavern, in the gray space."

"Then perhaps it is still there. Perhaps it was the price of your return."

The Treespeaker's words made a strange sort of sense...but Kath felt as if something of great value had been taken from her. Magic had become more important than she'd ever imagined.

Clutching her gargoyle, she stared at the small fire, remembering the fight in the cave, a thousand questions flooding her mind. "But what happened? What was that place? And the wolf with the red eyes? What was that thing? And why did I have the crystal dagger but not my sword?" The image of Danya crouched on atop the boulder flashed through her mind. "And what about Danya and Bryx? Are they safe? Is the wolf awake? Is Danya back to being herself?"

The Treespeaker held her hands up in supplication. "You chatter like a squirrel! Be at peace and I will try to explain."

Kath settled back, snug beneath the blankets, watching the firelight reflected in the Treespeaker's strange golden eyes.

"You needn't worry about your friends. The wolf is awake and the girl is healing. Given rest and food and warmth, they will be both be fine."

Relief flooded through Kath, she couldn't bear to think of them trapped in that awful place. "But what happened? How could a wolf have glowing red eyes? What was that thing?"

The Treespeaker shook her head. "Youth is always so impatient."

Kath tried to contain her questions, but it was hard.

The Treespeaker's voice took on the rhythm of a storyteller. "The elder trees of the Forest are thousands of years old. Their roots grow deep...and so do their thoughts. The great trees are rooted in the mortal world, but their thoughts delve into the gray veil, into the space between this life and the next. The trees dream deep, they dream long. But of late, a dark taint has crept into the space between, a poisonous strangler vine choking and distorting the dreams of mortals. The great trees are immune to the nightmares of mortals, but they warn of a growing evil, of a shadowy threat that could spill into the waking world. The Dark Lord seeks to influence the dreams of men by invading the gray veil."

Kath sat bolt upright. "That wolf was the Dark Lord?"

"A minion or a demon, but not the Dark God himself. He sends his minions into the gray veil to corrupt the minds of men, to bend their dreams to Darkness. To the great trees, this threat appears as a strangler vine, in the wolf's dreams the threat appeared as a great wolf, both are manifestations of the Dark." The Treespeaker added a sprinkle of herbs to the flames, a flare of golden light filling the hollow. "This war is waged for hearts and minds, not just for golds and swords."

The Treespeaker's words struck a memory in Kath's mind. "In the monastery, when I learned to use my magic, Master Rizel said much the same thing."

The Treespeaker nodded. "The monks have their own wisdom, rooted in a deep history. You do well to heed their counsel."

Kath stared at the Treespeaker, trying to read beneath her words. The tree-witch was no different than the monks, full of partial answers and cryptic replies. Kath felt as if she was caught in some grand design, a great tapestry of events, but she could only see the smallest portion of the weave, and yet so much depended on her choices. She needed better answers; she was tired of groping in the dark. Frustration spilled into her voice. "I don't understand. What was that place? What happened?"

"Your friends entered the gray veil, the wolf because of a head injury, the woman because of her magic. The Dark Lord used his minion to trap your friends within the veil. If they'd remained trapped much longer, their mortal bodies would have succumbed to starvation, their spirits forever bound to the gray realm. But chance, or fate, brought you to the Forest, one of the few places where a mortal might influence the gray veil."

Kath leaned forward, holding the blanket tight. "There are other places?"

The Treespeaker nodded. "A few. They say the gray veil is thin on the Isle of Souls, where fortunetellers can see the future and priests can hear the voice of their chosen god."

Kath shivered, remembering her visit to the Isle, the brightly colored tarot cards and the deep, raspy voice of Valin. She tightened her grip on her gargoyle. "So the Forest is like the Isle of Souls?"

"No, not at all." The Treespeaker smiled. "The veil is no thinner here than most places in Erdhe...but the trees are the difference. The great trees know the way to the gray realm. The trees dream deep, they dream long, their roots soaking up wisdom from both sides of the veil."

Kath remembered falling into the golden stare of the Forest. "So the trees showed me the way to the gray realm?"

"The trees and your magic."

"But why didn't I have my sword or my axes?"

The Treespeaker shrugged, an elegant gesture, firelight rippling along the length of her silver hair. "Who can say? Perhaps steel is not as potent in the gray realm. Or perhaps the gods gave you the weapons you most needed."

Kath's voice was a whisper. "The crystal dagger."

The Treespeaker nodded, her voice solemn. "Long have I yearned for such a weapon, for a chance at vengeance, but it comes too late for me."

Kath clutched the dagger. "What do you mean?"

"Having lost much, I gained more, becoming a part of the Forest, a servant of leaf and bark, yet I cannot forget the debt of the past."

"Then you knew of the dagger before I came?"

"The great trees have always known."

Another cryptic answer, Kath unsheathed the crystal blade and held it to the light. The milk-white crystal reflected the firelight but it did not glow from within. Kath wondered if she'd imagined the light.

"In the cavern, in the gray realm, this dagger glowed like a shard of frozen moonlight...yet now it seems no more than ordinary quartz."

"Some items of great power exist in more than one realm, waiting for a hero's hand. The crystal dagger is steeped in the Light. It glows like a beacon in the gray realm."

Kath stared, astonished. "You saw it?"

"I saw some but not all."

Kath considered all that she'd learned. "Ordinary steel would not have killed the demon-wolf." It was a statement, not a question.

"You learn well. The wolf was a thing of Darkness. It takes courage and free will and the Light to defeat the Dark."

Kath shook her head, struggling with her thoughts. "When the wolf died and I was stuck in the void, all I could think of was returning the crystal dagger to the world of men, back where it could make a difference."

"Perhaps the wielder is needed as much as the blade." The Treespeaker's words dropped to a whisper. "But guard the blade well, for friends and foes will both be drawn to its power."

A shiver ran through Kath despite the fire's warmth. She sheathed the crystal blade, keeping it close at hand.

"You should rest for you have done well. The trees dream easier. The mortal realm will not be enslaved by nightmares...at least not this time."

Kath felt the need for her companions, one in particular. "Where's Duncan?" Her face flushed red, but she had to ask.

The Treespeaker laughed like a rustle of leaves in the summer sun. "That man paces like an angry tree-leopard. I had to forbid him from the Heart Tree else you would not have healed."

A smile crept across Kath's face.

The Treespeaker added a handful of herbs to the fire. The flames flared bright green, releasing the scents of pine and spruce and cedar, and something else, something musky. "You have accomplished more than you know. The clan leaders witnessed the fight in the gray veil. They saw for themselves the threat of Darkness. Your bravery has swayed them. The next clan gathering will yield a different answer. The Children of the Forest will aid the white-eyes in the fight against the Dark." She bowed her head. "You have gained an ally for the Light. Perhaps in time, the wounds of enmity will heal."

Hope flooded through Kath, but then a strange languidness crept upon her. She felt suddenly tired, barely able to keep her eyes open.

"Sleep, warrior of the Light. You have won a great battle in the gray realm, but the true war will be fought in the mortal world. Having lost one battle, the Dark Lord will be even more ruthless in this realm." The Treespeaker made a sign of blessing. "Sleep with the peace of the Forest. Rest and prepare for the trials ahead. For in the immortal battle, you will need both the sword and the dagger if you are to be victorious."

Sleep claimed her. Kath surrendered to the deep hum of the Heart Tree, a brief respite before the coming storm.

45

The Mordant

Snowcapped peaks reared overhead, jagged and sharp as a gore hound's toothy maw. The Dragon Spine Mountains made a fierce barrier, dividing north from south, but the Mordant knew every barrier had its weakness. The knights put too much faith in their walls, man-made or otherwise. Walls were no stronger than the men who held them. Twist the right man and the drawbridge would fall, the gates thrown open wide. The Mordant laughed, his mirth echoing against the mountaintops. He'd stopped fighting for walls many lifetimes ago, now he fought for men's souls, a much more interesting game.

He rode alone, his horse picking its way up the chiseled switchbacks. A bitter wind howled down out of the mountains, carrying a breath of snow. The Mordant shivered, bloodstains clinging to his back, sticky and cold. He pulled the maroon cloak close, hiding the stains and the jagged hole in the silver surcoat. Clad in the armor of a dead man, he went in search of his enemies. The irony appealed to him. His enemies provided all the right disguises, first the Kiralynn monks and now the Octagon Knights.

His servant, Sir Raymond waited in a small cave at the base of the switchbacks with the bulk of their provisions and the extra horses. The Mordant would have preferred to bring the knight along, servants were always useful, but there was no easy way to disguise the traitor's marks branding his face. So the Mordant rode alone, eager to sow one last seed of chaos before crossing into the north.

Rounding the last switchback, he found the frozen keep looming overhead. An ugly piece of work, Cragnoth Keep was a single, stubby tower, thrust like a blunt finger pointing towards a frozen sky. The keep had none of the elegance of Castlegard, no soaring towers of mage-stone or fancy gargoyles, only brute stone wrested from the mountains. Made of massive blocks of granite, the squat tower straddled a tunneled passageway that led to the far side of the mountains. Legends said a single knight could hold the narrow passageway against all the hordes of the north. The Mordant shook his head at the absurdity. The knights loved their dreams of heroism almost as much as they loved their honor, both would be their undoing.

His horse plodded to the base of the tower, blowing twin plumes of mist into the cold. A knight clutching a spear approached. Hoarfrost clung to his thick brown mustache, his maroon cloak pulled tight around his shoulders, a thin shield against the cold. "Welcome, brother. What brings you to the frozen crag?"

The Mordant dismounted, making sure the wind did not tug his cloak away from his back. "My new posting. I'm here to report to the prince."

The knight sneered. "What deed earned you a posting to this frozen hell?"

The Mordant stamped his feet against the cold. "I fell afoul of the marshal. Guess I spent too much time whoring with the women at Bell's, so he ordered me to the crag." The Mordant shrugged. "I was gaining a fearsome reputation with the ladies. Maybe the marshal didn't like the competition."

The knight snorted. "That one-eyed bastard visiting Bell's? Hah! The marshal's only mistress is duty, a cold bitch like the crag." He gestured toward a cave opening chiseled into the mountainside. "Give your horse to one of the stable lads and then get yourself up to the great room. The prince is most likely there for the noon meal. He likes to eat with the men." The knight gave a half-hearted salute and returned to his post by the tunneled passageway, standing guard beside a great bronze bell.

The Mordant led his mount toward the narrow cave. The warmth of horses and the rich smell of hay offered a welcome relief from the bitter cold. A copper-haired stable lad rushed to accept his horse. The Mordant fussed with a saddlebag, taking stock of the stables. He counted stalls for two-dozen horses but only a handful were occupied. The numbers were deceiving. Sir Raymond had warned that the bulk of the horses were stabled below the tree line, leaving only a few for scouts and messengers. Cragnoth Keep was a defensive post. The knights of the crag fought on foot...safe behind their walls of stone, never guessing who walked among them.

The Mordant threw his saddlebag over his shoulder. "Where might I find the prince?"

The lad stroked the neck of the chestnut mare. "Prince Lionel is most likely in the great hall, supping with the men. You're lucky not to miss mealtime."

The Mordant smiled, pleased to gain the name of the resident prince. Sir Raymond hadn't been sure which brother held the posting. "You'll find a few apples in the other saddlebag, for you or the horse, whoever's hungrier."

The lad flashed a broad smile. "My thanks! Your name, Sir?"

"Sir Alynt of Wyeth." He chose a simple name, a common name, one that was easily forgotten. "And see that you take good care of my horse."

The lad bobbed his head and the Mordant strode into the biting cold, careful to keep his maroon cloak close. He crossed the small yard to the keep, surprised to find the ironbound door unlocked and unguarded; the knights grew lax with peace. Shouldering the door open, he startled a blond-haired knight dozing on a bench. A gust of cold wind blew in behind the Mordant but the knight misread the omen.

"Shut the bloody door." The knight coughed and sputtered, covering his laziness with a stern look. "Haven't seen you before. A new one, huh? Who you here to replace?"

The knight's voice held a thread of hope, proving the crag was a punishment posting, just as Sir Raymond had said. The Mordant kept to his simple tale. "No one. I got on the wrong side of the marshal and found myself posted to Cragnoth. Nearly froze my manhood off just getting up here."

The blond knight barked a rude laugh. "Wait till you take your turn standing watch atop the tower. Try taking a piss up there and it'll freeze solid." The knight's laugh held a cruel edge. "Welcome to the bloody crag."

The Mordant nodded. "Where do I find the steward and the prince?"

"Steward Ballard will be in the great room oversee'n the noon meal. Prince Lionel will most likely be there as well."

"Which way?"

"Only one way up and one way down." He gestured to the stone stairs. "The ground floor is for stores, the armory and supplies. The next three floors are the sleeping cells. The fifth floor is the great room and the kitchens."

"What lies above the fifth?"

"The sixth is for the prince and above that is the signal tower. You'll see plenty of the tower soon enough. Fresh knights always draw the coldest postings." The knight settled back on his bench, a lazy grin on his face.

The Mordant muttered, "Thanks," and made his way down the hall to the stairs. The tight stone spiral threaded up through the heart of the tower, the steps worn deep with centuries of use. Countless knights had tread this path, defending the southern kingdoms against his armies...and now the Mordant walked those same steps, unopposed...even invited, all for the sake of a silver surcoat and a maroon cloak. He shook his head. Time and decay had eroded a once worthy opponent; the Octagon did not deserve to survive the coming war.

The Mordant breathed deep, testing the air for Darkness. Such a potent mix of ambition, anger, cruelty and malice, all fertile ground for his plans. One thread in particular drew his attention, darker and stronger than the others. The thread he'd followed up the mountainside, the thread foreseen by the Dark Lord, his reason for coming to Cragnoth Keep.

He climbed to the fifth floor, following the Dark scent to the great hall. Heat and the tempting smell of spit-roasted meat announced the hall. The room took up half the tower, heat roaring from two stone fireplaces at either end. Trestle tables and benches ran the length of the room, crowded with knights in silver surcoats, great swords, axes, and weapons of all sorts kept close at hand. The bristle of weapons suggested the knights were not quite as lax as they seemed.

The Mordant paused in the arched doorway, studying the men, unraveling the tangled threads of Darkness. He counted thirty-seven knights, an even mixture of young men and graybeards, sitting in clusters at the tables. Six knights sat at the head table, but none of the threads of Darkness led to the leaders, making his task all the more challenging.

One knight interested him above all others. He sat at the far table, a large mountain of a man holding court with seven of the younger knights, each with their own Dark taint. The Mordant smiled, he'd found his fertile ground. But first he needed to pay his respects to the prince.

He entered the hall and crossed to stand before the head table. The dull murmur of conversation fell to a hush, the weight of stares following the newcomer. The Mordant stood before the table and saluted, fist to chest, keeping his stare on the blond-maned knight seated in the ornate chair. "Lord prince, I've been posted to Cragnoth Keep by orders of the knight marshal."

The prince wore no token of royalty, just a silver surcoat like any other knight, but he had the air of command, this youngest son of his enemy. "Do you come with a name, sir knight?"

"Sir Alynt of Wyeth."

Smooth-shaven with dark green eyes, the prince had a ready smile. "And your orders, Sir Alynt?"

The Mordant opened the pouch on his belt and handed the prince a folded parchment, the wax seal lifted from a message carried by the murdered knights. Fortunately the knight marshal had a simple hand, easy to mimic.

The prince gave the seal a cursory glance and then opened the parchment.

The Mordant hid his smile; mortals always saw what they wanted to see.

"Another disciplinary posting," the prince shook head in dismay. "And it says you have a shoulder injury. You're to be excused from arms practice for a fortnight."

The Mordant nodded, a necessary ruse, his skill at arms would not pass scrutiny.

"You'll be excused from practice, but we'll have no shirkers here. You'll take your turn standing guard along with the others."

The Mordant kept his voice humble. "As you say, m'Lord."

"Cragnoth Keep is a minor posting, but I expect you to serve with honor."

The prince had the voice of command...but the Mordant had the voice of deceit. He thumped his fist to his chest in salute and infused his voice with fervor. "Honor to the Octagon. I am yours to command."

The prince flashed a ready smile. "Then be welcome, Sir Alynt, every sword is needed at the crag." He gestured to a chair. "Join us for the noontime meal. I would know the men who serve me."

The Mordant took a seat and the murmur of conversation resumed like a slow tide. A steward brought a goblet and a plate heaped with roast venison, fried potatoes and leeks, all smothered in gravy. The hearty meal was welcome after the long cold ride. The Mordant plied his table knife, keeping his mouth full and his answers short. He made a point of knocking over a wine goblet, a show of clumsiness to support his tale of an injured shoulder, but otherwise he made himself small, a man of little note and less consequence. Talk at the table flowed around him, rumors of war, speculation about the red comet, and tales of skirmishes in the northern steppes.

The meal passed without incident. Afterward, the steward showed him to a cell on the second floor. Small and spare, it had a simple cot and a chamber pot, hooks on the walls for weapons and clothing. The steward issued him a sheepskin liner for under his cloak and a pair of leather gauntlets lined with fur, weapons against the cold. He talked the steward out of a spare surcoat, eliminating the need to hide the telltale bloodstains.

Safely disguised, the Mordant melted into the simple routine of the crag, eating with the other men, taking his turn walking the walls. He spoke little and listened always, biding his time, waiting for a chance to plant his seeds of chaos.

He drew lookout duty on the tower top, the cold wind biting his face like a pack of hungry wolves. Huddled beneath his maroon cloak, he stared for long hours into the north, watching for an enemy that had already breached the tower's walls. Amused by the irony, he walked the tower ramparts, circling the wood kept dry by thick tarps, wood that waited for a flame to announce the start of war...as if the comet in the sky was not warning enough. Mortals were so blind.

On his second watch, the Mordant got the chance he waited for. The big knight sought him out, Darkness drawn to Darkness. Built like a mountain, he stood over seven feet tall, broad shoulders, a square jaw, cruel eyes, a huge battle-axe strapped to his back. Given the man's enormous size, the Mordant wondered if the knight carried the blood of a Taal, another irony.

"Do you know who I am?" The knight's voice was a menacing rumble, a bully seeking to establish dominance.

"Few in the maroon do not know of Sir Trask and his great battle-axe."

The knight's eyes narrowed, his stare spearing the Mordant.

"I meant no offense. Your skill with the axe is legend, as is your strength. You have a following in Castlegard, especially among the younger noblemen. You should be a champion and a commander of the Octagon, not exiled to this frozen tower."

Trask grunted, his eyes burning with interest.

"Too many good men are wasted by the Octagon, wasted by the king and the knight marshal."

Trask grumbled. "Dullards lulled by honor."

The Mordant took the opening. "The Octagon is a hollow promise. We come from noble families, yet what do we have to show for it? A maroon cloak and a silver surcoat?" The Mordant scowled. "How dare they exile us to a frozen rock without even a woman to warm our beds?" The Mordant leaned close to the big knight, his voice flush with quiet outrage. "We are the third and fourth sons of barons and dukes and even kings. Nobility runs in our veins. We deserve better than this." He made his voice a whisper. "We have the skills to take what we want. Gold, women, land...it is all ours for the taking...if only we dare."

"You speak of treason."

"I speak the truth."

Trask grunted, his face guarded.

"You'll die here, you know. The knight marshal will never release you from Cragnoth Keep. You're too much of a threat. You'll die guarding this frozen midden heap."

The knight's eyes narrowed, listening but never agreeing.

"I know you want it."

Trask proved smarter than he looked, smart enough to remain cautious. He turned without answering and strode from the tower. The Mordant watched him go, content to plant the first seed.

Days passed and the Mordant kept to himself, eating in the great hall, sharpening his sword, burnishing his armor, watching Trask. He listened to the small talk, marking the undercurrents of discontent, but he said little, waiting for the seeds of chaos to take root.

He did not have long to wait. Heavy boot steps climbed the tower stairs. The Mordant kept his gaze on the north, his back to the stairs, hiding his smile.

Trask stepped behind him, a hulking presence. "Cold enough for you?"

A bitter wind howled across the open tower, but the Mordant just shrugged. "I'll manage...I dream of something better."

Trask stepped close, his voice a low rumble. "Still dreaming of treason?"

The Mordant breathed deep. The knight was thick with Darkness, ripe for the taking. "I know you want it."

Trask hissed, "And what if I do."

"Then reach for it. A single deserter would be hunted down and killed...but if enough knights turned, you'd have a force to be reckoned with." He turned and stared into Trask's dark eyes. "All that is needed is a leader."

"*You* would never get the numbers."

"Me, no. But I've seen the way the younger knights are drawn to you. They look to you for leadership."

Trask shook his head. "At best, I might persuade a third of the knights. It would not be enough."

"Then make it enough. Force the issue."

"How?"

"Cragnoth Keep is full of factions. A third of the knights, most of the older ones, are loyal to the prince. A third follow you. The rest are nothing more than sheep waiting to follow the strongest sword."

Trask nodded.

"So be the strongest sword, force the issue. Once the deed is done, once the blood is spilled, there will be no turning back." The Mordant lowered his voice. "And those who survive will follow you, damned for the deed whether they fought or not."

Trask whispered. "Open rebellion."

"*No,* a sword in the back. Treachery and stealth are your best weapons. Capture the prince and kill his loyal men while they sleep. Take the tower before the others wake."

Trask nodded. "And then the sheep will turn."

"Exactly, but they must prove their loyalty. Every man must have blood on his hands or there is no trusting them."

"How?"

"Use the prince."

Trask hissed, "You're a ruthless bastard, Alynt. I'm surprised I never heard your name before." When the Mordant didn't answer, the big knight rumbled, "And what do you get out of this, *Sir* Alynt?"

The Mordant hid the Darkness within, showing the knight the face of a young man hungry for life, desperate for freedom. "I get free of the maroon. I get a woman in my bed and gold in my purse. I get a better life."

Trask stared down at him, the decision hanging in the balance.

The Mordant pressed the point. "Women, gold, and land...escape from this frozen rock and a share of the plunder claimed by your axe. All are owed to you as payment for slights of the past."

Trask grinned, a bloodthirsty mix of menace and avarice. "I'll talk to the others."

"No." The Mordant's voice held a deadly edge. "Talk is a waste of time, a waste and a risk. Take command. Issue the orders and then act the same night. Any who do not agree must be killed. Fortune favors the bold. Reach for what you want or don't reach at all, there is no other choice."

Trask stepped close, towering over the Mordant. "And what if I decide to kill you instead?" His voice lowered to a growl. "One shove and you'd die, a simple accident."

"Then you'd have one less sword to serve you, one less chance of winning." The Mordant stood his ground, his face closed, hiding the Darkness lurking within.

The big knight began to laugh, the sound of crashing boulders. "You have guts Alynt, I'll grant you that. And I'll think on your words." Trask turned and strode toward the stairs, a mountain of maroon walking into the wind.

The Mordant watched him go, the threads of Darkness tightening around the knight like a hangman's noose. It was only a matter of time till Trask turned his cloak. The Mordant suppressed a laugh. His enemies gave him all the right tools, first the monks, then the forest, and now the knights. He'd set them all against each other, brother against brother, a grand dark divide...and all of it started with a few choice words. Deceit was the sharpest sword of all.

Two days later, the word was passed. A soft knock in the dead of the night marked the signal for the killing, each man assigned to specific murders. The Mordant wore chainmail under his silver surcoat, a long sword belted to his side, a dagger in his hand. Slipping down the hall, he counted two doors to the left. Rusty hinges issued a soft creak, but the snoring from within hid the warning. The Mordant crossed to the cot. Sir Carline slept, a loud rumble of snores pushing past his mustache, his breath heavy with garlic. The Mordant smothered a laugh, garlic never kept the monsters away. Kneeling on the knight's chest, he pressed the dagger against his victim's throat.

Sir Carline sputtered awake. "What is this?"

"A gift from the Mordant." He waited to see the fear in the knight's eyes and then slashed his throat. Blood spurted bright red, a wet, gurgling sound.

The Mordant cleaned the dagger on the blanket and then went in search of new prey. Muffled sounds filled the hall, but so far there was no clash of steel. He passed another conspirator, blood dripping from the knight's sword, a grin of revenge on his face. The Mordant nodded, intent on his own mission of death. He reached the next door and lifted the latch. Torchlight from the hallway lanced into the small cell.

Sir Belmort proved a light sleeper. "What is it?"

The Mordant hid the dagger behind his back and stepped close to the cot. "The prince is asking for you."

The burly knight sat up, peering into the dark. "What, now?"

The Mordant struck like a snake, the dagger plunging deep into the man's right eye. Eight inches of steel skewered the knight's brain. His legs twitched, thrumming against the bed. His bowels gave out in a rush of stink. The knight slumped dead, another satisfying kill.

Out in the hallway, the warning bell clanged.

The Mordant cleaned his blade and stepped out into the chaos. He kept to the plan, shouting above the clangor of the bell. "Fire in the great hall! Fire above!"

Knights rushed from their cells, some of them struggling to dress, most still in their nightshirts. More than a few carried a weapon of some sort, but they wore no armor, no chainmail, no shields, sheep already shorn before the slaughter.

The Mordant herded the sheep toward the stairs. "You're needed above for a bucket brigade. Be quick about it." He followed them up the stairs, spilling into the great hall...but there was no fire save for the flickering torches and the blazing hearths.

The knights gaped, milling in confusion. More than one indignant voice shouted, "What's the meaning of this?"

Sixteen conspirators ringed the great hall, all clad in chainmail, all with weapons drawn. The Mordant sheathed his dagger and drew his sword, taking a position at the top of the stairs. The undecided knights began to bleat. "Where's the prince? What's the meaning of this?"

Trask's voice boomed through the great hall. *"Silence!"* He glared at the knights, the half-moon blade of his axe dripping with gore. "The prince is captured! The tower is taken!"

The sheep refused to see the truth.

Sir Orrick, a tall thin knight, his white nightshirt hanging to his knees, stepped forward to challenge Trask. The old knight looked like a stork, ridiculous in his nightshirt, but he carried a great sword, his voice full of righteous rage. "Taken by whom?"

Trask loomed over the knight, a hulking menace. "Taken by me. Taken by men who renounce the maroon, men who prefer to live by the profits of their swords."

Sir Orrick drew his great sword, a hiss of steel. "Traitor!" He raised the sword above his head for a two-handed strike, but Trask was lightning-fast. The moon-shaped axe blurred, a wicked slash of silver. The strength of the blow sent Sir Orrick's head flying, hitting the far wall with a sickening thud. Blood sprayed from the severed neck, the body staggering for two steps before slumping to the floor.

A thick silence settled over the great room.

Trask shook the blood from his axe and glared at the rest of the undecided knights. "Sir Orrick kept his honor but lost his head." The big man sneered. "The rest of you have the same choice. Bend the knee and obey...or die."

Eleven knights sank to their knees, weapons placed on the floor in submission.

Trask laughed, a deep rumbling sound. "That's better." He gestured to two of his conspirators. "And now the test."

Trask circled the kneeling knights, his great axe in his hands. "Every man who joins will have a share of the plunder, a share of gold, women, and wine. But every man must also share in the risks." Trask growled a threat. "I need to know if I can trust you kneelers. I need proof you renounce the maroon."

The Mordant watched, pleased with Trask's performance, for every act of cruelty bound the big knight with threads of Darkness, making him more malleable, more susceptible to control.

Footsteps clattered down the stairs. Two knights emerged from the stairwell, dragging the captive prince between them. Bound and gagged, the prince wore nothing but a torn nightshirt. Blood on his forehead and a jagged cut slashing his sword arm gave proof that he fought rather than submit. The Mordant grinned, another noble son of the Octagon about to get his just rewards.

They dragged the captive prince before Trask, dumping him at the big man's feet.

The prince struggled to stand, muscles straining against his bonds.

Laughing, Trask transferred his great axe to his left hand and reached for a dagger at his belt. "Ah, the noble prince." He pressed the point of the dagger under the prince's chin, forcing his head back.

The prince glowered, his nostrils flaring wide, but he did not move away, he did not flinch.

Trask withdrew the dagger. "Very good." He turned his back on the prince and circled the kneeling knights, a prowling threat. Quick as lightning, he slammed the dagger into the nearest tabletop. The dagger quivered upright, the table shuddering from the blow. Trask glared at the kneelers. "Each of you will have a chance to prove your loyalty, to make your choice." He pointed to the dagger impaled in the wood. "Take the dagger and strike a blow against the prince. Not a killing blow, mind you, but enough so that each man has royal blood on his hands. Enough so there is no turning back."

The kneeling knights shrank into themselves. Nervous glances darted around the great hall, looking for a way to escape, or a reason to obey.

The prince glared defiant, his voice muffled by the gag.

One of the kneelers muttered. "It's not right."

Quick as an adder, Trask grabbed the dagger and thrust it deep into the kneeler's throat. "What did you say? I didn't hear you." A wet gurgle came from the skewered knight. Trask twisted the blade, holding the knight's head aloft as blood spewed from his mouth. Trask withdrew the dagger, letting the dead man slump to the floor. "Anyone else?"

Silence reigned.

Trask impaled the dagger in the tabletop and then pointed to one of the sheep. "You, Sir Dravin. You first."

The burly knight with long sandy hair rose to his feet and wrenched the dagger from the wood. Moving with sullen reluctance, he stood in front of the prince, indecision on his face. "This is hard."

Trask hefted his battle-axe, a sheen of blood on the moon-shaped blade. "Your honor or your head."

Sir Dravin scowled. He closed the distance in two quick strides, plunging the dagger into the prince's right side. A muffled scream echoed through the great hall. The knight withdrew the dagger. The prince slumped to his knees, a red stain spreading across his white nightshirt.

The Mordant hid his smile, knowing the first was always the hardest.

Trask chose another knight. "Sir Tallover."

The prince struggled to regain his feet, making a show of mute valor.

Sir Tallover accepted the dagger, but this time there was no hesitation. He plunged the dagger hilt-deep into the prince's thigh. Writhing in pain, the prince collapsed to the floor, a sacrifice to treason.

Each of the kneeling knights accepted the dagger. Each did the deed, earning the blood on their hands and the dark taint on their souls. Bound and gagged, the prince lay crumpled on the floor, ten wounds gaping open like bloody mouths. Only a twitch of his right hand showed he still lived.

Trask raised his axe in a two-handed grip. With one fell stroke, he took the prince's head. Blood gushed across the floor, a stain upon the stones. Trask kicked the severed head across the great hall and raised his axe in triumph. "We're blood brothers!"

The men raised their weapons and echoed the shout, "The Bloody Brothers!" Even the kneelers joined in the shouting. They capered about the great hall, drunk on violence, tasting their freedom, reveling in their Darkness.

Trask pointed toward the only remaining steward, an old man cringing on the far side of the hall. "You there, Simon. Break out the wine and cook us a feast! Use the prince's own stores, we celebrate tonight!"

The men cheered as the steward scuttled to obey.

Trask crossed the room to the Mordant. "You, come with me."

The Mordant followed Trask to the sixth floor. The door to the prince's chambers gaped open. Blood spattered the feather bed, blankets strewn across the floor in disarray.

Trask retrieved a goblet, and filled it with red wine from a skin on a side table. He lifted the goblet in salute. "To freedom! To plunder! To the Bloody Brothers!" He took a long swallow, wiping his mouth with the back of his hand.

The Mordant watched, letting the Darkness rise behind his eyes. "Cragnoth Keep is yours. What will you do now?"

Trask refilled his goblet. "Tomorrow morning we'll head down the switchbacks to the tree line and sack the stables. Once we're mounted, we'll ride for Navarre, raping and pillaging as we go."

The Mordant kept his voice low. "What if I make you a better offer?"

Trask swilled the wine and reached for more. "You? A better offer?"

The Mordant stepped close. "They say the eyes are the windows of the soul." He dropped his inner shields, letting the Darkness pour into his gaze. "Look into my eyes. Darkness knows Darkness." A thousand years of evil hammered into Trask's soul, an avalanche of dark deeds and dark thoughts. The knight fought back, struggling to reach for his axe, but the Mordant's will slammed into him. He made it rape, flaming pain through the knight's body, a brutal assault for a brutal tool. Claiming the knight, he branded his will into the mortal's soul.

Trask groaned in pain, sweat beading his face. Released, he staggered backwards and fell to his knees, fear etched deep into his eyes. "Who are you? What are you?"

The Mordant's voice rang with the strength of ages. "I am the Mordant Reborn! Kneel before me and serve."

"The Mordant!" The big knight cringed in prostration.

"Feel the strength of my Darkness and know your liege lord!"

Trask quaked, his face ghost-pale. "W-what would you have of me, lord?"

"Darkness rewards those who serve well. Hold Cragnoth Keep till the turn of the next full moon. Maintain the illusion that you are still knights of the Octagon. I will send reinforcements to claim the keep. My men will bring a thousand golds for each of your knights."

"A thousand golds!" Avarice gleamed from the knight's dark eyes.

"And double that for their leader." The Mordant nodded. "Once my troops arrive, you and your men will be free to pillage the southern kingdoms. I ask only that you continue to wear the maroon cloaks and silver surcoats of the Octagon." He lowered his voice and smiled. "Let your deeds be attributed to the Octagon. Let Castlegard be blamed for rape and pillage and slaughter among the southern kingdoms." He gave the big knight a conspirator's smile. "Gain your revenge on Castlegard by grinding their precious honor into the mud."

Trask rumbled with laughter, a wicked grin on his face. "They will hate that."

"Kill their honor and you crush the very heart of Castlegard."

Trask grinned. "A pleasure to serve, my lord!"

"Now rise." The Mordant's voice was a command. "You have men to lead and I must be away. I have an army to claim in the north."

Trask stood. "What orders, my lord?"

"Dispatch a rider to the base of the switchbacks. A sworn man waits in a small cave near the base of the first turn. He is ordered to attend me."

Trask nodded. "It will be done. Anything else?"

"I'll need your swiftest horses and supplies for the journey north. The rest I leave in your hands." The Mordant stared into the knight's soul. "I leave the keep to your command. Recruit, trick, or kill any who come to Cragnoth. Do your best to maintain the illusion that the Octagon still holds the crag...and then work your will on the southern kingdoms." He smiled. "May the Dark Lord's pleasure reign...over all the lands of Erdhe."

46

Liandra

Liandra felt the need for light, for the cleansing warmth of sunshine on her face. She walked alone along the parapet, staring down at the surrounding sprawl of her capital city, staring but not seeing. Her mind was elsewhere...wondering what transpired in the dungeon depths, wondering what answer the Master Archivist would bring. The queen shivered despite the warmth.

Summer was waning. All too soon the nights would grow long and cold, crowded with too many worries, too many nightmares. And always the queen remained alone, a tower of strength for her people, a pillar of virtue for her kingdom...but sometimes she longed for the shelter of strong arms. To take off the crown for even a single night would be bliss. Liandra shook her head, angry at her weakness, angry for even considering such a folly.

She paced the length of the parapet, the soft rustle of pale green silk providing a civilized contrast to the harsh clang of swords. Soldiers trained in the courtyard below, the ring of swords against shields evoking another worry. The recruiting went well, but Lanverness needed time to rebuild an army decimated by the rebellion. She wondered how much time she had.

Footsteps followed behind...heels ringing against stone, sure and bold. She knew he did it deliberately, so as not to startle. Liandra usually welcomed his company...but the footsteps heralded a possible nightmare. A fist of anxiety tightened in her stomach.

She turned and met his dark stare. His face gave nothing away.

The Master Archivist bowed low. "My queen."

"Is it done?"

The master nodded.

"And?"

"He held the crystal but there was no change, no red glow. The monk says he is not a harlequin."

Relief washed through her. Closing her eyes, she leaned against the cool stone of the parapet, drawing on the castle's strength. "Thank the gods." Danly was a traitor but her throne was not compromised by the taint of evil. She'd birthed a monster but not a demon.

"Majesty, Danly is still a threat. He must be dealt with."

The queen glared at her shadowmaster, weary of the topic. "We will not discuss this."

"But majesty, your line is thin, you have but one heir. As long as Danly lives, he is a threat to your throne."

She began to pace, the dark-robed master walking beside her like a persistent shadow. "Yes, Prince Stewart must wed, and the sooner the better. We have a bride in mind. We must open negotiations with Navarre."

"Yes, but majesty, sooner or later you must deal with Danly. Justice must be served and the threat to your throne eliminated."

She stopped and stared at him, anger warring with shock. Danly deserved death, but the thought of executing her own son was monstrous. "Would you turn us into a monster? Would you have us execute our own son?"

His face paled beneath the onslaught of her royal anger. He bowed his head, his voice contrite. "Majesty, I am only thinking of the security of your throne...and of your own peace of mind." His voice deepened. "Majesty, I know you too well. I see how the weight of Danly's fate gnaws at your mind. I would ease this burden from you."

She knew he meant well, but his open acknowledgement of her weakness stoked her anger. "Then think past the headman's block." Her voice snapped like a lash. "Danly will remain in the dungeon, awaiting our royal justice."

"Majesty, there is another way."

That stopped her. She stared at her shadowmaster, trying to see past his words. "You mean exile."

"Exile in itself would not be sufficient."

"What then? What short of death or a lifetime spent rotting in the dungeons will serve?"

"If Danly is allowed to live, then he must never be a threat to the Rose Throne." His voice dropped to a whisper. "Danly could be safely exiled if he were gelded."

"A eunuch! You would turn him into a eunuch?"

His face was impassive. "Majesty, it is the only viable alternative to the headman's axe. Gelded, he can never be king, nor can he ever sire a king."

She shuddered. "But what you suggest is torture. What man would live without his manhood?"

"The darkness of the dungeons has broken him."

Images of the dungeon assaulted her mind, too many nightmares.

"Majesty, put an end to the threat, an end to the agony of indecision. Absolve yourself of this judgment. Give Danly the choice. Let him decide between the knife and banishment or the executioner's axe."

She was weary of thinking of Danly. Weary of wrestling with a decision that seemed to have no acceptable solution. Her shadowmaster offered her a way out. A way to see justice done without killing her own son...but the alternative was almost as monstrous as the headsman's axe. How could any man live without his manhood? And how much more would her son hate her? She shook her head. "No!"

He started to object but she cut him off. "Danly will stay in the dungeon. And you will speak no more of this." She made her voice hard, a royal command. "Are we understood?"

He nodded.

"Then go. We grow weary of your presence."

His face hardened to stone...a flicker of hurt dancing behind his dark gaze. He bowed. "As you command." He turned and walked away, his footsteps as silent as a shadow.

She watched him go, tall and lean, his squared shoulders screaming of pride and determination, the one man she could count on, yet she parried his words with nothing but anger. If truth be told, he only tried to ease the burden she carried. Liandra let him get as far as the doorway before she called him back. "Lord Highgate!"

He spun, as if he'd been listening for her voice.

"Walk with us."

His long stride closed the distance between them.

Strong and silent, he walked beside her. Close but never touching, he gave her just what she needed. The queen gazed beyond the battlement, past the city, to the green fields in the distance. "The summer is waning. I fear a great darkness is coming."

"Yes, but as long as Liandra is queen, Lanverness will have a light to beat back the darkness."

For a moment, she let herself believe, she let herself hope...but she couldn't shake the shadows from her mind.

47

Katherine

Stroke and parry, Kath dodged the massive trees, fighting imaginary foes. She'd slipped away from the others, seeking a solitary glade, needing a chance to test her own mettle. Hidden from prying eyes, she danced the sword amongst the redwoods, executing all the classical forms. Slash of the Falcon, Thrust of the Dragon, she whirled and parried, her short sword issuing a deadly whisper. Leaping over a fallen log, she raised her shield against an imaginary blow. Pain lanced her left arm. She battled through the move but the ache persisted. Slowing to a stop, she sheathed her sword and shucked her shield, sweat dripping from her face. Her sword strokes were sure, but her shield arm ached. Rolling up her sleeve, she stared at the crisscrossing scars. A shudder passed through her remembering the demon-wolf's red eyes and the sharp bite of its teeth. The battle with the demon-wolf was supposed to be fought in the world of dreams but her scars were very real. Kath flexed her arm, grateful to be whole, but somehow the pain still lingered. And if truth be told, her arm was not the only problem. Slick with sweat, she tired too easily. The fight with the demon had taken its toll.

"Are you well?" Duncan glided from the trees.

Her startled surprise turned to pleasure. "How did you find me?"

"I'll always find you."

Kath felt her face flame red.

His stare dropped to her shield arm. She started to roll down the sleeve but he stopped her. "No, scars of honor should not be hidden." He laid a kiss on her forearm, amongst the angry welts. "It pains you."

"Yes, but not like a real wound...more like a shadowy pain."

"Let me help." He led her to a mossy patch beneath a grandfather tree. She sat upon the velvety green, her back to the great tree as his fingers kneaded the muscles of her shield arm. Strong and sure, his hands worked the pain from her arm with steady strokes. Kath groaned in pleasure. "Your hands are magic."

Duncan gave a throaty chuckle that held a promise of so much more.

The rumble of his voice sent a shiver down her spine. Kath stared into his mismatched eyes, the one cat-eye golden and the other sapphire-blue.

"Are you bothered by my eyes?"

"No! Not at all." She felt her face blush but refused to drop her gaze. "I like your eyes...they make you even more interesting...more alluring." Her voice deepened. "I'm glad I finally found you. You were hiding behind that black patch."

He released a long-held breath. "Just so." Duncan pulled her into his arms, settling her against his chest, his back to the great redwood. His hands continued to knead her sore arm. She leaned against him, safe and secure.

"As a child I wanted to flee the forest...but now I find myself wanting to stay."

"The forest feels like a sanctuary...a place for us."

He tightened his arms around her. "Just so."

The crystal dagger pressed against her side. "But duty calls us forward." She had to ask. "When we leave the forest, will you wear the black patch?"

"It's for the best."

She heard the regret in his voice and shared his sadness.

He parried her question with one of his own. "When we leave, we'll ride for Castlegard?"

"Yes, to warn the Octagon, to warn the king."

"Your father."

She heard the question beneath his statement. It was her turn for regret. "My father will not understand."

"Nor should you tell him. The truth will not aid our cause."

"But?"

His calm assurance surprised her. "Beyond the forest, duty must come first. Once we defeat the Dark, then we'll carve a place for ourselves." He held her close, his arms encircling her. "The knights will not welcome the wolf and Danya will not leave Bryx. When we reach Castlegard, I'll remain in the forest to guard them both."

She could not fault his logic, but it seemed like a deception...or a betrayal. He deserved better. "It does not seem right."

"Sometimes I wear the black patch for myself, but most oft I wear it for others. As long as the truth stays between us, it's for the best."

Kath sighed, realizing he'd lifted an invisible weight from her shoulders. "Thank you."

His voice held a gentle smile. "There is no need to hurry. We have all the time between."

She smiled, reassured by his words.

"You need to rest."

Kath nestled against him, savoring his solid warmth and his smell of leather. Content in his arms, she must have dozed. Sleep claimed her, but instead of a restful peace, she found golden eyes staring back at her, eyes of the forest, eyes full of sad wisdom.

Warrior of the Light! We bring you warning! The Ancient Darkness has passed beyond the sight of trees, beyond leaf and bark and root, climbing into the realm of rock and snow. Beware, for the Ancient Foe nears his domain! Wake and heed our warning!

Kath woke with a start. "*No!*"

Duncan sat up, his hand reaching for the dagger at his belt. "What is it?"

The vividness of the dream beat against her. "I had a dream, a nightmare." Understanding struck like a knife in the dark. "No, a warning." Kath gripped the crystal dagger and turned to stare at Duncan. "The Forest sent me a warning." She struggled to recall the exact words. "The Mordant has climbed beyond the sight of the trees...into a realm of rock and snow."

Duncan followed her words. "He's climbed beyond the tree line."

Kath gasped, "The Dragon Spine Mountains!"

"Unless the knights stop him, he's nearly reached the north."

Fear and sadness gripped her in equal measure. "We've lingered too long."

Duncan stood and offered her his hand. "Come, we must warn the others. It's time to leave."

Kath reclaimed her shield. Together, they ran through the dappled sunlight. A single autumn leaf fell from the heights. Kath did not want to leave, but at least she'd have Duncan by her side.

48

Blaine

Green cloaked the forest, but the dawn carried a chilly bite, the first hint of autumn. Blaine shivered against the chill, more proof they'd lingered too long in the bloody forest. Unlike the others, he'd seen the truth of the Deep Green, nothing more than a tangled trap, a way to dull their swords and slow their passage. At least Kath had finally caught his urgency, even if her explanation made little sense. Blaine finished tying his bedroll and settled his great sword over his shoulder, eager to be rid of the forest, eager for a foe worthy of his blue blade.

His companions finished breaking camp. Duncan had his longbow strung, hovering close to the two women. Blaine was pleased to see that Danya carried her own bedroll. The girl seemed well enough, yet she never strayed from the wolf. Always keeping one hand buried in the wolf's thick fur, she kept her gaze averted, as if suddenly shy. Her reticence stung him, especially after the way he'd cared for her. At least Kath flashed him a warm smile. She looked fit for battle, her twin throwing axes strapped to her back, her hand on her sword hilt, but shadows darkened her eyes and fresh scars marred her shield arm. The forest had taken its toll and Blaine was glad to be rid of it. "Where's the monk?"

Sir Tyrone shrugged, "He said he'd be back."

Zith emerged from the depths of the grove, walking with the Treespeaker. The two had grown thick as thieves. Blaine scowled at the tree-witch, unable to trust her pupil-less eyes, eyes that looked blind but weren't.

The Treespeaker nodded toward them, a benevolent smile on her ageless face. "I have come to bid you farewell." Sunlight shimmered on her white-feathered cloak, casting a silvery glint. "May the blessings of the Forest be upon you." She stared at Kath as if words passed between them, yet nothing was said, more proof of the woman's witchery.

Kath offered her a reverent bow. "We thank you for your hospitality, for your words of wisdom, and your help in healing our companions."

The wolf yipped as if in agreement. Danya bowed low, her face solemn.

The Treespeaker smiled, her arms spread wide in acceptance. "By fighting the ancient Darkness, you have proven yourselves friends of the Forest. The blessings of leaf and bark go with you." She turned to Duncan. "Remember, Duncan Treloch, you are, and always will be, a son of the Forest." A green-robed attendant offered Duncan a quiver of arrows fletched with clipped peacock feathers, each arrow tailed by a single feathered eye. "Accept this token from your people. May your arrows always fly straight and true. Keep safe and return to us, son of the Forest."

Duncan accepted the quiver and bowed low, a faint flush on his normally stoic face.

The tree-witch turned toward the monk. "I have enjoyed our conversations. May your wisdom always be heard."

The monk offered a deep bow. "May the trees ever drink deep."

Blaine looked away, shunning the Treespeaker's strange pupil-less gaze.

"You do not want my blessing, knight of blue steel, yet it is freely given."

Blaine felt a prickle down his back. He scowled, refusing to meet her gaze.

"Our farewells have been said and you have tarried longer than you should." A troop of green-clad archers melted out of the forest. "These rangers will see you to the Forest's edge. The blessings of leaf and bark go with you. May the Light always vanquish the Dark and may your journeys bring you back to the Mother Forest."

The leave-taking was finally done. Unlike the others, Blaine did not look back. The cat-eyed rangers set a swift pace, leading the companions through the maze of trails. Beneath the birdsong and the rustling leaves, they jogged in silence, keeping their thoughts to themselves. Blaine carried two saddlebags over his left shoulder and a bedroll under his right arm, feeling more like a packhorse than a knight, but at least they were leaving the forest. Deliberately slowing his pace, he fell back among the others. His gaze strayed to Danya, to the sway of her long chestnut hair and her slender waist, the wolf pressed close to her side. The wolf-girl seemed healed, but something had changed. Her friendly smile was gone, replaced by a closed guardedness, a feral wildness shining from her brown eyes. Blaine tried to draw her out, but she seemed oblivious to his advances. Maybe if he grew fur and howled at the moon she'd notice him. Blaine barked a laugh, realizing he was jealous of a wolf. He reached for the hilt of his great blue sword, touching it like a talisman. Pride swelled through him, he was a knight of the Octagon, a sworn sword, but somehow his gaze always returned to the dark-haired girl.

They traveled for the better part of the day, taking meals while they walked, chewing strips of dried venison and handfuls of nuts. As the sun neared the horizon, they reached a small glade and found their horses cropping the grass. Saddled and tethered, they were tended by a handful of cat-eyed rangers.

One of the rangers approached Kath. "Your saddlebags are stocked with food, a gift from the Treespeaker." Without another word, the archers melted back into the forest.

Blaine snorted. "A frosty farewell."

Duncan said, "They're still wary of white-eyes." He settled his black patch across his golden eye, hiding his mixed heritage.

Blaine shrugged. "It matters not to me. I'm just relieved to see our horses." He found his stallion and gave the big chestnut a welcoming pat. The horses proved to be well fed and well rested, the spare saddlebags stocked with supplies. He tightened the girth and swung into the saddle, eager to be away. Kath took the lead, riding beside Duncan, setting a course toward the northwest.

He smelled the burned land before they reached it. With a single stride their mounts took them from the living forest into a land of burnt trees, like crossing into the realm of death. They rode close, their hoof beats raising small clouds of ash. Eerily quiet, the only sound in the charred landscape was the harsh staccato of a woodpecker. Naked and blackened, the trees stood like skeletons pointing toward an indifferent sky, a grim reminder of the Mordant. After the verdant forest, the charred ruin was a bitter blow, as if a deep doom had fallen on the land. Blaine urged his charger to a canter, eager to be free of the hellish ruin.

Charred trees gave way to charred fields, proving the cat-eyed archers had spoken the truth. The fire set to ambush the forest had turned back against the villagers, ravaging the farmland. Soot and ash dampened the drum of hoof beats as they rode through fields and vineyards blackened by the fire's embrace, so much destruction, so much waste.

They came across a burnt village, a flap of crows rising into a darkening sky, scavengers disturbed from a grim feast. Bryx loosed a mournful howl. Blaine found himself agreeing with the wolf. He stared at the blackened ruin, amazed that one man could cause so much desolation, yet there was never anything to fight, never any foe to face. It was as if they chased a dark shadow, following footprints of evil across the southern kingdoms, but never finding the source.

Twilight descended, but none of the companions wanted to camp in the fire-ravaged land. The moon rose full, so they pressed on, riding by the silvery light. They reached the main road and turned north, holding the horses to a steady trot. The blackened hell gradually gave way to rich farmland, vineyards and fields of grain ripe for the harvest. The road passed through an orchard, the horses' hooves churning the fallen apples into cider. Blaine breathed deep, relieved to be free of the burned stench, relieved to find a limit to the Mordant's shadow.

They stopped at the first inn, but kept to themselves, avoiding trouble, avoiding traps. On the tenth day, they came to the Snowmelt River, a cold torrent of slate-green water and white foam. A great stone bridge spanned the river, the proud banner of the Octagon flying from a tower turret, maroon on a field of silver.

Blaine straightened at the sight of the banner, a flush of pride rushing through him. He'd been gone too long, almost a full year, chasing shadows with nothing to show for it, never once blooding his sword in combat, a waste of blue steel. Pride and regret warred within him. He was glad to return, hungry for the brotherhood of swords...but doubt gnawed at him, knowing he hadn't earned his blue blade.

They slowed their mounts to a walk, hooves ringing against stone.

A knight holding a spear stepped from the shadows of the bridge. He wore a silver surcoat, a maroon octagon emblazoned on his chest, the hilt of a great sword looming over his right shoulder. Blaine did not recognize his face.

The knight's gaze passed over Kath and Duncan, settling on Sir Tyrone. "Brother, what brings you back to the Domain?"

The black knight halted his charger and gestured toward Kath. "The princess of Castlegard would see her father."

"Her father?" The knight stared up at Kath, confusion on his face. "The *Imp?*"

The guard did not recognize the girl...but then why should he? Blaine studied Kath seeing all the changes: the fit of leather to subtle curves, the axes strapped to her back, the sword belted to her side, the way she sat straight and proud in the saddle. The Imp had blossomed to a woman and bloodied her sword in battle; small wonder the knight did not recognize her. Blaine grimaced, thinking of the king's reaction.

Kath grinned at the knight. "Greetings, Sir Gentwell. Do we have permission to pass?"

The knight's eyes widened, "Yes, m'lady." He shook his head. "I mean, yes, princess." He gestured for them to ride through, a bemused look on his face.

Kath urged her mount to a trot, a smile in her voice. "Thank you, Sir Gentwell."

Blaine saluted as he rode past, but the knight made no acknowledgement, staring after Kath.

They clattered across the bridge, through the gated archway and into the lands of the Domain. The farmlands looked much the same on the north side of the river, amber fields of grain interspersed with orchards and stands of pine, but beyond the fields the Dragon Spine Mountains loomed large. Castlegard's Domain lay within the very shadow of the mountains, a constant reminder of the threat of war.

Blaine studied the countryside, searching for signs of the Mordant's passage, but he found none. The farmlands seemed peaceful and prosperous. Peasants worked the fields, harvesting the summer bounty. Great oxen-pulled wains clogged the road, struggling to bring the harvest tithe to the castle granaries, an annual store set against winter and war.

Blaine spurred his charger forward, catching up to Kath. "If the Mordant's passed this way, I see no sign of it."

Kath rode beside him, staring at the countryside. "It looks peaceful enough, I'll grant you that, but I can't help feeling we've come too late...that somehow the Deceiver is already at work, weaving treachery against the Octagon."

"Or perhaps he's afraid to show his face." Pride leached into Blaine's voice, "He's powerful but he's only one man. Alone he's no match for the might of the Octagon."

"In a fair fight, you're right." Kath shook her head, her face grim. "But evil never fights fair."

Her words set a splinter of doubt in his mind.

A chill wind blew down from the mountains, tugging at Blaine's maroon cloak.

Kath shook her head. "Either way, we need to warn the king." She flashed him a bright smile. "And besides, I would see home once more. We've been too long away."

Blaine returned her smile, eager for a glimpse of the great castle.

49

Samson

Grandmother Magda sat in her rocking chair, her knitting needles filling the kitchen with a rhythmic clacking. Tempting smells of fresh baked cinnamon cake swirled from the hearth, adding a cozy comfort to the refuge. Samson breathed deep, tempted to believe, but he knew it was all an illusion, easily shattered by soldiers in the dead of the night. They were running out of time, he had to make the others see.

Justin had called a council meeting to plan the next raid, the next act of defiance. The heart of the rebellion sat crowded around the kitchen table. Samson studied his compatriots: a bard, an ex-soldier, a silver-haired grandmother, a young man who led the orphan boys, a tanner rescued from the Flames, a man swayed by songs, and a skinny orphan lad who followed the bard like a shadow. A ragged handful of idealists pitted against all the might of the Flame God. Samson shook his head in despair. "You're gambling with our lives!" His gaze circled the table looking for support. "The risks keep getting worse! It's only a matter of time till they catch us."

"I don't see it that way." Justin pushed back from the table, the wood of the chair scraping against the flagstone floor. "We're making a difference. I can feel it in the marketplaces, in the taverns, and even in the temple square." The bard's voice held the strength of conviction. "The proof is in the rumors and the back-street gossip. The people are starting to think there might be another way, a choice beyond the Flame God."

Samson did not agree; the bard was beguiled by his own songs. "If we're making a difference, then why are there so few of us?"

Jack answered, mumbling past a mouthful of cake. "The people are afraid. We're not."

Samson shook his head, the boy had a bad case of hero-worship. "We can't keep doing what we're doing. We can't trade two lives for every man we save!"

Daniel, the big tanner, glared at Samson, his voice as hard as stone. "I know what it's like to stand in the stocks, to wait for death in the Flames." His knuckles cracked as his hands tightened into fists. "Innocent people are dying. I can't sit back and let that happen, can you?"

Samson felt his face flush red; he'd chosen the wrong argument, used the wrong words. Ignoring Daniel, he focused on the bard, his voice desperate. "They know about you, Justin. The soldiers are combing the city for bards and minstrels. They're arresting tavern owners and putting them to the question." He feared to say the words but someone had to. "The confessors will be the death of us." Samson glared at the others. "It's only a matter of time till someone talks. Our deaths won't make any difference."

Justin scowled, staring into the candle flames.

Ben crossed his arms, a stoic look on his weathered face.

Jack fidgeted and reached for another piece of cinnamon cake.

Grandmother Magda kept her head bent over her knitting, the rhythmic clacking and the steady creak of the rocking chair the only sounds in the kitchen.

Samson glared at his friends, his stomach clenched in fear. Instead of being the only realist, perhaps he was the only coward among the brave.

Red leaned forward, scratching the stubble of his first beard, his voice apologetic. "It's true, Harper, all the lads have heard the rumors. They're rounding up the bards and the minstrels. Soon there won't be any music left in the Flame God's city."

It wasn't the support he'd hoped for, but Samson took it as an excuse to leap back into the argument. "We can't keep doing what we're doing. The confessors will find us and then we'll all be food for the Flames."

The bard's voice held a touch of anger. "We can't just give up. We have to discredit the Pontifax and his priests." The bard pushed away from the table and began pacing in front of the hearth. "We have to change tactics. We have to do something spectacular. Something that will make the people take notice. Something we haven't tried before."

Samson watched the bard, praying he'd find another way. Spectacular sounded dangerous, way too dangerous.

"I say we kill the Pontifax." Ben leaned forward, his gaze unyielding, offering a soldier's practical solution. "We find a way to slip into the Residence and murder the holy bastard while he sleeps. One sword in the dark will solve all our problems."

"If only it were that simple." Justin shook his head. "Kill him and you make him a martyr. As a martyr he'll be even more of a threat. And then we'd have that beast, the Keeper, to deal with. There has to be another way."

Grandmother Magda looked up from her knitting, her stare keen despite her years. "Never forget we are fighting a religion. The people are seduced by the miracle of the Test of Faith. Reason alone will never be enough." The rocking chair creaked, keeping time to the clack of her knitting needles. "It will take a miracle to defeat a miracle."

Daniel's deep voice rumbled, "Fire to fight fire."

The old lady nodded, her steel gray eyes flashing in the candlelight.

The bard stopped pacing. "But how? What kind of miracle can we achieve?"

If the old lady had an answer, she did not say. The mood in the kitchen turned pensive. Justin resumed pacing, his face thoughtful. Samson slumped in his seat, watching the bard, resigned to his fate. Grandmother Magda kept to her knitting, her needles clacking to a steady rhythm, marking the slow passage of time. The candles began to burn down, melting to a waxy pool in the center of the table.

A knock sounded on the outer door.

Samson jumped, his heart hammering.

Frightened stares raced around the kitchen.

Ben reached for a cutting knife and stood poised by the kitchen entrance, his voice a whisper, "Expecting anyone?"

Justin shook his head, his face grim.

Samson cringed into his seat, waiting to hear the door crash open. Tension swirled through the kitchen but the knitting needles never broke rhythm.

The knock came again.

Ben sighed, "It can't be soldiers." He reached for a candle. "I'll see who's there."

They waited at the kitchen table, straining to listen.

Ben returned, his face guarded. "We have a visitor."

A tall man with a fair face and graying hair stepped into the candlelight. The stranger wore a long robe of midnight blue. "I am seeking a song about the Rose and the Lion. Have I come to the right place?"

Samson stared in surprise, recognizing the code but not the man.

Justin answered, "I know a sea chantey or two, but otherwise we only sing songs about the Flame God."

Tension drained out of the kitchen.

The stranger nodded. "I am Aeroth, a Kiralynn monk. I bring word from Queen Liandra. I have come to contribute the knowledge of the Kiralynn monks to your fight against the Flame God."

Relief flooded through Samson, desperate for any breath of reason.

The bard offered the monk his hand, his smile infectious. "I am Justin of Navarre and your offer of help is welcome, especially if you come from the queen."

Introductions were made and a chair was found. Ben set a slice of cinnamon cake and a mug of ale in front of the monk while everyone else crowded close, eager for news of life beyond the reach of the Flame God.

"I'm afraid the tidings are grim." The monk took a long drink of ale. "There has been a rebellion against the queen." Gasps rippled around the kitchen table. "The queen is victorious but Lanverness will need time to recover from the bloodshed. And after seeing the army of tents surrounding the Flame God's city, I fear the queen may have less time than she knows." He leaned forward, his gaze circling the table. "What you do here in Coronth is of great importance." His voice lowered. "I witnessed this morning's Test of Faith. I saw the brutal murder of that poor woman...and the frenzy of the crowd." The monk shook his head. "The religion of the Flame is an abomination. It reeks of the Dark Lord. Only the Dark God would countenance human sacrifice."

Jack gasped, "The Dark Lord?" The orphan lad stared at the monk, making the hand sign against evil.

The monk nodded. "The red comet foretells the rise of the Dark Lord. He reaches through to the mortal world, twisting the souls of men, setting brother against brother. My Order believes the war has already begun."

Ben said, "The rebellion against the queen?"

"Yes." The monk nodded. "And the religion of the Flame. This abomination must be stopped."

"But how?" Justin burst from his chair and began to pace. "We've tried using songs to open the people's eyes to the truth, but words are not enough. So we lead by example, freeing the sinners from the stocks, depriving the Flames of their grizzly feast. We've risked much to free a handful of sinners but the priests only increase the number of arrests." Frustration seeped into the bard's voice. "We save a few lives, but the dungeons bulge with innocent people waiting to walk in the Flames." He stopped pacing and stared at the monk. "If you know of some way to defeat this religion, we would gladly hear it."

Grandmother Magda looked up from her knitting, candlelight reflected in her silver hair. "It will take a miracle to defeat a miracle." The clack of the knitting needles underscored her words.

The monk stared at the old woman, his face thoughtful. "You have the truth of it. Religions are beliefs. They defy logic. The people will only be free when their belief in the Pontifax is shaken. You must strike at the very foundation of this so-called religion."

"But how?" Justin's voice exploded in frustration. "Unless the Lords of Light care to intervene, we are fresh out of miracles."

"The Lords of Light do not work that way."

"Then perhaps they should!"

Samson had never seen the bard so bitter...or so angry. Perhaps the prince had always understood the odds, yet he fought anyway.

The monk sighed. "The miracle of the Test of Faith is the heart of the Flame God's religion, the source of the Pontifax's power."

Justin nodded, his face still.

"Then you must strike at this miracle."

"Yes, but how?"

"From what I've seen, the most likely explanation is magic."

"*Magic!*" Ben made the word a curse. "But the wizards of old are long dead! Magic is gone from the world of men, wiped out during the War of Wizards."

The monk shook his head. "Not gone, just rare."

Ben stared, as if the monk had sprouted two heads. "You're saying the Pontifax is a *wizard?*"

"Not exactly. Does the Pontifax perform any other miracles? Does he do more than walk through flames?"

Justin answered. "Just fire. He walks through fire and on occasion he carries a child through the flames, both emerging unharmed."

The monk nodded. "Then I suggest he works magic, not a miracle."

Samson did not understand. "What difference does it make? Magic or a miracle, how can we stop either one?"

The monk smiled, but his face seemed weary. "It makes all the difference. A true miracle is the divine intervention of the gods, proof of their favor, proof of their existence. Miracles are extremely rare. Magic is something else entirely." The monk leaned forward, his voice thoughtful. "Magic is a latent talent carried by more than a few mortals. But in order to invoke that talent, most mortals need the use of a magical item, a catalyst that unlocks their hidden talent. These magical items are called focuses, rare artifacts left over from the days of high magic. Since the Pontifax can only do one type of magic, he must have a focus keyed to fire."

Ben had a stubborn look on his face. "So how does all this help us?"

"Without the focus, the Pontifax cannot work magic."

The rocking chair stopped. The knitting needles fell silent. Grandmother Magda stared at the monk, a shrewd look on her face. "Steal the focus and the Pontifax will burn like any other mortal?"

The monk nodded. "Just so."

Grandmother Magda smiled, but it was a cold smile, full of death and revenge.

A shiver slithered down Samson's back; old women should never look that way.

Ben asked, "So what does this focus look like?"

The rhythmic clacking resumed, the vindictive smile banished beneath age, as if the old lady was nothing more than a harmless grandmother. Samson shuddered, wondering if the others had noticed.

The monk stared at Ben, his voice solemn. "It will be something small, something the Pontifax can hold in the palm of his hand. It could be something precious or something common. There is no way to distinguish a focus by sight alone."

Ben's voice was a low growl. "Then how do we find it?"

"The Pontifax will always keep it close, something he jealously guards, something he is always touching, always holding...even when he sleeps, or bathes. And he will need to be touching the focus when he works his magic, when he walks through the flames."

"When he bathes, you said." The old lady pounced like a cat. "What about when he takes a woman? Would he keep it with him even then?"

The monk nodded. "Yes, even then."

Grandmother Magda nodded, a shrewd smile on her face.

Justin's voice was thoughtful. "There are rumors of orgies in the Residence. With the right accomplice, we might identify this focus...and perhaps even steal it."

The monk's words were a caution. "The Pontifax is bonded to the focus by a magical link. He will know if anyone so much as touches it. Sleight of hand will not work."

"Yes, but we have to at least know what it is before we can try and steal it."

The monk agreed, "Just so."

Justin smiled. "Then we have the start of a plan. We will steal this focus, whatever it is, and deprive the Pontifax of his miracle, proving he is nothing more than a fraud." The bard stared at the monk, his face thoughtful. "You've given us a way to steal his miracle. Perhaps the Lords of Light listen to prayers after all."

The monk kept his silence.

"Will you stay with us? Will you help us defeat the Pontifax?"

Samson held his breath.

The monk raised his right hand, displaying a Seeing Eye tattooed in blue on his open palm. "I have been sent to share the knowledge of the Kiralynn Order. In the right hands, knowledge is stronger than swords." The monk lowered his hand. "I can only tarry for a few days. Queen Liandra must be warned of the army ranged against her."

Samson had to ask, "But how will you get out? Soldiers seal the borders, arresting all who try to cross."

The monk stared at Samson, his hazel eyes giving little away. "The Order has its secrets."

Samson shivered; he did not want to know.

Justin intervened. "Then we'd best use the time that we have." The bard's voice held the lilt of optimism. "Ben, pour the ale, Jack, get more candles." He gestured to the dim glow in the center of the table. "We need more light. These have melted to nubs and we have much to discuss before the night is through."

Talk flowed around the kitchen table, full of plans, full of confidence...but Samson did not share the sentiment. He knew the monk's knowledge was a godsend...but he could not shake the feeling that doom lurked just outside their door. That somehow the knowledge came too late...for all of them.

50

Steffan

The city was full of sin, the confessions proved it. Steffan sat in the privacy of his solar, sipping Urian brandy and reviewing the confessors' archives, searching for clues to the rebellion. The scrolls made for interesting reading, a litany of thefts, betrayals, lusts, lies, cheats, and even murders. So many sins, so much fodder for the Flames, Steffan knew the Dark Lord was pleased. Religion was a wondrous tool, but Steffan dared not drop his guard. He needed to find the rebels and feed them to the sacred Flames.

Reading late into the night, he searched for patterns in the confessions, looking for an elusive figure, a bard who harped against the Pontifax. Rumors said he sang by night and disappeared by day, vanishing like mist in the dawn light. Such embellishments annoyed Steffan, making a myth out of a mere man. Like a hound to the scent, Steffan followed the whispers, plucking details from many different confessions, weaving an image of subtle rebellion. The people named him the 'Dark Harper', a bard dressed in robes of midnight blue or perhaps black. He appeared without warning in taverns scattered across the city, always arriving late and never staying long, hiding his face in the shadows of his cowled robe. None knew his true name, but many swore he had the gift of a master bard, that instead of strings his small harp was strung with pure emotion. Some even claimed the mysterious bard was Xel, the master harper reborn, a champion of the Light come back to walk the lands of Erdhe. Such superstitious prattle would have been amusing if the bard was not such a threat. Steffan knew the power of persuasion. He delved deeper, looking for answers.

He finished the last scroll but found no clue to the bard's true name. Setting the scrolls aside, he reached for a small ironbound chest. The chest held confessions of a darker sort, a chronicle of sins revealed through torture. Steffan had ordered the random arrest of tavern owners and bards, casting a loose net, hoping to catch a single prize. In the dungeon depths the priests worked late into the night, extracting truths with hot tongs and pincers, with iron maidens and wheels. The deep dungeons rang with screams while the acolytes scribed every pain-racked word. Confessions of the tortured were less coherent but far more damning. Pain yielded a torrent of secrets, a flood of hidden truths.

Beneath the torturer's tools, the tavern owners screamed their knowledge of the Dark Harper. They confessed to the Harper's presence in their taverns but they swore on their children's lives that they did not know his true name. To a man, they died without giving up the secret. Knowing the skill of the torturers, Steffan had to conclude that the tavern owners did not know his name. Somehow this bard slipped through the Flame God's city, harping his songs of rebellion, and then disappearing like smoke. The Harper was a cunning foe, but Steffan would flush him out. It was only a matter of time.

A knock sounded on the door.

Pip peered into the study. "Sorry to bother you, lord, but there's a woman asking to see you."

"A woman?" Steffan wasn't expecting anyone.

Pip grinned. "Long dark hair, skin as pale as fresh milk…" the boy's grin deepened, "and plenty of curves."

An image of the Priestess writhing naked in bed ambushed Steffan's mind. He took a moment to savor the lust…but then he poured cold logic on his dream. The Priestess was far to the south, on the Isle of the Oracle…not waiting at his door. "Did this dark-haired beauty give a name?"

"No, lord, but she begs for a moment alone."

Lust evaded logic. "Send her to me. And she best prove half as beautiful as you claim."

Pip flashed a grin, closing the door behind him.

Steffan returned the scrolls to the ironbound chest and refilled his glass with brandy. He settled in the large stuffed chair, his thoughts lingering on his one night with the Priestess.

A second knock sounded.

"Come in."

She wore a green cloak over a blue wool dress, a tumble of dark curls cascading down her back. Her face was pale as snow, her curves ripe and round and lush…but this woman was petite not statuesque, young not mature…nothing like the temptress of his dreams. Steffan kept the disappointment from his voice. "You asked to see me?"

"Yes, lord."

She curtseyed like a commoner but there was something charming in her wide-eyed innocence. "Do you have a name?"

"Yes, lord, Lucy, lord...Lucy Jonson." She stared at him with wide doe-eyes, as if her name was supposed to mean something, but it did not.

"Should I know you, Lucy Jonson?"

"Not me, lord, but perhaps my father?" She took a deep breath and then the story tumbled out. "My father's a good man, a pious man, a tavern owner. He pays his tithes and goes to temple twice a fortnight, but the soldiers came today and arrested him." Her voice sank to a whisper. "They dragged him off to the dungeons." Her voice broke. "He's all I have, my only family. I had to come and ask...to beg." She sank to her knees, a tear sliding down her cheek. "Please, lord, free my father?"

He sipped his brandy, staring at the girl, another grieving relative come to plead for a captured heretic...but few had the courage to approach the Lord Raven. "Why me?"

"Why, lord?" She seemed confused by the question.

"Yes, why come to me? Why not seek out the Pontifax or the Keeper of the Flame?"

Her eyes widened. "The *Pontifax*," her voice quavered, "would be like talking to a *god*." She shook her head, as if it was too much to consider. "And the Keeper," she shuddered, "the Keeper knows nothing of mercy." Her eyes flooded with fear, her voice dropping to a whisper, "and they say he does not keep his word."

The girl was amusing if nothing else. "And the Lord Raven? What do they say about him?"

She hesitated, her voice soft. "The Lord Raven is the counselor to the Pontifax. A powerful lord, but not brutal like the Keeper...a man who might show mercy." Her voice held a note of pleading. "And so I thought to try." A second tear slid down her cheek.

Her tears enhanced her charm...as sweet and beautiful as an unopened rosebud. "Yes, but heretics are only released for good reason." His voice deepened. "What reason can you give me?"

"I would do anything, lord." Her cheeks bloomed red, her eyes downcast.

And now they came to the anything. He smiled. "What do you have that I might value?" He sipped his brandy, waiting, enjoying the moment.

Her voice was a rushed whisper. "I know about the Dark Harper."

"What?" He sat up almost spilling his brandy. "What did you say?" Perhaps his loose net had caught a fish after all.

She cringed. "If I tell you what I know, will you release my father?"

It was not his habit to negotiate with commoners...but he wanted the information. "Do you know the Dark Harper's true name?"

She shook her head. "No, lord, but I know where he lives. He hides in plain sight during the day." She knelt at his feet, staring up at him with dark doe-eyes.

He could break her and take what he wanted...but those who confessed willingly deserved to be rewarded...and the life of one tavern owner was a cheap trade for the Dark Harper. "For that information, I will see your father released...though I cannot vouch for his condition. The priests are never easy on sinners."

She grabbed his hand and kissed it, urgency in her touch, tears in her eyes. "Thank you, lord, thank you."

He extracted his hand, his voice stern. "First, the information."

She nodded, her face solemn. "He lives above a cobbler's shop, on Rye Street, in the southwest quarter of the city."

"What does he look like?"

She shook her head. "I've never seen his face." She shrugged. "I only know where he lives because...another rebel bragged about it." Her face flamed bright red.

He wondered what else she knew.

"My father, lord?" Her voice held a note of urgency. "He's all I have in the world."

"Your father's name?"

"Petyr Jonson."

He rose and went to the desk. He found a sheet of blank parchment and dipped a quill in the ink well. "I'll send a note to the dungeons and have him released." The nib scratched across the parchment. "But if you've lied to me, you'll both dance in the Flames." He finished the note and fixed his seal to the bottom, a raven imprinted in red wax.

"Can you read?"

"A little."

He handed her the parchment. "Then see for yourself that the Lord Raven keeps his word." He went to the door and called for Pip.

The redheaded lad came running. "Yes, lord?"

Steffan retrieved the parchment and handed it to Pip. "Take this to the dungeons, to the chief priest on duty, and see to it that the tavern owner, Petyr Jonson, is released. Have a pair of soldiers escort him home and remain there on guard until they receive other orders." The lad nodded. "Be quick about it, time is of the essence."

Pip tucked the parchment in his pocket and disappeared into the hallway.

Steffan closed the door and turned to stare at the young girl. She remained on her knees, a sheen of tears on her face. He wondered what other secrets she harbored. Passion had a way of loosening a woman's tongue, and his lust had already been aroused. Crossing the room with a predator's glide, he stared down at her, his voice deep. "We were talking of anything."

Her voice was a hushed whisper. "Yes, lord, anything."

He used a single finger to brush the tears from her cheek, slow and gentle, a soft caress...a temptation and a question combined in a single touch.

She trembled but did not pull away.

He lifted her chin and traced the full curves of her ruby lips. He pressed and she took his thumb in her mouth with a gentle suck. Steffan smiled, stiffening with anticipation. Perhaps she was not as innocent as she seemed. Either way, he would give her a night of unbearable pleasure...and in the morning he would hunt a harper, crushing the rebellion beneath his boot heel.

51

Katherine

*C*astlegard! Great mage-stone towers soared to the sky like swords thrust straight up to the heavens. Knights walked the ramparts, proud gleams of silver in the afternoon light. Drum towers crowned with catapults anchored the castle's eight corners, commanding every approach. Between the towers, the massive outer walls stood like burnished steel, strong and stubborn and undefeated. Reflections of the battlements shimmered in the deep green moat, casting an image of enduring strength, an image that defied the very siege of time.

Kath's pride swelled at first sight of the sun-bright towers. A symbol of strength, a beacon of honor, the great castle called her home. Standing in the stirrups, she shouted the castle's name like a battle cry, *"Castlegard!"* Urging her horse to a gallop, she surged ahead, racing across the vast greensward, the two knights and the monk trailing behind.

Laughing, Kath reached the outer gatehouse and slowed her stallion to a walk. Two knights stood guard, maroon cloaks over silver surcoats. She recognized the older knight, his chestnut mustache drooping down past his chin. "Greetings, Sir Marin! A fine day to be alive!"

The knight stared wide-eyed, his gaze bouncing from her face to Sir Tyrone's and back again. "The Imp? Is it really you?"

She laughed. "Only a stop in a long journey but home nonetheless."

"The king will not be believing it." Sir Marin looked puzzled but he waved her through.

They clattered across the drawbridge and beneath the portcullis, a menace of iron spikes poised above. Kath led her companions through the stone labyrinth of tricks and traps that separated the two concentric walls, a gated pass-through, an archery crossfire yard, and too many murder holes to count. Rumors claimed the castle held eleven built-in defenses, but when they reached the inner gate Kath still only counted ten. She shook her head in wry amazement; someday she'd discover the elusive defense.

Passing through the ironbound gate, they entered the inner castle. The great yard rang with the clang of swords, the knight candidates hard at weapons practice. Kath studied the sparring pairs with a critical eye. The fresh-faced candidates still needed a lot of work. She shook her head and laughed; she'd learned a lot in her year away.

Stable lads rushed to claim the horses. A blond-haired boy with a gap-toothed smile took Dancer's reins. "Is it really you?"

"Yes, Val, I've come home, but not to stay." Kath swung down from the saddle. "Give Dancer an extra ration of oats and an apple or two." She claimed her saddlebag and patted the chestnut's neck. "He's earned it."

Word of her return spread like wildfire. Apprentices and masters from the forge spilled into the great yard, joining the knot of stable hands. The old veterans left their benches to crowd around. Greetings and questions came from every direction. "Show us your axes!" "Tell us how you killed the ogre." "Tell us about the fight in the forest!"

Tears crowded her eyes; she hadn't realized how much she'd missed her friends.

Burly and bald with thick sooty eyebrows, the master swordsmith bulled a path through the apprentices. "So, you've come back to us." His deep rumbling voice matched his muscled bulk.

Tears threatened but she forced them back. "I would not be here without the gift of the dagger hidden in my boot."

The big smith nodded, his voice a deep rumble. "You did the forge proud, putting our steel to good use." His dark eyes twinkled like polished metal. "The tale of the princess defeating the ogre is oft told in the forge."

Kath remembered long hours spent in the forge, watching as the smiths fashioned new blades from raw steel, their hammers ringing to the cadence of their stories. "So you got my letter."

"And the purse. The lads appreciated the golds." His voice deepened, the sound of rumbling boulders. "Few knights remember the hands that forge their blades. Both the deed and the remembrance were well done." He gave her a deep bow. "Welcome home, Princess Kath of Castlegard."

Her throat closed tight, a single tear running down her cheek. Her friends accepted her, swords and all.

A bellows boy broke the tension. "Tell us how you killed the ogre!" The clamor became deafening, a sea of smiles surrounding her.

Otto winked. "They won't be satisfied till they hear the tale from your lips."

Her grin was irrepressible. "Then I guess I better not disappoint them."

A ragged cheer greeted her reply.

A single voice cut through the revelry. "The king will see you now."

The banter came to a sudden halt. The knight marshal stood on the edge of the gathering, his face stern, his one-eyed gaze pinning her like an eagle hunting a mouse. Kath flushed, feeling like she'd done something wrong.

The marshal released her, his stare surveying the crowd. "Get back to work. There is nothing to celebrate."

Her friends dispersed, scattering to the forge, the stables, and the sparring yard. Only the two knights and the monk remained.

The marshal raked her with his one-eyed gaze. "The king will see you now." He turned, leading the way into the heart of the castle.

Kath threw her saddlebag over her shoulder and followed the stiff-backed marshal across the yard. The marshal's cold greeting shivered against her mind like a warning. Perhaps she'd made a mistake in returning home. Duncan had tried to warn her that the past had a way of biting the present, that home could become a trap, but she hadn't wanted to listen. She needed to warn the king, but perhaps a bit of caution was due. Easing the crystal dagger from the sheath at her belt, she slipped it into the pouch of her saddlebag. Sir Tyrone saw and nodded, grim agreement on his face.

A pair of knights saluted as they entered the King's Tower. Afternoon sunlight lanced through the arrow-slit windows, striping the stairs with beams of light, a reminder of the castle's military prowess.

They reached the top floor, a pair of guards snapping to attention as they entered the king's antechamber. Battle banners crowded the ceiling, a testament to past glory. Kath stared up at the familiar banners, so many memories, so many dreams.

The marshal knocked on the inner door. The king's voice replied, "Come."

They found the king sitting on the far side of the round table, maps and scrolls spread across the tabletop. He wore scarred battle leathers, his tanned face etched deep with lines of decision, his gaze as keen as his sword. A great bear of a man, the king's commanding presence dominated the chamber.

The marshal took his place, standing behind the king.

Kath and her companions bowed low.

The king's steel-green gaze bored into Kath. "So, you've disobeyed orders."

His words ambushed Kath. She struggled to find a reply but he cut her off.

"You were sent to foster with the queen with orders to return a princess fit to wed." His gaze raked across her, from her disheveled hair to her dusty boots. "Instead, you return a hoyden, a ruffian with axes strapped to your back and a sword belted to your side." He shook his head. "A hoodlum-girl who betrays her sex and her royal blood."

"That's not fair!"

"*Silence!*" The king's roar echoed against the tower walls.

Kath bit back her words, realizing she faced the king, not the father.

The king's gaze moved to the monk. "My daughter was sent to Lanverness, to the queen's court, yet she journeyed to your monastery for fostering. I presume you bring an apology from your Grand Master?"

Zith raised his right hand, displaying the tattoo of the Seeing Eye. "I am Zith, a monk of the Kiralynn Order. I accompany the princess for my own reasons. As to the Grand Master, he serves the Light in all things."

"A cryptic answer." The king's voice was a low growl. "I want an explanation."

The monk bowed, his voice measured. "It is not my place to explain." Zith stood statue-still, his face a blank mask.

The king's stare smoldered with anger.

Kath watched the exchange. Zith had warned her that the secret of the crystal dagger was not his to reveal. Knowing the monk kept silent for her sake, she could not let him endure the king's ire. "I went to the monastery of my own free will."

The king speared her with his gaze. "Yes, a willful child disobeying her king's commands."

Kath sputtered in rage.

The king turned his gaze to Blaine. "And what about you, Sir Blaine? Have you earned your blue steel sword?"

Blaine gasped like a fish out of water.

"At least you've not abandoned your charge, although your wits are in question." King Ursus made a dismissive gesture. "It's just as well that you've returned. Your blue sword will be needed. War is coming." The king turned his gaze to the black knight. "And you, Sir Tyrone. I expected you to have better sense."

Kath's anger exploded. "My lord, we bring a warning."

"A warning?" The king's shrewd gaze snapped back to Kath. "We have already had a warning. A monk from the monastery brought a strange tale, claiming that the Mordant has been reborn. That he seeks to cross over the Dragon Spines and regain his dark throne." He leaned forward, his voice cutting like a sword. "What more can you add to this tale?"

Zith intervened. "If you've heard from the monastery then you know the truth of our words. The Mordant must be stopped before he crosses the Dragon Spines. You must heed our warning."

"*Must?* You dare use *must* with a king! I am not a lackey for your Order." His gaze challenged Kath. "Well, daughter, what do you have to say about the monks and their warning?"

The question was a trap, yet Castlegard needed to be warned. She had to try. "We've seen firsthand the footprints of the Mordant's treachery. The fire that ravaged the farmland south of the Snowmelt is proof of his passage. The Mordant is not like other foes. The sword is not his first weapon. He finds ways to divide, to turn brother against brother, to make enemies of allies. This evil must be stopped before he crosses the Dragon Spines, before he gains a greater power."

The king sat back in his chair. "You followed the Mordant? Two knights, a monk, and a slip of a girl?"

The truth hovered at her lips.

"I wait for an explanation."

She had to try. "My lord, at the monastery I was shown a dire vision, a vision of a great battlefield where..." she stumbled on the words, "where you *died* and the Octagon was slain to a man. The best hope to avert this battle is to stop the Mordant from crossing the Dragon Spines." A note of pleading entered her voice, "I've come to warn you...and to ask for your help."

"You've seen a *vision?*"

She nodded.

"A delusion more likely, some mummery of magic." His steel-green stare stabbed into her. "Look at you! Instead of a daughter fit to wed, you return a sword-wielding ruffian! I'll be lucky to make bride-price for you!"

His cruelty cut her to the bone. She stared at the king who was also her father and realized that he would never see past his own blind prejudice. Her heart sank, her voice hoarse with bitterness. "My lord and king, you know the strength and weakness of every knight in your command...yet you know nothing of your own daughter." A thunderstorm moved across the king's face but Kath persisted. "Father, I am not such a riddle. I only want the same thing as you, to make a difference with my sword." Her voice dropped to a whisper. "If only you would only open your eyes and see me for who I truly am."

"My eyes are open!" The king's voice roared like thunder. "I see a daughter who does not know her place. A daughter who has spent too long pretending to be a squire, deluded by visions of glory. A daughter who refuses to obey. And now I've seen enough." He raised his voice to a shout. "*Guards!*"

Two knights burst into the chamber, fists saluting against chests.

"Escort my daughter to her bedchamber and see that she remains there." His gaze turned to Kath. "And the next time I see you, daughter, I expect you to dress in a gown as befits a princess of the royal blood."

Rage warred with hurt. He refused to see her, making her a prisoner in her own home.

The king turned his gaze to her companions. "I will speak to you later, monk. And the next time we talk, I expect answers." His voice hardened to a command. "Sir Blaine, Sir Tyrone, report for duty and take your turn walking the walls. Every sword is needed."

Kath's anger turned to bitterness; every sword was needed but hers.

King Ursus gestured a curt dismissal. "Now, go. Get out of my sight."

The guards stood close behind Kath, a looming threat, enforcing the king's will.

She gathered her dignity like a ragged cloak and gave the king a stiff bow, memorizing her father's face, her father's shallow-minded stubbornness.

Perhaps her cold stare reached him, for the king's voice softened. "Katherine, war is coming. You should have stayed safe in the south at the queen's court, learning to be a lady. I promised your lady mother I would make you a good marriage, but you make it hard, daughter, you make it so hard."

He would never understand. Kath fought to keep her voice from betraying her. "Yes, father, it is hard, harder than you know." She turned and followed the guards out of the chamber, throwing a passing glance to the two knights. Sir Blaine avoided her gaze but Sir Tyrone nodded, his face grim.

The guards marched her down the stairs, escorting her to her former bedchamber, returning her to her childhood, but that time had already flown, the bird would not return to the cage, gilded or otherwise. Kath's anger hardened to resolve, the time for obeying was long past.

The two guards took positions on either side of the door, their faces implacable. Knights chosen to guard the King's Tower were always the most loyal. Kath closed the door, shutting out the guards, shutting out the castle.

She turned to face her childhood. The chamber was just as she'd left it: a narrow bed with a thick eider quilt, a small night table with a half-melted candle, a writing desk stocked with quills and ink, a chest for clothes, a chest for scrolls, and a chamber pot. The only luxury was a worn tapestry on the wall, a battle scene showing the maroon knights triumphing over the Mordant's hordes. Crossing the chamber, she ran her hand across the tapestry, like greeting an old friend. She'd spent countless hours lying in bed, staring at the tapestry, dreaming of victory and glory...a dream denied to any girl-child. She laughed but the sound was bitter. Her lord father did not see her worth...but the gods did.

Kath shook her head in defiance and began to pace the chamber. She'd come to Castlegard to give warning, and to gain more swords for the journey north...and instead she'd become a prisoner of the king's narrow-mindedness. Duncan had warned her, but she hadn't wanted to listen. Castlegard had become a trap, a trap she'd eagerly run to. It almost had the twisted smell of the Mordant...but this trap had been set long ago. Prejudice divided her from the king, from the Octagon Knights, from those who should have been her closest allies, her strongest swords. The Dark Lord was devious beyond the telling. But she would serve the Light with Valin's help.

She crossed to the arrow-slit window to gauge the hour. The sun edged towards the horizon, a glory of gold and red marking the supper hour, a good time to escape. She had no time to waste. The traps and tricks that kept invaders out could also hold a prisoner in. She had to leave before her lord father's orders extended beyond the guards posted at her door...and that meant leaving this very night. The question was how.

Kath gripped her gargoyle and resumed pacing. The arrow-slit windows were too narrow, and besides, the mage-stone walls were impossible to climb. The guards on the door were incorruptible, so pleading or persuading would be of no help. There had to be another way.

Tightening her grip on her gargoyle, she realized the answer lay within her very grasp. The gods provided the solution! Her gargoyle gave her a key to any wall. But passing through the inner wall would just bring her into confrontation with the guards, while the outer wall offered a shear drop to an ugly death. The gargoyle was the key, but for which lock? The solution seemed just out of reach till a smile crossed her face. The floor held the answer. She could drop to the chamber below and slip out into the hallway. Once she reached the tower basement, she could use the secret passages to make her way to the stables.

Kath knelt, one hand on her gargoyle, one hand set against the mage-stone floor, praying there was no one in the chamber below.

A knock sounded on the door.

Startled, Kath scrambled to her feet, shoving her gargoyle beneath her leather jerkin.

The door creaked open, the smells of roast lamb and garlic wafting into the chamber. The tantalizing smells took her by ambush. Kath lowered her guard. Quintus, the master healer, appeared carrying a platter heaped with lamb and roast potatoes. "I thought you might want some supper." Clad in a brown robe the color of peat, he flashed her a broad smile, his unruly black hair falling into his eyes.

The sight of her friend and mentor nearly pushed Kath to tears. "Master Quintus, how did you..."

"The castle folk are speaking of nothing else." He set the platter on the desk. "Come and eat, you must be hungry."

The smells of lamb and garlic woke a ravenous hunger in her. She sat at the table and attacked the meal, savoring every bite. She mumbled past a mouthful, "Thank you."

He nodded, taking a seat on her scroll chest.

She watched him, wondering why he'd really come. She'd trusted him before, but her secrets had little consequence then. Much had changed. "You've seen the guards."

He nodded, his face solemn.

"The king's made me a prisoner." She tore off a hunk of bread, still warm from the oven, and sopped up the thick gravy. "I came to warn the king, but he won't listen." Anger flooded her voice. "He never sees me for who I am."

The master sat listening.

She remembered that about him, the healer was always a good listener. Needing to talk, the painful truth tumbled out. "He'd listen if I was a son."

"Yes." The healer's face softened. "He's a good king, an honorable man...but he is chained by convention."

"And that makes it all the more cruel." Kath shook her head, too much emotion in her voice. "It's hard to always be overlooked."

He gave her a conspirator's grin. "Yes, but you won't let that stop you."

A grin slipped across her face; he knew her too well. "You're right."

He nodded. "Now how can I help the bearer of the crystal dagger?"

She gasped, "You know?"

He chuckled. "Seek knowledge, protect knowledge, share knowledge."

"But how?"

"Those of us who serve outside of the monastery do not take the tattoo."

"So all these years..."

He nodded. "I served as Castlegard's healer, and I also served the monastery...and I mentored a young girl who showed great promise but was always overlooked." He chuckled. "Looking back, I see now that destiny's hand had marked you. But I confess, I never thought you'd be the one to wield the crystal dagger." His face turned thoughtful. "But then again it makes a certain sense, a certain symmetry. The Lords of Light have a sense of irony and who better to wield the dagger than a daughter of Castlegard."

"If only the king shared your wisdom." She knew the answer but she had to ask. "Do you think the king would see things differently if he knew the truth? If I told him about the crystal dagger?"

His face stilled. "Would the king ever give a woman, even his own daughter, a blue steel blade?"

Frustration rode her voice. "You monks always answer questions with questions."

"Perhaps that is because some students refuse to see the answers." He gave her a half-smile that she remembered from her days in the healery. "I'm waiting."

The bitter truth would not be denied. "No. He would never waste blue steel on a mere woman."

The healer nodded. "The king would see it as his duty to take the dagger from you, to wield it himself, or to give it to a champion of the Octagon. In his eyes, anything else would be a waste of a great weapon." His voice softened. "The bearers of the crystal dagger always choose their own paths. The secret is yours to keep or to tell. But I think you have done well to hold your silence with the king...much as it hurts you."

The understanding in his eyes threatened to loose her tears.

He clapped his hands against his thighs and stood, his voice full of optimistic vigor. "The Kath I knew would have a plan." He stared at her, his dark eyes full of mischief. "So how do you plan to beard the knights in their own castle?"

An irrepressible smile spread across her face. "With magic, and wits, and guile."

He beamed a smile. "I would expect nothing less." He gave her a half bow. "How can I be of service?"

She thought about her plan. "I *do* need your help." Reaching beneath her jerkin, she revealed the small mage-stone gargoyle. "I know how to use this."

His eyes glittered with interest.

"The gargoyle will let me pass through stone walls." Her hand curled protectively around the small figurine. "I never thought I'd need it to escape from Castlegard."

"The gods work in mysterious ways. How can I help?"

"Go to the chamber directly below this one and make sure it's empty. If there's someone there, get them out on some pretext, whatever you think will work." He nodded. "Then find Sir Tyrone, Blaine, and the monk, Zith. Tell them to quietly make their way to the stables. Have them get the horses saddled and I'll meet them there."

"Anything else?"

"No...yes." She needed information and the healer might be her only chance to get it. "The Mordant has to pass through the Domain to cross the Dragon Spines but the countryside seems peaceful enough. Have the knights reported anything unusual, any type of treachery?"

The healer looked thoughtful. "I'm not privy to the king's council, but there has been talk in the great hall that two knights have gone missing."

"Missing?" A warning shivered down her spine.

"Yes, they were sent to Raven Pass with dispatches from the king but they never arrived." He stared at her. "Do you think the missing knights have something to do with the Mordant?"

"I don't know. But whatever the Mordant does, it will be devious and deadly."

"Just so." The healer threw a glance toward the arrow-slit window. "The sun sets. If you're going to slink through the castle, you best do it while the knights are at supper." He gave her a conspirator's wink. "I'll meet you in the stables." He picked up her empty platter and turned for the door. "A thin excuse but it worked."

She couldn't let him leave without a last word. "Thank you..." she was going to say for helping, but the words came out differently, "...for believing in me."

He smiled but his eyes were solemn. "The gods marked you from a young age. I never doubted you'd find a way to make a difference." He opened the door and was gone.

The healer left behind the lingering smell of roast lamb...and a sense of optimism. Kath had to smile; with such friends she would find a way to move mountains. But first she needed to escape from her beloved castle.

She paced the length of the chamber, counting to one hundred, giving the healer a chance to clear the chamber below. Finished with the count, she gave her bedchamber a final glance, knowing she might never be welcome in the great castle again. She slipped a candle stub into her pocket and gave the timeworn tapestry a last salute. "Honor and the Octagon."

Throwing her saddlebag over her shoulder, she crouched in the middle of the chamber. Placing one hand flat on the stone floor while holding her gargoyle with the other, she took a deep breath and reached for the magic within. Stone pulled beneath her hand. Proud and stubborn and strong, the stone called to her. She fell forward, into the floor, submerged in mage-stone. Hard to move, hard to think...but she needed to breathe. Kath pushed forward, refusing to be trapped. A roaring sound filled her ears, and then she was through. She gasped for breath...and fell.

The floor rushed up to hit her.

She tried to get her feet under her but the floor was too quick. She landed with a hard thud, the breath knocked out of her, a sharp pain in her left ankle. Gasping for breath, she shook her head in wry amusement. She'd forgotten that one man's floor is another's ceiling. Pity she didn't land on the other bed but at least the chamber was empty.

Pushing to her feet, she tested her ankle, relieved to find it sore but not sprained. Her palms stung and she'd have a bruise on one elbow but thank Valin nothing was broken. Retrieving her saddlebag, she went to the door and pressed her ear to the thick wood. Hearing nothing, she eased the door open and peered out.

Torchlight danced along the mage-stone walls, but the hall was empty. Kath grinned, knowing the castle was her ally. She crept down the hall, hugging the shadows, slinking her way toward the stairs. Her doeskin boots whispered down the staircase, taking two at a time. Rounding the second spiral, she heard voices climbing from below. She ducked into the nearest corridor and hid in the shadows till the voices dimmed.

Twice she had to backtrack to avoid being seen, but her knowledge of the castle served her well. She reached the tower basement and sprinted down the empty hallway, counting six torches to the left.

Every trigger mechanism was slightly different. She pressed the raised metal octagon at the base of the torch...but nothing happened. Turning the octagon left and then right did nothing. Frustrated, she wracked her memory, wondering if she'd chosen the wrong torch.

Voices flowed down the stone staircase.

Desperate, she grasped the torch bracket and tugged to the right. A low grating noise came from the opposite wall. The thick wall slid back, releasing a long-held breath of stale air.

The voices grew louder.

Kath fumbled in her pocket for the candle stub and held it up to the torch. Shielding the small flame, she dashed into the secret passage and punched the raised octagon on the inner wall. The wall ground closed, sealing her into the subterranean passageways. She leaned against the inner wall, soaking up the cold solidness of the stone, relieved to have reached the secret ways.

The small candle cast a feeble light but Kath was undaunted by the dank darkness. The secret passageways were her private domain. She'd grown up exploring the underground vaults, roaming the castle like an invisible ghost. And now they'd help her to escape. Kath shook her head at the irony.

Descending the stairs, she shielded the flickering flame, protecting her only source of light. Cobwebs choked the passage, dust lined the floor, and darkness crouched close. She pushed through the webs, threading her way through the twists and turns of the great labyrinth. As a young girl, she'd often dreamt of finding treasure hidden in the passageways. She'd found plenty of rusted swords and faded shields, and in one strange cubbyhole, she'd found her mage-stone gargoyle. Smiling, she realized her good-luck charm was treasure beyond her wildest dreams. Whatever the reasons for the ancient passageways, Kath was grateful for finding them.

Turning right, she took the next two lefts, hoping her memory proved true. The passageway led to a narrow set of stairs. If memory served, the steps should open onto the last stall of the stables. She climbed the steps and found the octagon set in the wall. Sending a quick prayer to Valin, she pressed the raised octagon.

A low grinding noise came from the wall. A three-foot high section moved back, revealing a soft light. Kath breathed deep, relieved to smell the rich scents of horses and hay. She scrambled through the opening, thankful the stall was empty. The secret door ground closed, disappearing into the rear wall.

Kath peered into the long corridor. Castlegard's stables were a vast warren of stalls, holding over four hundred horses. Deciding brazenness was her best ploy, Kath walked down the hay-strewn corridor, her saddlebag thrown over her shoulder, trying to pretend she belonged.

Horses whinnied and nickered, munching on hay. Kath made her way toward the front entrance, listening for voices, hoping to find her friends. She rounded a corner and nearly collided with a stable lad carrying an armful of harnesses. The young boy issued a shriek, turned ghost-pale, and fled the other direction before Kath could say a word. The boy's reaction made no sense. Kath quickened her step, afraid the lad might raise an alarm.

She found her companions saddling horses, near the front of the stables. Sir Tyrone elbowed a big black stallion, fighting to tighten the saddle girth, while the monk fastened saddlebags to a sleek gray mare. The pudgy healer led a saddled roan stallion out of a nearby stall. Kath stepped out of the shadows, glad to be back with her companions. "I'm glad to see you."

Zith stared wide-eyed. "Why are you covered in cobwebs and dust? You look like a ghost."

She looked down at herself and found it was true. She laughed, trying to brush the sticky cobwebs away. "So that's why the stable boy took such a fright. The ghosts of Castlegard are rising from the crypts."

"If the ghosts can fight, you might want to bring them along." Sir Tyrone's voice held a bitter edge. "We're short one blue sword."

"What?" The black knight's words struck Kath like a douse of ice water. "Where's Sir Blaine?"

The healer handed her the roan stallion's reins. "I talked to him, but he refused to come."

A cold hand gripped her throat. "But he swore his sword to me! He swore an oath in the ruins of the Star Tower." She couldn't imagine taking on the Mordant without his blue blade.

The healer took the saddlebag from her shoulder and began fastening it to the back of the roan's saddle. "Blaine said he swore an oath to the king. That war is coming and his blue blade is needed here."

Kath shook her head in denial. "He's supposed to come with us. He can't desert us now." She felt like someone had plunged a sword into her gut. First her father and now Blaine, too much betrayal for one day. She stared at the master healer. "Where is he? I need to talk to him, to convince him to come."

Sir Tyrone gripped her arm. "You can't risk going back. If the king orders the gates closed, you'll never get out." His dark stare drilled into her. "We have to leave now. We'll make do without him."

The black knight was right, but Blaine's desertion felt like a deathblow.

The master healer said, "I'll talk to Blaine. Perhaps I can convince him to follow you."

It was a slender hope, but better than nothing. Kath nodded. "Tell him we need his strength, we need his blue sword." She found it hard to believe that Blaine would not be coming. "Tell him, I still believe the two swords will be true." Her stare pinned the healer. "Use those exact words, the two swords will be true." Bitterness crowded her voice. "Perhaps the words of the gods will convince him to keep his oath."

The healer nodded, his face solemn. "But which way will you ride?"

Kath considered the choices. "The king will expect us to ride north, through the valley, so that way is shut. Instead we'll ride south and choose another way to cross." She considered the eight strongholds held by the Octagon. "We'll have to bluff our way into the north." She whispered her choice in the healer's ear.

"I'll do my best to convince Blaine to follow."

Sir Tyrone swung up into the saddle. "Tell Blaine to ride fast. We can't wait for him."

The healer gave Kath a leg up onto the roan.

She stared down at her friend and mentor, wondering if she'd ever return to Castlegard. "Thank you...for all your help."

He raised his hand as if in blessing. "May the Light be with you."

Sir Tyrone said, "Are we ready?"

Kath shook her head. "Just a moment." Reaching back into her saddlebag, she reclaimed the crystal dagger, sheathing it at her belt. She also pulled a dark green cloak from the bag and settled it around her shoulders, pulling the deep hood up to hide her blond hair. "You first, Sir Tyrone. With a silver surcoat leading, perhaps there'll be no questions at the gates."

The black knight urged his mount to a walk. They exited the stables and rode out into the great yard. The twilight sky had deepened to purple, shrouding the castle in shadows. Kath kept her head down, hiding within the cloak's deep hood. So tempting to urge the horses to a gallop but they dared not draw unwanted attention. The ride across the great yard seemed to take forever, a trickle of sweat running down her back. Kath clutched her gargoyle, sending a prayer to Valin. They reached the great ironbound gate without incident and slipped out of the inner castle.

Sir Tyrone urged his stallion to a trot, entering the gauntlet of traps and tricks that separated the two concentric walls. Kath could feel the stares of sentries from the towers above, but if they navigated the gauntlet without a mistake, there would be no alarm.

Sir Tyrone led them unerringly to the gated pass-through. The clatter of hooves echoed in the pass-through, as if multiplying their numbers. Murder holes stared down like dark eyes watching from above. They passed beneath the last portcullis and clattered across the drawbridge.

A knight barred the final gateway. "Halt and declare yourselves."

Sir Tyrone slowed his horse to a walk but he did not stop. "Sir Tyrone on the king's business, escorting two travelers beyond the Domain."

Kath kept her face averted, hiding beneath her cloak.

Sir Tyrone kept his horse to a walk. The black stallion bore down on the knight.

Kath feared the knight would raise the alarm, but at the last moment he stepped aside. "On your way."

They rode through the final gateway and out into the greensward. Kath urged her horse to speed, desperate to get away. They galloped across the vast greensward, nothing but shadows in their wake. Reaching the forest's edge, Kath pulled up and turned for a last look. Moonlight silvered the towers of the great castle, a vision of strength and honor and pride, a bittersweet sight. Returning had been a terrible mistake. She'd gained her freedom but lost her father, her friends, and her home. The losses ached like arrow wounds to the heart. Kath raised her fist in a final salute, "Honor and the Octagon," and then turned and galloped toward her destiny.

52

Samson

Samson felt like his luck had finally changed. Full of restless energy, he couldn't wait to greet the dawn. He rose and dressed before the others, avoiding the creaking steps on the stairs, slipping through the shop door and plunging into the cobblestone streets. He roamed the city with a brisk stride, basking in the freedom of the early morning, watching the sunrise colors climb the dawn sky.

The city came awake as he walked: the clop of hooves on cobblestones, the ring of a hammer from an open shop door, the creak of a merchant's wagon, the smell of fresh baked bread, the rich tapestry of a city day. He took it all in, savoring every detail, feeling giddy or perhaps drunk, like a man who'd escaped a death sentence. He laughed, for the thought was close to the truth. The bard had finally listened to reason, agreeing to stop the raids while he investigated the source of the Pontifax's magic. Samson had gained a reprieve from worry, a release from fear. He knew the reprieve wouldn't last but he intended to make the most of his time...and that meant seeing his Lucy.

They weren't supposed to meet till noon but Samson couldn't wait. He roamed the streets, walking in aimless directions, waiting for a late enough hour to knock on her door. He thought about how they might spend the day, perhaps a meander through the spice markets or a stroll through the city's herb gardens. Perhaps he'd seize the chance to pull her close and savor the scent of lilac in her lustrous dark hair. Perhaps he'd even dare another kiss. He smiled, deciding to stop by a bakery and purchase two of the flaky pastries with golden raisins that she loved so much, an early morning surprise. Turning toward the street of bakers, he caught a glimpse of dark hair cascading down the back of an emerald green cloak. His heartbeat quickened, eagerness overcoming his surprise. Lengthening his stride, he closed the distance. "Lucy!"

She whirled like a startled cat, face flushed, hair tousled like she'd just spilled from bed. Her dark gaze met his, her eye's flying open wide.

"Oh, it's you!" The flush fled from her face replaced by a shock of pale white, as if she stared at a ghost.

And then he knew. Ice water rushed through his veins, freezing his heart. "What have you done?" His voice was a low rasp, parched of life.

She stumbled backwards, fear in her face. "I did what I had to...to save my father."

He gripped her arm, his voice like iron. "What have you done?"

"I went to the Lord Raven." Her gaze clouded, a deep blush blooming on her cheeks. "He was..." Her words trailed away.

His heart shattered. "I trusted you." He shook her, desperate for details. "What did you tell him?"

She pulled away, her voice a low whisper. "It's over Samson. Run and hide before they find you."

Cold gripped him like an ice-shroud. He let her go, a flash of emerald running down the cobblestone street.

And then he fled. He raced into the nearest alleyway, running without thinking, looking without seeing, needing only to get away, to lose himself in the twists and turns of the back ways. Despite the pain in his side, despite his ragged breath, he pressed for more speed but he couldn't escape himself. All of his nightmares came stalking, chasing him through the stink of the narrow lanes, catching him, consuming him.

He tripped and fell, sprawling face-first on the hard-packed dirt. Exhausted, he lay in a puddle of filth, a discarded man. His breath came hard and ragged from the long run...and then the sobs started. He cried a river. He shed tears for all of his mistakes, for all of his shortcomings, a flood of regrets. When the tears came to an end, when the fear and grief were both exhausted, cold logic struck like a war hammer pounding a spike into his mind; he'd betrayed his friends.

A different fear settled over him. A cold hand twisted his guts; he couldn't be the death of his friends. He'd made many mistakes but this one he could not live with. He stared up into the sky, a faint flush of pink still riding the clouds. Perhaps there was time.

Samson pushed himself to his feet...and then he ran, only this time with purpose. He took the shortest route, praying he was not too late. Scuttling between two burned out buildings, he dared a shortcut through the cobblestone streets before plunging back into the alleys. Rounding the final turn, he paused in the shadows, trying to control his gasping breath. He peered around the corner, afraid of what he might find...but there were no soldiers waiting in ambush, no red tabards. Hope flooded through him.

He raced down the narrow alley to the secret door. Releasing the hidden latch, he stepped into the cupboard. He stooped and gazed through the knothole, his heart thundering.

Soldiers crowded the kitchen.

Samson froze.

The captain barked a question. "Where's the bard?"

Grandmother Magda sat in her rocking chair, her bag of yarn in her lap, her knitting needles clacking. She stared at the captain, her face a serene mask, a harmless old lady. "There's no bard here, sir. Just a family of cobblers tryin ta get by."

The orphan lad, Jack, cowered in the corner, his face chalk-white.

"I'll have none of your lies, old woman. There's been an informer. Now where's the bard?"

Samson pressed his face to the door, staring through the knothole, unable to look away, afraid to watch.

Footsteps clattered down the stairs, more soldiers. "There's no one upstairs, captain."

Samson sagged against the door; at least the others were still free.

One of the soldiers paused on the steps, his boots striking a hollow note. He knelt and pried up the floorboard, discovering the cache of swords. "Swords here, captain! They're rebels for sure."

The captain growled an order. "Cut the boy, one finger at a time, till the old woman talks."

A soldier grabbed for Jack. The boy dodged behind the rocking chair. Grandmother Magda reached for her bag of yarn. Steel spun from the old lady's hand. "Run, Jack!" The handle of a butcher knife protruded from the captain's chest, the blade sunk deep. A scream sliced through the kitchen. The captain sank to his knees, a death mask on his face.

Chaos erupted in the kitchen.

Jack sprinted between the soldiers, lunging for the open door. Grandmother Magda yanked the butcher knife from the captain's chest. Turning, she hurled the bloody blade into the knot of soldiers. A soldier screamed, blood spurting on the flagstone floor. The old lady reached for another knife.

A sergeant bellowed, "Get the boy!"

Hands reached for Jack.

The boy struggled and dodged but the soldiers crowded close, grabbing him by the back of his tunic. The boy kicked and bit like a wild thing but the soldiers held tight.

Samson watched from the cupboard. He bit his lip to stifle a sob, tears running down his face, the taste of blood on his lip.

Grandmother Magda brandished a second butcher knife, a wicked gleam of steel. "Let the boy go!"

A sword snaked out, striking the knife from her hand. Steel clattered against stone.

Jack kicked and struggled, but he was caught tight.

The sergeant growled, "That's enough from you, old woman. I'd gut you like a fish, but the Lord Raven wants answers." He grabbed the old woman by the arm, pulling her from the rocking chair.

Grandmother Magda seemed to wilt, aging a thousand years.

The sergeant snarled a cruel laugh. "We'll have payment for our captain, bitch. You'll scream in the dungeons and then die in the Flames." He shoved her toward the other men. "Bind her hands and let's get out of here. Maybe the others will be back later. We still have a harper to catch."

The soldiers bound the old woman and the boy, herding them out into the street. They collected their dead and their wounded, closing the shop door behind them, leaving nothing but bloodstains.

Samson stood in the cupboard, staring through the knothole, staring into the empty kitchen.

The knitting needles had stopped...the knives had come out...the nightmare had begun.

53

Blaine

Swords clanged with a ferocious beat. Blaine attacked, giving in to a blind fury, the sparring sword becoming a blur in his hands. Stroke, cut, and parry, his anger raged, driving his opponent across the sparring yard in a relentless attack. Blaine pounded the other knight's shield, angry that he'd had to choose between Kath and his king. Beating the knight's sword away, he struck a flurry of blows, angry that Kath had left without him. Parrying a low slash, he leaped to the attack, furious that he'd been left to take the brunt of the king's anger. Stroke, parry, and cut, Blaine remembered the fierce blistering the king had given him the morning he discovered his daughter missing. At least he hadn't been able to tell the king where she went, spared that betrayal by ignorance. His anger blazed to a wild fury. Blaine threw himself into the fight, furious with his life. His sword crashed against the knight's shield, a mighty two-handed blow. The shield buckled and splintered, cleaved in half.

The battered knight threw down his sword. "I yield."

Blaine growled in frustration, "I'm done with this one! Who's next?" He yanked off his helmet, a rush of cool air against his face. Sweat ran down his forehead, stinging his eyes. He stood in the middle of the sparring yard, glaring at the other knights. He'd defeated five in a row, helmets and shields battered to ruin, but still his anger raged. "Come on, I'm just getting started."

No one took up his challenge.

"Surely one of you will cross swords with the lowly farmer boy!" Blaine raked the yard with his stare but they all looked away. He shook his head in disgust and stalked to the benches; the Octagon was not what he remembered. He ripped at the bindings of his armor, needing to get free of the steel cage but his fingers were suddenly too thick. Feeling suffocated, he clawed at the armor.

A squire rushed to help. Blaine let the boy loosen the bindings, removing the breastplate, gauntlets, and leg armor. Free of the weight, he retrieved his great blue sword, settling the harness across his back.

The knight marshal approached, a stern look in his one-eyed gaze. "Five victories, Sir Blaine, not bad...but you should guard against too much rage. We train knights here not berserkers."

Blaine nodded, biting back an angry retort. He'd obeyed his king yet he felt like an oath breaker, damned by the gods and men alike. Blaine felt the other's stares, a mixture of questions and recriminations. Turning his back on his brother knights, he settled his maroon cloak across his shoulders and stalked off.

He prowled the inner castle, seeking another outlet for his rage. He'd thought that sparring would ease his rage, seeking solace in the dance of steel, but instead of a dance he'd turned the sparring yard into a battlefield, acting the berserker instead of the knight. The one-eyed marshal had seen the truth of it. Blaine did not like what he'd become. Trapped by the maroon, trapped by the king, he saw no way to keep both oaths.

"Sir Blaine!"

He pivoted to find the pudgy healer running to catch up. Blaine had no interest in talking to the healer, the man had meddled enough, but before he could walk away, the healer said, "I have an ointment that could help that cut on your arm. Come with me and I'll see to it."

Blood seeped from a cut at his left elbow, a weak point in the armor. It was only a minor wound, but he hadn't noticed it. Disgusted, Blaine shook his head, another sign of the berserker's rage. "Let it bleed." His voice was a low growl.

He turned away but the healer grabbed his arm.

Rage flooded through him. He unsheathed his great blue sword and turned on the healer.

The pudgy little man stood his ground. "Do you want to kill me...or yourself?"

His rage evaporated, replaced by shame. Blaine lowered the blue blade. "I don't deserve this sword."

The healer leaned close, his voice a whisper. "The gods gave you a hero's sword for a reason. Come with me and I'll tell you how to keep your oath."

Blaine gaped at the healer, feeling like he'd just been pole-axed. "But how..."

"Shhh..." The master healer shook his head. "Not here. Come with me."

Walking like a man in a daze, Blaine sheathed his sword and followed. He did not believe the healer could help but he owed Quintus for turning on him with his sword. The least he could do was listen.

Quintus opened the door to the healery and ushered Blaine inside.

The scroll-cluttered antechamber was stuffed full of mismatched furniture. A large patch-ridden armchair sat in front of the cold fireplace, another chair sat in front of the desk, a cabinet filled one wall, stuffed full of scrolls, and a long workbench full of bottles and braziers stretched beneath the only window. A jumble of smells assaulted Blaine's nose, potions, ointments, herbs, musty scrolls...and owl droppings.

A giant frost owl perched by the scroll cabinet. Ruffling its feathers, it issued a greeting, "Whooooo."

The sound sent a shiver down Blaine's spine. He stared at the owl. "I forgot about Snowman. I saw another frost owl deep in the Southern Mountains."

The healer shrugged. "They thrive above the snowline."

Blaine settled into an armchair while the healer sorted through a collection of bottles and jars. Sniffing a bottle, the healer set it aside. "Frost owls are quite remarkable. They can glide for long distances, utterly silent in flight, and they're smarter than most people realize." Selecting a small amber-colored bottle, he removed the stopper, releasing a bitter scent. "Yes, this will do. Roll up your sleeve and let me see that wound."

Blaine peeled back the bloody sleeve and watched as the healer cleaned the wound. The ointment stung, but Blaine kept his arm rock-still. "What did you mean about keeping my oath?"

Smearing honey on the wound, the healer wrapped it with a strip of linen. "That should do." He stoppered the bottle and returned it to the workbench, settling into the patched chair by the fireplace.

Blaine's patience was running thin. "Quintus, what did you mean about keeping my oath? What do you know?"

The healer sighed. "The Lords of Light believe in free will, and so mortal men are given the chance to choose. Our lives are a series of decisions, to stay and fight or to run, to remain silent or to raise questions, to do the right thing or not. And sometimes the true measure of our lives comes down to a single decision. And that one choice defines us beyond all else."

Blaine shook his head, his voice stubborn. "No. There was never a choice. I am sworn to the king. War is coming. My blue blade is needed here."

"Then why don't you believe that?"

He hid behind his anger. "No! There was no choice."

"There is always a choice and always a consequence."

The frost owl shook his feathers. "Whooooo."

"I saw your rage in the sparring yard. You don't believe you made the right choice."

Blaine glared at the healer, refusing to answer.

"You must decide who you are." The healer's voice beat against him with a storm of words. "You can remain here, one of many knights protecting the southern kingdoms, or you can follow the princess north of the Dragon Spines and hunt the Mordant to his lair. You can stay here and obey orders, or you can take your hero's blade to where it is most needed."

Blaine stared at the dark-eyed healer, torn by the healer's words, torn by his own decision.

"What chance will she have without your blue sword?"

A knife twisted in Blaine's gut. "But I swore an oath to the king!"

"What about the oath you swore to Kath in the ruins of the Star Tower?" The healer's dark gaze bored into Blaine. "Can a sword be sworn to two masters?"

The words triggered a storm of memories. Visions from the Guardian Mist assailed Blaine's mind. He'd told the Guardian that he'd be true to Kath. He'd sworn to protect the bearer of the crystal dagger. "But I didn't really think she'd leave Castlegard." The excuse sounded weak to his ears.

"She had to leave or fail her destiny." The healer's voice softened. "Before she left, Kath said to tell you that she still believes the two swords will be true."

The two swords will be true! A shiver raced down Blaine's spine; she still believed in him.

The healer leaned forward, his voice urgent. "Only you can decide. Will you be a knight or a hero?"

"I dreamt of both."

"That is not the choice offered to you."

Blaine shook his head. Quintus spoke like some type of seer...or a messenger of the gods...not a simple healer. Blaine stared at the man, trying to see past the unruly black hair and the pale, pudgy face. "Who are you?"

The healer shrugged and smiled. "A messenger, a catalyst, a friend...but the decision is still yours to make."

The giant frost owl ruffled his wings. "Whooooo."

Blaine sighed. "Even if I wanted to follow, I don't know where she went."

"I know."

Hope sparked within him. "Where?"

The healer shook his head. "If you decide to follow, then you must swear to use the way stations."

"Impossible! The way stations are for the sole use of the king's messengers!"

The healer's face turned grim. "A fear has been growing in my mind, a fear that Kath walks into some kind of trap. If you go, you must find a way to reach her before the trap springs shut. You must ride hard, making up time by getting fresh mounts from the way stations. You must reach her before she crosses the Dragon Spines."

He'd been too late in the Guardian Mist; he'd sworn he wouldn't be late again. "Then I'll use the way stations." His words sealed his fate. If caught, he'd forfeit his maroon cloak and be branded a traitor. But somehow the decision felt right. Perhaps honor was more than a maroon cloak.

"And you'll leave this afternoon? You're already a day and a half behind."

The rage left him, replaced by resolve. "Yes, I'll leave this afternoon."

The healer closed his eyes, relief washing across his face. He looked at Blaine and smiled. "Then ride for Cragnoth Keep and may the Light be with you."

Blaine nodded and rose from the chair. "I've a hard ride ahead." He paused at the door and looked back at the healer. "Thank you...for the second chance."

Quintus smiled. "The gods gave you a blue blade for a reason. I knew you'd prove worthy of the sword."

54

Samson

Samson huddled in the cupboard, stunned by what he'd witnessed, afraid to move. Shadows lengthened, creeping across the kitchen floor and still he waited. At first his mind froze, refusing to accept what he'd seen, but then the guilt came, burying him like an avalanche. He stared through the knothole, into the empty kitchen, blood on the floor, the knitting needles abandoned, all proof of his guilt.

Crouched within his hiding place, he watched the shadows grow, a seed of a plan forming in his mind. He wrestled with the plan, quelling his doubts, asking himself what the bard would do. It seemed a thin hope, but better than nothing, a way to atone for his many mistakes.

Samson made his decision and opened the secret door, stepping into the kitchen. He stood frozen, listening, but no soldiers rushed to arrest him. The kitchen was empty, a hollow shell, a mockery of safety. The scent of apple bread still lingered, the ghost of Grandmother Magda.

He crossed to the cold hearth, stepping around the telltale puddle of blood and the gleaming butcher knife. His gaze avoided the knitting needles, lying abandoned on the floor. Loosening the stone on the side of the hearth, he reached deep into the hidden space. His hand closed on a bundle of dark wool, the Dark Harper's cowled cloak.

Replacing the stone, he searched the kitchen, stuffing a sack with the things he needed, a scrap of parchment, a quill, a stoppered inkwell, and a purse of gold coins. Giving the kitchen a final survey, he snatched up the butcher knife and tucked it in his belt. He took a last look and retreated to the cupboard.

The secret door opened onto the back alleyway. Samson peered left and right. The alley was empty of soldiers...or else they were hiding. Resigned, he took a deep breath and stepped into the alley, into plain sight.

His heart thundered but no soldiers came running. It seemed the enemy did not know everything.

Samson used the butcher knife to carve a crude x on the secret door, warning the others to stay away. Tucking the knife in his belt, he sped down the alley. Slinking through shadows, he threaded his way through the back lanes, always watching for the red of soldiers, the red of priests. Twice he doubled back, making sure no one followed; he carried enough guilt on his soul.

A noon sun glared overhead by the time Samson felt confident enough to approach the abandoned stables. Charred from an old fire, the front was blackened and caved-in like an old man's puckered mouth but the rear remained solid. Samson slipped around the side, searching for the loose clapboards. He knocked, using the code Jack had taught him, and then pushed the boards aside and slipped into the cool shadows. The stable smelled of burnt wood, moldy hay, and mouse droppings. His eyes adjusted to the dimness. A dark-haired lad stood guard, a pitchfork in his hands. Samson nodded. "Hello, Shiner. I'm looking for Willie and Red if he's around."

The orphan-lad grinned. "Somethin for the Harper?"

Samson replied, "Something like that."

"I'll see who's up there." The boy leaned the pitchfork against a post and then scurried up a ladder to the loft. Most of the orphan boys slept in the stable during the day and prowled the alleys at night, serving as eyes and ears for the Dark Harper. Samson hoped Willie was sleeping above.

The floorboards creaked overhead and two lads, one tow-haired and the other dark, raced down the ladder. "Lookin for me, Samson?" Tall and skinny, all arms and legs, Willie was a roof-rat with a knack for climbing. The tow-headed lad knew the rooftops better than the other orphans knew the back alleyways.

Samson nodded, relieved to see him. "I need your help."

Willie grinned a gap-toothed smile. "Somethin for the Harper?"

"Something like that." Samson looked at Shiner. "Is Red up there?"

"Nope. Might be with the Harper."

Justin was most likely in the red lantern quarter, sweet-talking the courtesans, spying out clues to the magic behind the Test of Faith. Samson doubted Justin would take Red to the bordellos but he could not afford to wait. "Shiner, you'll have to stand in for Red."

The dark-haired lad beamed a smile and stood straighter. "What for?"

Samson hesitated, basking in their trust, like a drowning man clinging to a last hope. But time was against him. Taking a deep breath, he plunged into the bitter truth. He told them about Lucy and how he'd bragged about the Dark Harper, desperate to be a hero in her eyes. In grim tones, he explained about Lucy's betrayal and the bloody scene in the kitchen. He confessed to hiding in the secret cupboard, watching while Grandmother Magda killed one soldier and wounded another, but in the end, both Jack and the old woman were taken prisoners, dragged off to the dungeons. Flushed with shame, he told them the truth, every damning detail. And as he talked, Samson watched as the light in their eyes turn to disbelief, then horror, then something cold and distant. His voice trailed to silence, condemned by the accusation in their stares.

Shiner, the older of the two, was the first to speak, his voice blunt. "Did ya rat on us? Did ya give us lads away?"

The boy's question drove a nail through his heart. "No. I never told her about you lads or about the stables."

Shiner stared at him, his gaze rife with mistrust.

The younger boy, Willie, still held a glimmer of hope. "If he didna tell, then the stables'll be safe."

Samson held to the grim truth. "They have Jack."

Shiner hissed like a cornered cat, but Willie replied with a boy's brash defiance. "Jack won't turn rat!"

Samson shook his head, his voice gentle. "They took Jack to the dungeons."

Willie looked uncertain, hovering on the edge of tears. Shiner's voice was old for his years. "Them priests'll make anyone turn rat in the dungeons...even Jack."

A stifled sob erupted from Willie, a single tear running down his cheek. Shiner crossed his arms, a brave front. Samson realized both lads needed an adult. He did his best to try. "I have a plan."

Shiner balked. "Ya ratted once, ya'll rat again."

Another nail to the heart but he'd earned every one. "I don't deserve your trust, but I've told you the truth...and I have a plan that might free Jack and Grandmother Magda."

"Why should we trust you?"

"Because if you don't they'll die."

Shiner crossed his arms, his voice angry. "We'll hear it."

Samson whispered his plan, showing them the dark cloak hidden in the sack. He explained the help he needed and told them what he hoped to achieve. Doubt shadowed their eyes, but it was the only plan he had. "So will you help?"

Shiner studied him, his stare full of accusation, full of doubt. "Will ya do that? Will ya keep yer word?"

Samson nodded, swallowing the fear churning in his stomach. "I have to. It's the only way I can undo all the mistakes I've made."

He waited for the judgment of a fourteen year-old orphan boy, desperate for another chance. The waiting seemed to take forever. Shiner nodded, his voice neutral. "We'll help ya. But we do it for Jack and Grandmother Magda."

Samson hid his relief, knowing he did not have time to waste. "Willie, you know the rooftops. We need to pick a place. Someplace open, like a square, but the buildings need to be tall and close together and the alleyways near."

Willie nodded. "Tha green market's yer place. Buildins on tha east are tall and close enough to jump. That'll be tha place for ya."

"Will you show me?"

"Sure." The boy's face grew defensive. "But um not stay'in."

"I'm not asking you to stay."

Willie nodded. Shiner said, "What 'bout the rest of us?"

"Wake the rest of the lads and send them into hiding. The stables won't be safe unless we get Jack back." Shiner nodded, his face grim. "Spread the word that the cobbler shop and the stables are no longer safe. Then send a runner to find the Harper. Tell him everything." Samson hesitated. "But don't tell him what I've got planned till after sunset...after sunset it won't matter anymore." Samson fell silent, waiting. He thought he saw a faint glimmer of respect in the older boy's eyes.

Shiner nodded, his gaze filled with an intensity beyond his years. "Get 'em back for us." The lad offered his hand.

Samson stared, wide-eyed. The offer contained more dignity than he deserved, a chance to redeem his mistakes. They shook, sealing a bargain between men, a bargain Samson intended to keep.

Samson's voice was hoarse. "Come on, Willie, we have work to do."

The tow-haired lad led the way out of the stables. Samson followed, trusting the boy's knowledge of the alleys. They threaded their way through the city, walking rather than running, trying to avoid notice. The vegetable market was crowded, wagons laden with the first harvest, the smell of ripe green hanging heavy in the air. Samson studied the timber and daub buildings surrounding the cobblestone square. Most were two floors high with workshops on the ground floor and homes above. A few had peaked roofs but most were flat, perfect for his plan. Samson nodded. "This will serve."

Willie led him to the eastern alley, pointing out a tall timber-framed house. "Easy climbin this one. See all tha handholds?"

Samson shook his head, he'd never liked heights.

"Watch." Willie scaled the house like a spider, making it look easy.

Samson secured his sack to his belt and started after the boy. He made it half way before getting stuck. Willie retreated back down, pointing out the handholds. With the boy's help, Samson made it to the top, pulling himself up onto the flat roof. Sprawling on the sun-baked shingles, he caught his breath, and then crept to the edge of the roof. Perched some twenty-five feet above the market, the roof provided a perfect view of the square.

Crawling away from the edge, Samson stood to survey the rooftops. The bird's eye view was very different from below. Stretched out in a line to the left and right, the buildings appeared as rectangular islands separated by gaps of three to five feet. A few had peaked roofs, and many had chimneys, but otherwise it was a flat landscape of shingled islands. He looked to the boy. "You know the rooftops better than anyone, what do you recommend?"

"Stay low and in ta middle. If ya can't be seen, ya can't be tracked." He pointed to the right. "Five buildings over has a back wall good for climbin. Six has a chimney ta shimmy down."

"Anything else?"

Willie shrugged. "Stay low and be quick."

"Sage advice." Samson knelt and opened the sack. He removed the parchment, spreading it flat on a shingle. Dipping the quill in the ink, he sealed his fate in writing. He blew on the parchment till the ink dried and then folded the note into a square. So much at stake, such a slim hope, he handed the note to Willie along with the purse of gold coins. "You know what to do."

The lad tucked both in the top of his breeches and then turned to go.

Samson needed to hear a friendly voice to bolster his courage. "Wish me luck?"

The boy turned and gave him a shy smile. "Luck." Willie walked to the edge and began to climb down. Before disappearing below the roofline, he looked back at Samson and said, "Watch your feet on the steep ones, the shingles can surprise ya."

Samson nodded and then the boy was gone. Alone, he sat in the middle of the roof, battered by his own fears, cowed by his own shame. Desperate for a distraction, he pulled the dark cloak from the sack and put it on. Assuming the mantle of the Dark Harper, he gained courage from the disguise.

He crept to the edge of the roof and lay flat, staring down at the market, staring down at people leading normal lives. A voyeur from above, he watched the crowd shopping for supper. People meandered around the wagons, dickering with the farmers, a few moving with purpose but most swept along with crowd. Samson realized he'd lived his life as flotsam, pushed and pulled by waves and tides. There had been a few choices along the way...and he hadn't done well with most of those. Perhaps this choice would make a difference, perhaps he could save his friends. A strange peace settled over him. Lying on the sun-baked shingles, he must have dozed in the warmth.

He woke to the sound of screams. Red tabards swirled through the market below. Soldiers with drawn swords flooded the square. The people panicked, running for side streets, scattering in all directions, trying to hide. A wagon overturned, spilling melons across the cobblestones, adding to the chaos. Women screamed and children cried, a stampede of fear. The soldiers gave chase...till a voice roared, "Let them go!"

A dark figure strode through the red. A long black cape swirled behind him, a lock of white hair at his temple. The Lord Raven had come. Samson shivered in fear, watching as the lord claimed the center of the square, issuing orders like a general.

Soldiers continued to pour into the market, the tramp of boots echoing against the cobblestones. They formed ranks around the Lord Raven, facing outwards, hundreds of wicked-looking halberds held at the ready.

Samson groaned; he hadn't expected so many. The numbers proved the Dark Harper was a true threat, but with so many soldiers Samson had little hope of escape. Muttering a prayer to all the gods, his gaze swept the square, desperate for a glimpse of his friends. *Only one prisoner.* His heart sank. Bound with ropes, Jack stood between two soldiers, but he found no sign of the silver-haired grandmother. He'd failed her. Perhaps the old lady was already dead, the knitting needles stilled forever...but there was still hope for Jack.

The tramp of boots stopped. The soldiers stood in long ranks of burnished steel and red tabards, a threat waiting for an order. A grim hush settled over the square.

The Lord Raven's voice rang against the stillness. "The boy is here, Harper. Come and claim him...if you dare!"

The dark-cloaked lord pivoted, staring in all directions...but he never looked up. Hope rushed through Samson; they weren't expecting him to use the rooftops. Perhaps his plan would still work. Pulling the cowl of his cloak up to hide his face in the deep shadows, Samson stood, a dark sentinel staring down from the edge of the roof.

A boy crouching under a wagon was the first to spy him on the rooftops. *"The Harper!"*

A murmur of surprise rippled through the people as others looked upward.

Samson waited for the Lord Raven's stare. He took a deep breath, hoping his voice would pass for the bard's. "The deal was for the boy and the old woman."

The Lord Raven laughed, confident and mocking. "There was never a deal...only an offer." He held the folded parchment aloft as if in proof.

"I want the old woman released."

"The old woman killed a soldier. She'll pay for her crimes. But the boy," the Lord Raven shrugged, "the boy I'll trade for the Dark Harper."

At least his disguise was working. "Let the boy go."

"Come and get him."

"Where can I go? I'm a bard not a bird." Samson stood still, waiting, hoping.

"So be it, bard, we'll play your game of cat and bird." The Lord Raven issued orders. Soldiers rushed to obey, surrounding Samson's building with a ring of steel.

The trap narrowed but he still had a chance to escape over the rooftops...but only if they released Jack. "Let the boy go."

The Lord Raven bowed, a flourish of black and crimson. "By all means. Children are beloved of the Flame God." He gestured and a soldier released the boy, cutting his bonds.

Jack shrugged off the ropes. He raised his hand in a silent salute...and then he ran. Samson watched as the boy slipped between the rows of soldiers, darting into a side street, a streak of dark hair and grimy clothes. He followed Jack with his stare, hope growing with every stride, watching till he disappeared into alley. Relief spiked through him, at least the boy was safe.

"And now, bard, we have a deal to complete." The Lord Raven's words cracked like a whip. "The boy is released. The Lord Raven keeps his word. But what of the Dark Harper? You said you'd trade your life for his. Do you deal in lies or do you save those for your songs?" He gestured to the market square. "The people are waiting. Show us the value of the Dark Harper's word."

Samson realized he had an audience. A thousand eyes stared up at him, watching from crowded doorways, from open windows, from storefronts, from the shadows beneath the wagons. Young and old, rich and poor, they witnessed the contest between the raven and the bard.

"Come, Harper! Prove your worth!" Samson realized the Lord Raven played to the crowd, his words loaded with mocking. "Will you come down or must I send the soldiers up? Show us the value of a Harper's word. Do you stand for truth or lies?"

Samson staggered backwards, realizing the trap. He could run, and try to evade the swords, but he could never evade the words. The Lord Raven set a fine trap, laced with barbs as strong as steel. The Dark Harper had to keep his word or all of Justin's work was undone. Samson had to decide who he wanted to be. He had to decide if the masquerade was worth his life.

The Lord Raven's voice struck like a goad. "Make your choice, Harper, before I make it for you."

Samson felt the weight of the people's stares, he felt their hunger for a miracle...but he had none to give. He was just a simple man in a dark cape...but perhaps he could be more. He stepped to the edge and stared down at his fate. Faces stared upwards, full of desperate expectation. The hushed silence goaded him, making Samson realize he needed something to say, some words of wisdom or a clever rhyme to prove he was the bard. He'd never been good with words but somehow the words came anyway. "The Dark Harper speaks the truth." His strength flowed into his voice. "You can silence one voice but you can never stop the truth, you can never stop the music."

The sun chose that moment to set, spreading a glory of red and gold across the sky. Samson smiled, choosing to be the bard for one brief moment, for one glorious sunset. "I choose to keep my word." He took the long step. He took the long fall...and the Light reached out for him.

55

Steffan

Steffan watched the Dark Harper take the long step into nothing, the dark cape fluttering behind like a broken wing. The harper tumbled in silence, a wet thud sounding as the body smacked face-first into the cobblestones. Blood spattered across the stones, red as a banner.

Steffan swallowed his shock.

A sigh rippled through the marketplace. A child cried and a woman sobbed. Steffan surveyed the crowd, pale faces peering from windows and shop doors. Too many witnesses, the Dark Harper had cheated, stealing victory from defeat.

The Lord Raven crossed the square and nudged the body with his boot. The face was smashed to a bloody ruin, no way to distinguish the man behind the gory mess. "And so it ends. You sang the wrong songs, Harper."

He looked for the nearest officer. The man snapped to attention.

"Erect a stake in the temple square. I want the body impaled upright. Make sure the dark cape is secured to the corpse so there's no mistaking it's the Dark Harper. The body's to stand on display till it drops from rot." He raised his voice so the crowd could hear. "Let the people see what happens to rebels who dare oppose the Pontifax."

The officer saluted and two soldiers moved to obey.

Steffan turned, a swirl of black and crimson. He strode from the square, anger in his stride. Soldiers and citizens scrambled to get out of his way. Dismissing his guards, he walked alone through the city streets, weaving his way back to his mansion.

The mute giant, Olaff, snapped to attention, before rushing to open the door.

Steffan paused. "No visitors tonight."

The giant nodded, his bushy black beard contrasting with his shaved head.

Steffan passed through the door, his boots ringing on the marble floor.

Pip appeared from the depths of the mansion. "Take your cloak, lord?"

He let the lad remove his cloak. "Have Olaff bring the copper tub up to my bedchamber. I want a bath, Pip, and make it hot. And brandy. I'll have a bottle of the best brandy."

"And something to eat, lord?"

"No, just brandy." He entered his solar and poured a glass of Urian brandy. The amber liquor was smooth and strong, leaving a trail of warmth down the back of his throat. He drained the glass and poured another. A pile of scrolls from today's confessions waited on his desk but they could not hold his interest. He rose and stood by the window, watching the sunset sky. Streaks of red and gold fanned out from the west, a glorious display. The sky held the colors of the Pontifax, the colors of the Flame God. Steffan shook his head. The sky lied; the Dark Harper had won the day.

A knock sounded on the door. "Your bath is ready, lord."

He followed Pip up the marble staircase to his bedchamber. The copper tub stood in front of the double doors leading out to the balcony. Steam rose in lazy curls, the scent of lemongrass filling the chamber.

Steffan sat on silken sheets as the lad knelt to pull off his leather boots. He let the lad do all the work, nimble fingers easing bindings. Stripped of his clothes, Steffan stepped into the tub, the heat of the water easing his muscles. "Open the doors to the balcony. I want to watch the night fall."

The lad obeyed. A cool breeze blew in, carrying a hint of autumn.

"Now pour me a glass of brandy and you can go."

Pip moved a small round table next to the tub. He poured a glass of brandy and set a full decanter within easy reach. The lad served the brandy and then bowed, closing the doors to the bedchamber.

Steffan sank back into the heat, sipping the amber liquor. He watched the sky, waiting for the victory of night, the victory of Darkness. The day had not gone as he'd planned. He'd hoped to humiliate the Harper in front of the crowds. He'd expected the bard to run, trusting his soldiers to catch him in the end. Once caught, he'd planned to break the Harper in the dungeons, extracting the name of every rebel. He never thought the damned fool would jump. Draining his glass, he refilled it, the liquor taking a bite out of his thoughts. At least he'd broken the heart of the rebellion, spattered to a bloody pulp across the cobblestones.

He must have dozed, succumbing to the heat and the liquor. A scent roused him. Crushed violets and the musk of sandalwood, the scent teased his mind...evoking memories of the Dark Lord's Isle...memories of passion and pleasure.

The water had turned tepid, the sky darkened to a deep shade of purple. A gentle breeze blew in from the balcony, renewing the scent of violets. A figure stepped through the open doors. Tall and statuesque, she stood silhouetted against the twilight sky...an image from his dreams.

"Is it you?" His voice was deep and husky.

She stepped through the doorway, a soft whisper of silk. Her thin diaphanous sheath accentuated every curve.

"Is it really you?" He needed to hear her voice, to be sure he didn't dream.

She reached for a towel and stepped to the side of the copper tub. "Let me dry you."

Her throaty voice rippled across his skin, across his need. He rose, rampant, water falling like drops of rain. He tried to think past the wanting. "How did you get in?"

Her laughter rippled down his spine. "Your guard is a mute not a eunuch."

The touch of the towel was a tease, cool and gentle...when he wanted hot and hard. He stood statue-still, holding back, not trusting the temptress. "Why have you come?"

"To bring you a message from the Dark Lord," her voice deepened to a silken purr, "and to offer you an alliance."

"A message?" He tried to think past her touch.

"The Lord Raven has done well. But to earn the rebirth of a harlequin, you must do more than twist a single kingdom. The Dark Lord rewards those whose reach is long.

The Priestess licked a drop of water from his chest, a cat tasting cream.

He suppressed a groan. "My army stands poised to march."

"Then let them march. The time is right. Lanverness stands weak with chaos."

She abandoned the towel, using hands and lips and tongue. The Priestess did not play fair. His body railed against his will, but he remained statue-still, stiff as stone. "And the alliance?"

"The Mordant has crossed the Dragon Spines. We compete against a thousand years of evil. But working together, combining our strengths, we can conquer the heart of Erdhe before he can raise his armies."

She moved lower, doing something with her tongue, something that racked him with shivers, straining his control.

When he could speak again, his voice was hoarse. "What do you bring to this alliance?"

Her fingers trailed a line up his chest. Leaning close, her breath hot, she whispered the answer in his ear.

His eyes widened at her audacity.

She stepped away from him, standing within reach but not touching, a subtle torture. Her voice dropped to a deep husk, a verbal temptation. "Yours to decide. Shall I stay...or shall I go?"

Steffan knew he shouldn't trust her...but her plan had merit...and the ache of his manhood had grown unbearable. Desire dissolved doubt. He gave in and reached for her. Stepping from the tub, he carried her to the silken sheets. Her raven hair spilled across the pillow, her ivory skin bathed in moonlight. He drank her in, the softness of her skin, her lush curves, her scent, her deft touch. Everything about her was intoxicating, as if she wove a spell of desire...driving him beyond reason, beyond the edge of passion. He quenched his need in her, rough and hard...but she pressed him for more. Every touch was insistent, teasing, demanding, insatiable. His passion came in waves, better than any dream. Pain and pleasure melded into one, a maddening tidal wave of need. They spent the night sealing their alliance, straining every limit...all to the glory of the Dark Lord.

56

Liandra

T he queen took comfort in numbers. Sifting through the ledgers and scrolls, she counted silvers spent and golds collected, taking the measure of her kingdom. The revenue of the Royal Ruby mines had soared, owing to the popularity of the dark stones. The farming yields were up, a bountiful autumn harvest filling the granaries to the brim. Her investment in saffron had paid off handsomely and so had the import of Urian brandy. Her treasury was flush with golds, her kingdom prosperous beyond the telling. Such a pity the profits of peace had to be turned to swords. But all the signs pointed to war, a future she could not see any way to avoid.

A knock sounded.

The queen gestured and the page admitted her handsome son. Prince Stewart wore fighting leathers, his dark hair pulled back, exposing his chiseled features...and the scar marring the left side of his face. The signs of war were everywhere.

The prince bowed. "You asked to see me, majesty?"

She gestured to a chair across from her desk. "Yes, we have important matters to discuss."

He settled in the chair, his long legs stretching across the carpet. Without preamble, he launched into a report on the army. "The recruits continue to pour in and the training goes well. We push the men hard but they understand the need. Given enough time, we'll have a strong army to defend Lanverness."

"Time is one luxury we do not have." She fingered the strand of pearls at her throat. "But we called you here for another matter. One as equally pressing."

He stared at her, waiting.

"The Tandroth line is thin, a single strand easily broken. We have but one heir, and that heir is the general of our armies. We will not let our line fail. War is coming. You must marry and produce heirs. The sooner you take your bride to bed the better."

His face paled, coughing as if he'd swallowed a fly. "B-but Mother..."

She forestalled his argument with a raised hand, knowing all too well that young men were eager to bed but slow to wed. "We have found the perfect bride for you, the perfect daughter-in-law. She is of royal blood and comes from an extremely fecund family. She is brilliant as well as beautiful, with a penchant for finances, never one of your strengths. The two of you will make the perfect royal pair. You can manage the army while she manages the royal finances."

"But Mother..."

"We plan to write to King Ivor and begin negotiations for the royal wedding. The sooner you are wedded and bedded the better."

"King Ivor?" The prince looked like he'd been struck with a war hammer.

"Yes, King Ivor of Navarre. We thought to talk to you before starting negotiations.

"Your want me to wed Princess Jemma?"

Her royal son seemed particularly slow today. "Yes, of course. The princess proved her courage and loyalty during the rebellion. And she is a rare beauty. The entire court is captivated by her. Beauty is a valuable weapon for a queen, not to mention her skill with finances. She will make you a formidable wife."

"But I am in love with another."

"In love?" She stared at her son, always ambushed by his lack of maturity. "Love has nothing to do with choosing a future queen. Royalty marries for duty, for gain, and for progeny. We are not afforded the luxury of love." She shook her head. "Whoever this other woman is, you best forget her. Put her aside and do your duty to Lanverness."

"We are hand fasted, promised to each other at Midwinter."

"Hand fasting is for peasants! You are the crown prince of Lanverness. No one will ever hold you to some silly Midwinter tryst. You will do your duty to the crown and the kingdom, and that duty is to wed Princess Jemma."

His face pulsed with anger. "You have not even asked her name!"

"Her name is of no consequence. Princess Jemma has all the attributes we seek in a queen. We shall write to King Ivor and begin negotiations for the marriage."

The prince glared at the queen. "Yes, Mother, write to King Ivor...but ask instead for the hand of Princess Jordan, for she is the woman I love."

The queen sat back in her chair, shocked by the revelation. "The swordish one!"

"Yes."

"But she was attacked in the monastery and may not survive her wounds."

Grief and worry washed in waves across the prince's face. "She *has* to live." He shook his head, the scar pulsing along the side of his face. "Jordan will come back to me." He stood and began to pace the room, his hand gripping the hilt of his sword.

The queen had never seen her son so consumed with worry...yet reason must prevail. "Even if she survives, such a severe wound to the abdomen may mean she will never bear children."

The prince whirled, his face ghost-white. "How do you know this?" He stepped toward her but then stopped, his voice bitter. "Yes, of course, your famed shadowmen."

"Not everything comes to us through whispers. We share Princess Jemma's concern for her sister." She stared at her son, willing him to understand. "You must put aside your feelings and serve the kingdom. It is your duty." She tried to soften her voice. "Princess Jemma is the perfect match for you."

"Perfect except for love, Mother." His voice cut like a sword. "Duty makes for a cold bed. Clearly the vaunted Spider Queen does not need love, but I will have more than duty in my marriage bed."

His words struck like a slap. The woman buried beneath the crown erupted with long-held rage. "Do you think we do not know what it is to burn for love? To hunger for the tides of passion?" She reined her voice back to a cold anger. "You have no idea what we give up for the crown, what we endure for the throne, always putting the kingdom first. Even you, our heir, our first-born son, do not appreciate our sacrifices."

He threw his hands up in the air. "Mother, I do not wish to fight. Lanverness has never had a better ruler, never seen such prosperity, and all because of the brilliance of the queen. But in this one thing, I must have my way."

"One does not use the word 'must' with queens."

A knock sounded.

The queen glared at her son. "As the crown prince, it is your duty to serve Lanverness."

"Duty!" He shook with anger. "Duty keeps me here when my heart bids me to ride into the mountains to be by her side." His voice turned bitter. "But instead, I stay and I serve, for I have always been the dutiful son."

"Then set aside your feelings for Princess Jordan and marry the woman who should be the next queen."

"No. I will not gainsay my heart."

The knock came again, louder.

The queen's voice snapped with anger, "Who dares to disturb us?"

The door opened and the Master Archivist braved her wrath. "Excuse the interruption, your majesty, but the monk has returned."

The look in her shadowmaster's eyes broke through the queen's anger. "From Coronth?"

The Master Archivist nodded, his face grim.

The prince shook his head. "That's not possible! Even if the roads were open, the monk could not have ridden there and back in so little time!"

"Possible or not, the monk has returned and he begs an urgent audience with the queen." The master stood at the door, waiting for her approval.

The queen gestured. "Show him in." It seemed her day was to be crowded with arguments and ill tidings.

The master bowed. A short time later, he ushered the monk into her solar.

Her shadowmaster took a position by the side of her desk, a pillar of black. The monk crossed the room and bowed low, a mystery wrapped in robes of midnight blue.

The queen studied the monk, wondering at his secrets. "So you have returned to our court, Master Aeroth."

The monk's hazel eyes gave little away. "Yes, I bring news from Coronth."

"What did you find in the Flame God's city?"

The monk grimaced. "The so-called religion of the Flame is an abomination. Only the Dark Lord would countenance human sacrifice."

He told her nothing she did not already know. "And what of the rebellion?"

"I met with Prince Justin and his small band of rebels. They make a valiant effort but songs and a few lives saved will never be enough. They must discredit the Pontifax in order to topple this foul religion."

"And is there any hope that they will succeed."

"A thin hope." His face turned thoughtful. "From what I've seen and heard, the source of the Pontifax's power is magic."

"*Magic!*" The prince made the word a curse.

The monk nodded. "Magic itself is neither good nor bad. But the Pontifax..." the monk shook his head, "the Pontifax is a perversion. The man makes the foulest use of his magic, using it to deceive, to pretend to be ordained by the gods, to claim to work miracles. May the Lords of Light strike him down for committing such a blasphemy."

The queen was surprised to see so much anger in the normally stoic monk. "Yes, but what hope do the rebels have against this magic?"

"The type of magic displayed by the Pontifax is almost always associated with a small magical artifact left over from the War of Wizards. If the artifact is lost or stolen, then the Pontifax will lose his magic."

The queen smiled. "And the crowds will not tolerate the loss of their miracle."

"Just so."

"It seems an eloquent and just solution." The queen fingered the pearls of her necklace. "Why do you give the rebels such slim odds?"

"Because the artifact cannot be discerned by sight. And even if they discover the item, sleight of hand will not work. The Pontifax is magically linked to the artifact. He will know the instant anyone else so much as touches it."

She saw the nature of the challenge. "Prince Justin is quite resourceful. We will hope that he finds a way to succeed." She stared at the monk. "But we doubt this news is the reason for your swift return."

"I returned with all speed to bring you a warning."

The monks were ever the harbingers of ill tidings. The queen gestured for the monk to continue.

"The Pontifax has amassed a huge army. Judging from the number of tents, I'd venture to say that the army of the Flame exceeds thirty thousand swords."

"*Thirty thousand!*" The prince gasped, his face ghost-pale.

The queen shook her head in denial; the number was a death knell for her kingdom. "Too many swords. We cannot face that number alone." She stared at the monk. "Are you sure?"

He nodded, his face grim.

She looked to her son. "How many?"

"Not enough." The prince shook his head. "Including the constable force, Lanverness has seven thousand trained swords. We have another three thousand recruits in training, but even if the training was finished tomorrow, we cannot stand against an army of thirty thousand."

The queen returned her stare to the monk. "You warned that the Dark Lord wants our throne. How can your Order help against this threat?"

He raised his hands as if to ward off her stare. "The Kiralynn Order brings warning, we provide knowledge long forgotten, we advise...that is the nature of our aid."

"So you'll watch, and warn, but you won't get your hands dirty?"

The monk stood statue-still.

She needed the monks as allies, but given the numbers against her, she needed more than just warnings. She considered the pieces on the chessboard and took a chance. "Your Order seems to know much about magic."

The monk's eyes narrowed but he remained silent.

"We venture to guess that your Order does more than collect knowledge," the queen studied her opponent, "that it also collects magic."

The monk was a good player. He kept his face still as stone but his eyes gave him away. The slightest widening told the queen that her guess was true. She sat back in her chair, her voice a sword. "Perhaps the Kiralynn Order can provide some magic to even the odds against the Flame God's army?"

He raised his hands in protest. "Magic should only be used for peaceful purposes."

Her patience snapped. "But we don't have the luxury of peace, do we?" She pressed her argument. "And the enemy will not fight fair." She stood, piercing him with her stare. "Your Order claims to serve the Light. So how will you help Lanverness defeat this threat from the Dark Lord?"

He bowed his head. "The queen of Lanverness is indeed formidable."

"We need help, not platitudes."

"I will pass your request on to the Grand Master."

It was a start. The queen nodded. "We welcome the help of our allies."

The monk gave her a wary smile. "By your leave, I will see to the message at once."

She made her voice gracious. "You have our thanks, both for the warning and for the message." Liandra waited for the monk to leave and then went to stand in the casement window, needing to feel the sun's light through the dappled panes. She spoke with her back to her two advisors. "Thirty thousand is too many."

Neither man offered any suggestions.

She turned and made her decision. "We need the mercenaries of Radagar."

The prince looked shocked, the master nodded.

Prince Stewart protested, "You cannot trust bought swords."

"I don't propose to trust them, only use them." Pain throbbed at the back of her eyes; she did not need another argument. "Put the mercenaries in the vanguard of the army. Use them as a shield in front of our own soldiers. Blunt the enemy's weapons on the soldiers of Radagar. Mercenaries can be used without being trusted."

The prince shook his head. "If the center fails, the whole army is routed. I cannot trust mercenaries in my vanguard."

Her patience snapped. "We are the queen and you are the general. We will buy you an extra ten thousand swords. Surely with such grim odds, the general can find a way to use them!"

The prince flushed crimson under her glare.

She waved her hand in dismissal. "We have had enough argument for one day. You are dismissed."

The prince bowed. "Your majesty, I did not mean to argue."

His tone was full of regret. He was a good son, a young man burdened by great duties. She gave him a soft smile. "We know. We will speak to you tomorrow."

He knelt and kissed her emerald ring of office, a mixture of concern and wary stubbornness in his face. "Tomorrow?"

It seemed their discussion was not yet done, but she nodded giving him permission to leave. She watched him go, her son who was also a warrior. The Master Archivist moved to follow, but she called him back. "Lord Highgate, we would speak to you."

He closed the door and stood in front of the cold fireplace, his face composed, his arms behind his back, the counselor waiting on his queen. She studied the man, standing straight as a sword, his gaze keen, the perfect blend of strength and intelligence...such a temptation. So many sacrifices for her throne, for her kingdom, yet what did they accomplish? The woman buried beneath the crown railed for a taste of life...for one night of pleasure. She forced her mind back to the problem at hand. "Do we have a chance against thirty thousand?"

"The mercenaries may buy us some time but they are not the solution."

"Then what is?"

He hesitated. "You played the monk brilliantly. Perhaps the mysterious monastery will make the difference."

"A long shot. One we dare not count on." She sighed. "Pity we do not have a magic artifact to provide a miracle or two."

"Your majesty will think of something." He gave her a wry smile. "And if you don't, I will."

He was always her rock. She found herself returning his smile, her headache banished. "You managed to win the last game of chess, employing a devious gambit as we recall."

"A gambit I found in the archives. I need to read scrolls just to keep up with you."

She laughed. He was her most worthy opponent, her most ardent admirer, her rock. "We shall miss you, Lord Highgate."

He understood instantly. "Radagar?"

"There is no one else we can send, no one else we trust as much. Lanverness needs the extra swords and whatever else the mercenary court has to sell."

He nodded.

"And be careful with our golds. The royal purse is fat but not bottomless. We may have need of every gold before this war is finished."

"As you command."

She studied his face, his dark penetrating eyes, his confident mouth, the faint scar at his left temple. "The Rose Court will be a lonely place without you." Liandra fingered the strand of pearls at her throat. "How soon can you leave?"

"I'll need a day to make all the arrangements, to make sure the queen is well guarded in my absence."

Returning to the window, she stared down at the castle, wondering if she dared steal one night for herself, one single night of passion. "Lord Highgate..." she held her breath, afraid of the question, afraid of the answer. Liandra shook her head; she could only be the queen. "Lord Highgate, we command you to travel with all speed and come back safe to us."

She felt the heat of his stare. She turned. His dark gaze burned into her...as if he knew the question in her mind.

"Ask me." His voice was deep and hoarse.

Longing shivered through her but she could not forget the crown. She stared at him, torn with indecision...wondering if she could trust any man to accept a single night and not press for more.

"Even if it is only for one night, I would be there for you."

The perfect answer. She wondered if he would be perfect in bed. It had been so long. The need overwhelmed her. Her voice fell to a hushed whisper. "No one must ever know, must ever suspect..."

"Majesty, I am your shadowmaster...and I serve only the queen."

He stood confident and strong, his dark gaze blazing with need, yet he made no move to touch her, waiting on her decision.

Passion triumphed over duty. She went to her desk, to the hidden drawer, and removed the key to the secret passages. "Then come to us tonight when others sleep." She crossed the distance and pressed the key in his hand. "For a single night, we will take off our crown."

He knelt and kissed the hollow of her palm, tender and ardent, a promise of more.

A shiver of longing raced through her.

"Madam, you are always the queen."

She watched him go...consumed with thoughts of the coming night.

57

Steffan

Thousands marched to the beat of war. Aurochs horns loosed their eerie wail and red battle banners snapped in the wind. Helmets gleamed in the afternoon sun and red capes fluttered. Fearsome black halberds rode every shoulder, bristling with threat. The soldiers marched six across, a long multi-legged beast stretching to the southern horizon. The army of the Flame marched to war.

Steffan stood with the Pontifax on the rampart of the city wall, reviewing the troops. The Pontifax appeared as a vision of holiness, his golden robe gleaming like a second sun in the afternoon light. He gripped the ruby amulet and made the sign of blessing as the troops passed, proclaiming an omen of victory for the army. "Very impressive, Lord Raven, but have you left enough soldiers for our safety?"

Steffan nodded. "Of course, Holiness. The Fortress is held by five hundred of my best troops, more than enough to protect the Pontifax and control the city rabble." It was a half-truth. Steffan had left five hundred behind but none of his best.

"And you're sure this rebellion has been defeated?"

"The leader was a bard, known as the Dark Harper. His corpse rots in the temple square, serving as a lesson to the people."

The Pontifax made the sign of blessing over the soldiers. "And you think one rotting corpse is enough to kill the rebellion?"

"Just so, Enlightened One. Strike the head from a snake and the body will still writhe, but the snake is dead. You'll have no more trouble with the rebels."

"Let us hope your words prove true."

"I would not take the army south unless I knew you were safe." Steffan made his voice confident. "You have the confessors, the Test of Faith, and five hundred soldiers, plenty to keep the people cowed."

The Pontifax grunted. He tugged on his beard and glanced at Steffan. "The Keeper tells me that you plan to take the pyromancer with you."

Steffan kept his face neutral, the Keeper would meddle one too many times. "The pyromancer will be useful to me."

"I prefer to keep him in Balor, where he can best serve me with the Test of Faith."

Steffan made his voice humble, a petitioner begging a favor. "Enlightened One, it is your miracle of the Test of Faith that holds the people in thrall. By comparison, the pyromancer is a mere conjurer of cheap tricks. I would never expose your Holiness to the risks of the army, but I must have a way of influencing the beliefs of the men. By manipulating the Flames with color and scent, the pyromancer can give the army omens of victory. Belief in a god-inspired invincibility is a mighty weapon for any army, but it is especially essential for the army of a theocracy. Belief is the fuel for fanatics. Surely the temporary loss of the pyromancer is a small price to pay for the plunder of Lanverness?"

The Pontifax grinned. "The plunder of Lanverness. I like the sound of that." He stared at Steffan, a gleam of avarice in his eyes. "You have my leave to take the pyromancer south with you. But in return, I expect wagons full of gold, plunder and slaves."

"Gold you shall have in abundance...but not the slaves."

The Pontifax's stare snapped to Steffan's face. "Why not slaves? They've proven a valuable commodity."

Steffan drew on lessons learned from the Dark Lord. "There are two kinds of war, Holiness. In the first, the victors swallow their opponents, turning the conquered into slaves, serfs, and eventually citizens. The danger is that the culture of the conquered is imbibed, eventually tainting the conqueror. In some ways, conquerors become what they eat." He bowed to the Pontifax. "Coronth is a theocracy. We cannot afford to let our religion be corrupted by infidels, lest we lose what we already hold." Steffan gestured to the long line of red stretching below the city walls. "The army of the Flame will wage a pure war, where the culture of the conquered will never be corrupted by weak infidels." Steffan smiled. "We will sack the treasuries of our enemies, claiming their gold and their land for our own, but we will not wage a war of conquest...instead, we wage a pure war, a war of annihilation!"

The Pontifax stared at the long line of marching soldiers. "Is it possible to wage such a war?"

"For a theocracy, it is the only type of war."

The two men stood on the rampart, listening to the tramp of thousands, the sound of invincibility. The Pontifax said, "Has there ever been such an army in the southern kingdoms?"

"Not since the time of Igor the Cruel." Steffan swept his hand toward the horizon. "And even Prince Igor's army would tremble before the might of the Flame."

The Pontifax smiled. "Then you have our blessing. Return with the spoils of war."

Steffan knelt and kissed the ring of the Pontifax, taking his leave of the old charlatan. With a final bow, he left the rampart and made his way down the stairs, a swirl of black and crimson.

His retinue waited at the base of the stairs. An elite guard of thirty Black Flames stood alongside his squire, Pip, the giant Olaff, and Jellikan the pyromancer. Steffan wished the raven-haired Priestess waited as well, but the vixen had vanished with the first light, leaving as mysteriously as she came. He'd enjoyed their dalliance, but the temptress had best keep her bargain.

"Mount up, we ride to war." Steffan took the reins from Pip and mounted his sorrel stallion. He spurred the warhorse to a gallop and clattered out of the southern gates, leaving the others to catch up. His stallion raced the length of the army, his black cape streaming behind like dark tidings. Steffan laughed, he'd won the war of words in Coronth...now he'd try his hand at the war of swords against Lanverness. One lifetime was not nearly enough.

58

Justin

S oldiers did not bother guarding the dead. The dark cloaked corpse stood impaled on an iron spike, a lone figure standing vigil in the temple square. A night breeze lifted the cloak. From a distance it looked like dark wings flapping in the night, straining to fly free, but the corpse remained pinned, nailed to earth, a trapped soul.

Justin watched from the mouth of the alleyway. "You'll soon be free, my friend." He'd heard the bitter tale from the orphan lads. Betrayal followed by the capture of his friends and then finally the long fall. Samson had come late to courage but he'd found a way to make a difference with his death.

Stories about the Lord Raven and the Dark Harper consumed the city. The tales told how the Harper saved a lad from the dungeons and then cheated the Flames by jumping to his death. Some claimed the jump was a triumph for the Harper while others claimed the Raven had won, forever silencing the rebellious bard. Either way, all the tales ended in death. The story needed a better ending.

A lone soldier stood guard at the temple doors. Every turn of the hourglass, the guard walked a slow circuit around the temple. Justin waited till the guard turned the corner. "Now!"

Three men sprinted across the square. The breeze shifted and the stench of the rotting corpse engulfed them. Justin doubled over, retching his supper. Gagging, he wiped his mouth and joined Ben and Daniel at the corpse.

Justin gasped, "Get the cloak."

Ben growled, "The bastards nailed it to his body."

Justin swallowed the bile rising in his throat, cursing his weak stomach. He joined Ben at the grisly task. They pried long nails from the body, releasing the dark cloak. Unwrapped, the body proved a bloated ruin, the face a bloody pulp. Justin stared at the corpse, shuddering, finding no sign of his friend in the rotting horror.

Daniel hissed, "Hurry!"

Justin knelt and spread the length of canvas across the cobblestones while the two big men wrestled the corpse off the long cruel spike. The gruesome task proved harder than expected. The spike refused to give up its grisly prize. The two men heaved and the body came free, releasing a gush of foul odors.

Justin fought to keep from retching.

The men laid the ruined body on the canvas.

A whistle pierced the night.

Daniel hissed, "Quick, the signal!"

They rolled the body in the canvas, hiding the horror and muting the stench. Daniel and Ben lifted the ends while Justin carried the Harper's cloak. They ran for the alleyway, escaping into the back ways, thankful for the moonless night.

The city slept, leaving the streets deserted, but the conspirators kept to the alleys to be safe. They bore their grisly burden to the south side of the city. Jack and the other orphan lads waited in the shadows of the herb garden. Red stood with a shovel in his hand, a shallow grave dug beneath a small crabapple tree. Justin had chosen the spot, knowing how much Samson liked apples.

They laid the canvas-wrapped body in the grave and circled around to pay their respects. There'd be no tombstone and no coffin, just a pauper's grave, the best they could do.

One at a time, they took their turn saying goodbye. Shiner went the first. "Ya kept yer word. Ya saved Jack and for that we thank ya." The dark-haired lad released a handful of dirt into the shallow grave.

Willie, the roof rat, fought back tears as he dropped a fistful of soil into the grave. "Luck, Samson."

Red stepped forward. "Ya died a hero's death, ya died our friend."

Daniel, the big tanner, knelt, laying hand on the canvas-wrapped corpse. "You helped save my life when the rest of the city was afraid to do anything. I owe you my life, Samson Springwater."

They all looked to Jack. The dark-haired lad reached into his pocket and knelt, placing a bright red apple atop of the pale canvas. Jack stood back from the grave and shook his head, tears gushing down his face.

Justin went last. "Words are not enough but sometimes words are all we have." He stared down into the grave remembering Samson. "True courage means defeating your own fears. You showed true courage by coming back to Coronth and fighting the Flame God. In your last act, you saved a friend and preserved the honor of the Dark Harper. I'm honored to call you my friend." Justin smoothed the soiled cloak folded over his arm. "You will be missed." The bard tossed a handful of soil into the grave and then sang a parting lullaby. Sad and bittersweet, the melody spread a soothing balm over the small gathering of mourners.

When the last note faded, the friends dried their tears and filled the grave. They smoothed the soil flat, hiding footprints and any sign of burial, the small crabapple tree serving as the only marker. Their work finished, they disbanded into the back alleys, seeking bolt-holes for the night.

The rumors started the next morning. The markets buzzed with gossip about the missing body. Some said the Pontifax had ordered the corpse removed because of the stench. Others told tales of a grisly ghost walking the back alleyways seeking vengeance. Everyone had a story. Rumors ran rampant through the Flame God's city, waiting for a spark of truth.

Justin stayed in hiding, cleaning the dark cloak, washing the stench out of the wool and stitching the terrible rents made by the nails. Two nights later, he darkened his face with lampblack, tucked his small harp under his arm, and donned the cloak.

Hiding his face in the cloak's deep cowl, the Dark Harper prowled the back alleys, making his way to the Praying Maiden. Lewd laughter and lantern light spilled out of the tavern kitchen into the back alleyway. Climbing the stairs to the back door, he stepped into the bustling kitchen.

A woman's scream announced his arrival.

A pitcher of ale crashed to the floor, shards of pottery flying in all directions.

Cooks and serving lasses turned to stare, their faces pale with fear.

Bev, a gap-toothed serving wench, stammered, "I-is it really you, H-harper? Have ya come back from the grave ta sing for us?"

Justin nodded but said nothing. Keeping his head bowed, he strode from the kitchen into the great room, a silent wraith in a dark cloak. The kitchen folk followed, crowding the doorway, more than one making the hand sign against evil.

The Praying Maiden was crowded, mostly men, mostly working poor, drowning their sorrows in ale. They sat at long trestle tables, their stares dead and dull, beaten by drudgery, beaten by the cruelties of the Flame God...fertile ground for his songs.

The Dark Harper took his customary seat on the stool in the shadows by the door to the kitchen. He settled his small harp on his lap and ripped through a flurry of chords, loosing the music as his herald.

Silence followed, hanging like a shroud across the tavern.

Patrons stared open mouthed, gaping in shock and surprise.

The Dark Harper surveyed his audience, seeing questions on every face. He knew they waited for proof, needing more than just a man in a dark cloak. Music was the answer. His fingers ripped across the strings, loosing a melody of anguish, of burnt dreams and trampled justice. His tenor voice joined the harp, revealing the truth of the Flame God. Lyrics and melody wove together, exposing the lies of the priests, reminding the listeners of loved ones lost to the Flames. The bard used all his skills, plucking emotions with every chord. He sang of injustice, horror, and fear, discordant notes jamming together, the music tortured by the Flames. Holding nothing back, he gave them the truth and then he gave them the courage to change. Lifting the tempo to a rousing beat, he belted out ballads, tales of the rebels, of sinners freed from the stocks, of lives saved from the Flames. The rebels outwitted the soldiers, outwitted the priests. The music flowed free and proud. His fingers blistered across the strings, ripping into a rousing round of chords. His voice soared to the rafters with triumph, a victory of Light over Dark.

He stilled the strings and waited, letting the last note soar to silence.

The patrons sat stunned.

One man clanked his tankard against the table and others followed. The beat grew like rolling thunder, pride and defiance glowing from every face.

The Dark Harper let them revel in their courage and their hope. Then he bowed low, tucked the small harp close to his side, and slipped out the kitchen door.

The kitchen folk scattered, as if they feared his touch. But as he walked past, he felt hands reach out to see if there was flesh beneath the dark cloak. He smiled, hiding his face within the deep cowl, never breaking his stride.

Leaving the Maiden, he disappeared into the darkness, visiting three more taverns that night. By morning, a legend was born. The Dark Harper had returned from the grave, singing songs against the Flame God. The tale of Samson's death had a new ending.

Justin walked the back alleyways, thinking of knitting needles and the smell of fresh baked apple pie. Grandmother Magda always said it would take a miracle to defeat the miracle of the Test of Faith. Thanks to Samson's bravery, the rebels gained a miracle that night. The resurrection of the Dark Harper was a start...but Justin still had to find a way to free the silver-haired grandmother from the Fortress of the Flame...and then he'd discredit the Pontifax...one miracle at a time.

59

Katherine

The companions left autumn behind, climbing into winter, snow-capped peaks thrusting into a crystalline sky. The trail was just wide enough for a wagon, a forbidding passage of sheer drops, biting winds, and sweeping views. Jagged peaks stretched in a sinewy line from east to west, like the spine of a great dragon felled to earth. The Dragon Spines made a formidable barrier to the north, every crossing point held by the Octagon.

Kath swiveled in the saddle, surveying the long mountain trail, searching for a glimpse of Blaine. She couldn't believe he'd abandoned her, but there was never any sign of the blond-haired knight and his great blue sword. She bit back her disappointment and huddled beneath her dark-green cloak, a thin shield against the bitter cold.

The north wind howled through the mountains like a pack of ravenous wolves. The companions rode single-file up the switchbacks, the lead rider taking the brunt of the wind's wrath. Kath was thankful for Sir Tyrone's strong sword and Duncan's bow, but she worried about Danya and the monk. The old man had a quarterstaff tied to his saddle, but Kath had never seen him use it. Danya was a worry of a different sort. She glanced back at the wolf-girl riding in the rear. Huddled beneath her cloak, Danya seemed shrunken and withdrawn, as if she hid within herself, cocooned in silence.

Kath nudged her roan stallion, pulling even with Duncan's black gelding.

Dark hair tied back with a silver clasp, a black patch hiding his golden eye, he flashed her a brilliant smile. His smile warmed her like a fire against the winter wind, but his blue-eyed stare missed little. "You're worried."

She sighed. "Worried about Blaine, worried about Danya...and if truth be told, worried about Cragnoth Keep."

He nodded. "Blaine will make his own decision. From what you've told me, he never really did. He followed you because he was ordered to, not because he chose to."

His words held the truth but they carried a bitter sting.

"As to Danya," he glanced back at the wolf-girl, "something happened in the gray veil, something that frightened her...or changed her. But whatever it is, she's never mentioned turning back. She's been a good traveling companion and the wolf has proved a boon." He shrugged. "Give her time. She'll tell us when she's ready."

"I suppose, but I can't help worrying."

"Spend your worries on things you can change." He gestured up the trail. "How do you plan to get us past the knights of Cragnoth Keep?"

"Lionel is the best of my brothers, just five years my senior. He's the only brother who ever understood me." Kath gripped the hilt of the crystal dagger, her voice grim. "I thought I might tell him the truth."

Duncan raised an eyebrow. "The truth can be dangerous."

"Yes, but I can't think of anything else. And once we're across the mountains it won't matter." She tugged on the leather thong around her neck, making sure her gargoyle was safe. "But something nags at me, as if we're too late."

"I know what you mean. It's been too quiet for too long. In Wyeth and Tubor, and even in the Deep Green, we found signs of the Mordant's passing but none since we crossed the Snowmelt River." He shook his head. "It seems an ill omen, like a doom waiting to fall."

An eagle's shrill cry beat against the mountains.

Kath's gaze followed the cry, surprised to find a dozen eagles riding the wind, carving lazy spirals in the crystalline sky.

Duncan said, "That's odd."

"Why?"

"Eagles are very territorial. They only congregate when there's a rich food source."

Kath surveyed the snow-capped peaks, bleak and forbidding. "What would draw them here?"

"Eagles haunt the heights, but a dozen is a riddle." Duncan shrugged. "Seems you've run out of time to worry."

The horses rounded the last switchback and Cragnoth Keep loomed overhead. Squat and ugly, the tower blocked the top of the pass, a blunt finger pointing toward the sky. Made of brute granite wrested from the mountains, the tower held a signal post at the crown and a tunneled passageway at the base. A crude design, the frozen keep was nothing to look at, but Kath knew it had a rich history. Legends said that a single knight could hold the tunneled passageway against all the hordes of the Mordant. She hoped to explore the tower before crossing into the north.

The horses plodded into the courtyard. A knight wrapped in a maroon cloak guarded the tunneled passageway. He clutched a spear and pulled the cord of a great bronze bell. The deep-throated clangor seemed to toll a warning instead of a greeting.

Kath slipped from the saddle and joined Sir Tyrone, stamping her feet for warmth.

The knight had long auburn hair and a crooked nose, a morning star belted to his side. His glance darted between the companions, finally settling on Sir Tyrone. "What's your business here? And who are these others?"

The black knight kept to the agreed story. "Sir Tyrone, escorting three visitors to see Prince Lionel."

"You're here to see the prince?"

Sir Tyrone nodded.

The door to the tower banged open and three knights spilled into the courtyard. A barrel-chested knight with a great sword strapped to his back led the others. He surveyed the visitors and strode toward the companions, a smile on his face. "Tyrone, what brings you to the Crag?"

The black knight offered his hand in greeting. "Penross, I didn't know you were posted here."

"Been here a year now, a long frozen year." His gaze kept slipping to Kath. "But what brings you to the frozen keep?"

"King's business, we need to see the prince."

"To see the prince, huh." The knight stared at Kath, studying her face. Recognition dawned. "The Imp? The king's daughter here at the Crag?"

There was something about the knight's smile that Kath did not like. "Greetings, Sir Penross. I'm here to see my brother. Will you tell him we've arrived?"

"Afraid I can't do that. The prince is ranging north of the Spines. He took a squad out five days ago. Don't expect him back for another week." The knight gave her a crooked smile. "You must be cold after the long ride. Get your horses settled in the stables and then come up to the great hall for a meal." He barked an order to one of the other knights, "Dravin, tell the others we have visitors."

A large blond knight slipped back into the tower.

The wolf chose that moment to lope up the switchbacks, startling the horses. A frightened whinny echoed in the courtyard.

"A wolf!" Sir Penross drew his great sword.

The wolf bared his fangs, snarling at the threat.

Kath stepped between them. "He's no danger."

Danya dismounted, shouting, "Bryx, to me!"

Sir Penross growled, "What's the meaning of this?"

Kath answered, "The wolf is with us. He's tame."

"A tame wolf?"

Danya hugged the wolf, ruffling his fur.

Sir Penross shook his head. "That beast's not coming in the tower."

Kath nodded. "Fine. He can bed down in the yard. Just tell your men to leave him alone and there won't be any trouble."

The barrel-chested knight sheathed his sword, but he kept his stare on the wolf. "Get your horses settled and I'll show you up to the great room." His voice dropped to a growl. "And I'll expect no more nasty surprises."

Kath let the snide comment go unanswered. She led her roan stallion to a narrow cleft carved in the side of the mountain, grateful for the warmth of the stable, but the stench was appalling. Crowded with horses, some two to a stall, the stable stank of old hay and sour dung. Kath took care where she stepped, shocked by the slovenliness of the stalls.

Sir Tyrone growled, "I've seen cleaner pig sties." The black knight glanced at Kath, his voice apologetic. "Perhaps discipline is lax when the prince is away."

Kath nodded, but the state of the stable did not speak well of her brother. She brushed her roan stallion and then went to help with the packhorse, surprised to find Zith grooming Danya's mare. "Where's Danya?"

The monk shrugged. "She wouldn't come in."

Worried about the girl and her wolf, Kath returned to the courtyard. She found Danya staring up into the sky, the wolf turning in nervous circles at her feet. "Danya, what is it?"

The girl did not reply.

The wolf issued a low-throated whine.

Kath gripped Danya's arm. "What's wrong?"

Danya stared into the sky as if spellbound, her voice thin and distant. "The eagles."

A shiver raced down Kath's spine. "What about the eagles?"

"They've come for the dead...so many dead."

Kath gripped the girl, urgency in her grasp. "Who's dead?"

Danya shook like a wolf emerging from a pond. She stared at Kath, her eyes going wide, a flush spreading across her face. "What?"

"You said something about the dead."

"The dead?" Danya sounded confused. "I don't know..." She glanced up at the eagles, her face wary. "I was just watching the eagles...watching the lazy circles." She shrugged and stared at Kath, looking lost and frightened.

The wolf nuzzled Danya's hand, whining for attention.

The other companions gathered around.

Kath wasn't sure what to make of Danya's strange behavior, but a warm fire and a tasty meal could not hurt. "Come on, you need a hot meal and we all need to get out of the cold."

The ironbound door was unlocked, a cold wind following them into the tower. The big knight, Sir Penross, led them down a long corridor, and up a tight spiral staircase. The stone steps were worn deep with centuries of use, footprints of countless knights sworn to serve the Octagon.

The great hall took up the full width of the tower. Stone fireplaces at each end roared with welcome heat. Trestle tables ran the length of the room, clusters of knights sitting on the benches. A gray-haired steward roamed between the tables serving tankards of ale and steaming mugs of tea. Blazing heat and the tempting smell of meat stew drew the companions into the hall.

The conversation crashed to a halt. Twenty-two knights turned to stare. A mountain of a man wearing the silver surcoat of the Octagon slowly rose from the head table. He crossed the hall to greet them, a great axe strapped to his back.

Kath gasped, "Trask!"

The knight's voice rumbled like grating boulders. "The daughter of the king." He sketched a courtly bow, surprisingly graceful for his massive bulk, but his face held a sneer. "What brings the Imp to Cragnoth Keep?"

Sir Tyrone intervened, "The *princess*."

Trask flicked a glance to the black knight. "As you will." His gaze returned to Kath. "What brings the princess to the frozen keep?"

"I've come to see my brother."

"So Dravin tells me." His dark eyes glittered in the torchlight. "Prince Lionel is ranging north of the Spines. Perhaps I can be of help?"

Kath couldn't believe her brother would leave a brute like Trask in charge. "You?"

His dark gaze narrowed. "I hold the keep in the prince's absence." The seven-foot knight towered over her, a hulking menace, drilling her with his stare.

Kath held his gaze.

A log in the fireplace snapped, spitting a shower of sparks. The noise seemed to break the stalemate. Trask grinned. "You've had a long ride. Come and join us at the head table." The big man turned without waiting for an answer and led the way to front of the hall. He settled in the center chair. The others scrambled to make room for Kath and her companions.

Kath's gaze roamed the hall, realizing she knew only a handful of the knights.

The steward set bowls of steaming stew in front of each of them, returning with mugs of tea and a platter of biscuits. The day-old biscuits were hard but the stew was rich with chunks of venison flavored with garlic and rosemary. After the long cold ride, the hearty stew was more welcoming than the knights' reception.

Sir Tyrone plied the table with questions while they ate. "What tempted the prince down the mountains?"

Trask took a long pull from his tankard, wiping his mouth with the back of his sleeve. "Scouts reported sightings of the Mordant's forces." He shrugged. "The prince decided to give chase."

"But the crag is a defensive post. Why would the prince risk men north of the mountains?"

Trask grinned. "Maybe the prince got tired of defense."

Sir Tyrone asked, "Tired of defense?"

Trask banged his fist on the table and bellowed, "More ale!"

The elderly steward nearly jumped out of his skin. His tray-load of tankards crashed to the floor, spraying ale in all directions. The pale-faced steward bowed toward Trask, and then scurried to bring a fresh pitcher. His hand shook as he filled the knight's tankard.

Kath watched, surprised by the steward's reaction. She'd never seen such fear at Castlegard.

Sir Tyrone persisted. "What do you mean, the prince grew tired of defense?"

"He wanted a share of the glory." Trask's voice bristled with anger. "There's never any glory in defense. So he took a squad north, looking for a fight." He stared at the black knight, his voice a low growl. "Satisfied?"

Duncan leaned close to Kath's ear, his voice a whisper, "He lies."

Kath fought to keep her face still. Duncan's words sent a shiver down her back. Everything about Cragnoth seemed wrong, from the sloven stables, to the steward's fear, to Trask being left in command. It was like finding rust on a fresh-forged blade. Kath took a long drink of tea, studying Trask. The knight was freakish-large, like one of the giants of legend...or a Taal. She choked on her tea; the knight looked half-Taal.

Duncan thumped her back. "Are you well?"

Kath nodded, burying the thought. Trask was a bully, a braggart, and a brute but he was a sworn knight. Her gaze roamed the great hall. All the men of Cragnoth Keep were all sworn knights...but then why all the lies?

Duncan nudged her beneath the table.

She found Trask staring at her. "I'm sorry, I must have missed the question."

He gave her a shrewd stare. "I asked why you've come to Cragnoth Keep."

She reached for an answer. "My...father finally gave in."

"Gave in?" He shook his head.

"I've begged for years for a chance to see the Domain, to visit all the walls and towers, to see for myself where the legends were born." She shrugged. "Father finally relented."

His stare narrowed. "And this is your retinue?"

"These are my friends."

He glanced at her companions, disdain on his face. "Seems a weak guard for a king's daughter."

"Castlegard is at peace and we visit only strongholds held by the knights." She skewered him with her stare. "What's to fear?"

He gave her a surly smile. "I'd be pleased to give you a tour of the keep. The view from the tower top is impressive."

Kath repressed a shudder. "Perhaps on the morrow." She smiled. "It's been a long cold ride."

He raked her with his stare. "I'm sorry, but I can't offer you the prince's quarters without his permission...and we have no other quarters fit for royalty."

She shrugged. "Knights' quarters will do...but we'd like to stay together."

Trask scowled. "Penross, show the princess and her retinue to the third floor. There should be plenty of empty cells for them to choose from."

Sir Penross pushed back from the table and stood waiting.

Kath finished her tea and nodded to Trask. "Thank you for the hospitality of your table. I look forward to the tour on the morrow."

He gave her a leering grin.

Kath felt the weight of stares in the room, too much tension, too many lies. She swallowed a retort and turned her back on Trask.

The companions left the table and followed Sir Penross down the spiral staircase to the third floor. Torchlight danced against the curved stone hallway, distorting their shadows. The knight stopped at a narrow wooden door, one of many in the hall. "This one should be empty." He opened the door to a small cell and gestured to Kath, "Your Highness."

She ignored his surly attitude and glanced in the chamber. "This will do." She stood in the doorway, watching as her companions were settled. Duncan took the room next to hers. Danya, Sir Tyrone, and Zith were settled in rooms on the opposite side of the hall.

Sir Penross nodded to her. "Anything else?"

"What time is breakfast?"

"The first meal is served a turn of the hourglass after first light." He gave her a wry smile. "Sleep well, princess."

She watched the knight saunter down the hallway, a sense of unease shivering in her mind. Turning back to the room, she found a half-melted candle on the small nightstand and lit it before closing the door. The cell was small and spare, a narrow cot, a chamber pot, and hooks on the wall for weapons and clothes. Too restless for sleep, she paced the length of the chamber, mulling over the riddles of the evening. She couldn't shake the feeling of wrongness...or Duncan's warning of lies. But why would the knights lie? What did they have to hide?

Kath shivered against the chill. The small chamber was cold, especially after the heat of the great hall. Kath tugged the wool blanket from the bed...and found the stains. Old bloodstains on the mattress...and a deep cut from a sword thrust. *Murder in the night!* Kath shivered as the puzzle fell into place. Danya had given the first warning; the eagles had come for the dead. A cold certainty gripped Kath; her brother lay dead on the mountainside, his body flung from the tower after being murdered in the night. And those who murdered once would murder again. Kath did not know whom Trask served, but it was not the Octagon.

60

Liandra

A thousand times the queen thought to order him not to come, but each time the ache within grew stronger, a bonfire consuming common sense. Daylight faded to darkness and still she could not decide. Her indecision bled to her wardrobe, unable to choose a nightgown. The green sheer of Urian silk was too revealing, the dark red temptation of spider-fine lace too bold. Liandra finally settled on an elegant sheath of ivory silk, a perfect contrast to her long dark hair, an enticing shimmer of curves in the candlelight.

She ordered a platter of fruit and cheese and a bottle of her best merlot, not knowing if he'd like something to eat beforehand...or maybe afterward. Liandra shook her head, bemused by her own indecision. She was the Spider Queen, the White Rose of Lanverness. Tempting and teasing the men of her court, she twisted them to her will...but she never let them touch, never let them in. Only her husband, a marriage of pure politics, and that had ended with a hunting accident eighteen long years ago. A long time to last without a single kiss, a single caress, Liandra shivered with longing, eager for his touch.

Doubts assailed her. Surely this was a folly, a weakness of the mind, a road to madness. Liandra paced the length of her solar, raging a silent debate. She understood men all too well. They worshiped from afar, but once the prize was claimed, the goddess became a mere possession, something to be owned and jealously guarded, subject to the whims of the conquering lord. She'd never again suffer the yoke of a wedding ring, never again submit to the whims of a man. She was the queen, married to her people, wedded to her kingdom. The weight of the crown could never be removed...not even for a single night. She had to stop this madness before it began.

Crossing her solar, she reached for the hand bell to summon a servant...but the secret door swung open. Tall and dark, her shadowmaster stepped into the room.

She felt the rake of his stare, felt the way his eyes lingered at her curves, felt a blush rise to claim her face.

He stood by the hidden door, statue-still, his plain robe dark black, his voice deep and hoarse. "You summoned me, my queen."

His words rippled down her spine. She met his stare. Even now, he waited for her permission...as if he understood her concern. She held to her resolve, a thin shield of words. "We must always be the queen."

He nodded, his voice rough. "Always."

"The crown can never be removed."

"Never." His stare raked across her, lingering.

Her resolve weakened. She gave him an order, a test. "You cannot stay past first light."

He nodded. "As you command." His smile softened. "As you wish." He made the words a kiss...but still he waited, as if held captive by respect for her crown...or perhaps respect for her.

His respect melted her resolve. She reached out to him, unable to speak the words.

He crossed the room in three determined strides. He knelt and kissed her ring. "Always the queen." He turned her hand and kissed the hollow of her palm, a long slow kiss. "But also the woman."

She shivered with longing, her voice a throaty whisper. "One night for Robert and Liandra."

He made her name a prayer. "Liandra."

She shivered to hear it, to be just the woman.

He rose and cupped her face, a burning intensity to his touch. His thumbs traced her eyebrows, her nose, her lips, as if his hands memorized her face. He bent down, a soft kiss that became hard...a moment that stretched to infinity. She leaned against him, soaking up his strength...but he stepped away. She stared up at him, confused.

His hands hovered at the silken straps of her gown. He stared deep into her eyes, silently asking. She nodded, blushing with understanding. He eased the silken straps off her shoulders, a fall of silk, leaving her dressed in nothing but golden candlelight. He gasped, "My queen!"

She loosened his dark robe, leaving the black wool a puddle at his feet. The scars surprised her, too many to count, but otherwise he was lean and muscled, strong and hard despite his iron-gray hair.

He swept her into his arms and carried her to the four-posted bed, the massive gold-encrusted bed where she'd spent so many nights alone...but not this night. They started gentle and tender, discovering, exploring...but then the passion long denied came in waves. They rode the ecstasy together...and then the need gave way to pure pleasure.

Deft and sure, he knew just how to please. The candles melted to darkness and still they touched and talked. She fell asleep in his arms, sated and safe, cocooned from every care, a bliss of dreams.

She slept late, sunshine pouring through the casement window, a deep smile on her face. Content and happy, she reached for him but found him gone, and then she remembered her command. He'd kept his word, leaving at first light. The bed seemed a lonely place. The emptiness crushed her. Liandra regretted the command...but it proved he understood, that he knew she must always wear the crown. Memories of the night brought a rush of heat, a thrum of longing. Perhaps she'd found the rock she needed...a man to stand with her against the coming dark. Liandra wondered if she could be both the queen and the woman.

61

Justin

Bribery, blackmail, and begging, Justin tried them all. He plied the off-duty prison guards with liquor and tempted them with purses of gold. Befriending the soldiers of the fortress, he tried gaining access to the dungeons. He even dared to corrupt a confessor, offering the rum-soaked priest a wealth of golds if he would free the old lady, but fear of the Flames prevailed.

He found plenty of takers for his golds, winning small favors, gaining Grandmother Magda the comfort of a blanket and extra rations of soup. One guard agreed to smuggle an apple into the dungeon and another carried a small scrap of parchment scribbled with a few words of hope. His greatest victory was getting her name removed from the list slated for torture. The golds of Lanverness saved her from that horror, but despite all his efforts, the silver-haired grandmother languished in the deep cells, waiting her turn to walk the Flames.

The last of his golds went to the daily bribes, keeping her name from the top of the death list. Every morning he made the trip to the fortress, counting each day delayed as a victory, a race against time and his dwindling golds.

The Fortress of the Flame stood on the north side of the city, a brooding jumble of dark gray towers squatting like a malignant beast, waiting to swallow innocent victims. A monument to pain, the commoner's named it hell's parlor, a grim taste of hell on earth. Justin stared up at the grim walls, knowing the great stone beast rarely gave up its prey...but he had to try.

Walking with a limp, he kept his spine bent, a wad of wool beneath a dirty brown cape giving him the appearance of a deformed hunchback. The deformity drew stares away from his face, making him seem a harmless cripple, a welcome form of invisibility. Limping to the gate, he slipped the guard a silver. A familiar petitioner, the hunchback gained entrance to the fortress. Passing beneath the iron teeth of the portcullis, he entered the belly of the beast.

Justin kept to his disguise, limping across the cobblestone yard to the line of citizens waiting to purchase mercy for their loved ones. Bribery had become a thriving industry for the guards. He stood eighth in line, watching as the sun climbed above the walls, trying to ignore the nightmare of screams and muffled moans that filtered up from the dungeon.

Grim-faced soldiers patrolled the battlements and priests came and went through the dungeon door, intent on their grisly tasks. The line of petitioners stayed meek and silent, mice trying to hide from a fortress of hungry cats. Justin tried counting the number of red tabards but he lost track. The army had marched south but they'd left far too many soldiers behind, bribery seemed the old woman's best hope.

The pock-faced sergeant appeared at the dungeon doorway and pointed at Justin, a silent summons.

The others stared as he limped past, but there was no protest; the mice didn't dare complain. He followed the sergeant through the grim doorway to a small, spare room with bleak stone walls. Chilly like a root cellar, the room was empty except for a table cluttered with parchments and a single chair. A pair of iron manacles hung on the wall, a grim reminder that the small cell had other uses.

Justin stood in front of the table, keeping his back bent and his head bowed. Huddled beneath his brown cape, he was just another petitioner begging a favor.

Sergeant Jexel closed the door and sprawled in the chair. "Yer a stubborn one, hunchback, but yer golds are good." He tapped a scroll against his palm, a crooked smile on his pockmarked face. "Kept her name off the death list for another day."

Justin completed the ritual, pushing a small purse of coins across the table.

The sergeant spilled the coins into his hand, counting to be sure. "The old lady must really mean somethin to ya to keep payin." Satisfied, he tumbled the coins back into the purse. "Pity I won't be helpin you after today." The purse disappeared into the sergeant's belt, a broad grin on his face.

A cold hand gripped Justin's heart. "What'd ya mean?"

"Can't risk jiggin the death list anymore."

"But what if I pay more? Double the price?"

The sergeant shook his head. "Wish I could. But Clavin, a senior priest, has taken over. There'll be no more jiggin of the names."

"Can't Claven be...reasoned with?"

The sergeant scowled. "Claven's one of those holy types. Prances around like he's got a hot poker up his ass." He shook his head. "Not enough golds in all of Coronth to risk approachin a priest like that."

Justin's thoughts raced like a cornered mouse, frantic to save her. "But what if I pay ya to smuggle in a sleepin drought and claim the old woman died in the night? I'd pay ya a heavy purse of golds when I collect the body. A lot of golds for one frail old woman."

"Won't work." The sergeant shook his head. "No one in the dungeon escapes the Flames. There's never any bodies, never any graves. The dead are burnt, the priests see to it. Sinners all burn one way or another, only difference is, the live ones scream before they die."

Justin stood stunned, crushed by the raw cruelty of the Flame.

"Give it up, hunchback, there ain't nothing ya can do." The sergeant gave him a twisted smile full of bad teeth. "Now run along." His grin deepened to an ugly sneer. "There's others waitin for their chance to pay."

Justin turned and shuffled toward the door, pole-axed by the turn of events.

"By the way, hunchback. Since ya been good with the golds I'll give ya this one for free."

He turned to meet the sergeant's pitiless stare.

"The old lady's due to walk the Flames in three days."

A cold fist gripped Justin's heart. He had to find a way to save her...but it would take a miracle to get the old woman out of the dungeons. Justin limped from the fortress, his mind frantic with worry. He needed a miracle...and he had less than three days to find one.

62

Katherine

Halfway through the stone wall, Kath realized Duncan might be naked. The thought stole her concentration...and the stone began to claim her. Granite surrounded her with an immortal embrace. Panic seized her. Kath fought to control her magic, desperate to remain flesh, desperate to breathe. A roaring sound, like the beating of a thousand wings, surrounded her and then she was through. Kath staggered into the small cell, hungry for air, her heart pounding.

Bare arms and a warm chest caught her, pressing her against the wall, a knife held to her throat.

"Kath?" Duncan sheathed the knife but stayed close, keeping her pinned to the wall.

A quick glance proved he was only half naked. Muscles rippled across his chest, a line of dark hair disappearing beneath his belt. A blush heated her face.

"That's quite an entrance."

"There wasn't any way to knock." She tried to steady her breathing, tried to keep her gaze on his face...but it was hard to concentrate. "Check your bed."

"My bed?" His voice held an odd quality, a hungry smile spreading across his sun-tanned face.

Her blush deepened. "I found dried blood on mine...and a cut from a sword thrust."

"Murder!"

She nodded. "The reason for all the lies. Danya had the truth of it. They murdered my brother in the depths of the night and threw his body off the mountainside. That's why the eagles circle above...for the loyal dead."

Duncan sobered. "I'm sorry, Kath."

A cold fist gripped her heart. She couldn't think about her brother. "If they murdered once they'll murder again."

"Tonight?"

"I expect so." The musk of his bare skin was distracting.

His face turned grim. "I counted twenty-two knights in the great hall...and there must be others standing guard...too many swords against us. Any chance some are still loyal to the Octagon?"

"Trask wouldn't let them live." She considered the odds, twenty-two swords trained by the Octagon...and then there was Trask, a knight with the strength of a Taal. She shuddered. "We'll have to sneak out and fight only if we have to."

He cursed and took a step back, releasing her. "My bows are with my saddle. And an archer's not much good for close fighting."

She stared at him, regretting the distance. "But you can see in the dark."

"True." He ripped off the leather patch, revealing his golden eye. "But how does that help?"

She met his mismatched gaze. "I don't know, but we'll need every advantage."

He stared at her, a thread of tension running between them. Duncan closed the distance and leaned toward her, staring down, his gaze intense. For a moment, she thought he might kiss her...but instead he pressed his lips to her ear, his voice a husky whisper. "When we've won." And then he did kiss her, long and deep. His arms encircled her, pulling her to his bare chest. Kath answered his kiss, feeling his heat, feeling his heartbeat, breathless for more.

Without warning, he stepped away. His gaze smoldered. "Too tempting." He took a deep breath, a promise in his gaze. "When we've won."

She leaned against the wall, hungry for his touch, but instead she just nodded. "Till then."

He turned away, pulling on a black shirt, leather sliding over a ripple of muscles. "We need a plan."

Kath took a deep breath, trying to keep her thoughts focused. "We sneak down to the stable, saddle the horses, and ride through the tunneled passage into the north."

"They'll have a guard posted in the hallway, maybe more if murder is their plan."

She reached for one of her throwing axes. "I'll take care of the guard, you get the others. Rouse Sir Tyrone first, his sword will be needed."

"There'll be knights guarding the tunneled pass-through."

"I have an idea that might give us an advantage." She moved toward the door.

He gripped her arm, lightning in his touch. "Stay safe."

She gave him a quick kiss. "And you."

They opened the door and peered out, grateful the hinges were silent. Torchlight danced along the curved walls, proving the hall was empty, quiet as a tomb. Kath nodded to Duncan and crept down the hallway, hugging the inside curve. Nearing the staircase, she paused to listen. The quiet told her there was only one guard. Taking a deep breath, she steeled her courage, telling herself that the knights were all false. Still, it was hard to fight against the Octagon...if she was wrong, it would be treason. Kath weighed the axe in her hand and then returned it to the shoulder harness. Needing to be sure, she stepped around the curve.

A knight slouched near the stairs, one hand resting on his sword hilt. Recognizing the droopy blond mustache and the crooked nose, she decided to risk a question. "Sir Carfax, why?"

He gave her a squinty stare, his face wary. "Why what?"

She studied him, looking for telltale signs, her voice a whisper. "Why murder my brother?"

His eyes widened, his grip tightening on his sword hilt.

Cold certainty rushed through her. She reached for an axe. The blade whirled, a tumble of death.

The axe struck deep, embedding in his face with a wet thunk. He grunted and slumped to the floor.

Kath retrieved her axe from the bloody mess. *She'd killed a knight.* She stared down at him, an ugly wound, an ugly way to die, but he'd killed her brother, a traitor to the maroon.

Duncan joined her, a dark shadow slipping down the hallway. "The others are coming." He nudged the body with his foot. "I'll hide him in your cell."

Kath nodded. "Get the others to the stable. I'll clear the way."

Steeling her resolve, she slipped down the stairs. Her doeskin boots whispered around the tight spiral, her heart hammering.

Footsteps came from below...one man. The knight climbed into sight. Sir Penross sneered at her, "What..."

She loosed her axe, a whirl of steel.

The blade took him in the throat. Blood sprayed across the stairwell. Kath lunged for the body, lowering it to the stairs. Bile threatened to choke her. She fought to keep her supper down. Tugging her axe free, she wiped it on his surcoat. Blood spattered the walls, too much blood, too much death.

Her companions joined her, footsteps on the stairs. Duncan shook his head. "No way to hide this one."

Kath grimaced. "Time is against us. We need to hurry." She led them down the last spiral and into the long corridor, pausing at the outer door. Turning to Danya, she whispered, "Can you reach the wolf? Can you tell me how many guards are out there?"

Danya nodded. "Bryx is easy to reach." Her eyes glazed, as if in a trance...and then she was back, her brown gaze clear. "There's only one. Bryx says he stands by the dark cave-mouth."

"He must mean the tunneled passageway." She looked to the others. "I'll take care of the guard. The rest of you run for the stable and saddle the horses."

Sir Tyrone said, "I'll take the guard."

"No." Her voice brooked no argument. "My throwing axe is quicker, quieter. Anything else and the guard will ring the alarm bell."

The black knight nodded, his face grim.

Kath turned to Danya. "Can Bryx watch the tower while we saddle the horses? To give warning if the other knights come?"

Danya nodded, her face pale. "Bryx can do that."

"Good." Kath hefted her axe, an assassin's weapon. "I'll go first." Remembering her lessons with the Empty Knight, she stepped out into the frozen moonlight.

A lone knight stood huddled beneath his maroon cloak, guarding the tunneled passageway. The rope-pull of the warning bell dangled beside him, the greater threat.

This time she did not hesitate. Stepping toward the knight, she hurled the axe, a bright blade whirling in the night.

The knight lurched sideways.

The axe clanged against stone, a clean miss.

Kath stared, frozen in shock.

The knight lowered his spear and charged.

Kath stood her ground, reaching for the second axe. She hurled the second, but he deflected it with his spear. Stunned, she reached for her sword.

Something blurred at the edge of her vision. The wolf hurtled toward the knight, leaping for his throat. Man and beast fell to the cobbles. With a savage growl, the wolf tore the knight's throat.

"Bryx to me."

The wolf grinned at Kath. Shaking the blood from his fur, he trotted toward Danya.

Kath approached the body. His throat gaped open, torn and bloody. Luck or stupidity had kept him from ringing the alarm and now he was dead. Kath thought of her brother, food for eagles, and wished she'd killed him. She went in search of her axes. Pale moonlight showed a glimmer of steel at the base of the tower. Retrieving her axes, she raced for the stable.

The companions worked by lantern light, buckling saddles, tightening girths, and checking bridles. The horses whinnied in protest, milling in their stalls. Kath found the roan stallion and flung the saddle across his back, her fingers clumsy with the buckles. She elbowed the stallion, pulling the girth tight and led the horse out of the stall.

Zith struggled with the packhorse.

Duncan strung his short bow.

Out in the courtyard, the wolf howled.

Danya yelled, "They're coming."

"We're out of time!" A shiver of fear raced down Kath's spine. "Mount up and ride for the passage." She swung into the saddle and unsheathed her sword. "Duncan, open the gates in the passageway and get the others through. Sir Tyrone, stay with me. We'll hold them off till the others get free." She settled her shield on her left arm and spurred the stallion toward the mouth of the stable.

The stallion burst into the courtyard.

Knights spilled out of the tower, a chaos of swords. Kath charged, a war cry on her lips. *"Castlegard!"* The battle-trained stallion bulled into the closest knight, knocking him to the ground. A muffled scream came from beneath iron-shod hooves.

The alarm bell rang, loud and urgent.

Kath slashed with her sword, a spray of blood in the moonlight.

The wolf snarled, an ambush of teeth.

Sir Tyrone fought beside her, his great sword a swath of silver.

Horses clattered through the courtyard.

A man's scream split the night.

Kath parried a sword thrust close to her leg and took a blow on her shield. Pain thundered down her shield arm, but she fought through it. Parry and slash, she kept her horse moving, not letting the rogue knights surround her. The courtyard became a milling swirl of steel. Kath hacked at a mace, pulling the stallion into a tight turn to avoid a slashing sword. More knights spilled out of the tower...too many swords to fight. In danger of being surrounded, she slashed at a hand grabbing her leg and spurred the stallion away. "Retreat!" The stallion lashed out, hooves clearing a path. The wolf raced into the tunnel. She looked for her friends, but the others were gone. Kath galloped for the dark passageway, Sir Tyrone followed.

She heard Trask bellow, "Stop her!

A knight barred the tunnel.

Kath whispered to the stallion. The war-trained horse did not flinch.

The knight dodged away.

The stallion clattered into the narrow tunnel, a mouth of darkness. Kath rode low, hugging the stallion's neck, asking for speed. The passage was just wide enough for single horse, a tunnel designed to choke an army. She raced for the opening on the far end, a keyhole of moonlight, the north side of the Dragon Spines.

Hoof beats from behind her came to a sudden stop.

She turned in the saddle to see Sir Tyrone dismount. "What are you doing?" She pulled on the stallion's reins, slowing the horse.

The black knight grinned up at her. "A single knight can stop an army." He saluted her with his great sword. "I'll hold them here."

"No! We stay together!"

"They'll only follow. Better to fight them here." He hit his horse with the flat of his blade. "Now ride! You're not the only one to hear the voice of the gods."

The warhorse crowded behind.

Sir Tyrone turned and settled into a fighting stance, guarding the tunneled passageway.

Kath watched him through a blur of tears, a valiant swirl of maroon. She knew he was right, but it hurt. "Valin guard you!" She thrummed her heels against the stallion and rode through the moonlit keyhole, galloping into the north.

63

Tyrone

Tyrone stood in the center of the long passageway, claiming the tower as his ally. Two hundred years of honor besmirched by traitors...but the legends of Cragnoth Keep said one knight could stand against an army. Long and narrow, the tunneled passageway was designed to choke an army, to stop the hordes of the Mordant. Relying on the strength of legends, he'd turn the keep's defenses against the false knights, giving Kath and the others a chance to escape.

Ever since the god's voice on the Isle of Souls, he'd known this day would come, a last chance for glory. Raising his great sword in a final salute, he yelled, "For Valin and the Octagon." His battle cry echoed down the passageway, as if legions of knights stood at his shoulder. Tyrone settled into a fighting stance, his great sword poised to strike.

The enemy did not waste time. Hoofbeats echoed down the long narrow passage. The false knight urged his horse to a gallop, brandishing a sword but not a lance. Sir Tyrone smiled...and waited, studying the warhorse as it loomed large. Iron-shod hoofbeats rang like rolling thunder. The horse listed to the right. Tyrone stepped to the left and knelt, his great sword slashing at the horse's knees.

The horse tumbled in a spray of blood, throwing the knight.

A squeal of terror echoed down the passageway.

Tyrone scrambled to his feet and stepped past the struggling horse, avoiding the slashing hooves. A quick sword thrust through the gorget finished the false knight. Wrenching his sword free, he waited, using the dying horse as a bulwark.

The narrow passage stank of blood and death...a trap with teeth.

Warhorses balked at the tunnel's mouth. Rearing in fear, they refused to enter. The knights came at him on foot.

He waited, forcing his enemies to step around the dying horse. His patience was rewarded. As they dodged flailing hooves, he caught them off balance, his great sword slipping through their guard, quick and keen. The traitors' screams mingled with the horse's dying squeals, but the enemy kept coming. The living tripped on the dead. Bodies of his enemies formed a barrier, choking the passage. The narrow tunnel became a nightmare clogged with death.

The traitors proved relentless. They rushed him two at a time, forcing him back, gaining room to fight. Steel met steel with a ferocious clang. He parried their attacks and answered with his own. The fight became a blur. His sword grew heavy; his arms began to ache. Sweat stung his eyes. Tyrone staggered under a vicious blow but somehow found the strength to fight back. Every man he defeated was replaced with another, no rest for his sword. His strength waned; his breath grew ragged. Cuts slashed his arms and legs. Pain became part of the fight, but he refused to give up.

Tyrone retreated backwards, trying to buy more time. Every stroke was an effort. He hoped Kath and the others were well away. He prayed to Valin for the strength to fight...he prayed to be equal to the legend.

64

Justin

Time beat against Justin like hammer blows against an anvil. Three days to find a way to save Grandmother Magda, three days to do the impossible. Bribery had failed, and a forced rescue was impossible. He had to find another way. He needed a miracle...he needed an army...so he turned to his last hope, the people of Coronth.

The Dark Harper slipped through the back alleys, making the rounds of the taverns, singing against the Flame God. Drawing on all his skills, he reached for the people's fear and stoked their anger, trying to rouse the populace against the Pontifax. He sang of loved ones lost, his fingers rippling across the strings evoking emotions, evoking memories. He sang of wives, husbands, and children fair, all consumed by the Flame, kindling fed to a raging inferno of death. His lyrics exposed the lies of the priests and exhorted the people to rebellion. Soaring ballads magnified the deeds of the rebels. Softer melodies evoked the Dark Harper's rise from death, a miracle to fight a miracle. From dusk till dawn, he risked his life, visiting the rich taverns as well as the poor. Playing till his fingers bled and his throat grew hoarse, he urged the people to rise. With harp and voice, he brought the city to a fever pitch, to a boil of rebellion...but in his heart he wondered if songs would be enough.

On the morning of the third day, he rose early and went to the temple square. The Dark Harper's cloak was too much of a risk, so he settled for the lesser danger, a bright blue cape and the gaudy finery of a minstrel. Minstrels were becoming scarce in Balor, too many fed to the Flames.

Weaving his way through the faithful, Justin chose a spot near the fire pit, in the heart of the square. The position put him near the place where the condemned sinners were forced to stand, near enough to let Grandmother Magda know she was not alone.

The crowd began to gather, men and women and children, a mixture of peasant-brown and the brighter garments of merchants and artisans. Flashes of red mingled with the other colors, soldiers and priests joining the throng, a festival of spectators. Justin scanned the square, looking for Ben and Daniel and the orphan lads. According to the plan, they were scattered throughout the gathering, ready to fan any glimmer of rebellion, but try as he might, Justin could not see them. Individuals were lost in the tide of humanity, a milling sea of faces, a swell of expectations.

A drumbeat pounded through the square, the rhythmic throbbing of a monstrous heartbeat.

The crowd hushed, faces turning toward the temple doors.

The great brass doors opened, disgorging a flood of red-robed priests. The priests marched in procession, incense burners swaying, raising a cloud of blue smoke. The Keeper came last, a large bald-headed man in rich red robes, holding a flaming torch.

The procession wound its way to the heart of the square. Priests lined the raised dais, a cloud of incense billowing into the afternoon sky. The Keeper prowled toward the charcoal pit, the flaming torch held aloft.

The priests chanted, "Feed the Flames!"

The people echoed the chant, "Feed the Flames! Feed the Flames!" while swaying in time to the drumbeat.

Justin watched the crowd, sickened by their cheap seduction. Most looked avid for spectacle or blinded by devotion. Only a few were stone-faced or skeptical, way too few. Anger thundered through him, knowing this travesty could only succeed with the consent of the people.

The Keeper reached the pit and lowered the torch.

Fire erupted from the charcoal. Licks of flame shot skyward, sucking air like a great beast. A melting heat beat against Justin's face, forcing him away from the pit. The crowd moved as one, pressing backward, opening a space around the crackling flames.

The temple drums stilled.

The great brass doors opened wide. A single figure emerged, a shimmer of light in a robe of gold, a great red ruby flashing at the patriarch's breast. The Pontifax claimed the stares of the multitude, a vision of holiness. Making the sign of blessing, he descended the steps.

The crowd sighed as the Pontifax passed. Women reached out to touch the hem of his gown. Babies were held out in the hope of a special blessing. Men knelt and women swooned.

Justin watched the show, crushed by the people's delusion. His songs of truth seemed a slender foil against the pomp and lies of religion.

The Pontifax climbed the dais, benevolence shining from his face. He made the sign of blessing and then embraced the crowd with his voice. "My people! Beloved of the Flame God! You join me here today to renew the Test of Faith! Those who are pure will walk untouched through the holy Flames. The Flame God brings love to all who believe!"

The rumble of a wagon came from the north side of the square. The crowd parted to admit a flatbed wagon and an escort of soldiers, the sacrifice for the Flames. Justin steeled himself to see his friend.

The wagon stopped near the edge of the flaming pit.

Grandmother Magda stood chained to the mounted stocks. Barefoot and dressed in a plain white shift, her face was ashen, her silver hair a wild tangle, her eyes sunken to dark pits. Justin gasped in shock; the old woman had aged a decade. Her bright vibrancy was gone, snuffed out by the dungeon's cruelties.

Soldiers unchained the old lady from the stocks and helped her down from the wagon. They locked her wrists in heavy manacles, the chains dangling like weights between her hands, but they left her legs unbound. The lack of leg chains seemed a small kindness, but Justin knew the priests wanted a show. Sinners danced in the flames, providing a spectacle for the faithful. The calculated ugliness sickened Justin, but he kept his place near the front, determined to be a witness for his friend.

The soldiers prodded the old woman with their swords, goading the silver-haired grandmother to the edge of the flames.

Justin stared at his friend, willing her to look up, willing her to see him.

Grandmother Magda stood with her head bowed, a broken old women waiting for death.

Justin ached to see her look so frail and defenseless, but all he could do was watch, hoping the people would heed his songs.

The Pontifax raised his voice, gathering the attention of the crowd. "My people! A sinner stands before you. A sinner accused of plotting against the religion of the Flame. But the Flame God is benevolent, giving every sinner a chance to atone through the Test of Faith." The Pontifax made the sign of blessing. "Before this sinner walks in the Flames, we will take the Test of Faith ourselves! With this miracle we prove the benevolence of the Flame God!"

The crowd stilled to an expectant hush.

Justin watched the crowd. It seemed miracles never grew dull.

The Pontifax descended the dais and knelt by the Flames. While acolytes removed his gilded sandals, the Flame Priest stared across the length of the pit at the sinner. Grasping his ruby amulet, he bowed his head in prayer.

Justin studied the Pontifax, trying to discern the source of the charlatan's magic.

The Pontifax stared into the Flames, his right hand clutching the great ruby.

Understanding struck Justin like a lightning bolt. His source of magic had to be the amulet!

Justin felt the weight of a piercing stare. He turned to find Grandmother Magda staring at him, but the old woman's steel-gray gaze was not defeated, not cowed. Her gaze burned with a righteous vengeance. She nodded, acknowledging Justin with a thin smile and then she fixed her stare on the Pontifax.

A premonition shivered down Justin's spine.

The Pontifax entered the flames. The fire snapped and crackled, pulsing with a ferocious heat, engulfing the high priest. Justin had never been so close to the flaming pit. He watched amazed as the Pontifax trod the flames. Tongues of fire licked around the priest, yet he walked barefoot through the blaze, untouched by the unbearable heat. Beaming a beatific smile, he made the sign of blessing, the perfect image of a holy miracle.

The crowd moaned with ecstasy.

Justin watched, sickened by the false miracle.

A blood-curdling shriek split the air. Grandmother Magda lunged into the fire. Leaping through the flames, she swung her manacled hands toward the Pontifax, striking him across the face with the dangling chains. The chains struck like a weapon, smashing his nose and crushing one eye, leaving a trail of blood and gore. The Pontifax screamed, reeling backwards. He reached up to protect his face, releasing his hold on the amulet. The old woman's shift burst into flames, but she followed the Pontifax, grabbing the great ruby. Fear and panic ripped across the priest's face. He beat at the old woman grappling for the amulet, but Grandmother Magda would not let go. She clung to the ruby like a mother wrestling for her child. A nimbus of flames surrounded the two, the fire unable to touch either one. The Pontifax and the old woman fought a grim tug-of-war, grappling for the amulet amongst the roaring flames.

Gasps of shock ripped through the crowd.

Priests and soldiers gaped from the edge of the pit, spellbound by the struggle.

Grandmother Magda fell to her knees, but she held tight to the amulet.

Justin stood at the edge of the pit, close enough to hear the gold chain snap.

The old lady fell backwards, the great ruby clutched in her fist.

Fire rushed to claim the Pontifax. A scream erupted from the pit. Flames engulfed the Pontifax, igniting his hair and beard. The priest became a living torch. His skin blackened and blistered. His cloth of gold vestments melted onto his blackening skin. Howling tortured screams, the Pontifax danced like a sinner, writhing in the heart of the flames, a damned figure caught in the grip of hell.

The crowd stared transfixed, shock reflected on a thousand faces.

Justin realized the crowd needed to be pushed. He reached for his bard's training, making his voice a righteous roar. *"The Pontifax is a fraud! He burns like a sinner!"*

A scream belched from the flames, proving the bard's words. The Pontifax slumped forward, a charred mockery of a man, a burnt and blistered grotesque.

Screams ripped through the square. *"He lied to us!"*

"There is no miracle!"

"The God burns his priest!"

Shock gave way to anger. The crowd erupted in a frenzied mob.

Justin turned back to the fire, desperate to save the old woman.

Grandmother Magda raced for the edge of the pit, the amulet clutched in her fist.

At first the flames seemed to hesitate...as if confused, but then they pounced, the flames licking up her legs.

Justin fought to reach the old woman.

Madness exploded through the square. The crowd turned on the priests and soldiers, clawing at them with bare hands and teeth, a wild fury of pent up vengeance.

A blackened hand thrust from the flames. Justin pulled her from the flaming pit. The skin of her hand came away like a glove. Shocked and sickened, he ripped his cloak from his shoulders and wrapped her in swath of blue. Beating at the flames, he fought to save her life.

The square broiled with anger, a frothing sea of madness.

Ben and Daniel appeared at Justin's side. The two men helped Justin carry the old woman to the edge of the crowd, to a sanctuary of quiet in a sea of insanity. Daniel ran to find water while Justin cradled his friend. Her hair was burnt, her face blistered and blackened. She seemed small and frail, like a singed bird in his arms...but her eyes were bright. She smiled up at him, her voice a breathy whisper. "I figured it out. I stole his miracle."

Justin nodded, his eyes crowded with tears. "Yes, but we should have found another way."

She patted his hand, as if to comfort him. "No...had to be this way. The people...had to see the truth."

"But the price was too high." He wanted to hold her tight but he feared hurting her.

She shook her head. "Always mine to do." Reaching for his hand, she put the great ruby in his palm. "For you." She smiled up at him, a dazzling smile full of hope and happiness. "Now...I go...to my grandchild."

He held her...long after she'd died...humming a lullaby, tears coursing down his face.

They buried her in the herb garden, next to Samson, beneath the crabapple tree...while all around them, the city raged.

The vengeance of the gods descended on Coronth. Madness swept through the city. Mobs ran rampant in the streets. Stores were looted and priests were lynched. Pockets of soldiers retaliated. The Keeper retreated to the Residence, while the priests held the temple. The dead littered the cobblestone streets, too many to count. Chaos reigned.

Justin and his friends hid, watching the madness, waiting for an end to the chaos. Surely something better would rise from the ashes of the flame priest.

65

Jordan

Jordan woke to the morning light. She stared at the brightness streaming through the healery window, a pale imitation of the Light. She remembered the time between. She remembered the peace and how everything fit together, the vast complex pattern of choices. For one shining moment it all made sense. Surrounded by the Light, she'd held the answers to all the difficult whys.

Her memories broke like waves across a beach, knowledge and understanding receding with the tide. She clenched her mind and fought to hold on, but the knowledge slipped through her fingers like sand. The tide rushed out, leaving her stranded on the mortal side of the gray veil.

The knowing was gone...and so was the certainty, but an underlying feeling of conviction remained. The warriors of the Light were needed. She'd chosen to come back. A war was coming and her sword was needed below the mountains. The time for healing was done.

Jordan took a deep breath and turned her head.

A blue-robed monk sat on a bench, reading a scroll.

Her words were a whisper, her voice long unused. "I've come back...and I need my sword."

66

The Mordant

Nine horses died for the sake of speed. The Mordant crossed the Dragon Spines, intent on reclaiming his power, the unmade knight riding at his side. Wielding bloody whips, they rode each horse to death, till its heart gave out or its legs collapsed. Switching mounts, they left the mangled horses to rot. Dead horses marked a trail down the mountainside, through the old growth forest, and out across the endless expanse of grassland, a trail of sacrifices, a fitting trail of death.

The Mordant rode the last horse through the sea of waist-high grass. He held the pale mare to a slow trot, coaxing the horse to travel the last leagues. Sir Raymond ran by the horse's flank, clutching the stirrup, his branded face streaked with sweat.

They traveled north, beneath an endless vault of blue, the sun a disk in the cloudless sky. The steppes stretched to forever, a vast sea of grassland, the waist-high stalks bowing to the wind. Golden grasses rippled and flowed, a dull sameness stretching in every direction, flat and featureless except for the north. At long last, he glimpsed the wall. A crenellated wall sliced through the steppes, marking the border to his domain.

He'd built the wall seven lifetimes ago, raised by the sweat of human slaves. Built to contain his subjects as much as to keep out his enemies, the wall was forty feet high and twenty feet wide, a smooth roadway running along the top, protected by crenellated battlements. Stretching like an impossibly long snake, the wall divided the grasslands from the Mordant's domain. Leagues of stone mortared with sweat and blood, the wall was a marvel, yet it paled before the gargoyle gates.

The gargoyle gates...gaping openings in the wall, without doors or a moat, and yet the great statues loomed above like a gauntlet of horrors frozen in stone. A cadre of wizards had raised the gates, a full year spent weaving spells and imprisoning souls. When the task was done, he'd ordered the wizards beheaded so the feat could never be duplicated or undone. He'd shown his appreciation by entombing one wizard beneath each gate, a lasting tribute to their greatest work. Ten dead wizards entombed beneath ten gates, the stone marvels spaced evenly along the vast expanse of the long gray wall. Such potent magic was long since gone from the land, but the gates remained as a lasting monument to Darkness, a fitting entrance to his domain.

The mare stumbled and nearly fell, flecks of foam on her muzzle. The Mordant slowed the horse to a walk and watched the gates loom large. A slow triumph swelled within him. Reaching inside his mind, the Mordant prodded the trapped monk. *Awake, monk, I would have you see this.*

Leave me alone! I've seen enough of your evil.

He laughed. *You've seen nothing. I have not yet to come into my full powers.*

Leave me alone! I walk in the Light. I walk in the Light.

The monk had endured beyond all expectation, maintaining his sanity longer than any of his other hosts, but the stubborn mantra wore thin. *Come, monk, I offer you the chance to see one of the marvels of the ancient world. Rise up and see through my eyes, see what Darkness can achieve.* The captured soul could not resist the temptation of sight...none of them could. He felt the monk rise within him and stare out of his eyes. He heard the soul gasp with wonder, and well he should.

The gate was actually a short stone roadway, wide enough for three wagons, a breach in the long wall. A hundred feet long, the roadway was made of quarried stone and the sweat of slaves. The road was ordinary. The marvel was the gargoyles. Twelve gargoyles guarded the gate. Perched on top of ten-foot pillars, the great gargoyles appeared as monsters frozen in stone, rearing over the road. Beaks and claws, wings and fangs, each gargoyle was unique, a twisted mélange of real and imagined animals held locked within the stone, the embodiment of dark sorcery guarding the gates to the north.

The monk screamed within his mind. *I can feel them! I feel their torment! They scream with the pain of centuries. Set them free!*

The Mordant studied the soul trapped within his mind, amazed at the monk's perception. *So you can feel the souls of the damned? How interesting. You may have more value than I thought. But first you must willingly embrace the Dark.*

Never! I will never join such evil.

Then you will spend your days howling in a corner of my mind till there is nothing left but gibbering madness! The Mordant drove the monk back into the depths, lashing the soul with his mind. Slamming the walls tight, he imprisoned the monk in absolute darkness. Deprived of all sensation, the monk howled for all that was lost. The Mordant smiled, enjoying the music of the damned.

He kicked the mare to a faster shamble. The gargoyles loomed large. Over twenty feet tall, the stone monsters were exquisitely detailed. Clawed talons and gaping mouths, the figures stood upon their pedestals, frozen in mid-scream. The Mordant breathed deep, reaching for threads of Darkness, reaching for the souls of the men and animals ensorcelled within the twisted figures...but he felt only cold stone. Annoyed, he stared at the gargoyles. Strange that the monk could feel the souls trapped within yet he could not. Perhaps it was merely the sympathy of the damned.

The mare stumbled to the edge of the gate, head bowed, legs trembling, lathered and blowing hard. The Mordant pulled on the reins and dismounted. The unmade knight collapsed to his knees, gasping for breath.

The Mordant prodded the knight with his boot. "Pay attention." He gestured to the gargoyle gate. "This gate is the start of my domain. I return to reclaim my power but none in the kingdom have ever seen this face, the face that I wear in this lifetime. And so, the return must, by necessity, be full of rituals and tests, enough to eliminate any pretender." His stare drilled into the knight. "Heed my words and obey if you want to live."

The knight nodded, his sweat-glazed face bright red. "As you command, lord."

"A patrol will come for us. They will be wary of spies and pretenders. Ritual is our shield and our refuge. Ignore any taunts or threats. If you remain placid you will be safe. If you are questioned, say only that 'you obey the true Mordant'. Do you understand?"

"Yes, but lord, you wear the surcoat of the Octagon Knights. What's to stop the soldiers from attacking you?"

"Fear of the Mordant. My shadow is long in the north." He gazed down at his silver surcoat, the mark of the enemy emblazoned on his chest. "I often return cloaked as one of my enemies. The irony appeals to me."

The knight nodded, but he looked doubtful.

"Remove your weapons and hang them on the saddle." The Mordant unbuckled his long sword and dagger, hanging the belt on the pommel. "To greet the patrol with even the smallest dagger is a death sentence." The Mordant watched as the knight divested his many weapons.

"Stay on this side of the gate until I bid you to cross. The patrol must find a single man waiting beneath the gargoyles. Do you understand?"

"Yes, lord." The knight glanced up at the gargoyles, fear written across his face. "But lord, I've heard strange rumors about these gates, nasty legends. Knights have died here."

"The tales told of these gates are legion...most of them true." He laughed, enjoying the fear in the knight's eyes. "Wait here, while my heralds announce my return."

The Mordant turned, a swirl of maroon, and strode toward the gate. As he stepped onto the roadway, the gargoyles rippled to life. They remained fixed to their pillars, trapped within stone, but the magic awoke. Wings unfurled, muscles rippled, and claws reached for the heavens as if seeking vengeance. Twelve gargoyles reared on their pillars, releasing a soul-piercing screech. The unearthly wail split the blue sky, a paean of pain.

The unmade knight cowered to the ground, hands over his ears. The pale mare whinnied in terror, showing the whites of her eyes. The Mordant smiled, waiting beneath the writhing gargoyles, waiting to fulfill the dark destiny of his twelfth lifetime. He laughed, listening to the tortured screams. The howls of the damned announced the Mordant's return. He'd come to claim the Ebony Throne.

67

Katherine

Kath galloped down the narrow trail, Sir Tyrone's words pounding in her mind. The black knight claimed he'd heard the voice of the gods, but surely listening to the gods did not mean he had to die? It was not fair. It was not right. Rage and rebellion roiled within her. Kath did not like leaving friends behind, she did not like running. If the gods believed in free will then she ought to have a choice. And running wasn't her choice.

She caught up to the others and yelled above the pounding hoof beats. "Stop!"

Duncan stared back at her, puzzlement on his face, but he slowed his gelding.

Kath pulled on the reins, halting the roan stallion.

The others slowed, turning their horses, but Duncan was the one she needed. She answered his unspoken question. "Sir Tyrone stayed behind to make a stand in the tunnel, to keep the false knights from following. I'm going back to fight with him." She raised her hand, forestalling his argument. "With your bow and my sword, he might have a chance. But alone, he'll die. Will you come?"

"What about the crystal dagger?"

"I'm not leaving a friend behind to fight for me." Anger bled into her voice. "If the crystal dagger matters so much, then the gods can bloody well help."

Duncan nodded, "Then we fight." He flashed her a wry smile.

She loved him for it. Kath looked to Danya and Zith. "It might be safer if you keep riding."

Danya shook her head. "I'm coming."

Zith nodded, his face grim. "We stay together."

Her friends filled her with pride. "Then let's ride." She turned the stallion and drummed her heels, asking for speed, praying Sir Tyrone still lived. They galloped back to the keep, dismounting at the tunnel entrance.

A clang of swords echoed from the narrow passage, an answer to her prayers.

Kath reached for a throwing axe, keeping her small shield on her left arm.

Duncan strung his longbow, a quiver of arrows belted to his side.

She stared at his mismatched eyes. "Make every arrow count."

He nodded. "And every sword stroke."

She raced into the tunnel, following the song of swords. The narrow passage was murky with darkness, ripe with death and fear. Torches lined the walls but none were lit. Silver moonlight glowed at the tunnel's openings, a keyhole at both ends, providing the only light. Kath thanked Valin that Duncan could see in the night, trusting his arrows to thread the darkness. Any other archer would be just as likely to hit a friend as a foe.

The clang of steel led her to Sir Tyrone. He battled a knight with a mace. The mace attacked with a flurry of blows, strength against finesse, pushing Sir Tyrone back. Other knights crowded behind the mace, waiting their turn to fight.

A bowstring thrummed...an arrow took the false knight in the face.

"*For Castlegard!*" Her battle cry echoed in the tunnel. She loosed her axe, a deadly whirl. A scream told her the axe found its mark. Unsheathing her sword, she stepped next to the black knight.

His voice was hoarse, his breathing ragged. "Why?"

An arrow thrummed past her, missing her opponent but making him flinch. She leaped into the opening, her sword finding flesh. "Because I'm done running." She beat back a saber slash. "Because I hate leaving friends." Steel clanged against steel. "Because it's right." She settled into the dance of swords, stroke and parry, concentrating on the fight. Steel flashed in the murky dimness, the only warning. She raised her shield to take the blow. Her opponents had the advantages of reach and strength, forcing Kath to fight with quickness and skill. The narrowness of the passage hampered her movements. Her small shield took a beating, each blow shivering down her arm.

Arrows whizzed past. Most found their mark but others missed. The narrowness of the passage gave advantages to each side.

Sir Tyrone faltered. He crumpled to his knees, a strangled cry on his lips.

"*No!*" Kath rushed forward, ramming her shield into the false knight's face, forcing him away from Sir Tyrone.

Duncan yielded, "Go left!"

She pressed to the left side of the passage, hugging the wall.

An arrow sprouted from the false knight's throat. He clawed at the feathered shaft. Issuing a strangled groan, he fell.

"Stay!" Another arrow sped down the center...another scream.

A knight with a battleaxe charged up the passage.

Duncan's bow thrummed but his arrows lodged in the knight's shield.

Laughter bubbled from the big knight, a berserker's battle rage. The knight closed the distance. The battleaxe whistled toward Kath's head. She sidestepped the stroke but had no opening to attack. The knight loosed a flurry of blows, fast and strong. Kath danced away, taking a glancing blow on her shield. The strength of the blow drove her to her knees. A second blow splintered her shield in a shatter of shards. Her left arm went numb. Driven to the ground, she knelt, exposed to the axe. Desperate to live, she thrust her sword up, but the blade skittered off chainmail. The knight laughed, raising the axe for the killing stroke, a demon in the dark.

The longbow thrummed.

An arrow protruded from the knight's right eye. The berserker toppled forward, the axe falling from his lifeless hand.

Kath struggled out from under the dead bulk. Her whole body ached, a line of fire dancing down her left arm.

More arrows hummed overhead.

She hugged the wall, gripping her sword.

A wolf's howl echoed through the tunnel. Bryx loped to Kath's side. He grinned up at her and yipped. Kath nodded, appreciating the wolf's presence.

She peered down the passage, waiting, but the flood of knights seemed to have run dry. Bodies in silver surcoats littered the passageway, a swath of death...but the numbers didn't add up. She kept her sword ready, suspecting a trap. Staying close to the wall, she crept toward the south end of the passage.

A dead horse clogged the way, a glut of slain knights on either side. Sir Tyrone had fought well, a hero's effort. The passage stank of blood and piss and dung, a gallery of horrors. A fallen knight moaned, "Water. Give me water."

Kath shuddered and stepped wide.

A torch waved across the far end of the passage.

The longbow thrummed...but there was no scream.

The torch waved again. A deep, gravelly voice yelled, "Parley! Hold your fire and parley!"

"*Trask!*" She made the name a curse. She'd hoped to find the brute among the fallen...but he hadn't had the guts to risk the passage. "What do you want, Trask?"

"Come out and we'll talk."

The wolf snarled, a low rumble that echoed in the passage.

Kath agreed with the wolf. "I don't think so. What's your offer?"

"We're fighting for no reason, no gain."

A traitor's logic, she kept silent and let him talk.

"What if we each ride our own way? No arrows in the back, no pursuit."

His words reeked of treachery. She waved to Duncan. "Bring the others." Whatever Trask was up to, she did not want her forces divided. Better to have them in the passageway, protected by stout stone. Duncan moved up behind her, keeping an arrow nocked. The others came behind. Danya led the horses while Zith tended to Sir Tyrone. Kath raised her voice to a shout. "Fine, Trask, ride away."

"But how do I trust you?"

"So it's trust we're talking about?"

He laughed, a low menacing sound. "I think you should come out while you can. A princess can be a valuable hostage."

A loud crash came from behind them. A wall of flames erupted across the northern opening, sealing their escape. Dark smoke billowed into the tunnel, the reek of burning oil. The horses squealed. Danya worked to ease their fears.

Kath yelled to Zith, "Close the outer doors! Stop the smoke!" Pressing her cloak to her face, she studied the passageway, desperate for an advantage. They needed to attack instead of just defending. They needed to mount an ambush. Clutching her gargoyle, she considered the problem...and remembered her god-given advantage. But how to use it? She stared at the thick walls, wondering how much stone she could pass through. She told Duncan her plan. "Hold the passageway, while I take the fight to Trask."

He nodded, his face grim. "I'll protect the others but what about you?"

She shrugged and gave him a half-smile. "The gods will have to help." She turned before he could protest. Sheathing her sword, she slipped down the tunnel, trying to remember the dimensions of the tower. A quarter of the way to the south entrance, she gripped her gargoyle and pressed her hand to the eastern wall. Taking a deep breath, she reached for her magic. She fell into the wall, into stubborn stone, cold and hard. Granite embraced her, solid and sedentary, tempting her with permanence. She pushed forward, through the hardness, desperate for a breath of air, afraid of becoming trapped. The stone's grip tightened, seeking to hold her in an eternal embrace. Every step seemed harder than the last, the stone impossibly thick, perhaps she'd chosen the wrong place to try. Aching for air, she pushed through...and stumbled into a room. Gasping for breath, Kath stood trembling against the wall, trying to get her bearings.

Torchlight seeped under a closed door, providing a dim light. Weapons lined the walls. Spears and swords, maces and battleaxes, the edged weapons offered no help...but in the corner, she found a crossbow and a sheath of quarrels. She'd never loosed a crossbow but she knew how they worked. Sure death at close range, she smiled, knowing it was just the weapon she needed. Standing on the stirrup, she struggled to cock the bowstring, needing both hands to latch the string. Loading an armor-piercing quarrel, she kept her finger well clear of the tickler. She didn't bother taking more quarrels. One chance was all she'd get.

Kath listened at the door and then stepped into the hallway.

The outer door gaped open, moonlight shining in the courtyard. She crept to the doorway and peered out. An argument raged in the yard. Six knights stood clustered with weapons drawn, confronting Trask and four of his cronies.

One of the six, a tall knight with flaming red hair, pointed his spiked mace at Trask. "We're not going in that tunnel. The pass-through is a cursed deathtrap."

Trask's voice was a low rumble. "You'll do as you're ordered."

Kath held her breath, praying for bloodshed.

The red-haired knight hawked and spat. "We're done dying for you, Trask."

"Then stay for the golds. A thousand for every man who fights."

"Golds are no use to the dead."

A mounted knight burst from the stable, leading six saddled horses, a clatter of hooves on stone.

Trask growled. "Your hands are just as bloody as mine. Stay and fight or the Octagon will hunt you down like dogs."

The red-haired knight swung into the saddle. "We'll take our chances in the south." He spurred his horse to a gallop and led the others down the mountain trail.

Trask raged, hurling curses into the night.

Kath grinned, seven less swords to deal with. It seemed the gods lent their help.

Trask rejoined his cronies, his back to the doorway, peering into the tunnel.

Kath stared at the traitors. The odds were better but still grim, but if she killed Trask, the others might run. Steeling her courage, she stepped out into the courtyard. Her heart thundering, she raised the crossbow, her finger on the tickler. Slow and silent, she crept towards the knights, knowing distance was her enemy. Aiming low to compensate for the crossbow's kick, she focused on the small of Trask's back. Her heart hammering, she took one more step.

One of the knights yelled, "Look out!"

Trask spun.

She squeezed the tickler.

The crossbow bucked against her cheek, pulling to the right.

The quarrel missed Trask, slamming into another knight. The knight grunted and staggered backwards, staring down at a fist-sized hole punched in his chest. He toppled forward, his face a mask of surprise.

Kath stood frozen; the moment of advantage lost.

Trask stepped towards her, a mountain blocking out the moon.

She threw the crossbow at him, but he battered it aside with a gauntleted fist.

He sneered and reached for his battleaxe. "So, the princess plays at war."

Kath reached for her last throwing axe and hurled it at the traitor.

Trask's battleaxe flashed in the moonlight, a bitter clang of steel. "That's twice you've missed." He stepped toward her, a looming menace.

Kath backed away, drawing her short sword. The blade wavered in the moonlight, a thin shield against the hulking brute. She tried to think of some advantage but there seemed to be none left. "Why, Trask?"

He barked a laugh. "I had a better offer." The battleaxe rushed toward her, a keening whisper of death.

She jumped backwards, avoiding the blow, cold sweat trickling down her back. "What offer?" She scuttled sideways, trying to lure him toward the gaping mouth of the passageway, praying for Duncan's arrows, but the other traitors moved to block the passage. Kath angled away. Perhaps she could distract him with talk. "What offer?"

The battleaxe whirled, a circle of death. "I've felt the power of Darkness. The Octagon is doomed."

A shiver of certainty raced down her back. *The Mordant!*

He laughed, a sound straight from hell. "So you know him!" The axe slashed towards her neck, an executioner's cut. "I'll gift him with your head!"

Kath ducked low. The half-moon blade whooshed overhead, a narrow miss. She lunged, thrusting low with her sword but found only chainmail. She danced away before the axe could find her.

He roared in anger. "Stand and fight!"

Hoofbeats thundered up the switchback. Kath prayed the traitors did not return.

The battleaxe blurred, a mighty overhand strike.

Kath slipped on the bloody cobbles. Desperate, she raised her sword to parry the stroke. Steel clanged against steel. Her sword twisted from her hands, clattering across the cobblestones. She fell backwards, naked without a sword, staring up at Trask's leering face.

"And now it ends."

The axe rose for the killing stroke, a silver crescent in the moonlight.

Kath reached for the dagger in her boot, a thin chance.

The axe descended in a rush of silver.

Kath rolled to the right, narrowly escaping death.

The axe struck stone, shattered chips flying in all directions.

Hoofbeats thundered into the courtyard. A blond-haired knight galloped toward Trask, moonlight shining on his face.

"Blaine!"

He did not hesitate. His great blue sword struck like vengeance.

Trask whirled to face the threat, his axe blocking the blow.

Kath swore she saw sparks where the two blades met.

Trask disengaged and stepped backwards, his face twisted in an ugly sneer. "Farmer boy!" The battleaxe cut a vicious arc. "Come and meet your death!"

Blaine leaped from the saddle, the blue sword poised to strike. "Trask!"

The false knight charged, a mountain in motion.

Blaine sidestepped, but the half-moon blade followed, a wicked slash of silver. The blue sword met the attack with a fearsome clang. The two knights clashed. Trask loomed over Blaine, forcing him back. His mailed fist lashed out, smashing into Blaine's face.

Blaine staggered backwards, blood streaming from his nose.

Kath scrambled for her sword, fearing for Blaine.

Trask rushed in, a head-high swing of the axe.

Blaine dropped to his knee, a risky move. The axe whispered overhead. The blue sword lunged upwards, striking for the heart. Metal screeched as if in pain. The blue blade plunged through steel, through plate, through chainmail, through flesh and bone, the tip erupting from the traitor's broad back.

Trask grunted, disbelief on his face.

Blaine twisted the blade.

The axe clattered from Trask's hand. The monster toppled to the side, a clatter of armor smashing to the cobbles.

Kath stared at the slain knight, awed by the strength of blue steel.

Blaine put his boot on Trask's chest, tugging on his sword.

Footsteps rushed across the courtyard.

Kath yelled, "Behind you!"

Blaine wrenched his sword lose and whirled, a backhanded stroke. The false knight parried the blow, steel against steel, but Kath did not have time to watch. A second knight rushed at her, his great sword raised for a killing stroke. Too weary to dance away, Kath raised her short sword, bracing for the blow. She watched the sword flash in the moonlight, everything slowing to a frozen heartbeat. The blade descended for the kill...but then the false knight staggered, an arrow protruding from his chest. Issuing a strangled cry, he toppled sideways, lying dead at her feet.

She stared across the courtyard and met Duncan's mismatched gaze. For a moment, there was just the two of them.

"You took too long." His words were a whisper yet she heard them.

He saluted with his bow, standing guard at the tunneled passageway. It was only then she realized the clash of swords had fallen silent. Bodies lay strewn across the courtyard. She turned to Blaine.

He crossed the yard to kneel in front of her, extending the hilt of his great blue blade. "My sword is yours."

Kath shook with fatigue, her voice a whisper. "You came."

"I made a mistake."

"You had to decide."

He held the hilt of his sword toward her, insistent. "Will you take me back?"

She smiled through tears. "I never let you go."

He smiled then, and rose. "Are there others?"

"There must be more in the tower, perhaps a handful. They're traitors, every one." She gestured to the tunneled passageway. "We fought in the pass-through. Sir Tyrone held them off."

Blaine nodded, his face grim. "I'll check the tower while you get the others." He stalked toward the door of the keep, moonlight flashing on his blue steel sword.

Kath trembled with strain, weary beyond the telling, but she made her way across the courtyard to the tunnel.

Duncan yelled, "Hurry!"

She knew from his voice. Fear shivered down her spine. She sheathed her sword and stumbled up the passageway, nearly tripping over a body. Danya held a torch, a bright circle of light. Sir Tyrone lay still, his head cradled in Zith's lap, too many wounds to count.

Kath stifled a sob. She knelt by his side and took his hand. He felt cold, too cold. "Don't leave me."

He stared at her, a weak smile, blood leaking from his mouth. "You...shouldn't have...come back."

She shook her head. "I had too."

A wave of pain crossed his face.

She held his hand tight, as if she could anchor him to life.

The pain passed and he gave her a half-smile. "When the bards sing of your victory...tell them...my skin's black...not my armor."

Tears streamed down her face. "I know a good bard." She squeezed his hand, trying to hold on to him, knowing he was slipping away. "He'll sing it true. I promise."

He smiled...and shuddered...and then was gone.

A sob escaped her. Kath shook her head, numb with grief, weary from fighting.

They stayed with the dead knight, keeping vigil in the grim passageway.

Blaine came much later, wiping the blood from his great sword. "The others are dead." He stared at them. "Sir Tyrone?"

Kath shook her head, too numb to speak. Blaine sheathed his blue sword and helped them carry the black knight from the depths of the passageway. The moon was setting, but the stars were glorious, jewels against the velvet darkness, a night for heroes.

Blaine's voice was a hushed whisper. "There's nothing here but rock and stone. We can't bury him, but we can build a cairn."

Kath shook her head. "He'll have better than that."

They carried him into the tower, round the spirals and up to the great hall. They laid him on a trestle table, too weary to do more. Spreading bedrolls on the stone floor, they slept past sunrise, straight through to sunset. Sore and aching, they woke and had a quiet meal of cold venison, hard biscuits, and a brew of hot tea.

Kath sat in a haze of aches, weary despite the sleep, straining to hold the mug of tea steady. She looked at each of her companions, fatigue on every face. They'd fought well and endured much, but they needed to hear the truth, to understand the evil set against them. "It was the Mordant. He corrupted Trask, turning him to evil."

Her words sounded like a cold doom, casting a pall on the great room.

Blaine broke the spell. "Trask was always evil."

"But the Mordant woke the worst in him, unleashing the evil."

Zith stared at her, his face lined with grief. "So much death...and we haven't even crossed the Dragon Spines."

The monk had the truth of it. The trap at Cragnoth Keep had almost caught them...yet the Mordant wasn't even present, fighting with nothing more than a legacy of words. Kath wondered how they could hope to win against such evil...but she refused to give up. She drew the crystal dagger and looked at her friends. "Will you come with me into the north?"

Blaine was the first to answer, his voice full of conviction. "To hell and back."

Danya hugged the wolf. "Bryx and I are with you."

The monk whispered, "For my son."

Duncan just stared...bringing a flush to her face.

Kath nodded, struggling to keep her voice even. "Then tomorrow we hunt the Mordant," she sheathed the dagger, "but tonight we honor a fallen hero...we honor a friend."

The sun set in a blaze of glory, streaks of maroon and red fanning across the sky, as if the gods paid tribute. They carried Sir Tyrone to the tower top and laid him on the bed of dried wood reserved for the signal fire. Kath placed his great sword on his breast, his hands on the hilt. Blaine set a shield at his feet, silver emblazoned with a maroon octagon. Duncan spread the oil and Kath held the torch. Danya and Zith watched, keeping solemn vigil.

They waited till the first star appeared in the sky. Kath lifted the torch to the heavens, her voice a mixture of pride and sorrow. "We send Sir Tyrone back to the Light. A friend, a true sword, a knight of the Octagon...a hero whose skin was black. He proved the legend, restoring the honor of Cragnoth Keep." Her voice broke. "He will be sorely missed." She struggled to finish. "May the Lords of Light welcome him home."

She touched the torch to the pyre.

The wood blazed to life. The flames embraced the fallen knight, a wreath of golden light, a beacon against the night, the second star of the evening.

The wolf loosed a mournful howl.

Kath watched the flames grow, a light to beat back the dark. The signal tower was lit, fueled by a hero's bravery. The beacon blazed bright. The kingdoms of Erdhe were called to war.

Dear Reader,

Thank you for following Kath, Duncan and Blaine, through the kingdoms of Erdhe. Their adventures continue in the third book of the saga, The Skeleton King. More excitement awaits, so I hope you will read on.

I'd love to know what you think of my books and what you'd like me to write next (The Silk & Steel Saga is finished!). So tell me what you liked, loved and even what you hated. You can contact me at k_azinge@hotmail.com or on Facebook at Karen Azinger.

I'd love to hear from you.

And now I have a favor to ask. Readers have the power to make a book or a saga successful. The fate of The Silk & Steel Saga rests in your hands. Please support my books by posting a review on Amazon or Goodreads or any other social network. Even a one sentence review matters. I'd love to see my books on the silver screen, but that will only happen if you show the world you care. Thanks for your time and your support, I write for you. For Honor and the Octagon!

APPENDIX

CASTLEGARD

Three hundred years after the War of Wizards decimated the kingdoms of Erdhe, a group of knights banded together to protect the southern kingdoms from the ravages of the north. They claimed Castlegard, the great mage-stone castle left empty after the War of Wizards, as the seat of their power. Adopting the shape of the great castle as their symbol, they became known as the Octagon Knights.

To bolster their cause, the knights were ceded land running along the length of the Dragon Spine Mountains. Stretching from Castlegard all the way to the Western Ocean, this land became known as the Domain. A series of castles, keeps, and walls were built along the Dragon Spines, allowing the knights to control the mountain passes and deny access to the southern kingdoms. The Domain also includes the only iron ore mine in all of Erdhe to yield blue ore, the rare ore required to forge the knights' fabled blue steel swords.

As a sworn brotherhood of elite knights, the candidates forsake their lineage and their past when they win their maroon cloaks. Their symbol is a maroon octagon emblazoned on a silver shield.

KING URSUS ANVRIL, King of Castlegard and the Knights of the Octagon, Lord of the Domain, hero of the Battle of Raven Pass, bearer of a great blue sword named *Honor's Edge*.
>   -his wife, **QUEEN PHYLA**, died giving birth to their only
>   daughter
> -their children:
>>   **PRINCE ULRICH**, First-born son of the king, a sworn knight
>>   of the maroon, commander of the wall at Raven Pass, bearer of
>>   a great blue sword named *Mordbane*
>>   **PRINCE GRIFFIN**, Second-born son of the king, a sworn
>>   knight of the maroon, commander of Dymtower
>>   **PRINCE GODFREY**, Third-born son of the king, a sworn
>>   knight of the maroon, commander of Shieldhold

PRINCE TRISTAN, Fourth-born son of the king, a sworn knight of the maroon, slain while leading a patrol into the steppes

PRINCE LIONEL, Fifth-born son of the king, a sworn knight of the maroon, commander of Cragnoth Keep

PRINCESS KATHERINE, Sixth child of the king, also known as the Imp or Little Sister or Kath. As a female, the Octagon symbol of Castlegard is forbidden to her. Instead she uses the Anvril's ancient heraldic symbol of a red hawk attacking with talons outstretched on a field of white.

-his sworn knights and retainers:

SIR OSBOURNE, The Knight Marshal of the Octagon, right hand of the King, a hero of Raven Pass, a one-eyed man, he wields a saber as his weapon of first choice.

SIR ABRAX, knight of the maroon, champion of the sword, he wields a blue steel sword named Protector

SIR MALVOY, a fresh-sworn knight of the maroon

SIR MARIN, a knight of the maroon

BALDWIN, senior squire of the maroon, assigned to the King

OTTO, the Master Swordsmith of Castlegard's forge, responsible for the forging of all blue steel weapons

QUINTUS, the Master Healer of Castlegard

VAL, a stable lad of Castlegard

SIR RAYMOND, branded as an unmade-knight of the Octagon, exiled from the Domain of Castlegard on penalty of death

-the contingent of knights and retainers sent to Lanverness

SIR BLAINE, sworn knight of the maroon charged with protecting Princess Kath, he bears an unnamed blue steel sword

SIR TYRONE, knight of the maroon with skin the color of ebony, often referred to as the 'black knight'

SIR TELLOR, a knight-captain of the maroon, charged with leading the group to Lanverness and returning with a down payment of gold for the Queen's blue steel weapons

SIR KIRK, a knight of the maroon, sent back to Castlegard with dispatches for the King

CARL, a Master Smith of Castlegard's forge, sent to Lanverness to take measurements for the Queen's blue steel weapons

ALAIN, a squire of the maroon

TODD, a squire of the maroon, sent back to Castlegard with dispatches for the King

-the knights of Cragnoth Keep

SIR TRASK, knight of the maroon, leader of a dissident faction, sent to Cragnoth Keep as a punishment posting, champion of the battleaxe

SIR PENROSS, a knight of the maroon

SIR DRAVIN, a knight of the maroon

SIR CARFAX, a knight of the maroon

SIR CARLINE, a knight of the maroon

SIR BELMORT, a knight of the maroon

SIR ORRICK, a knight of the maroon

SIR TALLOVER, a knight of the maroon

STEWARD BALLARD, the head steward of Cragnoth Keep

SIMON, a steward of Cragnoth Keep

NAVARRE

The youngest kingdom of Erdhe, Navarre was founded less than four hundred years ago by a daring adventurer, Alaric Navarre, who rescued the youngest daughter of the king of Coronth from a band of sea pirates infesting the Orcnoth Islands. Gaining the king's confidence, and his daughter's hand in marriage, Alaric earned a freehold of land running along the Western Ocean where he later established his kingdom. His domain includes the Orcnoth Islands.

While defeating the nest of pirates, Alaric discovered a long-forgotten focus. The magic of the focus renders the royal house very fecund, enabling the queens to bear six to ten children in a single pregnancy. After using the magic, both the king and the queen become sterile. The focus is the secret strength of the royal house of Navarre, the bedrock for the succession to the throne. Alaric abandoned the convention of primogeniture, declaring that all of the tuplets have an equal chance to the throne. He instituted the practice of Wayfaring, a type of fostering where the heirs develop their greatest interests, striving to become excellent at a skill, a knowledge, or a trade, so that they can bring this knowledge back to Navarre and thus enrich the kingdom. After the Wayfaring, the King, together with the royal council, chooses the successor to the throne based on the talents, skills, and temperament that best fit the needs of the kingdom at the time. Navarre is well known for its uncommonly wise rulers...but with every great boon there is also a cost, the hidden focus brings with it the Curse of the Vowels.

The symbol of Navarre is a white osprey soaring on a checkered field of red and blue. The seat of their power is Castle Seamount, perched on a rocky outcrop on the edge of the Western Ocean. Navarre has always had close ties to the sea.

KING IVOR NAVARRE, the ninth ruler of the kingdom of Navarre
 -his siblings:
> **PRINCE IRWIN**, died of poison, believed to be a victim of the Curse of the Vowels
> **PRINCESS INGRID**, fell from the rigging of a ship and died, believed to be a victim of the Curse of the Vowels

PRINCESS IRIS, accused of murdering her two siblings, exiled to the Orcnoth Islands she murdered her guards and then disappeared

PRINCE ISADOR, Commander of the Army of Navarre, advisor to the king, nearly fell victim to the Curse of the Vowels

PRINCESS IGRAINE, Counselor to the king, court historian, tutor to the Royal Js

PRINCE IAN, Royal Bowyer, advisor to the king

PRINCESS IVY, Captain of a royal merchant vessel of Navarre

-his wife, **QUEEN MEGAN**, a princess of Tubor

-their children known as the Royal Js:

PRINCESS JEMMA, Wayfaring with the Queen of Lanverness to learn the way of multiplying coins

PRINCE JUSTIN, Wayfaring to become a bard, he receives permission from the King and Council to travel to Coronth to try and overthrow the Pontifax, also known as the Dark Harper

PRINCESS JORDAN, Wayfaring with the Kiralynn monks to learn the art of war, she remains locked in a healing coma, felled by the treachery of the Mordant

PRINCE JARED, Wayfaring with the Octagon Knights to learn the way of the sword

PRINCESS JULIANA, Wayfaring with Navarre's merchant fleet to learn the way of the sea

PRINCE JAMES, Wayfaring in Tubor to learn to become a vintner

PRINCE JAYSON, Wayfaring in the Delta to learn the secrets of a new water wheel

his retainers:

MASTER SIMMONS, the royal healer

DUNCAN TRELOCH, a master archer and trusted counselor, the companion of Princess Jordan's Wayfaring

LANVERNESS

Carved from the ashes of the War of Wizards, Lanverness is an old kingdom, steeped in tradition, often relying on its wealth of natural resources and the shrewdness of its rulers to grow in prosperity and influence. Never fecund, the royal line of Lanverness has been forced to branch out several times over the centuries. The Rose Throne is currently held by the Tandroths. The Tandroths nearly lost the throne when the last king of Lanverness, King Leonid, failed to produce a male heir. The king survived a revolt and forced his noblemen to accept his only daughter, Liandra, as the heir to the Rose Throne on the condition that she marry a peer of the realm. Liandra is the only queen to rule a kingdom of Erdhe. Under Queen Liandra's stewardship, Lanverness has become the wealthiest kingdom in all of Erdhe.

The symbol of Lanverness is two white roses crossed on a field of emerald green. The seat of their power is Castle Tandroth, rising from the heart of Pellanor, the capital city.

QUEEN LIANDRA TANDROTH, ruler of the Rose Throne, also known as the White Rose of Lanverness, also known as the Spider Queen, also known as the Black Widow Spider
> -her husband, **PRINCE-CONSORT DONALD TERREL**, chosen from among the noble families of Lanverness, Lord Terrel was raised up to be the Prince-Consort to the Queen on condition that he forsake his name and his lineage. He died in a hunting accident shortly after the birth of his second son. The heraldry of house Terrel is a red unicorn rearing on a field of green.
> -their children:
> **PRINCE STEWART**, heir to the Rose Throne, Commander of the Rose Squad
> **PRINCE DANLY**, spare heir to the Rose Throne
> **PRINCESS ASELYNN**, died at birth

-her councilors:
> **LORD HIGHGATE**, the Master Archivist, the queen's shadowmaster, right hand to the Queen
> **LORD WESLEY**, Lord of the Treasury

LORD TURNER, Lord of the Royal Guard, also known as the Knight Protector, responsible for the safety of the Queen

LORD SHELDON, the Lord Sheriff, leader of the constable force of Lanverness

LORD HELFNER, General of the Army of Lanverness

LORD HUNTER, a skilled diplomat, used as a roving ambassador to the other kingdoms of Erdhe

LORD BRADSHAW, the Lord Steward, responsible for crops and farms,

LORD RICKMAN, the Lord of Mines, responsible for the ruby, emerald and iron ore mines of Lanverness

LORD QUINCE, Lord of the Hunt, Warden of the Royal Forests

LORD CADWELL, Master of Letters, the secretary to the Royal Council

-her ladies-in-waiting:

LADY SARAH JAMESON, a distant cousin of the queen, principle lady-in-waiting

LADY MARTHA, a lady-in-waiting

LADY AMY, the youngest of the queen's ladies-in-waiting

-other members of the court:

PRINCESS JEMMA, a princess of Navarre, Wayfaring with the queen to learn the way of multiplying coins

CAPTAIN DURNHEART, a captain of the Rose Guards assigned to protect the queen

MAJOR TELCORE, a major of the Rose Army

SIR CARDEMIR, fifth son of the Duke of Graymaris, the seahorse knight, sent by the queen as an emissary to the monastery of the Kiralynn monks

CAPTAIN RANOTH, a captain of the Rose Squad

THOM BARKLEY, a queen's shadowman serving in the guise of a royal guard

TIMOTHY COLLINS, a queen's shadowman serving in the guise of a royal guard

JON DENT, a queen's shadowman serving in the guise of a royal guard

MASTER CARL, master baker of the royal kitchen
PAULUS, jailor of the dungeon
TALBERT, valet to Prince Danly

-the people of Pellanor:
MASTER SADDLER, a royal jeweler
MADAM STOCK, the madam of an exclusive bordello

CORONTH

The kingdom of Coronth was long ruled by one of the oldest royal families in Erdhe. Tracing their lineage back to before the War of Wizards, the Manfreds struggled to maintain their kingdom despite the aftermath of chaos and famine caused by the magical war. Their descendents ruled in an unbroken line for over a thousand years until a preacher of the Flame god brought a new religion to the capital city of Balor. Enthralling the crowds with the miracle of the Test of Faith, the Pontifax gained a rabid following. In less than a year, the new religion consumed the kingdom, making the Pontifax more powerful than the king. Ruling from the pulpit, the Pontifax declared that only a true believer of the Flame god could wear the crown of Coronth, forcing the king, his wife, and all of his children to submit to the Test of Faith. When the searing flames consumed the royal house, the Pontifax became the spiritual and secular ruler of Coronth.

The symbol of house Manfred was a golden lion rearing on a field of blue. The new symbol of Coronth is a golden flame on field of red, the symbol of the Flame god. The seat of power is the capital city of Balor.

THE PONTIFAX, the supreme spiritual and secular ruler of Coronth, also known as the Enlightened One, beloved of the Flame God
-his priests and counselors:
> **THE KEEPER OF THE FLAME**, Senior priest of the Flame, leader of the Confessors of the Flame
> **LORD STEFFAN RAVEN**, Counselor to the Pontifax
> **GENERAL CAYLIB**, General of the Army of the Flame
> **ALAN JELLIKAN**, Pyromancer of the Flame
> **CLAVIN**, a senior priest of the Flame

-the people of Balor:
> **SAM SPRINGWATER**, a baker accused of sinning against the Flame, killed in a Test of Faith, father of Samson
> **SAMSON SPRINGWATER**, son of Sam the baker, a former sergeant in the city guard who returns to Balor as a refugee plotting to overthrow the Pontifax
> **JUSTIN**, a prince of Navarre, a bard, the leader of the plot to overthrow the Pontifax, also known as the Dark Harper

GRANDMOTHER MAGDA, an old woman who has lost everything to the Flame God, a refugee who returns to Balor to overthrow the Pontifax

BEN OBERN, a former drill sergeant of the Rose Army, he volunteers to return with the refugees to Balor

RED, the leader of a gang of orphan boys

JACK, a member of the gang of orphan boys

WILLIE, a member of the gang of orphan boys, a roof rat

SHINER, a member of the gang of orphan boys

DANIEL, a tanner rescued from the Test of Faith, joins the rebellion against the Pontifax

LUCY JONSON, daughter of the owner of the Jolly Penitent tavern

BEV, a serving wench at the Praying Maiden tavern

OLAFF, a mute giant, a guard serving Lord Raven

PIP, an orphan lad who serves Lord Raven

SERGEANT JEXEL, a sergeant at the Fortress of the Flame

MERCHANT RASINT, a wealthy wine seller

MERCHANT GILDEN, a wealthy wine seller

THE KIRALYNN MONKS

Founded over two thousand years ago by a group of scholars, knights, and wizards, the Kiralynn Order has always presented an enigmatic face to the world, a face that is open yet closed. One hundred years before the start of the War of Wizards the monks withdrew from the southern kingdoms, retreating to their monastery hidden deep in the Southern Mountains. As if erased from the minds of men, the location of the monastery disappeared from the maps of Erdhe. The memory of the Kiralynn monks has slowly faded, becoming little more than legend and myth. Yet select rulers of the southern kingdoms still receive scrolls sealed with the symbol of the Order. History has proven that these scrolls contain an uncanny prescience. Kings ignore the advice of the Order at their own peril.

The symbol of the Kiralynn monks is a Seeing Eye in the palm of an Open Hand. Their seat of power is their mountain monastery. The motto of the Order is "Seek Knowledge, Protect Knowledge, Share Knowledge".

THE GRAND MASTER, the leader of the Kiralynn Order, his/her identity is a closely guarded secret
-monks and initiates of the Order:
>**MASTER RIZEL**, a Master of the Order
>**MASTER GARTH**, a Master Healer of the Order
>**BRYCE**, an initiate of the Order, he studied to take his vows to become a monk and a healer but was subsumed by the Mordant's Awakening, becoming a prisoner in his own mind
>**MASTER AEROTH**, an ambassador monk sent to the kingdoms of Erdhe
>**MASTER ZITH**, a Master of the Order, accompanies Kath as one of her companions

-visitors to the monastery:
>**PRINCESS JORDAN**, a princess of Navarre, sent to the monastery for her Wayfaring
>**DANYA,** a young woman who sought sanctuary in the monastery with her mountain wolf, **BRYX**

THE DEEP GREEN

The Deep Green is an ancient power reborn from the ashes of the War of Wizards. Rising from the ruins of a great city, the forest grows with frightening speed. Trees at the heart of the forest are giants, growing to more than thrice the height of normal trees, while the dense tangle of underbrush forms a nearly impenetrable barrier. The forest protects its own, a race of people with golden cat-eyes. Calling themselves the Children of the Green, the cat-eyed people live within the boundaries of the forest in a confederation of clans under the leadership of the Treespeaker.

Outside of the forest, the cat-eyed people are shunned as evil abominations, said to be born from the perverse mating of man with animals. The cat-eyed people are persecuted across the kingdoms of Erdhe, and often put to death by the 'white-eyes'.

THE TREESPEAKER, as old as the forest, she is a seer, a witch, the embodiment of the power of the Green. As the leader of the clans, she wears a cloak of snow-white swan feathers.
-her clan leaders:

> **CENRIC**, leader of Clan Hemlock, he wears a cloak of peacock feathers

> **AGATHA**, leader of Clan Aspen, she wears a cloak of blue jay feathers. She leads a faction that opposes dealings with the white-eyes

> **BRAN**, leader of Clan Ash, he wears a cloak of raven feathers

> **CAMILA**, leader of Clan Maple, she wears a cloak of orange kestrel feathers and is a member of the faction that opposes dealings with the white-eyes

> **DEREK**, leader of Clan Redwood, he wears a cloak of red woodpecker feathers and is a member of the faction that opposes dealing with the white-eyes

> **CONRAD**, leader of Clan Spruce, he wears a cloak of brown thrush feathers

> **LANA**, leader of Clan Oak, she wears a cloak of golden finch feathers

-her people:

>**JORAH SILVENWOOD**, a ranger of Clan Cedar
>**RONAH**, a ranger of Clan Hemlock
>**JENKS**, a patrol leader of Clan Hemlock
>**MARTYN**, an attendant to the Treespeaker

ABOUT THE AUTHOR

KAREN L. AZINGER has always loved fantasy fiction, and always hoped that someday she could give back to the genre a little of the joy that reading has always given her. On a hike in the Columbia River Gorge she realized she had enough original ideas to finally write an epic fantasy. She started writing and never stopped. *The Steel Queen* is her first book, born from that hike in the gorge. Before writing, Karen spent over twenty years as an international business strategist, eventually becoming a vice-president for one of the world's largest natural resource companies. She's worked on developing the first gem-quality diamond mine in Canada's arctic, on coal seam gas power projects in Australia, and on petroleum projects around the world. Having lived in Australia for eight years she considers it to be her second home. She's also lived in Canada and spent a lot of time in the Canadian arctic. She lives with her husband in Portland Oregon, in a house perched on the edge of the forest. Her seven book epic fantasy, *The Silk & Steel Saga,* is finished! This saga includes: *The Steel Queen, The Flame Priest, The Skeleton King, The Poison Priestess, The Knight Marshal, The Prince Deceiver,* and *The Battle Immortal.* Karen also published a collection of short stories, *The Assassin's Tear,* including two stories set in the kingdoms of Erdhe. She also published a book on writing, *Power Writing: Make Your Genre Fiction Soar!* You can learn more at her website, www.karenlazinger.com or at her Facebook page for The Steel Queen.

The Front Cover artwork was done by the Australian artist, Greg Bridges. Greg's artwork has appeared on the book covers of many well-known fantasy authors. His cover perfectly captures the Pontifax and the feel of the saga. To see more of his art or to contact Greg, visit his website at http://www.gregbridges.com/

The Map and the Back Cover artwork was done by a graphic artist from Oregon, Peggy Lowe. Her illustration of the two maps helps to bring the kingdoms of Erdhe to life. Peggy can be contacted at her e-mail address, peggy@portfoliooregon.com

This story continues in **The Skeleton King,** the third book in *The Silk & Steel Saga.*

www.ingramcontent.com/pod-product-compliance
Lightning Source LLC
Chambersburg PA
CBHW020919020726
47495CB00002B/252